DAWN OF UNITY

DAWN OF UNITY

LAST OF THE SEEKERS

1

NITISH SHARMA

BOUNDLESS ADVENTURER
PUBLISHING

Published by Boundless Adventurer Publishing

Dawn of Unity (Last of the Seekers, Book 1)

First edition October 2022

ISBN 978-1-7782142-2-6 (Hardcover)
ISBN 978-1-7782142-1-9 (Paperback)
ISBN 978-1-7782142-0-2 (Ebook)

Cover design and illustration by Jeff Brown Graphics
Interior Illustrations by Nathan Hansen Illustration
Regional map by Karin Wittig
World map by Daniel Hasenbos

Printed and distributed by IngramSpark.

nitishsharmabooks.com

For my family and friends.

No one achieves anything without guidance. A special thanks to these individuals who provided the following services:

Editors:
Ayesha Ghaffar (What Ayesha Reads)
Gabby D'Aloia (GCD Editorial)

Beta Readers:
Abirami Kirubarajan
Faizan Fahim (Bookaapi.com)
James Gordon
Meghalee Mitra
Mohammad Hamad (The Book Prescription)
The Book Gremlins

ICE OCEAN
BO...
NORHARRLAND
Nogrmork
Joröskögr
ASH
Fornmork
Cerulean
LAND OF THE Woods
BLUE ELVES
Hearth Mts.
REPUBLIC OF
FREEHOLD
Upper Free R.
FREELANDS
Serive Mts.
Iznachalnyi
Forest
Dichter-
wood
Blue Mountains
Lower Free R.
Free Woods
KINGDOM OF GURMANIS
Great Central
Wetlands
SAOMARHAD SULTANATE
Nor-
wood
North
Isen R.
Al-Khadra
Al-Gawf
Forest
Swamp
Al-Bunniah
Forest
Dava R.
Bì Sha
South Isen R.
White
Desert
Dasht-e-
Sharq
King's R.
Hamasheh
Omari Desert
Bashar R.
Dasht-e-
Marzaki
Green
Swamp
Herror R.
Roywood
Oghurk
Steppe
Alpennmos Mountains
Teichos
Varvaron
Qahil
Heights
Imperial R.
Iultsu R.
Hercyneiotia
Forest
RHOATHIAN IMPERIUM
Rhoathian
Wetlands
Kayiyb
Basin
Elysiania R.
Zanjī
Savanna
Al-Asfar
Desert
Avuan R.
Mrefu Jungle
GREAT MER
REEF
SOUTHERN OCEAN
ASE...

SEA
ICE OCEAN
Kidelak R.
THE TAINTED LANDS
Tainted Swamp
Dead Forest
Malnoc Forest
Vbeas R.
Great Guardian Wall
POTENTATE
h Steppe
ALTAN UULS
Öndör Gol
Ulorkash R.
MOKERJIN KHAGANATE
Mokerjin Steppe
Zhēnzhū Marsh
NICHIKOKU
HATORANDO Mts.
Yù Hé
Great Wall
Dashahai Desert
QINGUO
Shānzhi Forest
HUÁNG SHĀN
Huo Hé
OSACHA
GOYONARA
RALYAN MOUNTAINS
Tiāntáng Hé
Zhōngyāng Forest
Zhúzi Forest
Sikab Savanna
Phyllous R.
Vasuthar Desert
Eldarun Wetlands
Sylórien Forest
Baadh Marsh
A'ræn Corridor
Burning Desert
Greysynth R.
Thylakuil R.
HRINDNAGARA
Sacrasylvia R.
hanvyacas Jungle
ELDARUN DOMINION
Stone Forest
Vercotyl Forest
Brahputra R.
DWARVISH HEIGHTS
Stonehearth R.
Ligthyr Forest
Three Vines R.
NEW COMERLANDIA
SOUTHERN OCEAN
AICA

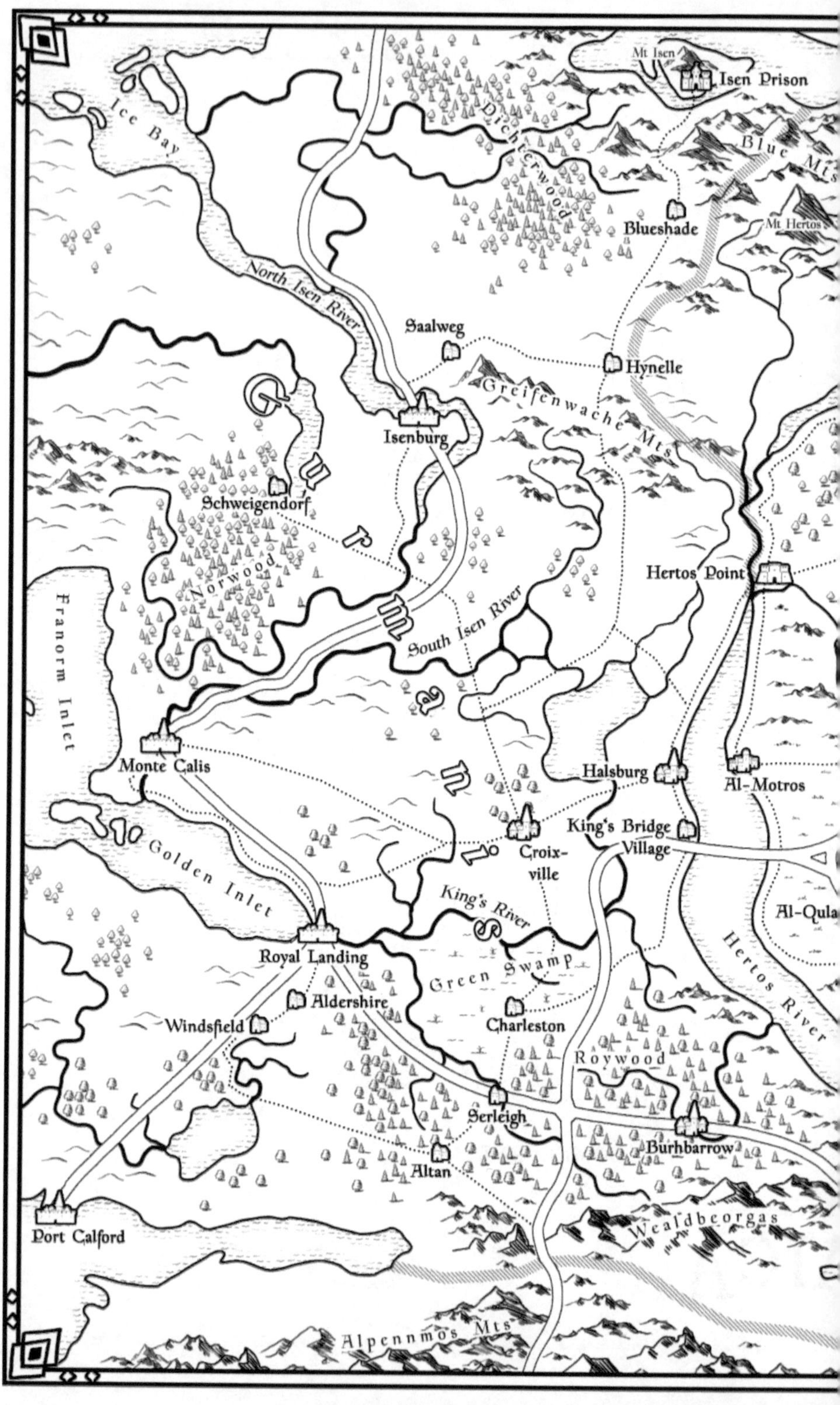

Ice Bay
North Isen River
Dichterwood
Mt Isen
Isen Prison
Blue Mts
Blueshade
Mt Hertos
Saalweg
Hynelle
Greifenwache Mts
Isenburg
Schweigendorf
Norwood
Franorm Inlet
South Isen River
Hertos Point
Monte Calis
Halsburg
Al-Motros
King's Bridge Village
Croixville
Golden Inlet
Al-Qula
King's River
Hertos River
Royal Landing
Green Swamp
Aldershire
Windsfield
Charleston
Roywood
Serleigh
Burhbarrow
Altan
Port Calford
Wealdbeorgas
Alpennmos Mts

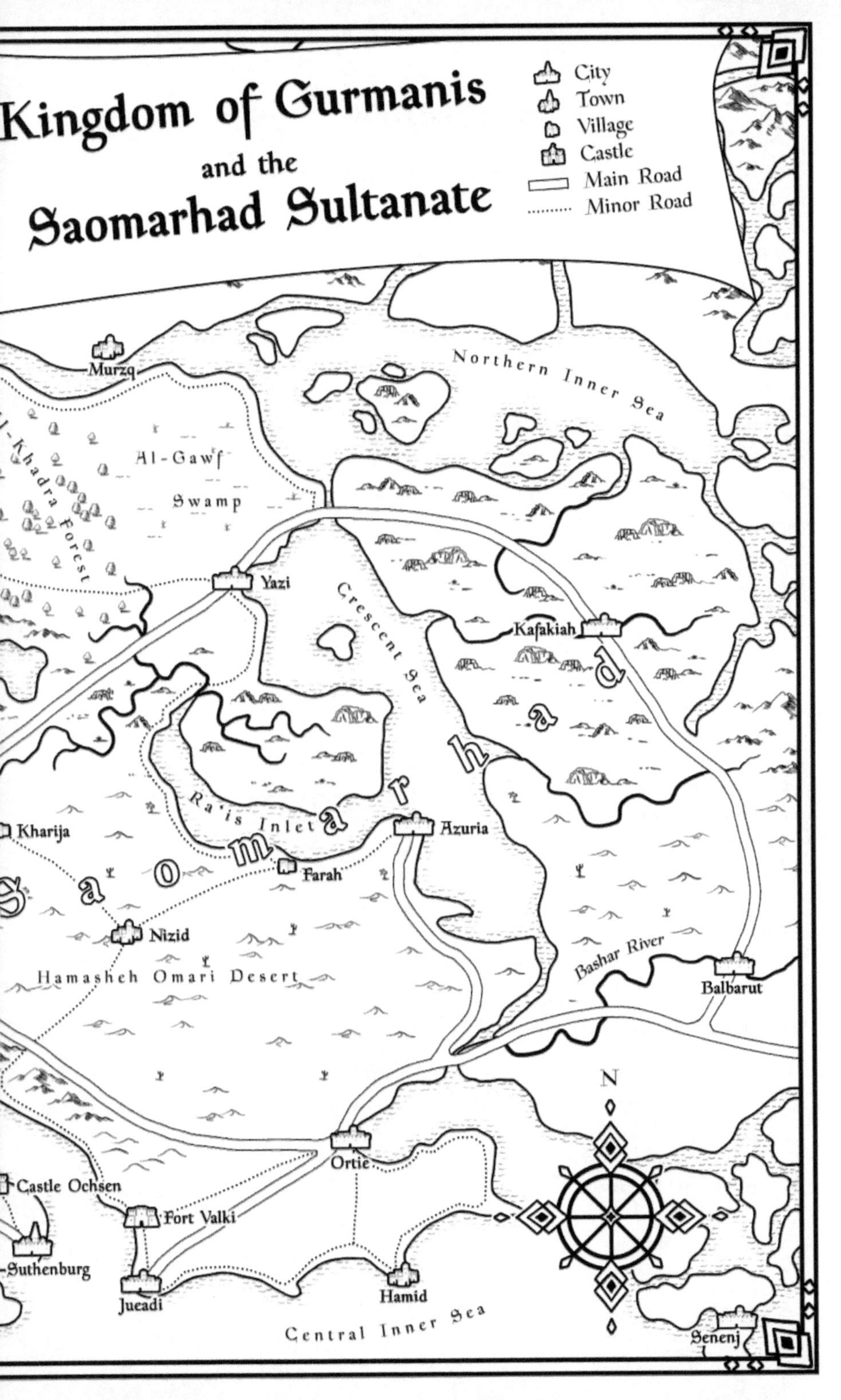

Kingdom of Gurmanis
and the
Saomarhad Sultanate
City
Town
Village
Castle
Main Road
Minor Road
Murzq
Al-Gawf
Swamp
Al-Khadra Forest
Northern Inner Sea
Yazi
Crescent Sea
Kafakiah
Saomarhad
Kharija
Ra's Inlet
Azuria
Farah
Nizid
Hamasheh Omari Desert
Bashar River
Balbarut
N
Ortie
Castle Ochsen
Fort Valki
Suthenburg
Jueadi
Hamid
Central Inner Sea
Senenj

Contents

Prologue

"DO WE NOT both believe in the Father? Is he not the one who created Erathas and all people?" the priest said. "Whether within Manianity or Alhurahism this is true. We disagree on who, Manis or Alhurah, is the true essence of the Father but wouldn't the Father prefer us to co-exist peacefully?" His long, robe-like alb billowed around him. He placed his hands over his chasuble and smiled at the grand imam in front of him, then offered him a sacred stole. "Manis is a being of praise in Alhurahism after all."

"But not one to be worshiped." The grand imam accepted the stole, and examined its embroidery, oval and petal shapes layered over one another to create a golden flowering sun. This was the symbol of Manis. "Tis a simple gift," the grand imam said as he handed off the stole to a nearby assistant and arranged his kaftan.

"To show my intentions are just that. Simple. Pure."

"For one-hundred years have our countries fought start and stop. How will this gift excuse the blood on both sides?"

"It will not, but you can agree that it's a start. Do I not stand before you, far from my home, standing in your Grand Mosque unarmed and without escort?" The priest gestured with arms spread wide at the massive, domed room. Huge pillars held it up decorated in colourful tessellations.

"You have shown either great trust or foolishness." The grand imam chuckled. "Your king wishes us dead. He shows no intention of peace."

"Your sultan is the same, is he not? Tell me, what does Alhurah say?"

"I only interpret what he wills. I cannot hear him. Such was… was for people of long ago." The grand imam led the Manis priest towards the Eternal Flame behind him, burring within a massive brazier. A power emanated from it, a type of Godly Magic. Long ago the idols around it had been smashed and Alhurah instructed that all should turn in its direction, if they could, to pray to God. "I am surprised the grand bishop did not come himself. Is there disagreement among you?"

"There is… tension. But all of us want peace. More than you know. The interests of the Church do not always align with that of the king."

"Nor do our interests always align with the sultan's. I do not represent all believers."

"So maybe we can start to talk of pe—" An earth-shattering boom followed by the jolt of an aftershock ripped through the mosque. Dust fell from the roof and walls marring the patterned marble floors and carpets. Shrieks and shouts tore through the mosque door from outside. The priest almost fell into the grand imam. Inside the large space, imams and civilians looked around and mumbled while children clung uneasily to their mothers and fathers. The door to the Grand Mosque opened and a Saomardrim soldier stumbled in, his padded and chainmail armor stained with blood. "Gurmians! They are here. They've snuck into the city an' are slaughtering everyone!" His voice echoed through the space, then his head snapped back. Coughing up blood, he fell forward and laid still, an arrow sticking out of his back. Onlookers in the Grand Mosque screamed and the grand imam held up his hands.

"Shut the doors. Quickly!" He glared at the Manis priest. "You. Seize him!" Two imams leapt forward and grabbed hold of the Manis priest. The man's eyes widened.

"You have the wrong idea!" The priest struggled against the imams' grip.

"You were a distraction. Meant to trick me!" The grand imam pointed a shaking finger at the priest.

"I had no knowledge of the attack! I was sent… I came to negotiate." The priest's face paled.

"Lies!"

"It is the truth!" His pleading eyes focused on the grand imam.

A booming thud against the Grand Mosque doors shook the building. A few more and the door cracked, swinging open. A dozen Gurmian soldiers flooded into the space brandishing swords, their plate and mail armor stained in blood. The men rushed forward, slashing and stabbing the imams and civilians inside. One man walked ahead of them. His blue-gold robes billowed behind him and a black velvet chaperon sat wrapped around his head. A cape with the symbol of his domain, an impaled man, draped almost to the ground. He raised a flintlock pistol and fired, striking a nearby woman in the head causing her to fall on her side; smoke drifted from the muzzle. With the single shot used he tossed the pistol aside and drew another then strode towards the Eternal Flame, unmoved by the carnage around him.

"Verräter," he spat at the Manis priest. The grand imam looked at the priest, and seeing no subterfuge in his eyes, he was released.

"Curse you, man of your king! Only a demon would do what you are doing now." The grand imam glared at the Gurmian lord. The Manis priest trembled as he scanned the room with wide eyes. His insides threatened to spill. Saomardrim men, women, and children lay slaughtered around the floor of the Grand Mosque, staining the patterned walls, floor, and carpets with blood. The screams of pain and mourning amplified upwards into the wide domed ceiling.

"All Saomardrim deserve to die." The Gurmian lord smiled. He raised his pistol and pointed it at the grand imam. The grand imam raised his hand and gestured towards the Eternal Flame. His eyes widened, skin tightened, and the anger in his voice seemed to shake the air between them.

"Those of the old days will come. Seekers who will end this war. They who can hear the voice of Alhurah. They who can contact him and travel to the godly realms alive. They will end this madness!"

The Manis priest looked between the lord and the grand imam. His attention moved to the Eternal Flame. The power that emanated from it grew stronger, pulsing with unbridled energy.

"And you!" The Manis priest shouted at the lord who had noticed the power in the Eternal Flame. The Gurmian lord raised an eyebrow, his grip on his pistol faltered, and the Manis priest continued, "I curse you! Manis be by my side. One of those Seekers will kill you for what you've done here today. This massacre will be avenged!" He turned and looked at the grand imam. Despair painted his face, pain from the blood spilt in such a peaceful place. He flashed a drained smile. Their attempt at peace was over, and now they'd die together.

The Gurmian lord fired his pistol.

Part One:
Empty Beginnings

Chapter One

LAUNCHING FROM THE crest of a mountain ledge he soared through star-lit sky, his wings stretched far outward resisting the glacial wind trying to shrivel his feathers. The bird of prey dived towards a grey castle nestled against the mountainside on an island in the Blue Mountains. It was surrounded by a deep almost circular ravine formed by the separation between the island and the mainland.

As he passed the light of the moon his shape shimmered a translucent pale blue. He made a mournful call, tilting his head at the castle. Mount Isen stretched tall in the northeast, a sentinel guarding the structure on its blue-grey slopes. All around him, a barren mountain landscape spread, covered in snow and ice. This remote corner of the world, frigid and empty, acted as a sanctuary for the beings the bird took the form of.

Gliding over a small chasm, only passable by a single icy stone bridge, he passed the two walls, the inner slightly higher than the second. Below in between the three keeps of the castle were crude gallows and a stockage where men and women hung, their chains dangling off their frozen bodies, their wrists bound behind them and wrapped in strips of leather.

He landed on a tower and hung his head for he knew what this place was and for whom he'd been sent. Watching a few unfortunate souls dragged towards wooden stakes, readied to be driven through, confirmed his knowledge of this place. It was Isen Prison, the most feared prison in Gurmanis, and it housed who he had come for. Despite the wind and snow, the prison stood, braving the elements, fulfilling its grim purpose as a place people were sent to die.

The bird flew high into the air. As he had done before with the other boy, he would do the same here. In an instant, he fizzled away, its form fading into specks of glowing blue.

Held by his arms, he stumbled up the set of stairs, shackles clanking around his ankles. Every muscle in his body throbbed with the echoes of recent pain and his vision blurred. The boy tripped and stumbled forward, prompting a grumble from the broad-shouldered guard who dragged him. The guard jerked him forwards from the top of the stairs into a long shadowy corridor carved through the rock deep underground, with barely two meters of space. The only visible light, a glow from a few blue-white crystals set into sconces.

The teenage prisoner, dressed in a short-sleeved tan-brown tunic and shorts with a thin vest overtop, had been securely bound. Shackles connected together by heavy chains hugged tightly around his neck, wrists, lower chest, waist and ankles, slowed his walk across the ragged stone floor, rattling with each step. Above the neck iron on his left side was a tattoo, half covered by the collar, that read **271**. Fresh red stains covered parts of his frayed and torn prison uniform.

Again, he slipped, his fabric strip wrapped hands catching his fall, and his guard cursed.

"If you'd walk right, I wouldn't have to drag you," the guard grunted. A frown cracked the dried grime on the boy's face, through the shoulder-length strands of his dark brown hair hanging in his face and that partially covered his ears. He slid his strip wrapped feet attempting to stand properly, feeling the hard leather sole and vamp underneath the strips. He glared at a second guard approaching.

"Night treating ya well?" the newcomer greeted, adjusting one of his metal bracers. The other guard nodded and shoved the boy into the damp wall. He slumped to the ground, scratching his cheeks against the surface, his chains clanking.

"I'm outta here come morning. Could use the rest ahead of the trek down the mountains an' to Blueshade. This filth's cell is a little further down the hall, DOM-37B. Think you can take him there?" The newcomer's green eyes scanned the sorry creature and he raised a bushy eyebrow.

"Did ya take him to the mages first? Don't want him crippled or diseased."

"I did, don't you worry."

"He's the one, one the warden likes. The boy, the youngest prisoner, ain't he?"

"Yea he's the one, killer of his own parents."

A flash of heat rushed through the boy and his eyes grew wide as numbing pain surged in him.

"What happened?"

"Warden's orders. Said today's a special day for the boy."

"An' you? Gonna join the army?"

The guard smiled. "Ya. Infidel Saomardrim will fear my blade."

"Leaving one hell, entering another." The newcomer shook his head.

"Better than this place."

The newcomer leaned close and whispered. "Warden's not right he is. He's got something wrong in the head what with the things he does to the prisoners."

"Quiet! If someone hears ya, we'll both be in serious trouble. Look, the people in here deserve this, as intended by the gods." The guard looked back down at the boy. "They're naught but murderers, thieves, rapists and madmen. Will you take him to his cell or not?" The guard gave the boy's chains a jerk, sending searing pain into his raw wrists and ankles.

"Yea, just keep your voice to yerself." The newcomer yanked the boy off the ground, and led him down the corridor. Hunched over and arms sagging against the weight of his restraints, the boy hobbled forward into a cell block and a new hallway. Two sub-blocks, cages, the bars intertwined in chains, contained a row of cells. Everything was still, mute, and against the dim light stray dust drifted in the air. The guard pushed the boy against the bars of a sub-block and keys rattled as he unlocked the door. The boy slid his face against the mesh covered square spaces between the bars and coughed.

An echoing metal grinding preceded the sliding of two bars; the guard kicked open the lower bar, which was always jamming, and swung the door to the sub-block open. He pulled the boy inside. They walked down the hall passing several cells until they reached cell DOM-37B. The guard slid open the solid metal door to the cell then swung open a second barred mesh covered door behind the first with a ringing creak. He threw the boy inside the squat rectangular space whose curved roof ran lower towards the back. It was barely enough space for a grown adult. Securing the boy in chains attached to the cell's walls, and with a last look of sickened disapproval, he slammed and locked the cell doors with a heavy echo. The banging of closing and locking doors did not faze the boy. He'd grown used to it. Left in complete darkness he could only whimper before he blacked out.

⁕

He woke to tortured screams echoing from somewhere under the cell block. Dim blue-white light illuminated the cell through the door's cracks. The light revealed the stone walls, their surfaces coarse and bumpy, less one wall which had alternating patches of smooth, as if it had been plastered over. A foul stench came from a hole in one corner.

He tried to lift himself from the ground only to crumple back down into a shallow puddle of water. Burning pain radiated from him as he shifted to adjust to the weight of his chains.

The boy huddled himself together and squeezed himself tight. He closed his eyes and tears started to form. *'Yea he's the one, killer of his own parents.'* His parents came to mind, their faces ones of love and compassion he had once known. He saw his father's weather worn skin, felt his firm touch. He saw his mother's calming smile and heard her tender voice.

Halfway between sleep and wakefulness, he spotted a shadow creeping towards him. The shadow echoed his image, its shadowy hair cut so that it followed the curve of its head and came closer together behind its neck. The shadow's round jawline stretched into a smile while the gash that was its mouth parted and it's curved nostrils flared. Panicked, the boy scrambled to one corner of his cell. Red eyes emerged and the shadow growled at him.

"No!" the boy cried. "Go away." Tears clouded his eyes. "I thought you were gone."

"Gone? How can I leave you? I am you!" the figure growled and its arms reached out towards the boy. "Murderer!"

"No…no…" The boy shivered. "Green fields, rolling hills, the forest on the cliff," he whispered, attempting to rid himself of the familiar vision. He saw his young self, his long hair neatly shaped and side-parted, eager to go to market the next day, the day everything went wrong.

"Memories of your home won't make things right. You'll ne'er make things right!"

"L-Laughter… children's…"

The shadow took hold of one of the boy's arms. "No longer king of your little treefort," it teased.

"William! William!" The boy lurched upwards, looking towards the cell door, his eyes wide. That was his mother, that was his name. Why did she have to die? Why could he not be with her? In here, he had time, time and little to do with it other than to work and think, but he'd not *have* to think of things, they'd just find him.

———

"If that's the case I won't eat. I'll feed my son first," Will's father said, standing resolutely before his wife. Will's mother looked at her husband, teary-eyed. From the other room a ten-year-old Will hid by the side of the door frame listening carefully.

"You don't understand, Trent! It's going to come; ya know that, then what? How're we going to feed the baby? Will? How will we feed ourselves if you insist on not eating?"

"I know it's gonna come." Trent held his wife's shoulders. "An' I told you I'll figure it out," he said tenderly. He touched his wife's stomach, gently tracing the new slight swelling. "The child is a blessing. Will deserves a brother or sister." Hearing this, Will froze. A little brother? Sister? What would that be like?

"Half a year ago the Smiths had to abandon their—"

"No, don't say it. I won't abandon my own blood."

"Then how? We can't make food out of thin air," Will's mother stressed.

"We could take Will and run away; heard many serfs from other villages who ran from their lords to freedom."

"But what kind of life will that be for Will and the baby? A life of fear? Where'd we run to? The cities wouldn't let us in and the lord's soldiers would hunt us. We'd die of starvation, sold into slavery or worse."

"I s'pose so…" Will's father reassured her, "we'll find a way."

———

Will shivered. He tried to remember the names of his friends, but they slipped from his memory except for one. The one friend who turned out to be traitorous. As fast as his image came it vanished from memory. The shadow knelt in-front of him.

"You'd kill him too if you could," it sneered. Will looked up at it. "Like you did them."

An image passed through his mind. He stood over the bodies of his dead parents. His mother was still alive; she gasped as blood seeped out around her.

"Wh-Why…" she'd groaned.

The shadow rushed at Will and put a ghostly blade to his neck. "Murderer!"

"Th-That's not true. Go away!"

"You can't escape yourself and what you did, you never can."

———

Ten-year-old Will woke from his bed, nothing more than a raised straw mattress, in a room that doubled as storage. He turned in his bed and opened his eyes. A distant sound didn't register to the half-asleep boy but he slid himself off and sat on the edge of the bed. His mother screamed. Will froze, fear making him hesitate. He rubbed his eyes. Someone shouted.

"M-Ma… F-Father…" Will's voice broke. His father screamed. He walked forward, trembling, and approached the door of his parent's room which stood half-open. Candlelight flickered as he peeked inside. A cold flooded over him and his heart threatened to stop. The entire world muted and blurred. His parents laid at the foot of their bed with several stab wounds, blood pooling around them. Will ran over and fell to his knees. The sound of shifting feet barely registered in Will's ears before he was thrown aside from behind. Will fell onto his back and looked into the face of the man who would haunt his dreams thereafter. A ragged black beard hung from the man's dark face, highlighted by splatters of blood. The man pointed a dagger at the boy, his dark wide eyes barely blinking, his face devoid of any emotion, and thick age lines across his forehead.

"He didn't tell me they had a son," he said flatly, his thin eyebrows pushing together. The man took a few steps forward. Will was too paralysed by fear to react. The man moved to strike, his bulky stature towering over Will, but as he raised his dagger he hesitated then sighed. He stowed his blade. "Your ma and pa were in it bad, boy. You'll join 'em yourself if you know what's good for ya." The man's eyes met Will's eyes for a moment, then he turned around and walked towards a small linen sack filled with coin.

"I'm not here to kill kids. Run off." Will stood and lunged forward. He wailed, a sound somewhere between anger and despair, and attacked the murderer. The murderer stumbled forward before shoving Will off him and into his parents' still bleeding bodies. The man huffed. He picked up the sack and fled from the room.

Will sobbed, knowing he had lost everything. A cold shaky hand touched Will's cheek leaving some blood on his face. Will looked at his mother's pale face; she struggled, barely alive.

"Ma... wh-what do I do?" Will panicked. He looked around and tried to rush away to find water or linens or something to help her. Before he had the chance to go, Will's mother touched his arm and he turned to look back at her.

"Wi-Will... l-listen..." she said with an exhausted and hoarse voice.

"Ma! Why..."

She coughed, splattering blood over her son's face. Will winced, but he couldn't take his eyes off his ma."

"Don't leave me! Please no... I don't know what to do..."

"Will." She smiled, staggering on her words, "Stay strong, Wi-William. He or she would have..." She placed a hand on her stomach, but lost her train of thought. Will looked over with watery eyes. She stared, lingering only a moment, then closed her eyes and lay still.

"No! Ma wake-up! No. No. Moth... er!" Will screamed and lost himself in his sadness. He hugged her body and laid by his dead parents stained in their blood. The only thing that marred the smooth pool of crimson on the floor was the murderer's knife. The world spun around him and blurred away along with the sound of his own cries.

———

Will sobbed, hugging himself against the bitter cold of his cell. He kept trying to remember the faces of his parents but they became obscured, blocked by some unseen veil. Instead, the face of the murderer sharpened. When Will was ten he remembered the man as a ghoulish looking monster, but he'd only been repressing the man's true face. Recently, it had become more vivid. After that night, his life was never his own to live. Cold-hearted, stoic men were all he ever knew thereafter. Men who never listened to him, never believed him when he kept telling them he was innocent.

———

He was a shadow himself, hollow inside, and he watched his body dissipating into a black red mist. He stood in his parent's room. Dizzy and confused, he stumbled towards the door. He was covered in blood. He fell. Tears filled his eyes. He crawled forwards, struggling to get up but crashed against the door frame. Struggling to stand straight, he looked back at his dead parents.

'Wi-Will...l-listen...' Will's mother spoke, but it was only in his mind. Will walked out the front door into the light of early morning. The sounds of chirping birds and blowing wind seemed muted. Will ambled down the main path to his village's center where the green rolling hills rose to the chapel upon them.

'S-Stay strong...' his mother whispered. Will reached the guardhouse and knocked on the door.

'He didn't tell me they had a son.' The distant voice of the murderer spoke. A constable opened the door and stared in surprise and concern at the bloody ten-year-old who had come to them.

"Home," Will said. They followed him back home and inspected the horrifying scene. They examined the dagger and noticed it matched with a set of daggers belonging to Will's father. They stared in disbelief at the boy.

The constables pinned Will's arms behind his back, and cuffed him in irons; the cold metal clicked shut tight around his wrists. All Will could do was stare at his dead parents oblivious to the dismay of the adults. He stared at the face of his dad. His father's eyes stared back, cold, lifeless and empty.

———

Will watched the shadow standing at the door of his cell. It looked outwards, away.

"Where has your life gone?" it teased, saying each word slowly and with care. "Bound to a small rectangular cell, the purpose of your life merely to sit and to work." It turned back to face Will and smiled, a black jagged twist in its face. Will stood, arms sagging, pulling against his chains. Streams of black mist shot out, emanating from the shadow and clouded his cell. Will coughed and tried to advance, but the cloudy mist engulfed him.

A cold hand clamped his neck. His breathing grew strained and glowing amber eyes widened ahead of him. They glared at him as if admiring a trophy. Will's insides tightened, his eyes stung, and his voice left him. He tried so hard to look away, but could not. Sweat broke out over his skin. Some unseen force made him stare into the eyes, the warden's eyes. His vision blurred and his forehead throbbed in pain. It spoke with both the voice of the warden and that of the shadow.

'You *are* guilty, you *are* dangerous, and you *are* a monster,' it growled, every cold breath smelling of feces. Will's eyes watered. Monster… monster…the word invaded his mind.

Isen Prison housed the worst of Gurmanis' criminals, people like him. Its denizens were murders, rapists, traitors, terrorists, and those who slighted the royalty.

Night after night, the shadow tormented him when he was younger. Every night Will woke in his cell and cried. The other prisoners seemed lifeless and would not speak to him. The guards looked at him only with disdain and a desire to inflict pain. Slowly, his thoughts and self-perception deteriorated. He was a boy in a nightmare; he was afraid all the time. Will told himself no one cared about him and he deserved to be in here. He was alone and he was worthless. He slowly lost one emotion after the other and only despair, stress and detachment filled the void. He was wicked, evil even. Why else would he be here? He was the shadow, a demon of the worst kind. That was why, like the other prisoners, he also learned to be silent.

"N-No…" Will spoke into the dark. "NO!" he shouted, his voice bouncing off the walls of his cell. The shadow backed away. "Go. Away." Will growled, glaring. The shadow smiled, floated backward, and faded. Will collapsed to the floor and gripped his throbbing forehead.

He listened to his own breathing and the faint noise of guards shouting at someone. Several thuds, a rod hiding flesh, barely reached Will's ears.

A filled wooden tray and cup slid through an open slit underneath the door. He looked at the hard, dark coloured bread and thin cold soup. Will pulled the meal forward and absent mindedly shoveled it in.

Laying back and looking at the grey floor, he caught sight of his scarred hands and ran them through his dirt filled, slimy hair hoping not to find any lice. They would clean the lice out when he got them. His hair fell back into the left side part it naturally kept.

A pain pierced Will from his left shoulder, his brand. He ran his fingers across the angry scar, traced its ⚡ surrounded by a circle, the mark that forever tied him to this dark place. Cuts had been opened over it from the torture he suffered hours before. He held his chest, feeling the other brand they had given him, slightly larger than the fist of an adult man, an 𝕸 for murderer. Will squeezed his eyes tight, resisting his thoughts and the memory those scars elicited.

Bound by leather straps on a stone table, Will could only look up at the snowy sky. He'd met the warden for the first time. A guard fixed a strap in his mouth; it separated his teeth and pinned his head to the stone. It hovered over him, the red-hot branding iron. The blacksmith brought it close to his face and the heat dried his skin while the tangy sent of burning metal filled his nostrils. He stared wide-eyed at the sizzling prod.

*"I won't lie… this will hurt a lot." Tears clouded Will's eyes, he struggled to no avail prompting three guards to hold him down on the slab. Another pulled up his prison uniform to expose his right arm and heaving chest. The guards wiped away grime and dust then the blacksmith lifted the branding iron and pushed it onto Will's chest. A second later another, smaller branding iron was pushed into his right arm. Yet another moment later, they pulled back his head to expose the left surface of his neck, and a mage dripped ink onto his skin before burning it into his flesh, forcing the ink to take the shape of **271**. The brands hissed upon his skin and the boy's muffled screams were carried away by the wind.*

Will exhaled. He trembled and held himself tight, chains clinking as he moved his arms. He squeezed his eyes shut and shook his head trying to push the memory away. His head pounded with a dull thud. Will pushed the palms of his hands against his forehead. He'd remember so much on days like today. Why? Why did his memories torment him? He exhaled again and opened his eyes. The sore feeling became apparent to Will again as he slumped against the cell wall and looked into the dark ceiling.

It was his sixteenth birthday today.

Alone in the dark, he cried.

Chapter Two

A FTER WILL HAD eaten, he pushed the empty tray towards the cell door and wiped any remaining tears. He crawled over to the corner of his cell and rose to his knees. Pushing lengths of chain out of his way and pulling up his tunic, Will urinated in the rancid hole. His cell grew thick with a nitrogenous stink before it thinned and dissipated. Will huddled against the back wall. He waited.

Shouting echoed outside as doors slid and swung open. A baton dragged against the sub-block bars, its clanging bounced off the walls, keeping in time with a hum. A hand reached in, grabbed the empty tray, and pulled it away. Will showed no reaction. He stared towards the grey ground ahead of him.

His cell door lock clicked. A guard slid the outer door open letting it hit the end with a ringing echo. Dim crystal light flooded Will's cell. He sat stoic.

The guard looked through the inner door bars and huffed. Behind him, in the hallway space between both sub-blocks, the cell block commander walked by with his papers holding a thin scepter with an octahedral crystal set on one end. Around him other guards unlocked cells and lined up the prisoners, collecting them outside in the sub-block. It was a cacophony of clangs, clinks, and rattles.

"Sun's up 271. Get-up," the guard ordered. He yawned and spat to the side. Bags sat under each of his grey eyes. Will touched the grainy floor and scraped up some dust as he stood. He pulled on one of the chains connecting him to his cell in order to hoist himself up. He hovered, taking a moment to steady himself. He blinked, face non-reactive, at the guard. The guard tapped on the inner cell door, signaling Will to shuffle forward and slide his shackled wrists through the upper tray slot. The guard was joined by another younger guard who leaned against the frame of the door and flicked dirt from under his nails. They acknowledged each other before the older guard adjusted Will's shackles.

"Cousins, uncles, brothers, sons, the men folk are nigh gone now from the countryside. All of em been conscripted into the war," the older guard complained. "I'm afeared they'll take my son when he's grown, they will. Back-up kid."

Will obeyed. The older guard unlocked the inner cell door and stepped towards Will to unlock the chains binding Will to the cell.

"War needs men. Who are we to deny the king 'is men?" the younger guard answered the first.

"Cause erelong they'll be none left on the farms. Army's good n' all, an' a crusade's redeemed a soul or two, but even the army can't keep it up without no farmers to work the fields, smiths to smith, hunters to hunt, tanners to—"

"Yea yea. I gets it."

"You just not got yer own family yet." The older guard loosened Will's leg irons and worked his way up to the other restraints. "I got a wife n' child to worry bout. Thing is, at the rate conscription is going, pretty soon they'll conscript women too."

"Ha! Come now, Fighters Guild given birth to plenty capable female fighters."

"Right but once the men folk are dead, then the women folk follow, what's gonna be left to fight for, eh? Children will be all that's left and the Saomardrim will run o'er them like they were ants."

"Yer fancy… what's they call it… reasoning."

"It ain't fancy. Common sense, plain and simple." The older guard huffed.

"Well here's some sense. We got prisons here and there with degenerates ready to fight. Men in here make up a few hundred, the women another hundred or so. Then we also got us."

"Sure, you and plenty of others wanna fight. But the prisoners in here, they're needed to get the crowdite and other metals. Still gotta supply the armies." The older guard finished removing the restraints connecting Will to his cell. He raised Will's arms and pressed hard on his wrist shackles, ensuring they were secure. Will flinched at the slight pain, and the guard examined his face.

"Been crying, have you?" he huffed, "I 'd think you'd forget that kind of thing."

Will stared blankly at him. The younger guard stepped forward.

"Remember this kid eh? 271? Six years ago, we took bets on if he would survive." The younger guard nudged his partner.

"That was 'afore we knew the warden fancied him and wanted to keep him alive." The older guard laughed. "Boy's still alive." The guard looked Will in the face. "You ought to die already ya know, no one grows old in this place, one way or another."

"He's sure as any to be run through with a Saomardrim blade, I think. Probably deserves it too."

"Sure. Come on, let's go." The older guard gripped Will's left arm and ushered him out of his cell. He pushed Will against the sub-block bars outside while the younger guard slid shut Will's cell doors. "Saomardrim prisoner camps are dotted around the country I hear. All supplying material for the war. I think with the amount of people supplying material and the army still not getting enough, means this war is in real bad shape."

"Who says the army's failing?" the younger guard huffed.

"You've heard, haven't you? King Duggan's been hiring more mercenaries cause the levies ain't providing."

"You hear about Fritz from the infirmary? Poor sod killed himself. Found out his village was ravaged, razed to the ground. All the men young an' old were dragged off to war and the women, children, and the elderly hanged. His wife, children, and father among them."

"The king did that?" The older guard's eyes widened.

"Ordered it. Villages who won't submit their share to the war will get it. Burdens eliminated. God be merciful to Fritz upon his judgement."

"Suicides go to the Underworld."

The cell block commander walked down the space between the sub-blocks. He noticed Will pushed against the bars and strode up to him. From across the bars, he glared at Will.

"271," the commander barked. Will didn't react, his eyes dead. "To attention 271!" The older guard shoved Will and he blinked, looking at the commander. "When I call you, you listen. A night ago, I got a right shouting from the warden. You know how it is boy. Warden takes you into his quarters and you gotta serve him well. If not, I get the flack for your idiocy. Got it?"

"Y-Yes," Will croaked. The commander shoved his scepter between the bars and jabbed it into Will's side. The crystal lit up, sparks jumping from it. Tendrils of pain shot through his muscles, tissues, and bones rendering him shaking in rhythmic shearing hurt. He stifled his shouts. The crystal fizzled out and Will gasped, panting. The commander took it away and grunted.

"Lost its charge. When the warden wishes something for you to do, you do it. If I get yelled at again, I ain't giving you a change of clothes when you come back, an' you'll just have to live naked, ya hear?"

Will struggled to stand, echoes of pain subsiding, but he nodded. The commander moved onwards. Will was dragged to the prisoner line and attached to it. He stood there. He waited.

Will shuffled forward, chained together and flanked by two tall prisoners, watching the heavy connecting chain ahead of him swaying. The chains rattled taut, urging him along. Will lifted his feet against the pull of his chains and let his arms sag. The prisoners shuffled from the cell block through three barred doors and entered into a large rectangular cavern. Sharp tapered stalactites and stalagmites grew out from the corners, from the wrinkled and fractured grey-blue roof and floor, barely visible through dim blue-white spell crystal light.

"Keep yer heads down till we get down, y'all hear an' don't you forget to pray to yer mistress if ya care for it," a guard shouted.

Will stumbled forward, following the motion of his fellow prisoners. He looked up, hesitating a look. This complex, a system of mines, was carved deep into Mt. Isen and weaved itself in all directions leading through numerous tunnels and spaces. At the far end, three huge metal barred cages attached to giant chains, one large central one and two smaller flanking ones, acted as lifts

The thick air, hazy with visible dust, held a hint of rank mine water. Sounds bounced off the wall reaching every person in this enclosed place and the heat of every body multiplied to fight the cold. Some prisoners in front of Will started to mumble prayers, directed to the huge statue of a female standing on a step higher than the central lift, jutting out from the wall recessed to accommodate it. The goddess of slaves, criminals, and the imprisoned stared down at the prisoners with an expression of insanity, her hair pulled back into a ponytail. She was a young woman wrapped in a straightjacket and chains and small fangs protruded from her lips and horns from her head. Will didn't understand this god because his parents had always taught him of Manis, the only inheritor of the Father's essence, the one most worthy of devotion, and through whom was the only way to the Father. The goddess depicted before him, in between wooden cross-beams, looked nothing like the allegedly benevolent Manis. Will frowned; in his mind Manis was anything but benevolent. Without warning someone shoved him. Will grunted and fell a little forward.

"Keep looking at the ground boy! You want to pray? Ya do so with your eyes on the floor!" a guard shouted behind him.

Will fixed his eyes on the ground. He shivered. Will and his fellow convicts shuffled towards the central lift and were locked inside. Will missed working in processing when he was younger because it was easier. The guards had initially put him there, where he would sort ore from rock, crush that ore with hammers and crushing machines, wash ore in troughs of running water with a brush, and roast ore in furnaces and pits.

The lift made a loud creak, and descended into the depths of Mt. Isen. They passed dozens of tunnels and caverns until they came to the lowest section. The air grew thicker and harder to breathe. They followed like sheep out and through a dim crystal lit tunnel, over a floor of wooden boards hiding drainage and ventilation pipes. Once they got to a larger, round cavern, not too far from the lift, they were pushed to their knees. The master miner, and his assistant approached and addressed the guards.

"Poor wretches," a guard teased. "Ore veins are of the hardest type. Can't put fire to it so you'll have to force it out with wedges. Gonna need every minute to reach yer quotas. Time to get to work." Guards systematically arranged prisoners along the length of the ore vein and linked each person to the other by chains adjusted to give the convicts room to maneuver. Escape by brute force was impossible in those restraints, besides, the convicts from

Will's cell block worked at the lowest level and the only escape was up, through lifts and guards.

Everyone received the tools they needed to work and were expected to mine all day. Any attempt at using the tools to attack a guard, prisoner or oneself was quickly thwarted. Guards roamed the interior of the mines whipping slow workers, assigning tasks or socialising with their fellow guardsmen. A mage, who could react fast to the efforts of any prisoner attempting to end their life, was stationed nearby. Prisoners dug, cleaned, and groaned.

As soon as a guard was satisfied with Will's position along the vein, Will started chipping and digging a space to insert a wedge. Dust flew back over his face with every blow. The sounds of clanking chains and of metal on rock echoed through the chamber. Clink, tick, clink, tick. Time dragged almost to a standstill here.

"Faster fool!" a guard shouted. Will froze and braced himself. The swish and crack of a whip hitting home broke the rhythm of their work and the prisoner beside him moaned. Will flinched. The prisoners worked in silence, without emotion. There were no fights, no socializing among prisoners, nor any other typical interaction another prison may have between inmates.

Will was chipping at a rock fold when a hand clasped his right shoulder and yanked him up. Will jerked, dropping his pick.

"You, you're coming with us." the guard holding him commanded. He was from another cell block.

"I didn't do… wrong," Will pleaded, his voice flat. The guard dragged Will out of the prisoner line. A second guard unlocked the chains connecting Will to the other prisoners then he took hold of Will's left arm and both guards dragged him deeper into the mine. Panic overwhelmed him, but his face was blank, hiding it. They dragged Will past other lines of prisoners, their blank faces focused on their own tasks. They entered a lift and took it up. Will stood between the two guards, head down, limbs drooping from his chains. His chest heaved and sweat trailed down his back.

"The boy stinks something awful."

"He's in his years of change, it makes it worse."

"You think if we dump mine water onto him it'll snuff out the smell?"

"I'm pretty sure that'll kill the boy."

"Maybe that's for the best."

"He's due to bathe soon."

"He's all yours then. I'm not blindfolding him and dragging him across the bailey." Will's heart raced, wondering where they could be taking him. They approached a smaller newer section of the mine and here the prisoner lines began to disappear. Further they went, Will's chains clanking, past rooms with wooden machines pumping water out of the slightly flooded tunnel they were wading through. They arrived at the entrance to a small round room where two guards and a sergeant crowded around, looking at the floor.

"Please, finish… work," Will begged, on the verge of delirium knowing the punishment that would come if he didn't finish. One of the guards holding him punched Will. He fell forward and coughed, clasping his stomach. The sergeant turned to Will, pulling him up.

"Be quiet, idiot!" he spat. A guard unshackled him.

"I-I… ah…" Will stepped back as the chains fell away. He rubbed his wrists where the irons had bit him. He'd always been shackled. At first their sight, weight, and restraining nature always tormented him and made him feel like the monster the warden loved to call him as. Over time they had become a normal part of who he was. Having them removed simply reminded him that they had been there.

The sergeant spoke again, "Climb down the ladder in this shaft." He moved to reveal a hole in the floor. "You'll fit in there. Go down. Tell us what ya find, you have two minutes or we smoke you out."

Will nodded, choked down his nervousness, and shuffled towards the shaft. The rope ladder disappeared into darkness. A guard ahead of him, who wore a faded blue sash across his torso, held up a glowing blue-white crystal set in a sconce. It flickered, gaining Will's attention, then darkened. The guard touched the crystal and blue-white light flickered back into existence, holding a steady dim glow.

Will hesitated, and the sergeant prodded him forwards. Will climbed into the abyss. He hit the floor with his feet, his grip-less leather soles almost slipping him; he could see nothing. Will took a few nervous steps, concentrating on not tripping, unable to walk as well unrestrained. A crystal torch was dropped down the shaft behind him. It flickered as it landed but was too thick to shatter. Will picked up the crystal torch and waved it in front of him to observe the walls. The space was no smaller than the cramped round room with the guards. They must have uncovered this room by accident as prisoners were mining. He searched for anything worth mentioning, feeling his way along the walls when his hand pushed against a hidden button. Stunned, Will retracted. The wall in front of him lowered making a soft grinding noise.

"What's going on in there?" a guard shouted. "Any mineral veins of worth?"

Will kept quiet. When the door opened fully, Will stumbled forward, unsure if he should enter. Inside the new chamber, a wide set of stairs led deeper into the earth. As Will left the last stair, his foot sunk into the ground, triggering a lose stone. The rumble of sliding earth echoed around him and he stared ahead as glowing blue lines and symbols swirled and formed on the walls. They took more shapes, images of warriors and creatures, and Will couldn't make much sense of them. Their light overwhelmed the light of his crystal torch.

Drawn were longships, mail armored men, large round shields, and prominently, an armored warrior holding up a longsword as he rode on the back of a half-bird, half-lion creature; a griffin.

The blue light turned red further down the hall where a round object sat on a pedestal. Above it, the glowing light traced out an imposing griffin on the wall.

Will walked down the vaulted hall past degrading statues of people he had no knowledge of and past two sealed doors he tried to open but could not. He approached the pedestal; the round gem captured his attention. No, not a gem, something more perfect, even flawless. About the size of a pearl, its outside reflected his image like glass and inside whiffs of coloured mist floated around. Overall, it retained a red look. Will tugged the object free and held it in his palm. He rubbed his fingers over its smooth glass surface. Slowly the object grew to fit snugly in his hand. Warmth radiated from it and up his arms, penetrating him like veins of heat and revitalizing every tired muscle. Will looked at it cautiously. It must be magic. It was valuable, perhaps. He'd have to give it to the guards. The object cooled a little, pulling away the warmth and energy it had given. Will hesitated; he wanted that again. Both shot back up his arms and filled his body. Will stood there and reveled in it. A decision made, Will stuffed the item into a fold in his tunic; he would not give it to the guards. He turned and retraced his steps.

Upon coming to the first room the door closed itself behind him. The guards above laughed. They'd thrown something down the shaft and it was generating smoke. Thick grey clouds packed the room and invaded Will's nose. He coughed, falling to the ground. He struggled to reach the rope, finding it hard to breathe. Then the world grew dark.

<hr>

When Will woke, the five guards were crouching over him and the room he was in glowed with crystal light. The guards, out of necessity and maybe even sport, had blasted the cave to get to Will. He coughed violently as he woke and someone pushed a waterskin to his lips. Will drank the cool liquid greedily only to have the waterskin pulled away and a guard shove his face back.

"Ahw, he didn't die." a guard grunted. Another guard re-shackled Will.

"You half-wit!" The sergeant grabbed Will by his tunic and brought the boy's face to his. "Look what you did! You destroyed the cave. You won't be getting any food for days. I will make sure of it. Back to your work boy, you've half a day to finish."

Will was surprised they didn't find the door but he was not surprised they blamed him for failure. His heart sank when he realised he had less time to finish filling his bucket and he'd be left hungry. Will gave the sergeant a hopeless and empty stare and was rewarded for it by being shoved to the ground. Cold metal bracelets clicked tight around his wrists, ankles, and neck. Will spit, blinked, and stared.

As the day was ending, Will gathered his mineral pail then ambled towards the exit. After depositing his pick and allowing guards to tighten and shorten his shackles, he showed his pail to the stone-faced guard who waved him along. Another guard lifted Will's arms and patted him all the way down to his toes and checked his hair and mouth. Will remembered the object he had found and held his panic back. Not noticing any reaction, the guard nodded him onwards, chaining Will to the prisoner line in front of him and then passed the boy through. Before they could move Will was grabbed and jerked back. He was turned to look at who had interrupted the entire post-work process. It was the guard who wore the faded blue sash. The guard's tan eyes regarded Will with a deep suspicion.

"You didn't find anything, did you?" the guard asked. His grip was accompanied by a slow burn, threatening to cast on Will. The man's voice was calm and collected, not harsh or uninterested like the guards normally sounded. This suspicious tone confused Will and he didn't know what to say. The other guard had missed the object and he was so close to leaving with it, but the sting of the burn reminded him of the rooms beneath the cell blocks, where men and women anguished, their existence known only by the screams.

The guard who had checked Will walked forward. "Naught anything on him. You sense something?"

"Maybe… nay… nothing." The guard pushed Will into the prisoner in front of him. "Move em' along." Will was ushered to his cell, chained to it, and left alone.

He sat motionless against the back wall. In silence a weight pressed on his ears, the sound of stagnant air. Water plopped onto rock in a perfect rhythm, echoing through the cracks of his cell. It was a tapping he'd grown accustomed to.

Straightening himself, he took the pearl out and studied it. In the dim light within his cell the object emanated its own soft light, and a shifting mist swirled about its center. Will thought about his mother's few charms; this was nothing like them. The pearl warmed him again, giving him energy. It was as if his muscles were tightening and expanding, allowing energy to flow. Will became suddenly aware of himself. He looked over his body. Why had he been born like this? Like a monster, like everyone saw him as? The thoughts of the shadow that had revisited him a day ago surfaced.

Will's eyes followed the swirling of the mist inside the pearl. It drifted towards his cell door. A shape took form. In awe, Will watched his mother come closer and smile.

"William." She raised a cloudy hand to his cheek.

"M-Ma…" Will spoke, looking up at her light translucent form, his locked emotions struggling to feel something.

"You aren't a monster. You aren't worthless and beyond saving. You are my son. My able son. Your life is precious and worth living." She hugged him and kissed his forehead. Her touch was like a soft feather barely touching his skin and her nose nestled next to the gradual curve of his own. He stared at her wide-eyed, trembling. The apparition faded. Will sobbed into his arms, making himself small. His heart sank and his breath thinned.

Then something changed in him, something shifted within his being. The feelings he was used to started to push back, as if they were fighting something else. A sense of loss, less painful than emptiness and despair, filled him. Remembering his mother's fruity voice, her pleasant face, her tender touch forced him to smile. Maybe he did have some worth left.

Will looked up. He looked at the pearl. The source of his sudden comfort pulsed in his hand. He tossed it aside, huddling in the corner and feeling loneliness and despair surge back. What had he felt? Had he smiled again? He didn't remember what a smile looked or felt like. He could not smile. What was that object? Will hesitated. He looked down at a finger on his right hand. It rested inside an unknown pocket between the vest and tunic of his prison uniform. His eyes grew wide, feeling the new well-hidden cavity. This object was magic! Will swore there was no pocket before. He stared at the faintly glowing object then looked away. He skulked into a corner of his cell. Will shrank back looking at the ground.

A distant shout of pain tore through the air making him shudder. What a stupid object. It was like the shadow readily teasing him with the things he could not have nor feel anymore. Manis must be punishing him. Wasn't it enough that he was here? Why all the dreams and memories these past few days? He didn't want to remember; it made everything worse.

The mysterious object still glowed in the corner of his cell. He crawled towards it and picked it up, hesitating as he did. He placed it securely in his new pocket then curled up in a corner, unable to go back to sleep. Fine then, he'd play along, torment after all was supposed to cleanse his sinful soul. The screaming intensified. He waited. His purpose was to be a person who sits in a cell.

Chapter Three

WILL PUSHED A mine cart full of rock and ore towards a cargo lift. Sweat rolled down his face and his sticky, slimy hands slipped on the cart's handle. He'd been working for hours at a stubborn ore vein trying to hammer iron wedges in between wall rock and vein to rip out chunks of ore. Will pushed his cart to the lift and shoveled the rock and ore into the lift tub. Two conversing guards stood beside Will and waited for him to finish.

"They say there's much resolve in the Saomardrim lines. The fighting will last a long while, might come up here," a guard with a bent nose and growing stubble said.

"Hey! Don't joke bout that." The second guard, a scar through his thin mustache, shook his head. "If the Saomardrim come here *we* will be caught up in the fighting. I don't want no part in the war."

"Bah, this was once Saint Sir Isen's fortress-monastery. It had ways to flee, holes behind water, others behind shit," the bent nosed guard said, not worried about being overheard.

"I'm not sliding down a shit tube." The scarred guard gave his friend a warning stare.

Will hesitated and adjusted, listening idly. He bent down for another scoop, his arms straining with burning pain as he lifted his full shovel. His chains clinked as his legs trembled with effort.

Scarface snapped his fingers. "Come on boy, you can shovel faster than that!"

Bent nose shifted the belt under his bulbous belly. "Ah, he's near the princess' age. Wish she had married that Rhoathian Imperium prince. War be over if she had. Them legions are endless. She was just a child when the Saomardrim killed the queen."

Will made a raspy cough, spitting out saliva and dust.

Bent nose yawned then lowered his voice. "Scouts report that heathen ships were sighted heading to Kolotovagrad."

"Saomardrim corsairs! Manis' balls… no. They'll be in this area for months."

"We're well hidden. Warden ordered no lights lit from sunset."

Scarface groaned. "Wish it would've been over when the grand marshal campaigned—"

Will missed the lift tub causing rock and ore to spill over the guards' feet. Scarface growled and shoved Will to ground. The shovel fell on his chest, winding him.

"Screwy prisoner." He kicked at Will.

The flaring soreness in Will's arm hurt more than the guard's kick. He'd lifted the wrong way, bending his arm painfully. Will spit out dust from his mouth stifling any attempt at a cough. A dramatic and painful magical procedure awaited him if he did since the warden would not let him die of dust and fume inhalation. Will stood, grasping the lift tub to help him. He'd slide down a shit tube if it meant freedom, there was no question in that.

Before he could continue his work a new guard approached and ordered the others away.

"Come on, you've work down with the women." He yanked Will up by the arm, detached him from the prisoners, and dragged him towards the lift. They traveled down, deeper into the mine and exited into a long tunnel. At the end it opened up to a large round section. Female prisoners lined the room, digging for ore. All resembled him, dressed in rags, chained together, empty and emotionless.

His guard led him towards the back and down a step into a flooded corner. There a few women and two men worked.

"Needed some extra hands. Seeing as you can fit in tight spaces—" the guard shoved a bucket into Will's chest— "get to it." Will waded into the flooded section. Cold and stinging water lapped up to his knees, and rendered the fabric wrapped leather sole and vamp around his feet soggy and spongy. Will bailed the water out with his bucket, hoping that he wouldn't leave this job like last time. He'd spent a week in the infirmary for the blisters and rashes he'd gotten. Will bumped into a woman, who gave him a blank stare.

A few hours passed and still the flooded section was no-where near clear. When the prisoners were allowed a five-minute break, Will slumped against a dry wall and stared at the grey-blue ground. Everyone did the same.

"Dobroslav!" a female's voice screamed. Chains clinked as she stood, holding her pickaxe in her hands. She was not more than twenty, with long black hair, a pale face, her eyes wide and her body shaking. She ran and stumbled forwards. Guards nearby approached.

"I-I found it, found it! It! Dobroslav's plans! His cell, I found it, escape!" she shouted. Will's pearl grew warm. Heat crawled up his arms and torso and into his head, as if telling him to focus. The guards surrounded the girl and shouted at her, ordering her to calm down.

"No. You want to keep me here!" She swung her pickaxe erratically around her. The guards tried to find an opening; one came too close. The girl swung the pickaxe into his side, finding a gap in his armor. The guard grunted and the pickaxe flew out of his side and from the girl's grasp. It crashed into another guard's head. The man fell backwards. She ran, stumbling over her chains. The guards lunged at the girl. Six? Eight? So many were on top of her, crushing her. Will shuddered and turned away.

Working again at clearing the flooded section, Will tried not to pay attention to the muffled screams and moans of the girl. She was gagged and chained to a mine cart filled with rock. Will fixed his focus on his work, feeling a little pity.

Prisoners dropped their tools and clambered against the walls in sudden fear. Will turned and looked back at what drew their attention; the shadowy figure of the warden had appeared. The insignia: a crown flanked by a sword and a feather, the Kingdom of Gurmanis coat-of-arms, with a pitchfork in the center was unmistakeable to Will. Two of the warden's personal guards, covered from head to toe in mail and plate with pointed helms revealing only their eyes, flanked him. Will's chest heaved painfully and he too clambered back against the mine wall. Cold fear shivered up his spine.

The warden sauntered forwards, his cloak billowing back. His amber eyes seemed to glow as if piercing out of his dull grey-white skin and the zagged scar that ran through the right side of his face. Guards pulled the gag off of the struggling girl. She looked up silent, cowering in the sight of the warden. He ran a hand over his neatly cropped hair and hissed, showing his yellowed teeth. He crouched down to face the girl, his lamellar armor bending, and extended a hand to her cheek.

"Skyla, no no no, Skyla," his vile voice emerged, deep and taunting, his lips bordered by his light beard. "You replaced my last man… I enjoyed you but you had to go and run. Always struggling and making trouble. Alas, you didn't get far now d'you?" the warden asked. Will's heart tried to break free of his ribs, as if the warden's voice was pulling it away. The warden's eyes were pinned on her. Skyla stared at him trembling, not speaking. "Did you?" the warden shouted. She whimpered and nodded. The warden slapped her across the face then stood. He sighed and turned an evil eye to everyone in the area, his amber irises glowing.

"It's always going to be from one of you, isn't it? One of you dangerous offenders who reject my mercy and betray me." His thick squarish face observed the prisoners. "I am sure you saw what she did. Now she needs to pay. I need to remind you all about the punishment for breaking the rules. Attempted escape is of the most atrocious of infractions.

"You are all here and you are all alive because I allow it to be. That is a mercy! You should all consider yourselves lucky. Out there in the free world you would all suffer a thousand times more than you would in here. I protect you! To attempt escape is to disrespect me and my generosity. No one takes advantage of my generosity. Now, who wants to help me?" Nobody dared to move. The warden's eyes fell on Will. "You."

Will's temperature spiked, his heart skipped a beat. Instinctively he tried to slide back, but a guard dragged him forward, unshackling Will from the line. He threw him beside the girl. Will looked at Skyla. She looked back at him broken and scared then adverted her eyes. A pickaxe landed before Will with a thud.

"Show your fellow inmates what happens to those who disobey me. Kill her." The warden smiled, clearing air from his heavy-set nose. Skyla cried out and tried to escape but she was held down by a guard. Will looked up at the warden. The warden's stare foretold Will his future if he disobeyed. Will stood. He grabbed the shaft of the pickaxe and brought it in front of Skyla. She was on her back, held down. The fear and panic in her face shred right through Will and he trembled, conflicted between his painful future if he disobeyed and the look in the girl's face. The warden placed a cold hand on Will's shoulder and clamped down. The air between them thickened. "You are a murderer Mr. Farmer; you have done this before." The warden waited then let go of Will and stood back. "Do it."

Will raised the pickaxe. Before him was a girl, older than him, and she had committed a crime. She had surely suffered immense horrors here. He couldn't do it.

Warmth radiated from inside his tunic, his pearl heating up, and the faint image of his father came to his mind and a memory. Six-years-old, Will was terrified. He'd heard the girl crying and screaming and despite his racing heart and shaking limbs, Will had startled the man trying to kidnap her, and ran back into the village with her.

Trent had tried to calm his shocked and shaken son. *'Always protect those in need, Will. Manis looks kindly on this, an' that is what truly makes you noble… knightly.'*

Will could not do this. He dropped the weapon and a quiet resolve washed over him as he braced himself for pain.

"I see." The warden's wide lips sagged and his thin slanted eyebrows knotted together. He grabbed the pickaxe and stood over the girl.

"Wait! Please, please spare me! I won't do it again an' I'll do what you want. I won't struggle anymore. Spare me," Skyla sobbed. The warden showed no emotion. "Mother, my sister, my brothers, I want to see them again."

"Skyla of Crownmoon you have been found guilty of attempted murder and attempted escape. Your punishment is death and will be carried out immediately. You attacked my man with this axe so consider this a punishment equal to the crime." The warden brought the weapon down without mercy, once, twice, again and again. Skyla screamed trying to cover herself with her shackles to no avail. Will witnessed in front of him the result. Crimson blood flew through the air finding both Will's and the warden's face. Finally, Skyla stopped moving and lay silent. The warden stopped, bent down, and lifted her bloody face with eery gentleness. He brought her lips forward and brushed a greyish-white finger over them, he sighed. He stood and kicked her limp body sideways; she fell into Will. Her blood pooled out over the mortified boy. Someone pulled Skyla off him and pulled him up.

"Leave her there," the warden ordered. "What a waste." The warden sighed. He threw the bloody pickaxe in front of Will and turned back to the prisoners. "Do any of you think I like doing this? D'you think it fills me with joy to punish you like this? You all brought this life upon yourselves when you broke the king's law! This punishment is a release for your souls so that Manis might convince Judeicar, god of order and justice to judge you mercifully. Obey an' all will be good; that is all I ask of you." The warden turned to face Will, who shivered and shrunk back. As soon as his eyes met the warden's he looked away to the floor as if showing respect. "Disobey—" The warden lifted Will's chin so that the boy could look at him. Will's insides twisted and tightened, his eyes stung, and his voice left him. "Disobey again and you will suffer the consequences." The warden's eyes narrowed. He turned Will's face to Skyla's mutilated form. Will could not stop himself from shivering.

Chapter Four

FOUR DAYS LATER, Will waited in line until it was his turn, then gave his bucket to a guard and stepped over to another to be searched.

"This is not right. It's not nearly enough!" the guard with Will's bucket said. Will turned, his heart slowed and his chest tightened.

"No." Will was grabbed by a guard and struck with a baton. His world started to spin as his wrists were pinned behind his back and he was dragged off. He was taken back into the prison buildings, and deep within the earth, past the cell blocks. The agonising wail of prisoners deep within grew louder as they descended. Will's guard slid open a heavy metal door which revealed a fire and crystal lit hall, flanked on both sides by large barred walls. The stench of blood, decaying and burning flesh wafted up Will's nostrils. Will stilled, knowledge of this place assaulting him. His guard nodded to another who wore a face mask.

"Help?" he asked.

"Only if I stay." Will's guard smiled, offloading the burden of escorting Will to the new guard. He wrapped a face mask around his mouth and nose. The two guards took hold of Will's arms and dragged him down the hall. Will dangled between them, legs and chains scraping against the floor. Behind the barred walls were large cells filled with bloodied prisoners chained and bound in all manner of ways, to the walls, strapped on racks, chairs, or bound by pillory. Masked guards tore at their skin, beat them, whipped them, burned them, their tools of torture numerous. None of the wails of the unfortunate men and women fazed Will.

"So, what's the news from the south?" one guard asked, shifting to get a better hold of Will.

"King Duggan was in Highcliff village showing off his new sword."

"Fascinating… is that all?" A man crashed into the barred wall, sliding against it, his eyes dead and saliva dripping from his mouth.

"Nah, you don't get it, twas smoking green! He calls it Heretic's Bane. Forged by some smith in Suthenburg then enchanted by his court mage. The thing constantly emits a corrosive poison."

"Fine, what's it matter?" A woman's scream overpowered the space, cut short by a choking gurgle.

"What's it matter!? He rounded up Saomardrim prisoners from the latest campaigns and showed off his new weapon. The infidels died screaming an' melting and burning by a few mere cuts. He killed at least a dozen with that thing. King Duggan is an 'ero he is, he protects us against those Saomardrim." The guards slid open a door at the end of the hall and dragged Will into a new room. Flanking this room were a row of slender mesh-linked cages. The guards marched Will to one of the cages, unlocked and opened it, and pushed the chained boy in. The door slammed shut.

Will blinked, his eyes heavy and his limbs aching. He tried to keep his legs from buckling under him with no room to sit. The guards idled between the cages, oblivious to the wailing around them. In cages across from him, two male prisoners stood still and silent, no expression on their faces. Another prisoner mumbled incoherently and played with his fingers. One of the guards hit his cage, shaking it and screamed at him for silence. The prisoner shrank back like an abused animal. A female prisoner stood in the cage furthest from Will. The torturer would come for him soon. Like the reception room for some twisted doctor, the patients were lined up, waiting for their turn to be admonished.

Will rested his forehead on the door of the cage against the mesh, staring at the ground. The scream of a brutalized prisoner from within the senior torturer's room tore through the air. The caged woman screamed and broke into a sob. From the door leading to agony, the senior torturer, face covered in a black mask, appeared and tossed a bloodied man out. He looked over the convicts in their cages.

"The boy next," he said with a stoic voice. Will was dragged into the torturer's room and his wrists were fixed to a stake above his head. They yanked his vest off him then pulled up his prison tunic. Will closed his eyes as he knew what was going to come next. He had many scars from the whippings he'd received and in the atmosphere of this prison, not many had fully healed. A voice sounded close behind him.

"I am a very superstitious man, prisoner. You did not reach your quota after doing so for years. It was about to be a record. Pray tell me, what happened?" The cold voice of the warden silenced the room. Even the guards around them shifted uneasily.

"Bad luck," Will dared to whisper, trying to keep his insides from erupting.

"Bad luck? Are you sure about that boy? Or was it something else, something you are hiding from me?"

"I-I don't… what y-you… 're talk… bout." Will stuttered, struggling with the longest sentence he'd spoken in ages. The warden approached Will and placed a cold hand on his back. He ran his hand over the scars Will bore, the warden's leathery touch giving him sickening goosebumps. The warden leaned into Will's left ear.

"So many marks, so much pain. I remember when you were a small boy some six years ago. You had a growth spurt some years back, didn't you? I remember how silent an' submissive you were back then as your reality started to sink in. You *tried* to resist me, with anger if I remember, when it became too much for you. I did not expect you to return into being a rebellious, resentful, irate one. I'd thought that was only temporary, I'd thought I removed such feelings from you." Will made no sound. "You know something Mr. Farmer, you are a handsome boy, and at this age in life you could have even been married. Ahh the things you could have enjoyed. Freedom to live and love. I am trying to help you. Has all that I have done for you not mean aught to you?" The warden placed his cold hand on Will's cheek, brushing it backwards into the boy's hair and ear. Will's skin recoiled and he fought the urge to gag. "Just look at that fine face, have I e'er scarred it? Have I e'er let you die? You and I have a special bond Mr. Farmer, don't hurt me, you don't want to hurt me. Tell me the truth and we can avoid pain." The warden removed his hand and backed away. Will shivered. He gripped his fingers into fists.

When Will was younger, the warden would claim how kind he was to him. Will believed him. He had rationalised that he was a criminal, a bad person despite knowing he didn't kill his parents. Maybe it was something else he was being punished for, something he'd done in childhood and now Manis had sent this man to punish him. He had accepted the punishment he received was justified, that it could redeem him and the person dealing it out cared about his redemption. Some part of him still believed that false narrative.

"I did everything… in a day. Promise… there's n-naught. Please l-let me go." Will pleaded, pulling himself inward.

"Do not lie to me boy! For I will extract the truth!" the warden shouted. Will recoiled fearing the warden would blow-up in anger, the expectation like pin pricks underneath his skin. "I hear word of a strange glow coming from your cell. It isn't blue-white, so you didn't steal a spell crystal. What have you stolen?" He had brought the pearl out in his cell and it had given off a glow; he hadn't thought it intense enough to leave the cracks of his cell. For a few days he reveled at the warmth it gave him and battling the dejected memories it triggered in him. New feelings had begun to take hold in him. Not happiness, worthiness, and belonging yet, but feelings he had forgotten existed. A sense of resolve radiated from within; he couldn't give it up.

"I don't know," Will insisted and closed his eyes. "P-Please… don't…" He knew it was coming. His body tightened as if preparing for the burn.

"Defiance!" the warden growled. "Please don't? So, you've found a rebellious voice once more."

"N-No…"

"Give me a whip."

As if his stomach had broken like a popping bladder, Will shrunk back, his face losing all colour. The warden turned to a guard and grabbed his whip.

The first strike hit home on Will's back. He cried at the pain trying to hold back his inevitable screams. One by one the metal studded leather hit drawing blood and tearing his flesh. Each strike burned and stung with such intensity. Sweat and tears streamed from Will's face as he grunted and wailed. He took a loud breath in and his muscles strained and flexed. The warden looked at him with pleasure as he threw all his might into the blows, Will's blood found the man's face. When it ended Will fell to his knees his shackled wrists causing his arms to stretch. His back was a mass of hot pain and blood dripped on the floor around him. He gave into the pain and blood loss, throwing himself into the cloudy dizziness it brought. His skin throbbed in time with his racing heart. The warden grabbed him and whirled him around. Will screamed in pain from the twist of his wrists against his shackles. The warden eyed Will. His face was livid, but his eyes betrayed his desires.

"I've had just about enough of you! Get him against the wall an' search him," the warden shouted, shoving Will back. A guard yanked Will off the ground and shoved him into a corner. Will's brain settled and he became more aware of his surroundings. Searing pain still stung him. The other guards surrounded Will as one took away his chains and stripped him. He faced the wall. They removed his clothes and rifled through them.

"Straighten up boy," a guard ordered. Will did so and exhaled nervously; he'd left the pearl in the pouch but they hadn't found anything yet. Relief, confusion, and sadness came over Will all at once. He had lost the mysterious object that had helped him feel again. A guard pulled up Will's hair and looked behind his ears.

"Squat." Will's eyes teared. He shivered, embarrassed and humiliated. Cold air nipped at his skin and all eyes were on him. He squatted.

"Cough." Will did as he was instructed.

"Turn around." Will turned to face the guards, revealing to them his chest and arm brand.

"Those brands amount to your worth Mr. Farmer. Practically nothing." The warden scoffed. Will's cheeks reddened; shame bleeding through. He was powerless to resist such evil men. A guard lifted Will's arms and checked under his armpits, checked again behind his ears and combed through his hair.

"Open your mouth." Will did so and the guard checked inside. Finally, they forced him to squat again and the guard checked between his legs. Will covered his cold body with his arms as if they were clothes.

"Very well boy." When the warden came close to Will's face, Will's insides tightened, his eyes stung, and his voice left him. Will tilted to stay back against the wall. "But I am watching you, following your every move. I know you are hiding something."

"Wh-Why d'you torment me… so much?" Will croaked, forcing himself to speak and surprised he had done so. The warden raised an angry eyebrow.

"Now you talk back to me? Truly, where has this rebellion returned from?" Will waned under the warden's intense amber gaze. "Because tis my job and I am effective at it," the warden answered. "Get him a new tunic and take him from my sight." With that the warden turned and strode out of the room.

When the guards had re-dressed and re-shackled him, Will touched the right side of his waist and felt a pouch slightly bulging with a small object. The pearl had returned and his body surged with tension as if someone else would notice. The guards shoved him forwards, making Will stumble. It… it had returned.

Sore, his skin still stinging, the bite and weight of his chains mocking him, Will lay in his cell. A prisoner moaned and cried as a lock clicked open.

Today he'd been paying too much attention to… what? Dobroslav! Skyla came to mind, that day, Dobroslav and escape, how could he *not* listen to it? In the days after Skyla's death he'd overheard more talk of this mysterious Dobroslav. A cell once housed that man who had carved plans all over it. Once he'd escaped, guards had plastered it over.

He wasn't serious; his cell could not be Dobroslav's. Will's mind raged; this was not the cell. There is no escape. I will die in here. He lay on his side and brought his legs towards his torso, chains dragging and clinking, his arms before him and closed his eyes.

'At first, he was rough… just pushing me around… Wi-Will, he tortured the animals. He killed them slowly and I could see that… that h-he enjoyed it.' Saul's voice, his once best friend pierced through his mind.

"Y-Yes…" Will agreed with the lies, a nauseous swirl surging in his stomach.

'He was angry. He boasted about stealing from others an' tried to get me to join him. He'd tell me how much he hated each person in the village and how he'd… k-kill them.'

Cold sharp pain gripped his chest as he saw his parents corpses in a pool of their blood.

'H-He saw… it as a betrayal. He hated them for it…' Saul's voice pounded against Will's head. he reached out for his pearl, seeking its comfort. He moved his fingers across its surface, taking in its warmth. He had had enough. His life was going nowhere and day after day he only served as the warden's plaything, and a target for the guards. He was rotting in here.

Why? Because he was evil, because he deserved all of this, because although he was not a murderer, he had done something to enrage the ever-cruel Manis. He saw it in the guards' eyes, what he was to them. Saul told the court exactly what he was. They saw a monster… monster… a word the warden loved to describe him as. It sucked his body dry hearing the word. He was a monster, he was evil… No he was not. Will hugged himself. He wasn't, he wasn't, he repeated in his mind as if telling his ten-year-old self not to think those tormenting thoughts that followed him as he grew. *'Then why are we here?'* His ten-year-old self asked back. Will whined and exhaled. A shiver rattled through him as he gripped the coarse ground. He was suffocating, wanted, no needed all of this to end. The walls of his cell closed in on him.

Dread entered Will's mind. Clouded in memories of his attempts to escape.

Ten-years-old, trying to drag himself through a grate into the abyss that surrounded the prison.

Twelve-years-old, turning his pickaxe on himself.

Fourteen-years-old, a careless torturer and a sharp four-pronged tool he could take.

The chaotic images flashed through his mind. He had to find a way. He could try dropping a rock on his head... yes... that would crush his skull and kill him before anyone could stop him. Will trembled, a rock, all he needed was a rock... rock... rock.

He tried to sleep, his mind still provoking him, no escape, not this cell, die in here. A horrid scream echoed from below, but it didn't faze him. His thoughts raged over the screams; escape, cell, death; escape, cell, death, rock, rock, rock...

Will stood, crying and shivering, advancing. He slammed his cell door and the echo bounced off the walls around him. Anger wafted off his small frame in thick waves. Frustration threatened to wither him, his vision blurred, and his head pounded with pain. He slammed the door again and screamed. A guard pounded the door from the other side.

"Stop it 271!" he shouted. "Don't make me come in there!" Will backed away and collapsed onto his knees, defeated and swallowed by his misery. He bent forwards and pressed his face into his hands. Hair fell around his fingers. Tears pooled below him. These feelings, his reactions to them, had resurfaced as raw as they were when he was ten. His pearl glowed intensely, radiating its heat.

'I-I'm s-scared... I want ma; I want her back I want pa back. I wanna go home.' It was his voice, but ten-years-old. He didn't know what home meant anymore, it was a hollow word to him.

In the orchard upon a low hill grew the apple tree he and Saul owned. Will jumped back down and grinned at a worried Saul.

'But I didn't fall.' Will picked up his basket of apples. 'You would ne'er let me be hurt and I would ne'er let you be hurt.'

'Sure.' Saul smiled back. Saul's face darkened their home blurred forming metal bars and mesh-link across his vision instead.

"No… isn't home anymore," Will whispered. "Can't go back. Don't have any friends… anymore… those I did… hate me now, fear me."

He was feeling very lost…' Trent's voice surged forward riding a wave of warmth brought out by Will's pearl. *Life is precious. In each of us is the lord an' killing hurts God… No matter how hopeless it seems you must remember all the good you have felt and done… You are a good person; you make mistakes but you learn from them. You have to be brave Will. Be brave, strong, and resilient.'*

"I am a monster… murderer… killed my parents. I should hate myself." Will repeated the things he'd told himself when he was younger. "B-But its not true. I didn't kill my parents but one man out there did." He gritted his teeth. Right now, he only wanted to never see this place again. When free he might deicide to seek out that man, but it was a hopeless endeavor. He'd not achieve anything, except for wandering the vastness of Gurmanis ten times over. If he ever saw that man by some chance or magic, he would kill—

We're evil. We did something to deserve this,' Younger Will spoke.

"I…" Thoughts of killing his parent's murderer seemed to confirm young Will's words. He didn't know what he would do… but he'd do something. Will's pearl glowed as if acknowledging the idea. "If only I could leave."

B-But you said there's no home anymore.'

"I'll find somewhere to go. Anywhere but here."

I'm afraid.'

"So am I."

Will's reddened eyes blinked; his pearl glowed eerily. Grasping it in his palm its warmth shot through his arm. Escape. His father could have never imagined the endless suffering he would go through, there was no favourable end to look forward to here. If his life was so precious why was Manis allowing this? There was nothing in his life.

"What is the point in living just so others can see you suffer? I have no future dad… I have nothing, and not you nor ma anymore." Escape meant embracing death. In that he saw a warm and welcoming light. Yet he also saw the green grass of home. Escape meant leaving. In that he also saw a warm and welcoming light. There was no green grass anymore, but he'd find somewhere to go… somewhere.

Will looked at the stone walls of his cell. No one cared for him, no one would miss him. Either this cell was Dobroslav's cell or… he'd die.

Will crawled over to the hole and stuck his hand in pushing through wet semi-solid waste. He pulled out a small, thick, weathered metal wire he had once found. On many occasions he thought to defend himself against the torturers with it, but never followed through with the idea for fear of retribution. Will scraped the back wall of his cell. At first only light scratches appeared, but then he caught onto something and the plaster revealed itself. Amazed, he scraped again with fervor and more plaster chipped off. Finally, after an hour of feverish work, he stood up and examined the layer. Nothing.

A stone wall stared back at him, no words, no drawings, no evidence of an escapists' master plans.

Will's heart sank and he threw the wire to the side. He fell back, chains clanking, laughing at his pathetic attempt. He pulled his knees to his chin and cried. He held his head in his hands. He saw himself growing, year after year, shrivelled and forgotten for when he'd finally lose his youth even the warden would abandon him.

A storm of viscous wind swirled, wrapped around him, and tightened. It suffocated him. Light flickered through it. One faint, warm, welcoming light teasing him with a rush of air to revitalize his sore lungs.

Will looked across his cell to the metal wire. It had been sharp and durable enough to scrape away the wall, so it would work for this. Shivering like he was naked in the snow, Will picked up the wire, pulled back the shackle on his right arm, and exposed his wrist. The sound of his heavy breath and pounding of his heart filled his ears. He faintly smiled. Suddenly an intense yet calming heat came over him as a wave and stopped his trembling. As if a beam of light had entered his cell Will looked up and gasped.

"One more try." A powerful voice overwhelmed him. His pearl gleamed with energy. Will scrambled against a wall, his heart skipping a beat, wire held out, and he stared at his cell door. No light or person was there. He looked at his pearl and wondered if it had spoken. He felt usually calm then, as if he were basking under the sun in the wheat fields nestled beside his father. He could almost feel the warmth.

As the heat and voice faded, he gripped the wire in his hand. Will scratched the wall again removing more plaster, throwing his urine to clean the wall, and soon he reached a layer that refused to be chipped away. Will squinted through the dark, feeling the wall. He traced the outline of a word. He couldn't read it but he was sure it was a word. He found Dobroslav's cell. Will fell back, panting, containing the urge to scream for joy as his limbs shook. His pearl glowed warmly.

Will imagined himself free, the idea filling him with a kind of ecstasy. One thing was for sure, one thing he could latch onto to fight despair, for the first time since the day his parents were murdered, he had hope.

Chapter Five

THE GLACIAL GALE was like claws clenching him every time it blew. Will shivered irrepressibly, thin ice spreading over his skin. He held his pearl in his hands, soaking in what warmth it gave as it pulsed in time with his heart. Locked hundreds of meters above the sea in a cage jutting out of the north keep of Isen Prison, Will knew they'd not let him die, but It didn't help him cope.

The gale threw the occluding mists upwards which hovered in place when the wind stagnated. Will leaned against the door of the cage, back as far as he could from the bars, his chains clinking as he shifted. Months had passed before he was able to reveal Dobroslav's complete secrets. He worked at night, whenever possible, under the dim warming glow of his pearl and with a sharp gem he'd smuggled out of the mines. Resolve filled him. Dobroslav was not a myth. He'd left manifests, predictions, charts and maps. Though Will could not read, he studied the maps with the upmost care.

Will could not keep his mind from his cell to where he'd found a key, Dobroslav's spare. In a time before the prison's current practices, Dobroslav had made two keys. Will found the spare key fossilised and fused to the inner edge of his privy, wrapped in stone, plaster, and organic matter. He'd tested it, fearing it would break, but it had been well-preserved. When the lock clicked open his heart nearly stopped. He'd eased himself against a wall, holding the unlocked shackle and stared at it, his breath thick, relief and possibility flooding his mind.

Yes, he carved over them, he told himself for the tenth time. He'd memorized as much as he could. Will needed to act soon. Hope and confidence slowly returned to him the more he prepared fuelling the motivation that helped him survive the last few months.

Something in the sea made Will stir. He slid towards the bars and squinted in the diming light to where five ships faded in and out of view within the mist. He'd not seen a sailing ship before. Will clutched the bars, his breath blowing through them, and his pearl in his other hand. If only they could save him. What a stupid thought. No one would save a murderer. His pearl brightened, radiating light, but Will's attention was locked on the ships as they were obscured by the mist.

Twenty-four hours later, Will pulled off the last of his chains and the neck iron, the scars on his wrists and ankles stood out, marring his white skin. Will rubbed his wrists, his skin refreshed by the stale prison air. He secured his pearl. His mind spun, a mix of emotions. He had to try. He didn't care if he died but he wouldn't let the warden decide his death. It had to be soon, it had to be now. He was going to escape. His heart raced and sweat beaded on his skin.

The guards had already finished their first rounds. Will paced back and forth in his cell, concentrating on walking correctly unrestrained. He spoke simple phrases, remembering how to piece sentences together without hesitation. As he paced, he realised the flaw in his plan, his barred cell door was covered by the outer solid metal door hiding the lock on the outside. He could unlock the barred door but not the outer one. Will resisted failure and doubt clawing its way up from the back of his mind.

The thump of a guard's footsteps made Will flinch. He mustered up his courage, coming up with an idea. Will unlocked the barred door, through the upper tray slot, then took his chains and knocked repeatedly on the door making loud reverberating clangs. The footsteps outside stopped before growing louder. Will stepped back, crouched, and curled up. His back faced the door and he held his chains tightly to his chest. His foot shifted and his ears twitched as the sharp click of his door preceded it sliding open.

"271 what in Manis' name are you—" Will's inner cell door creaked open. "What…"

Will swung around tossing his chains as if they were a whip, standing and stumbling towards the guard as he did. The chains slammed into the man's face, causing him to shout. Will thew his chains around the man and pulled with all his strength. His body groaned in protest. He fell backwards, but brought the struggling guard with him who screamed through airless breaths.

Will spun over and hit the guard with his chains. Three hits to the head, left the man limp, blood dripping from his forehead. Will hesitated, thinking he had killed the man. He scrambled backwards, his breathing difficult, and stared. The man's chest heaved and Will shook the thought away. He dug into the guard's pockets and found a leather strap, a gag, and affixed that around the man's mouth, bound his wrists behind his back, then collapsed again to the ground. His actions had quickly depleted his overwhelmed body. If he wanted to escape, he had to be silent and use less force. Will searched through the guard's belongings once more and retrieved the man's keys.

Will eased open the door and closed it behind him, locking it shut. He crept along the sub-block, through dim crystal light, careful not to wake the sleeping prisoners. Even in the late hour, the screams of tortured prisoners rang out below. Will stopped. He looked through the bars at the hallway between the two sub-blocks and made-sure no other guards were around. Satisfied there were none he crept onwards.

Before the door out of the cell block, in the separating hallway, another door led into a small armoury and store room. He needed a disguise if he was to continue but as Will approached the door of the sub-block his heart sank. The door was closed. Will pulled, but it didn't budge. It could only be opened from the outside. Why had the guard closed it behind him if he was the only one around? Then he noticed the door wasn't locked, it was jammed. The lower bar, that the guards kicked to open, had latched itself into a locking position. He tugged at the door to no avail. The spaces in between the bars were mesh covered; he could not reach through.

He tugged hard at the door. It was not locked, he had to be able to open it. His heart raced and his actions bordered on hysteria. His escape could not end here, not when he'd just started. Will threw all his energy into pulling at the door. The bar gave way, bending enough for Will to pull open the door with a loud metal creak that vibrated through the cell block. Will cursed. Somebody had probably heard that.

He stepped out, rushed across the hall, and into the armoury. On one side of the room a bundle of tattered and torn guard tunics sat next to clean ones. He found a small size uniform that most guards wore. It was the typical uniform of Gurmian soldiers. The chainmail went on first followed by the thick warming tunic. Will fingered the faded blue fabric, but the emblem in its center still proudly bore the Gurmanis coat-of-arms, modified with three black lines in the center and the sides of the tunic. He placed the uniform over his prison tunic and unwrapped his feet to slide on the boots. Will then strapped on thin dented plate armor over his arms and legs, giving him weight. He touched his neck where the number **271** was tattooed. He ripped a strip of fabric off one of the tattered tunics and wrapped it around his neck so it covered his number hoping it looked believable as a scarf.

"Anyone in there?" a rough voice asked. Will flinched. He threw on a helmet, attached a sheathed dagger to his belt, and prepared his voice to be as mature and adult as possible.

"Aye, I am in here."

The man entered wearing a matching uniform. "The door was open; lost yer uniform eh?" He chuckled, giving Will's uniform a second glance, "Warden will have your hide if he finds it. That new one doesn't fit very well though, you're small eh?"

"Aye," Will said. Waiting for an answer, he eyed the exit.

"Well, better get back to your post."

Will nodded and started to leave.

"By Manis you sound young, take your helm off, and let me look at your face."

"I should get back."

The man frowned and crossed his arms. "This ain't time to disobey your superiors'. Take that helm off." The scowl on the man's face foretold Will of retribution if he did not listen. He reluctantly pulled the helmet off. "How old are you?"

"Eighteen, sir," Will lied. "My friends say I look young for my age." Will held his breath. He didn't recognise this guard; he hoped the man was a new guard who had never heard of the fabled William Farmer, the youngest prisoner in the prison. The guard scrunched his forehead and gave Will a curious inspection.

"Yer not in the right place, I think. Dangerous offenders cell block's no place for you. Get em to transfer you to the guard's barracks. What were ya doing here anyway?"

"I… ahh… I was relaying a message from the commander to the cell-block captain," Will said. The guard scratched his head.

"Fine. You seen another guard down here? Our patrol is o'er in half-an-hour and he should meet me by the lift."

"I've seen him sir." Will wanted to keep the man from looking for the guard he knocked out.

"Where then?"

"I saw him I did. He was leaving, said something bout a mate topside." Will focused on using the words and style he heard guards using all the time.

"Blast it, why's he gotta get us in trouble so much? Thank-you, now get going out of here."

"O-Of course."

The guard nodded and left Will, but stopped when he noticed the broken door. "What's wrong with sub-block B? The door's been broken open?" He turned to Will.

"Ahh…" Will hesitated, thinking of an explanation. "Ya know that door is broken, don't you?"

"No. I came down here to look for my friend."

"Ask anyone who works down here. It's always been in bad shape. It's embarrassing…" Will scratched his hair more out of nervousness than trying to act embarrassed. The guard laughed.

"What d'you do?"

"I locked myself inside. Had to break it open."

"Ha! You did that?"

"If it's unlocked, opening it from the inside ain't too hard." Will steadied himself with relief that the man was buying his explanations. "You won't tell the commander, will you?"

The older guard smiled, showing his yellow teeth. "I saw naught a thing." He turned and left, and Will clutched his chest letting out a breath.

Will made his way through the halls. He grabbed a messenger bag and paper from another store room, so he could stick to the idea that he was relaying messages.

Will exited the super-blocks bypassing the three super-block doors without any trouble. The guard there didn't ask any questions, more interested in going back to sleep. He walked up a ramp and past a barred gate, coming up from the floor into a common room where all the super-blocks terminated. At one end of the room stood a large lift system. A cage with heavy iron bars rested at the bottom of the lift attached to a length of thick chains. A disinterested guard sat near a large lever and he took a tired glance as Will approached.

"Going up?" he asked. Will nodded. The guard stood and unlocked the cage. With a metallic creak, he slid the cage door aside allowing Will to enter then closed the door with a loud thud making Will shudder. Giving Will a brief look he pulled the lever back and a ticking played as gears ground and the cage ascended. Will held onto the bars and looked through the square spaces between them watching as he left his level of cell blocks... alone. Confidence batted with doubt. He was running out of time and the lift's laborious crawl set him on edge. The cage stopped. Will tensed. The cage rattled behind him and he turned to see the back of it open. A tall, moustached guard walked inside, carrying a box of the crystals the prison used for light, but they were all dark. The lift ascended once more.

"Night treating you well?" he asked Will.

"Yes... it's quiet."

"It's always quiet. Outside the cell blocks ya can't hear the screaming from below."

"That it is." Will tried to end the conversation by keeping his responses short and uninterested.

"Several blocks had their spell crystals fail. These ones I'm taking to be recharged."

"Um-hm." Sweat formed on Will's brow.

"My last day's tomorrow, I feel great! They're moving me south to the front with a handful of other men."

"That's... that's good."

"I know..." The man let out a sigh of relief, "Can't wait to see our king. Rumour is that he'll be leading a battle or two 'afore he returns to the capital from his latest tour. They say he wields a magical sword, what's its name?" The man took a second to think. Will found this information familiar, he scanned his memory for where he may have heard it before. "Heretic's Bane!" The man snapped his fingers causing a jolt to shoor through Will, but he maintained his composure. "That's it. I will go out there and fight and claim riches. Then I'll return home an' find myself a girl. Wait... what was the colour of that blade? Everyone was pointing it out..."

"Green," Will said without thinking. The lift jerked to a stop at the middle level.

"That's right! That's what it is." The man walked out of the cage. He looked back as the guard nearby slid the door closed again. "You seem familiar… that voice, yer size… were you there when we dropped that boy into that hole?"

Will remembered all too well. "No… I'm not stationed there," Will said as the lift slid from view.

In the final minute of the lift's ascent it shook every time a rumbling distant boom radiated down. Will clasped the bars to maintain balance and tried to calm his sudden racing breath. What was happening up there?

Will exited the lift at the top level. The door to the outside was meters away, but now the booms were crashes, thuds, and explosions. Will wandered out of the lift, urgency replaced with caution. Guards rushed from the left, running towards the door.

"Open it. Quickly!" the warden shouted, leading his guards. Will froze, stomach hardening, and his body hair went taut snaking up his limbs. The door was right there, so close, and now he could not leave with his prime tormenter standing between him and freedom. Will knew the warden would recognise him.

"You!" a guard shouted at Will, making him jump. "Go to the west keep. Wake everyone!" The doors swung open, allowing dim light to flood inside and cold mountain air to surge through the openings of Will's helm.

Will followed the men into the immense, limitless air around him. His legs quivered and his feet dragged over the snow as men rushed past him and thuds shook everything. A ringing burst though the light-headed clot in his mind. Force pushed him, snow, dust, and smoke falling over him. Will ran sideways, shielding himself with his arms. His mind jolted back into focus. Cannonballs and flaming stone crashed into the bailey hitting the keeps and walls. Guards rushed to take control of the cannons and arrow guns above. Guard dogs barked eagerly. Will looked back at the eastern keep entrance, the northern and western keeps rising higher behind it. A fragment of stone had almost hit him.

Will forced himself forwards, but stumbled. For so long his life was contained within the four walls of his tiny cell and the mines. To be dragged across the bailey in chains was one thing, but to stand in it so free and unhindered, Will almost collapsed with the sense of being so exposed and threatened. Will steadied himself and settled, moving onwards. Cold wind cut across his skin, a thin and stale mountain air, stinging him, amplified from what it had been in Will's cell. The bailey of Isen Prison was a nauseating smell of rot and blood.

As he rushed through a fence gate in the chain-link fence enclosing the eastern keep, there was chaos all around him.

"I will not let these Saomardrim corsairs enslave what is mine!" the warden roared from atop the inner wall. "Send men below to the water and drive them away!" Snow fell in thick flakes, sliding off Will's face. The Saomardrim here? Will wandered aimlessly, strikes missing him. His heart raced and his body heaved. Focus! Focus! He tried to remember what his next move was. The inner wall, that contained the prison, obscured freedom beyond.

Will rushed towards the western keep. A cannonball crashed into the wall above him. Will gasped and stumbled away, bits of rubble and dust striking him. The courage and resolve he'd mustered earlier dissipated, as he imagined the torture the warden would inflict. Skyla's gruesome death flashed in his mind. No. Focus. The postern gate Dobroslav had promised was nowhere to be seen. Will ran through every rare moment he'd been brought to the surface in his mind searching for a clue that could help him. They led him across the bailey when they took him to bathe. Where was that? He was blindfolded every time; they were hiding something from him. The guards always stood in front of him when he bathed, hiding were the discharge for the water led to. Maybe this was the postern gate.

They'd dragged him across the bailey this way; he struggled to remember his steps. Searching around the right wall of the western keep, flinching every time a cannonball hit the bailey, Will brushed away snow to reveal a cellar door. He pulled it open and followed a tunnel until it opened into a room. The sound of a waterfall echoed in the underground cave illuminated by blue-white light. The waterfall plunged vertically from the roof to in between several showering stalls then drained out from underneath via a stream. One could pull a lever on each stall to divert the water at the center into a stall. The image was like a snapshot into Will's mind. The dread of his ever-dwindling time encouraged Will to look for something that would reveal the passage. He hoped he hadn't made a mistake. He walked the length of the space, even feeling the walls for something that would open the passage. He followed the stream to where it disappeared behind a wall. He dipped his hands into the waterfall, in between two stalls, gripping something. *'It had ways to flee, holes behind water…'* Will remembered the words, then pulled.

A loud grinding and sliding startled him. Where the waterfall turned into a stream and disappeared, a passageway revealed itself. Will looked around, fearing something else had happened. He stared at the open passage for a few moments, not fully comprehending that this must be the last door to pass through. Someone grabbed and jerked him back. Will whirled around to face a guard.

"Saomardrim saboteur!" the guard held a dagger to Will's neck. "Wait… who the hell are you?"

Will stared dead at him guessing an alarm had been set off. "I…" Before Will could come up with an excuse, the guard sheathed his dagger and ripped Will's helmet off of him.

"You're 271! How d'you… it doesn't matter."

Will struggled with the guard who pulled Will away from his freedom. He couldn't let this happen. Will tried to draw his own dagger, but ripped himself free instead and darted for the stream passage. The guard followed and seized him again. Will tripped, landing beside his helmet. He took the helmet and spun onto his back. He launched it at the advancing guard, hitting his face. The guard tumbled into a stall. Will retrieved his helmet and bashed the guard's face with it. The guard moaned and fell limp. Will took the guard's wrist shackles, and with some difficulty, dragged him towards a vertical pole on one of the stalls guards chained him to while he bathed. He attached the guard to it. The guard groaned, but Will rushed out of the cave. The man's screams for help echoed behind him as Will ran through the passage, so close to freedom.

The passage opened to a small ledge overlooking the deep canyon around Isen Prison, its black pit lightless at night, and he knew if he slipped and fell, he would never come back. He leaned forward, hands resting on his knees, panting from the adrenaline.

A smoking bridge hung in front of him, impassable. On the other side a thin path disappeared as it wound down and behind rock. Likely, it was hit by the corsairs. Thuds and explosions, loud again, were slowing but Will noticed the lights within the canyon below marking ships. Puffs of smoke propelling cannonballs from them. To his left one bridge led from Isen Prison, and the prison's gatehouse loomed above it. He had to get on that bridge which curved downwards to the mountains on the other side.

Where the prison wall met the canyon edge, a small icy ledge arched around the side of the prison's base. It ran not far under the bridge. With the postern gate road impassible, there were no other options.

Will pressed himself against the wall's base, looking away from the abyss, and shimmied sideways. An exchange of fire thundered overhead. Will paused, catching his breath and briefly squeezing his eyes shut as rubble tumbled past him. He shimmied over to his right where the road was, slipping ever so dangerously as he did.

Will climbed onto the bridge, surrounded by smoke and clouds of entrained snow on either side.

"Down there! Saomardrim attacker!" someone shouted from atop the wall.

Will jolted into action running as fast as he could. A large arrow bolt missed his head. Three mounted guards from the tower at the end of the bridge galloped towards Will, blocking his way forward, one wore a blue sash. Will skidded to a stop as the men dismounted and angled their spears at him. The horses nervously moved back towards the tower, so close.

"Congratulations. You did it Mr. Farmer! First-rate!" the warden mocked above the dying sound of exchange fire. Will turned to the ramparts atop the outer wall. "Get back here now less the Saomardrim kill you," he roared. An explosion from below shook the air and the warden smirked. "Finally my guard do something right. You have nowhere to go. So, tell me prisoner, how exactly did you think you were going to survive out there? How were you going to survive in this cold an' dark land full of predators and chased by my men?"

"Anywhere is better than here!" Will screamed, his breath visible. Fear rose in him. Men shouted from below and the clang of steel grew louder.

"To think I focused so much of my time on you. You, not any other prisoner, I cared for most. I wanted to save you from the Underworld! Now this is how you repay me. Surrender yourself and die with some dignity. Let us all go back to sleep, won't you?" The warden waited. Will swayed as a spear pressed against his back.

"N-No!" A frigid gust of wind sheared across his face making him shiver. He was trapped between the prison, guards, and the heathens below.

"Then know that I have warned you." The warden walked out of view. The gates of the prison opened. Unable to run away and not willing to go back Will fell to his knees, defeated, his heart sunken and anticipation of a horrid end dawned on him. The warden sauntered out, holding an arming sword, a dark expression shadowed his grey-white face emphasised by his glowing amber eyes. He stalked towards the boy, his blue-grey cloak whipping behind him in the wind. A dark aura seemed to hover around the warden as if he had become the harbinger of death.

"You should have complied." The warden towered over him placing the tip of his sword under Will's chin, pricking his neck. "Go back to your cell." The warden's breath floated past his face.

"I won't." Will's mind lost focus and he stared into nothingness. It was over. A quick death was what he hoped for. Keeping his sword close to Will's neck, the warden paced around him.

"Why don't you get it? You must pay. Just like the lights you extinguished from the world so too yours must be slowly snuffed out." His tormenter stood behind him. "This is where you belong." The warden kicked Will sideways. Will fell onto his back, gasping at the pain. The warden's sword lunged forward and ripped into his skin, carving a shallow cut. A line of warm blood trickled down Will's face and stomach as he screamed in agony.

"You're the spawn of Kalshaimar," Will spat.

"You are a murderer. You are his beloved." The warden made four quick strikes, scarring Will yet again. "I am the only thing in this world left for you. How could you even dare to leave me? No one but I will care for you. That is what you do not understand boy. How can you leave me? You can't!"

The warden kicked Will towards the edge of the bridge and stabbed into Will's right leg, twisting the blade. Will screamed as flesh wrapped around the cold metal and jolts of pain racked his body.

"You are a monster, Mr. Farmer. Something to be tamed. I am justified. It is a cleansing to be rid of vermin such as you and a purification of your soul! I am the vessel for Judeicar's Justice." The warden pushed the tip of his arming sword lightly into the center of Will's chest and slowly pulled down towards his nether regions. "You are special… different. It seems you've successfully resisted me."

Will glared at the warden. A wicked smile spread across the warden's face. "So it seems then you never completely ended up like the others, hollow inside, voiceless, without desire other than to serve me." The warden removed his sword before it reached Will's lower stomach.

Anger raged within Will. He shot forward with such speed and strength that the warden stumbled back. Will grabbed him, filled with an urge to destroy the vile man. The warden pushed Will off him towards the edge of the bridge. He stood and raised his sword. Will swung his left leg at the warden's, tripping him and grabbing hold of him. Now the warden was at the edge, above the battle below. Will held the man's life in his hands.

"Kill me then! It is what you're good at!" The warden sneered. Guards approached Will from all sides. One neared but Will skirted out of his reach as an arrow gun bolt arched over his head and sent one guard flying back. He'd let go of the warden, without thinking, but another guard lunged forwards just in time and grabbed the warden. Will rushed forwards, diving behind the end of the remaining guard's spear before he could react. The spear cut him as it passed. Will clamored to the ground and scrambled to a horse.

Tendrils of rope, entrained in pale magic, slithered over him squeezing tight around his waist, neck, and limbs. Will pulled forward as hard as he could, straining to break free of resistance. The warden behind him laughed. The horse ahead whinnied and stamped around, terrified of the men's battle. Will raised his hands, exhausting his burning limbs as he reached out towards it. The spear armed guard, he who wore the sash, was a mage.

"No… don't leave…" Will moaned. The chestnut rouncey spun around, plowing his hooves into the icy ground, his nostrils flaring. Will was pulled back. He stumbled, falling to his knees. His body numbed but he tried to slide forward, tried to break free, tried to reach his dagger. He was so close. Pain raged from his wounds, pounding with every strained breath.

"Time to come home Mr. Farmer. Pull him in." The warden inhaled, refreshing his lungs. A gust of wind blew Will's hair back and soared over his ears guiding crystals of frigid ice to shear across his skin. He latched onto his pearl, feeling its calming aura. His pearl had given him strength, comfort, and it had cleared his mind. He begged it now to impart strength to him one last time, but it gave him nothing. He managed to draw his dagger and cut the rope, freeing a leg, but that took all his strength. Freedom was just ahead where the mountain flanked path curved downwards. On the side of the road he saw a translucent falcon perched on a ledge. It wasn't real. It must be some sort of spirit. The bird tilted its head.

Will collapsed in a heap, shivering, his dagger slid away and he closed his eyes, accepting death. He had failed. He just wished he could have died his way, and not the warden's way. To have a choice in his life, that felt good. He'd die alone on a mountain, hated, forgotten, but it would have been peacefully. He was dragged back. Will's pearl boiled, singing his side. An intense yet calming heat came over him.

"The strength to resist evil has shown how brave you have become," a powerful voice said. Will recognised this inner voice as the one from his cell. He couldn't imagine who or what it was. Why did it overwhelm his senses when it spoke? *"Be delivered."* His pearl was pulsing, slowly lighting and dimming and Will imagined drawing its strengthening power into him. As he did his limbs resisted again. Will pushed himself up against the mage's pull. With all his strength, he pulled. He snapped his right arm free, then his left. The magic wavered, having extended the rope beyond its strength, and Will stumbled ahead.

"Stop him you idiots!" the warden shouted. Two men advanced. The translucent bird flew forwards, a swath of blowing blue mist rushing past Will's shoulder, tickling his face, and barreling into Will's pursuers. Will scrambled ahead, taking his dagger, and reached out to calm the spooked horse. He locked eyes with the animal and some unseen understanding passed between them. The horse relaxed. Will grabbed its reins and spoke soothing words as he climbed up on it. The warden cut down the bird, shattering its blue frame, and strode towards Will. Will wasn't sure what to do, but he nudged the rouncey's side and begged it to go. The horse started to trot, sped up, then launched into full gallop, away from the prison. They entered onto the mainland mountains at full speed.

The voice, the bird, and these events, was something maybe… helping him?

Chapter Six

OVERWHELMED, WILL FOCUSED on balancing atop his horse until it slowed its pace. The dark of the night kept him from seeing the road but his horse, well acquainted with traveling Isen's Path, did all the navigation for him.

Will tried to spot something recognisable in the dark. Rubbing his eyes, he squinted through the increasing snow and hail as a powerful gust of frigid wind rushed over him. Will groaned. Weary, still bleeding, and in pain, he clutched his pearl against his chest, letting it warm him against the howling cold. It sealed his shallow wounds, but they could still scar.

As he'd rode down Isen's Path, a surge of joy consumed him. He had done it, left prison, confronted the warden, and as he rode, half-believed it wasn't real. His mind wandered, halfway between sleep and wakefulness.

Weaving through the Blue Mountains took time; night became day, and warming sunlight crept over Will's face as he descended into the foothills. Will tested the reins of his horse, recalling how to ride. His horse huffed, refusing to make things easy.

He figured that he needed to confirm his direction soon, otherwise he could simply ride off into some forest and never be seen again. Will discarded the armor he wore and kept only the tunic and pants. Figuring it would be pretty obvious, he also turned his tunic inside out to hide the Isen Prison guard symbol at its center. He kept his dagger, knowing of its utility. Boys having such a weapon wasn't uncommon.

Will descended onto a sloping ridge. He looked across the land to the south as the sun's rays cast light over it. Will stood there watching in awe at the lands he was so unfamiliar with. Nestled against the foothills was Blueshade, the last place of civilization before the ascent up Isen's Path. Will had passed the village when being transported to prison. He'd circle around it.

Freedom. It had long been a foreign word to him and now that he had it, he didn't know what to do with it. Being un-bound by shackles, bars, and guards frightened him. This was the first time in six years he'd travelled this far. At times he couldn't feel his legs. Freedom was a feeling he no longer understood.

Even though he knew there would be no home for him in Gurmanis, he had still escaped. Fleeing the grip of his prime tormentor had driven him thus far. Yes, that was worth it. The thought of what the warden would do to him made him clutch the reigns of his horse and tremble. He begged to himself not to be recaptured.

Will crossed the open hilly landscape. Stony soil supported short green grass which swayed lazily under the blue sky. The wide-open expanse was covered with boulder sized glacial erratics, distant windmills, and a castle atop a distant hill. It unnerved Will. He could be seen for hundreds of meters in any direction but luckily, he had not encountered any other guards.

In a moment of realization he registered the green of the grass and the fragrance of fresh air. He had never seen or smelt such things in a long time. It was an overload of distant chirps, the sound of an occasional breeze, and if he looked too long, green flooded his eyes.

As he rode, the sparsely green land grew brown and then black. Fresh, sweet air gave way to the choking bitterness of soot. Will travelled over a large area of blackened crop fields all hugging a system of streams in the distance. His horse's hooves sank into a thin layer of ash. Small fires crackled in the distance discharging pillows of smoke into the sky. Someone had burned everything in sight, but for what purpose?

Will steered his horse to a stream, dismounted, and crouched to take a drink. His horse did the same. He coughed up some of the water and spit out grains of ash. His stomach growled; he'd been travelling for at least two days since Blueshade with nothing to eat or drink in that time. Nothing green and edible had been left. He sighed, remounted, and travelled on.

As the hours passed, Will wondered why he had not seen any more Isen Prison guards. Surely, they dealt with the Saomardrim by now and hadn't given up. Will knew the warden was the last person to give up when slighted. The burned carcass of a village came into view. He risked getting close, doubting people would still be there.

Will rode unsteadily into the village, past blackened smoking houses. His horse huffed, turning abruptly and Will realised the ground was littered with burned corpses, warped and smoking. Though the sight gave him pause, he pushed on. At the central crossroads a half-standing well sat in between several husks of houses. Will tied his horse to a post and wandered from house to house, looking for food while he navigated around corpses of men, women, and children. He dusted away the floors looking for a cellar that might have survived the fire finding only one house whose cellar contained scraps of pickled vegetables. A single small jar remained, the rest had been looted and at the back of the cellar lay the mangled corpses of a small family. A shiver rushed up Will's spine, images of Isen Prison's torturers came to mind. Will rushed outside with the jar, eating what he could before moving on from this horrid place.

Two more days passed. In that time Will had avoided two groups of soldiers, not from Isen Prison, but dangerous to him nonetheless. One group wore foreign armor and carried oddly shaped bows and curved swords. He had long left the stretch of burned land and his surroundings grew greener as he moved south through a valley flanked by steep mountains. One night he stared at the stars, mesmerized, blurring and giving him a migraine if he looked too long.

The sun began to set. Will stopped at a squat farmhouse. Peels of white daub hung from its walls, rotten joists lined the frame, and the thatched roof was pock-marked with holes. A large pile of refuge leaned against one side of the house. The garden out front, maybe once a humble array of colour, was now neglected and overgrown, coloured a dying green.

To his surprise the barn doors were unlocked. Will tied his horse nearby, out of sight, then crept into the barn and threw himself on the hay that lined the back floor and wall. *Just some time's rest; no one will mind.* He drifted to sleep.

The sounds of an opening door woke Will the next morning. He hobbled to the barn entrance and rubbed his eyes. Through the twilight, candlelight flickered from inside the farmhouse and a woman walked within. Will held his breath and crept to his horse, mounting it and moving onwards.

Will arrived at the outskirts of Halsburg a few days after. As he rode past a windmill along a stone fenced road and towards the buildings outside town, people buzzed by him, moving this way and that. Carts, carriages, and horses lumbered by in front of him. Above the busy scene stood the towering stone walls of Halsburg. Large vertical green banners displaying a white castle hung from the walls. He neared the town center and the bustle caused his rouncey to huff in annoyance. The sun drifted ever lower in the sky.

He stopped before entering the gathering crowds and gripped the reins of his horse, a cold sweat forming on his brow. There were dozens of people and so little space between them. Will fought his growing discomfort. He shouldn't be scared of this, but he was. Confined for so long with a few lifeless prisoners had made him adverse to such a larger, freer gathering of people.

Will pushed forwards. As he entered the crowd a few people looked up at him, or were they glaring? Will tensed. They were judging him. They knew who he was. He felt as though the bars of a cage were forming around him and he stood in the courtroom he had once been in. They saw him as a wild beast, as a monster. Will's head pounded; this throat dried up, and his vision blurred. His horse made a muffled, distant snort. Unaware of himself, he was sliding off his horse.

"Steady yourself boy, don't want to lose yer horse now?" a man said, his voice louder. A hand pushed on him, straightening Will's body. Will jolted back to the present. The person who helped him had come and gone.

Will urged his horse to go a little faster to a tavern outside the walls. The noise of the crowd kept assailing him, rendering himself dizzy and disoriented. Finally the crowd thinned. He rode under an arch connecting the tavern to another building across the street and looked up at the two-storey structure, observing the stone at its base, the wattle and daub storey above, the overhang between the two, and its tiled peaked roofs. Two children were in its square tower, excitedly looking out over the countryside.

Will tied his horse to a hitching post in the small stable. He looked up at the tavern and questioned his own motivations. If someone recognised him, then— Will's stomach angrily protested his line of thinking and his dry mouth agreed, but then he realised, he had no money. Will hesitated, looking at the water filled horse trough in front of him. He took a few unsure steps forward then leaned over and drank. The brackish, bitter taste assaulted his tongue, threatening to make Will gag, but to his dry mouth this water was paradise.

"Great Manis!" A woman gasped. Will spit out the water and stumbled, falling backwards. His body trembling, he stared at the woman, expecting to be screamed at and beaten, his muscles tightening as if expecting it. The elderly woman's skin stuck to her bones. She laughed, then seeing Will's terror, her smile dropped to a frown. "Hello. That is for the horses, not for you."

"No. I…" Will stammered.

"You don't look to be in good shape. You seem hungry an'… tired. I am Abigail. My husband and I run this here tavern. What's your name?"

"Wi-Will."

"Let's get ya up Will." She extended a hand, smiling. Will hesitated, unsure what danger the gesture hid, but seeing her smile convinced him to take the hand. That smile seemed so distant, like it was meant as something he could trust. A hint of warmth teased him, or maybe that was his pearl which had decided to impart a soothing energy to him. Abigail helped Will off the ground. "You look like you could use a bath. Where're your parents?" Abigail raised an eyebrow.

"I lost my parents."

"What… I am so sorry. D'you have any other family?"

"If I do, I don't know where they are." Will thought about it; if his grandparents, whom he had never met, were still alive, he could only imagine what they would think of him. They would assume he'd killed their children. His own family hated him, like so many others. "They probably wouldn't have me anyway," Will mumbled.

"But they are your family. No one will e'er love you as much as your parents. Surely someone in your family would care for you? Where're you going to then?"

"To the south. I'll find something there."

"Well Will, I'm sure you were just thirsty. Could have come inside though, yer not a horse."

"I'm sorry." Will hung his head. "I have no coin."

"That all?" Abigail scanned Will's face which turned red when his stomach growled.

"Oh my!" Abigail laughed. "Let's do something bout that."

Will looked up at her, unsure. "P-Pardon?"

"You look like once you get a hot meal in yer stomach you'll be in good shape. Then you can work the cost off. Go inside. Talk to Norman, should be behind the bar. He'll get ya something."

Will had no intention of trapping himself in a tavern. He cursed his foolishness; he should have kept going south. But he was starving. Will nodded and entered the tavern. He lowered his face, not knowing if news of an escapee had arrived yet. The thick smell of alcohol mixed with fresh vegetables drifted up Will's nose. A barmaid swerved to avoid a drunken patron trying to grab her dress. She smiled and laughed, giving the man a wink. People were talking and laughing amongst their friends and a group of men played a game with dice in one corner. A bard stood on the other side, playing a lute and singing a song.

Across from Will, a long bar table sat below a set of ascending stairs that led to a balcony overlooking the room. Children tossed a large feather that drifted down past Will as he navigated through people and under chandeliers and flowers hanging from the rafters towards the bar table. Will instinctively took note of the exits and the demeanor of every person in the room. These thoughts helped combat the noise. He sat on a stool and waited. Will tried to bring up a memory of being in such a place with his father. What had his dad said? The elderly bartender, Norman, finished with two men sitting on Will's left then approached.

"A little ale and the special please, sir," Will asked Norman, repeating what his dad said so long ago.

"There're no specials here boy."

"Then can I have… I want…" Will hesitated. Norman raised an eyebrow and tapped his fingers on the bar.

"We got ale, weak stuffs all that's left right now. Are ya trying to get something to eat?"

"Yes." Will nodded, feeling himself go red with embarrassment.

Norman sighed. "For two silver I can get you a small bowl of bean pottage, a slice of bread, an' a slice of ham."

Will nodded then realised he forgot Abigail. "W-Well I—"

"Oh, it's that now is it? I'll tell ya the same thing I tell all blasted vandals like you: no coin means no service. Get out you!"

"Abigail sent me."

"Don't ya bring mi wife into this! I ought to—"

Abigail trudged over, wiping her hands on her apron. "I sent him dear. He was drinking from the horse trough."

"Bothering customers' horses more like! Vandal he is."

"I'm not a vandal," Will muttered.

"Right, I've dealt with your kind 'afore, always stealing food an' drink, looking unsavory out-front and scaring the chickens out-back. Law says I can beat you outta here."

"No! Don't do that Norman. He's just a boy, look at him. He's in bad shape."

"If we let every needy-looking vandal go, we won't make enough for the Aids, Dues, Tithes, nor anything left to eat."

"Business has been tight, but not so bad. Not like the farmers in the area."

"The lord would do better helping his people refurbish their houses and enrich their fields."

"I promised him some food and drink Norman. Help is thin what with a single barmaid so he'll work the cost off." She propped her hands on her hips; her words were final.

"Arrg! Fine." Norman sighed. He retreated to a back room. After some time, he returned and put Will's meal in front of him. Abigail stood by her husband, cleaning earthenware. Will started right into his food grateful for a hot and hearty meal after so long. The savory aroma of the pottage warmed his nose and made his mouth water. The thin layer of oil over the ham softened his lips and tingled his tongue. He'd not eaten like this in years, even the bread was soft and fluffy.

"You look thin kid. Have you not eaten in days?" Norman asked.

"I ate but last morning," Will lied, speaking softly, not wanting to start a discussion with the man. Norman examined him.

"You're young aren't ya? Where you headed?"

"South." Will looked at his food already having eaten half of it.

"Of course, the rich and warm south! Hardly anyone left here since people started moving south." Norman grumbled, "Or sent to the front."

"Norman!"

"What! It's true. Remove the scarf boy. It ain't cold in here." Norman looked at Will expectantly.

Will touched the scrap of fabric that passed for a scarf. "I'd prefer to leave it on."

"It's fine Will." Abigail poured him some ale and slid the drink toward him.

"So, Will, where're you from then?" Norman asked.

"The southern farms sir," Will answered.

"Ah! Farmer by trade. No good harvest they'll be this year, not when the king burned the western fields and the Saomardrim burned the eastern fields. We narrowly escaped we did," Norman grunted.

"Don't you worry for the spoil sport there," Abigail teased. "We're alive and the locals still have fields in the north."

"Soils not right in those fields. What you doing so far north?" Norman wiped crumbs off the hairs on his chin.

"It's… complicated."

"Is it?" Norman asked with force.

"Don't interrogate Will!" Abigail came to Will's rescue.

"Just want to know bout the scrounging stranger you invited to our tavern."

"I am sure if he doesn't want to talk bout it then it's best not to ask. Its good to have someone to fuss o'er since our daughters were married and our son was conscripted into the army."

Will blushed. These were kind-hearted people and Will wanted to believe that. So was the warden, something in the back of his mind told him. No, Will shivered.

"It's been hard since the taxes were raised again." Abigail sighed. "Especially the Aids, some benefit for the war or something. We're all nervous."

"Not right it is." Norman pounded the bar table. "Now prices in town has gone up, rationing doubled. Ain't enough to go around for the kingdom, all being sent to the army. Harder and harder it is to source food n' drink for the tavern."

"They want to conscript Norman now too." She frowned.

"And if they did, I would give those demon worshiping Saomardrim a right beating I would! I'd run each one through the chest!" Norman tried to make his older self seem stronger and more muscular.

"Such ill talk is not good."

"Oh, I know you have a weak spot for em."

"They look like you an' I." Abigail sighed and shook her head.

"But they got evil inside."

"True they don't worship Manis and so they are doomed to be disfavoured and misled. But to purge evil we ought to talk it out of them. I don't like all this blood." Abigail shuddered. "I'm afeard every day I'll get a letter telling us our son's been killed or worse, I'll get naught a thing." Abigail clasped her husband's arm. "They say that a certain Lord Richrit led a battalion on a forced march into enemy land. He accomplished naught."

"He wasn't in that battalion."

"I keep telling myself that." Abigail stepped back to compose herself.

"Some dodge the draft if they're a member of the Fighters Guild. It's worldwide, got no stake in this war." Norman let loose a frown. "Halsburg's next I reckon. It's been attacked crusade after crusade."

"We can do naught but hope."

"Hope? Or you could join—" Norman leaned close to Will and whispered, "She came out from the west. She and her men routed the local lord's forces. Lorna, Underworld's Angel of Retribution. Fitting name ain't it?"

"Shoosh!" Abigail slapped Norman's arm. "We're proper folk, not rebels." She turned to Will. "I apologise for this talk Will. We'll give you a moment to yourself." Abigail and Norman migrated further down the bar, leaving Will with his meal. He leaned over his food and took a drink of ale. The bard started another song, one with an upbeat rhyme and a lively rhythm, strumming her lute. People tapped their feet and clapped to it, but Will tried to drown out the noise, not able to enjoy the atmosphere. A faint memory of festivals in his village came to mind. With Saul they'd even questioned the bards, awed by their talent. He longed to feel such joy again. When the cheering and applause let the bard bow, the sounds returned to a simmer.

The tavern door burst open and four soldiers entered bearing the Isen Prison coat-of-arms on their uniforms.

"Bartender! Rum an' whatever's freshest for me and my friends here." They commandeered a table and sat by the door.

"Of course, sirs, coming right away." Norman answered over the noise. Will froze, now he couldn't leave. There was no other exit and if he stayed more guards might come and he would be trapped. The guards were loud enough to hear from where Will sat.

"We'd have caught him if we'd passed through the Saomardrim ravaged lands and Hynlle you know," a guard spoke.

"You questioning my leadership, eh?" the leader pointed at his junior.

"No sir, it's just that we'd have him. 'Afore that farmer an' his wife told us they figured someone had slept in their barn…"

"I'll cut out your tongue if you continue! I lead us and I have a feeling we'll catch-up to him erelong."

"Yes, sorry sir."

Will pushed the food he hadn't finished aside and took a drink of ale. If he couldn't leave then he had to take Abigail's offer. Will signaled to her.

"Finished, Will?" she asked once she strolled over. Her lips curled into a frown and Will realised he was letting his fear show. "Something the matter?"

"Y-Yes. I'll help now." Will tried to smile.

"Splendid! Why don't you come out back?" Abigail led him behind the bar towards the kitchen. Will looked down, not daring to glance back towards the Isen Prison guards. Norman passed them with a tray of food.

"Huh, didn't run off with a free meal." Norman huffed.

"Far from a vandal," Abigail teased.

"Well get him back there quick. These guard types seem to be full of em selves."

Will followed Abigail into the kitchen, a small space with a hearth on one end, long counter tops along the walls, and hanging herbs and cooking ware. A table stood in the center of the space. Will spotted a back door on the far side. That was how he could leave. Norman hobbled in.

"Shite guards. Good lord." He cursed. "Hope the kid was taught some cooking then." Norman glared at Will. Will backed away towards the door. These were such kind people and Will *could* imagine the torture the warden would inflict on them if they were caught with him. Also, the longer he stayed the greater the chance the guards would realise he was here.

"I am putting you at risk," Will croaked, choking on the last word. "I don't deserve this."

"What nonsense is this?" Abigail furrowed her brow.

"I am sorry, thank-you for yer kindness. I-I can't stay—" Suddenly Norman was on top of the boy. The older man grabbed Will's arms, twisted them behind his back, and slammed Will against the central table with surprising strength. Will shouted as his face hit the table, pain radiating to the back of his head.

"N-No… please." Will groaned. Norman shoved Will's face against the table, his hand in Will's hair, tightly pinning the boy's head in place.

"See what you brought into our house? Some criminal! He's trying to get a free meal he is. I knew it!"

"Stop Norman!" Abigail stood, horrified at her husband's sudden action.

"Boy's some thief or fighter he is. Delinquent. We here are a good n' honest family. Kid you ain't leaving without paying."

"This… this is a misunderstanding."

"Listen here Abi. Them guards were going on about some escapee, they were. A boy. Told me he came this way."

"Oh my God." Abigail gasped, looking with fearful eyes at Will. Norman pulled Will's scarf down. The number **271** stared up at him.

"Prisoner tattoo! He's the fugitive." Norman removed his hand from the back of Will's head. "What is it boy? What d'you do?"

"Let me go." Will groaned, he struggled to get out of Norman's hold.

"Answer the question then!"

"I-I'll ask… bring the guards." Abigail trembled.

"Yes! Get em back here."

"It's not what it seems." Will begged. "I don't want trouble, just let me go!"

"You think to implicate us an' then we'll simply let you walk? Don't you dare suggest we're like you. What is it then? What did ya do boy?" Will struggled. He managed to push back against Norman but the man noticed and shoved him sideways against the table. "Don't you move!" he shouted. Will teared. If Abigail brought the guards he'd be brought back to the warden and his final hours on Erathas would be agonizingly slow. Merely imagining the pain threatened to make Will convulse. Abigail hadn't moved. She stood rigid on the spot.

"I knew you were some sort of vandal when I saw ya! By Manis you should have listened to me Abigail."

Their kindness had been great. Will figured he owed them an explanation but he knew they wouldn't believe the truth.

"Ok!" Will shouted. "I-I am… falsely blamed." Will cried, his heart sank.

"Get those guards Abi!" Still, she didn't move.

"P-Please don't take me back there! Take me anywhere, any prison, just not there… please." Will begged.

"You're going to go right back where ya came from." Norman yanked Will off the table and pulled him straight.

"I… I can't… y-you can't…" Will's mind swirled and his vision blurred. The warden's shadow seemed to be standing in front of him. It laughed. Will's eyes widened and his stomach sank. "I can't…" Will tossed himself backwards, pushing Norman back and breaking free. The sudden action overcame the old man and he staggered. Will turned and raised his hands. "Let me go," he dropped his hands to his side, "or kill me." Will started to back away. Norman lunged. Will countered, catching the man's arms and shoving. The old man flew backwards and fell against the wall with a thud. Abigail screamed. She drew a nearby knife, trembling and crying, and pointed it at Will, moving to her dazed husband.

"I-I didn't mean to…" Will froze, unable to process what was happening. Norman touched the back of his head. Blood stuck to the fingers he pulled back. Will backed away and fled from the tavern.

Will stepped out into the twilight, light headed. He tried to steady himself and spot his horse.

"There!" Abigail cried behind him. She stood with the Isen Prison guards who rushed forwards.

"You there! Stop in the name of the king!" It was the leader of the soldiers. Will raced towards his horse. His heart dropped when he saw a guard standing there attending to the horses.

"I got him sir!" the man shouted. He stood between Will and his horse. Will skidded to a stop trying to keep his balance. Their eyes locked, like a predator preparing to lunge at his prey. "You surrender peacefully, you hear? Though the warden will kill ya anyway. Slowly, till you beg. Then he'll kill you even slower." The guard lunged, drawing his sword as he did. The blade tore Will's side open and threw him to the dirt covered ground, he screamed and shook, his attacker's blade pointed at his chest.

"Move this thing aside now!" the leader roared, he and his men were stuck behind two oversized carriages. Will's mind raged. He couldn't go back and let the warden slowly rip him apart. He crawled back. The guard, confident Will couldn't do anything more, opened up.

Like a flash of light, Will spun around and launched himself upwards. He let dirt fly from his hands towards the guard. The guard shielded his eyes too late, dropped his sword, and staggered back. Will took the initiative. He scrambled forwards, picked up the guard's sword and swung it at the weaponless man. The blade caught on a gap in his armor and lodged itself in his side. Will pulled it free, allowing blood to splatter.

Shock filled Will but the shouts of the other guards broke him from his trance. Will mounted his horse and galloped past the advancing guards, forcing them to dive to the sides. Will had the advantage, riding faster into the growing dark.

Chapter Seven

HIS BREATH VISIBLE and his eyes heavy, Will rode into the Village of King's Bridge at night. After hitching his horse near the village entrance, he staggered down the stone stairs along the Hertos River and crouched to clean his face. Will sat on the steps and stared at his reflection in the water before turning to gaze across the river. The other side was obscured by fog.

The memories of every person he'd had to hurt to get away and stay away from Isen Prison lingered in his mind. He'd wounded guards; he'd wounded Norman. Will stared at his hands seeing blood on them under the light of the moon.

The rays of the sun rising over the tiled and thatched peaked roofs of the village buildings warmed Will the next morning but what woke him was the click of locks, slamming of metal doors, the feel of jagged stone aggravating his sore skin, and the shouting of guards. Will trembled on the stairs, panicking. Someone shouted his number, hatred thick in his voice.

But then the sun tickled his cheek and he jerked his eyes open. His panic dissolved. He staggered but managed to stand, stumbled on the steps, and looked across the central crossroads of King's Bridge Village.

Dozens of people moved through making the small village resemble a bustling city. Merchants, soldiers, craftsmen, farmers, and citizens of all types strolled through. Many beggars, orphans, infirm men and women, were mixed within the crowds. They all walked about a central square flanked by blocky buildings.

Scaffolds hugged almost every building in sight. Some buildings were half destroyed and rubble lay at their bases while tarps stretched over their roofs. It seemed the village had been devastated recently but was on the mend. Indeed, Will could see many rural peasants and serfs flooding into King's Bridge Village bringing with them little of worth other than crying babies and makeshift packs of meager possessions on their backs. '*Saomardrim raid*', he overheard someone say. '*Came as fast as a gust of sure wind an' enslaved those not killed or escaped. The lands were left devastated, blackened with ash and soot.*'

Carts and carriages of all sizes rolled across the roads and through the central square. Small simple wooden carts, belonging to more fortunate laborers and farmers, rumbled down the paths. Towering around them were larger, boxlike, domed and peaked roofed craftsman and merchant carriages, some of their products hanging off their sides. Dwarfing them all were massive oversized carriages, some with an additional level of height, pulled by unusually robust horses. Some resembled miniature homes.

Will did not stay. He walked along the edges of the crowd, unintentionally keeping a building to one side so he could see as much as possible. He avoided soldiers and constables, not only because of a fear they'd recognize him, but also for a general fear *of* them.

Will approached the bridge, which connected both sides of the river. Checkpoints, towers, and platforms stood at various points of the bridge to render it as a border fort and a taxing point for ships and pedestrians. A churning watermill hugged one side. Last night's fog had faded and revealed the land on the other side where another village sat, its style similar to the peaked roofs of King's Bridge Village, but with something foreign. Some of the houses were roofed in domes. A domed structure flanked by a tower, both emerging from a square base, stood taller than the other buildings, like a chapel. This Saomarhad village was also recently damaged.

No one would hunt him in Saomarhad, but with what he had been learning about this war between the two states it would probably be best not to go there. He was their enemy which was equally as bad as being a fugitive. Saomardrim corsairs had attacked Isen Prison, seeking him and the others as slaves, likely also an unpleasant future. Besides he could never blend in effectively amidst a culture he did not know or understand.

To the bridge's left, on a rocky outcrop jutting out of the middle of the river, stood a small castle matching the design of the village buildings and to the bridge's right, on another piece of land, stood another castle similar in design to the Saomarhad village. The majority was in a state of decay.

A man wearing the simple brown alb of a Priest of Manis stood atop a raised platform preparing to speak to a gathering crowd. Two stoic soldiers stood at his flanks wearing white surcoats over mail, and plate over their limbs. Their surcoats bore the symbol of Manis, yellow on their clothes, a flowering sun. Behind it was a simple red T-shaped cross.

Will remembered the symbol from when his village lord, Lord Jerold, had permitted some families to undertake a pilgrimage to the Grand Cathedral of Manis. These soldiers were templars, the same order that had protected and guided his family on the journey.

The priest's voice rung with zeal, "You ask, I hear you, what is the heathen land of Saomarhad like? Hear me now for I have seen these lands and they are repulsive! Know that Saomarhad is inhabited by demons of all sorts. Giant gold hoarding ants live in its mountain caves, the trees of its forests grow toxic meat, and its people practice the dark arts of magic to turn humans into dwarves and pygmies! You have heard of the sand seas deep within but do not think them places of God. Demons roam them. Huge sand serpents and giant scorpions are at the beck and call of evil magi! Saomarhad is no place for the faithful, tis a land of death!" The crowd mumbled amongst themselves. People looked at each other and back at the priest in disgust. Will took in what the priest said; the image of giant ants and snakes scared him. Against his better judgement, he stayed to hear out the man.

"Repulsive! Repulsive indeed. We hear you!" a man shouted.

"The people are far worse I tell you! Hear now the truth of their kind. Saomardrim are pagan idolaters for they follow not the words of our lord Manis or those of the great Father, no, they follow their false god Alhurah! They create idols of the false god and store them in their mosques where they revere these pagan images! They worship fire! Alhurah was no god, no Wise Lord; he was a demon in disguise. He was a power-hungry ruler, a trickster. He led the Saomardrim not to salvation but to Kalshaimar!"

"He is Kalshaimar incarnate!" a woman shouted. Will frowned. Was Manis any better than this Alhurah? Wasn't it Manis who'd abandoned him in Isen Prison when he was naught more than ten?

"That may be right I tell you! Know the sultan is no better for he takes after the demon Alhurah as well. The sultan is a despotic ruler, autocratic, cruel, and repressive. His whim is unrestrained. Know a dear friend, who was forced to live under his rule before he escaped back into the graces of God, told me that all in the sultanate are his servants. There is no freedom!" The crowd cheered again. Freedom? Will remembered his life on the lands of Lord Jerold. Was that freedom? He and his family could not leave their lord for fear he'd recapture them. Their jobs were to serve him, they couldn't decide not to, not unless they wanted to bear retaliation.

"Manis teaches morality and we practice this by proper etiquette, faith, and structure. I tell you that there is none of this in the lands of the heathens! There is a culture of lasciviousness and sexual immorality there. Hear me when I say I have witnessed polygamous families, huge palace harems, the very way they carry themselves is immoral!" The crowd booed and jeered. Will wondered if this priest had actually been to Saomarhad. They were at war, weren't they? This man did not seem like a warrior so how could he have survived? Then again, his soldiers seemed capable.

"What do we do priest? How do we please Manis an' save our country from these infidels?" a man asked.

"I know some Saomardrim an' they do not speak about their kinsmen as you do!" a woman argued.

"Lies! Lies and doubt are the weapons of the Saomardrim!" the priest began. "They sow the seeds of confusion so that we falter in our defense against them. They have no notion of proper war. They do not follow the peace nor the truce of God so they do not refrain from attacking holy men and women, the unarmed, children and holy property nor do they refrain from warring on holy days and restricted times. They do not care for our faith. Do you not see that they mean to destroy all of us!" He gestured to the border castle ruins. "We must defend our faith and our very lives! Manis punishes our sinful ways and our doubt in his supremacy by sending these infidels to kill us. That is your proof of my words. Listen not to the infidels!"

"The king is right! The king fights them!" a woman shouted.

"The king cares naught for his people. He is a tyrant!" a man countered.

The priest, undeterred, continued. "The king is graced by God! And through him God works to protect us. Take heart for God's hands will guide us to victory and he will watch o'er the faithful. Fear not for he is on our side not the Saomardrim's. We must do all we can to help the king. For those capable take up the flowering sun of Manis and fight alongside your kinsmen against the infidels. For others go and tend to your fields and your forges. Supply our armies with the food and the tools necessary to win!" Upon the finish of the zealous speech, the crowd's cheers erupted to a new level. As the priest stepped down many peasants strode up to him and thanked him. A handful accepted a flowering sun symbol from him. A handful more left the crowd looking discouraged, some storming away. Will looked towards the Hertos River and the Saomarhad side. A new fear enveloped him. The Saomardrim must be really evil. To think he had even considered going to their side.

⚍

Stretching before Will was the dense green forest known as the Roywood, the only place Will thought may be safe. His father had taught him survival and hunting but how long would that last him? Soldiers, bounty hunters, brigands, and wildlife were some things of concern. The Roywood had plenty of these dangers. So dense were some of its trees that no human had ever managed to explore the deepest parts of the forest where some say only dead trees, bramble, thorns and dark magic existed. In forgotten crags and dense old growths of the world goblins roamed. Worse, were the tales of tall bipedal rats, rataven, who feasted on naughty children. None of these did Will want to see.

He let his horse free, knowing he could not support it in the forest even if the animal wanted to stay with him. Will didn't know how far he should walk so he followed a small winding stream, thinking it was a good idea to stay close to drinkable water. He found a small clearing dotted by colorful flowers, mushrooms hugged the edges of trees, and leaf debris floated with the wind. At one end, lonely ruins stood, grass creeping up its lower sides and flanked by two withered birch trees all bathed in rays of sunlight. The architecture resembled nothing in Gurmanis. Its stone was greying and stained, and overgrowth covered it, winding within and out. A delicate yet robust structure, its stonework was artistically placed, with arches and accents as if it were tree branches, and small half-destroyed domes.

As Will neared the ruins, his pearl heated up, pulsing, slowly lighting and diming. Confused, he thought naught of it and forced the rusted ruins door in. A swarm of blue, glowing, and translucent butterflies rushed out and fluttered around him. Will almost fell back, but he steadied himself as the creatures landed on his limbs, his head, and his shoulders. Some hovered around him still, all acting as if attracted to him. Then they flew around the ruins, some starting to fade; others hurried into the trees as if on some vital quest to relay an urgent message.

Will had never seen such bizarre creatures, but they seemed harmless. Undeterred, he entered into a small, dark, damp room which held only cobwebs and dust. He frowned; this was just another type of prison. He quivered from memories the place triggered.

He set right to work crafting a crude stone spear and collecting food and water, thankful he'd kept his dagger which made all this work easier. He made a fire in the night to keep warm. This clearing became his camp.

Will knew he had to be alone. If it was like this then it was what Manis wanted. Living just to survive, not a single other purpose. As he spent his days in the forest, he built up strength through constant upkeep of his camp, foraging, and hunting small animals.

He took to fishing after, of all things, stalking and watching a bear to learn how to and where to best capture fish. He was moving downstream to return to camp with a few small fish when he saw a drenched bird, a lanner falcon, flailing wildly in the shallow water. It was a young bird without much meat on it, but it would make for a single meal. Will approached and the bird, entangled in roots and muck, made a shrill chattering sound. It locked eyes with Will. He sighed, poor bird. Will waded in and carried the falcon onto dry land without difficulty. Leaving it with his smallest fish and assuming it would dry off and recover.

A few days later, Will was about to go looking for food again when a shrill screech made him look up. The same lanner falcon that he had saved swooped down to him and dropped a large fish at his feet. It perched on a low tree branch nearby. Amazed, Will stared at the bird. It tilted its head, as if expecting something. Grateful for his luck, Will cooked the fish, but the entire time he spent doing it, the falcon watched him. Day after day the bird returned with more food and soon it started to make its home in the trees nearby. Will didn't understand why it was sticking around or why it didn't fear him. It began to come closer, then ate from his hand and allowed Will to stroke it. Will began to talk to it as if they were friends. It helped him maintain his voice and kept him sane.

A week passed and Will lived on. He sat by his fire, which illuminated the twilight around him. He poked at it with his spear, adjusting the logs within. Why couldn't he return to simpler times? Why couldn't he be treated mercifully or respectably anymore? Norman wouldn't have attacked him. All he wanted was not to be looked at with distain or suspicion. He believed he had the potential to do good with his freedom, but if no one believed in him nor let him try, he was nothing. He wanted to go back, back to a time when he was William Farmer, son of Trent Farmer and Saydie Farmer, when he was loved and cared about.

His pearl grew warm and when Will took it out, it pulsed. He watched its light fight for dominance with the light of his fire. As he lived, memories still came to him, triggered by this object. A glowing blue butterfly flew past his cheek. Will turned and looked towards the ruins that he had made his home. Butterflies swarmed around the ruins, some landing on top. Among them a glowing blue orb formed, like a fire, but it wasn't a fire, it was light.

Will sprang up and hefted his spear in his right hand while keeping his pearl in his left. The glowing orb took a shape. A female faced the ruins, but she wasn't alive. She was a glowing blue-white figure, translucent and slender with long strands of hair and pointed ears. Will cautiously circled around her as she ran a hand over the stonework. Then she stopped, turned, and smiled at Will. She approached causing him to raise his spear and take a few steps back.

"Wh-What are you?" Will asked, filled with awe. She was beautiful. "You're a sylgahon." A female elf straight out of his childhood stories. It surprised him that he recalled the word. She pointed to the pearl in Will's hand.

"It called me back to the home I built for a bairnling, a Child of the Forest. This is a spiritual place blessed by that child's presence. Then humans slaughtered us both."

"I don't understand. I didn't call you here, but the pearl did?" Will looked at his pearl. The sylgahon walked to Will's fire. She sat beside it and offered Will a seat. Cautious, Will neared but did not sit.

"In my time there were such objects held by revered people. I knew not much of it for this spiritual place was my home and I cared not for such matters. But I can share what I know and what I now know."

"You are some sort of spirit." Will eyed the sylgahon carefully, remembering tales of spirits told in his village.

"It seems I am. I never passed on I guess." She frowned. "You can talk to me through that object otherwise the spirits would be silent to you unless you were elven, for we can hear their songs." Revered one? What did that mean? He was hated, not respected. "Such objects, I think, attracts spirits. Treat this forest well and perhaps the spirits will protect you in kind. Look." She pointed to the ruins, the birch trees had bloomed with leaves of soft glowing white. Similar trees around the clearing had done the same. "It called me here, so now I may up-keep this place once more. Gurmanis, as you call it now, is a land striped of its magic and spirits. One day, perhaps both can thrive once more. Curious, would you enable this rebirth?"

Will's falcon screeched a warning call from above. A wolf's haunting howl shook the leaves of the trees and a violent gust of wind extinguished Will's fire. Will stowed his pearl, his senses on full alert, and scanned the tree line. The sylgahon faded. Will's heart hammered away but he held firm to the spear. His pearl burned.

"Will the power of your object into your weapon," the spirit's voice spoke. Will imagined the red light of his pearl engulfing his spear and to his surprise, his pearl did just that.

A low growl drew Will's attention down in front of him. A grey-black and white wolf bared his teeth at him. Will lowered his spear at it. The wolf stalked closer, the desire for blood gleaming in its eyes. Will moved to his right and backed away while the wolf jumped at him, mouth wide. Will thrust his spear forward and hit the wolf on its underside. The impact threw the wolf aside. It cried out and landed, but turned and growled again, then it whimpered and struggled to remain standing. Its underside burnt, a ghostly red mist rising from its wound.

Will readied himself for another lunge but he stopped. The trees rustled around him. An arrow whizzed past Will's hand, drawing blood and making him drop his spear. The wolf advanced to half a meter close, despite its burn, and again bared its teeth. Will raised his hands, involuntarily, and stared fearfully at the wolf. Now seeing his prey was helpless the wolf prepared to lunge. A whistle echoed through the camp.

"Vuko! Down boy!" a hooded man ordered as he walked into the camp clearing. The wolf backed away, still watching Will. The man tossed his green-blue cape around him and sat beside the fire. He put his bow down then flicked dirt off his light breastplate. He warmed his hands over the embers of the fire. Will looked on, not sure what was happening, noticing the arrows in a pouch strung over his back, the falchion sword, dagger and hatchet on his belt, and the pistol on the other side.

"Nice place ya have here." The man motioned to the ruins. "High Elven Empire, thousands of years old, the high elves are long lived an' they make things to last." The man pulled away his hood and examined Will. He turned back to the embers and took out a flint and tinder from his belt pouch to start the fire anew, taking a moment to brush a hand over the thick line of black hair rising between his shaved sides. A small beard and mustache defined his face and across his nose, a scar supported his weathered appearance. "Boy are you worth a lot but ya don't look it. Some advice, make it harder for trackers to find you. Staying close to water is far from original."

"Y-You're… a bounty hunter," Will said through a cough, finding his voice.

"Ostobaság! Comes with a lot of perceived dishonor. I am just a man making honest money. When it comes to finding criminals like you, isn't that a service to the kingdom?" The bounty hunter grunted. "So much praise I e'er got."

"Who are you?"

"Ugrin Vadász, once a King's Ranger and now a mere tracker of filth." The man stood and kicked the dirt at his feet into the fire, diming it. Will tried to move but Vuko barked at him, threatening to advance.

Will froze. "What now?"

"Now? Now I will take you back up north, that's where they want you." Ugrin huffed. As he walked between Vuko and Will, the wolf backed away to give his master space. "Hate sending off someone so young to die, they'll most likely kill ya, but I know what you have done so I don't think anyone's losing anything here. Except you and your head." Ugrin laughed. Will glared at him as he approached. Will's hand had been discreetly at his side, his dagger hidden behind the curve of his right leg.

"I didn't kill anyone. I didn't kill my parents," Will repeated for the nth time; he knew not how many people he had told this to.

"Right, right," Ugrin dismissed. When the bounty hunter got close enough, Will calmed his tense body. He hoped he didn't get himself killed if he missed the blow.

A gust of blue rushed from behind and the sylgahon took form in front of Ugrin. Vuko whimpered, the animal's burn flaring. Ugrin's eyes widened under the sylgahon's glow and he fell back. Will gasped.

"Leave this place!" the spirit sylgahon demanded. "This is a holy place, your fight defiles it." It didn't seem like Ugrin had heard her.

Ugrin drew his falchion. His face hardened. "Begone spirit! This is a blessed blade!"

"Run," the spirit said to Will. "Do not return, and thank-you for bringing me home." The stream of red on his spear faded. Will didn't understand any of this, but as the spirit and Ugrin began to fight, he didn't stay to think. He ran, as fast as he could. After that night he never stayed in one place for long.

<hr>

Will always moved south, unaware of the direction at the time. He made countless shelters but none were ever home for long. It had been nearly a month since he escaped from Ugrin. Will shivered at the memory, how he empowered his weapon and the ghostly form of the sylgahon. He had tried many times since to will the magic of his pearl into his spear, but to no avail.

To keep himself from boredom, he kept a schedule in mind that involved gathering, hunting and building. Long nights and boring days felt faintly familiar to prison. On such nights and days he battled to keep himself from going mad. He'd talk to his falcon. He had already told it his entire life story and everything that made him hurt inside. Will wondered what it thought, if anything, at the times he cried in front of it.

Will found himself within the territory of the forest town of Burhbarrow. He continued to keep away from roads and trails. In the territory of

Burhbarrow, there were plenty. Many times, he stumbled onto any number of old dirt trails and one time he narrowly missed passing peasants.

Months passed, his birthday as well. The year came to a close. The forest taught him survival and strength.

Will crept along the edge of the forest road hidden by the thick underbrush at the base of the large hardwoods around him. Will's stomach let out a loud grumble. He clutched it and cursed; silencing it was beyond his control. Warmth radiated from the pouch at his waist. His pearl beamed; it had been doing so since he woke and Will didn't know why. He halted and crouched behind a broad bush, shifting his spear. Ahead, dragonflies skimmed the surface of a pond at the base of several large trees, leaving ripples radiating from their impact, reflecting sunlight. Moss, leaves, and other debris coated rocks and wood in the pond or floated on its surface. A mist hovered above the water shimmering in the sun's rays. Between a growing broad-leafed plant and a green mossy rock, half in the water stood some sort of animal.

No larger than a fox, it seemed to Will to be drinking. That was no problem; it would be distracted. Will crept towards it, stepping lightly across the underbrush. He was a meter away when he realised the creature didn't have any fur. The creature stirred and it slid around, spikes lifting off its scaly backside and its long reptilian tail sliding out of the water. A long sharp stinger trailed at the end of the tail. Its face came into view, frog-like with yellow eyes and long thin lips carved across a broad face. Its underside was equally as broad, lighter than its predominantly brown-green dorsal side. Bat wings lifted out of the water and it stretched them to their full length. The creature seemed to have gained size, larger than Will had thought, at about half his own size.

The creature snarled, opening its mouth to reveal yellow sharp jagged teeth and a long-forked tongue. Will froze, his insides hardened. He'd never seen anything like this before. He hefted his spear and stumbled a few steps back. The creature shrieked, a wailing vicious cry. With great speed it leaped from the water towards Will. Will dove to the side before the creature's snapping maw could catch him. It landed on the ground and slithered around, shrieking again. It leaped. Will thrust at it, hitting its side and deflecting its maw. The creature recovered, barely hurt. It blinked its eyes, snarling, ready to leap again.

Will ran, his heart racing as he dashed past trees and over hidden roots. There was no way he was going to kill that thing. The creature shrieked behind him and he turned back to see it gliding like an arrow towards him. Will's falcon swooped out from the sky and tackled the creature in midair, then swooped back up. Will turned and stumbled forward, falling through the treeline and rolling onto a hard-packed wide dirt road, right into the heavy hooves of a startled neighing horse.

Chapter Eight

METAL GLINTED FROM the horse's rider and a man's voice commanded the horse to calm. Will scrambled to his feet and took a few steps away.

A mounted knight, his horse carrying saddlebags of supplies, stood before him blocking the road. The brown palfrey he rode neighed angrily then huffed. The knight froze and paled, staring at Will through wide eyes. Will held his spear out, instinctively angled at the stranger.

"So, this is what passes for a highwayman these days? A ragged boy with a stick?" The knight let out a mocking laugh. "Am I being robbed?" He stroked his pointed goatee, his straight mid-length brown hair catching in the wind.

Will did seem wild with his scruffy hair and dirt-covered body.

"I-I'm stealing… n—" Will choked on the last word. He looked at the forest line, not hearing the shrieks of the creature he had faced. But it could still be there, between him and his camp.

"Are you daft? I am a knight, trained to kill, so you would be very unwise to threaten me."

No! He wasn't trying to steal from this man. But Will noticed too late that he had angled his spear closer to the stranger.

"You are truly a fool, I will feel bad killing you." The knight dismounted his horse and drew his longsword, standing taller than Will. He moved easily in his complete set of armor including chainmail and padding underneath a surcoat and plate bracers, greaves and pauldrons. A great helm hung off his horse. Light gold and engraved designs decorated his armor but it had seen better days. Regardless of the armor's age Will stared in awe and fear.

The knight laughed, a hearty chuckle that boomed through the forest. His deep voice almost making Will drop his spear.

"Now you see me in full, right? Come now, before we begin, think about what you are doing I am sure you don't want to die. You can't hope to fight me as you are." Will grimaced and gripped his weapon; if he was going to be attacked then he had to defend himself. That creature was still waiting somewhere in the trees and facing a man seemed better than facing whatever that creature was. Will rushed forward, but not towards the threat. He thrust his spear at the knight's palfrey. The animal reared and charged east so fast that Will had to jump back into a tree to avoid it's crushing hooves. The knight frowned.

"Very dishonorable. Alas"—he shrugged— "It seems you will not back down and I will need to teach you a lesson." He spun his longsword in his hand and advanced on Will.

Will attacked, thrusting with his makeshift spear. The knight blocked Will's spear lunge and countered. Will blocked, but shuddered back under the force. Attacks came in endless waves. They parted. Will held his spear with two hands, angled upwards, his feet apart. The knight took a moment to observe. He lowered his longsword, angled it downwards, and rested his off-hand near his thigh. Will lunged. The knight swung upwards. His sword forced the spear away, up and to Will's left. Before Will could react, the knight reached in towards the spear shaft. He grabbed it, forced it downwards and lunged with his sword point angled at Will's neck. He let Will stumble backwards, unharmed, pulling the spear from his hand and tossing it aside. He smiled and paced away.

"Don't get me wrong, I will kill you if I have to but I will regret it, though not by much. It seems a shame to kill you, young outlaw as you are." The knight stabbed at Will, almost a teasing gesture then swung. Will jumped back, swiftly drawing his dagger and knocking the sword aside. He rushed in, close under the knight's sword. The knight gasped, shoving Will's chest before any injury could be inflicted. Will fell, scrambled up and pointed his dagger towards the threat, unsure how to best use it.

"That was a fancy move boy." The knight aimed his longsword at Will's throat then attacked again, his armor creaking.

Much to Will's own surprise he saw the move coming and dodged, his reaction time more than he knew he had. Will thrust his dagger while the knight rightened himself but the blade bounced off mail. The knight turned and swiped too close to Will's neck. Startled, Will stumbled backwards.

"You do know that I am not even trying, right?" The knight toyed with him, chuckling in amusement. Will's face turned red. He charged aggressively and traded simple blows. "I will give it to you that you do have some skill, surprising for being so spent," the knight commented between blows, "Yet there is so much you lack, for example, what will you do if I do this?"

Will made a defensive stance, expecting to receive an attack to his right. It was a feint. The attack came from the left. They froze, the knight's sword centimeters from Will's head. Unexpectedly, the knight shifted, striking the hand that held the dagger and sent it flying to the ground. He flipped his sword as he swung, hitting Will's head with the pommel. Will stumbled back, dazed and ready to collapse. It was over, he'd be killed. The knight grabbed Will's neck and pushed him to the ground. Will whined but gave in to the force.

Sir Robert Gilios sighed and crouched to the boy in front of him. This assault was what he got for desiring to return to the front alone. As Grand Marshal his personal battalion had offered to escort him, but he was uninterested in such pomp and his motivation for such norms had dried up.

"Manis forgive my violation. Forgive me as well boy." Sir Robert's hand hovered over Will's face and he hesitated before turning Will's face forward. Sir Robert felt the boy's warm cheeks, sliding his had over them and against Will's round jawline. His eyebrows were only slightly curved and Sir Robert imagined if the boy smiled he'd look even younger than he must be. The knight saw his own son in this boy. His face was so similar, especially his eyes and stature. Sir Robert's heart had almost stopped when this boy startled him, he'd thought, just maybe, that his son had somehow returned. But now the knight noted the distinctions in this one's face, like his nostrils, mouth, and hair, alas.

Sir Robert pulled away the boy's scarf and traced a scar band around his neck as if something had been clamped around it too long. It led him to a tattoo, **271**.

"A prisoner number. Who are you boy?" Sir Robert pulled back Will's clothes to reveal the Isen prison brand. "You are the one who escaped Isen Prison, aren't you?" Sir Robert had heard tales of an escaped prisoner in these parts. He pulled away more of Will's clothes and found the brand on his chest, faded and stretched as the boy had grown but still visible. Sir Robert brushed his hand over the ▉. "Murder. You are a murderer." Sir Robert spit out bitter taste. He took a pair of shackles from his tunic belt and fastened them on the boy's wrists. Will moaned, waking. He blinked open his eyes and stared at Sir Robert who looked back imagining for a second his own son waking. For a moment the boy looked completely clueless, then his eyes widened as Sir Robert lifted him to his knees.

"Please… don't take me back they will… h-hang me…" Will croaked.

"That is not my concern boy. I am doing my duty to my king."

Will clutched his bound hands together in a fist and looked down. His dark brown hair dropped over his face. "I'm not the person you think I am; I don't want to go back." His frown and pleading eyes cut through Sir Robert's heart. In his career he'd seen many forms of fear in the faces of men, women, and children. This one looked just as genuine.

"You have sinned boy and for that you have been sentenced by the king, you must now bear those consequences. They say you are dangerous, yet all I see is a withering fool."

"I'm innocent! Take me anywhere but Isen Prison, please."

"What is wrong with this particular place?" What was he supposed to know about that place? He returned his attention to the boy. "I am sorry. If you are innocent then God will help you." Of course a criminal would try to avoid responsibility.

The boy kept pleading now dazed and in a panic. Sir Robert plunged his longsword between the chains connecting Will's wrists into the ground, pinning him there.

"Mercy!" Will cried, tears forming in his eyes, he held his fingers out as if reaching for the knight. "Don't take me back I beg you!"

"Calm boy, first you will go to Burhbarrow." The town of his long-time friend Lord Dillion was close, deep in the Roywood. Dillon's people persevered through attacks by bandit gangs and neighboring lords, rebuilding each time. The wall was naught more than ruins now, being reclaimed by the forest. Images of the town's wattle and daub buildings camouflaged in creeping green vines, and flowers in window sills, hanging off buildings, and lining streets coloured Sir Robert's mind.

"B-Burhbarrow…" Will's eyebrows rose and his eyes wavered. Sir Robert turned and searched through his supplies finding a vial of healing tonic. Dillon's castle stood on a small hill, larger and taller than the other buildings.

In higher concentrations the healing tonic could do more than heal. He spread it on a strip of cloth and pushed the cloth over Will's mouth and nose. Will's whined, unable to struggle against Sir Robert's firm grip. Will fell into unconsciousness and Sir Robert pulled out his sword. He looked into the sky perplexed with his fate.

"Great Manis what test is this? Why have you presented to me the boy who escaped so suddenly and at this time? What is it you want from me?" Sir Robert spoke. Lord Dillon will want him too; poor lad was in a lot of trouble but he was standing there determined, such resolve in him. His stance and movements could use work, but there was something the boy could work with in them.

A criminal they say? Dangerous? Violent? Violent was up for debate, the boy did just attack him. And all that about not being guilty. He sounded so broken. Sir Robert pitied the lad. It did not sit straight with the knight to send this boy to his death, to be responsible for another child's death after his son. Then again it was not his fault the boy was to be executed; he had killed. *'We are all killers'.*

After his son and wife had been lost to the plague some summers back, he'd experienced one stress after another. First, the king sent him to re-join his men and then Princess Elizabeth ran away. The girl, in her young age, had always looked up to him. Now the boy who escaped runs into him unexpectedly. Perhaps Manis had ordained this meeting as repentance for him not being there when his wife and son needed him most.

Searching the criminal, Sir Robert unveiled a round red object from his possessions. The knight held it to the light. It had a perfectly round form like glass with mist swirling around inside. The mist swirled slowly at first, then faster, and the object began to heat. It burned and he threw it to the ground shaking his singed hand. What a weird object, the first thought that came to his mind was dark magic but this thin boy didn't seem like one so dependent to such addictive magic. The knight drew a handkerchief from his belt pouch and approached the object. He wrapped the cloth over it and picked it up, but could still feel the heat emanating from it. Concluding it was sufficient enough not to burn him, he stowed the object.

The knight picked up the boy and threw him onto his back, bending forward to support him. Not too surprisingly, the boy was light for his age. A screech from the trees caught his attention. A lanner falcon perched up top, pruning its feathers. Curious, he wondered. Sir Robert carried the boy east to find his horse.

Will woke to a bright light glaring in his eyes. He groaned and tried to get up but his body would not listen. Soreness and constraint wrapped around his mouth and he realised a hard strap of leather had been tightened there, separating his teeth. His wrists, neck, and ankles were bound in shackles connected to the wall. Panic swelled in his chest; he was back in Isen Prison. Smooth stone formed the cell, not rough. On the wall across from his cell was a large green crest, a bear head with crossed swords behind it, it was lined in yellow. Inside the cell Will was laying on his side, on the floor, but there was a raised straw mattress, a stool, a slop bucket, and a bucket of clean water. A small barred window let sunlight and fresh air in. This was not Isen Prison.

Will shifted and pain shot up his limbs and his heavy head lolled to the side. His vision grew blurry and Will blinked to regain focus. The voice of the warden echoed in the back of his mind; words from the nightmare he had. His execution. He'd seen and felt himself be flayed, ripped, burned, and mangled. Blood had filled his eyes and pounded in his ears while his skin had torn open. Will trembled and held back tears and nausea. He'd soon face these tortures. Determined footsteps grew louder to the left of his cell.

"Out of my way!"

"Sir, please! My lord is glad that you've found him, but he insists no one is to see him."

"He ran into me, looking to rob me!" Sir scoffed. "Lord Dillon's chamberlain greeted me. Dillon has not even seen me but he spouts orders regardless. He has changed." A man came to Will's cell. He stood at the barred door, his white cloak swaying; he was a fully armoured knight!

"Open it," he demanded. The guard opened the door and closed it after the knight entered. He stood sturdy and tall over Will, his complexion gleaming and his skin smooth with good nourishment. He stared down at Will.

"Well you are finally awake boy. You have been out for hours and were quite ill, though it wasn't clear what was wrong with you. You have the Lord of Burhbarrow's magisters to thank for your quick recovery." The man detached his sword belt. "I hope you do not mind if I take your stool." The knight pushed aside his white cloak and sat on the stool in the cell. He met Will's eyes. Will looked up at him in wonder noting his straight hair, messy fringe over his forehead, and the middle-sized goatee-like beard on his chin. Wait, he was the knight on the horse!

The knight brought his hand forward causing Will to slide away, shoulders tight. The man placed his hand on Will's forehead and then on his cheek, making Will sweat and tense. The knight withdrew his hand.

"I am glad to see the fever is truly gone. I am Sir Robert Gilios," he started. "I found you robbing me if you remember; brave or insanely foolish to face a knight especially when you have been evading the law for a year."

Will bit his gag. He wasn't robbing the man! Will thought of his falcon and its fight with the creature; he hoped it had survived.

"Will. Yes, I know your name. I know of you, and these quarters will be slightly more comfortable, you see. You are in the town of Burhbarrow. The local lord is a man of caring, whether it be a noble, peasant, or criminal, he always respects life, no one is executed here. Though he insisted on restraining you like this, to appease anyone reporting to the king."

Will observed the knight's surcoat, four red and blue quarters made a check pattern with a golden phoenix over the torso.

"You defeated a guard in Halsburg…,"

Will winced at the memory.

"… and escaping the inescapable is already an achievement. You are brave, challenging me in the forest as you did." Sir Robert sighed and rubbed his goatee. "Lord Dillon will send you back to Isen Prison. You'll be punished, his chamberlain says, in numerous ways; you won't die quick; you won't enjoy your final days. This is a terrible end. *I* want to make good use of you so I offer you this choice: die a criminal or serve your country in this war by becoming my squire. I will give you one hour to decide. Think on this well boy, few get a second chance as the one I am giving you." Sir Robert smiled at Will who could only stare up wide-eyed at the man.

"It really is excessive in the way you are being kept. Even if you managed to escape Isen Prison I doubt you can repeat it here." Sir Robert looked away in thought stroking his beard, and then he turned back at Will and put a hand forward. Will flinched and tried to back away. Sir Robert smiled again. "I am not here to hurt you boy, take the hand and sit up, lying on the ground won't do anything good to you."

Will stared at the knight's hand looking on with uncertainty. He hesitated, but clasped the hand. Sir Robert pulled Will up and Will straightened himself against the back wall. "That strap need not be on, what will you do? Shout the bars away?" As the knight bent forwards Will shuffled back again. The knight smiled and reached for the strap, detaching it at the back. He threw it aside. Will rubbed his sore jaw and looked at the knight.

"Wh-Why are you doing this?" he asked. The knight stood to full height once more and responded in a soothing voice.

"I pity you boy. Murderer you may be, a killer of his own two parents, but how the king's men plan to torture you to death, no one deserves. I find you peculiar, you are not what I expected. I saw when you fought me, potential skill."

Will wasn't convinced.

"I want to help you, Will. Think on my words," Sir Robert said. The knight picked up his things and left, leaving Will in awe of what had happened.

A squire! Any other knight would not give the slightest attention to any boy like him let alone ask him right out to be a squire! He could not be serious. Of all people, a knight, offering him his life. The only nobility Will knew of was the manor lord of his village. He rarely showed himself to the people and only sent his tax collectors. Knights, like the nobility, were the same. They were nothing but villains who basked in their wealth and power not ever caring about the people who fed them.

But what choice did Will have? He did not want to die; he would at least have a chance with the knight. This knight seemed sympathetic, he offered to help him, not hurt him. Everyone wanted to either hurt him or were helping for their own needs, but wait, what about Abigail and her husband? They had helped him selflessly, though they did not know who he was. Maybe that knight had some other motive, but what he was suggesting could be genuine, and in that case this was Will's only hope. Will's head spun with confusion.

No! It was all a trick! Just like the warden's words, how the man had always told him that he was the only one who cared about him. How he said Will needed to stay with him in order to be safe. The warden said that suffering, torture, and working in the mines were how he thanked him. This knight was doing the same. He spoke honeyed words to bring Will to him, then the knight would hurt him, as the warden had, and he would suffer. Images of the warden, Isen Prison, all of it flooded his mind and Will began to wither, shaking and crying and feeling old punishment as if new. An intense yet calming heat came over him, it had not spoken to him in months but Will knew what was coming.

"Do not rebuke those who seek to emulate mercy as the gods do," the powerful voice spoke. Will exhaled and pulled his legs to his chin trying to suppress his tears.

Finally, the hour was up and a guard came to fetch Will. He left the shackles around Will's wrists and ankles, a chain connecting them. The man herded Will from the dungeons to Burhbarrow castle's higher floors. Ladies and lords stared at him as he passed, noting Will's drooping stature and the clanging his chains made. He was led to a large door which the guard pushed him through.

"The prisoner, my lord Gilios," he said.

"Bring him forward." The guard led Will forward and left. Sir Robert observed Will for nearly ten seconds while Will stood there awkwardly, limbs sagging from the pull of his chains.

"Come Will, be seated," Sir Robert said, pointing to a seat by a table that held mid-day meal. Will stumbled, interfered by his shackles, and sat down. Sir Robert sat as well. The room was huge. A large bed sat to Will's left and a fireplace with a sofa and table in front of him. Other doors led to a bathroom and servant entrances.

"Please eat Will, you look hungry."

Will hesitated, wondering if the kindness was a trick. He looked at the food on the table. A feast sat in front of him: vegetables, bacon and leek pottage, fruits of various sorts, cheese, cream and butter, and the whitest bread he had ever seen. All were arranged on a wooden board in an artistic manner with the pottage in bowls.

Will tasted the pottage letting its warm liquid linger in his mouth. The carefully spiced and cooked dish pricked his taste buds the moment it touched his tongue. Sir Robert watched. The knight moved for a jug of yellow juice, startling Will with the movement. He stopped eating and recoiled. Sir Robert smiled as he filled his pewter cup and resumed observing Will. Will hesitated, shyly taking small bites and occasionally looking up at the knight.

"What is your last name Will?"

"I don't ha'e one, everyone used Farmer or Trentson," Will answered through mouthfuls.

"Really? A serf's last name is his profession so you are a farmer's boy, Will Farmer. That is an honest profession. It is from them we are able to eat such food. Trent was your father's name?

"Yes." Will nodded.

"Have you thought about my ultimatum Will?"

Will hesitated. "I have a ch-choice sir?"

"Of course you do."

Will looked at the knight sat across from him waiting for an answer. Will tensed and sweat formed on his face. Was he really being allowed to choose his own fate? It wasn't a trick or a lie.

"You have had time to think on it yes?" Sir Robert prompted. The knight took a sip of his drink. Will looked down at his shackled hands, dizziness overcame him. "Are you alright Will?"

"Y-Yes. My answer is yes. I wish to serve you. I don't want to die." Will looked up and forced the words out trying to sound honest and confident, though confidence felt foreign to him. He'd thought about this. This man was the only person who'd ever shown interest in not hurting him, but Will feared he was false, so Will would be false. Say yes now. Run later. That is, if the knight was actually false. When the knight did not answer right away Will grew nervous.

"So, you value your life, good, we all should," the knight said, calming Will. "There are some who wouldn't care. I have seen many horrible things to prove that. Zealous people moved by conviction or faith to martyr themselves or those fallen to the deepest despair and driven too far. Such things have always made me question Manis' teachings on a variety of subjects. Much recently, Judeicar's Justice, the torture encouraged on criminals by Judeicar and Manis."

"I ha'e no choice. Should I leave you I've nowhere to go. You can protect me from the king's men too," Will said.

"Ha, I doubt, not for long."

"Please, I have no other options. And you've gotten yourself in this now. I want… to… aid you if you'd give me the chance, I want to serve you rather than live as I had. If you'd give me purpose, I would please you. I'm not who everyone says I am. Maybe I could prove that?" Will was half sincere. He did want, so very much, to show everyone in the kingdom he wasn't the monster they thought he was, but his words may also convince the knight. "Please be merciful; please don't send me back to Isen Prison."

"But understand this Will Farmer, should you betray my trust you will not live to tell the tale."

"I don't understand." Will frowned. "You're a knight. I'm a peasant. You're supposed to hate me."

"What!" Sir Robert laughed wholeheartedly, "I don't hate you because you are a peasant. Not all knights are the same Will. Many are like that and many are nobler. Indeed, many are rich and have fighting men while some knights are too poor for proper armor."

"I see, my lord," Will said, but not fully believing it.

"Call me Sir Robert or Master."

"Yes, Master." Will resumed eating, his shackles making a loud clanging noise. Sir Robert lifted Will's pearl holding it by a cloth.

"My pearl, Master…"

"Yes, it is remarkable. What is it?"

"I found it in some tomb the guards threw me into. I swear, I don't know what it is."

"I had the Burhbarrow court mage check it; it is not dark magic like necromancy, witchcraft, or blood magic. He tells me it is probably nothing but a malfunctioning spell crystal containing a weakened old spell. Nothing of concern, in his words." Sir Robert handed the object back to Will and observed how the object did not burn Will's hand. "Guardsman!" Sir Robert called. The man who had brought Will entered and waited for orders.

"Yes, my lord?" he asked.

"Take Will's shackles off for him if you will, the noise disturbs me and I do feel very irregular dining like this," Sir Robert said.

"My lord Dillon ordered me not too sir… if I may speak freely."

"Dillon, who is too busy to see me since I arrived, of course, proceed."

"Sir I respect you greatly. I've heard of your battles and the men and I hope that we'll fight alongside you one day."

"Such words are kind of you guardsman."

"So, I feel I should tell you what Lord Dillon says. Lord Dillon says the boy is not to be trusted sir. He says you're a fool for trusting him. He's worried for your reputation sir, allowing a criminal to squire for you… sir." The guard cringed at his own words. A slight anger filled Sir Robert's face.

"I do not care of what Lord Dillon thinks, I will deal with him and take full responsibility for the boy. What has happened to my friend? Does he spy on my affairs now? Are you to report my conversation to him? It seems gossip is more important to you than your integrity."

"But sir he's a murderer! Killed his own…"

"Release him guardsman," Sir Robert ordered. The guard hesitated then nodded.

"Aye sir." He rushed forward and unlocked the shackles, took them away, and was dismissed by the knight. No one had defended Will before. Nervous warmth tingled his insides, did his master truly care?

"Now I would like to know a little bit about your side of the story, Will. Leave not a detail out."

Will sat quiet, his breath catching in his chest. He could not find the words. The knight smiled. "You can trust me. I want to help you."

Will made himself small, hugging his body as if he was shivering. "I-I…" Will mumbled. The blood drained from his face, a grave cold look, and he looked down and away from the knight. Sir Robert stood, walked over to Will, and crouched to the boy's level. Will backed away on instinct, fearing the worst. Sir Robert slowly extended a hand and gently placed it on one of Will's shoulders. Will looked into the knight's eyes and the knight examined his.

"God knows I can see the misery in you William."

"Wi-William…" Will stuttered.

"I want to understand what happened and I want to help. As your new master that is my duty. I am being genuine."

Will's mind raced. It had been so long since someone had addressed him by his actual name. His mother's voice calling him echoed in the back of his mind. Will tried to discern whether he saw the warden's face or the knight's. It filled him with so much pain, despair, and shame to think about everything he had escaped yet he did want to believe this knight was true. When he was ten-years-old he'd told everyone what had really happened. No one had believed him. What did another attempt matter? Reluctantly, with much hesitation, Will relayed his story.

He told the knight about his farm, friends, and parents. He told him about the murder and the court. And finally, about the prison and the mines, the horrors and Skyla's death. Will struggled through it as injurious memories assaulted him.

With difficulty Will was convinced to show Sir Robert his scarred and gouged skin, all for five seconds before Will pulled back his clothes. The deepest cuts and scars stained his back making grooves across the boy's skin. Sir Robert traced his fingers over them. On the boy's stomach and chest scars criss-crossed, some more faded than others. All of them told the story of a boy growing-up at the right hand of warped desire. Sir Robert thought in silence for a long moment, staring at nothing, and Will feared he'd done the wrong thing.

"I am really only a commander now," Sir Robert spoke. "For political power we will need to look elsewhere. I need to know if he knew since he's been a judge in the past. I should get you a new set of clothes. We will need to talk with Lord Dillon."

Lord Dillon, a large aged man, sat proudly on his throne. White hair flecked his short light brown hair. Sir Robert approached him as men-at-arms eyed Will cautiously. Will wore a new tunic and a scarf to cover his number.

"My friend Dillon. What a pleasure. Finally, I get to see you." Sir Robert made a shallow bow.

"It's Lord Dillon to you!" he howled, his face turning cold. The green of his velvet robe emphasised the coat-of-arms of Burhbarrow embroidered on it. Will wondered how many bears Lord Dillon and his men had killed to clothe the lord. Around the top of the robe at the neck, the arm cuffs, and the leg cuffs were trimmed with fur. Maybe that's why the coat-of-arms of Burhbarrow displayed swords behind a bear. Will smiled at the connection he'd made.

"Dillon there is no need for formalities among friends now is there?"

"You are ruining yourself Robert. This boy is not worthy of your teachings."

"And who is to decide that? Anyone is worthy of knowledge."

"Would you resort to teaching lowlifes? This boy has committed many serious crimes. And have you forgotten about your own duties? You have a war to command!"

"And that is an advantage to having this boy squire for me Dillon. I will have an assistant and someone to watch my back." The knight remained stoic in the face of his furious friend.

"Boys must become pages then squires, it takes years of practice and they must be of noble birth Robert. You know that."

"This boy already has potential skill. It would be a waste to have him killed."

"But why taint your name like this? Why must he be squired to you?" The lord slammed his thick fist down on the arm of his throne.

"Because no one else will take pity on him. There is a great history of suffering in him. It has replaced the evil inside of him."

"I trust your judgment Robert, though you base his skill on guesses, but today you have left me with few options. To elevate a sinner and peasant to squiredom is scandalous at best and deadly at worst. If I let you both go my own worth will be questioned. He should go back to where he belongs."

Will frowned. He wanted to belong, except as far away from Isen Prison as humanly possible.

"You of all people should understand life is valued. Are you blind Dillon?" Sir Robert raised his voice, "He was ten-years-old, ten, and was sent to Isen Prison! Do you know what they did to him in there? He has shown me the scars to prove it. He was tortured, barbarically. How is that acceptable?"

"It is acceptable because he extinguished the lives of his parents! The sinful must pay as if they have entered the gates of the Underworld. It is so they might be shown mercy in the afterlife and to adequately serve justice."

"I have come to doubt such scriptures, my friend. They contradict with Manis' mercy. Why has the world chosen to deal with suffering with suffering ten times worse? Does it make sense? Dillon I still believe he is a good person."

Will warmed at the thought of his master saying that. Lord Dillon huffed at Sir Robert and his eyes swept over Will with judgemental hatred. "Look straight boy!" Lord Dillon snapped. Will raised his face to eye level. He tensed; it was as if Lord Dillon were judging his soul. He observed the lord's wrinkled face, his narrowing eyes, and his thick brown eyebrows. Will blinked. He remembered this face, faintly, but he knew he knew it.

"I was one of the judges at your trial. I remember your case. Back then, for a second, I believed that one so young could not do such a thing. The others wanted you hanged but I thought I could save your pathetic soul. He deserved to be hanged, has he told you Robert, the greatest of his sins? 'Tis a little-known fact; his mother was pregnant with child when he savagely killed her!"

Will froze, his face paled and his eyes wavered. It came back to him, that curse that with it brought pain, but now he felt a kind of impending betrayal. Sir Robert, what would he think, say? Lord Dillon grunted, acting as if Will were a foul creature. Sir Robert took a moment to take this in. Lord Dillon waited for a response. Finally, Sir Robert stepped forward beside Will.

"All of us stand under the watch of God. Will it suffice for me to stand aside and let this boy be destroyed? In Manis' eyes it will not. By God's will I found him and learned of what he has suffered. Manis is merciful even towards the most twisted, so should we be as well."

Will turned his head to face the knight. After that, still? Lord Dillon glared at the knight.

"He admitted to the crime. The courts have his signed confession." Lord Dillon sat back in his chair, dismissing the issue.

Will shivered. The memory of the man who interrogated him entered his mind. Sir Robert wavered. He weighed the new information.

"I will make my own judgement based on the boy's character now, not his past character." Sir Robert scratched his beard and looked Will's way. Will was looking towards the ground, his hair hanging over his face. "I do not believe he deserves to die, not after the kinds of zealots I have encountered in the war. Is it not the duty of a knight to protect the weak and defenceless? Is such a thing void if he who suffers has sinned? When I stand before Manis, I cannot say that I stepped aside because it was inconvenient… no. Had he been a sinner, he is not the same now. Willing to serve, willing to redeem himself, I will permit him that."

Lord Dillon frowned and pinched the bridge of his nose. "You are far too chivalrous, far too pious. Robert I will give you and this boy until tomorrow morning to leave my home, the boy is banished from here forever and if you insist on helping him then you too are banished. Ladies will whisper in the corners of castle halls, calling my worth into question for this."

"Very well Dillon, goodbye old friend," Sir Robert said as firmly as he could.

Lord Dillon turned, "Goodbye friend."

When the pair exited, Will froze at the door. Sir Robert walked forward before realizing Will had stopped and turned back. Will stared at the knight, his heart filled with sadness.

"A-After that, you don't throw m-me away?" Will asked, baffled at the knight's defence of him. Even if he was young the knight should see him like others, a monster.

"Did you want to kill your own family? Your own younger brother or sister? Did you enjoy it?" Sir Robert asked in a firm and serious tone. Tears came from Will's eyes and he stuttered, "No, No! I didn't do any of that! I ne'er would do that! I ne'er would want to! I wanted to be an older brother. I…"

"Did you confess?"

"I… I…"

"Did you?" Sir Robert spoke with force.

"He wouldn't stop asking me the same question, he kept saying I could go home. His face… it was… half of it was melting into a black mist, black veins, yellow eyes, grey skin…"

"Answer the question!"

"Yes, I did! I did and I lied!"

"How can I ever trust you now?"

Will looked at the knight, panicking. This man was his only hope to escape his miserable life. "I was chained to the chair and table… he sucked the life from me and I couldn't cry nor speak. Even breathing was difficult. As if he were clutching my insides, he caused me pain, though he didn't touch me. He warped my memories, feeding me lies. He threw me against my chair, shouted centimeters from my face… he…"

"Impossible."

"Please! You must believe me! I confessed because I wanted him to stop." Things were blurring and spinning for Will. Sir Robert's hands came down on Will's shoulders, Will, still panicking, threw them off.

"They said you were dangerous yet you turned out mannered. They say you are a monster yet you do not appear a demon nor do you have the qualities of one. You are asked questions and you drive everything out of you repeating the same words again and again, and thus you *appear* sincere and sorry. Your scars bear witness to the torture you suffered. Whether you killed or not, you are and have paid for it."

"I remember all of it every day; it's too painful to remember, but I can't stop remembering. That lord brought up the pictures that haunt my dreams. I ne'er wanted what happened, I feel such a loss."

"Will, that is over."

"I know, it all is!"

"No Will, it *is* over. Forget and move on."

"You don't understand!" Will screamed, holding his head, "I can't!" He exhaled, wiping his face and stepped back from Sir Robert. Composing himself he said in a confident tone, "But I will try to move on." Sir Robert looked at the broken boy in front of him with empathy. After a moment he smiled. The knight opened his arms. unsure, Will stood still.

"Come, William," Sir Robert invited. Will hesitated then took a few steps forward and closed the distance. The knight embraced the boy. Sweat broke out across Will's brow and his heart raced. He tried to escape the unfamiliar gesture. Instead, the knight shifted to rub Will's back, and sighed, "I don't know what you were, but why don't we work together and build you into something new."

Will stared over the knight's shoulders wide-eyed. This was a hug. It felt more foreign than familiar but it started to calm him and he wished against all hope he had the strength to move on.

Part Two:
A War Long Waged

Chapter Nine

WILL HAD NEVER seen a city with more canals than roads. Suthenburg was built on islands within a lagoon at the mouth of the Hertos River. An immense palace and cathedral stood out above the rest of the city. Both made use of arches and spires, giving a sense of height and fragility, yet strength and awe. Scaffolding clung to the palace, in places neglected. Clearly the city's wealth had been lessened by war.

Buildings flanking the main street scattered the sun's rays, under whose alternating light and shadow Will rode, following his master. He found himself surrounded by stone, wood, and people. Stone, wattle and daub houses with multiple storeys towered above him, connected at times by clotheslines or bridges and archways. People made way for him and his master by retreating under building overhangs, allowing them a wide berth to travel by, showing respect for the knight.

Will rode on a small brown rouncey and his master on a larger palfrey. As they navigated the streets a shrill bird's call made Sir Robert and Will glance up. A falcon circled close by, and swooped low towards Will. Will gasped and pulled on his horse's reins. The horse reared up in protest, abruptly spinning around. The bird missed him, swooping up again. Sir Robert veered around and laughed. The bird landed on top of a storefront sign ahead of Will and his master. The young lanner falcon tilted its head, made a low chattering noise, and focused on Will, expecting something. He recognised this bird, noticing its distinctive colouring. It was the falcon from the Roywood. He was glad the bird still lived. Sir Robert turned back to examine it as Will rode up beside him.

"It seems to like you." The knight stroked his beard. "It has been following us since the Roywood. Do you know this bird?"

"I saved one in the Roywood. I told you…"

"I remember. It is a lanner falcon, the squire's bird."

"Squire's bird?"

But Sir Robert didn't answer. He shifted on his palfrey and stared at the bird.

"Does it have a name?" Sir Robert broke the silence.

"N-No…I…"

"You should give it a name." Sir Robert smiled. The bird groomed itself as master and apprentice rode forward. Will looked at it as he passed under. The bird eyed him keenly.

"You do what you want when you want, don't you?" Will mumbled.

Will followed Sir Robert into the cathedral upon the knight's insistence. The stone vaulted roof towered above him, coloured windows let in light of red, green, blue, and yellow. Sweeping arches reached across the room with intricate stonework decorating their surface. Small statues depicting religious stories stood at intervals among coloured tapestries. So high was the ceiling that Will wondered if it reached the Overworld. In fact, it made him dizzy, he was not used to such heights, yet he was in awe, humbled at its sense of scale.

Sir Robert had moved to the altar and was on his knees, whispering a prayer. Will stood waiting. He could run now, but where would he go? Besides, Sir Robert had not yet turned out to be false.

Will looked back at the altar and frowned. The flowering sun of Manis was on full display. He remembered his mother and father taking him to church service long ago. His mother had explained how he should pray and to carefully hear the words spoken by the priest giving the sermon. He would never pray again. He would never ask Manis for anything.

Along the road to Suthenburg Sir Robert told Will about everything: politics, history, and even about the plants around them and their healing or nutritious natures. The knight had been unexpectedly enthusiastic about delivering his knowledge to Will. It was like Sir Robert had been revitalized by the confidence brought on by a new purpose and set of goals.

Sir Robert had talked about the war as well. As Will had been in isolation, he had little knowledge of this war, just the bits he'd heard from guards. Will only listened, thinking if he should run or stay. A part of him had slipped into another mindset. He absorbed all the information the knight told him hoping to retain it so he could start to show his diligence to Sir Robert. Will tried to persuade himself, he needed to show the knight he was not only thankful for his mercy and protection, but he was worthy of it. When Sir Robert finished his prayers, he stood and turned to face Will.

"Don't you wish to pray?" the knight asked.

"No, Master," Will answered.

"You ought to pray and give thanks to Manis; it has been a long journey."

"N-No…" Will looked down. In prison he had little reason to pray to any god, half asking Manis why he was punished and half cursing Manis for his situation. Prayer seemed a lot more important back in his childhood on his farm. In prison, where none of his prayers were ever answered, prayer seemed to lose its importance. He didn't believe a caring and merciful god would have let him or anyone else suffer through the horrors he'd faced.

"My master used to say we ought to talk to Manis as both our friend and our mentor. We connect on a personal level as friends yet show him due respect as our master, our shepherd. One should always speak truthfully to him."

"Yes, master." Will looked away, worrying about how the knight would interpret his defiance.

"I see. Perhaps over time you will find the lord again. Come, let's move on."

Will followed his master out. No, he would never reconcile with Manis.

The two rode through the bustling city streets, alongside canals where anything from small rowboats to cargo barges sailed, to the palace. People from all walks of life passed, some walking and others on horses or carriages. As they advanced in and out of small side streets and the main street, Will noticed the number of the impoverished sitting on the curbs: beggars, infirm, orphans. An old woman stumbled up to Will and put her hands out towards him, mumbling. Will looked at her, not understanding what she was saying to him. As he moved, the crowds naturally forced her away.

They rode under a bridge connecting two buildings and out into a small square. Children ran about followed closely by their parents. A large group of them found it fun to cheer while chasing their horses. Their laughter sounded foreign to him. Will tensed. He cursed to himself, keeping his eyes on his master and away from the crowds and children. He could not brush away his discomfort, there were too many people. The children kept pace with them and clung to their horses, little hands grasping at Will's and his master's tunics.

"That's a big sword! It's a good sword?" a young girl asked Sir Robert looking at the knight with wide eyes. The knight laughed.

"It's a fine sword alright but very dangerous and very sharp!" Sir Robert said, causing the girl to gasp.

A boy spoke, "It better be a good sword, did ya kill many Saomardrim with it? Will ya?"

"I hope I do not need to kill many people with it; it would be unfortunate."

"It isn't unfortunate. It's holy!" The child grinned, convinced. Sir Robert frowned.

Master and apprentice neared the palace, riding over two canals and up an ascending street. Sir Robert dismounted to the remaining children who had followed. Dirt was smeared on their shy faces and their clothing hung like rags. When the knight came close, they looked down, not meeting his eyes, each knowing their lowly station. Sir Robert knelt to them and spoke with them. He took some coins and put them in the children's hands closing them with his own. The children barely smiled and when the knight was finished, he remounted.

"What were ya doing, Master?"

"Showing a bit of kindness, Will. Charity is encouraged by Manis. These children have little, they, we, everyone deserves to have a good safe life. Everyone deserves to live in dignity, Will. These children and their families instead live-in squalor due to their poverty driven these days by the war. It saddens me that those children must abandon childhood so that they may survive in a life where they were and are afforded very little. Of course, you now know what kindness and mercy is don't you Will?" Sir Robert smiled. Will looked down, taking the knight's advice to heart.

Palace men-at-arms snapped to attention and waved Sir Robert and Will through the palace gates. In the courtyard they were mobbed by several servants who helped them off their horses and delivered their supplies to the knight's room.

"I will need to speak to the baron of Suthenburg. He is a resolute man when it comes to tradition." Sir Robert glanced at Will. "He may not agree with my decisions but its by his leave all will gather for war."

"Here?" Will asked.

"At Castle Ochsen, the castle owned by the baron. Before you wandered into my path I was coming back from the final preparations for an attack on Al-Motros, in Saomarhad. We will be going to the front in a few days so I will have to coordinate with the baron. I would expect most of the men-at-arms and lesser knights have already mustered at the castle. The higher knights and nobles are coming to this city to attend a farewell feast. Morbid, if you think of it in another way." Sir Robert laughed. "We will go too."

"What should I do while you speak with the baron?" Will was unsure of the tasks required of a squire.

"Your duties of course! Unpack our supplies and when you're finished find the training yard. It shouldn't be hard. It is at the center of this castle adjacent to the garden. I need to ensure you know how to fight, that is, if you are to go to war."

"Y-Yes master." He was hardly able to defend himself, much less fight by the knight's side. War was not an inviting prospect... the knight hadn't yet been false... Will feared what would happen to him if he stayed as much as he feared what would happen if he parted with the knight.

<hr>

When Will finished unpacking he found the training yard, but his master was still in war meetings.

The training yard held sandbags on poles, wooden structures, and many other things he had never seen. The jousting yard stretched twice the length of the training yard farther away. Something hit the back of his head.

"Ouch!" Will yelped then turned.

"A rule: always be attentive. No enemy will play fair Will; given the chance, they will skin you alive. So, you must do so first," Sir Robert said.

"I'll have to kill people?" Will wasn't sure about skinning someone alive. An image flashed through his mind. He lay chained to a board, on his back, the torturer shearing the flesh off the wailing man ahead of him…

"Yes, you will, but remember the knightly ways laid down by the first knights and lords of our kingdom. They are there to ensure you don't abuse your station. Protect the weak and defenceless, give aid to widows and orphans, speak truth always, kill only in defence and when forced, be loyal to your king and lords but firstly your king, and always defend and respect a woman's honour, keep faith in God, and live by honour and for glory."

"But not all knights follow that." Will remembered those less valiant, like Lord Jerold and his knights. Will and his childhood friends had built a castle, really only a wooden treefort, he smiled. Convincing the uncompromising lord took all the children, a couple of years, and many tears. Not wanting to remember Saul, Will shook the thoughts away.

"This code is ancient. Different knights have different ideas about what it tells us to do, and so not all follow one version of it. My father and my teacher taught me the code as I have told you, they have always followed it this way and so now I teach you the same. "Come," Sir Robert gestured, "Have you fought with a sword before?"

"My dad taught me a little, long ago." He thought back to when he was young, in the fields, he and his father and two wooden swords. Will stressed the first part hoping it would impress the knight.

"Hmm… your father was a farmer…"

"He used to be a watchman until he met my mother, taught me a little bit."

Sir Robert nodded and examined Will's body. A familiar fear crept in, like the stares of hatred from those looking at him caged in the Royal Landing courtroom. Like the warden's stare. Wicked eyes looking at him with a mix of lust and distaste, the man salivating at the savagery to come. A tremor spread across Will's shoulders and he was on the verge of withering until the knight finally spoke.

"You have some muscle I think," Sir Robert said. Will released a breath. "At some point we will need to work directly on refining your strength and endurance. Both will be important in a fight. Of course, as you use a sword you will naturally build both up. That's what our focus will be on. Building up your strength and endurance while learning technique."

Will gripped his sword tightly and nodded. Sir Robert laughed.

"Hold it closer to the cross-guard."

He blushed and adjusted.

"I will go over basics first. Get a proper stance then I will show you the three guards, high, middle, and low," he demonstrated. "Knowing how to quickly change to any position is important since you can start an attack from any one. When you fight, keep eye contact and remember to breathe properly; tiring yourself out will result in failure." He lifted the wooden sword and so did Will. "No Will. keep your hips and torso parallel and legs slightly bent."

Will corrected himself, the awkward stance already had his muscles straining.

"Okay, let's practice." Will missed a lot of blocks, and Sir Robert's sword sent bursts of pain through his body. His master's attacks seemed unstoppable. Sir Robert emphasised that crippling an enemy was at many times a better way to end a fight, after all, an enemy who couldn't fight was defeated without a kill. That seemed like a better situation to Will who was still unsure about drawing people's blood with this knowledge.

For a long time, Sir Robert helped Will perfect his defence. The knight next taught Will offence. In a real fight, Sir Robert explained, one had to dispatch the target and move on quickly. Sir Robert showed Will how he could attack from the various sword guards using the body to put force behind one's attacks, allowing the weight of his body to deliver it.

Will readied a stance and waited some seconds before moving in for an attack. He thrust, what he thought was quick, but Sir Robert expected it and sidestepped. Will tumbled forwards; the knight elegantly grabbed Will by the back of his tunic, spun him around, and tossed him to the ground. Will coughed as he landed onto the dirt. Heat surged into his face and he looked up. The knight laughed.

"If that is how you are going to attack, I suggest you make your peace with God before you go to battle, because you won't come back!" Sir Robert offered a hand to Will. He took it and was pulled up to his feet. "In your stance!" Will stood as Sir Robert walked behind him and with his feet, pushed Will's feet in the correct position. He grasped Will's arms molding them into the corrected positions. The knight stepped away. He walked over to a stake with sandbags tied around it and dragged it in front of Will.

"This is a pell. You will attack this. Focus on the correct footwork and technique. Strike hard. Don't stop until you collapse."

Will nodded, determined. He swung at the pell, once, twice, and onwards.

⁓

Will dropped his practice sword. He fell onto his knees and hands, hair falling over his face. Drenched in sweat and panting he spit on the ground, letting lose volumes of saliva. His arms throbbed with pain, heart raced, and his tongue vibrated with his ragged breath. Will collapsed to his side.

"An entire hour, non-stop. Very good." Sir Robert smiled. He gave Will a waterskin and the boy drank greedily between heavy breaths. "Remember to time your attack. Do not leave any part of yourself a target for your opponent. Search for an open flank."

The afternoon approached; they had practiced almost all day.

"You learn fast Will. Many men have at least a couple years training but you swing as if you had at least one year already. There are many places you still need to master though. One day when you are ready, I will teach you some advanced moves and then maybe you will even be able to defeat me!"

"Very good Master." Will didn't believe him, but appreciated the encouragement.

"You should clean our clothes and armor then bathe in preparation for the feast. I will send a new tunic for you."

"Yes Master."

"At the feast the nobles may intimidate you but don't let them trick you into returning their advances with an unpleasant response. I know of quite a few stories of nobles acting with no restraint getting inferior seats in the next feast and sometimes banned entirely!" Sir Robert laughed.

"I will master." Will smiled at the image of drunk and erratic nobles.

"Good… and listen… don't wander away from the castle until I come find you…" The knight stared hard at him. Will nodded one last time.

Will took their clothes and armour to the baths and cleaned them, then he bathed himself. He rubbed away all the grime and dirt off his hair, face, and body, hopefully Sir Robert had not minded. Afterwards he dressed himself in a blue, red, and gold camlet-silk tunic bearing his master's crest. Blue and red quarters made a check pattern, the lines between the quarters formed a white cross behind a golden phoenix over the center, an extension of his master's surcoat design. He wrapped his scarf around his neck and placed his pearl in one of the tunic's pouches. The silk's lightness and smoothness imparted a sense of cool refreshment he'd never had in the rough linen he was used to wearing.

Will walked back towards his master's room. He'd parted his hair on his left side and had neatly shaped it. It felt so light, a first in a long time for him. Will stopped. Someone stood in his path. Standing under a large arch that led out to a balcony, looking out at the city, was a girl; about Will's age. For a moment he stared at the back of her head, noticing her long reddish-brown hair, a small strand of it tied around the back of the crown of her head, coming together at the center. She was so… a strange fluttering warmed in his chest. He didn't understand why he stood there and kept staring at her back.

The girl turned, as if she had sensed someone watching. Her thin eyebrows rose then her lips parted as if she was going to say something, but she hesitated, staring at Will. A light breeze flowed in from the balcony, sending a fragrant vanilla sent past him. He tasted it on his tongue, paralysed. The girl's expression changed into a neutral smile, her lips stretching to the sides. He became fixated by her face; her healthy complexion and brown eyes gleamed.

"Who are you?" she asked. "I've never seen you around here." Her voice was toned and unbroken, regal even. She smiled again and Will's heart skipped a beat. He stood awkwardly on the spot for a little too long, then he smiled and walked closer.

"I come from… from…" Where did he come from? The answer was lost to him.

"You can't forget your hometown," the girl prompted. His hometown. Did it have a name? He couldn't remember.

"Aldershire," Will said, the word stunning him. That was his hometown, so long ago. He frowned.

"I don't recognise that place. I come from Royal Landing."

"It's south…" Will spoke as if in a trance, his mind automatically remembering things long shrouded. "South of Royal Landing among the hills and alder trees."

"I like that description." She angled herself towards Will. "Royal Landing is naught more than smoke and stink among the smell of the salty sea." She sighed. "It's home though. Pardon my rudeness but, I notice the crest on your tunic. Who are you?"

"I'm a… a squire." As the word rolled off his tongue and floated towards the girl, his world seemed to slow a little. He *was* a squire.

"I know that crest now! You're… you're a squire to Sir Robert, aren't you?"

"Yes." For a moment Will was caught by the sight of the curves of her body. He followed them, her thin delicate body… but she did have a slight build. Why was he fixating on this? Somewhere in the back of his mind, his conscious told him to stop… but… he couldn't.

"Sir Robert refused to train any pages or squires since he… then that means…" In an instant the girl's expression darkened. The gleam he'd seen in her eyes vanished and her lips pinched together, lowering towards her chin. The change threw Will out of any trance he might have been in. Now she was intimidating. Now she was judging him and fatigue spiked in him. The shadows around them seemed to darken as Will's heart sunk. He realised his mistake. He'd freely admitted to her who he was, who everyone thought he was. She had heard of him. All tasteless rumours.

"I just… I mean you look… no! I mean…" Will blushed, still trying to navigate this foreign attraction he felt. He lowered his voice, scratching the top of his head. She'd hate and fear him now and she'd leave; that beautiful face. "Wh-Who are you?"

"Me?" she sighed, a hint of annoyance in her voice, "I came to admire the city. I was told the view was unlike any other city in Gurmanis."

"Is it that good?" Will smiled, hoping if he kept talking, she wouldn't leave. He walked forwards, his closeness making the girl back away. Will looked out over the city. Suthenburg's buildings seemed to create a sort of patterned form, cut up by streets and canals, stretching far. Awe overcame Will. He'd never seen a city from this height.

"The streets and canals are like vines wrapping around each building." Will rested his arms on the railing. It was beautiful, but around its edges sat thick walls held by slanted triangular stone braces and a wide round citadel. These massive cannon batteries contained the beauty within.

"The canals make shapes out of the islands they isolate." The girl came up to Will's side, gripping her left arm with her right. "There is a planned form, almost as if God was painting it, yet tis the creation of man. Imagine what it'd look like from higher up. From a bird's eyes." She flashed a weak smile that didn't reach her eyes, cautiously keeping her distance. Will felt her tensing. As if on que, Will's falcon flew into view over the balcony making long wails. "Imagine being free to go and do what you want, like a bird can. So much to see and to experience." She hesitated then gripped the railing and relaxed a little, mirroring Will. She looked briefly at the falcon.

"I've heard the world is a big place but I've seen very little of it." He stared out towards the city and she at him. Will looked her way and she smiled faintly before looking out towards the city again.

"But it's not everything you think it is," she said, half to herself. "There are many dangers" —she took a brief glance at Will— "and many realities I have neglected to face."

The girl looked back at Will, seeming to stare and take in the boy's features.

Will, his arms now crossed in front of him was smiling and in deep thought, lingering on the words the girl had said. He was small amongst a vast and unseen world. The scale of the city from his height was only the surface and he'd never know every part of the city just like he'd never know every part of the world. In his childhood it seemed to be enough, he in his own bubble. In prison it had been extremely small. What did it seem like now, he wondered? The girl had not left, but why? His words had kept her and maybe she wasn't so ready to judge him.

"The weight of it all seems overwhelming. The past... the world." Will shivered. "How do I prove what none want to consider?"

The girl inhaled and Will saw her eyes waver. "Changing minds is no easy thing. Once alone reality challenged me to consider what I knew not." Unsure to what she was referring to Will looked back at her and he saw it, the hint of fear in her face, fear of him. She let go of the railing and backed away.

"I must go now. I am a healer for the army. Please do not tell anyone I came here; I am not s'posed to be in the castle." The girl turned to leave, hesitating to show her back to Will. Will straightened, turned, and met her face.

"I hope you do not need to tend to me!" Will smiled but the girl turned quickly back around, as if fearing his advance.

"Yes, I hope not," she answered plainly and left the balcony. Will watched her go. Her face lingered in his mind. Who was she that could get him to feel so strange? It was hard to describe the mix of nervousness and warmth he was feeling. He wasn't used to these feelings nor understood what they were. He didn't know how to deal with them.

Chapter Ten

WHEN WILL RETURNED to the room he shared with Sir Robert his master was not yet there. He took a seat on a chair beside a dresser and thought about the girl he'd met, but she soon faded and Will's mind emptied on instinct. Unbeknownst to him, he slid his wrists and ankles closer together and dropped his head. Aside from an occasional laugh or thump of footsteps from outside, it was silent. He waited.

"Good to see that you're still here." At his master's voice, Will gasped and, in an attempt to escape some immediate threat, he tried to slide away only to fall onto the ground. How long had he sat there? He didn't know.

"M-Master." Will fumbled with himself trying to get back up. "I'm sorry Master."

"No need. I startled you."

"You? Tis not my fault?" Will tightened, elbows pinned to his sides. Confused Sir Robert approached him. Will moved back. The knight held up his hands.

"Are you alright? Nothing scraped?"

Will shook his head.

"Good. I don't think you were thinking of this room when you were sitting there, were you?"

He frowned.

"Come let's go. It is time to get you looking presentable for tonight's feast."

"But the clothes…"

"That is one part of making you presentable. First, we need to go see the court mage. I will convince him to get rid of your number." Will froze then quivered. He touched his scarf. He hadn't thought of the number on his neck, nor had it crossed his mind when taking a bath. Sir Robert offered a hand and Will looked at it with hesitation.

"Come. It's about time you parted with it."

"B-But master, removing is… illegal."

Sir Robert smiled. "I am sure the court mage will have reservations about it…"

As Sir Robert explained how he'd convince the mage, clearly pleased he'd come up with the plan, all the knight's words seemed muffled for Will. He touched his number and his mind emptied. A darkness took hold of him and he imagined shapes taking form. A small dark room. Metal clamped him around his wrists, ankles, neck and chains around his waist. He was younger. The swish of a tunic brushed across his cheek. A small idol sat upon a table, a young woman in a straight jacket and chains, driven insane.

'Xylryna is an image of you Mr. Farmer. She's a monster, just like you.' The warden sneered.

Will stared at the idol, her thin pupils, wide enraged eyes, and sharp fangs and horns scared him and he imagined himself looking like her. 'All convicts must take her image. Because indeed, this is what they become.'

"… But I am sure I can convince him. Afterall Will, does it seem like I care if it is illegal to remove your number?" Sir Robert's voice propelled Will back to the present and he warmed at his master's comment. Will's pearl began to burn. As if outraged, it flared, bringing sharp pain to his side and Will reached into the folds of his tunic, clasping it, feeling its heat. He took it out. It was glowing and the mist swirled faster than it had ever been. Slowly, a strand of its magic snaked out of the object and floated towards Will's number.

Sir Robert watched wide-eyed at the light show happening in front of him. The magic flooded around Will's number, **271** visible through a translucent red magic.

At first a stinging boiled on his skin, and then a sharp pain. He whined, trying to muffle the desire to scream. The number on his neck started to fade. Sir Robert, seeing this, did not intervene. Instead, the knight sat Will down and gave him something to bite on. Finally, the number was gone and the magic of the pearl retreated into the red object. The burning pain on his skin cooled and Will felt the area his number had been. It felt no different. He stared off into space. Sir Robert pulled up a chair and sat across from Will, eyeing him with great curiosity.

"That thing… it's more than what the Burhbarrow court mage credited it for. Are you sure you don't know what it is?"

But Will didn't answer. He stood and walked towards a mirror. It was the first time he'd seen himself clearly in a long time. Will stared at his white skin, not believing that the number was gone, he kept tracing over where it had been.

"Will?" Sir Robert asked.

"What is it Master? My pearl."

"So, you truly don't know?"

Will turned to his master and shook his head.

"I feel like I should take it." Sir Robert stared at Will, as if trying to find deception in his expression.

"N-No… please don't Master." He didn't know what it was, but it had helped him when it mattered. After a long moment Sir Robert nodded and stood.

"Fine. It didn't hurt me when I had it and it seems to be helping you, but be sure I will be speaking with all mages I come across. One of them must know something."

Will followed Sir Robert down a wide arched corridor towards the great hall. In his new clothes Will was out of place, the impending exposure to all the nobles invited to this feast increasing his nervousness. He had never worn such expensive and richly colored clothes, never learned to carry himself as a noble, and now he was going to dine with them. He wrung his hands at the thought of how he would be perceived. Sir Robert's directions on proper etiquette, as they walked, were not making him any more confident.

"… So then be sure to use only your right hand when eating your food. A belch or two signals a happy guest but let it get out of hand and you will irritate everyone. You can eat with your fingers but sling your napkin over your right shoulder so it's easier to clean them. Of course, you can use a knife or spoon to… wait…" Sir Robert stopped and Will almost crashed into him. The knight spun around, his camlet-silk bliaut swaying. His worrying expression made Will all the more nervous.

"Wh-What?" Will asked.

"We did not get you your own knife."

"I could use a dagger…"

"No, no, no that won't be seemly. Have you not listened to anything I just told you?"

"Sorry Master… I am trying." Will hung his head.

"Head up! Confidence Will!" Sir Robert sighed. "Never mind it, we can share my knife." The knight smiled. "I will be given one at the feast due to my status." The knight adjusted the twisted silk chaplet around the top of his head, in his colours, then turned and walked onwards. Will followed close behind. At the doors to the great hall stood two guards, a butler and two other servants, one holding out a bowl of water and the other a towel. The butler bowed at Sir Robert and politely gestured to the bowl. Sir Robert washed his hands then dried them, stepping aside to allow Will to do the same then the butler walked into the great hall. Will fingered his own chaplet, same as the knight's. It sat uneasily on his head.

"Announcing Grand Marshal Sir Robert Gilios, now in the direct service to King Duggan Chas." The butler made a low bow to the nobles in the hall and stepped aside to allow Sir Robert and his squire to enter.

They entered into a wide space flanked by tall pillars holding up a vaulted roof. Light shone through tall windows outlined in blue curtains. The walls themselves were decorated with colourful murals and tapestries. Banners of Suthenburg hung between the pillars.

Will stayed close to his master trying to hide his face, which he knew was flushed with embarrassment as they walked down an isle between long tables parallel to the isle. Did he have to announce his master? Now all the nobles present were staring at him. The Baron of Suthenburg was especially interested, and their gaze was judgemental, in contrast to the fine clothes they wore. Will couldn't name all of the types of fabric but within their tunics, bliauts, houppelandes, tabards, jerkins, kirtles, surcotes, and other dresses many types of cotton, silk, and furs were likely woven.

The lords, ladies, and knights muttered and scoffed as he passed them towards to the high table. Will's ears twitched, taking in even the slightest of sounds.

"Him, un escuier?"

"A disgrace! Baseborn, lurdan."

"Murtair."

"Nyet, he does not deserve this." The tone of the conversations were cruel but he was just trying his hardest to serve. They couldn't see that. They saw him as refuse. Will broke a sweat and did his best to ignore them. These nobles were very powerful and it was clear his presence had insulted them.

Most nobles wore elaborate hats including chaperons, chappeaus, burlets, wimples, and chaplets. Most of the women had arranged their hair using hair nets and hennins, shaping their hair in a variety of ways.

Will and his master approached the high table where the Baron of Suthenburg sat in the center with his wife and children and the city's archbishop to his right. At the baron's feet stood two large grey mastiff dogs scrutinising anyone who dared approach. Behind the high table hung a massive colourful tapestry showcasing the founding of Suthenburg with the city's coat-of-arms, also that of the baron's, front and center. A fish overtop an anchor and with a banner that twisted around the two. A yellow pale over blue formed the background.

Sir Robert stopped in front of the high table and bowed to the baron which Will copied.

"Grand marshal, you may take the seat on my left with your... what is it? Squire?" The baron's keen eyes examined them. Sir Robert hid a frown. To be seated on the left told him the baron was not thinking highly of them.

"As you wish." Sir Robert took his seat and Will took the seat on Sir Robert's left. At the high table, Will had a view of the entire hall as the final guests settled in at the low tables. Many stared at him and exchanged quiet conversation with their fellow nobles. He brought his hands together over his lap, looked down and twiddled his fingers, making himself look small. His heart raced. The baron leaned towards Sir Robert.

"You understand, Sir Robert, the consequences of bringing that boy here. Many in my hall this hour do not agree with his presence but all tolerate it because you are the king's Grand Marshal. I urge you not to make his presence more noticeable than it already is and to leave with haste when I withdraw." The baron's voice was laced with a passive-aggressive threat.

"If it is at your behest, we will withdraw in a timely manner," Sir Robert answered. Will realised how bad he made his master look. Dark thoughts tried to surface in his mind, the warden, chains, bars, walls slowly materializing.

"I thank-you for understanding. When you are with your own men come time to depart, the boy will not be so forward, if you know what I mean."

Sir Robert nodded and turned away. He looked at Will staring down and trembling. The knight put a reassuring hand on his shoulder, making Will look up at him with fearful eyes.

"Try to relax, Will," the knight said. When everyone was seated, the baron motioned to the butler who rang a bell. Doors on the sides of the great hall swung open and a dozen or more servants walked out carrying platters of food, all beautifully arranged and decorated. To the high table came the most extravagant of foods and displays of various birds, farm animals, and game doused in thick sauces and gravies, garnished with various vegetables like turnips and leek, sitting on a bed of cabbage.

Various types of salted, spiced, and stuffed meat glistened topped with lemons and limes. A tower of colourful fruit was placed down next to various cauldrons of soups including pottages of meat, fish, and vegetables, some more liquid and others chunkier. There was bread whiter than what Will had eaten in Burhbarrow. Pastries and pies loaded with all sorts of things such as soft cheeses. A tray brimming with assorted cheeses and nuts, various fruits and warm plums in cream lay to his left and oatcakes lay beside them. He spotted honey wine to drink warm or cold.

The cooks had used the most expensive of spices imported from the east, including various salts, peppers and sugars, sage, mustard and parsley but also saffron and gold leaves. The taste of such food spoke to the care in preparation as each and every dish had a unique take, and many courses were assured. A nef, shaped like a sailing cog, was placed in front of the baron holding extra salt, spices, cutlery, and cloth napkins.

Will watched as the servants set food and drink down according to the status of the noble present. Things came first to the high table then to the lower tables directly below the high table. Food was placed down the line until those furthest from the high table received the least flavourful cuts of food last. Additional spices and seasonings were given only to the most important and those at the high table, dined with porcelain plates and porcelain bowls, while the least important dined using pewter or wooden bowls.

"Friends!" the baron demanded attention. "Tonight is a feast to honour our duty to go to war and see the king's work done. All day have my kitchens and their ovens been at work to bring to you the most appetising of food."

When all the food sat on the tables, the arch-bishop rose from his seat and led a prayer to which everyone clasped their hands and bowed. Will followed suit, but saying no prayer. Finally, only when the baron took his first bite, did everyone start to eat.

This experience was unreal. At first, Will did not know where to begin with the variety of food before him.

"Sir Robert," the baron spoke after a bite of seasoned stag leg. "Tell me, what are your thoughts on the recent muster? In your experience, will enough lords, knights, and their retinues come? I know the Royal Forces are already at Castle Ochsen."

"Indeed, they are. As this war continues, I have noticed a decrease in the lords and knights who answer the king's summons."

"Bah! Traitors," the baron spat.

"I would not presume that." Sir Robert placed a slice of spiced capon on his plate. "I think many lords are merely disgruntled with the progress in this war. They see their lands in turmoil, worsening with each passing day as they are commanded to increase their levies. It removes serfs from farms, and peasants from artisan professions and mercantile endeavours. All of this loses them money."

"Yes, I am well aware Sir Robert. However, loyalty to the king is paramount. Since the previous sultan's defeat, we have regained all the lands taken from us. There is a feeling of surprise. King Duggan and indeed many nobles think that the Saomardrim are spent and fragmented. There is an open frontier to the east, so the king says. That the Saomardrim could not hold onto it clearly shows they are weakened and their lands open to us."

"Sultan Yazid the second is a unifier of his kinsmen, if stories are to be believed. His defence will be difficult to break."

"But necessary. By conquering his heathen land, we will obtain more than enough wealth to settle all debts and repopulate this kingdom."

"I hope so Lord."

Will realised he was not being served. The others around him happily accepted food and drink but nothing came to Will; in fact, the servants seemed to be trying to keep their eyes off him. Sir Robert tapped his fingers on the table; he stopped the man serving him.

"Your poor service is noted. My squire has not received anything so serve him before you serve me anything more," the knight demanded. The servant looked to the knight then to the baron. The baron leaned towards Sir Robert.

"I do not agree with the boy, Sir Robert. You cannot expect me to serve him. If he will eat then he will eat what you give him for I do not wish to alienate so many nobles as you have. If you were not grand marshal, I would have the boy under the table where he is unseen to eat the scraps with the dogs." The baron leaned back and tossed some of his leftovers below to his mastiffs.

Sir Robert looked at Will's worried expression. "Sorry Will, I did not think it would be as bad as it is," he whispered.

"I hurt your reputation Master, I wound you. I should not be here. If it pleases his lordship, I will eat under the table."

"You will do no such thing!" Sir Robert recoiled. "Here." The knight handed Will his knife. "Eat from my plate, it is no problem."

"But Master…"

"I have made you my squire out of my own accord. There will be difficulties, but I am fully aware of them and I am ready to deal with them. Pay no mind to my reputation. Simply sit, eat and learn."

Will nodded and ate from his master's plate conservatively.

The feast continued on. Though nobles still stole a disgusted glance or two at Will most became absorbed in their own conversations and paid him no mind. Sir Robert occupied himself with the baron discussing the war and the kingdom but would take a few moments here and there to instruct Will on manners at the table or how to assess the actions and words of the nobles. Will learned of the complex political games the nobility played their entire lives. He carved meat and poured wine for his master.

A troop of travelling musicians and jesters entered the hall providing a lively serenade including the long notes of a rebec formed from the sliding of its bow, and supported by the short notes of a cittern strummed at an even speed. But it was the pounds of the tambourine and drums which emphasised a lively beat. A flute supported the melody. The jesters, musicians, and dancers provided fitting entertainment that reminded him of the plays put on in his village when he was younger.

"Baron." Another knight's squire bowed to the baron of Suthenburg at the high table. The baron padded his mouth and gestured for the young man to continue. Will examined the three squires who had approached over the din of melodic music. A numbing tension grew in his muscles.

"We feel obligated to introduce Sir Robert's new squire to our masters." The eldest squire bowed. "If you and Sir Robert would be willing, we wish to host his new squire for the night is almost at a close."

"Huph." The baron smiled. "Why not? Sir Robert let your charge go with them and we will retire."

Sir Robert looked between the squires and his apprentice. "Perhaps it is a good idea."

One of the boys gave Will a smile that set off alarms within him. Maybe it wasn't a good idea, but Sir Robert was already standing. Reluctantly, Will left with the three squires, smiling at them but not knowing what to say.

"What is your name?" the youngest boy asked.

"Will."

"A serf name," a boy scoffed.

"You should use the full iteration, William," the eldest advised. The three squires had surrounded Will as they left the hall.

"Who are your masters?" Will said, then tried to mimic their speech, "I am honored to be engaging them. They must be esteemed." No honor, just fear. One boy snickered.

"Right this way." The eldest gestured down the hall. Will scratched his hair. The eldest squire whirled around, causing Will to crash into him. With a scowl he shoved Will to the ground and jumped over him. Will's chaplet fell away. He grabbed Will by the shirt while the others circled around him causing tension to rise over the burst of dull pain.

"You don't belong here, not where we live. Look at you! The level you are at and the level we are at!" The leader glared at him through agitated blue eyes. So, there would be no introductions with anyone.

"What d'you mean level?" But Will knew. The lords and ladies at the feast had sent their squires after him.

"The peasant does not even understand common tongue! You have hurt us all gravely." The eldest laughed letting go of Will in the process. Will scrambled to his feet.

"What are you talking about? I have not troubled you." Why did his master allow him to go? He was in deep peril now.

"You have ruined what a squire, no, what a knight is. A criminal serf can be no squire!"

Will raised his hands. "I just want to serve my master. M-Maybe I am unworthy but... I could prove to you that—"

"All you prove to us is how out of place you are. If you think you are worthy of being a squire then prove it! Fight me, I will even make it easy for you." The leader unlatched his weapon belt and threw his dagger on the ground. He stepped back and took a stance, "There, no weapon. Come at me!"

"I don't want to fight you. There is no need."

"Are you admitting defeat? A knight needs to be strong. Coward!" the boy taunted. "I guess everyone's right, you *are* naught more than a murderer."

"You're wrong I am—" The unruly squire punched Will clear in the face causing Will to stumble backwards. All three boys laughed. They approached him, jeering at him, raising their fists. Will's head spun, dizzy from the impact. The squires blurred and grew in size. Isen prison guards cornered him. One guard taunted him;

'Come on boy! That all you can take? We ain't started yet!' the guard spit at him.

'Don't punch him in the face again, we don't want the warden to see any lasting marks,' another guard warned.

'He's got nothing. Let's teach him what happens when he wanders into the wrong place.'

"P-Please... I made a mistake!" Will cried. "Took the wrong tunnel. Don't..." Will made himself small, thinking the prison guards were going to punish him. The squires looked at each other and laughed. The older one advanced and punched Will in the gut then followed up with several other blows. Will's arms were pinned to his body, his chains restricting him any chance of defending himself… no…Will realised, he was not chained and these three were not the guards. The leader took another swing at Will's face but to even Will's amazement, he stopped the punch halfway. The surprised squire retracted and took another swing. Will stopped it and punched the boy in the stomach. The squire coughed and staggered back. His friends tried to help him but he shook them off.

"You'll pay for that you little lowborn wretch!" He punched Will in his stomach. Will coughed up blood. He recovered in time and prepared to attack, but the squire interrupted him with a kick. Will tumbled to the ground and rolled out of the way of another kick. He stood and lunged for the boy. Will pushed him to the ground and threw some punches before being grabbed and pulled off.

"In Manis' name, my lord what is this!" A middle-aged priest glared at the four with wide eyes. He was clutching Will and had a hand out to discourage the others. Will spit blood, he must be the most injured.

"We are teaching him a lesson, Priest."

"This is unseemly! Manis would ne'er forgive any of you."

The priest pried Will away as the squires looked on in disgust.

⁓

Will stared at the altar as the priest tended to his wounds, they were not serious anyway. He sat upon an oak-pew.

"Thank-you, sir. Who are you?"

"I am a Hicel, a Priest of Manis, but what is *your* name?"

"It's Will, sir."

"Will, is it short for William?"

"I guess." Will saw the man more clearly now. He wore a brown alb with a hooded scarf which draped over the right of his back. He reminded Will of Aldershire's priest, Prior Albert.

"So, you are the boy who escaped? A challenging task, how d'you do it?"

"I found a key sir. The guards were also dense."

Hicel let out a warm chuckle.

"Sir I was… ah… wondering."

"Yes?"

"Why does Manis cause me so much suffering?" He remembered all the times during his imprisonment when he'd called out to him. Manis never answered. Will's faith had slowly eroded, and he'd stopped calling out, cursing Manis instead.

"My boy, God does not cause suffering to his children, he has the best interests for them. He cares and knows of your suffering and feels it in equal measure. Manis died for all the evil in the world. When times of great need come on his people, he comes to liberate them."

"Then why was I forced to live in that prison? Why does he not protect me from people who wish to hurt me?"

"Manis wishes for you to make amends for your crimes and he must punish you as well. You must suffer your punishment as given, for God has instituted our king to maintain order. Manis has bestowed the Divine Right to Rule upon King Duggan whose laws God expects you to follow. Your punishment, under the law must be served."

"But I am innocent!" Will frowned; if Manis was all knowing then he should know he was innocent, and Will was sure Manis knew. But Will *should* blame the king. The priest's cold justification for his imprisonment was somewhat true. The laws of the king allowed him to suffer as he had. Hicel hesitated; he didn't seem moved.

"Accept the truth and submit to Manis. Learn to repent."

"I don't need to repent, and I don't have faith."

"You must, child. Trust in him and he will reward and help you. Believe in him and you will find clarity. He lies inside you no matter your station or situation, learn to confide in him in all things, sins or otherwise, and he will forgive and purify you. We were all created by the Father and since Manis is his son Twas from his image that we were created. Who you are, is an imperfect reflection of him. Repent and refine. Try to speak to him with faith."

"And if he does not answer?"

"Believe in him, the Father, Mother, and Son. Speak to him with compassion, kindness, humility, gentleness, and patience. Have faith in your words and his power, he will answer. Has he not already answered? Are you not here? With his help you have escaped, and he has given you a master who will care for you."

"No, Manis doesn't care for me. I escaped on my own and I found my master through luck. Manis had no part in it."

"You may have doubts in him but I assure you he is planning something for you. I will tell you something about Sir Robert. In this age where people care for only themselves there are some people who would care for strangers should they need aid. Sir Robert is that kind of man. His lands had no poverty and little crime. When he joined his host, he never executed his prisoners or sent them out of the range of his command, because he knew if he did, they would be treated inhumanely. Sir Robert is a man of great virtue; he is a moral knight of which these days are a rarity. Such quality should be admired and thought upon."

"You don't speak of the same Manis. I learned in my childhood and by listening to my master that Manis is merciful. Yet he also demands severe punishment for the sinful. I don't understand. He is not merciful, not kind and loving to all."

"Manis looks after your afterlife as well, child. Because of your choices he suffers as he watches you sin and be punished, but tolerates it because it will save your soul. Judeicar, god of order and justice, told him that he will only judge those who have been adequately punished for their sins in their physical life. If not, they would taint the Overworld with their souls. Manis demands severe punishment because it is the only sure way Judeicar will agree to judge the soul. The mercy of Manis allows even sinners the possibility of ascending to the Overworld and live alongside him. This is universally acknowledged; all lands follow Judeicar's Justice."

"Then Manis shouldn't listen to Judeicar."

"There are many gods, sure, but Manis is the worthiest of devotion for he is God. Only what he affirms is worth following."

"He is worthy of nothing."

"You are confused and you grieve because you will not admit to your crimes. You cannot start on the path to obtain Manis' mercy if you do not repent. Your soul is tainted."

Will glared at Hicel. He shook him away and stood. "You don't care! You're like everyone who thinks I am a—"

"You are a murderer, child. Your image is that of a monster." Hicel stood and approached. "Repent. Save your soul."

"Stay away!" Will shouted. The priest sighed and smiled.

"Sorry my child. You misunderstand me. Please sit." Hicel gestured to the pew. Will didn't sit. "Your suffering is painful, I know. You feel it is unjust. If you cannot yet find faith then think upon how your suffering can be used for good."

"What d'you mean?"

"In suffering there can be a message of compassion, unity, and comfort. Learn to become gracious, understanding, empathetic, humble. You know of darkness; how can you grow from it?"

Will frowned, still not understanding. Hicel smiled. "Think, William. Think about what you can do with your free life. After all, as I said, Manis has brought you here and maybe for a reason. What can you do to help those in the world around you? From your experience, what do you most want?"

"To ne'er go back. For all my nightmares, memories, and pain to disappear."

"And for others? Your master?"

"I don't want people to hate me. I want to serve my master loyally and to prove myself worthy to everyone."

"These are genuine. But to repent you must search further."

"I-I... I don't... I don't want anyone else to suffer as I did."

<div align="center">~~~</div>

Will didn't tell his master about the fight. He feared upsetting the knight and disappointing him by having further tarnished his reputation, so he ignored the fact that his master had suggested he go with the squires in the first place.

The next day Will continued to train with his master. After that day's final meal, Will found himself sitting on the floor beside his bed with his knees pulled up to his chin. He shared the room with his master. Of modest size, but larger than any other space Will had slept in, the room held two beds arranged perpendicular to one wall. A window overtop a wooden side table separated the two.

Sir Robert came into the room. "You're doing it again Will... Will?"

Will looked up expressionless. "S-Sorry... master... I can't do it. I tried but I can't."

"Try..."

"I've been trying already... I-I feel more comfortable on the ground. It's colder... and I can sleep better." Will tensed, hoping his master would not shout at him. Instead Sir Robert smiled warmly.

"Keep trying. Remove the covers if you have to. I don't want to leave you on the ground." Sir Robert offered Will a hand. Will took it and stood, then took a seat on his bed. Sir Robert took a seat on his own bed, across from Will.

"Master."

"Yes?"

"I'd like to know. Noblemen, the higher nobility I think, have manors an' castles, where are yours?" Sir Robert raised an eyebrow.

"Where is this question coming from?"

"It's just that... well the other nobles in the city all have estates."

"Very well." Sir Robert stroked his beard. "The short of it is that I gave-up my lands. I gave-up my retainers, and abandoned a portion of my remaining wealth. I lived along the Golden Inlet northeast of Royal Landing and ruled the fiefdom of Dustan. The land there is... quiet, rustic, and traditional, picturesque. My manor was perched atop a small hill overlooking the Inlet and the village I ruled over. Gilios is a renown name. My ancestors aided Lady Eleanor, Templar of Manis in her victory against the Rhoathian Imperium. Quite a bit before her my ancestors also had a part to play in Saint Sir Isen's campaigns. Nowadays I am the... the only Gilios left."

"Why'd you give up yer lands?"

"I lost it to a tragedy Will, a tragedy. A new family rules it now ending the historic line of Gilios forever. It is my fault and I cannot discuss this. Refrain from bringing up my past ever again Will." Sir Robert sighed.

"Sorry Master."

"I will tell you one day, as you once told me everything about yourself..." The knight blew out the candle and adjusted himself in his bed.

⁓

That night a storm of nightmares raged through Sir Robert's mind. Will's questions had provoked memories of those he'd lost. Before the sun was fully up, Sir Robert woke, with a jerk, sweating. The knight clutched his forehead, his brain pounded against his skull. He looked to Will. The boy was sleeping on the floor again. It was not easy for the boy. He wondered if Will would ever have a normal life again.

He rose from his bed, lifted the blanket off of Will's bed, and gently put it over the boy. He would continue to help and teach Will; a familiar fatherly feeling swept through him. Emmeline would have cared for him. She had that personality. He remembered her care for the children of their servants and those of their village.

Sir Robert crept over to his bed. He sat, staring at Will. He remembered the face of his son. They were at their manor along the Golden Inlet. His boy was six and already a page. He laughed as his mother tried to hug him and Sir Robert watched on with the boy's master.

'He will become a great warrior Robert, I see you in him,'

'With your training I am sure!' They laughed. Sir Robert lay on his bed looking at the ceiling as Will shifted. Another memory came, He had been fighting rebels near Port Calford. There'd been a break in the fight and a solemn looking messenger arrived. He took a letter from him and read it:

Dear Sir Robert Gilios,

I am sorry to bring this bad news at such a time but as you know famine and plague are ravaging everywhere north of Royal Landing. It has hit your manor. Your son has been taken by the plague four days ago, your wife two days after. I am deeply sorry friend.

Sir Scott Gills

The shock had almost become the death of him. He would never forget that letter; in fact, he had kept it among his personal belongings to this day. He'd failed as a husband and as a father that day. He failed to provide for and protect his family and was not there to see them go. Because of the tenant of loyalty to one's king he had to stay while his son and wife were buried, separated from the normal procedures because of the plague. He had gone once to see their graves and after that had never set foot on his old home again, and swore off almost all his holdings and wealth. From then on, he'd spent years in King Duggan's service, protecting the king's daughter and completing tasks appointed by the king with not much purpose in life.

He remembered the painful dreams he had back then, of such vicious imagery they were, only God could truly describe. He saw his son, Ferand, in the arms of his mother as the last of the food ran out and the faithful servants had given up the last of what they had, to see their young lord survive. His son took his final breaths, eyes on his mother as they closed for the last time. He saw his wife, Emmeline, her face scarred by the signs of the blight as she called out the knight's name with her final breaths, tears leaving her eyes.

He remembered the day four days after leaving his home, how King Duggan had summoned him. When Sir Robert walked into the king's study, the sovereign was finishing a discussion with an overseer in details of rebelling peasants and the need for more workers in mines and in craftsmanship to support the war. The king was burning uncooperative villages. He had hanged the elderly and children while conscripting the youths, men, and women. Sir Robert had protested, other lords had as well, but the king refused to listen.

In the wake of Sir Robert's loss and the loss of his lordship, King Duggan still had use for the talented knight. He'd made Sir Robert the grand marshal and allotted him a personal regiment. All while saying but seven words pertaining to the death of the knight's family. Sir Robert pushed the lack of sentiment aside and took the position. Princess Elizabeth showed a great deal more sympathy. Sir Robert smiled as she expressed her condolences.

Later Sir Robert found out by letter that she had run away, and the king ordered him to find her. Now those sorrowful and monotonous years were suddenly broken when a boy decided to ambush him on the forest road. It gave him a greater purpose than being servant to the king, even if the purpose was not entirely clear. Will seemed both grateful and willing to please him, like his own son... but unlike his son.

Ferand's smile, inherited by his mother, flashed in his mind. Those expectant eyes filled Sir Robert with warmth. "I am sorry Ferand," Sir Robert whispered. Manis forgive me." He looked to Will. "He takes some of your traits... but reflects my own loss. If this is God's will then I will follow."

Will shifted and a tear ran down Sir Robert's face. He let those heartrending memories fade away.

Chapter Eleven

WILL CONTINUED TRAINING. Occasionally, knights, ladies, squires, pages, and servants would pass through along the edges giving him all manner of looks. It discomforted Will, having so many eyes on him. Suddenly a practice sword hit him on the hand. The throbbing sting made Will drop his own sword and exhale.

"Your attention is escaping you Will." Sir Robert raised an eye-brow. "Your mind is wandering."

"No Master… maybe I'm just tired."

"In battle fatigue, distraction, or hesitation will get you killed. You seem to hesitate quite a bit."

"Sorry, Master."

"We will work on it. That is why we are training." Sir Robert noticed something and looked past Will. He smiled, and strode by. A well-groomed knight, his brown hair tied back into a ponytail and a small goatee on his chin, walked up to Sir Robert. They shook each other's hands.

"Sir John. I was wondering when you'd arrive."

"Robert! We did not get a chance to talk, it's been long," Sir John exclaimed.

"Yes John it has been. How is your family?"

"They have been well, despite their worry about me getting mustered for war. The oldest is well on his way to becoming a squire, and the youngest shall soon become a page. It seems such little time that we have with them. They grow up fast."

"Ah, but they are still young! How is your daughter? Wife? The baby?"

"All are well. My wife and daughter are taking care of all while I am away."

"You should always keep them close John, always." Sir Robert grimaced. "What of your squire?"

"Ah yes. Alex is somewhere in the palace. He's been instructed to un-pack but I feel he is more interested in other matters. You know how it is with young men and courting young women. No doubt he has gone to find her."

"Is he still set on the baron's youngest daughter?"

"Hah! When has he ever not been crazy about her! He is nineteen now and he tells me soon he will be knighted, despite having much to learn. He tells me that when he is a knight, he will ask the baron for his daughter's hand."

"He is lucky to have found love." Sir Robert smiled.

"Ahh but you have been busy too Robert. I have heard you got a new squire." Sir John glanced at Will. "Look at you two; you make quite the picture right there, learned knight and youthful squire!" Sir Robert smiled and Will blushed.

"Yes, a fast learner and a loyal one at that."

"It is hard for me to understand why you made him your squire Robert. I may not have. I have known you for a long time and we have fought alongside each other in countless battles so I have grown to trust you. I will trust you now."

"That is refreshing to hear."

"Yes, well he has not stabbed you in the back yet. People *can* change after all. I hear the boy is brave. He held his own when some of the other squires challenged him to a fight. Lord Pankratz's retainers were gossiping about it at the palace gates. One of his many squires got punched by yours."

Will's heart jumped to his throat at the mention of the fight.

"Those squires attacked you? Why did you not tell me this Will?" Sir Robert asked.

"I guess I didn't want you to worry Master, I handled it."

"That you did! Faced those squires well enough, they won't be troubling you so soon though you may have angered their masters," Sir John started, "But be wary for enemies made within the nobility, more often than not, are enemies made for life. Say, now that you have a squire, perhaps we'll resurrect the old days Robert. With you, me, Białek, and Dillon. Adventure! Maidens! Danger! Youth uninhibited!"

"Having squires is a responsibility." Sir Robert laughed.

"Who's to say they won't want to join in?"

"Then we may yet have such a time in the coming battle."

"Fighting side by side once more!" Sir John darkened. "I am glad you're back Sir Robert. I know it's been… hard…"

"Think nothing of it."

Sir John nodded. "My men-at-arms came with me. I sent them ahead to Castle Ochsen."

"All are prepared for battle?"

"As you and King Duggan have requested. But do you have all you need Robert?"

"I will fetch some supplies from the city. That is all."

"I can have some of my men-at-arms do that for you. Perhaps Alex can help."

"You don't need to concern yourself. I have a squire. I'll send him."

A jolt rushed through Will, confidence filling him.

"In that case we might see each other later? For a drink? We must catch-up on things."

"But I have so much to teach the boy."

"You were never a teacher Robert."

"I slowly came to realise why I wasn't" Sir Robert smiled at Will. "But his improvement seems to speak well for my lessons."

Will scratched his hair awkwardly.

"Later, perhaps, we can have a drink," Sir Robert said.

"That's what I wanted to hear! I shall see you tonight." Sir John parted and Sir Robert turned to his apprentice.

"Now Will you tell me everything going forward, ok?"

"Yes Master." Will bowed his head.

***

At the end of the day, Will set off to fetch their personal supplies while Sir Robert got a drink with Sir John. Will beamed at being given an opportunity to show his loyalty to Sir Robert. He would not fail his master. He hurried into the city and bought the supplies, even managing to get a discount, leaving Will with extra gold. He stopped outside of the shop and looked towards the streets filled with people, thinking on the happiness that was filling him. It was so foreign and returned to him so easily when he was not paying attention.

Will walked towards the canal where he had left the gondola Sir Robert gave him. It floated, tied to a post on the stairs leading to the waterway. He put the supplies inside and prepared to board.

"Sir, what a modest boat you have there but by yer clothes you do not look modest at all," a honeyed voice said so close to Will's ears that he seized up then whirled around. A boy around fourteen or fifteen stood there, his hair a messy mop of brown, similar to Will's but shorter, and his clothes in need of repair. The boy bowed. "Sorry sir for startling you. I'm a boat boy, so the locals call us, and I offer service to well off people such as yerself. If you wish it, I can help ya go anywhere for a small fee."

"I can manage myself," Will said with caution, unsure if he should smile. He turned away then an intense yet calming heat came over him.

"Accept," the powerful voice said. Will turned back.

"It's my livelihood, sir. I've got a baby brother an' a sickly mother and I have no father. Died in the war he did. I provide for 'em, sir, only way I know how." The boy dropped his head. Remorseful, having refused, Will remembered the charity Sir Robert gave to the poor children when they'd arrived in Suthenburg. He could help this boy now; he did have the extra gold.

"Very well. You can take me back to my master. What's yer fee?"

"Why tis a small fee, sir." The boy looked up and smiled. "Ten bronze coins is all I ask."

"I only have gold. Will one gold coin do?" Will beamed inside understanding how generous he was being. The boy hesitated then nodded, joy radiating from his face.

"Y-Yes of course, sir! Thank-you. I will see to it that you return safe!" The boat boy gestured towards the gondola and boarded when Will had settled in. He rowed them down the canal following its curve. They passed under bridges and beside ramps and stairs. Buildings and baloneys were partially covered in green creeping vines in this area of the city accented with colourful flowers and stonework.

Will was not accustomed to this situation. Should he speak? He had with the girl in the palace, but what should he say? On their left another gondola neared, a hooded figure rowing it. Will realised they were alone.

"I-I think you missed a turn." Will watched the boat boy stop rowing. Will was grabbed from behind, a hand planted firmly across his mouth. Their gondola rocked to the side as someone boarded. Will's shouts came out as muffled gasps. His attacker tied his wrists together, then gaged him. The boat boy leaned over and snatched all of Sir Robert's gold from Will's side.

"We're too heavy." The hooded figure was turned away from Will, but he sounded masculine. He shoved the supplies off the boat and Will's heat sunk as he watched them splash into the water. The boat boy rowed on.

"Look at all this gold! Its great!" The boat boy grinned. The man shoved his head.

"Just get us to the drop off point." He turned to face Will. They locked eyes. The sense of urgency that seemed to radiate from the man's eyes was something familiar to Will. "You be quiet ya hear, if you know what's good for ya."

Will remained silent just as prison had taught him. His muscles tightened, ready to receive some sort of punishment. The evening reached its peak and Will knew he was late to return. What might his master say? He had trusted Will on a simple errand that he had failed. He'd been kidnapped for trying to help someone out. Even when he tried to emulate his master he failed. He was lost too, being taken into a secluded network of canals. Will's once excited demeanor crashed and familiar despair crept over him. Shaking, he resisted the involuntary urge to wither.

As they took the left turn at a T-junction, the man's eyes and his guttural voice swirled in Will's head. He knew this person from somewhere. *You'll join 'em yourself if you know what's good for ya.'* A shiver soar up his spine and heat fled his skin, realization dawned on him.

"F-Furm… A-Auldershre." Will glared at the man, his vision fuzzy. Will stumbled as he tried to approach.

"Stay down." The man shoved the tip of a dagger centimeters from Will's neck. Will burned, anger surging and memories of his home flashing and blending in his mind. Will looked upon his face, the eyes, the voice, he still remembered them. Will made muffled noises, trying to speak through his gag. The man rolled his eyes, shoved Will's head back, and ripped the gag off.

"What?" he growled.

"Do you remember me?" Will's nails dug into his palm, cutting his skin.

"Of course I don't know you."

"You don't remember! Why would you? My family was only a way for you to fill yer pockets, naught more!" Will screamed against tears. The man pushed the dagger deeper.

"What're you yapping about boy?"

"You came to my farm seven years ago, south of Royal Landing. You don't remember breaking in and murdering my parents or how you left me an orphan!"

The man looked on befuddled.

"What's that have to do with you?" He thought for a moment. "Parents… you must have been that boy. Shite luck, Manis the devil. That's what he meant."

"Who meant what?" the boat boy asked, but Will raised his voice.

"You ruined my life!" Will was frantic but the murderer only laughed.

"You don't know the half of it, do ya boy? Your parents didn't know what they were doing. They tried to increase their income by buying textiles from a merchant who sold it to 'em cheap, they sold it for double. But one day the merchant didn't come."

Stunned at the words Will wavered.

"Wh-What are you talking about?"

The gondola turned into a right curving canal.

"Probably, thing was, they didn't know. Merchant they were dealing with was a fraud. Stole from the lord of your village a variety of things. The lord found out and the merchant was hanged. Lord didn't wish to pursue the buyers, mostly cause they were impossible to track. But yer parents were a different story. Bought an object that was dear to that lord, a jewelled necklace, an heirloom? Belonged to his daughter. I was hired to deal with the issue."

"Lies! They knew naught of the merchant trade."

"And that's why they got themselves into this mess. They should've known something was suspicious. Were desperate to make more gold, probably couldn't feed ya or something."

Will thought back to the discussion he had overheard when his parents talked about how to feed a new child. They were already hard pressed for gold. "Lord Jerold's a prideful one, ya know," the murderer huffed. "Didn't want the embarrassment of being robbed by his own serfs, sent me to find and collect what was his, an' to permanently evict your family. Lord Jerold also did a piss poor job in keeping records of who lives on his land. He didn't mention you."

"What's going on huh?" The boat boy looked between the two. "What's all this about?"

"I told ya to do your damn job!" Then the murder snorted and laughed. "Small world this. I ken this poor kid, we go way back."

"B-But you left me alive." Will couldn't believe the story he was hearing. It seemed so farfetched to be true.

"I should have killed you too, the lord berated me for leaving you alive but things seemed to work out by themselves."

"K-Kill?" The boat boy's eyes widened, but the murderer glared at him and he continued rowing.

"The constables," the murderer cleared his throat, "who you led to your parents the next morning, were convinced you'd killed them yerself. We ran with that story an' let it play out. The entire village saw it as the truth. People will eat up any shite you serve to them so long as they're angry, afraid, or sad. They did fear you and they did hate you for what the constables thought you did. Perfect it was, troubled boy tainted by demons kills his own parents in a night of rage."

Will shivered and he slid back. He felt bars form around him and he was in the Royal Courts again, ten-years-old. His best friend stuttered untrue words and Will glared at him, half enraged, half devastated. Will's ears tingled as each lie Saul uttered cut through his heart like a blade. Chained, caged, and gagged, all he could do to stop Saul was to scream inside.

"E-Everything... it w-was all because..." Tears formed in Will's eyes and he shouted, "Why couldn't he ask—" The murderer shoved his hand across Will's mouth.

"I was hired to do a job an' I did it."

Will's pearl grew hot and red in his pouch. He remembered everything, his whole life playing for him. The pain and grief at the sight of his dead parents. The fear on his first day in prison, the emotion that overcame him when he was free, and the hatred harboured by the nobles.

"You're not gonna get anything else from me. You want..."

The murderer smiled and lowered his tone, "That's what you want isn't it? Revenge? Look. I figured you ought to get an explanation. That's all you're gonna get."

The gondola entered a square canal whose south end was attached to a parallel canal and whose north end rose up along a set of stairs. At the top of the stairs stood seven men. The two closest to the center were covered in mail and plate with a mail aventail that revealed only their eyes. They bore three black stripes on their armor except for the blue-grey cloaked man in the center, whose face was hooded. Two glowing amber eyes peered out.

Will gasped and fell back, his muscles shriveled and his chest heaved. The murderer caught him before he fell off the gondola. Tremors burst through his body.

"Finally, where he said to meet." The murderer pointed to the men. "Take us in."

"I thought we were just going to rob him an' toss him in some alley. You didn't say we were gonna give him to someone." The boat boy paled. "He's rich… look at his clothes." He gestured to Will. "Kidnapping is years locked up and tortured… or we'll hang."

"The pay's big. You don't got guts, then jump in the water. Don't need you no more."

The boat boy swallowed and parked the gondola along the side of the stairs while the murderer left to speak with the men. Will steadied and propped himself up, watching the boat boy anchor the gondola.

"L-Listen!" Will whispered. The boat boy ignored him. "I'm squire to the grand marshal." That made the boy pause and hesitate a look at Will. "If you l-let me go I won't tell anyone of your part in this."

"He is mine! Take your gold and give him to me!" The warden's deep voice sent shivers through Will. He held the urge to vomit and raised his voice.

"Please."

"Did he really kill your parents?"

Will nodded. Ten constables rushed into the courtyard above the canal in between the warden and Will.

"You all! Constables, stop! What are ya doing here so close to curfew?"

"None of you matter." The warden sneered. He and his men drew their swords and forced their way forwards. The murderer shoved a constable aside and bolted down a side street. The boat boy scrambled from Will's side and stumbled on shore skidding to a stop in front of two constables. One thrust his man catcher polearm forward, clamping it around the boy's neck and shoving him to the ground. The other pinned his torso in place. Will grasped his longsword and drew the blade, gripping the handle. He rushed on shore and followed the murderer, cornering him in a dead end.

Saul's betrayal, the ire of his village and the judges, the lust of the warden, Norman, the girl, and those he had hurt to find some sense of peace rushed through his mind. His parents' smiles faded with their lifeless corpses. All of it because of what this man falsely painted on him. He drew forward his longsword and channelled his anger into it, acknowledging the revenge he sought. His body aflame with heat he screamed and thrust the blade forward, tears streaking along the edges of his eyes. To Will's horror, the blade flew over the murderer's shoulder. The murderer thrust his dagger, primed to lodge it in Will's lung. A pistol ball zipped into the murderer's temple and he collapsed, forcing Will to stumble back. The killer lay there bleeding and lifeless.

"Drop the sword boy and hands on yer head! To your knees!" the constable who had fired ordered. Will dropped his sword and complied, not once breaking eye contact with the dead murderer before him. He was a mix of emotions. No relief or satisfaction, nor sadness, he just was.

Sir Robert came two hours later and found his apprentice in a stockade beside the boy who'd robbed Will in another. Served him right. They'd not talked to each other. Both were also chained by the neck, wrists, and ankles to a pole behind each stockade.

"He thrust his sword at the man sir; couldn't tell whether he agitated the man or if he was defending himself," explained the constable who'd detained Will.

"And what was said?" Sir Robert asked, his horse grew restless beside him as a constable tried to calm it. Darkness crept into the sky.

"Didn't hear but the boy…"

"Squire," Sir Robert corrected the man.

"Your squire accused the man of murder."

"Whose?"

"His family's. Shot the man before he could kill your squire."

"You did well sergeant. I won't leave him through the night, I will be taking him. How much is the fine?"

"You're a knight, but this violence ain't right. Three men injured from those other brigands, but they fled. Anyways, Fifty silver." Sir Robert nodded and counted out the fine. He handed the coins to the sergeant and then strode to his squire. Will stared at the ground. The warden's return was overshadowed by the murderer. He thought people had stopped hunting him; it had been like a weight lifted off his shoulders. Knowing the man who tormented him for six years was still looking for him terrified Will. As he heard his master's steps, he bit his lip.

The holes of the wooden stockade for his head and wrists held him tightly and he had been standing in a hunched over position for so long it rendered him drained and aching.

"Will, what can I say," Sir Robert started dismissively. "I asked you to retrieve supplies, it was a simple task."

"It wasn't my fault, I was robbed, got lost…" Will answered.

"He *let* you go, you told the constable, you *could have* run off. There was no need to escalate things."

The boat boy tilted his head, mouth agape, but didn't say anything.

"But he was…" At the sound of his master's sigh Will stopped.

"Will, I am helping you towards a different life. Had you not been wearing your tunic with my crest, these guardsmen would have handed you over to the sheriff and he would have had you on your way to Isen Prison. I could do nothing to help you then."

"I know Master. I want to prove myself worthy of…"

"You have no need to prove me anything Will, you just need to do as I say, that is all."

Will nodded his head. "I couldn't run away. I felt I had to face him, I felt like I was defending my family's name."

A constable unlocked the stockade and chains. Will collapsed into his master's arms, head falling over and a ragged groan spilling from his chest. Sir Robert guided Will to the horse. He helped Will onto it then mounted himself up.

Sir Robert signaled the sergeant. "Here. Silver for the other's release and another for his family. Hold him for a few days then let him go."

The murderer's voice crept into Will's head. The man's explanation for why he had killed Will's parents bothered him. Had his parents known that they were buying stolen property? They'd been so desperate that they'd not fully considered the deal they made with the merchant. The murder of his parents was ordered by a man who didn't care about them, who saw them as mere cattle, and whose power was too great for him to challenge. He didn't feel like enacting vengeance; perhaps he should as that's what other people would want. Instead, powerlessness and exhaustion overcame him.

Regardless, a weight lifted from Will's chest at hearing the truth and the murderer's confession filled him with relief. Even though many would still hate him and blame him, it wasn't true, he wasn't who people thought he was. As a squire, he resolved right then and there to demonstrate who he really was. If he followed his new master faithfully, maybe he'd gain power like the knight had. That way he could change things and even prevent others from falling prey of King Duggan's systems and Judeicar's Justice.

"You had better hold on so you do not fall," Sir Robert said. Will brought his arms around his master's waist and rested his head on the knight's back. They moved over a canal and towards the palace.

His duty as a squire came first right now. He would serve this knight who'd been so kind to him as loyally as he could. He knew now that this knight was *not* false. This knight was nothing like the warden. He'd fight this war and he'd kill Saomardrim, though he feared if he could kill with intent. He'd make a name for himself so that he could properly settle, without the nobility's distain, into his new life. Sir Robert had not approved of his actions. The knight always seemed to choose his battles, waiting for the right moment to exert authority or energy. He'd thought running was the better option. Will disagreed. Facing the man who'd destroyed his life had freed him more than anything. But still, he had to make amends with Sir Robert.

"I am sorry. I was foolish," Will admitted.

"No, you had a right to confront him. It was dangerous but your right nevertheless. He admitted to killing your family. Besides, I shouldn't have sent you alone."

"He was the man, and I didn't force him to confess."

"I wasn't thinking that and truthfully Will, you couldn't force anyone to do anything."

"I know." Will frowned. One day though, Will knew, he would have the power to take initiative, he just needed to learn how.

Chapter Twelve

THEY DEPARTED SUTHENBURG early the next day, and rode north then northwest into a hilly region, with the Hertos River on their right. Will rode alongside Sir Robert who headed a small column of soldiers sent to see them safely to Castle Ochsen.

Ahead, on the highest hill, Castle Ochsen rose into the sky. With its keep on the highest peak, the sides of the keep as well as the outer bailey wall, facing Will, were pointed and seemed to almost cut through the sky. At the base of the walls, around its entire length, a slanted brace had been built making it resistant to undermining, cannon fire, and gave the castle a more mountainous shape.

To the north of the keep a bridge connected to a tall cylindrical tower, slightly higher. Around it, at regular intervals, drawbridges lay open as if people could walk out onto them and jump off.

They approached the southeastern entrance, where makeshift barricades enclosed a field of tents and the many soldiers who occupied them. Soldiers dashed around the camp, packing supplies, readying arms and armor, and engaged in various other essential tasks.

A familiar fear crept up on Will. There were so many soldiers, so many guards around him. He veered a little closer to his master and kept his eyes downwards, only daring a few quick glances.

"We will be going to the port and board our ship," Sir Robert said, seeing Will's distress. "Once you see how many ships are docked in port and offshore you will get a sense of how many thousands of men are here."

"Th-Thousands..." Will's face paled. "That many?"

"You come from a village; I doubt you have even seen one-hundred people in the same place. Yes, there are many people ready to go to war today."

Several large, armored carriages in one section of the camp caught Will's attention. Some were simple wood and metal boxes while others were large and enclosed. The walls of the carriages were lined with holes with the tips of weapons poking through, holes for shooting. They were armed with cannon, arrow gun, and their presence were fearsome. One man shouted to another inside. From inside, a tube-like shaft poked out. Suddenly it spit flame.

Will spotted a section where foreign men, dark in skin and wearing colourful foreign clothes, sold supplies to soldiers.

"Who're they?" Will asked his master. "They don't seem part of the army."

Sir Robert looked their way. "Those are Saomardrim merchants."

"Saomardrim! But they're the enemy."

"You will find out that this war is not so simple. A few Gurmian and Saomardrim contacts still persist in a peaceful manner. One such contact is trade and if the supplies are good, safe, and cheap many will have no quarrels trading with our enemy."

Sir Robert and his retainers approached the barbican of the castle and were quickly waved through. They crossed a bridge towards a walled island under the hill where the southeastern wall stood. Passing through the island bailey, equally as busy and populated as the camp outside, but housing officers, they crossed another bridge and began the climb up a winding path built into the side of the hill. Under a bridge above hung a massive blue and gold banner with the symbol of Gurmanis on it, similar to the various other smaller flags and banners on the castle's walls and towers. It bore a crown flanked by a sword and feather, backed by a white cross and with a crown in each of its four corners.

Once they'd climbed all the way up the winding path, they encountered the outer bailey's gatehouse. Will looked down towards the Hertos River where something burned on the shoreline. A structure resembling a large naval ship was lying on its side, half in the water and half on land. Men scrambled around it trying to put the flames out. A large leather tarp partially covered it.

"When we get settled in, I will speak to the castellan. You should set out my armor as you will be helping me dress. It is your responsibility as my squire." Sir Robert instructed.

"Yes master."

The outer bailey was filled with more fighting men and their support staff including craftsmen and servants, women and children, even a few opportunistic Gurmian merchants. The soldiers here however were of higher rank and mixed with lesser noble soldiers and knights. Many people were gathering supplies onto carts and sent them through the gatehouse that led to the castle port.

Groups of knights and nobles rode in with their retainers. Large parties accompanied each. Some knights, Will recognised from Suthenburg and others he did not. All had armed men with them, squires and pages, male and female servants, and some even brought their war dogs.

"As we go towards our ship, we walk among them dressed and prepared, thus we give their morale a boost," Sir Robert started. "We must show confidence and power through which the men will feel as they see us. As their commanders, they will look to us for guidance. A little bit of a show yes but just as vital to success."

"Walking among them armored?"

"Morale is the key Will, not so much the display of wealth and power. When you come down to its core, a battle is a contest to see who will break their formation and flee first. High morale encourages cohesion and confidence which prevents panic that can break a formation and lose us a battle. Understand?"

"I think so." Will nodded.

Sir Robert led his group even further into the castle through two more gatehouses, a bridge linking them, into the inner bailey. Here the highest-ranking knights and nobles prepared to be deployed.

Sir Robert left his retainers and led Will through the final gatehouse into the innermost bailey, which was no more than a small courtyard for the keep. They were greeted by the castellan. He had servants take Sir Robert's and his squire's horses to the stables, and other servants took their things into the keep.

***

Will kept in stride with his master who stood tall ahead of him, their cloaks flowing in the costal breeze restricted only by their heather shields which bore Sir Robert's full crest. The technical names Sir Robert had taught still whirled around in his mind: pauldrons, couters, cuisse, greaves, sabatons, arming jacket, poleyns, plackart, too many for him to remember.

In heavy armor Will was reminded of the descriptions, paintings, and even of Lord Jerold' knights. Most commoners rarely saw a heavily armored knight. Will's awe when he first met Sir Robert in the Roywood, wearing his lighter armor, paled in comparison to now. In heavy armor Sir Robert looked wealthier and more imposing than ever before. Even the decoration on his armor reflected the wealth he still had after forfeiting his lands, and his position as grand marshal. Painted into the edges of the armor was the red, blue, and white of the Gilios family.

Will wore mail, a surcoat, and plate for his legs and arms. The pieces were once the knight's, those that fit, and the rest the castellan had procured. Confidence and a sense of power came over him as he stood in the new armor, feelings that had long been ripped out of him. He was ready to do anything. Will found the confidence to voice his gratitude.

"I feel… you know… confident, secure. Thank-you Master… I hope I can live up to your faith in me in battle."

"That you will do Will if you remember your training. Play it safe. I'd rather you stay alive, there will be many opportunities to prove yourself at a later date."

"Yes Master." A coldness spread through him. Death, it was something he'd thought of in his life but he knew that no matter how close to death he'd been brought, he would never be allowed to die. That was how it was in Isen Prison. Now there would be no twisted warden or evil guard to preserve him. Despite the finality, this new situation was better.

Will's mind lingered. He remembered now the descriptions of the Saomardrim and their land, especially from the zealous priest in King's Bridge Village. Their bold ferocity when they attacked Isen Prison surely meant they were skilled warriors. Will's confidence quickly sank.

"Is there something else on your mind?"

"This is really happening then?" Will asked. "We are going to fight the Saomardrim? I heard things about them… bad things. Is it true they practice dark magic? Are we to see giant ants and snakes?"

"Where did you learn that nonsense from?" Sir Robert huffed. "I think I will let you see for yourself what the Saomardrim and their lands are really like. Fear is natural Will. You go to a land you cannot imagine."

Sir Robert and Will reached the stables in the innermost bailey and found their horses armored up in the knight's colours. Each horse wore plate armor over their entire body. Out from the armor hung a length of cloth so only the lower part of the legs could be seen.

Sir John and his squire, Alex, entered the stables. Both were fully armored and wore Sir John's colours, blue and green with the image of an elk. Sir Robert greeted his fellow commander,

"Sir John you have arrived and in good time. We are to ride out towards the ships."

"Yes, I saw your retainers ready to escort us," Sir John replied. The two knights continued to talk and behind them Will loosely paid attention. Alex came to Will's side and nodded a greeting to Will with a smile. Will returned the gesture and his body seized up as if the warden was coming to punish him. The last squires who Will had met were ready to kill him. Will hoped Alex wasn't one of those squires. Could that smile be like the warden's smile? A smile that hid a world of hurt.

"I should start by offering my apologies." Alex made a bow. He had a clean-shaven face and short wavy hair. "The actions of my fellow squires were uncalled for and they should not have acted as they did."

"I accept your apology," Will said, relieved that Alex did not hurt him.

"I am pleased to hear that." A sincere smile crossed his face.

"It wasn't your fault. You don't need to apologise."

"What one knight, squire, or page does affects the reputation of us all. Many have forgotten this."

Will remembered how ill he thought of Sir Robert when the man first offered to take Will as his squire. He distrusted him. Now Will knew the truth. Sir Robert cared. If there was any doubt it had slowly eroded away due to what the man had done for him, taught him and given him.

"You've not forgotten?"

"My knowledge is a result of my master's teachings. I owe Sir John my profession and I work to honour him." Alex, like all nobles, had that regal tone of talk and a way with words that made him sound sophisticated and intelligent.

"Squires," Sir John called, "Let's mount up." Sir Robert, Sir John, Alex, and Will all mounted their horses. The knights rode tall black destriers, expensive and muscular. The squires rode smaller coursers, fast horses with less muscle but by no means cheap.

The squires took position behind their masters and held up their banners. Behind them Sir Robert's retainers had mounted and each held a banner with the flag of Gurmanis emblazoned on them. They rode forward towards the inner and outer bailey.

"Respectfully, you look nothing like the descriptions of you I have heard," Alex spoke as they rode.

"You mean the descriptions on the wanted posters." Will frowned.

"And the words my fellow nobles use for you. I do not care where you have come from. Anyone willing to fight the Saomardrim threat is fine enough."

"Thank-you."

"I hear they have removed the bounty on your head and your wanted status because you now serve Sir Robert."

"Really…" Will said with unease, surprised he didn't care more about having the bounty removed. It hadn't stopped the warden. He didn't want Alex to speak further of this.

"You are very lucky to serve under the grand marshal. His command has been the most effective. He captured Al-Khadra forest in northern Saomarhad. Indeed, it is difficult to conquer and maintain control over a dense forest, but your master did it."

Will tried to copy Alex's noble speak, "I am respected to serve him. He has been the single man who had heeded." The group entered the outer bailey and the men around them cheered and bowed to their grand marshal. Alex laughed, sensing Will's change of tone.

"You have a long way to go before you can blend with the nobility. I hope we can fight alongside each other or practice together, there is much we can learn from each other." Will warmed at the thought of gaining a friend. The group began to cross the bridge towards the port, Castle Ochsen at their backs.

"Me? What can I teach you?"

"Do not lower yourself; there is a lot you can teach me even simply by observing you fight. My advice is to keep your eyes open and attend to what you are doing, what others are doing. Do not over-extend. Do not rush ahead. You will come to understand what I mean."

"I'll do that." Will smiled. The group turned to the right and began to slope down into the castle port. Across the busy space hundreds of ships sat either docked or anchored off-shore. Huge warships with tall masts towered above him dawning the colours and symbol of the Gurmian navy, a shark over the crown with crossed feather and sword. From left to right, the blue water that was the Hertos River painted the horizon.

Stretching from northwest to southeast, land not visible across it, and darker blue where it was deeper. A number of seagulls glided overhead, screeching.

All around the port, armored men marched onto ships, dragging bags and barrels on board. Horses neighed in displeasure as the most stubborn ones were strapped to a harness and lifted by crane onto transport ships.

"Ah! witajcie!" A man teased as he approached on foot. His blue tunic, outlined in red, and a flowing cloak with the Gurmian navy symbol on it caught in the river breeze. The man adjusted his tricorn hat and wicked sweat from his light mustache and beard. The riders stopped their horses. "You'll be upon the Swift Spear this time, she who is in command of all these hunks of wood. Fastest and deadliest ship you'll ever find!"

"Henryk, *you're* leading the navy this time eh?" Sir John laughed.

"I *am* the admiral."

"Who knows if the ship is sea worthy," Sir Robert said.

Henryk griped the rapier hanging at his belt. "How dare you insult my ship. I tell you, on my ship if you make such a comment, I will toss you overboard myself, grand marshal or not!"

Sir Robert put his hands up in protest. "Relax Admiral Białek, it was only a joke! It has been a long time." Sir Robert grinned.

"This campaign just gets better." Sir John signaled for the squires to greet the admiral. "Alas Alex and I will go upon a different ship. The reunion between friends must wait."

"If it was not for the meagre salary the king gives me," Admiral Białek waved a hand dismissively, "I would have added some more cannons and fix up the hull. King Duggan had me leading assaults on the southern seas."

"Well, I am sure once you get a bit of wine in you, you will tell me all about it. Are we ready to set sail?" Sir Robert asked.

"Almost, as soon as the last bit of cargo is hauled on. The boatswain is doing some final checks, should not be too long." A lanner falcon swooped low in the air, flying around the group and catching attention from below.

"Hold out your arm Will," Sir Robert said. Will did so. The lanner falcon came for another pass and gracefully landed on Will's arm. He tensed, almost shaking it off, but the falcon was calmer. It flicked its head at Will and blinked. Many in the crowd gasped and mumbled to each other. Will blushed.

"Amazing," Alex said. "Is that your bird?" The bird blinked at Will.

"I guess it is." Will sighed, unsure at calling the bird his, but clearly the bird did not want to leave him.

Will and his master left Alex and Sir John, and Admiral Białek who went ahead. The falcon flew off and Will rode up alongside Sir Robert, remembering to keep his banner held up tall. Will observed the groups noting how many of those present were not much older than him. The army was not like he saw among the older nobles and knights in Suthenburg. Likely, the same composition made up the Saomarhad army. The old may declare a war but it was the young who fought it, and died in it. It seemed unfair.

Sir Robert and Will rode down a set of stairs and onto the boardwalk being careful to avoid busy soldiers. They eyed the blue and gold command ship, the Swift Spear, frigate class, demanding a prominent place among the other warships.

"Sir Robert!" someone called amongst the crowd. The knight stopped and looked towards the noise. As a group of sailors dragged barrels off in one direction, from behind three men strode forward. Their dress was different than that of the army. They were Templars of Manis. The templars approached and one came forward, an older man near fifty with brown hair cut into a bowl shape and a thin u-shaped moustache, bowed to the knight.

"So you must be Sir Guarin Delacroix. When I heard the Templars of Manis were accompanying the army I was surprised," Sir Robert spoke.

"And how so? As is our duty, we have been ever fighting against the enemies of Manis." Sir Guarin scratched his chin, fingering the few strands of hair that passed as a goatee.

"Yet how zealously you do so tarnishes the honour of Manians."

"Mon dieu! I heard of you chevalier… I did not expect to be insulted upon meeting you." His eyes narrowed over his squat nose. His master's bluntness stunned Will too.

"Oh… sorry, perhaps I was too sudden. How many Templars do you bring?"

"Some fifty."

"And you will help us in the assault?"

"No, there is a relic within Al-Motros we wish to collect. Our primary goal is such. Worry not; once we are in, we shall not be in your way."

"Templars. Helpful as always." Sir Robert sighed. Sir Guarin raised an eyebrow.

"With this current attack should we not push our advantage further? What say you Sir Robert?"

"I think we should be cautious, Sir Guarin. In my campaigns in northern Saomarhad I saw not spent and fragmented foes, but a fierce people, who can coordinate when they will it."

"And plotting, qui. Templars relayed a message from a dying spy which claims that the sultan is planning something terrible."

"I have heard. We get information from Ortie. Still, the full picture is not known, so we should remain cautious."

"Yes, well your martial skill is recognised throughout Gurmanis. You do not share the king's initiative, dommage." Sir Guarin looked at Will. "For now, at least, you still remain loyal. The same cannot be said for the nobles who did not muster here. Have you heard aught of Lord Gregor?"

"Yes, I have." Sir Robert adjusted, appearing to be frustrated with the middle-aged man.

"He's leading the lords who petition King Duggan for peace. Ha! Saomardrim need not to be treated with peace."

"There is frustration everywhere Sir Guarin, among those lords and the commoners."

"And what is your stance? You still fight."

"I do, but I do so not out of a desire to put Saomardrim to the sword. I do so because it is my duty."

"Because you are a broken chevalier Sir Robert. Because you actually, willingly, gave-up your lands yet the king could not let you go. Non. He made you grand maréchal. There. We are now even." Sir Guarin bowed. Will shifted, uncomfortable. "My ship awaits, I hope to speak more of our plans soon, Sir Robert." The knight nodded and the templars strolled towards their ship.

"Leaving their more peaceful duties of pilgrim, priest, and relic protection, they have killed many Saomardrim." Sir Robert frowned, watching the templars leave. "Though at this point none of us are innocent of that. We have all killed many Saomardrim, and the Saomardrim have killed many of us. Sometimes I do wonder if Lord Gregor and his coalition of nobles has a point. Peace would better serve both nations I think."

As Will and his master neared the command ship, Will could not help but to stare up in awe. The masts stood towering above him, its ropes and sails moving slowly in the wind. There were even men at the top; Will thought them mad. The two dismounted in front of the command ship and Will handed off Sir Robert's banner to a servant then boarded the Swift Spear.

People rushed around, running and talking and doing any and every task. Many wore rough sea faring clothes, others, fewer in number, wore navy uniforms.

The ship set off north as the wind changed direction. It filled Will with a little bit of fear when in all directions he could no longer see any land, only water. He had lived his entire life land locked; this was very new. After a while standing over the side of the ship looking at the open water and all the other ships following, a sickly grumbling feeling welled up in his stomach. He remained stuck to the edge of the ship, constantly worried he'd spew vomit over the side.

Sir Robert was at the front of the ship scanning the horizon for the enemy, but Will couldn't understand why his master was also scanning the sky. What threat would come from there? They sailed for hours, the day coming to a close. Will had spent most of the day standing on the edge of the ship or wandering about the lower decks. It felt better to be inside a cabin. The small, mostly bare space felt familiar to him, safe. Those feelings eased his sickness.

Sir Robert and Admiral Białek sat across from each other in the admiral's cabin. To one side a large globe sat on a stand bolted to the floor. A low shelf held scrolls and books and displayed on top, a set of model ships in jars accented the room. A dresser sat at the other end beside a curtain separating a cotton mattress, covered in expensive coloured fabrics, set into a polished wooden frame.

Some walls held diagrams, maps, and nautical charts. Scattered across the table between Sir Robert and Admiral Białek, were similar items. A bottle of light blue wine sparkled between them. The admiral took a sip from his cup then thumped it on the table.

"You'd better like that wine, Robert. It's the last I have. Pfft," Admiral Białek said.

"Is something wrong Henryk?" Sir Robert took a sip of wine.

"There is a war going on. Isn't that worry enough?"

"Perhaps. As an admiral in the Royal Forces—"

"Royal Forces! Have you seen the men aboard my fleet? Before the muster padded the fleet with whoever supports the king or does so out of fear, most of my men are mercenaries! That's why I can't get more Imperium wine, Itympia Brew that is. All the coin's going to mercenaries. Remaining Gurmian men are volunteers sent by various nobles, not Royal Forces. The king is focused on his land battles."

"I am sorry its that bad."

"It get's worse." Admiral Białek sighed and rocked back in his leather chair. "Robert if you saw what I encountered in the Inner Seas down south, you too would be concerned. Eldarun Dominion warships."

"High elves? That far from home?"

"Princess Elizabeth's marriage fell through when she ran away. The Imperium pulled its offer of marriage and alliance, then reached out to the sultan. Did you ever find her?"

"No." Sir Robert grimaced. "I lost her in the south then the war needed my attention. Since then, I've had trackers and King's Guard looking for her. I get reports frequently. She was tracked to Altan, then Charleston. No word after that."

"Well, it looks like the king doesn't care anymore."

"Don't say that Henryk. He does love his daughter."

"Well, he's moved onwards. Negotiations with the high elves have started, an elf ambassador has arrived. King Duggan, no, all of us need more money. Just look at all the debts the king's amounted. He took out loans from the All Ocean's Trading Conglomerate's banks and you know how much interest the Conglomerate's banks demand."

"So, we're at a military *and* economic loss now."

"Tak." Admiral Białek nodded. "I and many others don't like this business with the Dominion. Very long ago before Imperium rule even, humans rose up from slavery and kicked out the elves. Dang elves have been but-hurt ever since. They're always trying to get a backdoor into the resource rich lands that is the metropolis of the Imperium. That backdoor is Gurmanis. Of course, the king wants to fight, out of vengeance for his wife and a desire for domination."

"You speak treason Henryk," Sir Robert warned.

"Last month I sailed the Inner Seas on a defensive mission against the Saomardrim. I saw Dominion warships standing off against several Imperium warships. No shots were fired, mind you, but God's mercy I feared they would. Trust me Sir Robert. Both the Dominion and the Imperium see Gurmanis and Saomarhad weakening. They're lying-in wait until both nations war themselves out of existence. Then they'll fight each other for the scraps. None of us will be alive to see it."

⁕

It took another day of huddling in his cabin for Will to finally feel healthy enough to go to the upper decks, with the intention of standing there without feeling sick or exposed. The sunset glowed a warm orange, as he exited the lower decks. Will caught the attention of some of the soldiers. One bearded, tall and muscular man came forward. He glared at Will and crossed his arms over his chest. Tensing, Will dropped his gaze.

"So, you're the grand marshal's squire huh?" the man spoke.

"Yes sir." More men noticed what was happening and stepped forward. They'd backed Will against the door. Their disdain-filled eyes stared down on him, judging him. Will's vision blurred. The Gurmian soldiers shifted between what they were and the form of Isen Prison guards. Will's heart raced, his skin paled, and he broke a cold sweat. He trembled and held back tears, trying to shake the image of Isen guards cornering him against the wall of the mines.

"He's our lord's squire. We ought to show him respect, or leave him alone," another man said. Where was Sir Robert? Will prayed the knight would come and save him before he withered.

"No. That boy's a sinner. Familicide. It's a bad omen having him around," the bearded man argued.

"Not all o' us are clean either. Men oft join this crusade to cleanse their sins. Boy could be here for that reason."

"As a squire." The man huffed. "Fine. Why're you here boy?"

"I... I..." Will tried to find words but only parts came. Voices crept into his head. Isen guards, the warden.

125

"Well, boy?"

"Look, you've terrified him."

"Ha. He's going to war. He ought to be terrified."

"I... I-I want to... serve my master," Will spoke. "H-He's good to me."

"He's good to all of us," a young man spoke to the others. "And we ought to remember that and not accost his squire."

"I will p-prove myself... I will. I'm not... not what you think," Will gave in. He hung his head and accepted that he was going to be hurt now. Instead, the bearded man laughed.

"Then I'll be watching. Kill Saomardrim. Prove to yerself, an' to us, that you know who it is you actually need to kill. Manis' mercy." The group of men left him. Astonished, Will looked up, blinked his wet eyes— then was thrown backwards by a shockwave. Wood tore apart and splinters flung into the sky. Men shouted.

"Boats spotted! Sloops I recon. To starboard!" the man on top of the crow's nest screamed out. Will scrambled to his feet. He froze. Panicked. Unsure how to react. A man noticed him.

"Squire! Get to the top deck and to your master's side. Go!" he screamed. Will stumbled forward then broke into a sprint, running past men rushing to their stations. He ran to the top deck where the ship's steering wheel was. Sir Robert and Admiral Białek stood there. Admiral Białek calmly gave orders.

"All hands-on deck! To your stations!" the admiral shouted.

"Will!" Sir Robert shoved a telescope into Will's arms.

"Master?" Will asked, panting and mistaken.

"We're under attack by two Saomarhad sloops. Spot them for us."

"Me? But..."

"Henryk, he's yours." The admiral nodded and Sir Robert rushed off deck to oversee the gunners. Will watched him go then looked at the admiral, dumfounded.

"Well look through it then!" the admiral ordered. A cannon ball smashed into the side of the Swift Spear, another hit the water nearby. Will looked through the telescope in the direction of the attack. Two sloops were on the retreat. One closer than the other.

"Which one is closest boy?" Admiral Białek asked.

"The left one."

"Target to port!" the admiral shouted to his men. "Distance?"

"Ah..."

"Quickly!" Will didn't know what to measure distance with.

"He's close... I mean..."

"Na Boga!" The admiral sighed. "Think of this ship. How many?"

"Four." The admiral shouted the correct distance and the guns fired. Cannon arced over the water and crashed into the closest sloop, it erupted into flame. The men cheered. "Good work boy."

Will nodded. The Swift Spear gained speed. It parted with the fleet and pursued the second sloop.

"Now. Tell us exactly when the last sloop is two ships distance from us," Admiral Białek instructed. Will watched carefully as they approached. The sloop fired back, trying to shake the Swift Spear.

"N-Now!" Will shouted. The Swift Spear fired at the sloop, smacking into its side. It burst into flames. Will could see Saomardrim jumping off and into the river. The Gurmians cheered.

"Brawo." Admiral Białek smiled. He took the telescope from Will. "You learn and adapt quickly. I see Sir Robert noticed that in you." Henryk leaned towards Will and whispered, "If you're ever looking to ditch the knight, I could use a cabin boy aboard this vessel." Will turned red.

<hr>

Standing on the top deck, Will fixed his eyes on the grinning man beyond his shield. The men surrounding them cheered for the grizzled Gurmian soldier. The soldier also held a shield and a practice sword. Will tensed, his muscles tightened.

"Breathe Will," Sir Robert said, standing to the boy's side. "The shield is the best defensive tool to have but you have to be able to withstand the force of a strike. Remember the stance I taught you."

Will gripped the center-grip of his shield then inhaled. He adjusted his own practice sword. The Gurmian soldier lunged. As per his master's instruction, Will tried to predict where the blow would land and adjusted his shield accordingly. He blocked the attack, then another.

"Good. Now charge him," Sir Robert ordered the soldier. Will panicked, that wasn't a part— The soldier charged, throwing his full force behind his shield. Will raised his own shield to meet him. They crashed into each other and pushed.

"Keep steady. I doubt you will get into this situation in battle but for now at least we can test your strength." Sir Robert crossed his arms and smirked. The men around them cheered on the grizzled soldier. Will's muscles strained as he tried to push back against the man's strength, but Will was giving ground, breaking a sweat across his face, and turning red. The soldier growled and shouted. With a last surge of energy, he pushed forwards and threw Will backwards. Will slid against the ground. The men around them clapped and shouted gleefully, and the soldier raised his hands, taking in the praise. Sir Robert helped Will back up from the floor.

"Good try. Let's leave the shield for now and you can try the bow. We can have a target set up."

<hr>

A few days later the Gurmian fleet had passed the King's Bridge. Sailing under the ruined bridge had been a tense affair with everyone standing at their stations and cannons primed. The Saomardrim had not fired, visible standing by their shore batteries and with their flag silently fluttering atop their border castle, but it was obvious the Gurmian fleet had been spotted.

One day passed without any further problems, and even the waters were calm and the current favorable. The next day, the favourable travel was quickly interrupted. Large wooden shapes appeared ahead of the fleet.

"It's the enemy! Saomarhad ships. They're in range. They're firing!" hollered the man on the crow's nest. Cannon fire erupted and water splashed up by the ship. A cannon ball hit the ship flanking the flagship. Sir Robert cursed.

"Their speed is commendable." he mumbled.

Admiral Białek emerged screaming from his quarters onto the upper deck, "All hands-on deck! To your stations! I want galleons and frigates covering our man-of-wars. All boats full speed!" Henryk made his way to the wheel and Sir Robert took Will to the bow of the ship to a siphon-like gun mounted on the deck.

"This is a flamethrower, it has fire that sticks, when we are in range turn this lever and stamp the piston below repeatedly. Keep turning to fire. Aim for the sails and stay safe, these men will help you." Before Will could protest, Sir Robert ran to the wheel to join the admiral.

A sailor looked at Will and advised, "Only fire when your master tells us to boy." Will nodded and tried to stifle the panic rising in him. More cannon fire came crashing down missing their ship and flaming rocks arched through the sky. The two fleets came so close now that Will saw the Saomardrim savages up close. They appeared as normal humans, only darker and with different clothing. The Saomardrim soldiers wore a brown tunic with green and gold lining over light chain armour. Their helmets were slightly pointed and a chain aventail ran down the back of their neck. The heavy class soldiers wore plate or lamellar armour that covered everything except for their eyes. A small coloured plume stood up on their helmets. Each warrior carried a different weapon including maces, polearms, ranged weapons, and curved swords.

"Fire!" Henryk shouted. Will turned the crank and aimed for the enemy's sails. Flame erupted from the weapon, shaking it and threatening to make Will lose his grip. He gripped it tightly to avoid losing control. The flame stuck. Sails burned. Men tried to throw water on the flames, but the fire kept growing. What a weapon!

"Fire to port!" Henryk commanded. Will did not know what port was.

"To port boy! Port!" yelled the sailor. He pushed Will to the left and he fired.

"Engage the flagship. Line those cannons up." Henryk ordered. He kept a calm demeanor despite the happenings around him. The Swift Spear turned gently to port diagonally so its right side faced the right side of the other ship. Fire and cannon burst out of both ships, shaking everything. As quick as the

Swift Spear was it missed the fire from the Saomarhad ship just barely. She was able to sink the Saomarhad ship.

"I want a path cleared to their destroyers so ours can engage them! Fly the flag, frigates to our sides, engage targets and gunboats on their starboard to provide support!" The Swift Spear straitened and headed directly towards the enemy destroyers. Around her, Gurmian ships engaged frigates.

The sounds of battle drained voices out. Cannon balls crashed with ships and flame rose everywhere. Ash and smoke filled the air and Will found it hard to see. Smoke stung his eyes. A cannon ball hit the side of their ship then another on deck. Will was launched back by the impact. He scraped his arm on the deck. Burning lingered for a few moments. Muffled voices shouted around him.

"Fire! Fire!"

Will stood. Saomardrim men swung from their ship to Will's. Will drew his longsword. They charged and Will made ready to strike the first man. He gripped his sword, certain he could do this. Unease surged, but he tried to remember his training. Will took a stance. His muscles tightened. He inhaled. Before the first man could get to him, the man was tackled by a Gurmian soldier. Another Saomardrim man advanced and swung his sword at Will. The boy countered, stabbed, and Will's sword point bounced off mail. They traded blows. He needed to find a weak point. Suddenly the ship rocked again and the Saomardrim man lost his balance. He fell to the ground, exposed. Will steadied himself but hesitated, afraid to make the killing blow, his hands clammy. The man started to stand. An explosion launched Will and the Saomardrim back across the deck. Will staggered to his feet in heavy confusion and panic. He ran across the deck trying to find Sir Robert.

"Abandon ship!" someone yelled. A series of flaming rocks hit the ship followed by at least five cannon shots. The Saomarhad destroyers had hit the Swift Spear. Heat ripped at his skin; he was on fire! He tried to douse it but tripped over himself and fell off the ship into the water, feeling his organs lift against the fall. Will struggled to stay afloat as his frantic movements only helped the water overtake him, which seemed to pull him as if he were trapped in lard. Fear rose in Will as he began to sink. A row boat mounted with an arrow cannon, floated over to Will and a man pulled him out of the water. There were two men on board, one gunner and one pilot.

One of them looked at his face. "You're hurt." Will traced a cut run along his neck. The man washed it away and gave Will a damp towel to clot it. The two men and Will approached three enemy boats.

"Hold on!" one of them said while the other manned the arrow cannon. He fired. A puff of smoke and fire accompanied an explosive boom. Flaming arrows arched to the first ship's mast; it went up in flames. They turned to avoid cannon fire only to move straight into a volley of arrows.

"Duck!" The rower moved fast and turned to the ship's side. Will's adrenaline peaked. From water level the chaos of the battle took a new meaning. A friendly ship glided across their view and crashed into the enemy ship ahead of them. The impact was so powerful that the enemy ship rolled over to its left, right into the water, sending a huge wave and splintered wood across Will's view. Will and the men approached. Sir Robert was the one who pulled them off the row boat.

"Welcome!" Sir Robert grinned. "Look about you, we have won! The enemy is routing." Cheering rose from all the remaining ships.

<hr>

After counting their losses, the Gurmian fleet formed up again and made for their destination. Surprisingly, the Swift Spear had survived its encounter with the heavily armed destroyers. As its namesake suggested, the Swift Spear had rammed a destroyer, rallying other Gurmian ships to its side. As Sir Robert and Will reboarded the ship Admiral Białek boasted in great detail, and maybe great exaggeration, of how his ship was the pride of the fleet.

The late afternoon brought fog, clouding up the view. This did not bother the admiral who smiled as he observed his crew from the wheel. Sir Robert followed by Will came up to him.

"The blasted fog is making it dreary. Why so content admiral?" Sir Robert asked.

"We are here Robert."

"Here? I cannot see anything."

"Hear the birds? Smell the smoke? Halsburg is upon us. Climb the mast and take a look. Crew prepare for our docking," Admiral Białek finished.

"In my age such heights of climbing are impossible. Could you go up there?" Sir Robert asked.

"Me… um…"

"It's not hard, use the checkered ropes." Will walked over and grasped the ropes. He started to climb. Halfway up he looked down then immediately looked back up as his stomach flipped. Taking a breath Will continued until he was in the crow's nest. The man there helped him up. Looking out towards the land Will saw Halsburg. It's crumbled husk was a glowing fiery scar.

"What do you see Will?" Sir Robert screamed.

Will answered in a voice his master could not hear, "Destruction. Death."

Chapter Thirteen

THE ONCE PROSPEROUS albeit threatened town Will had seen upon fleeing Isen Prison, now lay in near ruins. Much of it burned, the buildings half standing and the harbour a wreck. Smoking rubble lined the streets under ruined houses, shops, and guild halls. The dead were piled onto carts, ready to be taken away and buried. The air was choked with the smell of charcoal, ash, and burning flesh.

Sir Robert and Will walked across the docks, their plate armour gleaming in the sun, and made their way towards the harbour master's office to meet with the town's commanding official. Groups of civilians, men, women, and a few children, wandered, stood, or sat at the sides of the streets. Some stared with no aim, not reacting to any sound, prod, or discomfort. Others muttered to themselves. Still others cried and wailed. A sobbing girl hovered over the lifeless, burned body of a man. A woman bandaged around the head and in an arm sling was carried by a man and another woman. Two boys walked silently with an injured dog limping behind them. Will blocked them out, focusing on keeping pace with his master.

As they ascended a flight of stairs on the docks, they came into an open area facing the river. A few dozen men, women and children, were bound to poles, all Saomardrim, all dead.

"What is this!?" Sir Robert spoke, outraged. Judging by the blood on the corpses, they had been tortured to death.

"Master, one is still alive." Will pointed to a group of Gurmian citizens crowding around one of the poles where a man still moved.

"Come, quickly," Sir Robert strode towards the group with Will close behind. People in the crowd jeered and laughed at the bloodied and tortured man. "Who ordered this?" Sir Robert demanded. The citizens bowed and one of them stepped forwards.

"It was Lord Hellmuth."

"Where is Lord Hellmuth now?"

"He left with most of the surviving townsfolk to Croixville my lord."

"Get me a medic, the rest of you clear out." The people looked surprised. "Now!" They hurried away and Sir Robert examined the man closer.

"Wh-Why…" the man groaned in common tongue. He was covered in blood, wounded by gashes left by a lash, gouges left by a rod, and burns. "Wh-Why d'you p-purge us… I lived a peaceful existence among you. I worked with you, I traded with you… I had pride in the kingdom I lived in… I wished to see it prosper."

"You are a citizen of Halsburg?"

"Y-Yes."

"And so were the others?"

"Y-Yes…" A medic made his way over.

"You may yet live. Medic," —Sir Robert turned to the new man— "take him off this pole and treat his wounds. Inform the man in charge of the harbour guard that no Saomardrim or prisoners or otherwise are to be treated like this. Come Will." Sir Robert continued to make his way to the harbour master's office. Will avoided looking at the gruesome scene.

<hr>

In the harbour master's office, a simple room with bookshelves and racks surrounding a large map table, Sir Robert and Will met the knight in charge of the town.

"Grand Maréchal," she greeted. Sir Robert's brows drew together.

"Who are you?"

Will regarded her plate armor, the lower half covered in cloth and a blue sash across her torso. The sides of her hair were braided and tied in hair nets. She wore a small round escoffion from which a long cotton veil covered her brown hair, reaching her mid-back.

"Lady Clémentine." She flashed a faint smile. "I lead the battlemages who helped defend the town. We were sent by the arch-mage in Schweigendorf, and I rushed to aid my husband."

"Who is he?"

"Sir Dion… I am afraid he's dead." Lady Clémentine rubbed her temples and sighed. "The Saomardrim showed no mercy."

"It appears we indeed have come too late." Sir Robert grimaced. "I am sorry."

"That you did, forthwith the town was leveled, granted we were able to save some citizens and sent them to Croixville, Dieu merci. Some are still here to care for our soldiers."

"I heard Lord Hellmuth went with them. He should be here managing what remains of his town. When will he return?"

"Lord Hellmuth left. He demanded I come but my role here was to lead the mages in the town's defence. I will not leave. I will avenge my husband."

"Was Lord Hellmuth the one who ordered that mass execution?" Sir Robert's eyes narrowed.

"Yes. The townsfolk pulled the Saomardrim residents out of their quarter and tortured them before they evacuated the city, after that the Saomarhad Sultanate attacked."

This confused Will. First, he saw Saomardrim merchants selling to Gurmian soldiers, now he found out the Saomardrim lived in Gurmanis too, and they even had their own quarter. He thought they were the enemy. So why were they being treated like enemies one minute and friends the next?

"The army is here now. We will take control. Ensure there is no more killing such as I have just witnessed."

"I will ensure it."

"Very good, Lady Clémentine." Sir Robert gave the lady a piece of paper which she read.

"The king can't be serious! Attack Al-Motros? We barely have the ability to exert order on all the town yet."

"I know, but the king's word is law. I hear he is eager to advance east into what he considers is the frontier."

"I have heard such ideas. Halsburg should show however that the Saomardrim are far from beat."

"We must formulate an attack. Prioritize gaining order in the town and set up an encampment for the men."

Sir John, Alex and Sir Guarin entered.

"I don't believe the king understands what has happened here. We were attacked in the last day. Our supplies, soldiers, are all gone and many are dead. We barely have enough defences to hold this town, much less enough equipment to attack one. In addition, my battlemages are exhausted."

"Lady Clémentine, if you would like to tell this to the king then be my guest. Remember, we bring more men and supplies."

"Right, oui, we will make plans tonight." She sighed. "I will take my leave."

"A moment my lady. I have a concern to raise with you." Sir Robert gestured her to a side room. Lady Clémentine nodded and followed Sir Robert. Will shadowed from behind. "My squire has something I want you to see. I have had a mage in Burhbarrow look at it and one in Suthenburg, but none know of it. You perhaps may, if you come recently from the university."

Will flinched, caught off guard by his master revealing his pearl to strangers.

"A magical possession mayhap?" Both looked expectantly at Will. Supressing his blushing Will reluctantly presented his pearl. It gleamed a soft red, radiating warmth. Lady Clémentine brought a hand forward.

"Take care my lady. The object burns all but him," Sir Robert warned.

Nodding, Lady Clémentine lifted the pearl from Will's hand without touching it. The object floated towards her palm where it stopped. Flashes of red tried to swipe at her palm but Will swore he saw some translucent barrier holding the danger back.

"It is unusual. I do not sense any magic taught to any legal mage, but it does not appear to be dark magic. Manis forbid your squire holding something so vile. Incroyable! Even now it fights against my magic. How did he come by this?"

"Will," Sir Robert prompted.

"I found it in a tomb? I think." Will didn't want to say anything more. It meant going back and remembering. His pearl was his secret. Why did Sir Robert have to inquire? And when did he speak to a mage in Suthenburg about it? He hadn't let him know.

"It's not Mortal Magic or Spiritual Magic, that is for certain. Yet it is more similar to Spiritual Magic thus evolutionarily older. It chose him mayhap." Lady Clémentine floated the pearl back to Will's hand.

"Is it a spell crystal? The Burhbarrow mage suggested that possibility."

"No, I do not think so, no." Lady Clémentine lifted her hand and rubbed her thumb against a finger. "The object generates its own magic, rather than a spell crystal which only stores magic and needs to be acted on."

"Should it be destroyed?" Sir Robert asked. Will clenched it tight. Never!

"Let him keep it, he is not a mage so I doubt he could use it. Remember that magic should only be used to serve others in a capacity acceptable by Manis, it should not violate the natural order. Know this and you will not falter."

Will still wondered how he empowered his spear with his pearl when facing Ugrin and Vuko. Somehow… he could use it. He'd never tell them.

"It may help him in more ways than is obvious. Regardless, only Manis knows."

Sir Robert told Will to fetch their horses, set them up in a stable, then find the knight in the main camp. An encampment had been constructed in the middle of the harbour district for the most fortunate. A larger camp held most of the army outside the walls. The rubble had been cleared away to the sides, resulting in a flat area. Round and oval tents, printed with the blue and gold of Gurmanis or the colours of their respective lords, sat amidst sturdier wooden structures built into the sides of half-destroyed buildings.

Will, having finished his work, searched for his master within the busy crowd and found him talking with someone in a black ash-covered apron, a blacksmith. Will walked up and waited behind his master.

"Will, how long were you there? Make yourself known." Sir Robert had turned and smiled at Will.

"Yes Master."

Sir Robert waved Will over. The knight stood over a wooden cart filled with black rock. It looked familiar to Will, but he couldn't name it. A logbook lay on top.

The knight and blacksmith talked about the lack of steel they had. Sir Robert suggested mixing the more plentiful iron they had with crowdite but the smith shook his head, such an alloy would be too unstable. Iron arrows and blades wouldn't pierce Saomardrim steel, so the knight told the smith to reserve his metals for weapons.

Crowdite, Will's mind leapt into action, his brain familiar with the word.

"You know how to read and write yes?" Sir Robert's voice kicked Will out of his thoughts.

"I don't know how to do either, master." Will frowned.

"Really? You told me your father taught you many things?"

"My da didn't know how to read or write, my mother did."

"Oh? That is less common among serfs. How did she learn?" Sir Robert stroked his beard.

"She once worked as a maid in a noble's household. She said she learned there."

"So, she taught you?"

Will frowned, hesitating.

"She started one year 'afore…" Will exhaled, frustrated with himself. "Started one year before she died. We didn't get too far," Will said firmly. He was a squire now. Sir Robert had told him he needed to stop hesitating. Though it was painful for him to speak about what he'd lost, and what had happened to him. He had to at least *start* pushing past it.

"Very well." Sir Robert opened the logbook and looked through the entries. Will watched him write. "I will need to teach you to read and write at some point, won't I?"

"Master, what's crowdite?"

"It is a metal that starts as a dark grey mass, easily mistakable for any common rock, but when it is refined it becomes the darkest of black. The colour is not noticeable when put into an alloy." Sir Robert motioned to the black rock.

Will looked again at the rock and his body seized up, sweat trickled down his back. He remembered. In addition to any other metal, mineral or gem prisoners in Isen Prison dug up, Will and his fellow inmates dug out much of this metal. Will took a step back on instinct, battling his memories of the mines. He never knew or cared what the metal was for.

"Wh-What does it do?"

"It resists musket fire at a distance. It helps to prolong the co-existence of armor and guns."

Will looked at his own armor.

"I suspect there is some crowdite in there too," Sir Robert said. The same metal Will had slaved over now protected his body. "An armor of this metal would get very hot in the sun and would be heavy, pure crowdite is that way. There seems to be no weakness to its resistance ability if used in the correct amount and in the correct alloy."

"My lord," the blacksmith started, "I didn't know ya knew so much about smithing."

"I have only a little knowledge, nothing to brag about." Sir Robert turned to Will. "We are finished here. Let's tour the camp. As a commander it is important you assess the mood of the men. Make sure your camp is functional, the men prepared and satisfied, and everything else falls into place. War, after all, is ninety percent logistics over battle. Come, let us finish our work."

It was almost evening meal time when the knight and his squire had finished touring the camp, inspecting its various people. They were about to return to the command tent when a soldier rushed to Sir Robert and spoke to him. The knight nodded and signaled Will to come forward. The soldier returned with others bearing a stretcher upon which was a wounded man. They placed the stretcher at Sir Robert's feet. Will remembered the man. It was the Saomardrim his master had saved. The knight spoke to the wounded groaning man whose voice was strained. Sir Robert frowned and nodded. He turned to Will.

"He is dying, Will. The healers have done all they could, and tell me there is no hope. Within the hour he will die. They say it will be a painful death towards the end. This man wishes me to end his life for he considers me an honourable man. He hopes the Father will forgive him if I kill him. He has agreed for you to take his life." Will stared at his master in shock.

"I-I can't k-kill him," Will stepped back. Sir Robert drew his dagger.

"It is a tragedy but he wishes a quick passing instead of the agony he will endure should we let him die from his wounds. It is what he wishes and it is for us to respect. I need to know before the battle that you can take a life Will. If you hesitate in doing so, in battle, your life will be taken."

Will paled. His vision blurred and the warden stood in front of him. *'Show your fellow inmates what happens to those who disobey me. Kill her,' he ordered. Will shivered and his muscles stiffened. Skyla cowered on the ground and looked at him with fear and panic. 'You are a murderer Mr. Farmer, you have done this before.'*

"No," Will said.

'Do it,' the warden shot. A hand touched Will's right shoulder and Sir Robert pressed his dagger into Will's hand. His vision sharpened; Sir Robert's grim face came into view.

"Give him peace and show me you can defend yourself when the time comes. Show me you won't hesitate." The knight nudged Will forward and Will lowered to his knees in front of the man. The Saomardrim smiled at him and reached out to touch Will's arm. He gave Will a tired nod before coughing up blood. The gashes, gouges, and burns over him had been bandaged, but the bandages were soaked red. There was no fear nor panic nor despair in his eyes. He wanted to die; he was ready to die. Will thought back to the naval battle on the Hertos River. He had hesitated there and almost drowned. Sir Robert had a point. If he hesitated, if he let his past cloud his mind in battle, he'd be killed. Will brought the dagger over the man's heart.

"I am not a murderer," Will said.

"In this age, it seems in the end we all are. What kind of murderer is what separates the noble from the evil, the heroes from the villains," Sir Robert said, his presence a firm support behind Will. Will tightened his grip on the dagger to stop himself from shaking. Everyone was watching. The Saomardrim weakly clasped Will's wrist.

"Astaghfirualhurah," he croaked. Will let out a breath and pushed the dagger into the Saomardrim's chest. The man coughed and exhaled then smiled, closed his eyes and laid still.

"The boy did it. He killed the Saomardrim. Least we know he knows who the enemies are," one of the soldiers said.

"Take him and bury him," Sir Robert ordered. The men carried the Saomardrim away and the knight helped Will to his feet.

"You did well." Sir Robert sighed. "I would have preferred if it had not come to that."

"I should've killed her." Tears welled up in Will's eyes. Sir Robert raised a suspicious eyebrow.

"Who?"

"Skyla... she would not have suffered if I'd made her passing quick." Will gripped his hands into fists.

"I see."

"I understand what you're teaching me. This war is inevitable. We have to fight it because tis our duty to do so. How we fight it is up to us. We can be just an' merciful, even in death, or we can be like the warden... twisted and relishing violence."

━━◈━━

When night came, all the commanders, Sir Robert, Lady Clémentine, Sir John, and Sir Guarin huddled around a table with a map of Al-Motros. Will and Alex stood behind their masters alongside the late Sir Dion's seven-year-old page, whom Lady Clémentine intended to send back to his family, when the chance arose. All three were told to observe the battle planning.

From Lady Clémentine's hand a small flame grew and she lit a candle on the table.

"Al-Motros is a heavily defended town," she started. "The arid mountains and canyons to its east give it natural protection from there. The south is vast farmland along the coast. God grants us luck, before our arrival, another Gurmanis force led by a group of northern knights starved out

Motros Castle north of the city. Such coordination they had that they fended off all attacks from the city to try and dislodge them. They now hold Motros Castle and are watching the northern approaches to the town." The three knights regarded the lady, Sir John surprised, Sir Guarin un-amused, and Sir Robert with admiration.

"You have examined the situation carefully." Sir John smiled.

"Of course, they do not teach nothing at Schweigendorf mages university, and none of Lord Hellmuth's remained here. I gathered all I could."

"Regardless," Sir Robert gestured to the map, "it is best if they stay within the castle. If we are attacked from the north, we will quickly lose the battle."

"The same could be said for the south," Sir John protested. "The northern approaches are covered in arid mountains south of the Al-Khadra Forest." The knight pointed it out on the map. "The farmlands to the south make for an easier approach for any relief force."

"We have word other Gurmanis forces are holding any Saomarhad reinforcements in the south." Lady Clémentine informed them. "We are well positioned to capture the town."

"The safest way would be to starve them out, like our chevaliers did at Motros Castle. Would save lives too," Sir Guarin suggested, growing agitated at their lack of options.

"No, we do not have the time. The king wants this done as quick as possible," Sir Robert pondered. "King Duggan is no fool. He knows the Saomarhad are in no position to provide support to Al-Motros, so he is using that to his advantage. If we take the town now, we have a good chance of holding it. I would prefer to do so with as few casualties as possible."

"Our main problem are the cannons protecting its west." Lady Clémentine pointed to the harbour front of Al-Motros.

"We could rush them," Sir Guarin suggested.

"No that would be foolish! There are too many guns, they can deal with our numbers," Sir John answered.

"We could contact our allies in Motros Castle, get them to fein weakness and try to draw Saomarhad troops out of town to recapture their castle," suggested Lady Clémentine, again stunning all but Sir Robert. Will wondered if it was uncommon for women, even noble women, to be in the army. Evidently, they could be mages, even in leading positions.

"Time consuming." Sir Robert stroked his beard. Will decided they must be doomed either way they approached. "I don't want to disrupt Motros Castle; it is the only thing dissuading a relief force from attacking," his master continued, and Will agreed.

"There's no way! Al-Motros is impenetrable," Sir John concluded.

"What about this, we send a force to attack from the south and while they are distracted, we attack from the west. We can send scouts to take out their communication lines and silence some of their cannons. A two-pronged attack and a bit of stealth can win this," Sir Robert suggested. Will admired his master's thought process.

"If they try and flee, we will be positioned to push them towards Motros Castle and surround them. They won't go east into the mountains; it will slow them down and they know we will catch up to them if they do that," Lady Clémentine said.

"Do we have enough men?" Sir Guarin asked.

"Oui, but barely enough. Scouting teams report Al-Motros hosts one thousand defenders, our host is about nine-hundred, not incapable but troubling."

"Very well it's settled then, we attack in the morning," Sir Robert settled the discussion.

<hr>

While the commanders worked out numbers Sir Robert stepped outside the tent. The knight looked over the camp, at the mass of men under his command among pockets of crackling fires, and scratched his goatee.

"You seem stressed Robert," Sir John said, walking towards him.

"Is not every commander stressed before a battle?"

"Only the skilled ones." They both laughed.

"This is an important battle for you Robert?"

"Yes."

"If you don't mind me asking, why?"

Sir Robert looked towards the command tent to ensure Will was out of earshot.

"The king has shown discontent that I am training a criminal instead of finding his daughter. It was in another letter."

"How long has it been?"

"A year. If anything, the king is happy Will is with me rather than running amuck assaulting and raping his daughter, his words not mine."

"Ha, I can't see that boy do anything like that." Sir John looked back to the tent and noticed Alex talking to Will while pointing out things on the map. The page was trying to stand on his toes to see the map. "Alex seems to like him as well I think." Sir John shifted. "Do you really think the Saomardrim sent Hashashin to kill the queen?"

"It's impossible to ever know the truth now. Elizabeth will carry that pain with her all her life. Queen Liliana was a firm woman, but she loved her daughter, and Elizabeth loved her."

"Only you could have so much insight on her Robert." Sir John smiled.

"I came across Duchess Lena. She implores me not to forget about Elizabeth. When the queen died Duggan became less than interested in his daughter, she said. It hurts the duchess to have seen Elizabeth so alone." Sir Robert frowned.

Sir John smirked. "Don't offload your stress on me Robert."

"What a friend you are. I hope wherever she is she is safe. If she were not who knows what would become of this kingdom. She was the only one, aside from her mother, who could control her father. She has spirit and a will to act."

"Control the king? What are you saying Robert?

Sir Robert gave Sir John a grave look. "You know."

"I do." Sir John sighed. "I've brought my last levy to this campaign. If the king demands another, there'll be no more people to work the fields."

"But we must continue forward. As is our duty… right?"

"Maybe Robert. Get some rest; tomorrow will be long."

"You rest too John, don't worry for me."

Sir John smiled and walked back into the tent.

Elizabeth, where are you? Even my men could use the charm your mother gave you. Both of you could brighten anyone's day. Sir Robert looked up into the stars.

Chapter Fourteen

WILL STOOD ON the deck of the Swift Spear and looked towards Al-Motros. The distant echo of an explosion accompanied a huge rising flame and a cloud of smoke rising from the town. The crackle of tearing wood, stone, and metal made Will's ears twitch. The shockwave of the distant explosion brushed over his face. He was sailing closer to the town, closer to the fight.

He inhaled the sharp tang of burnt gunpower intertwined with the river breeze. Memories of the frantic battle on the river tried their best to show him that he'd done this before, but as Sir Robert had said, this was different. He'd prove himself. He'd show everyone he could do this. He'd show everyone he was worthy of being Sir Robert's squire… or he'd die. Will shook the thought away. Stay close to the knight, no heroics, don't hesitate, Will repeated his master's instructions in his head.

Sir Robert walked out on deck. Will's master was head to toe in plate armor and Will wore a surcoat over mail with plate armor. Both bore a shield on their back. Sir Robert walked the length of the vessel encouraging the men. But Will stood fixated on Al-Motros and battling his twisting gut that warned him of the impending inferno.

"Don't be the first to die." The voice of Admiral Białek over his shoulder did not affect Will. "Keep your wits about you, keep the goal in front of you and survive. The first battle is the most challenging." The admiral paused. "Fear in battle is normal, nie, vital, but don't let it cripple you."

His falcon swooped down and squawked and Will gave it a scratch. As if knowing what was coming, the falcon launched itself into the sky and glided away.

As they closed in, the large cannons protecting the harbour came into view. Some were smoking piles of twisted metal. The docks of the port stretched out towards the ships. Behind them stood the wall of the town. On top, Saomardrim soldiers rushed to ready the town's functional artillery.

As soon as the ships came into the range, the Saomarhad artillery fired. Cannon barrels erupted, launching smoke and flame behind cannon balls. Will's heart skipped a beat. He stepped back as cannon balls crashed into the water and into the ships. One broke the surface of the water close to the Swift

Spear and sent river spray across Will's face. He used the railings on the side of the ship to steady himself. A few Gurmian ships had already landed and men poured out onto the docks en masse. But not all landing craft were as lucky. Will watched as cannon balls sent men flying in all directions, rendering landing ships into nothing more than smoking chunks. The Gurmian ships responded with cannon and catapult.

Will disembarked from the ship, longsword drawn, and followed his master to the approaching enemy. He stopped. The sounds and sights stunned him. He lost his grip on his sword and looked forward, uncertain of his next move. A musket ball pinged off a barrel nearby and he gasped, but it jolted him back into focus. Will brought his sword up and tightened his grip on its handle. His face hardened and he exhaled a measured breath.

Men on both sides shouted as they engaged each other in melee. Will was not in the thick of the mass, but on the flank, his master beside him. Cannons from the ships made a thunderous volley. The shots pounded the walls of Al-Motros above the heads of the attackers. In his helm Will could hear his breath. The sounds around him beat at his helm, amplifying all input. The ground under him shook, more violently any time a cannon ball smashed into the wall. Will trembled. Everywhere in front of him was the clash of steel.

"Do not give up, men! Fight for God and kingdom so that our families can live in peace. Defeat these stragglers and get the gate down!" Sir Robert shouted over the cacophony of sound. Two groups of Gurmian soldiers charged from the landing ships carrying two long siege ladders. They were guarded by men holding shields on each flank. Saomardrim archers and gunmen shot at them. When the groups got to the wall, they pushed the ladders against it and carefully started to climb. As quick as they ascended, they were shot down. The enemy hurled naft grenades during the second attempt. Hot, sticky fire bathed the attackers. Men screamed and flailed and burned as they tumbled to the ground. Some leaped into the water in a vain attempt to douse the fire. Will's chest throbbed, his heart raced, his arms trembled, and his breath came in heavy heaves. He was unable to turn away. Suddenly, his master was beside him and held his shoulder.

"Stay close, focus. The enemy is ruthless but we will win the day." Will nodded. His master turned and shouted to the men, "Forget the ladders, focus on the gate, and get explosives over there!" Sir Robert pointed to the gatehouse. Will watched the knight effortlessly engage a charging enemy.

Will gripped his longsword and advanced. A Saomardrim shielded swordsman charged Will. The enemy shield bashed and the impact took Will by surprise. The world spun for him as he stumbled backwards. Regaining his vision, he intercepted the Saomardrim's sword. The two traded blows. Will trying to find an opening and to keep up with the attacks. He parried and forced the man backwards. Seeing an opportunity, Will thrust his sword. The man dodged only to be hit by an arrow from the wall. Will drew his shield and turned towards the wall, shield up.

What was he doing? He should have drawn his shield much earlier; his stupidity had nearly gotten him killed. Three arrows hit the shield, straining Will's arm. Holding the shield close to him and angled towards the wall, he ran for cover, sliding into place beside his master. The knight made room for his apprentice then turned and nodded to one of his captains.

"Detonate the explosives!" the knight ordered. A pile of explosive barrels sat huddled against the city gates. Friendly troops lay dead amongst the barrels with Saomardrim arrows sticking out of them. A flame ignited and then sizzled. The Saomardrim troops on top of the wall frantically shot arrows down and screamed in their language. A cannon ball ripped apart a chunk of wall and was flung towards Will. Sir Robert grabbed his apprentice and yanked the boy to him, holding him tight as Will fearfully saw what had missed him. A bit too aggressively, Sir Robert pushed Will back.

The rubble had doused the flame. Saomardrim troops cheered from atop their wall. Across from Will, a blue-robed, short-caped woman stepped out and pointed one of her hands towards the gate. A flame swirled into existence in her palm and it launched forwards.

An enormous, deafening explosion sent fire and wood outwards. Sir Robert shoved Will behind their cover. The port shook violently, sending shockwaves through Will's body. The Gurmian troops cheered. A few mages, shielded behind Gurmian troops, approached the remains. They pushed their hands forward casting a burst of pressure which cleared the rubble away. The Gurmians charged. Panting, Will looked at his master.

"Pay attention! Focus Will!" The knight's voice seemed muffled; the explosion had temporarily deafened him. Saomardrim troops filled the gatehouse gap. Sir Robert dove into the gap behind his men.

Will charged. He fixated on a swordsman and swung his longsword. The blade caught the swordsman off guard and hit his armor. Will deflected a counter then thrust at the man's side through a gap, tearing flesh and splattering blood on them both. A mace came out of nowhere and smacked Will's side. Pain shot through his waist as he fell into the wall. The enemy readied to hit Will's head. Will threw himself to the left, avoiding the strike, and scrambled up. He sliced at the man's legs and pushed forwards, trying to keep track of his master.

From behind them, a horn sounded and three templar landing craft opened the door to their hulls. Armoured, mounted knights, gleaming in the sun, charged onto the docks and towards the destroyed gate, sword, spear, or lance drawn.

"Deus le Volt!" they shouted in unison. Sir Guarin led them forwards.

"Fall back!" Sir Robert shouted, pulling his stunned apprentice to the side. The Gurmian troops dove to the sides of the gate, making way for the charging knights to ride towards the gap. Will watched as the mass of white, black, gold, and red rushed mere centimeters past him. The rumbling of the ground almost toppling him and tearing his chest apart. Templars crashed into the Saomardrim in the gap, sending some flying backwards and trampling others. They split from the gap to the northwest. Sir Robert regrouped his men and advanced.

Will ran through the gate and onto the main street. An explosion nearby sent embers flying at him, scorching his armor. He parted with the main force and stood beside a building. He panted, trying to maintain his composure. Sweat dripped down his face, sprayed onto the inside of his helm by his hot breath. His heart beat wildly. Will tried to catch his breath but the heavy smoke made him cough.

The street ran eastwards towards the center of the city. It was flanked on both sides by smaller side streets and blocky stone buildings. There was a bridge ahead, overlooking the street and an arrow gun was mowing down the masses of Gurmian attackers. Cannon balls arced overhead pounding the city, reducing buildings to rubble, and setting fires.

The Gurmian troops advanced behind mantlets, large wooden siege shields, firing through holes at the enemy. Three mantlets were mounted with a flamethrower.

The Saomardrim were retreating, most missing the arc of flames as the mantlets advanced under arrow gun fire. The Saomarhad arrow gun fired back, lodging arrows into its wooden surface, and stopping the Gurmian advance. The flamethrowers kept the Saomardrim back.

Will advanced with the men behind the mantlets as he searched the crowd for his master but all he saw was smoke, rubble, and shouting men. He looked towards the bridge where his master and some allies were advancing on the arrow gun.

War cries snapped Will back into action. Saomardrim charged head first into the line of flamethrower mantlets under the cover of musket fire which pinged off those mantlets covered in crowdite. They held shields but this did little to protect them. They rushed through the flames, engulfed in red-orange. In their final moments of life, they cut down the flamethrower operators as Gurmian troops left the safety of the mantlets, now unhindered by the arrow gun, to engage the enemy.

Will followed the men out of the siege shields and met a boot to his face. The impact shook his head. He tumbled to the ground, dazed. An axe swung through the air towards him. Will held up his shield. The axe smacked against it, again and again. Wave after wave of straining muscles, shaking bones, and sharp rhythmic pain, wore down his stamina. Frantically, his mind raced. How was he going to get away? His shield cracked. The axeman stopped and kicked Will's shield aside. He stepped on Will's shield arm. Will screamed in response and the axeman raised his weapon over the exposed boy. Will got hold of his longsword and swung it blindly at the man's legs, hitting armor. The distraction made the axeman hesitate and Will kicked at his legs, toppling him. Will stood and plunged his sword into the man's back.

Desperately, Will searched for his shield and when he saw it, he ran for it. Two shielded war hammer wielding men intercepted. One swung at Will who sidestepped into the other one, crashing into his shield. The man pushed Will backwards on the ground, rolling to his right to avoid more war hammer strikes. He stood. Shocked, Will backed away.

He faced two men dressed in armor similar to the Gurmian soldiers. They didn't wear Gurmanis colours, yet their faces were clearly Gurmian. There was a symbol on their armor, something that resembled a flower in side view with a sword across it. Bewildered, Will shouted to the men.

"I'm on your side!" he screamed, but his voice was drowned out by a nearby explosion. Debris flew over him. The men closed in. They swung on different sides. Will blocked one then the other. To avoid more left attacks, he charged to the right. Will's longsword sliced one's stomach. The man from the left attacked. Will turned and blocked. He swung at middle guard only to have his sword bounce off the man's shield. Panting and gripping his sword Will backed away. The man seemed to tower above him.

Sir Robert lunged into the man, toppling him. Will looked up into his master's frantic eyes.

"Did I not teach you anything Will? Never leave yourself vulnerable to attack! In attacking to your right, you forgot about your left!" He shouted the last word over the din of explosions.

"Sorry, Master," Will answered through heavy breaths, turning red. "H-He… they were Gurmian!"

"Mercenaries."

"But they tried to kill me!"

"Mercenaries for Saomarhad." Sir Robert looked up to the sound of a horn. Will stood there in stunned silence, panting, unable to understand what his master was saying. Gurmian troops advanced towards the town square as men rushed in from the docks, thundering past the knight and his squire.

"Advance and take the square! We almost have this town." Sir Robert shouted. The men cheered. He looked at Will again. "Have strength Will, this battle is not yet finished. If you see men not in our colours, kill them. Don't lose your shield again!" The knight pointed to Will's shield not far away. Will nodded and scrambled away to gather it.

They advanced up the street, through the souk, and to the town hall, meeting only minor resistance. The group of men who'd attacked the south of the town arrived and engaged the enemy. As they did, a large group of Saomardrim from the northern mosque charged in. Sir Robert's men turned left and formed a line to meet them. Spearmen with shields raced to the front and the rest formed the rear. Mantlets protected the flanks to force a direct attack. The speed of the regrouping maneuver amazed Will.

The Saomardrim charged the line and many were impaled by spears. Their weapons clanged against shields.

Will stood by his master. He held tight onto his cracked but still useable shield. They were surrounded by allies. As one they surged forward against the Saomarhad charge. Will was forced to follow. The deafening shouting only encouraged his own voice. Will let out an impassioned war cry. His heart raced, his limbs shook, his lungs drew in sweet cool air, then he crashed into the enemy.

Dust choked air invaded his throat. Sweat stung his eyes. Blood pounded in his ears. Yet, he moved onwards, instinct driving him to survive. Will lashed out with his longsword hitting one, two, three Saomardrim. His blade bounced off armor and found gaps. Strikes found him. A sword drew blood on his side, a hammer crashed into his arm. Arrows whizzed by him and he could not see his master. A large mace-wielding Saomardrim advanced on him. Will ducked as the heavy head neared. Will flanked, striking from the right. The mace hit his shield and Will tossed it aside. He cut at the enemy's side, dodged, then sliced. He drew blood, causing the man to fall back. Will thrust, feeling the blade tear through flesh. He held his sword steady, against the resistance, then tore his blade out, splattering blood. It flew past his helm and into his mouth. Will spit out the bitter spray.

A horn sounded and the Saomardrim broke ranks, retreating towards the mosque. Will, his armor covered in blood and bent in places, staggered forwards towards his master, Sir John, and Alex. He finally relaxed, catching his breath while the rush of adrenaline subsided.

"We need to push towards the mosque, but the street is narrow." Sir John informed through heavy breaths.

"That's not ideal. Is there no other street?" Sir Robert asked.

"Urban streets in Saomarhad are curvy with many private roads and dead ends. We could try but we risk getting turned around or lost."

"If we are flanked in that narrow street we won't last."

"Agreed. We should split into three. You and I lead the main force on the most direct path. Two other nobles will lead men on the closest street to the left. Alex and Will can push on the right."

"Will knows nothing of command and I hesitate to let him go without me."

"Alex is well experienced in this, he will command the men and will watch over the boy. By advancing on the sides as well as the center we reduce the risk of being surprised by a flanking action."

"Then we do it." Sir Robert drew his shield and shouted at his men to regroup.

"Robert." Sir John touched the knight's arm. He smiled under his helm. "Seven."

"Ten." Sir Robert laughed.

"I defeated twelve," Alex boasted. Both knights laughed. "What of squire Will?"

"I… I wasn't counting. Was I s'posed to count?" Will panicked.

"Worry not. We regroup and advance," Sir Robert said. The knights pushed on and Alex signaled to Will.

"Follow me and stick close," Alex instructed. Will nodded and pushed away the fear that threatened to creep in.

Alex met with other commanders and reorganised the men. They advanced to the right of the narrow street, in a tight formation. At first, they faced no resistance though they could hear the clang of swords and shouts of men to their left, where Sir Robert and Sir John pushed forwards. Without warning, a wave of Saomardrim ambushed them, pouring in from the smaller side streets.

"Shields up on the flanks!" Alex shouted. The column came together and the men obeyed the order. Saomardrim weapons slammed onto the shields. Alex pushed to the front of the line and engaged with his sword, staying behind his shield. Will copied him and protected his right flank. A spear pushed forcefully against Will's shield several times, causing him to push back. Will jabbed with his longsword hitting armor and pushed forward, catching the spear from below. He tossed the spear to the side and slashed at the enemy, striking flesh. The man fell back and another Saomardrim took his place.

Despite the fierce resistance of the Saomardrim, the column pressed forward and around a curve into a Saomardrim barricade. Archers and gunmen launched arrows from behind it. Naffatin soldiers fired fire-grenades from ballistae on the flanks, pinning Alex's column in place. Will narrowly missed a musket ball.

"Shields forward!" Alex shouted. The men created a shield wall and when Alex gave the order they charged forward into the barricade as musket men were reloading. Fire licked their shields and arrows bounced off them. A few men were hit by a lucky sharpshooter. Will shouted a war cry and followed Alex into the barricade.

Saomardrim rushed in from two side streets, pinning the Gurmians in front of the fire. Will was tossed aside and fell into a building. Outside the cohesive Gurmian formation, Will was not noticed. He caught sight of the barricade's flank. A grenade ballista operator wildly fired and reloaded. He was exposed to Will. Will tensed. He looked between the Gurmian formation and the exposed Saomardrim. There was no way the formation could move forward. *'No heroics.'* Will heard his master's voice in his head. But if he took out the grenade ballista operator, the Gurmians could charge forward. *'Don't hesitate,'* his master's voice said.

Will gripped his sword. Heart pounding and fear sharpening all his senses, he advanced on the exposed enemy. Breathing heavily, creeping closer, he readied to attack. A meter away, one of the Saomardrim warriors spotted him. The exposed Saomardrim turned to him, moving to draw a pistol at his belt. Saomardrim behind the enemy raised muskets. In a blitz attack, Will thrust his sword at the enemy, striking his side. He followed with a slash across the man's face. Howling, the man fell into his grenade ballista, a primed grenade falling to his side. Musket shots flew towards Will. One hit his arm, another his leg, another his side. With each Will staggered. He flung his shield up. Three shots pinged off its crowdite surface. Will tasted blood, felt sharp pain in his side, but he kept advancing.

The primed grenade exploded. Will was flung sideways, lobbed against a building and crumpled into a heap. The echoing vibration made Will come to quickly and he ripped his helm off to make it stop. His head spun and sweat… or blood clouded his vision. The sent of burned flesh stung his nose and the gritty taste of burnt dust dried his tongue. Will stood and stumbled forwards. Throbbing pain threatened to make him collapse.

"Squire William has done it!" Alex's muffled shouts seemed distant. "Everyone! The barricade is down. Charge!" Will collapsed behind rubble as the wind of men swooping past him infiltrated the gaps in his armor and cooled his burns. Some men patted him, cheering as they passed. Were they cheering him? Alex stood over him, a proud smile spread across his smoke-blackened face, visible under his helm.

"You did it Will!" Alex shouted. He grabbed Will's arms and pulled him up. Will stumbled into the young squire and looked at him. Will's eyes were watery, tears teasing the edges.

"I…"

"You blew up the barricade and got us out of that tight spot." Alex pushed Will's right arm over the boy's chest. "Your duty is fulfilled. Steel yourself. Chaotic, painful, I know. But now we must regroup with the marshal and my master. Come, I will lead you." Alex pulled him forwards.

The column broke into a coordinated charge and crashed into the right flank of the square. Men from both sides fought in front of the mosque. Its tall minarets, now damaged by stray cannon fire, loomed over the bloodbath below. Saomardrim soldiers rushed civilians inside as the people, at least fifty or so, ran through the fighting to the mosque.

Will encountered a solider desperately urging an old Saomardrim man to reach safety, but his steps were strained and slow. Will leveraged his sword, its point hovering as the solider lunged. Will parried, striking his armor. The solider held Will back with his sword as he shielded the old man with his arm. Will frowned, they'd lost and were no threat. He backed up and lowered his weapon allowing the men to retreat unchallenged.

Will raised his head, his heavy breaths mixed with saliva. All around him people from both sides lay mangled and disfigured. Occasionally the odd arm, leg, or head was left without a body. Blood soaked everything. It quickly hit him, the overwhelming shock at seeing so much carnage. His stomach threatened to empty its contents and his legs failed. An immense dizzying wave overtook Will, but he managed to steady himself. He touched his face, seeing blood on his fingers. The shouts of his allies compounded with the crash of their axes against the mosque doors and the wailing of women, infants, and children within.

As Will lumbered towards the mosque his allies broke through the doors, but the panicked screams were cut short when his master's voice demanded calm. Inside men, both soldier and peasant stood between their woman and children and the Gurmians. Fear mixed with determination in their expressions. Alongside them were a mix of Saomardrim troops and Gurmian mercenaries. The mercenaries held up their shields, protecting their clients and the civilians behind them. Will could go no further. He fell against a water fountain in front of the mosque, revising his idea to drink the bloody water within. He massaged his forehead, running a hand through his moist hair. It wasn't long before his master's voice jolted him to attention.

"This battle is over," Sir Robert announced to those outside the mosque. Gurmian troops cheered, victorious, and gathered closer to the knight. "The governor has agreed to surrender. We will not spill blood in this holy place. Allow the civilians to pass and take with them their supplies. There will be no pillaging." Sir Robert emphasised the final point. "Any living enemy soldier is to be captured and brought to Admiral Białek for logging and internment. You will be rewarded in turn. The mercenary Compagnie de Fleur nor the governor of Al-Motros is to be bothered. They will escort the civilians out of town." Gurmian troops walked past Will beginning to herd the Saomardrim into civilian and non-civilian groups. Sir Robert, hissing as he squeezed his arm, approached Will.

"It's a relief the governor decided to surrender. Further fighting would have ensured all his people's deaths. Indeed any force he can muster will not retake this town. I should share with you some of that intelligence and teach you how to interpret it."

Will was unsure if he should smile. The battle was over. Hearing Sir Robert say it finally seemed to calm his raging body. He nodded instead.

"We will regain this town, inshalhurah," the governor, a man in a fine armored robe shouted to Sir Robert. "Your enemies will know of your quality when next you meet them." he pointed.

"As I have heard, they already have," Sir Robert smiled, shouting back. When the governor turned away Sir Robert addressed Will. "A surrender not without vitriol."

Sir John strode to them. "Robert. Sir Guarin is clearing up small pockets of resistance and Henryk is already sorting all the conquered supplies."

"Good. We have won this day. Secure an area for the encampment. I want a full inventory of all our supplies, rations, and troops. Prepare a funeral for tonight." Sir Robert coughed and caught his breath. He turned to his apprentice.

"What happened to you!?"

"Th-There was an... explosion... I... broke the barricade..."

"What barricade?"

"I-It was…" Things blurred and Will fell. Sir Robert caught him, his capable hands supporting him.

"Steady. You're alive and well. Now you can face any battle knowing to expect the unexpected." Will blinked sweat and tears from his eyes. The knight dug into a break in his armor and produced a handkerchief allowing Will to wipe the blood off his face. The knight looked at Will's right side and noticed blood seeping through his squire's tunic. Sir Robert pressed the area, Will flinched and groaned.

"Pain," Will said. Sir Robert examined it.

"It is a cut or a puncture. Not too deep but something broke through the mail. At least the burns aren't so bad. Get that wound looked at."

"Yes master. Armored knights always seemed so invincible."

Sir Robert laughed. "Armor does not make you invincible; it only makes you more survivable. Fear, pain, the urge to lose my stomach, invincibility in armor. I felt the same way in my first battle though I was younger than you."

He focused on his master, trying to ignore the carnage around him, but Sir Robert was pulled aside by a group of soldiers. Will, exhausted, slid against the fountain and laid back. The sun broke through the clouds and onto his face. He held his chest and tried to calm his chaotic insides.

Chapter Fifteen

WITH MOST OF the town structures burning or destroyed, the troops pitched tents in the central square. Soldiers shuffled about, some holding tools, others talking or carrying boxes of supplies. A man's melodious call rose from the mosque. A call to prayer perhaps. Sir Robert had ordered that the Saomardrim civilians be allowed to retrieve their possessions and pray at their mosque before they were expelled from the town. Sir Guarin was not agreeable with Sir Robert's orders. He argued that the Saomardrim had to all be killed, no mercy, like when they'd destroyed Halsburg. Sir John, Alex and a few hundred men were watching the civilians and keeping them protected from anyone in the Gurmian army who wished to harm them. They also made sure the Saomardrim civilians did not turn on their Gurmian conquerors.

Will trudged through the crowds in search of the medical tent. He noticed some of the men around him looked at him differently. Word of how Will blew up the barricade had spread through the camp. He knew he didn't blow it up, but those men who looked at him with disdain, now looked at him with respect.

He bumped into someone. Will staggered back and looked up, his body stilling. It was that girl he'd met in Suthenburg. She wore a black robe with a yellow flowering sun of Manis on it, backed by a eight-pointed white cross.

Guilt and discomfort gnawed at him, but he also hoped he could talk to her again. She scrambled across the ground, regathering the medical supplies she'd dropped in the collision.

"Sorry sir, I wasn't looking," she said. Will helped her with the last items, moving closer to her. She looked up.

"That's ok, it was my fault I promise." Will smiled. He was stained in blood; he worried how he might look. The girl brushed past him to leave without saying a word, sending her vanilla scent flowing past his face.

"W-Wait! What's yer name?" Will grabbed her arm.

"Don't touch me!" she screamed. Will frowned, letting go. They stared at each other awkwardly and Will thought she looked sorry for a second. Her voice cooled. "Don't come near me, I want naught to do with you."

Will's lips trembled and he broke a cold sweat. Suddenly the warden was before him, hating him, telling him the same hurtful things, all untrue.

"I just wa-want to know your name, I'm sorry I grabbed you suddenly," Will whispered.

"You need not know my name; it isn't important to you."

"But why? I won't hurt you; I don't want to hurt you." Will held out his arms, showing her his palms.

"I am sorry if you got any ideas at Suthenburg because of me, but I don't want you near me."

"You were willing to know me in Suthenburg 'afore you found out what people think of me, but I'm not that!"

"Don't be a fool; I don't want to know you! Don't get any ideas. What was said in Suthenburg was a moment of weakness on my part. It was a mistake." With another awkward pause she turned and bumped into a taller, older woman wearing the same flowering sun on her clothes. Her hair was covered in a nun's wimple. She looked down in disapproval at the healing girl.

"Ms. Godfrey I was on my way back…"

"I will not have my charges insult a squire! Per'aps you commoners can't see very well but this boy you've been honoured to meet is a squire." Ms. Godfrey scowled.

"I know now Ms. Godfrey. I just…"

"There is no excuse! This attitude is deplorable for you, a girl with the talents you have." She turned to Will. "My lord, excuse my charge here. May we have the honour of your name?"

"I am Will… er… Farmer, squire to Sir Robert," Will answered shyly. Ms. Godfrey turned to the healing girl, her brows knit in anger. The girl looked up with an innocent smile.

"Sir Robert's squire, the man who you an' all others here owe their job to, distasteful, most distasteful."

"But he is not noble, he is a…"

"I'll not hear it! Insulting Sir Robert's squire is insulting our grand marshal himself. Be gone, you are fired."

"Ms. Godfrey… no, you can't do that! I need this job… I-I am sorry!" The girl panicked.

"The war's no place for peasant girls who dishonour their betters. Return to yer parents and tell them you need to be taught manners."

"Wait… she doesn't need to be dismissed," Will interrupted, half feeling sorry for the girl, half just wanting her nearby. "I am sure it was a mistake; she can be forgiven."

"But what would your master think, my lord? Disrespect in a warzone could mean death. Per'aps we should go to Sir Robert himself. After all, he has been the party disrespected here."

"No! Please do not take me to Sir Robert, Ms. Godfrey. I should not have been so rude. I will make amends," the girl begged.

"Ah, at the possibility of facing discipline from your betters d'you show some humility." Ms. Godfrey crossed her arms.

"There's no need to trouble my master, especially after battle. It need not be pursued. My master will understand," Will explained.

"Very well." Ms. Godfrey nodded. "Seems your job is saved." She directed towards the girl. "We will take our leave my lord."

"I need your help." Will raised his right arm to reveal the wound he had received. "I am in need of a healer." Will blushed at the thought of this girl being his healer… just so he could linger around her… a little.

"Right away my lord. My charge can make amends this way." Ms. Godfrey looked at the Suthenburg girl. "Take his lord to the private tent and treat his wound."

"No… you have to be kidding Ms. Godfrey. I won't do it." The girl stood firm. Ms. Godfrey fumed red. She grabbed the girl's right shoulder.

"Do not insult Sir Robert's squire! Know your station girl or I will toss you into the Hertos river right this instant! I swear Manis forgive me; you are uncharacteristically defiant right now. You will follow my orders!" Ms. Godfrey gave the girl a slight shove. The girl frowned.

"Fine." She shot Will an irate glance which eluded her superior. "This way my lord." The girl directed Will giving him a fake smile. Will followed.

"Can't I get your name now?" He smiled.

"Silence," the girl snapped, limiting any further talk. She took him into a subsection of the camp separated by crude fortifications. The flags and banners flying from the top of tents and repurposed buildings bore the same yellow flowering sun backed by an eight-pointed white cross as on the girl's clothes. Around him, other healers took injured soldiers to tents and buildings to treat their wounds. An oversized covered medical wagon, branded with the symbol, rolled across the way. Armoured men-at-arms and knights led it on. They passed through a check-point towards a large tent, under the watch of two armoured sentries, wearing black surcoats over mail, with the same peculiar symbol.

"Where are we?" Will asked. "Who are these people? You're a healer…"

"We are with the Knights Hospitaller. They deal with the health of our men, aside from other things like running food banks and orphanages." The girl stopped at the entrance to a large tent and turned around. "Keep that in mind. Those armed men will be watching you." Then she hesitated, regarding Will carefully. Will tensed, his heart twisting but his brain panicking. He tried to keep the eyes of the warden, in his mind, away.

"D-Did you really…" the girl croaked, then she pressed her lips together. "Why does the grand marshal train you?"

"He's a good man. He does not see me as e-evil," Will said without thinking much about it. In truth he was just grateful for Sir Robert, the reason he was chosen didn't matter to him. "I strive to serve him well for that is my duty."

The girl let slip a slight smile, then regarded him some more as if she were searching for something, her eyes glistening. She tossed aside some hair that had fallen over her face, frowned, then pulled open the tent door.

"Don't touch anything," she said flatly as Will followed her inside. He frowned, sick of being treated as a threat. He was directed to sit on a bench. Another girl stood at the table on the other side. She looked surprised to see Will with the Suthenburg girl.

"Keira bring me alcohol, stitches, and bandages," the girl instructed, more annoyed than angry now.

"Oh… yes right away," Keira said. She grabbed the materials off the table and walked them over. The two girls stood over Will making the boy feel small and defeated. Will stared at them in silence.

"What are you waiting for? Take off your tunic and mail!" the Suthenburg girl said.

"Oh right." Will stood and started to remove the layers of clothing he had on. Keira giggled; the Suthenburg girl glared at her.

"Don't Keira. Keep quiet…" The Suthenburg girl diverted her gaze. "He's not a good person."

"I will need some help reaching the straps on the back."

"Keira help him." Keira helped Will remove the tunic, chainmail, and the gambeson underneath. "My lord. I heard of what you did in the assault. You saved the men in that column an' we're all grateful for it,"

"Yes… thank-you." Will blushed, scratching his hair. The Suthenburg girl's eyes lit up, acknowledging the feat.

"Someone did not properly fit and do up the gambeson, that might have contributed to receiving the wound," Keira observed as she put the armor to one side.

"Properly donning armor is such a basic thing for a squire. Most pages already know how to do well before they become a squire. Just another reason why he shouldn't be here." The Suthenburg girl scoffed. Will frowned, Keira gasped.

"My lord, forgive my friend—"

"I don't want his forgiveness, give me the alcohol." The girl directed Keira. "You," she looked to Will, "sit." Will sat and revealed his wound. It was like the girl was conflicted, trying to decide if she should hate him or accept him as he was. She sat close to him and poured the alcohol onto the wound to clean it. The sting made Will flinch. She brought the stitches close and he looked away, gathering all courage he could not to let darker thoughts overtake him. She began to close the wound. The girl blushed. "Why did you save the column?" she asked.

"Why wouldn't I? Really, I stumbled into it, but there were few options."

The girl nodded. "It would be the selfless thing to do… or…" There was a silence between them. "The marks of punishment on your skin mark who you are, God," she said sourly. Her insults were not lost on Will. It was already uncomfortable enough revealing his scars. Keira watched the work. Will tried to relax.

"You're good at this. Thank-you," he said, looking at the side of her face, so close to him that he could feel her warmth.

"Be quiet, I am working."

"You still haven't told me your name,"

Keira opened her mouth.

"Don't say it, Keira. You might be the most obnoxious boy I have ever met."

"You're telling him my name!" Keira said.

"That's different… I mean…"

Keira crossed her arms and sighed.

"I t-think I know why you are so aggressive towards me. I'm not who you think I am, I only want to know more about you. The things you talked about in Suthenburg, for example, I want to know more." Will gave the girl a smile. She was so close, touching him, and Will didn't want her to step away. He wanted to talk.

"As I said, I don't want to associate with you. I'm almost finished here, leave after I'm done. How much more of a hint do you need?"

Will frowned, defeated again. Keira gave him a sympathetic look. The Suthenburg girl continued her work, applying salve to Will's burns.

"Accept my apology for her my lord. The battle was fierce an we've been put near collapse with all we've had to do."

"We have," the Suthenburg girl whispered. "You are covered in dust and soot. You fought hard."

"I did the best I could."

"For yourself?"

"For my master." For himself, of course that was a part of it, but she would not understand. "He is happy with my efforts."

"Is Sir Robert really so approving…?"

What was this girl trying to say? She looked up at Will, searching and assessing, blushing. Then she finished bandaging his wound and stood to clean her hands. Keira and Will watched her as the tension in the room thickened.

"You don't deserve to be squiring for Sir Robert. He is a man of virtue, honour, and integrity. You are not. So many lives were lost in this war, some closer to me than others." She glanced at Keria who gave her a supportive look, then she turned to Will who stood. Keira cleaned up and collected Will's armor. "That there must be Saomardrim on one side and murderers on the other does no one any good. The less… the less of those like you free to endanger others the better."

"Can't you understand that I don't want to hurt anyone I don't have to." Force grew in Will's voice. He was growing tired of the girl's comments.

"I fear how you've tricked Sir Robert."

Will's insides swelled at the words. "You're wrong to think I should not serve him. He accepted me."

"Don't fool yourself. Go."

"I…"

"Keira what is Judeicar's Justice? The tenets Manis emphasize?"

"Stop it. Stop degrading him; it's not right and it's going too far." Keira frowned.

"Just say it."

"He or she who has sinned against his or her peers should be shunned, ridiculed and made to realise his or her sin. They should no longer speak; they should suffer painful words. Wear away the sinner's mind and imprison, cut, rip, burn, shock, and create for them all pain physical and mental. Thus, they will be made to realise the severity of their actions and their sinful soul can start to be cleansed."

"Exactly, he deserves it." The girl finished wiping her hands and threw the towel beside him.

"As I see it, I am of a higher ranking than you," Will tried to say with authority.

"Oh really? So, what are you going to do? Force me to tell you everything? Fine, order it." The girl stood to full height and stared down Will. Keira glanced between the two, wide-eyed and still holding Will's armor. Will looked at the girl's judging eyes; they held a familiar aggression. The warden's voice swelled in his mind.

'I don't think you understand Mr. Farmer, I am your master now, you are my property an' you will obey me.'

The stench of the warden's polished boots threatened to knock his ten-year-old self out. 'Pathetic. Herded around without a care. D'you feel like a dog boy? You are a dog! I will break you; ya know that don't you. How hard it must be surrounded by adults who want to hurt you an' others who offer you no word.' The warden kicked Will then pushed down with his right foot on Will's back.

"You have been warned. DO NOT talk to the prisoners; do NOT disobey the orders of my guards. Stop crying. STOP CRYING!" the warden shouted. He crouched and gripped Will by the neck forcing the boy to stare into his pleasure filled face, centimeters away.

'A monster. Keep that in your mind boy. Remember that I am the only person who cares for you now. You can ne'er be loved by anyone else; no one will accept you. I will keep you alive, I will keep you close, you are mine… mine… mine…'

"My lord are you okay? Yer face has lost all colour?" Keira's voice entered Will's mind. Will blinked; he caught the aggressive glare of the Suthenburg girl and stepped backwards, holding his neck. The girl let her expression slip, a slight look of concern.

"No… I mean yes… I mean…" Will took his armor from Keira. He looked at the Suthenburg girl for a moment, tears forming in his eyes. She seemed unsure. Then Will rushed out of the tent, the Hospitaller section, past the sentries, and to a secluded part of the camp. His mind spun and his body shivered. *'Mine… mine… mine…'* The warden's words kept playing through his head. He tried to shake them away. Will collapsed to the ground, his hair falling over his face. He spent the next ten minutes alone trying to shake the warden from his mind.

<hr>

Will approached his master's tent. He waited outside unsure of how he should enter. He wanted to speak with his master about that girl. He wanted so much for this girl to talk to him, he wanted to know her name and if she felt the same way he did. He wanted to know what he was feeling because he had no idea. It was foolish. The girl did not like him anyway, but more importantly what if his master got upset at him for thinking of things other than his duties. Would the knight cast him away?

He took a deep breath and called for the knight, "Master? Can I come in?"

"Will? Of course, come in!" Will walked inside and sat across from his master who was seated on a chair with a small table in front of him. Sir Robert was reviewing ledgers while he stroked his sword with an oiled cloth.

"Why so downcast? We won; you should be happy."

"I am, it's just…" Will avoided his master's gaze.

"What is it Will?"

"No, it's not important."

"Will I am here to guide and help you. A bond between master and apprentice should be strong, you can tell me anything." Will built up his courage. He did not know who else he could talk to; there *was* no one else. He hoped his master had the right guidance for him.

"Ok… there is a girl…" Will forced the words out.

Sir Robert chuckled. "Oh, is there now? And do you like her?"

"I… I don't know what it is. I feel… I feel like I want to talk to her… but she won't talk to me." Her image floated into his mind, her smile from Suthenburg warming him.

"Then you need to grab her attention and tell her how you feel Will. When I met my wife, Emmeline, she wouldn't say a word to me. I tried hard to start a conversation with her, but back then in my youth, I was very awkward. She was visiting my manor when my father still ran it. I declared my love and she gave me her handkerchief to wear on my armor. She thought it a game!"

"Really?"

"Yes. At twenty-one, I was knighted and I saw her there alongside Sir Sylas, the man who was courting her. At twenty-three I took part in my first joust as a full knight against that man. Emmeline came to me before our final match after Sir Sylas had sent her away and refused to accept her handkerchief, as was his right. Dejected, she gave me her handkerchief instead and I showed her the one she had given to me in our youth."

"You kept it?" Will imagined how much she meant to the knight.

"Yes, I never forgot about her." Sir Robert smiled. "I lost the joust, knocked clean off my horse in the third pass." The knight laughed at the memory. "Sir Sylas scoffed at my offer to shake his hand. I attended the after party for a while then retired to the gardens where Emmeline found me again. She confessed that she did not love Sir Sylas. She confessed that she knew I had feelings for her when we first met and she had feelings for me too, but she made a joke of it because she was unsure."

"Then everything worked out?"

"I took her home. I told her I would not court her until she broke things with Sir Sylas. When she did, we spent time together and we never felt more alive. But because I did not tell her the truth in the beginning, I spent years away from her and I almost lost her to another man. Had I told her the truth, had I been surer of myself, who knows what good may have come from it." Sir Robert sighed, "And how many more years I could have spent with her," he whispered.

"That story is encouraging, but this is more complicated..." Will was embarrassed to admit the real issue.

"How?" Sir Robert discarded his oiled cloth and placed his sword across the table.

"She thinks I am a murderer; that's why she stays away from me."

Sir Robert frowned. "You need to show her she is wrong."

"But how?" Will couldn't understand the knight's logic.

"That is something you will have to find out on your own Will, only you can win her heart. I have found actions seem to be better in this situation. Show her you have compassion and that you have changed and are willing to better your life, and the lives of those around you. Or maybe you should find a way to tell her your most sincere truth, like you did in Burhbarrow, it worked for me."

"D'you think I feel like you did with Emmeline?"

"I think you simply find her attractive." Sir Robert smiled.

"Thank you, Master." Will felt a little more confident. If his master could be so bold then why couldn't he? The problem was, despite how lightly Sir Robert addressed it, Will was labeled. It was unfair how people judged so readily, yet labels helped protect people from potential danger. He wasn't a danger, couldn't they see that? All he knew is he wanted to know more about this Suthenburg girl and he would pursue her until she saw him in another light. But if she still disliked him… what would he feel like then?

Will pushed aside the door covering of Sir Robert's tent, holding the knight's great helm he'd been charged to see to the smith for repairs. The last of the day's light fell over the ruined town and people were preparing for the final meal. Across the space he saw Admiral Białek, Sir John, and Alex approaching. A hand grasped his shoulder and jerked him around. He tripped over himself, Sir Robert's great helm clanging against the ground. Will scrambled away and looked up. A man, an armored one with black stripes on his tunic, grabbed the boy. Will could only see his eyes, as the remainder was covered in mail and plate. The man lifted Will up, turning him to face the bigger threat. Will trembled, sweat formed on his brow, tears teased his eyes. His legs gave out but someone steadied him.

"We meet again." The warden sneered, his mania reaching his eyes. Light black veins snaked up the warden's face and his eyes glowed a brighter yellow-orange.

"Hold it! Put him down!" Sir Robert demanded; sword drawn. The warden's men gripped their weapons while the one holding Will squeezed him tighter. Admiral Białek, Sir John, and Alex rushed forwards, drawing their weapons and surrounding the intruders.

"One of you is Sir Robert I assume? The Grand Marshal?"

"Who are you and what reason do you have to be assaulting my squire like this. Put him down." Sir Robert stepped forward; his sword ready to strike.

"I am on business of the realm. This boy is wanted for escaping Isen Prison, my castle. He is a murderer." The warden grimaced.

"He is under my care and protection therefore you have no right to take him, you are bold to come here and challenge me."

"I have every right; he is mine," the warden reveled. A wave of sickness crashed over Will.

"Yours? He is not a slave. You no longer own him. Will, do you know this man? Who is he?" Will looked to his master, the warden's presence rendering him unable to speak.

Sir Robert stared at Will giving him reassurance. Will began, but the warden turned swiftly around and gave him a foreboding look, foretelling grave punishment.

Will forced it out, "He's the warden of… Isen…" Will staggered on his words.

The warden frowned and faced the knight. "Appointed by the king himself. This boy is property of the king. Will you steal from the king? *You have no right to refuse me!*"

"I am the grand marshal appointed in confidence by King Duggan; I am keeping him for the king," Sir Robert challenged the warden.

"I ha'e come too far to be turned away!" The warden drew his hands into fists.

"You can try to take him but you won't get far." Sir Robert raised his longsword towards the warden. The warden eyed the knight and raised a hand, he and his men turned. Will panicked and struggled against the guard's grip, his eyes watering. The warden walked into Admiral Białek's pistol.

"Not smart. You'd do better if you let the lad go," Henryk warned. Alex, Sir John and Sir Robert circled around the intruders.

"You are making a grave mistake knight!" the warden shouted. He jerked Will away from his guardsman and grabbed the boy's neck. "We will see each other erelong; I can assure you that boy." the warden spat into Will's face. "You've felt the contempt for you? Do people not see you as human? Do they not accept you?"

Everything that had happened to him including Norman's attempt to capture him, the noble's distain, the squires' attack, all the soldiers who had doubts in him, and the Suthenburg girl's ire flooded his mind.

"I told you, didn't I? None will e'er accept you, *except* for me." The warden looked briefly at those surrounding him. He was right. Will had faced such hardship but… but there were those who *did* help him and even believe in his worth.

"You're wrong!" Will growled, courage evaporating as quickly as he had gathered it. The warden threw Will to the ground. He and his men departed and Sir Robert lifted his squire.

"It's alright. He won't take you while I still breathe. *He* is the warden? *He's* the man you told me about?" the knight questioned. Will nodded. "He is a demon. I am beginning to think King Duggan's judgement is waning. Go to our tent and compose yourself; I will be there shortly. Alex, help him."

Will sat alone in his section of the tent he shared with Sir Robert. He was curled up, his chin on his knees, trembling. He'd been so close to the warden again and so suddenly. The warden had followed him from Suthenburg, would he hound him everywhere?

A sudden blast pushed him into the air with deafening force and his tent fell over him. Will gasped and ripped the tent open. He crawled out and slid onto his side. Will drew the dagger at his belt and scrambled to his feet. Where was he? Where was the warden. He'd resist that man to the end to preserve what he had. He was going to kill him. Will gripped his dagger, but the warden was nowhere to be seen.

Was it the Saomardrim? He expected hordes of enemies to be slashing and killing at pleasure but only bombs fell from the sky. Everything was on fire and the bangs of explosions mixed with screaming. Dirt flew up into Will's face and he brushed it away. He could barely breathe, smoke blinding him. Will looked up and as a mass of smoke parted, he could see large oval-shaped structures floating in the sky. They dropped bombs, cannon balls, and sprayed flames everywhere. This was why Sir Robert was searching the sky before! The enemy was flying, impossible! They were ships? In he air! There were three dropping bombs. One exploded by Will and sent him flying again. He crawled and stood.

"Master!" Will shouted. Was Sir Robert in the tent? Will rushed to the ruins of his tent and dug through it. Nothing. His master hadn't been there. He had to find him or at least get himself to safety. He ran straight ahead.

The whole camp was in chaos. People ran and shouted, others withered on the ground in the throes of death. He ran around a corner where cannon balls confronted him, pounding in quick order about the ground. In a split-second Will heard one right above him and sprinted forward but he could not stop. More slammed down and Will kept moving. A tower crumbled to his right and he switched direction, darting to the left. A cannon ball landed to his right and Will adjusted again. Putting his arms up to shield himself he dodged cannon and debris all the way down the street. Sliding under the cover of a shop doorway, Will was able to catch his breath. The death machines loomed over him. His body was littered with cuts and blood. The pain became apparent. Ahead of him, people ran from all directions.

A thunderous explosion sent stone and debris flying above him. Will looked up to see a huge grey stone barreling towards him. As Will was about to move a blue robed, caped warrior appeared and shot his arms to the sky. A light blue ward unravelled above Will and blocked the stone.

"Get out of here young master!" Will looked at him startled but nodded his thanks and ran past the mage.

Running closer to a crossroads Will ducked and ran past falling cannon ball explosions. One landed ahead and blew up. Unable to stop quick enough, Will ran straight into it. His skin burned as he was launched back the way he came. The fire and force ripped through him like sharpened claws. When Will landed he rolled over to his side and clutched his torso. His skin had been shredded off and blood dripped down his hands. Will moaned and coughed. He looked towards the crossroads, to his surprise the Suthenburg girl was running past until she caught Will's gaze. His face must have been one of immense pain, because the girl stopped and looked at him, unsure of herself. Will looked on in a silent plea for help. Then the girl, having made up her mind, ran towards him and Will turned to lie on his back groaning and still clutching his bloody stomach. The girl crouched down over him and gasped at the sight.

"Look what you got yourself into!" she said. Will groaned, not finding words. The girl tried to lift Will, cannon fire and explosives still blowing up around them. Will tried to aid her by slinging his arm over her shoulder, which she briefly looked cross about. The girl lifted Will to a standing position but Will's legs gave way and he fell, prompting the girl to crouch to catch him.

To the best of her ability, the girl brought Will under an overhang. She placed him on the ground and he found his voice.

"It's bad…" Will groaned.

"I don't know how to treat this," the girl said. She looked at Will, sweat breaking across her brow. He noticed her worry seconds before it disappeared.

"Then leave me and go get help. I can't walk."

The girl hesitated for the briefest of seconds then ran off towards the crossroads. She made it to the center and an explosion erupted too close to her. She screamed and fell, not moving on the cobbles.

"NO!" Will cried as something exploded by him and the walls of the overhang came crashing down. Then there was black.

Part Three:
The Two Seekers

Chapter Sixteen

WILL AWOKE ON his side in a grassy field. Beside him, the embers of a campfire crackled next to a tent, and a horse grazed nearby. He turned to lie on his back and realised his wrists and ankles were bound. A rope stretched from around his wrists to a tent pole, holding him in place. White bandages were wound neatly around his arms and legs. A cut throbbed on his neck and a massive bandage was securely fastened around his stomach, now sore and aching. He wore his damaged tunic. Will remembered the carnage of the previous night.

A boy emerged from the tent, as old as Will but with darker skin and short black hair ending in fringe. The boy moved effortlessly; his muscle suited him well. The slight beginning of a moustache was visible on his face as was stubble around his chin. He stretched under the sunlight staring at the sky for a moment, then at Will.

He took a few steps back and his right hand went towards a sword at his waist that wasn't there. Will's muscles tightened, his vision sharpened. The two stared at each other for a long moment taking in each other's features. Relaxing, the foreign boy spoke.

"You are finally awake. I carried you on my horse for a day," he said.

"Who're you? Where am I?"

"You are in my home…" he started. Will noticed he had a Saomardrim accent. "You thought we would let you take our town without counter? You like our new airships don't you." He smiled. "The ingenious use of hot air generated from fire to lift the airship into the sky, and if the fire falters, mages can keep it alight."

"You're Saomardrim! Why am I here?"

"You're here because I found you alive. I admit, I was late to the battle, it was over and most of your countrymen were already taken away, but when I arrived, I saw you, still alive among the dead. You were gravely injured. I am taking you to Ortie, the capital, to pay for your crimes against us."

"Crimes?" Frustration grew in him, blamed yet again for things he didn't do. Now he'd been captured by the enemy, at least this boy wasn't the warden… he hoped.

"You are a squire by the look of your clothes but we aren't ransoming anyone this time. You attacked our lands, killed our men, and raped our women, so you must pay for these crimes."

"I ne'er touched a woman, ever." But killed his men? Will hadn't realised until now if he'd killed anyone during the battles he'd been in, because he was too busy staying alive. The warden's laugh lingered in his mind and he steadied himself against it.

"Don't you lie! All Gurmians are liars!" the boy spat. The Saomardrim grabbed Will. He pulled up his tunic to reveal Will's chest, and the brand fused on it. "M for murder. I saw it. How does a murderer become a squire? Or did you kill a squire and steal his clothes? Do they allow any common criminal into the Gurmian army? Your people must be desperate." The Saomardrim gave Will a hard, disapproving look.

"I'm not a murderer," Will said.

"So what? You decided to brand yourself? For fun?"

"You wouldn't understand." Will frowned. The Saomardrim let go of Will's tunic.

"It doesn't matter anyway."

The Saomardrim started to pack up his camp. He attached his gold lined lamellar and mail armour to his brown tunic and added a weapons belt and red sash. The boy wielded a one-handed war axe, a curved kilij sword, and a curved djanbīyya dagger. He adjusted his flintlock pistol and what looked to be round pottery with rope sticking out of its top. He also held a light crossbow and bolts. Will guessed the boy was a skilled fighter.

"What's your name?" Will asked.

"I am Ahmed ibn-Iqbal Sharfi son of the Emir of Hamid." Ahmed smiled proudly.

"What is an emir?"

"An equivalent to a lord, as you use." Ahmed strapped on his pauldrons, adjusting the rerebraces below, then his bracers. Will felt his tunic pouch and found his pearl gone.

"Where is my pearl? D'you take it?" Will growled. Ahmed lifted Will's pearl out of his pocket.

"This I think I will keep." He held it up to the light.

"Give it back!"

"You're in no position to make demands. Besides it will be safe with me after your execution."

Will swallowed. If it was what Manis desired then it would happen, he had to accept that. But whereas before he had nothing to leave behind, now he had his master, and maybe that girl. Now leaving this world early filled him with dread.

"I have one like this. Curious? These pearls have some powerful magic in them, did you know that?" Ahmed ran a finger over the pearl's smooth surface.

"No," Will lied, not trusting the boy.

"Curious…" Ahmed eyed Will, not accepting his answer.

"You speak good common tongue."

"It is the language of commerce and scholarship is it not? I have been educated well. Are squires well taught?"

"I'm told they are."

"What do you mean? Have you not been educated?"

"I've been taught enough," Will lied again, not wanting to reveal his situation to the boy.

"Interesting answer." When Ahmed was finished cleaning his camp, he snuffed out the fire pit then took Will's rope and attached it to his horse's saddle beside a spare sword nestled next to a saddlebag and a rope noose. He unfurled the noose. Will watched him and didn't break eye contact as the boy slid the noose over Will's neck, weaved it between Will's bound wrists and tied it to the saddle. After securing a rolled mat over his horse's saddlebags Ahmed mounted and rode forward. Will got up as the rope tugged his arms, and his neck, but with slack. He scrambled to keep pace with the horse, stumbling as he went.

Ahmed ate a breakfast of dates, oranges, nuts, and some hot liquid. Will's stomach grumbled as he watched. He realised he had nothing to eat when he was out for a day.

"Will you let me starve to death Ahmed?" Will asked, testing the foreign name on his tongue.

"Of course not, I would fail in my duty if you died." Ahmed tossed a date at Will who almost missed it. Will examined the fruit, smelled it, and took a little bite. It didn't taste right, but Will was hungry, so he ate quickly.

"I will die anyway." Will frowned.

Ahmed laughed, "You know, you did not tell me your name, what is it?"

"It's Will."

"Will…" Ahmed tested this name on his tongue.

They travelled for a day, few words spoken between them, and Will's stumbling started to tire him. His wrists and feet burned from the pull of the ropes. Sparse dry greenery stretched far around them, hugging hills over which they traveled.

"When will we stop?" Will asked.

"Over this hill there is a small lake, we will make camp there. I would have travelled further on to the caravanserai but it will soon be dark and we cannot risk travel at night for fear of bandits or worse, Banu Murtād," Ahmed answered.

"What is a caravanserai?"

"It's a fortified inn for caravans, merchants, and travelers to rest at. I suppose you do not know very much about my land being the Gurmian squire you are."

"And if I were to tell you who I was a squire to?"

"It won't matter. I don't care if you are the squire to the king, in fact that would make a stronger statement. Just walk quietly and accept your fate."

Ahmed made camp by the lake and once again restrained Will to his tent, putting him inside when he noticed approaching storm clouds. He refilled his waterskins. Ahmed shared a supper of his hot liquid, colder now, and some preserved meat. Will did not even see Ahmed start a fire but it was lit. Will rolled around his side of the tent trying to find a comfortable position as thunder crackled outside.

"Would you stop rolling? Sleep! It's already disturbing enough with the thunder and rain," Ahmed said, frustrated at Will's indecision.

"If you remove the ropes 'twould be easier!" Will suggested. Ahmed laughed.

"You people are not very smart, are you? I am not a fool."

"I could still strangle you with this rope."

"And then where would you go? You do not know this land and any other soldier would kill you on sight."

"Least back home soldiers have sense to investigate 'afore killing. Ya know, figure out who I am an' what I've actually been doing."

Ahmed raised an eyebrow at Will. "Rational… not… bloodthirsty."

"Bloodthirsty?" Will frowned. "Where'd that come from?"

"That's what the sultan calls your people; savages and child killers. He says every word your people speak is an attempt to bewitch us. Your kind has virtues of courage and fighting, we can give you that, but it's not much different from the virtues of animals."

"Virtues of animals?"

"Animals have strength and can carry loads so not much different than your kind. The Gurmians are bellicose, treacherous and uncouth."

Will did not grasp all the complex words Ahmed described, but his tone reminded him of the zealous preacher in King's Bridge Village long ago. He repeated some of the same words.

"From what I hear the Saomardrim are no better. Your kind is lascivious and immoral. Sexual immorality runs rampant in yer land. The way you carry yourself is equally as vile. Look!" Will held up his bound limbs. "D'you call this proper?"

"You are my enemy. Why would I give you use of your limbs?" Ahmed looked at Will as if the reason was the most obvious thing in the world. Will thought it made sense.

"I guess so."

"All you say is false. Your people are simply ignorant. If you took a single moment to study the true culture of Saomarhad you would realise our superiority. The proper way of living is achievable only by emulating us."

"Why d'you get to say what's the better way to live?"

"I don't say it; it is the words of Alhurah. His words are law; his words are the truth, the way. Submission to him is the true way to paradise. The Father and Alhurah are the same and Alhurah is the only way to the Father. All others hold no claim. They may be powerful, but are not God."

"Manis' words are the truth, the way. He..." Will hesitated. What was he saying? Manis never helped him in any way. Manis shunned him, rejected him and took pleasure in seeing him suffer. Manis did not care.

"I get the feeling we're just repeating what we have always been told. All of it interpretations on the words of God," Ahmed said.

"I think so too." Will really didn't believe in all this.

Ahmed adjusted himself so he could speak to Will easier. There was a gleam in his eyes, an expectation or want of something.

"Wh-What do *you* think of me?" Ahmed asked. Will hesitated. How much should he be telling his enemy?

"When I saw you this morning... I was... afraid. Saomardrim are s'posed to be demons an' demons look twisted and rotted." Images of the murals in his village church came to mind. Demons were fiery, twisted, wore fleshy black armor, and horned.

"Do I rot?" Ahmed huffed.

"Not that I can see."

"I was told your country is cold, dark and surrounded in evil's fog. I was told it was populated by fanatical and warlike people who are slow to develop and backwards in every way."

"I don't even understand all these ideas." Will frowned. He was at war because he had no better choice. He didn't fight because he believed he was marching against pagans, no, he just wanted to please his master and shake the labels that had been glued to him. "I don't want to fight anymore than I have to," Will admitted.

There was silence between the boys for a few seconds before Ahmed broke it, "So... our leaders do not speak the truth."

"Maybe," Will hesitated to admit it.

"Or you are an exception." Ahmed's brow furrowed in confusion.

"You could also be."

"You could lie, I have yet to see the truth. How did you get to the front?"

"Why would you want to know that?"

"Merely curious. You said I should figure out who you are did you not?"

Yet when Will looked at Ahmed's expression, he could have sworn Ahmed had another motive. "Luck I guess." Will chose to be vague.

"War is hardly lucky."

"Well, it was a step up for me." Will hesitated, not wanting to say more, but Ahmed seemed to expect more. "I was a farmer…"

"You don't sound sure. There is more to it, isn't there?" Ahmed looked curiously at Will as if he was trying to read him.

"There isn't anything more…" Will hesitated, "I…"

Ahmed shook his head. "If you're not going to tell me the truth, I would rather not hear your lies."

"How…"

"I am done with you, go to sleep." Ahmed curled into his bed roll. Will was stunned at how Ahmed had read through the lies, he hadn't even finished speaking, but he decided it was best not to ask. He could cut the ropes somehow and run away like he did from Isen Prison but this Saomardrim had a point. This was not Gurmanis; Will had no idea where anything was and he stood out too much here. He would have to find another way. There would be another chance.

Will laid on his side. Sir Robert and the Suthenburg girl came to mind. He hoped they made it out of the attack and that they still lived. He had to believe that. Thinking they were gone, especially Sir Robert, made him tremble. It would be like reliving the murder of his parents all over again and he couldn't bear that. He'd be alone. Again.

<hr>

After riding the next day for several hours, the two arrived at the main road heading south. Around them the ground had grown progressively flatter. Shrubs and grasses replaced most trees upon this vast savannah. Ahmed listened to the wind, taking in the calm. Something was wrong. The rustling of tree leaves were all he heard. Not a single bird was singing and… Will coughed and stumbled forwards, almost falling into Ahmed's horse.

"The air tastes funny," Will said. Ahmed stopped his horse. He scanned over the landscape, checking for anything out of place. A gust of wind blew over them and Ahmed's nose twitched. He recoiled at the smell of smoke… smoke? He swiveled his horse to the south and noticed plumes of billowing grey rising into the sky.

"Wait," Will said, "d'you hear that?" Ahmed focused harder, concentrating and extending his senses.

"The sounds of a battle. I hear the booming of cannons," Ahmed said, sweat forming over his brow.

Ahmed led Will down the road towards the sounds and smells. They approached a ridge, overlooking the road as it turned and descended downslope. Ahmed leaned over the edge as Will pressed beside him; below them a stretch of flat farmland was marred by masses of people. There were two sides, each firing with arrow, bolt, and bullet, preventing the other side from hand-to-hand. Armored war carriages from either side charged each other, firing flame and cannon.

The ground shook under the boys' feet as they watched the battle from afar.

"Gurmians and Saomardrim are fighting each other," Will stated the obvious.

"And blocking our path south." Ahmed frowned. The shaking under their feet grew louder and louder. Ahmed turned, looking north, a large armored Saomarhad war carriage and some horse archers rode towards the ridge. Will walked back, putting Ahmed's horse between the carriage and himself. Ahmed stepped forward, confident there was no threat. The carriage came to a halt beside the boys. It stood at least two men tall, was covered in metal plate over wood, and had an arrow gun at the back, a swiveling cannon on top under a domed roof, and a cannon over the driver in front. There were holes in its walls for soldiers to shoot all manner of weapons out.

The driver signaled to Ahmed, "As-salāmu alaykum,"

"Wa alaykumu s-salām," Ahmed answered.

"Soldier," the man referenced Ahmed's armor, "Are you taking that boy south?"

"I am."

"You'll have to cross the desert. The main road's been taken."

"Is that battle lost?" In response, a huge explosion shook the earth and blurred Ahmed's voice.

"Just about it seems. We're going southeast to cover the retreat. Move east towards Nizid."

"I will do that."

The driver nodded and whipped the reins. The war carriage thundered forward, a handful of horse archers following.

⸎

They spent another night camping, saying very little to each other. As they rode onwards over the next few days, the air grew dryer and the ground sandier and more arid. The savannah gave way to rocky outcrops gradually growing larger into distant tan inselbergs and mesas. A layer of sand teased their feet, and became entrained by the wind. Will took in his surroundings, noticing a drop off into outcrops that arose from dunes of sand.

"That's the desert then?" Will asked, "There's so much sand, where does it all come from?"

"What? You don't know what a desert is?" Ahmed asked astonished, "How long have you been fighting my people?"

"I think you already know all that."

"I do. You seem to also think all the people of Saomarhad are Saomardrim do you not?"

"That's what Gurmians call you."

"The term is actually Saomarhadians which include the majority Saomardrim, Oghurks, Perssyans, and Zanjī, as well as smaller groups. I am Saomardrim."

"How did you guess what I think?" Will didn't consider asking what these majority groups were.

"I can figure it out. Come to think of it, you're making it too easy." Ahmed smiled.

Will shook his head. "What d'you even mean? I told you nothing, how are you…" Both boys looked up, responding to a shrill call. Will's falcon, circled above and landed in front of him. The bird hopped close to Will but stopped and looked back when Ahmed flicked the alignment switch on his pistol, pointed at the bird.

"No! Don't!" Will cried, falling to his knees so he was at a better height to the bird.

"What is this? We don't have time." Will carefully brought the bird closer to him.

"It's my bird."

"Why do you have a bird?"

"I don't know… I just… do?"

Ahmed holstered his pistol. "Be off with it."

Will waved the bird off. Ahmed got back on his horse, shaking his head. The horse jerked forward and pulled Will to his feet.

⚬⚬⚬

Waves of hollow heat crashed into Will, scorching his skin and taking all moisture with it. The sun's oppressive rays beamed down from the blue cloudless sky without end. They rode downwards through passes amongst wind polished rounded rock that seemed to melt into sand, grain by grain. On the edges of the desert, they approached a village, Kharija, built onto the flats of tan sandstone emerging from the sands, but upon seeing it, Ahmed's heart leapt from his chest. The sun played tricks on his eyes by showing distant unreal puddles of water, at its center the smoke and flames from the burning village rose, breaking the illusion. Ahmed spurned his horse faster, dragging Will along.

They made their way down the main path of the village as cries and wails of saddened people filled the smoky air. On either side some of the village upon the rocks rose above them. Buildings burned and crumbled. Shattered stone, wood, and fire littered the ground. Some of the rock had collapsed, not naturally, onto the buildings below. The grain storage, ghorfas, build into one face of the rock was charred by ash. Even the mosque that sat perched upon the highest point was severely damaged.

A man aiding another injured man limped by. Another man sat against a pile of rubble. His skin was burned and melted. Debris was, in places, wedged into his skin. Flies flew around him and he did not move.

"Baba! Baaba!" A child's hopeless shriek made Will and Ahmed jump. The sobbing boy clasped the bloodied corpse of his father. None seemed present or available to console him.

Above the carnage a fort stood. Thick streams of billowing black smoke, its foundation hot orange, rose from shattered towers and domes and from its airship tower. Will and Ahmed approached beneath a bridge which linked the flanking rocks. There a mother cried over her little dead son, a young girl in tears holding on to her leg. A soldier crouched to console her.

Ahmed dismounted and approached while Will stared around himself unsurely. Ahmed addressed the soldier,

"Wh-What happened here?"

"Alhamdulilhurah. You, lad, of the army?" he asked in a low voice, his face scrunched in distress. Ahmed nodded.

"Gurmanis attack."

"Out here? How? They can't march armies this far…"

"Not men on foot, men in machines in the sky."

"That would mean they have airships!"

"Aywa." He nodded. "This is the carnage of one. The bastards were hitting the fort. Already stray shells hit the village. As they left, they bombed it completely. No one survived the fort attack. I was lucky to be away from it when it happened along with some of my mates. All those brave men and boys martyred in there, commander too."

"Have you sent a man to warn that Gurmanis now have airships? Their production was supposed be a secret."

"Evidently, our enemies have excellent spies. Yes, sent a man to Farah, he should have arrived; a bird will take the message to the capital, inshalhurah. This has been the story so many times. Gurmians have no mercy. They attack, pillage, and burn then blame us to justify their actions! In every settlement they hit military targets as stray shots cause massive civilian casualties, then some turn and burn the residences!"

"I have heard of this. Gurmians rain into our lands to the edges of the deserts. Lands are left covered in ash and soot. Survivors are taken by Gurmians to be sold in the slave markets of the Dominion and the Imperium," Ahmed said.

"Persecutors, the lot! This young lad here was running an errand with his sister moments before the attack, and then when he heard the explosions and saw the shadow, he pushed his sister out of the way, now here he is."

Ahmed forced himself to glance at the dead boy, much of him had burned. His mother looked up at Ahmed, tears streaming down her soot-covered face and soaking the umber shayla wrapped around her head.

"He was my boy! My child! He was so kind, so brave, how could they do this!" She thrashed her chest. "They are monsters! His father was at the fort, he is dead too. How will we survive, me and my daughter?" She pressed her hands over her forehead and swayed. Her pain stabbed into Ahmed's heart.

Then the woman looked past Ahmed to Will, who was standing shyly beside Ahmed's horse. The change in her expression sucked the heat from Will's skin. Her face filled with anger. She stood, prompting her daughter to let go. She pushed past Ahmed. Will took a few steps back before the woman shoved him to the ground, stepped on his chest, and pulled the noose around Will's neck tight. His face burned as his strained lungs and burning neck struggled to function. He grabbed the noose, trying to free himself but managing nothing.

Ahmed jumped to action. He detached the rope attached to his horse, to prevent the startled animal from running and dragging Will. He and the soldier got hold of the woman and tried to pull her off of Will. Her grip held firm.

"You and your ilk are beasts! Monsters, murderers, demons! Alhurah curse you kafir; how could you do that to my family. We wanted nothing of the war yet you brought it to us!"

"Stop Ni'ja! Sabr! You're not a killer, think about your daughter. I am your friend, I will help you find a new, happy life, Alhurah willing!" the soldier pleaded. "Your son, your husband are martyrs, they will be welcomed at the Father's side." Ni'ja let go and crumpled on her knees, crying into her hands. The soldier clasped her shoulders, and her daughter cried over her dead brother. Will rolled over gasping for air.

Ahmed pulled him up. "It's time we leave," he said firmly. Reattaching Will, Ahmed rode out of the village.

Will, feeling ashamed, spoke when they were a distance away. "D'you mean Gurmians did that?" Will asked. Ahmed abruptly stopped his horse and dismounted. Anger flaring in his eyes, he grabbed Will by his collar and shoved him against his horse. The animal neighed and swayed.

"You mean all that death? Yes! Only they would do this." Ahmed growled. Helpless, all Will could do was push at Ahmed's stomach with his bound hands. "Your leaders all hide in their castles and order their men to persecute innocent Saomarhadians!" Ahmed shoved Will again. "Alhurah will not leave you unpunished!" Ahmed lifted his other hand and stretched his fingers as if he was going to claw Will.

"We're not all like that…" he whispered. Will glared into Ahmed's eyes and gripped the Saomardrim's stomach, causing Ahmed to flinch. "I don't know a whole lot about this war, why people are fighting or what battles have been fought." His master had always been so neutral about the war, except for an occasional doubt. "I only know that those people who are good seem to stand out a little more."

"Good people? What good people? I have heard what they say. Gurmians praise their king. That man who want's Saomarhadians extinct!"

"The king was ne'er a good person." Will frowned. "B-Besides… your people have hurt Gurmanis in equal ways. Blood has been spilt on both sides. If my master is right, for several waves of crusades and jihads. Your people raid the countryside constantly burning all homes, food, and even children. I know there are good Gurmians. We… we don't deserve yer hatred." The boys stared at each other, allowing a few tense moments pass them.

"I know…" Ahmed sighed. "I am educated enough to know it is not so simple as good and bad. There are more innocents than there are mad men. If only your countrymen were like you Will." Ahmed let go of Will and Will saw a hint of sympathy in his eyes. "Let's forget it. It won't help us any further if we talk more about what happened."

Will had never been so thirsty in his life. The arid air sucked all moisture from his body and the sand shifted so much that Will kept falling and stumbling. Rock had vanished, surrounding them in dunes. The air seemed to swirl at the edges of sand dunes, as if water. When he could go no further, Ahmed gave Will the water he so desperately required. Will groaned on his side as Ahmed forced the water in his mouth. The wind picked up, tossing swirling sand in waves around them. Will pushed his hands through the sand, lifting some and letting the rest flow between his fingers, the grainy texture scratching him. He looked in every direction, sand, sand dunes, and more hot golden sand.

"This is such a lifeless place. Goes on forever like an ocean! No, it's exactly like an ocean, like the Hertos River, so very hot and lifeless."

"That makes no sense." Ahmed laughed. "The Hertos River is a river, not an ocean. And if the sand stretched on forever there would be no ocean, or river!" Will fell on his back and looked into the sky.

"The sky is yellow, I can't see the blue." The once blue cloudless sky had vanished. Light shimmered off golden grains of entrained sand, yellowing the sky.

"Are you okay, Will? Is the heat getting to you?" Ahmed laughed again.

"Soon we will see giant snakes and scorpions rise up from the sand to eat us, ridden by dwarves and pygmies." Will knew their fate would be a terrible one. Ahmed looked at Will, stunned with disbelief.

"Now I know the heat has gotten to you. You're speaking complete nonsense."

"Even the wind is no saviour. The wind is hot and it brings sand with it."

"Yes, feel that wind Will? A sandstorm is coming and if we get caught in that, we will be buried alive! There is a rocky outcrop not much further, it is used at these moments for travellers to rest in."

"I can't go further, too tired," Will croaked.

"We have to!" Ahmed strolled back to his horse and wrapped cloth around his head to make a turban. He covered the lower half of his face with it and stuffed the tail into his armour.

"Stay close to the horse's behind and it will help."

Will snorted.

The two trudged through sheets of sand entrained by the wind. Low periodic howling wind grew consistent by the time they arrived at a set of massive yardang rock structures poking out of the landscape, semi-buried in sand. The tan sandstone sat quietly in the rising sandstorm, a wooden scaffolding, fitted with fabric tarps, holding it up and marking it as a rest camp. A cave was carved into the rock, empty with only the scattered remains of a campfire inside. A small stream ran from one wall to another, providing only a trickle of groundwater.

Ahmed bound Will to the back of the cave, then secured everything else. Will slumped against the cave wall. Though they were protected by the small enclosed space, there was no way he was going to escape now. The sandstorm raged, in full force, in the darkening sky. Ahmed entered with supplies and waterskins. He ripped his turban off.

"You are strong, Will. You lasted." Ahmed fetched the rolled mat from his horse and observed a flat round dial in his hand. He looked in the direction facing the cave entrance then unfurled the mat over the ground. Will watched with intrigue as Ahmed recited words of his language then went to his knees to prostrate.

"What are you doing?" Will asked but Ahmed didn't respond. He came upright on his knees and whispered before bring his hands together over his face and as if he were wiping it and ended with a deep breath. Ahmed stood and rolled up his mat.

"Prayer, wasn't it?" Will guessed.

"We've come safely so far and I am thankful to Alhurah for it." Ahmed took his mat back to his horse and returned with a pouch and two cups. He took a seat by the fire pit and placed a thin stick within. Will laughed to himself, how was he to make a fire last with that?

"Bismilhurah." Ahmed whispered then extend an arm and chanted, "Multiply vitalif ignahar ignahar extend." A fire blasted up.

"You're a mage!" Heat rushed from Will's face only to return as the fire settled into a steady flame.

"A mage in training that is," Ahmed answered. He took a cone of sugar out of his pouch and split it in two, placing a half into each cup.

"Now I know how you saw through my lie and read me. It was because you are a mage."

"Yes, a mage can read people's physical reactions and energies. I have trained hard to be able to read one's bodily functions and energy changes, it can be intensive. There is a change in both when people lie or do—"

"What's it like being a mage?" Will was enthused. The mages at Isen Prison would have hurt him if he tried to talk to them.

"It takes effort." Ahmed adjusted the strength of the fire. Will frowned, hoping to have learned more. Ahmed poured water into each cup and stirred the mixture.

"You can make fire?" Will imagined being able to wield such power. Ahmed said nothing. "How?"

"I'm not going to tell my enemy. You are not a mage anyway." Ahmed offered Will a cup. Will grabbed it, eager to have his thirst quenched. The taste of the yellow liquid was sweet with a slight sourness to it, utterly refreshing.

"You're not a dark mage, are you?"

Ahmed looked hurt. "Never! I am not so vile."

"I was told the practice of dark magic is common in Saomarhad," Will said.

"More lies." Ahmed scoffed then took a sip from his own cup.

"You know a lot about our pearls…"

"I only know as much as I have told you already." Ahmed took his pearl out of a pouch at his waist. "So odd. I have sensed the attraction between yours and mine for some time. It may sound strange but it led me to you in Al-Motros."

Will shrugged, finishing his drink. He settled in for sleep pleased at least for the balanced temperature.

Ahmed looked into his pearl and memories filled him. Shapes of people appeared within and Ahmed's mind drifted to a time when he was young.

Chapter Seventeen

"ONE DAY, INSHALHURAH, this will all be yours Amir, and your brother will be by your side to support you." Five-year-old Ahmed looked up with wide eyes at his older brother, who was only a youth himself. Their mother always joked about how similar they looked with the most obvious difference being that Amir kept his hair shorter than Ahmed's.

"As you wish, Father," Amir answered. They stood on a balcony, high up in the palace. The boys' father spread out his arms. Below them, stretching far, was the town of Hamid. Its blocky stone buildings, peaked and tiled roofs, and domes and spires like an urban jungle.

"This is the town I have revolutionised, with God's guidance. I gave it a souk, madressa, hammam, maktaba," Iqbal glanced at Ahmed with a smile, "And even an observatory."

"The astronomer's teaching me." Ahmed grinned.

"The people love and respect me Amir. Why is that?"

"Because you have done so much good for them Baba," Amir reasoned.

"Yes. Because I cared for their needs as much as I have cultivated our relationship with the sultan. These efforts are for you to continue."

"Yes, Baba."

A servant approached Iqbal and whispered to him. He nodded. "I have business to conduct."

Ahmed and Amir were left alone. Ahmed looked up to his brother who observed Hamid, deep in thought. Amir was so calm and knew exactly what to say or do. One day Ahmed would be just like him. He'd show Amir, he would. Ahmed pulled his brother's arm. "Amir! Look! Look!"

Amir smiled. He took Ahmed in his arms and hugged him. "How many times will you keep pestering me."

"Aaaamir!" Ahmed wined. He pulled out a sheet of paper. "Look!"

Amir took it. "What's this?"

"Ulgan's Fist. Constellation named after the high orc god."

"I know that! Why are you riding it towards me?"

Ahmed grinned. "I can fly!"

"Good, because I thought you were saying you're stronger than me qazam." Amir tapped Ahmed in the chest causing the younger boy to sway.

"I'm stronger than you too."

"Not ever." Amir laughed.

"Why were you so bored when father was talking to you?" Ahmed asked. Amir frowned.

"You shouldn't worry about it."

"Tell me! I want to know."

Amir sighed, "Our father expects me to rule Hamid after him. I'll try my best to fulfil that."

"But you don't like it. Why try?"

"No… that's not it. Liking and being bored are two different things. Baba says it's my responsibility, my duty as the eldest to rule. He is an emir and I will be someday. It is his dream and his wish."

"But do you want to?"

"I don't know, someone has to. Besides, we could do anything we wanted. But… there is responsibility and duty, to rein us in and stop us from going too far. It's not a bad thing, it's the right thing… I guess. We should consider what is best for all, not ending what we want… just… you know."

"I don't understand."

"One day you will."

"I want to watch the city."

"Of course you do." Amir lifted his younger brother onto his shoulders and they watched the sunset over the city.

By the age of seven, Ahmed's life would change.

"You can't catch me little brother! I'm too fast!" Amir rounded a corner. In the souk, Ahmed and Amir chased each other around stalls and people, despite the protests from their bodyguards.

"Wait Amir. I can't run as fast as you!" Ahmed yelled in reply as he bumped into a woman in a scarlet hijab.

"Sorry!" But Ahmed's apology was lost in the noise and color of the souk. Ahmed ran as fast as his legs would take him. He ran into the narrow arcade and dodged three jar carriers. Amir made a sharp turn to the right and disappeared around the corner. Ahmed made the same turn, but ran too wide and tripped onto an ornate carpet being shown to customers, scaring a cat as he did. He slid on the fabric, much to the frustration of the livid merchant and startled customers. Ahmed stumbled forward, running into another intersection of four halls. He stopped. He looked in all four directions trying to get a sight of his brother amidst the loud dense crowd. Amir peeked out from behind a barrel. Ahmed caught a sight of him and grinned, running to his older brother. Amir stuck out his tongue and ran away, ahead of Ahmed. Ahmed jumped left to barely avoid a man with a box of pears and dashed through the souk, under a horseshoe arch, and into the open air.

Ahmed found himself in a large circular section with a shadirvan fountain in its center. He stopped running and looked around for Amir.

Amir revealed himself at the far end. "Over here little brother! You can never catch me." He teased.

"Wait Amir! Let me win sometimes, I never win!" Ahmed yelled back, frustrated. Amir waved his hands and made a face. Ahmed threw his arms to his side. He squeezed his hands into fists, but as his motion stopped, puffs of fire emerged from each fist. Amir watched, wide-eyed. Ahmed released his clenched fists and fire beamed from them. He was thrown back as fire ignited fabric over the fountain. Flames wasted no time in engulfing the entire section of the souk. People screamed and ran in every direction away from the fire. The boys' bodyguards came running behind Ahmed but were cut off by a burst of flame.

"Ahmed!" Amir screamed as he jumped over flame and into the center of the souk's section. Ahmed remembered the fear that overcame him. He was in shock about what he had done. He didn't fully understand what he had done. He couldn't bring himself to move. Amir tackled him to the ground and pulled him up. He shook his younger brother.

"We have to go Ahmed. Come on! Move!" Amir dragged Ahmed as they stumbled towards the guards. The commander yelled to his men, they surrounded the boys and quickly moved out of the rising flames. As the group rushed out to a waiting carriage, people with water buckets were hopelessly trying to douse the flames. Behind them six green robed men came forward with water tanks on their backs topped by a glowing crystal on each. The last thing Ahmed saw was water surging forward from the tank hoses and the robed men chanting indecipherable words.

On the trip back to the palace, Ahmed sat beside his older brother, head down and trembling. Amir was quiet, the guards were quiet, and Ahmed didn't know what to say.

Ahmed sat on the edge of a flower bed in the courtyard of the palace, head down, as the shouting of furious merchants shook him. They'd mobbed the palace minutes after the brothers had retreated within. Amir was standing beside Ahmed, sweat breaking over his brow. Their mother, Rafia, rushed outside, adjusting the chador over her hair, followed by female servants. When Ahmed heard Amir call her, he looked up, tears forming in his eyes, and rushed to embrace her.

"What has happened?" she asked, fear and worry in her voice. Ahmed trembled in her embrace.

Amir tried to explain, "A-Ahmed… Ahmed burn—"

Iqbal, flanked by his captain of the guard and arriving from the ramparts, caught sight of them and he strode over, fury in his face.

"Ahmed!" he snapped. Ahmed's heart skipped a beat at the voice of his father. He let go of his mother and turned to face the raging man. Baba had never been so mad. Amir shifted uncomfortably. Iqbal pointed to the ground in front of him. Ahmed walked forwards and hovered in place. At the sound of his name again, he looked up at his father.

"You foolish boy! Who told you to ignore your bodyguards and run amok in the souk? You burned it all! I have all the city merchants outside threatening to involve the Merchant's Guild. Wages and wares have been lost by the hundreds. Thank God no one was hurt." Iqbal's tone was harsh and unforgiving. His voice could be heard throughout the intricate and lavish palace.

"F-Father we… I…" Iqbal slapped him across his face and Ahmed clasping his throbbing cheek, shook.

"Don't mumble. Speak sense!" It was the first time his father had used force with him. Shame made him to drop his head, and he cried, unable to hold it in.

"Father," Amir came forward. "It was my fault. I told him to follow me into the souk and I taunted him too far. He cast fire. I take the blame."

Iqbal's face softened, remorse replacing the anger. "My son *cast* fire?" He looked to his wife who stepped forward, equally as stunned, but there was recognition between them as if they had talked about the topic of magic before.

Magic arose in individuals from their biology. Lucky were those who obtained magic from Alhurah. Sometimes magic appeared in every generation of a family, like in the elder species. In humans it was more common for magic to appear every two to four generations.

Ahmed was sat down with his parents and his mother explained to him how her family had a few magi in the past. They'd considered the possibility that one of their sons would one day awake to magic. Ahmed could never forget the day he left home, at the end of the fasting month. A tall man wearing a green velvet and mulham Robe of Honour gifted by the sultan, lined in gold and silver metallic threads and accents came for Ahmed. He wore a tiraz around his right arm inscribed with a commendation from the sultan and was accompanied by robed soldiers foreign to Ahmed. The man was Grand Vizier Master Mahad Oman who Ahmed had seen on occasion when his family were guests of the sultan.

"Very good." Master Mahad smiled, resting a hand on his scimitar, as Iqbal kissed the man's other hand. Amir followed. Master Mahad gestured to the scroll held by one of his guards and he handed it to Iqbal. "Our sultan's commendation of your continued efforts in this city Emir Iqbal, and promise of dinar to help recover form the souk."

Ahmed winced, remembering the horror. His father accepted the scroll and bowed his head slightly. Ahmed hesitated, holding his one small bag of what he could take. Rafia kissed next, then it was his turn. He came forward. Master Mahad had a long black beard showing signs of grey. His ashen eyes regarded the boy as if to determine if he was worthy. Aside from the simitar at his waist, he also wore a dagger, and a guard held a finely made wood staff beside him. Ahmed came close. Master Mahad tossed his cloak back then clasped Ahmed's shoulders, giving him pause.

"There is no need son." Master Mahad smiled. "In you is God's gift, your family is well pious to the state, and you will *earn* my respect."

Ahmed looked up at him, nervous anticipation filling him, then dropped his bag and ran to his father, bowed his head and cried.

"I'm sorry Baba, I don't want to go, don't make me! I'll be good…" Ahmed begged. The thought of leaving was like a swirling tugging in the pit of his stomach. Iqbal bent down and held his son's left arm.

"No Ahmed, this is not a punishment. You are a special boy destined for great things! With Master Mahad you will become enlightened. You will learn to do things none of us can ever hope to do. You will become capable and wise; this is for your future."

"But I'm scared, Father. I don't want to leave. I don't want to lose you."

"You are not losing us Ahmed; we will see you again. Have faith in God. Now clean those tears and be the strong son I know you are. You must stay strong for at least your mother, who will help take care of her when I am gone?"

"I will," Ahmed answered, determined. Iqbal stood and gestured to his son to go. Ahmed, however, neared Rafia. She was already in tears when he came before her. She knelt to Ahmed and hugged him.

"I will protect you Mother. I will keep you happy, I promise."

"I will miss you so much," Rafia answered.

"No Mother, I have memories of you and your lullabies and stories."

"Ahmed, I love you." She hugged him tighter then let her son go to stand by her husband. Ahmed now stood before his brother. Amir was like his father. He stood almost emotionless. Ahmed looked up at him and unsure as to what to say he hugged Amir. Amir's eyes widened then he hugged back.

"I will miss you brother. Will you miss me?" Ahmed asked, voice trembling.

"Of course, I will miss you! It will be lonely when you are gone." Amir laughed but it didn't hide the sadness in his voice. "Figures, of course it's you who gets the magic in the family. I kinda envy you."

"I don't know what I am. What if… could I be a mutant?"

"Of course, you're not! Don't say that. I think it's cool once you learn to control it that is. Don't let me hear of any more burned souks around you while you're away."

"I promise there won't be any."

"Good."

"I will come back, then we can play again!"

"Yes, we will." Amir laughed. He turned and signaled to someone further behind him. A servant rushed forward holding a brown-gold cloak. Amir presented it to his younger brother. "Take this. This was mine when I was closer to your age."

"I remember," Ahmed said looking at its faded color.

"I just thought… take it as something to remember me by, while you're out there and until you come back. I heard it is much colder in the north than it is here. This will keep you warm."

Ahmed took it and put it on. He grinned and held out his arms displaying it in full.

Amir laughed. "You'll grow into it qazam," he said, seeing how the cloak extended a little past Ahmed's legs. Ahmed took it off and wrapped it up.

"I love it brother, thank you." He turned to leave.

"Ahmed!" Amir called, Ahmed turned to face him, "If anyone causes you any trouble tell them who your big brother is, I will find them!" Both boys smiled. Ahmed picked up his belongings and walked under the robed arms of Master Mahad.

The master mage adjusted the sash across his torso and the wrappings around his waist. "What we go to now is not an end it is a beginning, one that will see you become capable. I have high expectations for you. You will serve your sultan with piety and skill. Now come, we have much land to travel." As he and his new master walked out Ahmed looked back at his family, still hesitant to go onwards. He was afraid, but now having said goodbye to his family and taking in his father's encouraging words he looked out north as if to determine his direction into the future.

***

Ahmed jumped up from his bed roll, striking his head on the cave ceiling. He rubbed his now throbbing head. As his drowsiness cleared, his thoughts focused. Was it all a dream? It must have been, but when did I fall asleep? He looked to his side to see Will still sleeping soundly even in the bite of his ropes. Ahmed flexed his fingers, watching sparks fail to light, sleep inertia's effect on mages. Once he was fully awake there would be no problem. Ahmed peered out of the cave; the desert sun peaked up over the horizon. Hot and humid air hit his face as light pushed darkness away and gold turned to blue in the sky.

***

Sand blew past the boys as they left the camp and travelled over the dunes. Both remained silent. Will stumbled along, trying to cover his face with bound hands when gusts of wind threw sand at him. Though it was early in the morning, the sun blazed as if it was at its peak. The heat was unbearable to Will. he peered over the horizon to the southwest and noticed pyramids far off into the distance, almost vanishing behind the swirling air as if water.

"What is that?" Will asked. Ahmed turned and looked southwest.

"Soleb," Ahmed said without looking at Will. "Those are pyramids of the Aegyp Empire, built during the Ancient Eon, when the land looked different." He smiled. "Incredible that such things last." Will turned back.

"What is magic?" Will asked, wondering about last night.

"Why do you want to know?"

"Can I do magic?"

"You don't have the potential." Ahmed laughed.

"Well…" Will grunted. "Saomardrim are rude."

"Magic Potential. The innate ability of a mortal to produce magic. It is the sum of power and energy and there is a static amount of power in all of us at birth."

"Meaning?"

"The amount of power you have determines how potent your magic will be. Even non-mages have power however their stores are so low that it is improbable they will cast. Some people have more power and can be adept at a few specific forms of magic. Alhurah has gifted some people with a lot of power, these mages can thus generate much magic."

"I don't understand."

"Think of… blood. You have an amount of blood in you. Within that blood is… say… red colour. How red is your blood?"

"Red…" Will winced.

"Not red enough to perform magic. Therefore, not enough to access your Magic Potential"

"So I'll make my blood redder."

"That's an oversimplification. Power can be extracted and quantified, yes, but to call it material or tangible is too easy. Power can be converted into magic, though not always at a one-to-one ratio, until the body exhausts itself from continuous conversion. Magic is the tangible expression of immaterial power."

"I don't…" Will inhaled sand and coughed. He mis-stepped and fell face first into the sand. Ahmed stopped his horse and dismounted. He took a waterskin and brought it to Will. The Gurmian boy sat up on his knees and wiped sand from his face. Ahmed presented him with the waterskin.

"You don't understand but you still ask." Ahmed smiled, impressed. Will drank greedily until Ahmed pulled the waterskin away. The young mage took a seat beside Will and they faced the pyramids of Soleb far in the distance.

"Thought you said no breaks." Will frowned.

"To be honest, I've never seen Soleb's pyramids. One break is no issue, and you're not going anywhere." The two boys looked off into the distance.

"What's energy then?" Will asked.

"What?"

"You said Magic Potential is the sum of power and energy."

"Energy allows for power to magic conversion. Each person's energy is dynamic, changing depending on that person's physical and mental strength and stamina. Energy determines how long one can continuously cast magic."

"That's why you're a warrior." Will wiped sweat off his forehead. Ahmed nodded.

"Devoted mages work to keep themselves able and healthy because if they can increase their energy then they can increase their casting times."

"It's not blood that magic comes from. That was a comparison."

"Yes. Magic comes from internal tissue, where power is thought to be stored. It seeps through some sort of network." Ahmed raised his hand and cast fire. The fire took shape into a small snakelike dragon and whirled around, chasing its tail. Glowing embers emanated off of the dragon which made a quiet airy roaring sound. Will's eyes grew wide.

"Did that just roar?"

"It did." Ahmed smiled. "When I was younger it always seemed that I had an inexhaustible amount of magic. Now I know there are limits. I know my limits."

"I-It made a sound!"

"Yes!" Ahmed laughed. "There are four schools of magic: illusion, extension, combative, and restorative. What you heard is the movement of air. Easy to cast." A gust of dry wind blew Will's hair into his face. He pushed his hair out of the way with his bound hands. The fire dragon turned into two. Each eating the tail of the other and revolving in a circle. Then it disintegrated, blending with the hot air. "Know that no matter how hard you try it is impossible to create something from nothing. I took the heat in the air, what we breathe, and fuelled it with my power to create fire. Elemental magic is simple. What you need for casting elemental spells is all around us, everywhere."

"What else can you do?" Will asked, his interest peaking.

Ahmed picked up a handful of sand. He whispered foreign words, "Multiply arderrafol." The sand started to vibrate. Grains began to divide and replicate themselves. Soon so much sand was present it started to spill from Ahmed's hand. Then it suddenly stopped. "To extend and make more of something you need a base, like that handful of sand. That is the seed. From the seed you can use the elements around you and your own power to create more but to a certain threshold. Soon what you need or your energy is exhausted. It's like a plant, it can only grow so tall, and its growth is determined by the materials around it."

"I wish I could have more power."

"The natural world can increase one's power or fortify it. There is magic in nature. For example, if you stand close to a river you may find your water element spells are more potent and you can more effortlessly cast them. There is also magic within spirituality. Faith, enlightenment these things mean more to a mage than a non-mage, they can be harnessed."

"Right… but I have to be a mage already."

"Yes, you do. When I first discovered I was a mage… I was afraid. I thought I was a demon, a mutant, or some sort of monster."

Will winced at the last word. Ahmed stood and returned to his horse and Will stood as well.

They roamed onwards, deeper towards the heart of the desert. The sun rose higher in the sky and Ahmed wondered how naïve he'd been long ago, back when he was afraid of his magic.

Ahmed and his new master had travelled half the length of Saomarhad in a north direction escorted by the grand vizier's mounted guards, who Ahmed realised were mages, some holding the flag of Saomarhad up high. He kept to himself, talking little as he rode alongside his master.

They reached a village, Al-Qula, on the outskirts of the desert, its buildings seemingly refracting under the light and heat, in the distance. Ahmed wanted to break the silence, less he continue to let uncertainty wear him down.

"Ma-Master?" Ahmed asked.

"Be not uneasy Ahmed, speak," Master Mahad answered without looking back.

"What am I? No one has told me since… since the souk. Am I some sort of demon?

"Ya Alhurah! No Ahmed! You are a mage, wizard, a magi. Magic is a gift from Alhurah. You can use powers not everyone can use."

"But how do you know? Was it because of what I did?"

"You must feel ashamed for what you did to Hamid's souk; you should be as it was very foolish. Were you not a mage and not a nobleman you would be charged with arson." Ahmed bowed his head. "What you did was not under your control, what happened is what we call your awakening."

"What is that master?"

"It is the point in a mage's life that he or she first learns of their power, first uses it. Do you follow?"

"I think so."

"Unchecked, a person's awakening can be very destructive, sometimes fatal. We are still working on how better to detect a person's affinity to magic so we can predict their awakening and prevent mishaps like burning down souks."

At the center of the village stood a gnarled tree in front of the mosque, a square building with a domed roof and a single minaret. Flanking the path they saw a little girl, not more than seven, sitting against a building. She sobbed, clutching a miniature clay bowl. Master Mahad dismounted and set his horse nearby then walked towards the girl with Ahmed close behind.

"Alhurah knows what is in your heart and your pain. Look up child." Master Mahad stood over her. The girl looked up, her face dripping with tears. "Why do you cry?"

"My Mama. They put her in a cage outside the mosque and she sits in coarse clothes. Everyone spits on her and hates her."

Ahmed and Master Mahad looked behind the gnarled tree and saw the cage. The mother sat within, curled up with her head down, dressed in a burlap hijab and abaya.

"Who put her there? Why?"

The girl wiped her face. "Baba did. My mean aunties said we were not Baba's children and convinced him that Mama gave birth to a dog, a cat, and a log of wood."

Master Mahad huffed. "What a man who is easily convinced of such foolishness. Who is *we*, child?"

"My older brothers, one is eight and the other is nine. Will you help us?"

"I don't know how I might convince your father it is impossible for any pious woman to give birth to a dog, a cat, and a log of wood save by Alhurah's will."

"Baba swore he would free Mama if water turns gold, birds talk, and trees began to sing." The girl presented her miniature bowl. Within was that looked like golden water. "I put gold powder I got by trading Mama's one gold ring to the mason and gold dye into water." The girl smiled, but it barely reached her cheeks.

"You are a smart girl." Master Mahad laughed and Ahmed agreed. "What is your name?"

"Nahla."

"Alhurah! A beautiful name. But where will you find a talking bird?"

"We waited for entertainers to pass by, they come every year. I sent my brothers and they… they got a talking bird."

"Oh really?" Master Mahad crossed his arms. "Alhurah hates the liars and those who cheat and steal. He is always watching and knows what you do."

Nahla sobbed again. "Sorry! We'll return the bird, but we want our Mama. My brothers take good care of it."

"How will you find a singing tree?"

"I don't know!" She almost dropped her golden water, catching it before it spilled. Master Mahad crouched down to her and smiled.

"Come with me child to the tree in front of the mosque. Gather the villagers. I shall help you free your mama, but only if you and your brothers take this talking bird back to the travelling entertainers and apologise for kidnapping it."

Nahla nodded and Master Mahad helped her stand. She rushed off to find her brothers.

"Master?" Ahmed asked. "What are you going to do?"

"Come and watch closely Ahmed." They went to the gnarled tree and stood under its branches. Soon the space was filled by villagers, many taking a moment to laugh and spit at the mother in the cage. Two veiled women in particular lingered around the captive woman and jeered at her plight.

"Do you think those women are her sisters?" Ahmed frowned; he'd never treat Amir like that.

"Perhaps." Master Mahad raised his hands for silence when all were assembled, requesting that the village imam and the father of the siblings to come forward, and directed Nahla and her brothers to stand beside him, their talking songbird with them.

"People of Al-Qula I am a humble traveller who has come to solve this rift between a man and her wife."

"What right do you have to interfere in my affairs?" the father grunted.

"I was pleaded by Nahla to help. Imam, I know of the issue here. The challenge put forth by Nahla's father is mine to attempt because I represent her."

The Imam thought on this. The caged mother stood and griped the bars, daring a look. Her sisters fell silent, whispering among themselves. "I say we hear out this man. There was no rule that your daughter could not seek outside help."

The father grunted, but stepped back to allow Master Mahad to continue.

"That caged woman will be free upon the words of her husband made before all the village and before God if he receives golden water." Master Mahad gestured to Nahla and she held out her miniature bowl. The imam and the father examined it; its sheen convinced them.

"This is nothing!" the father shook his head. "It is a trickle."

"You did not specify the amount," the imam countered.

"Next for you we have a talking bird." Master Mahad gestured to one of the boys, who held out the bird in its cage. He whispered something to it.

"H-Hello! Hello! H-How are you?" the bird spoke, flicking its head. The crowd mumbled to each other, pointing at the bird.

"How could children find such a bird?" the father scoffed.

"Hmm," the imam scratched his chin. "When you brought up talking birds it was right after those entertainers passed by, so such an oddity was on your mind. It is here, that is all that matters."

"Lastly," Master Mahad quieted the crowd. "A singing tree."

"That tree?" the father sook his head. "It will not sing."

Master Mahad tapped Ahmed's shoulder and he looked at his master, figuring this was what he needed to pay attention to. His master didn't move and only smiled. A wind picked up around them, subtle at first, then a soft breeze. The tree behind them moaned, singing a steady note then increasing and decreasing in pitch as if it were a song.

Surprise flooded over the villagers. They laughed and clapped and demanded the caged mother be set free. The imam ordered it to be done. The mother's children ran to her, embracing her as their aunties tried to flee.

"Those are the ones who are guilty." Master Mahad pointed at them. "They convinced you of what is impossible." He directed to the father. "And you were fool enough to believe it. I will leave you now to determine their fate."

Master Mahad then took the three children to a nearby caravanserai where the entertainers were staying. The three dropped their heads, admitting and apologising for kidnapping the talking bird, and returned the bird. Despite the anger that followed, the three were forgiven so long as they spent that evening serving the caravanserai patrons food and cleaning up afterwards.

Ahmed and his master returned to their horses, which they parked on top of a rise marked by a solitary green and healthy tree. Master Mahad patted his horse.

"You tricked them Master… but… you saved her," Ahmed said, breaking the silence.

"Many small villages like this rarely have a resident mage so yes I was able to trick them, but you said yourself Ahmed; I saved that woman. I quashed injustice, thank God."

"So, when you said this is what we were, you meant we could save people?"

"Ahmed you are observant and a quick learner. Magic does not make you a demon rather it is a force you can use to change things around you; you can choose to use it for good. With such power we have a great responsibility to use it in a righteous way for if it is used in an immoral way, magic can bring great destruction, agony, and chaos."

"Should we go back Master?"

"You miss your family, don't you Ahmed? Your silence on this journey is telling."

"Yes master. Why must we be taken from our homes to study magic? Why can't I learn with my family?"

"You must be fully committed to learning magic and there are benefits of learning within a community of mages, this is crucial."

"But what can one do with magic? You make it sound so great. Can I make people—"

"Never Ahmed! Never! To control free will of any living thing is a path that will open what we call the Dark Magics of which sorcery, witchcraft, blood magic, and necromancy are sub-schools. They are a mutation of Alhurah's gift. These magics are by nature addictive. Reports we have tell of such people hearing malevolent whispers of shayāṭīn in their heads urging them to use more of this inhumane magic. The Imperium's Imperial Inquisition and witch hunters elsewhere hunt down and kill dark mages. They are uncontrollable and dangerous. Akin to the servants of Kalshaimar. A dark mage must be purged straight away!"

Ahmed's mouth dried and his master's expression lightened. "You will learn to use magic practically and properly. The magic you will lean is the use of creation, not its alteration nor to mislead. We can create energy from materials that already surround us. This is permitted, but we do so with containment and control. You will better know the Father's creation through proper use."

"I don't understand, I can do things? There is something inside me?"

"You will understand in time Ahmed. Know that for this world wizards are their scholars, leaders, explorers, and watchers. You are one of these people and will do many great deeds. Murzq is where you will learn. All mages of Saomarhad are brought there to be taught the proper use of magic. Poor or rich you will study together. Many graduates will leave Murzq as battlemages, agricultural mages, or various other professions. You, I suppose, will return to your family and serve your community."

Will and Ahmed stood by a peculiar yardang, rounded as if it were a sundial. Ahmed observed its shadow, comparing it to a map and compass to confirm their path. He stood dismounted.

Will scratched the sandstone. "It's so rough. How'd the sand get all stuck together like that?"

"Its only a rock." Ahmed sighed. "Badawī tribes use this rock as a meeting point and to orient themselves in the desert."

"Where are we going again?"

"To the capital, I told you."

"From camp to camp?" Will blocked a gust of sand with his arm.

"We will stop in Nizid, the Heart of the Desert." Ahmed noticed glowing from his pack. He dug into it and produced the two pearls. He observed them, the pull of their almost magnetic attraction to each other. They glowed a faint red, slowly pulsing in unison with the speed of a beating heart at rest. Ahmed looked at Will, who also observed.

"How did you find yours?" Ahmed asked.

"I found a tomb... or something. When I took it, it shrunk to fit in my hand."

"I see..." Ahmed nodded.

"How d'you find yours?"

Ahmed hesitated, unsure if he should explain.

"If you lead me to my death, least let me know a little more bout this object... if you know."

"Everyone wanted to do something about fire; every boy seemed to like fire. I wanted to do something different. For research about light magic, a complex form of magic that is said to be the closest to the magic of God, I went to a restricted section of our library. A friend…" Ahmed hesitated. "Waajid, one of the best students who held a lot of respect, taught me how to get in. I found a book. It was thick, boxlike, and had false pages between which was my pearl. It shrunk to fit my hand as well."

Ahmed remembered wanting to put it back. It glowed more brightly and warmly in his hand. Images appeared within it. His brother was shown, with a smile on his face. Stunned, Ahmed wondered if he should ask someone about it but then they would know he had gone where he should not have gone. He would wait on it, once he'd examined the artifact some more.

Ahmed put away the two pearls and mounted his horse.

"We need to adjust our direction, but we are getting closer to Nizid," he informed. They moved forwards again.

Another memory came to Ahmed. He'd quickly took notes on a book he thought would be most useful and exited into the library courtyard. His pearl had burned, then started to pulse, slowly lighting and diming. A gust of wind blew from behind and something swooped over his shoulder. He followed the figure to the top of the howz fountain in the center of the courtyard. There stood a blue glowing, translucent falcon staring at him. It tilted its head. Ahmed hesitated. What was that? Was it some sort of spirit? His mind raced through all the spirits described in one of his textbooks but none like this came to his mind. Before Ahmed could further investigate it faded into specks of blue light blowing away with the wind.

Ahmed wiped his forehead of sweat and rode onwards. The solitude of the desert, despite Will's occasional coughing, helped him think, as solitude always did.

———

In a small fishing boat, shivering beside his master, he looked up at a town built along the contours of a steep three-hundred-meter cliff rising above the sea. They would get up via lifts. This far and isolated town, Murzq, sat under falling flurries, a bewildering sight to Ahmed.

Among blocky houses, steep stairs, ramps, and domes stood mage towers culminating in The University of Magi, headquarters of Saomarhad's Mages Guild of which he was now an initiate. Two rivers ran through the town and emptied into tall waterfalls. Flanking the waterfalls, on both sides, were two massive statues of the Hajjar brothers who'd founded the university, Mu'taz and Umar. Each held a staff and a large fire torch, powered by a spell crystal, placed in such a way that it made it seem as if they were making the fire from their hands. It all intimidated him.

Over the nine years he'd spent at the school, Ahmed had learned everything a scholar and a soldier would. He'd become educated in astronomy, geography, history, and could wield a variety of weapons. He'd also learned math, science, as well as enchanting and alchemy. But most of all he became proficient in many schools of magic. The things his peers could not master, would be achieved by Ahmed. Master Mahad had made him his personal apprentice, and Ahmed learned he had been forwarded to the sultan as a candidate for the next grand vizier.

Ahmed's focus on his education and refining his magic kept him occupied for most of his days. His drive and purpose was to become the best he could be, to return home and show his family, especially his father, how capable and wise he had become. That was why even until the age of ten Ahmed had stayed alone within the alchemy labs, library, and observatory, speaking only when he needed to, and only with teachers and like-minded students. Most students even respected that attitude. One day however, that all changed.

"You are not supposed to be in here servant!" Ahmed entered the observatory, a round room atop of the tallest tower of the university. The walls were decorated in complex blue, green, and yellow tessellations which seemed to glow when moonlight hit them just right.

Responding to Ahmed, a boy turned to reveal his slave clothes. They looked like normal servant clothes from the back but the front bore a yellow X with a S on it. The same marking was fused on to the skin of each slave underneath their clothes. Behind him the dome was open and observation and measurement instruments receded.

The boy, maybe a year younger than Ahmed, was as dark as Ahmed but his hair was cut close to his skin. The boy moved away from the balcony and bowed his head. His sunken face and glassed-over eyes told Ahmed he was overwhelmed and exhausted.

"Sorry, I wanted to see the stars is all," he stammered.

"Just for the stars? I could have you killed for being here." Ahmed's tone was harder, now that he knew the boy was a slave. Ahmed had never paid much attention to the slaves and servants in Hamid or Murzq, mainly because they never crossed his path in the way this one had.

"I don't see them often, and people say they are nice. They don't let us out very much and I like the breeze."

"You talk too much." Ahmed huffed, but he was glad to find someone interested in the stars as much as he was, even if he was a slave.

"Oh… I'm sorry…"

"You know, those stars are not simply lights in the sky but may contain other worlds! It's what the scholars think." Ahmed strode over to the balcony past the boy and looked out at the vast sky.

"S-Sky reading does not interest me much b-but flying does."

"Sky reading? No, it's astronomy. We are working on flight but you didn't hear that from me."

"W-We are! I heard mages can fly but not non-mages. Can you fly?"

"No. Flight is limited for mages; most can just hover since it takes a lot of energy. If I could I would fly to the moon and the sun!"

"I would like to fly someday but…" The boy lowered his head, and with it his enthusiasm deflated.

"What is your name?"

"Shoran."

"Well Shoran, I think you and I will be great friends!"

Shoran's head shot up with eyes wide. "F-Friends? B-But I am a slave and you are a mage… er… sir." Shoran stuttered looking both amazed and nervous.

"So? It will be good to have someone to talk to about non-academic matters once in a while. I won't tell anyone you come here; I promise. I can talk to you about the stars."

"O-Okay… sir."

"Not sir. I am ten-years-old, you make me sound fifty. I am Ahmed." Ahmed smiled, putting Shoran at ease. Ahmed's friendship to Shoran was kept a secret for two years.

Since he met Shoran, Ahmed's outlook had changed. Where once before he rarely talked with the other students, now he spoke with them often. Ahmed made a few more acquaintances, but Shoran was his best friend and the one he spent the most time with. They'd play, explore the town and countryside, and make Ahmed skip class. By this time Ahmed had forgot about his past life at the palace with its intricate walls and lavish green gardens. The sounds of nightingales, doves, and fountains. The smile of his older brother. Ahmed may have forgotten his family entirely if he hadn't found his pearl, which helped him remember them again.

"The Father and Alhurah are the same then?" Shoran asked standing by a twelve-year-old Ahmed, looking in awe at the large tapestry depicting the father as a light.

"You do not know him?" Ahmed raised an eyebrow.

"I'm not allowed in the mosques." Shoran frowned. Ahmed pointed to the far-left panel of the tapestry.

"There is the Father gifting Godly Magic to the legendary beasts: The Elder Dragons, the Alpha Whales, the Phoenix, and the Great Owl." Ahmed pointed to each panel as he explained. "Alhurah learns new forms of magic. He stumbles upon dark magic and realises how evil it could be. He hides these results but Kalshaimar," he pointed at the next panel, "discovers them. That panel shows Alhurah teaching the High Elves how to use Mortal Magic, a lesser type of magic. Lastly humans learn magic by copying their elven overlords."

"Wow… I…"

"Stop teaching the slave!" Ahmed and Shoran turned away from the tapestry. A thirteen-year-old boy stood there and he always walked around with two of his friends, standing with him now. Judging by the sureness on their faces, they were here for trouble. Shoran frowned and dropped his head to respectfully avoid eye-contact.

"Waajid," Ahmed addressed him. Waajid approached Shoran.

"You have no business entertaining him. In fact, he should be working somewhere and not talking to you." Waajid grabbed Shoran's collar and pulled Shoran to him. "What you doing talking with the likes of us huh? You're nothing but a slave and we are mages! Maybe I should leave you with a good-sized scar or… better yet, why don't I turn you into a rodent?"

"I'm sorry Master… please don't turn me into a rodent." Shoran begged, fear in his voice.

"He can't turn you into a rodent, that's not possible. That isn't possible," Ahmed said.

Waajid glared at Ahmed. "I got this. We have class soon so you go prepare and we'll deal with him."

Ahmed hesitated. Up until now his friendship with Shoran had been secret. They'd been careless. Caught in the halls they had been seen and now Waajid was going to beat Shoran. Fear stiffened Ahmed's body. What was he to do? He looked between Shoran and Waajid, between his friend's terrified look and the older boy's pleasure filled glare. He inhaled and grabbed the arm Waajid held Shoran with. Ahmed gathered his courage and shot Waajid a serious look.

"Let him go," Ahmed said flatly. Waajid's mouth hung open, lost for words. The older boy's friends advanced.

"You care about this slave? What's gotten into you Ahmed? Below me you got what it takes to go far here." Waajid's expression grew harder. "Remember that you hurt Laiq because of your overconfidence and pride. You promised me and yourself that you won't make the same mistakes again. Looking out for this slave will derail you, you can't be around him!"

Ahmed frowned. He hurt Laiq when he was nine because Waajid was challenging him and he let his pride get in the way. He was showing off and as a result, Laiq spent weeks recovering and Ahmed's guilt had driven him to complete isolation, until Waajid made him promise to study hard and learn to control his impulses to ensure he'd never hurt someone unintentionally again. But bringing up Laiq was a low blow; Waajid didn't bring him up often. Ahmed let it pass.

"I know you're just looking out for everyone Waajid but you can't hurt him. I won't let you." Ahmed gripped his free hand into a fist to keep his courage from emptying. Waajid laughed and let go of Shoran.

"I am looking out for you! My respect for you just dropped right to empty Ahmed. The heck!?" Ahmed realised it was futile to keep this up any longer. As he and Shoran grew older it was getting harder to keep the secret and if he did nothing what if one day the university sold Shoran to someone else? He'd lose his friend. Warmth bloomed from his pouch. His pearl glowed seeming to give him the strength to continue.

"Shoran is his name and he is my friend," Ahmed said with conviction.

"Then here's what I say to those foolish words!" Waajid cast a ball of pressurised air and blasted it at Shoran. Ahmed stepped between the two in time and blocked the blast, absorbing it with a spell of his own. Ahmed glared at Waajid. The older boy snorted. "Fine, have it your way. Consider yourself officially shunned. Master Mahad will hear of this too!" Waajid and his friends turned and stormed off.

His master did find out about the friendship and he was disappointed. Ahmed remembered standing in front of his master trying to keep himself still and telling him why he liked Shoran and why he wanted to remain friends with him. Afterall, Alhurah desired slaves to be treated well, even as close to an equal as a slave could get. Master Mahad would not allow it. Such a relationship was unseemly and the master mage promised Ahmed he would soon find another person to sell Shoran to. Ahmed was heartbroken and that night he held back tears, unable to sleep.

A few days passed and Ahmed could not find Shoran. Frustrated, he tried to see his master again to demand what had happened but Master Mahad refused to see him. Exhausted from searching the entire university Ahmed fell onto a bench, buried his face into his hands, and held back tears. They had sold him! Ahmed had finally made a friend but because Shoran was a slave, because they considered him nothing more than cattle, they refused to let them be. An intense yet calming heat came over him,

"Lose not hope for fate's path is unpredictable," a powerful voice spoke. Upon inhaling air for his next breath there was an unexpected yet refreshing sweetness in it. It collided with the warmth brought on by the voice and seemed to sharpen and steady his mind. His panic subsided and for a moment he believed he could deny all who would want to separate Shoran from him.

As the heat cooled an image flashed in Ahmed's mind… the main courtyard at the entrance to the gardens behind the university. Ahmed stood and rushed to that place. When he stepped into the sun, Shoran was tied up with his wrists behind his back and his ankles bound together with rope. Three older boys stood around him kicking and jeering at him. Ahmed ran forward.

"Waajid!" Ahmed lunged for the older boy casting a wave of energy at him. Waajid turned too late and was flung back, along with his friends, before they could react. Ahmed rushed to Shoran's side, but as he was about to reach him, Ahmed was thrown back by an energy pulse. Waajid stood over Ahmed while his friends dragged Shoran off to the side.

"You are worth no more than him, you know. If you defend a slave you are no better than one." Waajid scoffed. "Hasn't been enough that no one will talk to you in class? Give it up and I will excuse you tossing me."

Ahmed stood and glared at the older boy. "Shoran is my friend and what you are doing is wrong…"

"He is a slave!" Waajid shot.

"He is my friend."

"He is worthless!"

"He is human, so says Alhurah."

The two boys stared each other down. Waajid scoffed and spit to Ahmed's side.

"You taint the title of mage."

"Let him go," Ahmed demanded, his anger boiling.

"No."

"Let. Him. Go."

"Make me," Waajid glared at him. Ahmed cast a gust of air but Waajid blocked and countered with a swath of flame. Ahmed cut the attack in half so the fire fizzled out safely to his sides. He cast a pulse of energy that Waajid caught and held as it pushed him a few paces backwards. The older boy formed ice from the air and shattered it into shards, sending them Ahmed's way. Ahmed cast a blue spherical ward around himself that absorbed the ice but Waajid did not wait. He followed up with a powerful gust of air and pushed it between his hand and Ahmed's shield. Ahmed strained to keep the shield stable. Classes had ended and an audience of mostly young students began to form. Suddenly Ahmed's shield shattered and he was thrown back onto stone. He landed hard and shouted at pain that ripped through his side.

"Ahmed!" Shoran shouted. One of his captors kicked him. Shoran grunted and shouted again, "Ahmed he's coming!" Ahmed looked up. Waajid pushed a towering wall of fire towards him. He planted his hands on the stone, forcing the stone in front of him to shoot upwards, creating a wall that blocked the fire. Ahmed let the wall fall and stood, panting and sweating, he stumbled back towards Waajid. The older boy laughed.

"Is that all you got? Maybe I was wrong about you when I thought you would go far. What are you afraid of? Are you even trying to hurt me?"

"I don't want to hurt you. I want you to stop. Please stop and leave my friend alone."

"Not a chance. I want it to be clear," Waajid addressed the crowd. "Slaves don't have anything to do with mages. In fact, we're better than any non-mage! Magic is a gift from God! If any slave tries to infect us like that one has done to Ahmed, they will pay for it." Disbelief flooded over Ahmed. The boy who'd once pulled Ahmed out of his guilt and made him promise to do and be better had allowed his own skill to fill him with poisonous pride. As if a hive mind, Waajid's friends started to beat Shoran. Ahmed roared and cast a wave of flame rumbling towards Waajid's face. The older boy blocked too late. Waajid screamed as the flames sheared across his cheek, burning his flesh. He fell to his knees.

"S-Sorry!" Ahmed looked wide-eyed and terrified. Ahmed approached him. "End this please. Call off your friends and let Shoran go." Waajid shot out his arm making Ahmed panic. No magic came. Waajid turned, his burn festering. A dark expression crept across his face. Magic shot out of his hand in the colour of black, whiffs of white, blue, and purple within it. The black mist enveloped Ahmed and pulled him to his knees. It stung at his skin and made his muscles twist in pain. Ahmed grunted then groaned, tearing up.

"Wh-What…" he barely made out. Waajid stood and towered over him.

"You know what, it's better like this. First, I will make sure you can't cast ever again then I will be the number one student here. Look at what I learned! You don't even know how it feels. It feels so good." Waajid spoke as if he were high on some euphoric drug.

"D-Dark magic…" Ahmed groaned, shocked.

"Let me go!" Shoran shouted. He tried to escape but was pulled back by Waajid's friends. The crowd mumbled and shouted. Some boys stepped forward but Waajid threw out his other arm in a threatening motion, dissuading them.

"No one interfere! Ahmed is not like us. He disrespects what it is to be a mage and we should all hate him for that." Waajid glared at Ahmed. "And I gave him enough chances." Waajid tightened the tendrils of dark magic around Ahmed's body. He could feel them start to cut at his skin, eager to squeeze their way into his core. Could Waajid strip him of his magic? He panicked. Magic was everything to him; it couldn't be taken like this. Ahmed tried to cast but the dark magic canceled his attempts. He struggled to break free but the tendrils held him firmer and firmer to the ground.

"Zilyumi zilyumi, magic mrtallat, magic mrtallat," Waajid chanted. A group of adults pushed their way through the crowd, Grandmaster Mahad leading them. The Arch-mage cast a shining ray of light at Ahmed. The dark magic tendrils seemed to hiss as they evaporated away. Waajid turned to Mahad and attempted to counter but the master expected that and cast at the stones around Waajid's feet. The earth shot up and pinned him in place. Waajid hissed at Master Mahad. Ahmed looked at him and swore he saw a whiff of black mist leave his mouth. He couldn't believe it. What had Waajid done? What did he plan on doing? He had become something twisted and vile… no, Waajid was young and he'd made a mistake, he couldn't be too far gone. Master Mahad helped Ahmed up while a group of campus security with him secured Waajid in a tight grasp and others captured his friends.

"This is unbecoming of such keen students of magic," Master Mahad said.

"Ahmed is the traitor, master. He refuses to listen to you! He's friends with that slave," Waajid hissed.

"What you have learned and become addicted to in the darkness of the late hours of night, is much worse Waajid. So much worse." Master Mahad gave the boy a remorseful look. He turned to Ahmed and cast healing magic over the boy. Its warmth dulled his pain. "Free the slave from his bonds then the rest of us can leave." The campus security dragged Waajid away through the crowd of astonished students. When Shoran was freed from his bonds he staggered towards Ahmed who cast at him, helping Shoran dull his pain.

"Leave him, Ahmed," Master Mahad ordered. Everyone was now looking at Ahmed. he inhaled and built up his courage.

"No, Master."

"No?" Disdain flashed over his face.

"Shoran is my friend and if I leave him now you will sell him off and I will never see him again."

"He is a slave—"

"He has a dream… a dream to fly."

Shoran's cheeks flushed red.

"Do not argue with me Ahmed."

"No master. I want to free him and to free a slave is great in Alhurah's eyes."

Shoran looked at Ahmed with shock.

"That is not your decision to make Ahmed. In God's name stop this!"

"I am Ahmed ibn-Iqbal Sharfi al-Hamid, son of the emir and I demand the freedom of this boy. I will buy him from you if I must and if you refuse, I will gain the support of Sultan Yazid."

"Defiance!" Master Mahad scoffed. "Boy, I am better friends with the sultan than your family is. Do not think I won't hesitate to throw you out of this university!"

"So b-be it." Ahmed gulped. This was his life; he did not want to be thrown out but he did not want Shoran to be taken away. Master Mahad sighed.

Three days later Ahmed drafted a letter to his father and sent it. Three weeks later Shoran was free. Waajid was never seen again.

———

The desert gradually grew rockier as they travelled on. Rocky outcrops stretched further outward and a road was soon visible. Small yellow-tan rock buttes gave way to larger inselburgs and eventually mesas and canyons. The sand they were traveling on became coarser and harder changing into desert pavement.

Ahmed adjusted himself on his horse. He and Will entered a canyon, its entrance marked by small alluvial fans. Built into the sandstone flanking each side of the entrance was a statue. One was of an armoured Zanjī, her two-handed curved sword pointing downwards. The other was a Saomardrim man, dressed in a thawb and turban, holding out a map.

As they traveled deeper the canyon sides rose into towering stone walls, sometimes funneling sand and wind at them and sometimes blocking it. Though the lack of exposure brought some comfort to Will, the maze they were in brought its own uncertainty.

Not long after entering the canyon did the sky grow dark. Ahmed found a sheltered rise on the canyon side overlooking the desert dunes some distance away. There he finally let Will drink more water.

Once Will was asleep, Ahmed stepped out of the tent and sat, cross-legged, upon the rise. He could just see the desert under the light glow of the moon and stars. With an astrolabe in hand he adjusted it's dials and compared his readings with the stars. Absorbing the solitude, he observed and wrote under the glow of a spell for near an hour. Ahmed wondered if this war was worth giving up a moment like this, sitting on a rise in the middle of the desert, under the moon.

"This plan... the one you're bring me to. What is it?" Will spoke. Ahmed looked back. Will had woken and was on his knees, as far from the tent as his restraints would allow.

"You probably should not know."

"I don't like surprises."

Ahmed sighed. "There will be many Gurmians, any we could take from the front and on raids. Their deaths will be made a show of."

"A show... like..." Will twitched.

"Your last moments will be the sound of Saomarhadian devotion in defence of our state. Anger, hatred, pride, but it won't be drawn out." Ahmed sensed Will close off his mind like a wall unbreakable against anything outside. It was familiar to Will. Ahmed smiled as genuinely as he could. "Want to sit?"

"I suppose."

Ahmed detached Will from the tent and sat with him on the rise. He'd hoped to have the night to himself, but he pitied Will for the death that awaited him.

"So, why are you dragging me to the capital? It doesn't seem like a noble's job?"

"It is my sultan's command. I am loyal to him."

"You're days must be filled with plenty." Will scratched the sandstone. "Do you have a manor?"

"My family rules a town."

"Oh."

Will was impressed, Ahmed could sense. "Days of acting to hold and gain position and power, wearing a face for each interaction which was never my genuine self, I never felt much for these things." He'd learn to be more appreciative of his scholarship and magic. "Look." Ahmed pointed to the stars. "God's creation is greater than all on Erathas. There may be countless worlds out there."

"No one expects a serf to achieve anything worthwhile, so we are left alone and free in our off time, but tis filled with uncertainty." Will followed Ahmed's eyes to the stars. "Suddenly our lord could piss off another and all our lives would be at risk, or we may not have enough to eat or for the taxes.

Sickness is common. Work is tiring." Will lowered his voice. "I had only ten years." He gritted his teeth.

Ahmed shifted as the noise around him dulled. *'A captive? Why a captive?'*

'The task is not important. It is only to please the sultan and to show you in favourable light and your adherence to the state,' Master Mahad explained.

'With your permission I will depart right away.' Ahmed was eager to please the sultan.

'There is more. A detachment of the Templars of Manis, who make for Al-Motros, will attempt to steal a relic.'

'What kind of relic master?'

'Archeologists and explorers have recently discovered it. The templars long knew of it as well. Not even I can understand it but we cannot let it into the hands of our enemies at least until we discover what it is. The object is locked by a magic seal in a box that has been moved into the town. You must retrieve this and bring it to the sultan. Do not open it.'

'As you wish.'

'Is something more on your mind?'

There had been, and there still was.

'Master… you have been watching over me and training me separate from the other students. I know you want me to become grand vizier after you step down from the position, inshalhurah.'

'That is my wish. It is an honour.'

'It is and I am very humbled that you have chosen me. As grand vizier I will be Sultan Yazid's highest advisor.'

'The second most powerful person in the sultanate. It is what you want Ahmed?'

'It is.'

Ahmed knew all his training and preparation was amounting to this. To replace his master as grand vizier. But unease echoed at the back of his mind. He'd not return to Murzq and would abandon his life as a student, a scholar, and even part of his identity as a mage. He'd become a politician. As the son of an emir, it was not a foreign concept to him and Master Mahad had continued to teach him that which the nobility knew, but still, he was so frustratingly unsure. Amir would not second guess himself. Amir followed his duty. Ahmed resolved to do the same. This was his chance to prove himself.

"What are you trying to say?" Ahmed asked Will.

"Let me go. I am not a threat to your country." Will whispered.

"Then you would swear to never take up arms against us? I hear to the knightly class one's oath is sacred."

"I-I can't…"

"You should have lied." He would not have let Will go anyway, but Will seemed so lost, as if he'd given up. That apathy to his situation, this night, sent a cold through Ahmed. Without any word Will dragged himself back into the tent.

In the morning they rested in the shade of a canyon. The canyon walls were coloured in a pattern of orange and shades of tan. Ripples were preserved, cutting through its sandy matrix.

Ahmed observed the two pearls, The pull of their attraction to each other and warm pulse of their magic. He was in deep thought, moving from one memory to another, book to scroll to lesson. He'd never learned about these objects. He noticed yet again that Will's pearl moved towards the boy only slightly, as if trying to reach him.

"Hold out your hand," Ahmed ordered.

"Why?" Will asked.

"I have a theory about these objects." Ahmed turned and smiled. "By now, if I wanted to kill you, I would have."

Will held out his bound hands, presenting his right hand.

"Face your palm towards me."

Will did so. Ahmed took Will's pearl and levitated it. He tried to access its magic, to make it show him what it showed Will. Instead, the pearl shone a rage fuelled red. It released waves of magic and red electricity. Flaming and zapping it threatened to lose control. Ahmed tried to tame it, pumping his own magic into it, but the pearl resisted, blocking all invasion.

"What's happening?" Will shouted. "I feel… it's like a tingle."

"Will, focus! Focus on the magic, draw it towards you!"

"I can't do that!"

"Visualize it." Will tried to do what Ahmed said. At first nothing happened, then red electricity shot towards Will's palm.

"N-No!" Will shouted. Before he could move out of the way the electricity stopped ahead of Will's palm, curled up into a little whirlwind, and crackled peacefully. It calmed down. He glared at the magic in his hand, shocked, sweating, and suddenly dizzy and tired. Ahmed looked back, equally as stunned. "But I'm not a mage." The magic disintegrated.

"No, you are not. But it seems you have a connection to this object allowing you to access some sort of magic."

"Some sort?"

"Not Mortal Magic; it isn't possible."

"What can I do?" Will's eyes widened; he was eager.

"Nothing," Ahmed admitted.

Will frowned, his eagerness extinguished in seconds.

"As fast as that moment came it died. I don't sense anymore useable magic in you now. Good. Having a mage as my prisoner would make things difficult."

"Just when I thought I could do something really special." Will sighed.

"We move forwards." Ahmed stowed the objects and readied his horse.

This mysterious magic had helped him find Will in Al-Motros. Ahmed remembered the difficulty of navigating the rubble as he rode over dead, mangled, burned and melted bodies of Gurmian soldiers and non-combatants. Saomarhad soldiers were rounding up any survivors for the long ride to the capital. Civilians cleaned up rubble, sweeping the streets, and scrubbing blood and burned flesh off the cobbles.

It had made him quiver. This was the first time he'd been so close to the war. Ahmed had never cared for the war. Sure, he'd hear news of it, but he was more focused on his studies. He accepted the news and the descriptions of his enemies, without much thought. To him, he had studies to focus on, they were more important to him.

"Can we stay in the shade?" Will asked. Ahmed swerved and pulled them closer to the canyon side. He let his horse navigate and turned back to his saddlebags. He touched the relic he had recovered, near the top of his saddlebags. Its magic sent a tingle through his hand. The relic contained in the box seemed to attract Ahmed's pearl. His pearl grew brighter anytime he brought it close. On the box was a peculiar engraved symbol Ahmed had not encountered before. A round object, like his pearl. A four-pointed, diamond inlayed, star overtop the circle. A flame burning out of the top of the symbol.

He'd found it in a dead Templar of Manis' hand. Its strong magical signal had guided him to it, but it was a similar signal that led him to Will half-buried under rubble. Seeing Will's pearl, exactly like his and attracted to his own, Ahmed had made up his mind; he was going to take this boy to Ortie.

Chapter Eighteen

AHMED HELD UP his arm to shield his face from a scorching gust of wind. The floor of the canyon, only three meters in width, rose and widened. In the distance, the canyon walls separated and a large mesa drew closer. At the top stood the town of Nizid, rising out of the sandy desert and canyons surrounding it. To the east a large rock arch connected the town to three tall towers where a number of airships were docking and undocking as they were made ready for war.

Built from sandstone and wood, the pale tan-coloured walls blended in with the desert. Special stone was used to make the palace and mosque. The mosque's minarets stretched to the sky, towering above the town and was only dwarfed by the castle sitting atop its own rock arch. The four minarets marked the corners of the gold-domed structure, similar in style to the Al-Motros mosque, but weathered by sandstorms. Many colourful girih patterns decorated it and other important buildings. Will and Ahmed came out of the canyon and into the space between the canyons and the town mesa. They passed a few oval-shaped ghorfa, to which workers and a mage guided sliding desert skiffs loaded with grain. They could see the skiff docks under the walls on the mesa ahead of them. Ascending the path up, they were allowed through the gate.

Unease seized Will. People stared, but did not ask questions after looking at Ahmed with all his weapons and soldier's gear. Despite its location in the desert, the town was bright and colourful. It hosted many different people from all over Saomarhad. Southerners, mixed with northerners, mixed with desert tribes of all sorts. People rode horses, camels, and carts and carriages of all sizes. Peasants mixed with craftsmen and merchants while stray cats navigated through the crowds.

Various colours decorated the tightly packed streets, fabrics hung across open spaces for shade, and plants adorned building ledges. Even in the most hostile of biomes, life had erupted and prospered, after all, Nizid was a town of both culture and military. It was the center of the desert built north of the desert's largest oasis and over a large network of near surface water.

The boys wound through the winding streets under shade bearing fabrics and projecting latticework mashrabiya windows. Blocky multi-storey buildings flanked them built of tan and orange sandstone alternating in layers. They passed the madrasa, maktaba, and a park.

Riding under an archway they entered a square whose sides were lined with rows of cages and carriages around a central stage. Several merchants laid claim to groups of cages and had set up shop around them. Will stumbled forward as Ahmed abruptly turned to skirt the furthest side of the square. Will could see people, young and old, men and women, chained in the cages. On the stage other unfortunate people stood shackled while a merchant auctioned them.

"Slavers," Ahmed said without turning. "Many Gurmians who cannot be ransomed are either killed or sold into slavery."

"My fate will be the former."

"That could be better or worse depending on the master."

"I am no… no stranger to being bound and caged…"

"What?"

"What kind of master would you be?" Will looked at Ahmed's back. The Saomardrim boy hesitated.

"I don't take slaves," he said flatly.

Ahmed talked to the city officials, using his master's name and the sultan's writ to give him creditability, at the citadel, and got Will locked in its dungeons for the night. At least the dungeons were underground so cool air refreshed him. No sand blew into his face and he was allowed unbound. Will never thought he would actually like the cold.

⁓

Ahmed walked through the streets and descended into a network of roads winding underneath roads above him. As he walked, he observed people, carts, horses, camels, and a group of performing Romani as he took in the evening air. He stopped by the souk where he found some tropical dried and seasoned meat for the remaining journey. As he browsed, the merchant attending him eyed Ahmed.

"You're not going to take anything without paying, will ya?" he asked.

"No." Ahmed looked up from his browsing. "Why would I?"

"Huh, were you been all this time?"

Ahmed didn't answer.

The merchant sighed, "Much trade from the east is tied up in customs nowadays, then what's let through is claimed by the army, the emirs, and the sultan, for the war. Had to raise my prices, so did many around the sultanate I hear, less we lose every dinar we make to resupply. Times are tough for us all."

"Only because of that?"

"Well, lands have been left in desolation after each Gurmian attack. Can't farm burned land and the sultanate's not got a lot of farmland…"

This Ahmed knew. In the center of the sultanate connecting east to west, arid land stretched far and wide. But there were vast greener spaces. "… Also, mind, emirs continue to increase their levies, cause only so many slaves can graduate from the military schools. People are getting pressed into action all over the place, sons, uncles, fathers, brothers. God be praised that most are told to defend their homes. Don't think our sultan really wants to take Gurmanis land. Still, we suffer."

"Sultan Yazid will make deals with far eastern powers. For more trade." Ahmed was sure of it.

"I have yet to see it young man." The merchant laughed. "That could be as hard as fighting this war. God forgive me if he wills this war. I just want peace. Many businesses would do better for it. You seem like a good sort. Still, are you taking or buying soldier?"

"I will buy."

"Fifty fulus."

Ahmed held in a gasp. "Sure." He handed the merchant the bronze coins. It discomforted him that this merchant had suspected he was going to demand his wares. He was reminded of Al-Motros, Ni'ja's village, their desolation, and the anger that had racked him. War was not an easy business and Gurmians were unrelenting, but his people couldn't simply lay down and be conquered.

Ahmed walked down an alleyway, curving to the left, underneath several arches above and to the right. He'd arranged to sleep in the dungeon's guard quarters as he did not trust the guards with his captive. He had to keep his eyes on Will, the boy was his chance to prove himself to the sultan, and he would not fail. A shuffle of feet behind him made his body stiffen. The assailant ran up a few strides, grabbed Ahmed's neck, and pushed the tip of a dagger into his back.

"Dinar, dirham, fulus, now!" he growled. Ahmed closed his eyes and silently chanted a spell;

"Sakkhuaya vitalif sakkhuaya." The mugger let him go holding his head and trying to regain his balance.

"Must you always use that spell? It makes my head so heavy with hurt."

"Shoran! It's good to see you." Ahmed said, recognising the voice. He turned to embrace his friend in a delighted hug. "Don't do that Shoran, I could have killed you."

"But you didn't! What are you doing here Ahmed? I thought you were still in Murzq." Shoran's eyes glowed with happiness.

"I was but the sultan tasked me with presenting to him a prisoner and a valuable artifact recovered from Al-Motros."

"A prisoner? What a strange request. Is it someone important?"

"I can't say too much about him, Shoran, because I don't know what everyone else is supposed to know."

"That's fine. I trust you. There seems like no end to this war. More and more men come every day. I blame all the attacks by Gurmanis. It seems Al-Motros was only part of a larger plan. After its capture more assaults quickly overwhelmed much of the river defences. They captured the main road to Ortie from the north."

"I know, that is why I am crossing the desert instead."

"I should have known, you always plan ahead."

"That, and I saw the road overrun. Have you been in an airship yet?" Ahmed couldn't forget his friend's affinity for flying.

"Yea, I went with the force that surprised the Gurmians at Al-Motros and Halsburg! They had no chance. I hate that we had to bomb our own town. I told you about the kind master I had when I was really young? He lives in that town. I hope he made it out."

"He was the one who first bought you as a slave."

"He was compassionate and fair. He may have bought me but I have come to forgive him. It was he after all who sold me to the mages, that led to meeting you." Shoran smiled.

"And Halsburg?"

"The Gurmians retreated there. We leveled the town. No one survived."

"We should catch-up. I bet you have gathered quite a few stories now." Ahmed wouldn't let the chance to talk to Shoran go by, and he had the whole night if they wanted.

Shoran blushed, "I haven't been at war for long and only in an airship once. Most of the time I spent training for the inaugural flight."

"That is still more flying time than I ever had, you need to tell me about it!"

"Here?" Shoran glanced around at the secluded alley.

"Somewhere better. How about the paradise gardens of Nizid? Ruea Bāgh? We can talk over something to drink." The two walked a short distance to Ruea Bāgh, a large rectilinear garden close to the citadel, lush with desert plants among fountains and canals. The two boys passed by a baradari stage in the central courtyard where a number of people listened to a late afternoon poetry performance. They passed the central fountain and towards a corner where latticed jali screens separated the garden into smaller private sections. In a number of the sections people were spending time together, some talking, others drinking coffee and tea, and a few smoking from hookahs. The two approached a merchant who had been allowed to set up a coffeehouse. They ordered salep, a hot milk drink with cinnamon, and a plate of makshufa, hard almond candy, then chose a section cornered off by jali and sat across each other.

"When you're up there it's as if all the world can be your domain," Shoran spoke. His smile beamed at Ahmed who could feel the strength of the boy's enthusiasm. "Everything is so small but so different. You can see roads and buildings, even entire towns and cities and it's hard to describe how the constructions look from the sky. Roads are networks, built-up areas are rigid and straight, farmlands have order and fields are almost all the same size. The largest of forests looks like fur on the skin of the earth, and oceans… actually oceans just kinda look the same as they do from the ground, big and blue." The two laughed.

"Perhaps the army should hire an artist to go up there and see." Ahmed smiled.

"Yeah! Then all the world would know how awesome it is."

"I am glad it's all you have dreamed of." Ahmed took a bite of makshufa. It wasn't made with more quality ingredients, like it was back home, but it still passed, sweet and nutty.

"It's all thanks to you Ahmed." Shoran looked away and hesitated. "I-I need to thank you again," he muttered.

"You have already thanked me…"

"B-But you don't understand how much it means to me…" Shoran looked up at Ahmed, tears teased the edges of his eyes. "I thought I would die a slave. I spent years working for my masters watching those my age free and carefree. I wished so much to join them. Some masters were harsh to me, others not, but you… you made me your friend. You treated me as an equal, educated me, everything. Then on that day you freed me… you can't imagine how grateful I am."

Ahmed's eyes shifted. "Shoran, I know I…"

"I shouldn't cry." Shoran clenched his fists.

"No, it's natural. There is nothing wrong with it." Ahmed blushed, not so able with emotions.

"I don't know how to tell you how much I have felt. I was so happy that I could be the master of my own life, as frightening and alien as that first was. And you are my friend, I ne'er imagined anyone would care about me, but you did. You made my dream come true. I feel ashamed I can't give the same to you."

Ahmed had used his influence to get Shoran into the airship academy, to train. Shoran hadn't believed him until he received his recruit kit.

"So long as you are happy, I am happy. I spent most of my time alone in Murzq until I met you. Our friendship more than repays me."

"Thank-you." Shoran wiped away his tears. "You're rising even higher now, aren't you? A personal request from Sultan Yazid, what's the end goal?"

"In his and Master Mahad's eyes I have always been destined for the position of grand vizier."

"Your hard work paid off."

"Inshalhurah… but…" Ahmed slid his fingers over each other.

"But?" Shoran raised an eyebrow.

"The prisoner I am escorting…"

"The one you can't say exactly what for or speak much about?"

"Yes. He's our age… he drinks so much of my water." They both chuckled. "But he's not what we were told Gurmians are like, and it doesn't seem like he's had a good life. It unnerves me." After spending time travelling with Will he realised Will was not so different from him. They both had limited knowledge of this war and both had not participated in it… until now. His duty was to bring Will to the sultan… to death. All he needed to do was his duty.

"Forget him. He's just an obstacle on your path to greatness."

"Is greatness all there is worth achieving?" Ahmed wondered.

"What else is there in a world of ambition? The power of such ambition might even spark much change, positive change."

"Or commonly such power overcomes decency and reason and brings about ruinous change. It seems you have become more well spoken."

"You rubbed off on me. Ahmed, you want this?"

Ahmed hesitated. The question was the same he had asked his elder brother long ago. "I knew something like this was coming, that's why I studied hard and practiced any chance I could. I do want this… I-I do."

"Then don't doubt yourself."

"I need some time to not think about it." Ahmed took a sip of salep.

"If you have time before we part. Why don't we play Tâb. I remember what you taught me and I know a few tricks now. That'll get your mind off of it."

"Sure." Ahmed smiled. As Shoran fetched materials for the game, Ahmed slid a finger against the table. "Alhurah if this is your will…" Ahmed sighed. "You are most gracious, most merciful and all forgiving. Guide me with the knowledge of the Father, he who is all knowing."

⁓

Late was the hour when the Emir of Nizid, Emir Qasim, summoned Ahmed to his great hall. Ahmed entered into an octagonal room; each face marked by a pair of arches from which hung a lantern and adorned by red curtains. The upper level, three arches per face, hid a balcony that encircled the room.

The emir was nearing sixty-years-old, with barely a tuft of grey hair. He wore robes of silk that were coloured red, gold, and green, laced expertly. Ahmed was half asleep when he arrived.

"As-salāmu alaykum," Ahmed said, bowing his head slightly.

"Wa alaykumu s-salām," Emir Qasim answered, sitting upon a raised cushioned chair flanked by potted plants. In the arch behind him hung his banner bearing three crescents, sand blowing across them "I heard that you were in town. What I have heard of you is pleasing, you are a talented young man."

"I am honoured, Emir Qasim."

Emir Qasim gestured Ahmed to a cushioned space beside him, past the howz fountain in the center of the room. "I must ask how your master,

Mahad Oman is? He and I are old friends and it has been some time. I know the hour is late but the day had me occupied. I must know."

Ahmed took the seat. "My master is in good health; he recently left for Ortie via the Crescent Sea."

"Alhamdulialhurah, but unfortunate he will not be passing through my town. As stoic as ever I assume?"

"If it pleases you." Ahmed gave a vague response, not wanting to inadvertently insult his master. The emir laughed.

"He helped me a great deal, your master. If it were not for his mages, Nizid would have been overrun by feuding desert tribes. I am forever thankful and I am ready to provide his apprentice with all the help I can give."

"I am glad to hear that, I will inform you if I need your aid."

"Come now boy, let me bestow my generosity and expression of thankfulness at least once with a small gesture. Have a drink with me!" Ahmed smiled and accepted. Servants brought in a small table and chairs along with a fruity drink garnished with a bit of lightly alcoholic wine.

"I am sorry my lord but I cannot drink this. It is not permitted."

"Come now, Alhurah will not smite us for such a small thing; a little from time to time is no problem."

"Still…"

"Very well, very well." The emir laughed and signaled his servants to get Ahmed a drink without alcohol. The emir also took a pipe and the two talked and drank for some time, occasionally laughing at an odd remark, or at Ahmed's ignorance of Nizid.

"I am thankful to have my master; he has guided me well thus far. But of course, he too does not know everything," Ahmed said.

"Master Mahad? No. Impossible! I have spent much time trying to think of something he knows not of. What is it he knows nothing of?"

"My master longs to see places now out of his reach. There is also an object he knows nothing about."

"You are discrediting your master, Ahmed." Emir Qasim laughed, "What is this object? You better show me the proof!" Ahmed retrieved his pearl and placed it on the table between them. Emir Qasim looked at it and gasped. "I have never thought to see something like this; it fits the stories spoken by the badū!"

Ahmed leaned forward astonished, "*You* know of this?"

"I am not saying I am completely sure but based on the descriptions I have heard from a popular badawī storyteller as a boy; I believe this object is very rare, and possibly very powerful."

"What is it?"

"Long ago in the Ancient Eon, the early species of mortals looked to connect with God through one of their own. This person was chosen by the gods and given an object, quite like this. This object, called a Seeker's Stone, was a device that allowed that mortal, later called a Seeker, to travel freely between the Underworld, Baseworld, and Overworld without having to die. The badū recall some other powers were utilised with this stone but they never specified what those powers were. The stones are said to hold the essence of magic, power, of Alhurah in them, maybe even the Creation Magic of the Father."

"What was a Seeker's job? He seems to be a glorified priest."

"Oh no! A Seeker was more than a holy person. There was a Seeker for every major empire of ancient times and each had the job of being the bridge between the immortals, mortals, and spirits. They were expected to be a neutral party but ironically were also expected to see the gods' will be put into action. However, they slowly came to an end."

"An end? How so?" Ahmed didn't want to miss any detail.

"Near their final days the last ten Seekers fell to corruption. Each one believed himself greater than the other and they fought for power. Disobeying God, one by one, they killed each other until only one was left. The gods were furious. The final Seeker, the champion, was banished to the Underworld along with his ten companions. The gods stripped them of their Seeker Stones and ended the existence of Seekers.

"In the Underworld Kalshaimar noticed them and gave them a chance to leave. For many years Kalshaimar and his spawn collected enough power to release the ten. To leave the Underworld, the ten became shadow mage knights, the first of their kind. These dark knights were able to travel between the Underworld and Baseworld at will making them powerful servants of the god of death. The champion became the commander of the ten. To this day the mystery still remains: where are the eleven and what might they be doing?"

"This sounds like a tale you would tell to frighten a child. It can't be true."

"A young learned lord like yourself has surely read some of the ancient histories or the scriptures of these gods; you know what Kalshaimar can do."

"But this? I have never heard of Seekers and otherworldly travel."

"Few have. If only you had the time I would take you to a badawī tribe and you could listen to their stories. All I am saying is that pearl of yours matches the descriptions."

⚬⚬⚬

Amongst the grey stone, cold, and damp cell in which Will was in he found it easy to fall asleep, but remaining asleep was another matter. Sweating and trembling, a night's peace for which he searched did not surface.

He smashed against the walls of his tiny solitary cell. Squeezed into an upright position, the eleven-year-old boy could barely sit in the cell. Hysteria gleamed from his eyes.

"Let me out! Please. Let me out!" he cried, begging for anyone outside. "I'm scared… voices… there're voices everywhere." On both his sides, some distance away, other prisoners screamed back and banged on their cells, some of the adults already insane.

Will looked at his hands. They melted, boiled, and bled. Liquid flesh crawled down his hands, wet and runny.

"N-No... no..." He fell backwards against a wall.

"William... come inside now..." his mother's voice called him. Glowing green eyes, black pupils thin and sharp, emerged from the wall in front of him. Terrified he punched at the eyes trying so hard to make them disappear. A prisoner screamed in agony close by, another spoke in garbled phrases.

Will screamed and smashed at the cell again. Anger broke free and he tried to push at the locked hatch at the top.

"Please... help me..." he sobbed. A snake slithered over Will's body and hissed at him. Behind it, the cell started to flood. Will could feel his mind breaking down. Weeks alone were quickly taking their toll, and all for accidentally dropping his pickaxe down a mineshaft. Someone above entered into the top cell. Electricity jolted down conducting through Will's body; he screamed, saliva leaking out of his mouth, until it stopped. The hot energy boiled and burned him, and the smell of smoke filled his solitary cell, choking him.

Will jolted back to reality. He woke in a cold sweat, panicked and hysterical. The warden was crouched in front of him.

"What's wrong?" He reached out for Will. Will screamed and scrambled backwards. The warden advanced and Will lunged for him. They wrestled, the warden pinning him face first on the ground of his Nizid cell.

"It's me, Will! Ahmed! Calm down!" Two Saomardrim guards rushed to the cell but Ahmed waved them off. Will sobbed and Ahmed adjusted, pinning Will's arms behind his back. "I... everyone heard the screaming. You were having some sort of nightmare. Th-That was not a nightmare." Ahmed looked at him with the same helplessness and fear etched in his face as Will had felt.

"Leave me be!" Will shouted and struggled against Ahmed's firm grip.

"Dreams are especially susceptible to magic; they are magical things in fact... they leave blurry but readable images... Did that really..."

"Leave me be!"

"I am sorry; I must do my duty, if you were... um..." Ahmed cast healing magic over Will. He was no expert in such mental damage, but it would calm Will.

Ahmed slid off of Will and took a seat in one corner of the cell. He'd sleep here and make sure Will would be alright but shame still gnawed at him. If he had any empathy, he should let Will go free, after witnessing what had been done to him, but he couldn't. He needed to finish this task, hand Will over to the sultan, then forget about him.

The sun was at its highest and the sandy desert seemed to spread in all directions forever. Rays of heat beat down on Will paired with the gusts of wind sending sand speeding over dunes. Ahmed was comfortable in his place on top of his horse. Sometimes he would dismount to lead the animal over the especially deep sandy areas. Ahmed took a long sip of water. Will longed for some but he knew Ahmed would not give him much as he had already finished his water.

"You seem content here," Will commented.

"Not fully but yes, why would I not be? I am in my home away from the war in the peace of the landscape." Ahmed smiled, a sudden enthusiasm on his face. "You can't worry for any war, person or country here. Here the silence is pure and the sea of sand endless. All you have is the time to think, to wonder and to enjoy the Father's creation."

"Not fully?" Will held in a laugh, smirking a little.

"It's nice, for a while, but the south is where I am truly home."

"But I thought your people were desert warriors."

"Another lie or exaggeration by your king. It is true that Saomarhad is mostly semi-arid to arid and there *are* large sandy and rocky deserts, but that is only on the surface. There are forests, plains, mountains and savannahs. In the northeast there lies the world's largest wetland. In the south are jungles. Most people have been through a desert in Saomarhad because it is central to all overland trade routes."

"I don't know what all those things mean."

"Of course, you don't." Ahmed chuckled.

"Is Saomarhad big?" Will asked, curiosity overcoming him.

"Big? Far larger than Gurmanis. It stretches from the Hertos river in the west to the Himeveralyan Mountains in the east that separate Saomarhad from Hrindnagara. It stretches from the Southern Ocean to the Free Lands in the north."

"How do all those lords stay loyal to the sultan?"

"Not lords. You already know the sultan rules over the sultanate. He has many emirs who rule over emirates or important cities and towns. Each emirate, except for important urban emirates, are divided into satrapies ruled by a satrap. Then into eyalets ruled by a pasha. Eyalets are divided into sanjaks ruled by beys. Further divisions form towns, villages, hamlets, etcetera." Ahmed looked back at Will to see if he understood. Will gave Ahmed a confused look. "Never mind."

"What class are you then, or do wizards have their own class?"

"I am a nobleman as you say. There is no special class for mages however the grand vizier position tends to go to a mage."

"Right, you told me, everyone seems to be of a higher class then me."

"You should not worry too much about classes. In Saomarhad there are ways to rise."

"Yeah but now I won't get the chance to."

"Right." Ahmed's horse slipped and he adjusted. Will was tugged forward.

"Can I have some water now?"

"No, you finished yours."

"I hate the desert." Will sighed.

As they climbed over the top of a sand dune, below them stretched dunes pock-marked with water filled depressions. Greenery persevered in the inhospitable heat and wind, rooting around the water. At its center under a cluster of broad-leafed trees sat an oasis and a small rest camp, bordered by a low rock face, all around its circular appearance. On one end small streams of water plunged into the oasis, emerging from within the rock.

The idea of fresh cool water lubricating his tongue made Will forget his surroundings. His foot hit a rock, twisted with a sharp jerk, and he skidded, dropping to the ground. His noose pulled tight, taking some of his air as he scraped his arm along the abrasive sandstone. Will grunted, an airy sound as air flooded back into his lungs.

Ahmed dismounted. "Are you okay?" he asked.

"M-My arm... leg." Will heaved.

"Here, I'll help." Ahmed slung Will's left and uninjured arm over his shoulder and led Will across the final steps to the oasis and to a crevice cut into the rock.

"Th-Thanks." Will whispered as he stepped inside.

Ahmed refilled his waterskins, shared the food he had bought, then made sure his horse was comfortable for the night. Alone in the dusty atmosphere Will held his injured arm, his sleeve reddened with blood. Ahmed entered with a bag of surgical equipment and vials. He treated Will's leg.

"Your ankle bones feel fine and I cleaned up the shear on your leg." Ahmed pulled back Will's sleeve and cleaned Will's arm wound. Will watched him work under his Isen prison brand. It never let him forget who he once was. Ahmed refused to look at it. Once bandaged Will pulled his sleeve down and frowned as Ahmed cleaned up the equipment. It was a nice gesture but Will would not be alive to see it heal. He wondered if Ahmed could rid him of his brands, like his pearl removed his prisoner number.

"Can you remove my brands?" Will asked. "Maybe your magic could?"

"No. I don't think that's possible." Ahmed frowned. "Those wounds are too deep. If a mage had intervened early then... maybe. One could use illusion magic to hide them, but such constant use of magic would probably kill him, and be sinful besides."

Will was going to bring up the story about his pearl but thought against it. A prisoner tattoo was designed to be permanent. Ahmed's magic could remove it with great difficulty, perhaps, but Will's pearl had removed it easily. If only his pearl would decide to remove his brands. He'd like that.

"It's too bad both our kingdoms fight. I would have liked you otherwise," Will said, still grateful for Ahmed's healing gesture.

"Yes... too bad. I would have liked you too." Ahmed stared to the side.

"They say you worship the god Alhurah. You consider him worthiest of devotion."

"We do. Mages are considered to be gifted by God, so long as they don't practice dark magic or illusion magic. Illusion magic, like dark magic, mutates nature and seeks to mislead. This goes against the Father's creation and is forbidden."

"My master told me how the war began one-hundred years ago. He said it was the Saomarhad who attacked first under Sultan Biazid."

"Ha! You have an ignorant master then." Ahmed laughed. Will frowned and glared at Ahmed.

"How d'you think it started?"

"King Lundy started it. He attacked first."

"Of course, you would say that. You don't have any proof."

"You don't either."

"My master told me. He does not lie." Will said with a straight face.

"That is a naive answer. Even if your master did not lie, he could have been misled."

"Maybe… it can't be." Will did not want to think his master was not as knowledgeable as he thought.

"The truth is more complex. During King Lundy's and Sultan Biazid's time there was prosperity. There were friendly relations between our peoples and merchants did much business between us. The citizens of both our nations even celebrated shared festivals together. It was the royalty, the nobility and our religious institutions that saw a benefit in war."

"I don't understand."

"Of course you don't. You were a commoner, so politics were far away from you. I remember my home and Ortie so long ago. I like the variety there used to be. Men and women from all over and all colours together. The scents, sounds, feelings. It's not that it's gone, but it's increasingly strained now."

"I want to understand. I am a squire now. I should understand."

"You'd accept the ideas of an enemy?"

"I would consider them."

"Those in power, one-hundred years ago, of both our nations stockpiled weapons and levied fighting men. They grew anxious and did not see much wealth that the merchants were obtaining. On the other hand, our religious institutions mistrusted each other. The common people too. Zealots easily angered the masses and this soon became a problem for our leaders. Idle words repeated frequently became truth. Acts of violence, by both sides, once small turned into conflict. Jermecida, the holy city, was closed off to all Gurmian pilgrims. That city, mind you, is an important site for adherents of both Manis and Alhurah. Each side violently expelled the other from their lands. A crusade was called by your grand bishop and the war began."

"So, the nobility wanted to start a war because they were bored?"

"They saw a chance to gain more land. In both our nations not a single piece of land was unclaimed, and the nobility continued to grow. They needed land to hold power. But the common citizens did nothing to ease tensions. They were galvanised by zealot preachers into distrust. At one point this war was fuelled by an idea that it was religiously right, now it's strayed from that, but there could still be those who disagree. I have observed that most times it leads to corruption."

"Then is there really a point to all of it anymore? My master said this war is draining Gurmanis of life and income."

"I don't know. In truth I spent long studying hard and improving my magic. I don't know what it is like for the people in Saomarhad. I'll tell you this though, I have heard of your king and no doubt he wants the extinction of me and my people. He sees us as all you have heard spoken of us. Perhaps he sees an opportunity to claim our lands for himself and his lords."

"You know this?"

"I think this. Why else would a man be so driven to war despite the harm it is doing to his kingdom if not for his personal gain, and that of the classes that benefit him the most?"

"Like your sultan."

"No. Sultan Yazid fights to protect his people."

"Then what kind of man is he?"

"They call him Rashid al-Din, the rightly guided of the faith. His father was an unparalleled warrior and frequently led Saomarhad's armies himself. Many said he took after Sultan Saadiq al-din, the greatest sultan of these crusades. Sultan Yazid remained in the sultanate and endeared himself with many influential people. He is a warrior, but he prefers not to fight, at least until King Duggan brutalised his father. Even in his youth he enacted policies and reforms that strengthened the sultanate. When the previous sultan died all the territories he gained were retaken by King Duggan and because Sultan Yazid had done so well strengthening the sultanate when his father fought, it remains strong."

"My master told me that once King Duggan was a man of piety and honour, liked by his people. But that changed when his wife died. I don't know, I was too young to understand what kind of man he was before." Will was reluctant to believe the king was ever a commendable man.

"You show him no love nor any loyalty?"

"I have no reason to. His rule, his systems, in the end they ruined my life."

"You've surprised me Will. This much I will admit. You were nothing like what I expected Gurmians to be." Ahmed stared at him.

"Nor did I expect the Saomarhadians to be like you."

"Now we talk as if we were friends. If only, in another reality, we were. You are uneducated but you ask many questions and that is important. But... why are you so curious? Why are you open with me?"

"I don't know. Maybe it's because I'm realizing the trick that was played on me. Manis left me in prison, made me suffer all those years, then gave me hope, gave me a new life. Now I go to die again. Or maybe I like talking to you." Ahmed looked at him with surprise. He turned away; his brows knit in concern.

"Enemies… enjoying discussion. I have an idea of your past Will but, please, don't make me regret my duty. I don't want to feel bad for bringing you to God. One day this war will end as all things do, and on that day our people may once again be friends," Ahmed laid down, resting his head on a small pillow.

Will thought, if captive and captor could have such a relationship then how come their people couldn't? Ahmed was right; peace would come, but Will could not die before it did. He had to try to escape. After all, he was a captive and speaking of duty, this was his duty.

Chapter Nineteen

EETING THE MAIN road as the two neared the southern edge of the desert, the way to Ortie gradually grew wetter. Low mountains stood to the right of the boys, their rocks casting shade on the road. The desert hugged the roots of the foothills, the wind pushing sand up its sides, and sparse greenery battled against the encroachment.

Ahmed rode at the head, leading Will along. They came to a slope in the road which curved southeast then eastward, greenery in the far distance. Outside that curve, Ahmed noticed the ruins of a maqam built into the side of the rock, a squat square holding up a small dome. This shrine had been co-purposed into a toll booth. Among the ruins lay several dead men in between piles of broken, jagged rock. Ahmed's horse huffed its displeasure. He stopped and dismounted, bending to investigate.

"What do ya think happened?" Will asked.

"Banu Murtād, apostates. Must have robbed the toll booth." But Ahmed had his suspicions. Why was the booth in ruins? That seemed like too much effort for mere theft. He examined a dead murtād more closely and noticed his sword wound was filled with sand. Could the wind have really filled it completely?

A whiff of air brushed past the boys, sending a spray of sand across their faces. Ahmed sensed something; the magic signature was— The sand around them coalesced into globular masses, as if generating their own wind. Rock piles lifted and merged with the masses. From nearby desert dunes, more sand formed into shapes. Humanoids, some more rock, others more sand, took form. They held curved swords of fast flowing sediment.

Ahmed drew his one-handed axe and kilij. His horse reared and Ahmed cut Will from it. The horse galloped through a gap in the encroaching sand warriors.

"The sand's rising up!" Will screamed over the sound of swishing sediment. "You were wrong. The desert is as they say!"

"Quiet! I don't know what's happening. This isn't normal." Ahmed screamed, taking a stance. The sand warriors were coming closer. Ahmed figured the Banu Murtād's attack disturbed some awry magic, or maybe there was a mage in the fight who had mis-cast a spell, or this was an unfortunate coincidence, it didn't matter right now.

"Unbind me an' give me a weapon. I can help. There're too many!" Will begged, presenting his bound wrists.

"No, you will run!"

"I won't, I have nowhere to go. Please. At least let me defend myself!"

"Ok! Ok!" Ahmed waved his hand over Will and the ropes binding him unraveled. "Get a sword," Ahmed ordered. The young mage waved his hand over his own sword. The blue glow of a field enchantment flickered over his kilij before stabilising. Will presented a dead Raider's scimitar and Ahmed cast the same enchantment over it.

"Whoa." Will smiled.

"You need magic, a blessed weapon, or an enchanted weapon to fight monsters and spirits." Ahmed eyed the sand warriors as they closed the distance. "Field enchants have limited charges, make each strike count!" The boys were surrounded; there was no escape.

One, mostly stone sand warrior lunged for Ahmed. Ahmed blocked the overhead cut, his blade connecting with the swishing sand. The monster was swift. Ahmed traded blows, backing into Will.

Will stabbed though the sandy gut of a warrior. It burst into a cloud of sand, burying him. He covered his eyes, adjusting at the last second to avoid a strike from a mostly sand warrior. Will traded blows with it. He swung in an arc, felling two warriors and coming back-to-back with Ahmed.

Ahmed pushed his kilij through the sandy face of a warrior. The warrior behind it shot out an arm. A stream of sediment barreled towards Ahmed. He cast a blue ward. The sediment connected with the ward, covering Ahmed's field of vision. Ahmed cast a wave of fire forwards, bursting several warriors into clouds of sand. He charged forwards, parting from Will.

Will slashed through one, two, three. Though they were numerous, the sand warriors were reckless. Will blocked another and traded blows with it. Catching it unaware, he stabbed through it. Will turned to avoid sand spray. Another charged him. He raised his simitar to block. Instead, the sand blade fell through his simitar. He moved. The sand blade hit his side, cutting but not deeply. Will glared at his simitar, its glow diminishing. Heat fled from his face and more sand warriors were forming.

Ahmed lodged his axe in the head of a warrior. Turned. Sliced through two warriors. Cast a wave of sand back at another group. Turned. Lodged his axe in another. As the clouds of dead sand warriors dissipated around him Ahmed looked towards the desert and the mountains. Dozens were forming. He lit and threw his spherical pottery. One towards the mountain and another towards the desert. They exploded, shaking the air, shocking Will, as shrapnel flew outwards. Still more sand warriors formed.

"Ahmed! My sword won't work!" Will screamed, dodging sand blades from left and right. Ahmed knew they would not last much longer. He sheathed his weapons and chanted a spell,

"Iihphagan Arderrafol." Ahmed closed his eyes. His magic extended far across the landscape, through the air, and under the earth. He searched for the awry magic assaulting them. Something seemed off under the fringes of the desert, from the source of the tremor.

"Iogr Bhiyalij— No." The air was too dry, no water under them, it would not be enough to wet the sand and prevent the warriors from forming. Will was being overwhelmed on all sides. They had to run. Ahmed's pearl burned, lending him power. Shocked at the unusually energetic jolt it gave him, he did not have time to question.

"Iogr Bhiyalij!" Ahmed shouted, throwing out his arms. A swirling ring of water rose up from the earth in a torrent around him and roared outwards, parting around Will and crashing into the sand warriors. It wetted the foothills and fringes of the desert, rendering the sand over the awry magic heavy and unable to lift. The water seeped within the earth, aided by the power of the pearl, attacking the awry magic with healing magic. But Ahmed could not sense if the awry magic was healed. The magic of his pearl diminished and so did his enhancements.

Ahmed took a moment to breathe, panting and sweating, shocked at his magic. His pearl cooled and he turned. Will's simitar arched towards Ahmed's head. The young mage threw a pulse of energy outwards, making Will stagger.

"Wi-Will…"

"I'll take my leave, Ahmed. I've stayed too long," Will said.

"As I've said before there is nowhere you can go, Will. You do not know this land as I do and you will stand out. You will be killed or enslaved before you make it to the coast." Ahmed spit, sweat sliding down to his lips. He drew his kilij.

"I still have to try! I have to do my duty."

"Your duty? I see, I understand. But I will do mine as well."

Will pushed forward. Ahmed walked backward. Ahmed stared firmly into Will's eyes assessing his next move and Will stared back. Ahmed ducked and Will swung were he used to be. They traded blows, wind throwing sand at them. Ahmed feinted. Will didn't react to it then Ahmed attacked and Will countered. Ahmed switched direction at the last second, striking Will.

"You may have some fight but I still have more skill than you!" Ahmed taunted.

"We will test that!" Will swung forward. Ahmed blocked. As soon as he heard the clang of blades he pushed at Will, drawing his djanbīyya. Will sidestepped. The two traded blows. Will blocked them, but was forced back. Adjusting his footing, Will lunged. The mage dodged. Like a flash of light, Ahmed pushed forward with his djanbīyya and ruptured Will's hand. Using magic, he slowed the speed and the dagger made a small incision instead. Will screamed and clutched his hand; he dropped the scimitar and fell to his knees. Ahmed propped up Will's chin with his djanbīyya and smiled.

"Consider your test successful. I am more skilled than you. You *are* coming to Ortie."

<hr>

Will, bound to Ahmed's horse and stumbling behind him, was in awe of the dense and colourful city of Ortie, capital of the Saomarhad Sultanate. He had to stay close to Ahmed's horse to avoid being crushed and trampled by the scores of people flooding around them. The sultan's palace's round shapes, colourful girih patterns, and gold made it stand out over the city on the peak of a hill, in the northwest. Its stone with hues of blue, red, and green and the top golden domes shimmered and reflected the light of the sun. The same style was present on the mosque, hospital, barracks, and government houses, the most prominent locations in the city.

They entered from the east gate and descended down a road curving north, riding under a few archways, a bridge, and shade bearing fabrics as they pushed through crowds who gave Ahmed's horse a wide berth. The streets twisted into a maze and Will hoped Ahmed knew where he was going. His gaze hovered between watching where he was walking and looking back at people who were staring. Ahmed kept shifting the horse's reins.

Unlike Nizid, whose buildings were composed mainly of sandstone and little wood, the buildings of Ortie, and other coastal cities in Saomarhad, were built of different stone and more wood. Unlike the flat roofs of the arid cities, many of Ortie's roofs were tiled and slanted to let rainwater flow down them. Being a city between the desert, the farming regions, and the coast it shared the styles of many places. The two boys began to ascend the streets towards the sultan's palace after passing through an inner-city gatehouse.

A pair of sentries led Will and Ahmed into the palace. They ascended a small set of stairs under a double arch into a courtyard surrounded by a two-story arcade, a balcony along the second level. The courtyard held two howz framing the entryway, flanked by circular towers, into the main building

Ahmed dismounted his horse as men of the sultan's guard, the Immortals, marched out and formed lines on either side of Ahmed. He seemed a bit distressed as he watched the tall intimidating Immortals form ranks. Their decorated gold trimmed armor shone under the sun and brought out the green, brown, orange, and red fabric that accented their armor. Most intimidating was their face mask, a mechanical mold of a man's face covering their own, topped in a turban with a metal spire and plume. It was thought the Saomarhad sultans recruited such elite warriors from among the most skilled, tallest, and strongest of the Saomarhad army and from the best of the elite mamluks, ghilman, and janissaries. Ahmed's hold was firm, tugging Will forward, sweat ran down his face.

The sultan emerged from the entryway; to his right stood Master Mahad, holding his staff, and to his left, the grandmaster of the Immortals, Barbas Abudi. Barbas was a Zanjī from the southern emirates. His skin was darker than the others. The sultan's black beard and moustache were trimmed neatly, highlighting his strong jawline and fading higher up his face. He wore an elaborate turban which wrapped around his neck and shoulders. His silk robes possessed the symbol of Saomarhad, a yellow sun with a green crescent moon, its points aimed upwards, and a star in between. The bottom of the sun bore two crossed swords. A cloak flapped in the breeze behind him. But above all his thick, upward slashed eyebrows, piercing kohl-lined brown eyes, and the hard wrinkles flanking his nose, gave him an intimidating and experienced look. Barbas stepped forward.

"Before you stands Sultan Yazid II Tairf Rashid al-Din, protector of all Saomarhad." The sultan smiled and stepped ahead of Barbas.

"Ahmed Sharfi, you are welcomed in my home! And who is this westerner you have brought with you?" The sultan's voice was rich and firm.

Ahmed pressed a fist to his chest and bowed his head slightly. "My lord, Sultan Yazid, I am honoured. This westerner is an enemy I found at the front and have brought him here to face justice."

"Mashalhurah! There were many prisoners, and you have done well, as I asked. We shall show everyone the Saomarhad people will not stand idle while we are slaughtered and tortured. Alhurah the Wise Lord, and the faithful are not to be underestimated," the sultan proclaimed, "Guards! You two, take the boy to the dungeons."

"Yes sultan." The guards walked forward, cloaks blowing back. Will looked into the masks of one of the Immortals who approached him. The Immortal's eyes looked back at Will with a cold dead stare. They seized Will's arms in a clamp-like grip. He shivered, cold and clammy, as he was dragged into the palace looking back at Ahmed with a frown.

"B-Be careful…" Ahmed mumbled too loudly, a slight sunken tug on his chest.

"Compassion even for the enemy. In many cases it might be taken as treason young Ahmed." Ahmed tensed, realizing what he had spoken.

"I would never think of that my sultan."

"I hope so. Have you acquired the relic from Al-Motros?"

"I have." Ahmed took the box containing the powerful relic from his horse's saddlebags and presented it to Sultan Yazid. The sultan smiled and accepted it. He passed it on to Master Mahad who hid it within his robes. Ahmed watched it disappear, wondering about the magic within and the symbol drawn on it. There was an unease in him that told him the relic meant something, but that he'd not see it for a long time.

"It shall be kept safe and studied." The sultan turned to Master Mahad. "You were right about him, my friend. Now that I see him before me, your praise does him credit."

"Thank-you, my sultan. He is my finest student," Master Mahad praised Ahmed and heat rushed to Ahmed's cheeks.

"I trust you. I hope he will guide me as well as you've advised me. Mahad, your friendship during the time my father was at war and we strengthened the sultanate was invaluable."

Master Mahad nodded. Sultan Yazid turned back to Ahmed. "Now you must be tired having travelled so far, rest, then come to a feast in celebration of our victories."

"I am honoured, my sultan." Ahmed made a slight bow of his head. Sultan Yazid turned and left with his Immortals in his wake.

"You have done well Ahmed, your powers have strengthened greatly," Master Mahad exclaimed.

"Thank-you Master." His master turned to join Sultan Yazid and Ahmed followed close behind.

———

The guards dragged Will down below, letting him bump and scrape himself along the walls, stumbling with every step in an attempt to keep up. Many of the cells were packed with men, women, and children captured from the front. Some whispered amongst themselves, others sniffled or cried, others still maintained a deathly silence.

The Immortals dragging Will took him to an empty cell where they took off his ropes and clamped his left ankle in a shackle attached to the cell walls. The guards shoved Will inside and left him alone in the dark.

Will sat, staring at the ceiling. So, this was it, any time now they would come and execute him. It was a short-lived life as a squire and a cruel joke Manis had played. He stood and walked to the bars, holding them for support and hung his head. He gripped the bars and bared his teeth. When he gained his freedom, then when he met his master, he had hope he could become someone of worth. He had hope he could contribute to his master's goals. That was his new purpose and he is and had been so thankful for that opportunity. Yet only a few weeks later he'd proved himself a failure. He could not escape Ahmed and now he was going to die like he thought he would when he was in Isen Prison, behind iron bars and bound by metal.

Frustrated, Will shook the bars, grunted, then fell back against the rear wall. He pulled his legs to his chin and hugged himself tight. The walls of his cell seemed to be moving in on him, crushing him. He shivered. The warden laughed in the distance. Tears formed in Will's eyes and he cried softly. The warden's shadow appeared over him. It called him a monster and a failure. Then Will descended further as his vision darkened and his head grew heavy and he was ten-years-old again.

———

He stood deathly still and looked at his hands. His right palm was forced upwards, and his left downwards. Two iron shackles were locked shut around his wrists, rigid metal connecting them pulled against the two lengths of chain snaking tightly around his waist, their rattle ringing in his ears. His heart sank, shame gnawed at his core. The sentence imposed on him echoed in his mind. Two more shackles shut around his ankles pulled upward by the heavy connecting chain attached to his waist. The guard attending him thrust up his chin to expose his neck. Will's ears tingled; acutely aware of what was happening to him, it felt unreal. The guard clamped shut an iron collar around his neck pulling it down by its chain which he latched to his waist. Finally, the chains were strapped to a metal clamp, fitted under his chest.

The guards pulled him out of the cell. He shuffled forward, head down, down a dimly lit stone corridor to a line of waiting, similarly bound convicts. He was a dog on a leash, bound like a slave, humiliated, dangerous and unpredictable. The way they shackled his wrists left him unable to move his arms even a little. He was limp, like a dead fish.

He was pulled into the line in between two men and was connected from the waist, neck, and between his ankles to the prisoner in front and the prisoner behind him.

Will and the men shuffled forward, like cattle, chains dragging along the ground, to a waiting prison carriage. He was shoved into the carriage and further into an internal chain-linked cage, then locked inside.

———

Will jerked against the wall. Squeezing his eyes shut and gritting his teeth he tried to banish the relapse, cursing in his mind for being so weak to his past. Movement to his left caused him to panic, and fear propelled him to reality. The outline of a female sat across from him.

"Y-You!" she said. She came forwards, her chain clanking. "I don't belong here… I… I don't want to be in here," she cried, fear in her voice. Then her voice grew cold. "You should be comfortable here."

"Wh-What?" Will retreated. She lifted from the darkness revealing brown hair, white skin, and a healer's tunic. "… Will."

Will looked on dumbfounded. The girl from Suthenburg and again in Al-Motros was in front of him, in his cell. "You know my name?" Will blushed.

"Yes, you told my superior, remember? Alas I s'pose I should tell you my name as it won't matter after tonight, you wanted so much to know, I am Jillian."

"Jillian, I like that." Will thought he saw a smile.

"I should have stayed home, then I would not have been in this situation. You should be quite comfortable. If you try to hurt me, I will fight back," she warned, making Will frown.

"I don't want to hurt you."

"You are a murderer. You should pay for your crimes. I mean how could you kill your entire family and not care?"

"But how d'you know if I have paid for it or not?" Will glared at her. "You don't know what it's like to be blamed and punished for something you didn't do."

"You can't own up to your crimes. You killed your entire family. That's unforgivable!"

"I don't make this up! Every day sitting alone, afraid, and miserable surrounded by death, suffering, and pain. What right do you have to accuse and hate me so much? I would ne'er hurt the people that I loved!" Will shivered. He made himself look small. "I was ten an' I didn't understand anything that was happening to me. Everyone was angry, everyone hated me. The warden and his guards enjoyed hurting me and I could not even go to the other prisoners for help. They were all quiet, lifeless. I was trapped, suffocating. Every day I wanted to die… they wouldn't let me…"

A moment passed before Jillian spoke. "I… I… don't know what to say. I didn't realise this is what you would say…" Jillian frowned.

"People judge. They hate me before they understand me. No one deserves what I went through. You said Sir Robert made a mistake caring for me, you said I don't deserve him. He accepted me when no one else cared to, showing me much kindness and I care not and know not why he did it, but I know it was right!"

"You talk so strongly, determined your words are true." Jillian shrunk back, embarrassed, uncomfortable, ashamed. "I would not know such things."

"No one e'er did. I am innocent. I know you may not believe me but tis the truth. Please don't call me such things, I am not those… I am not."

Jillian clasped her forehead and tilted her head up. "Ya know, I was wronged by someone whose title you bear. So many people in the war have. It's difficult to trust anyone again." Jillian shuffled forward, coming close to Will.

"Sitting with a boy who claims he is innocent when the kingdom tells me he is not. Waiting for my death in the darkness of this cell with nowhere to go. I guess there is naught more to do but listen. Tell me your story, Will." She was suddenly eager to hear.

<hr>

The sultan sat upon a heightened platform on a low cushioned chair underneath an elaborate semi-dome arcade bearing multifoil arches. His family sat around a low table, a sofra. To his right sat his wife, partially veiled, and to his left sat his eldest son, Ahmed's age, a strong and clean young man. The sultan's youngest son was beside him, as well as his three daughters.

All the sultan's guests, from lucky commoners to emirs, were seated on cushions set upon elaborate carpets of many colours. At the edges of the space a few palace cats lounged. Each guest shared a sofra, around an open floor, where women and musicians performed exotic dances to foreign music. Servants and slaves served the guests şerbet, ayran, and other drinks while some guests smoked from tall hookahs. Serious looking Immortals stood at the back of the sultan ahead of latticed jali and the curtains, fabrics, and plants that decorated the space. They revolved around the party on constant guard. Grandmaster Barbas stood close by, stoic and imposing.

Ahmed recognised it all as he entered the great hall underneath the tessellations of gold, blue, green, and purple. It had been so long since he had attended one of his sultan's feasts. Ahmed wore a fine golden-brown bisht robe over his thawb, unburdened by the armor and weapons he'd left in his room, and had covered his head in a patterned keffiyeh and black agal.

He pressed a fist to his chest and made a slight bow of his head towards the sultan, then took his seat by his master on the heightened platform at the viziers' sofra. Ahmed eyed the dancers as they spun around in colourful saris; all of them wore yellow except for the lead dancer in the center. The kathak style they performed was well suited for the sultan's court. He could get used to this. The dancers from Hrindnagara, a great kingdom to the east, repeated the chorus of the song they danced to, marked by rapid pounds of a tabla and the long hums of a stringed sarangi.

An ambassador brought gifts to the sultan; Ahmed could overhear their conversation.

"I am honoured to be invited to this powerful and culturally rich city on behalf of Maharaja Viraj and bring you good wishes, Sultan Yazid, furthermore at this grave time," the ambassador spoke.

"I am pleased you could make it, ambassador. My forces ensured the voyage into our waters would be safe for you and your delegation. I am disappointed your king could not come himself."

"The maharaja must deal with many internal issues before he can consider aiding you in your war. Refugees are flooding in, fleeing from conflict in Qinguo, while the desert is ripe with a spreading cult."

"I understand, there is much demanded of a king and he needs to be active in solving issues that arise. Nevertheless, this war is reaching an end, once Gurmanis sees our resolve; it is only a matter of time. Have you received the books and scrolls I sent for the Grand Library?"

Ahmed stopped listening at the mention of the library. He wanted to see the place one day; it was said the Grand Library of Hrindnagara, located in its Vasuthar Desert, hosted all the knowledge in the world. Master Mahad had talked of it long ago. He was enthusiastic in going himself but national matters kept him from it. Ahmed wondered if his political life would take up all his time as well.

"Once, northern Hrindnagara was the domain of the Highal Sultanate," Master Mahad informed Ahmed. "Since then, the land has been unified as Hrindnagara. Maharaja Viraj Suryachandra, they say, is a man of peace. Negotiations for allies in this war is wasted with him, but the sultan believes we may get supplies and trade concessions if not military aid."

"Are we so beat that we need to look to other nations?"

"After one-hundred years of war? We are getting there. But others wait for an opportune moment." Master Mahad pointed to a man on one side of the room. He wore an elaborate purple toga. "Sisenna Postumius Damasus, from the Rhoathian Imperium. Since the marriage proposal for the Gurmian princess was called off, the emperor has sent his ambassador to the sultan."

"The sultan wants to ally with the Imperium?"

"The Imperium does not want allies. Sisenna is here to wait. Wait for the war to destabilize the sultanate so the legions can claim it. However, Sultan Yazid is not called the rightly guided of the faith for nothing. We will not destabilize."

"But the threat is there. The longer this war continues the greater chance there is someone like the Imperium will destroy us. It's been one-hundred years, master, the time is coming," Ahmed reasoned. A rush of heat made him pull at his collar.

"That is why we are here, Ahmed. To ensure Saomarhad survives."

Servants and slaves flooded into the room carrying silver, gold, and painted ceramic trays and bowls off which savoury aromas spread. A multitude of dishes were set before the diners including spiced lamb, mutton, and fish complemented with pilaf, meat and vegetable stuffed pastries, flatbreads, various colourful meza including a herb and bulgur salad, ground fried chickpea balls, a chickpea tahini dip, and sauces of yoghurt or barely. Meat, fish, grain, and vegetable soups and stews complimented the dishes along with kebabı and köfte of lamb, chicken, beef, and camel. The sultan drew from all areas of the sultanate and the cuisines within it. From the deep south dishes with chillies, mangoes, plantains, and cassava were served.

"Bismilhurah." Ahmed spoke after the guests chanted the same. He pulled forward a buraniyya of lamb, fried eggplant, gourd, and onions spiced with coriander and saffron.

A servant offered Ahmed fruit and cheese. It had been a long time since he had this treatment. Back then he was a child and he always wanted to go elsewhere. At these parties he would sit by his mother, and his brother would be sitting by his father, who would tell Amir things about noble life and procedure. Ahmed noted many times when Amir cared less about it. But now that Ahmed was older, he understood the political importance of these parties.

"Ahmed when the executions are finished, I shall teach you the magic I have left to teach." Ahmed's master turned to him, wiping sweet and sour honey-lemon mutton harīsa from his lips.

"What do you mean *left* master?"

"The sultan is impressed with your courage and bravery. He has heard of your strength and what you did to those Banu Murtād. You have exceeded what was asked of you."

"How could he have learned of that? It happened recently."

"Who do you think tipped the Banu Murtād off to your location?"

"What! The sultan sent them to attack me?"

"He sent Grandmaster Barbas to suggest to those apostates that a young man and a captive were coming through with a valuable relic. Barbas offered them freedom from the power of the law."

"If I died?"

"We knew you would succeed, Ahmed. You have passed all the tests the sultan has required of you."

"The boy helped me master. He defeated as many of them as I did."

"Don't humour yourself! This victory is yours."

"Master, we didn't fight the Banu Murtād." Ahmed frowned. "They were dead when we arrived. Some sort of magic went awry there and we were attacked by sand warriors."

"Really?" Master Mahad raised an eyebrow. "But you defeated them."

"I did."

"Then that is all that matters. The sultan is pleased and has decided to move ahead with my recommendation. You are to become his grand vizier"

"Now? At such an early age?" In truth Ahmed was thrilled, he could have hugged the sultan… but that would be unwise… very unwise.

"I am getting old, Ahmed, and have taught you all I can. It is now time for you to make your mark in building a stronger sultanate. As I watched you grow and improve in university, I knew you would be the one to replace me. I could see you had much determination and the will to train and refine yourself. This has made you wise and powerful." Master Mahad took a talisman off his neck and handed it to Ahmed who received it uneasily. "This is a sacred object. It is said that many generations before, Alhurah gave it to the first magi. Now it has fallen to me to give to you. Keep it safe."

"Yes Master." Ahmed sensed its aura; it drew him in and warmed to his touch. "What will become of you once I take your position?"

"It is my duty to guide you through the politics of the sultanate over your first year or two in office. I cannot let you take the position blind to what is expected of you. It won't be magical teachings, rather more focused political teaching that I will give you. In addition, of course, to the politics you're acquainted with. After that I will return north."

"I wished to return to my family after my schooling master, at least briefly."

"Of course Ahmed. After the executions you can return to Hamid for a few weeks to be with your family. You can tell them the good news; they will be proud."

"Thank-you Master."

As soon as the first dishes had come deserts were served. Ahmed decided to avoid the pastries, balls of dates and nuts, and various nutty halwās for a sweet semolina cake he'd never tried. Its soft syrupy texture melted in his mouth. Everything seemed perfect.

In the dungeons, Will finished his story to the upset, paled face of his listener. He'd described his life to her like he had with Sir Robert. The knight had suggested being forthcoming. Was it too much? Despite the things he felt around her, she'd been so averse to him. Maybe telling her was a mistake and he feared he'd troubled her. Will stopped talking and there was a moment of silence as Jillian internalized what she'd heard.

"I... I didn't realize... did all that r-really happen?" Jillian spoke softly.

"Why? You don't believe me, do you? Why would I make all that up, because I thought it was fun? I have proof! I can show you..." Will choked on the last words. He hoped Jillian didn't actually want to see his wounds. Now she accused him of not only being a murderer but also a liar.

Jillian shook her head and held up her hands. "That's not necessary. I am sorry... I don't... all this... I don't know what to say."

Will frowned, curled himself up and looked away.

"I couldn't hope to understand this. I've felt trapped before, unable to decide my own fate... but nowhere as near as that."

"Sometimes the worst thing was waking up in my small dark cell." Will stared into a corner. "I'd curse myself for waking up. Waking up was the hardest thing to do because I knew I was going nowhere and I was alone. That reality hit me everyday. I thought I deserved it and I couldn't forgive myself for being there. I hated myself. I could have ne'er lived to old age in there."

"After everything that has happened, it seems I have been wrong about you. Wrong about what I thought you had been through anyway. I am such a heartless person, I treated you so horribly." She flashed a weak smile.

"You assumed I was what everyone thinks I am. That justified what I suffered, in your mind."

"Not to the lengths of torture you've described to me."

"You quoted Judeicar's Justice in Al-Motros."

"It's severe, yes, but its not meant to be indulged in. It's also meant to be proportionate to the crime. Not like how this warden decided to do it. God fearing men and women would not go to such lengths," she said, bitterness in her voice.

"Fear of God means little to such men as the warden. Tis no argument."

"Maybe you're right." Jillian sighed. "But I judged *you* too readily."

He could tell part of her was still cautious. She may have thought his torture was reprehensible but that did not speak to whether or not he'd killed his parents.

"I understand why people hate me. They, like you, liken me to a demon. But because of that they won't give me a voice to explain. They won't hear my side or even consider the idea that I'm not guilty."

"No one trusts the words of a criminal; I don't mean you. They will never think such a person could change or repent in some way. They want it gone, out of sight, out of mind. After all, forgiveness takes tremendous effort so tis easier to walk the path of vengeance. Thus, justice is weighed higher than mercy and mercy is harder than forgiveness."

"Justice should not occlude mercy," Will mumbled.

"You're surprisingly well read for a serf." Jillian smiled, blushing.

"My father and mother made sure I knew how to speak and think if not read or write."

"It shows. Our grand marshal saw something in you." Jillian relaxed.

"I have naught left but him to look forward to. In this war I don't serve the king, he has brought me naught but hurt. I serve my master, the one who brought me dignity."

"I see. The k-king… he's that bad."

"He's responsible for the warden. I heard he's done so much more besides."

"My mother was a good judge of character; she would know what to think. She taught me loyalty to family was paramount." Jillian sighed. "Evidently I am not the best example. I don't think she nor my father would want me working in the army." Jillian smiled. "I like your idea. A world without mercy leaves us all for the worse. No one, not even the worst should suffer as you did." Will looked at Jillian, awed. For no one to suffer like he did, he wanted that too.

Down the hall a loud click and creak preceded the shouting of the guards. Captives moaned and begged from within their cells as the Saomardrim guards jeered and laughed. Will stood and clutched the bars, pushing against them to see what was going on. Jillian slid into a dark corner, making herself small. A tied bundle of lettuce leaves entangled with prunes hit Will's face as a guard passed. He fumbled with it, catching it and falling back beside Jillian. She hesitated, unsure of the closeness, but accepted the larger portion of the meal Will offered her.

Finishing the last of the scraps Jillian slid even closer, cried, and clutched her clothes. Will shivered in his corner. He sensed her despair, telling himself to do something, say something. He didn't know what to do or say to comfort the girl. Will tensed, moved his hand forward, and touched Jillian's right shoulder. The girl looked up, without trust. Will's heart sunk and shame overcame him. He turned away, fighting the feeling of the walls closing on him, and the warden's faint taunting voice. Suddenly Jillian snuggled up against Will's side. He paled, resisting the urge to slide away. Jillian gripped his arm, she was trembling, then dropped her head onto Will's chest. His heart raced, fearing her touch. I-It's like his master's hug, Will tried to convince himself. He calmed a little and boldly, but hesitantly, brought his arms around her, trying to mimic his master's hug. The two youths spent the last night of their short lives, with only each other.

Ahmed made for his quarters, walking down a vaulted palace walkway whose curves were decorated in jali. He was stopped by a palace servant.

"Grand Vizier Mahad requests your presence, my lord," he said. Ahmed thanked the man and turned around. He yawned, the feast had been long. Ahmed was allowed into his master's room. His master stood with his back to his apprentice, hunched over, hands on a table, reading a set of documents.

"Master." Ahmed greeted him. His master turned, stunning Ahmed with what he saw. Bags hung under Master Mahad's eyes; his wrinkles were more prominent, and his eyes scarcely blinked. "Master, are you okay?"

"I am tired is all, Ahmed," he said. Ahmed nodded cautiously. He'd never seen his master so drained before. Master Mahad stressed many times that tiredness and drowsiness were a danger for a mage because these things supressed magic. His master worked often too, splitting his time between the sultan's side in Ortie, the side of his students in Murzq, and at times vanishing somewhere without notice.

"If I may ask, do you see to the war?" Ahmed motioned at his master's desk. Master Mahad shook his head.

"There is a rising shadow in the east. The high orcish Wardens report that forces in the Tainted Lands are becoming bolder and conduct more raids against the Great Guardian Wall. A fleet of lesser orcs has gathered to the north of the Tainted Lands. They move west."

"Do events so far away in another country concern us?"

"You are wise enough to know not to underestimate Kalshaimar's spawn within those cursed lands."

"But no force has broken through for hundreds of years." The revelation of such a threat had Ahmed on edge.

"Perhaps it is a minor fluctuation. Regardless, other matters call for your attention. The sultan is holding a meeting with me and you are invited to attend."

"The sultan wants me to attend?"

"Yes, I can see the reaction in your eyes. You will get used to being in the sultan's service." Master Mahad placed a reassuring hand on his shoulder.

"Oh, yes master," Ahmed said shyly. He followed Master Mahad to the war room, a room off of Sultan Yazid's study and attached to the library and main garden. Master Mahad strode ahead, standing tall and resting a hand on his scimitar. For a moment, Ahmed found himself back when he was young, walking behind his master to some meeting with nobles or scholars. He wondered upon the duty of pupils to follow their masters and the duty their masters had for their pupils, but he reigned in his thoughts before they could wander, as sometimes they easily did.

At the doors to the sultan's study, they waited to be allowed in, then several of Sultan Yazid's generals emerged. They pressed a fist to their chests and made slight bows towards Master Mahad, who returned the gesture.

The last general paused. "Grand Vizier, the sultan will see you now," he said. Ahmed and Master Mahad entered into the study, a large space, just the foyer surrounded by shelves of books and scrolls. Behind the Sultan hung a map of Saomarhad and a long low table lay stretched out in front of him. The sultan sat on a low cushioned sofa.

Sultan Yazid looked at Ahmed and Master Mahad, "As-salāmu alaykum," he greeted.

"Wa alaykumu s-salām," Master Mahad replied, pressing a fist to his chest and bowing slightly. The sultan gestured to a seat on his right. Ahmed made the same gestures when the sultan's eyes landed on him. Feeling the pit of his stomach tingle, he hesitated.

"Come take a seat Ahmed, you are among friends." The sultan gestured to a seat on his left. Ahmed took the seat.

Sultan Yazid nodded. "Bismilhurah. I have been told that Saomarhad remains strong… but vulnerable. If only my father were still alive, he'd know exactly how to strike the Gurmians effectively. Rivertown… the last Gurmian sortie." The sultan paled then pounded his fist on the table. "The Gurmian king refused to surrender his body and instead, God curse that king, hung him from the walls of his capital and let crows pick at him."

Ahmed heard this story when he was younger. It arrived a week or two after the fact as news to Murzq. The Gurmian king was a wild and vile man who did not even respect the dead.

"God will preserve his soul in paradise," Grandmaster Mahad said, giving the sultan a reassuring nod. "Despite a few sieges you have advocated a policy of defence."

Sultan Yazid sighed. "But as I have seen more of our people martyred, I realised Gurmians will not stop. They want to eradicate us. That is why we attacked them in Halsburg and Al-Motros. That is why we pushed them inland."

"And you have done well in this policy. Alhurah instructs that we must fight the transgressors, but if they cease then there need be no aggression. Still unbelievers do not relent and we have bore their violence for a long time."

"My generals say I should press our success and attack. I am not King Duggan; I do not want to eradicate Gurmians. I do want vengeance for the treatment of my father and for my people who have suffered their inhumane aggression. I want to protect them."

Ahmed wondered what his sultan thought inhumane meant. Sure, he had heard all the stories of savage Gurmanis attacks but he swore he could remember a few equally savage Saomarhad ones.

"I must meet aggression with aggression. It is the only language they know."

"Has all negotiation failed?"

"If only it were easy like when we went south Mahad. The Zanjī welcomed negotiation, the Gurmians do not." The sultan scoffed, he rubbed his mouth and chin. "Of the ambassadors I have sent before, some never returned. All others brought no breakthrough."

Master Mahad leaned towards him. "Tell us what the generals have said. You know I am here to help you Yazid." The sultan nodded, flashing a smile.

"A general suggests allying with the imperium to control the southern entrance to the Inner Seas. Superior Gurmian ships threaten Ortie, we've been blockaded before, and they sunk a refugee ship, few survived. Then in the Holy Land the massacre at the Grand Mosque of Alhurah still angers locals. Ya Alhurah! Gurmian's know no bounds."

Ahmed remembered the Saomarhad retaliation he'd heard of after the massacre. His countrymen had decimated stretches of Gurmanis land, and all the settlements on it. Massacring hundreds. In fact, a civilian jihad was conducted in response. Gurmians deserved it though, didn't they? How could they kill so many in the Grand Mosque and Jermecida, it was a site significant to them as well. Ahmed frowned, uncomfortable and disgusted.

"Alhurah will punish those who have transgressed. He will be most merciful to the victims."

"But It should not have happened Mahad! I should have stopped it! Astaghfirualhurah, astaghfirualhurah."

"We must take this severe lesson with care. We will punish those responsible. Ahmed, am I right?"

Ahmed jumped at his name, not expecting them to consult him. He considered his words. "I would face the ones responsible, inshalhurah. All who follow Alhurah would not hesitate to retaliate for this sin." Ahmed calmed at seeing the sultan smile, but Ahmed wondered how they'd determine who was responsible. Surely the Gurmian king held blame, but how many would they kill who had no part in the massacre in order to get to the king? Ahmed imagined killing Will, who was ignorant to everything. It didn't seem right.

"Surely Al-Motros is ours again, and Halsburg?" Master Mahad tried to bring up the mood.

"Mashalhurah!" The sultan nodded. "The Gurmians hold Croixville. I know you try to ease the stress off my shoulders Mahad but for every success there is another problem. The siege of Fort Valki is strengthening. A large Gurmian force may be able to take it."

"Their attacks continue as sure as ever, if something is not done soon an invasion will be imminent." Master Mahad frowned. It seemed desperate to Ahmed. Maybe waging war was the only way they could preserve their way of life. He'd not realised how dire it was, Alhurah help them.

"We could use an ally," Sultan Yazid said. "When there is in-fighting in Gurmanis some Gurmian lords would ally with us. King Duggan had quelled that division and has made such an option unlikely."

Ahmed raised an eyebrow. Ally with Gurmian lords? Why had he never heard of that? Before he met Will he would have thought the idea impossible.

"We need to send a forceful message; one King Duggan will understand." Sultan Yazid started. "The executions will do that. No matter how I may justify it, this act is cruel but I am left with few options."

Ahmed remembered seeing Kharija aflame from an airship attack. The pain of Ni'ja was deep and it had cut into him too. His people must be avenged; they must have justice. He had also seen Will's guilt in that moment, even though he had nothing to do with it. Vengeance and justice meant killing innocent people and it brought more suffering. Was that the only path? The executions were to include non-combatants. Were their deaths justified?

"Both kingdoms have been fighting for a long time. This war cannot last much longer," Master Mahad suggested.

"Ahmed, what do you say?" Sultan Yazid asked. Ahmed thought before answering.

"I think your plan sultan could be excessive." Ahmed gasped at himself; he was out of place.

"How so, young Ahmed?" The sultan's face tightened.

"Your plan proves to them that we are beasts. They have done similar things, they are the bestial ones, but those crimes will be forgotten when your plan takes fold. You could empower them to attack with greater violence." He couldn't believe he dared to disagree with the sultan's plan. In Murzq he had doubts too, but now he was more confident about those doubts. This plan seemed too far a step. As if agreeing with his assessment, Ahmed felt the warmth of his pearl.

"Or we could stagger and enrage them, forcing them to deplete everything they have left. I see this plan is vital." The sultan looked to Master Mahad for approval, but he looked to the side and scratched his beard.

"But is vengeance by blood, justice by blade the only way to end this sultan?" Ahmed heated up. Why did that come out of his mouth? "I-I never thought much of the reports that came to Murzq about the war, I was busy, but now it seems violence has only brought more violence. Gurmians are a warlike people but could they not be reasoned with?"

"We have tried that already." Sultan Yazid waved the suggestion aside.

"But you have not gone to King Duggan in person." The suggestion stunned everyone. Master Mahad looked between his apprentice and the sultan.

"You would advocate risking your sultan at the hands of the man who pinned the previous sultan, my father, to a wall and fed him to crows?" Sultan Yazid raised his voice and looked at Ahmed with fire in his eyes.

"S-Sultan I…"

"No Ahmed Sharfi, you do not understand what loss is nor do you know what you speak of. Be sure that we fight for our right to exist, and no matter in what form King Duggan will not agree to peace. Even if we had peace, could I face the soul of my father? Of the people martyred in this war? Men, women and children? No, I could not. I am their sultan and it is my responsibility to see justice served. We must punish Gurmians for what they have done."

Ahmed caught the warning stare of his master and looked down, silenced. He was a fool; he should not have spoken so personally about the sultan.

"It is settled then." The sultan stared hard at Ahmed, his eyes warning the boy. "You are not a leader Ahmed. You do not understand. As sultan, I have a responsibility to uphold Alhurah's law and provide protection, and I am failing at it. Nor do you understand what it is to lose a father... I-I won't ever forget what King Duggan did to him."

Ahmed stood. "I am sorry, sultan. I spoke too far out of turn."

"Forget it. There is another reason I called you Ahmed." Ahmed took his seat again. The sultan placed a letter on the table. "I received this a day before Ahmed came into the city. It tells me of spies in Ortie and worse than that, traitors. God curse those who dare aid Gurmanis in the murder of our people. I have shared this information with my rangers and tasked them with rooting out these spies and traitors. Ahmed, I want you to accompany the rangers, your words here have given me the reason for it. Bring me these enemies dead or alive and you will have my trust."

"As you command sultan," he vowed for he did not want the sultan to distrust him.

"I will also postpone the executions until this task is complete. I do not want these enemies to ruin my plan." The sultan stood followed by Ahmed and Master Mahad.

"Al-ḥamdu l-ilalhurahi rabbi l-ʿālamīn. God is with us in all our endeavors." The sultan excused himself.

"Your challenge of the sultan's plan was daring Ahmed but if we do not question the actions of our leaders then nothing can change." Ahmed nodded. "Let's go to bed now. I feel these next days will be significant for us all."

Chapter Twenty

WHEN THE SUN rose over Ortie, immediately after the first call to prayer, the city sprang to life. Ahmed led his horse from the stables to the courtyard. There he met the rangers, distinguished by their tan-brown uniforms with touches of green, a reflection of the arid landscape of Saomarhad. Ahmed approached the leader.

"As-salāmu alaykum," Ahmed greeted.

"Wa alaykumu s-salām," the leader answered. "You must be Ahmed. I am Aarif Ibn Vafa al-Zara leader for this mission. I s'pose you've been briefed on the situation?"

"There is a group of Gurmian spies in Ortie and they may be involved with a number of traitors in the city." Ahmed relayed the information he'd been given.

"Right, we have an informant in the souk who should lead us to these spies, inshalhurah. Are you ready?"

"I am."

"Good. Take this first." Aarif handed Ahmed a thin rectangular slab of wood. Carved into it was the seal of the sultan. "This gives you police-like authority. Since my superiors instructed me to give it to you, I trust you will be responsible with it?"

"Of course."

"Let's go then." Ahmed, Aarif, and his group of four rangers mounted their horses and rode into the city. As soon as they left the sultan's palace, dozens of people mobbed them. All around them, beggars, the infirm, orphans, and other desperate people, pleaded with the rangers for aid. Aarif ordered them back.

"Why are there so many?" Ahmed asked.

"All these people have little now because the war has taken much from them. This is not our concern right now. We must keep moving." The rangers and Ahmed broke away from the poor. They wove through crowds of people as they approached the souk.

The Ortie souk, an outdoor market, was broken up by long rectangular, stone vaulted and dome roofed buildings, arcades, in which merchants could sell their wares. It was the busiest place in the city both as the main center of business, and its location below the main mosque where crowds came to pray five times a day. The entrance archway was covered in an overhanging chhajja behind a courtyard decorated at the center with a shadirvan. As the group entered the souk Ahmed looked up into the vaulted ceiling of the arcade as a bird flew in through the open windows. He followed the bird to the ground where it snatched a scrap of food and flew off, away from the dense crowds. Along his left and right, shops and stalls were lined up in neat rows. Merchants called out what they were selling. Fabrics and carpets lined the walls and ceiling of the souk. Fragrant smells of exotic, multi-coloured spices dominated the air. Ahmed and the rangers dismounted when they could go no further on horseback. They left two rangers to care for the animals.

"Our informant sets up his shop in the main courtyard beside the sebil. You will know him by the faint smell of hashish," Aarif huffed.

"Hashish?" Ahmed raised an eyebrow.

"He is not a legal seller per say, but he does help the rangers and for that… well, you can be kept in confidence, right?"

"Of course. What kind of man is he?"

"You will see him soon enough." The group exited the crowds of the indoor section and entered the souk's main courtyard. At its center sat a large fountain, a sebil, playing host to bathing birds at its base, with stalls set up around it. A gap between the stalls provided access to protruding pipes, which dumped water into the base of the sebil. The courtyard was surrounded by the domed openings to more of the indoor sections. The flag of Saomarhad flew on top of the sebil and the dome of the mosque with its spires peaked out behind.

They came to a stop at a spice merchant's stall. On the table were uniform piles of various spices from all over the world. The man behind the stall wore robes of brown laced with yellow and his head was covered by a turban. Aarif merely rolled his eyes and commanded the man's customers to move, coming to a stop in front of him. The smell of hashish grew stronger now.

"Hello there, rangers! You must be eager to buy my aromatic spices from around the world, pushing through all my customers like that!" he said.

"Drop the act, Faris! We all know your spices are fakes." Aarif growled.

"Shhh! You will let my customers hear." Faris whispered.

"You make people very sick with your product. I should alert the muhtasib of this souk to your activities."

"Now, now, there is no need to get the police chief involved…"

"He would shut down your shop with one look at your spices… and when he finds your *other* wares, he would throw you in prison. Perhaps I should shorten the process and arrest you now."

"Easy! You do not need to be so harsh… and loud!" Faris looked around, casting fake smiles at his potential customers.

"Tell me what you found out!" Aarif demanded.

"Come with me, somewhere we can talk in private." Aarif nodded and followed Faris to one corner of the courtyard, signaling Ahmed to follow. They walked to a door, which Faris unlocked, and entered into a small room facing the courtyard through a window with latticed jali screen. Faris took a cushioned seat across from Ahmed and Aarif and removed the cloth around his head.

"Enough of this Faris. Why all the secrecy? What have you learned?" Aarif asked.

"You are looking for the Eyes of the King, these Gurmian spies. They are deeper within the city than we all thought. A Gurmian face even during war is not uncommon here, so it makes finding these spies difficult."

"Gurmian people are tolerated here? Aren't they our enemies?" Ahmed asked.

"Mainly merchants still operate in the souk and the harbor markets but a few dhimmis also exist," Aarif informed. "Go on Faris."

"My point is... I don't know where the spies are."

"You had one job to do Faris! Are you telling me that your worth has decreased?" Aarif glared at him.

"Calm good ranger, God may shroud some information from me but allows me to find other important things."

"What then?"

"Recently, the wealthiest merchant of this souk, Huzaifa-al-din ibn Waqas al-Ortie, nicknamed the merchant prince, has been receiving Gurmian guests not seen with him before."

"Huzaifa practically runs the souk and the Merchant's Guild."

"Yes, a powerful man. Since that meeting the souk has changed. The merchant prince's men have been seen guarding shipments of crates coming into and out of the souk."

"That is not necessarily suspicious," Aarif argued.

"It wouldn't be except I have tracked the origin of these crates. I snuck into the office of one of the merchant prince's lieutenants and found a document that indicates Huzaifa is getting the crates from Gurmanis."

"From merchants, yes. You said yourself it was common for Gurmian merchants to do business in the city."

"Except the men I saw with the merchant prince were no merchants. They seemed more like mercenaries. I checked with the Fighters Guild. There is no record, on the books, that Huzaifa obtained mercenaries. Many Gurmian merchants in the souk have recently become distant and nervous after these events. There was talk that a few had visits from Huzaifa's men."

"Very well, we will follow up on these leads. Though you haven't found the location of the spies you have provided us with some information of use. You have done well Faris, you will not spend your worthless, fraudulent life in a cell this time."

"I do all for my sultan as he is our protect—"

"Shut up, Faris! You lying fool!" Faris bowed and the three exited the private booth.

Aarif gathered his rangers together. "We will split up. Ahmed, you will go to the northwest section of the souk. I will go southeast and the others will take the other two directions. Walk among the crowds and get a sense for what has changed in the souk. Pay particular attention to the Gurmian merchants." The rangers and Ahmed parted to begin their investigation.

Ahmed walked through the wide domed corridors and open-air courtyards of the northwestern section of the souk. He weaved his way through the crowds of people and the lively discussions between merchants and their patrons. In fact, at least three different merchants tried to convince Ahmed he needed things he'd never needed before. Ahmed came to rest beside a pillar. He leaned back against it and observed the scene before him. Nothing seemed out of the ordinary. This section of the souk was mainly for domestic merchants so he wondered if that was why Aarif had assigned him this quarter. Maybe Aarif expected spies to be uncommon here, making things easier for him.

He noticed a group of muhtasibs at a stall further down the corridor on the corner of a crossroads. They were speaking with a Gurmian merchant at his stall and had him surrounded. The Gurmian was sweating, arms crossed and he broke eye-contact frequently when he spoke to the policemen. Ahmed approached the scene.

"Why are you not wearing your zunnar?" The lead muhtasib, identified by his taller bork hat than the others and kaftan over his lamellar armor, shook an orange-yellow linen belt in front of the Gurmian.

"Huzaifa-al-din does not mind. We are treated fairer by more people this way."

"Huzaifa's authority does not supersede the Pact of Caliph Umayyah ibn Kalil nor Sultan Yazid."

"I wear it outside the souk. Huzaifa is the merchants' patron, I was confused."

"Put it on now and there will be no punishment. Now, let me be clear, I won't tell you again. We have the authority to search your wares and we have already told you why, and we have the warrant for it, which we have already shown you. Step aside and let us search!" the lead muhtasib ordered.

"I have naught to hide, but my wares are delicate. I beg you, allow me to tour you through them so they do not break," the Gurmian pleaded. As Ahmed approached, he noticed the Gurmian was selling a wide selection of clay pottery. Ahmed walked up to the lead muhtasib and presented his wooden seal of authority. Better not talk of spies and traitors yet. "I am investigating things that have caught Sultan Yazid's attention. What has this man done?" Ahmed asked while the Gurmian fitted his zunnar around his waist.

"We received reports from other merchants about this new arrival. He's been seen selling more than clay pots and plates. Some say he's been selling weapons." The muhtasib turned to the merchant and glared at him. "That is a serious charge and he refuses to cooperate." Ahmed was taken a little aback. Aarif did not expect him to stumble into something so serious a charge as this right away. Dhimmis selling weapons during war was not a way for non-Alhurians to remain trusted.

"I told you I am only selling pottery. I don't have the connections or the funds to secure weapons. I am an honest man. I set fair prices, I treat all people well, and I pay the jizya on time. Talk to the merchant prince, his men can vouch for me."

"We are under the authority of the city. Huzaifa is not of concern in this investigation."

"If you have nothing to hide then why not cooperate?" Ahmed asked the merchant. The man scoffed.

"Tis a matter of principle. You are attempting to undermine my business by showing my fellow merchants an' customers a search that will damage my reputation. Furthermore, you will destroy my wares!"

"What if I search? I can do so without a scene or damage to your products."

"Who are you?"

"He has the authority of the sultan!" the lead muhtasib growled.

"I can use magic to sense items similar to your pottery. Anything dissimilar I can easily pinpoint." If the man had weapons their location would be obvious.

"This is not a negotiation." The muhtasibs stepped in between the merchant and his stall. "Do what you can." Ahmed stepped into the stall and took a hold of one of the clay jars.

"Bismilhurah," he whispered and focused on the material. Using magic, he sensed the minute details of the jar. Extending the magic, he closed his eyes and let his sense creep from one product to the other feeling through it the shape and texture of similar clay objects. He sensed vague grey shapes in the back shop. Most of them were pottery. The man had objects that felt like furniture, paper, ink, he had a bag with him, a sack of grain or was it animal feed? Nothing seemed out of place. His magic highlighted a false wall in the back but he could not see beyond it. It was too far and too thick. Ahmed opened his eyes and wiped the sweat from his brow. He put down the clay jar he held.

"There is a false wall in the back," Ahmed said.

"A what? You lie!" The Gurmian panicked. "There is naught of the sort."

"You go with him and search it," the lead muhtasib ordered one of his men. Ahmed and the police man entered the back shop and Ahmed pointed out the false wall. They pried it open to reveal a large rectangular crate. The two dragged it out to the front of the stall. Ahmed examined the sides and noticed a craftsman's marking on it. It was from Saomarhad according to the mark but it looked like it had been written over an older mark. Ahmed could not make it out. The visible mark had the initials 𝓂.

"I suppose this is more pottery?" the lead officer asked the Gurmian. The merchant fell to his knees and clasped his hands together.

"I have ne'er seen that before I swear!"

"Now we know why you were so nervous."

"I was nervous because you Saomarhadians have your bias against me an' my kin. I have heard the unfair treatment towards dhimmis especially of Gurmian ancestry. I pay all the taxes and I do honest work I swear. Have mercy," the man pleaded. The muhtasib scoffed.

"Pry it open." Two policemen pulled open the lid of the crate, pushing aside the tails of their turban helmets. Inside under the packing was a row of muskets with ammunition visible beneath. "You are under arrest for treason against Saomarhad. Seize him!" Two policemen grabbed hold of the merchant by each of his arms and pulled him up then away

"Let me go! I didn't know!" The merchant tried to pull away, forcing the muhtasibs to drag him.

The lead muhtasib turned to Ahmed. "Thank you for your help, young man. We should get these muskets back to the garrison and search the rest of the stall for anything else."

"I will need to know where this crate came from. There are rangers with me who will want to know too."

"If this concerns the sultan it goes much higher than a man illegally selling weapons."

"Something like that." Ahmed nodded.

The muhtasibs' tower was south and across the street from the souk connected to the market by a bridge. There, Ahmed and the rangers talked with the market police chief. Further examination of the crate and interrogation of the merchant revealed the merchant prince's men had told him to receive a shipment from the silk market. The merchant had refused and thought it would be the end of it. Ahmed felt bad about the situation because treason's punishment was death. Unless they could uncover information that would say otherwise, the pottery merchant did not have long to live.

Ahmed and the rangers rode around the south end of the mosque down busy small curving streets towards the silk market. The market was recessed behind the docks proper and wedged between buildings, in alleyways covered with wooden roofs built between the buildings. One courtyard was open to the sky with a modest sebil at its center where a girl fetched water for a cat. Aarif rode beside Ahmed, holding paper with the drawing of the craftsman's symbol and initials _JM_ on it. They dismounted and walked around a ninety degree turn into the silk market.

The market was a less decorated version of the souk with fewer stonework. The silks and carpets that hung from the walls and ceiling of the souk were more numerous here. It reminded Ahmed of the souk in Hamid, the one he had burned down during his awakening. Ahmed frowned. He kept his hands close to his sides. He did not want to make a mistake here, even if he knew he had improved in magic since he was that young.

"There is one weaponsmith who works at the docks. He's through the silk market and sets up shop near the arsenal. He can tell us who's symbol and initials these are." Aarif reasoned. The group exited the silk market onto the docks, a series of platforms connected by ramps and stairs leading to the water and wooden jetties. They turned south and approached the buildings that made up the north section of the arsenal. Facing this side were private houses, one of which held the weaponsmith's workshop. The Saomardrim man worked outside molding an axe head. When he noticed the rangers, he greeted them.

"Welcome. Can I help you?"

"We are here on the business of the sultan." Aarif showed the man the symbol and initials. "D'you know who's these are?"

"I have not seen this before. They're not local, that I know. They seem like something from Azuria I think."

"It was found on a shipment of muskets. Could this merchant have a ship sending them here?"

"He would be a rich weaponsmith. Either that or his work was transported with the work of others. There is one such ship, I just submitted an order to the captain for sale in Senenj. Maybe the ship came from Azuria, I can't remember."

"Where is the ship?"

"North, between the water and the wall of the zoo."

"Thank-you, you have been very helpful. God be with you."

"Anything for the sultan's rangers. God be with you as well." The rangers and Ahmed walked along the docks towards the north past workers, crates, cranes and alongside all manner of ships. The sultan's palace rose above the city in the distance. They spotted the ship as they approached and it was one of Aarif's men who noticed the three Gurmian men speaking with workers unloading the ship. Beside them were two of Huzaifa's men. Aarif acted quickly and split off the rangers. He went with Ahmed and the two discreetly approached the enemy rangers from a vantage point. Aarif took a seat at a bench and Ahmed made himself seem busy inspecting a pile of crates. The idea was to make themselves look like soldiers expecting shipments. The two observed the Gurmian men. When they finished ordering the workers, they turned to the merchant prince's men who escorted them aboard the ship.

One of them entered with the rangers while the other guarded the ramp. Aarif signaled Ahmed to sit beside him.

"The others will see if they can find more contraband unloaded on the docks. We need to get into that ship and see if there are more weapons inside."

"How will we do that?"

"I will distract the guard; it will be more convincing if I do it. He might laugh you off because of your age. Act like an inspector, youth in the police force and the army are put to similar tasks. Act the part and they won't be likely to second guess."

"I understand."

"If they leave, tail them, we will tail you." Ahmed nodded and took a position close to the entrance ramp. Aarif walked up confidently to the guardsman and greeted him. The man clasped the hilt of his sword.

"I am on the business of the harbor authority. This ship is not properly documented. Can you step aside and answer some questions?" Aarif ordered.

"Why did they send a ranger and not a policeman?" The guardsman raised an eyebrow and observed Aarif from head to toe.

"They are tightly staffed today. There is much happening in preparation for the executions of the Gurmian prisoners. I am helping out. I used to work here before the army." Aarif explained and the guardsman grunted.

"Then maybe you don't know whose protection this ship is under, Huzaifa-al-din. All has been taken care of so I wouldn't cross the merchant prince if I were you." Ahmed watched from his vantage point as the two talked. Aarif slowly took a few steps to the side forcing the guardsman to involuntarily turn to keep the conversation going. He was not looking at the entrance ramp. Ahmed took his moment and dashed forward and onto the ship. A few workers were scattered on deck but they paid no mind to the boy who looked like a soldier. Ahmed strolled below decks and acted like he was reading labels and checking papers. He noticed the Gurmian men and the other merchant prince's guardsman not too far away from his position. He could hear them speak.

"The weapons have all arrived," the guardsman spoke.

"Good." The talking Gurmian turned. His clothes were a little different and his lower lip and upper forehead had small cuts. Maybe he was their leader.

"I don't know why Huzaifa is allowing this. We are at war and this is treason."

"Is your merchant prince having second thoughts?" the leader asked.

"He awaits you in the center of the souk. Go and talk to him."

"Oh, we will go do that."

Ahmed smiled. He'd found the first traitor: Huzaifa-al-din, merchant prince of Ortie and leader of the city's Merchant's Guild. The Gurmians and the guardsman exited to the upper deck. As they passed, Ahmed retreated into the shadows and slipped out when they were out of sight. He observed the crates they had been looking at and noticed the symbol with the initials ⅋ on it. He shifted through the space looking over papers left on a desk. He found a scroll and unraveled it. Ahmed looked around to ensure no one was watching then leaned in to read. It was a ship manifest and Ahmed skimmed down the list of items the ship held until he reached a line that confirmed his suspicions.

30 crates of weapons. Stopover from Azuria, origin from Isenburg. Gurmian craftsman mark removed.

Huzaifa was importing illegal weapons from Isenburg in Gurmanis. He was bringing them in on his ships mixed with other cargo a few crates at a time. Those Gurmain men must be the spies.

Ahmed took the manifest with him and rushed out to the upper deck, following discreetly behind the three spies who were led by the two guardsmen towards the souk. Ahmed hoped Aarif and his rangers could see him as he tailed the spies and traitors back into the city. Through tight streets Ahmed blended with the crowd and followed the natural flow towards the souk being careful not to break line of sight. He followed them into the souk's hallways. People made room for the merchant prince's men and soon Ahmed found himself in a large central courtyard deep in the center of the souk. He sat on a nearby bench and using magic he extended his sense of hearing to where the spies waited while their escorts disappeared inside a building. A moment later a man wearing red, blue and green clothes lined in white and a white turban came out to greet them.

"Huzaifa, we finally meet." The lead spy shook the merchant prince's hand.

"God willing. His good fortune upon you," Huzaifa said.

"We do not follow your god."

"Sorry, it is habit. Perhaps you should for Alhurah bestows great boons on his faithful. He is worthiest of faith."

"The only boon we need is your cooperation."

"You have it in full ranger. Sultan Yazid drags on this war for no other reason than to seek vengeance. Revenge dries out the soul and drags he who seeks it to ruin. The sultan is the leader of my country and if he is ruined so is the country. My business would shatter if such a thing were to pass."

"Then what we propose is the only way. The word is spreading. Heralds turn the people's opinion against him. Only when he is gone can there be peace."

"I do not understand your aim. You would put King Duggan on the sultan's throne? I hear he wishes death to my kin."

"He wishes no ill will to your people. What you have heard are lies from the mouth of your wretched sultan. King Duggan is benevolent. He will liberate your people and there will be peace."

"I know that, you have already convinced me."

Ahmed had his confession.

"Get all the weapons in place throughout the city. When the time comes both Gurmians and Saomarhadians will need them. We can speak further inside." The two men retreated into the building leaving the remaining spies outside. Ahmed also noticed the increased presence of the merchant prince's armed men and not a muhtasib in sight. He was deep in Huzaifa's territory. Ahmed fled from his seat to inform Aarif and the other rangers.

People in the souk dove to the sides as nearly a dozen police men armed with spears, shields, swords, and bows rushed into position. People talked among themselves, wondering what all this was about. Aarif, Ahmed and the other rangers took position at the head of the column with the market police chief. They drew their weapons and the chief signaled his men to advance. From all sides, police rushed into Huzaifa's courtyard, surprising his men. He couldn't see the Gurmian spies.

"By order of the sultan, lay down your weapons and surrender. You and your leader Huzaifa-al-din are all under arrest for treason against Saomarhad. Surrender and we will not attack," the police chief ordered. The commotion drew the merchant prince forward. Huzaifa glared at the police chief.

"You have no right in my souk to threaten me and my men. I have command here, not you!" Huzaifa growled.

"This order is with the authority of the sultan, he who owns all this land. Surrender."

"You have no proof."

Aarif presented the manifest Ahmed had found. "This was found on your ship Huzaifa. It states that you imported weapons from Isenburg and removed the craftsman's mark from it, replacing it with one from a craftsman in Azuria."

Huzaifa looked around at the muhtasibs and the sultan's rangers, and at his own men.

"I have done nothing wrong. I deny these charges! I will surrender, then the truth will come out." He held up his hands and spoke loudly so that his men could hear. They sheathed their weapons.

"Where are your Gurmian friends?"

"They are long gone ranger."

"I am sorry Aarif." Ahmed frowned. "I tried to alert you as fast as I could."

"We will find them in time," Aarif reassured. "You betrayed the sultan, your own kin. The punishment for that will be death." Aarif glared at Huzaifa.

Aarif's men seized the merchant prince and pinned his arms behind his back. The muhtasibs seized Huzaifa's men.

"You think the Merchant's Guild will let that happen? I have powerful friends within and they will prove my innocence." Huzaifa laughed off the man's threats.

"Why? Why did you do it?" Ahmed asked. "You were smuggling weapons form Gurmanis and distributing them throughout the city using clueless Gurmian merchants in your souk to hide them, so they would be difficult to trace. Were you planning on a rebellion or are there more Gurmian sympathizers than we thought?"

"Ha! You are so ignorant of the situation boy. Forget about any sympathizers or traitors or spies. Worry about the people! Those who have suffered the murder of their loved ones and the exploitation of their livelihoods."

"Exploitation?"

"The sultan's men come and claim anything they want at no cost. For the war they say, for our protection. Some protection if the people are starving because they've taken all!"

"What d'you care for the common people? You are secure with your wealth," Aarif shot.

"Do you think me some self-entitled wealthy merchant who stands above his people? I hear the concerns of those in the souk, especially the dhimmi merchants who must suffer discrimination because people blame them for the war. Sultan Yazid maintains the Pact of Umayyah even when such things as wearing the zunnar has elicited attacks and discrimination against Gurmian dhimmis. I instead keep the peace with them. I involve them in the affairs of the souk. That is fair."

"Yet you used dhimmi merchants to hide your contraband."

"I did no such thing." A coy smiled stretched across Huzaifa's face. "Some dhimmis would beg for the chance to strike back at the sultan who does nothing end their suffering."

"But your wealth is threatened too," Ahmed said. "Should the sultan fall without stability your business would be dismantled in the chaotic aftermath."

"Nothing is so simple, boy. Look around! Business is already being dismantled." The man had a point. Ahmed hesitated. This war, he has seen, led to death, suffering, and uncertainty.

"The sultan wants to protect his people."

"Bah! By continuing to fight, he only promotes more violence and war."

"Get him out of here," Aarif grunted. Ahmed watched as the men dragged the traitor away. The sultan was aggressive and *did* want to continue to fight. He came partly from a place of anger, the fact he wanted vengeance for his father, but he also came from a noble place. He truly wanted to protect his people. It was also true what the merchant prince said about the dhimmis.

Ahmed remembered how the pottery merchant was so worried of discrimination and retribution from the muhtasibs. He did not need to worry about sympathizers, spies, or traitors? Were the people of Saomarhad so against the war that they would pick up weapons and rebel?

The east section of Ortie was a dense place of twisting maze-like streets, bridges and tunnels, and served as a residential quarter. Ahmed walked down a crowded street, under shade bearing fabrics, arches, and mashrabiyat towards a small city square. He climbed upstairs onto the upper terrace of the square. There a long rectangular howz fed by a small water fountain emptied into another howz on the lower terrace. Ahmed sat on a bench flanking it.

Once Ahmed had told Aarif and his rangers about the conversation between the lead spy and the merchant prince, Aarif had zeroed in on the fact that the spies were using heralds to turn the opinion of the people away from the sultan. He guessed if they could track down the heralds who were saying such things, they might discover more spies in the process. Ahmed was sent to search the residential quarter with two other rangers who weren't far, but they had split from each other to search more effectively. So far, Ahmed had heard a few men give speeches about how great this war was and how urgently the people needed to support the sultan, nothing traitorous, nothing going against the sultan's narrative.

Ahmed still had to admire the planning of the spies. It was increasingly being revealed they were arming the city and using its people as those who would go against the sultan. By controlling the narrative, they controlled the people's minds. Deep in this thought Ahmed barely noticed the herald, stepping up to the raised platform behind the upper howz, ready to give yet another speech on subject matter Ahmed had already heard so many times. A crowd gathered in front of him quicker than Ahmed expected.

The man's voice had a zealous tone and rung with conviction, "Hear me good people of Ortie, good people of our divinely favored land! I stand here to deliver to you a warning! The Gurmian king, King Duggan, is a tyrant and he will not stop until he sees us wiped from this world. If he takes more cities and if he advances deeper into our lands then he will continue until there are none left.

"I have heard your concerns! I have heard your protests! But this war has brought us much suffering and there has been much death and destruction. Why should we fight? Why should we not try for peace? Well, let me tell you that even if we try for peace the Gurmian king will never accept. He wants nothing more than to see us all dead! Our duty is to fight them in any way we can. Take up arms! Tend to your fields! It is our very existence we are fighting for!

"Gurmians have committed on our divine soil vile depraved acts of violence! God has cursed us for our inaction to respond! Curse the infidels for they go against the will of God! Let us drive them back and pray that this will please Alhurah and that his favor finds us and grants us victory!

"You say, how can this war be the will of God? How can more violence please God? I say that this war is an honour! Death in service to the lord, there is no greater glory! Be sure that this is a jihad we are fighting. This is a battle between asha and druj, truth and deceit! To stand on the side of asha we must avenge the barbarous acts committed by the Gurmians!

"Praise to the sultan for he has found the strength to fight against them! He is the man who we should all aspire to be. He is like Sultan Saadiq al-din who when Gurmians had almost destroyed us in the Holy Land, unified us and crushed the Gurmians by the will of God! Let Sultan Yazid lead you in jihad against the infidels, those bellicose, treacherous, and uncouth barbaric people. Let no one tempt you to give them quarter for you must resist the temptation that weaves itself unseen. Gurmians will either bow to our superiority or they will be put to the sword!"

The crowd cheered him and a few even pledged their services towards the war effort. Ahmed scoffed and looked away. This herald was not speaking against the war or the sultan, far from it. The afternoon dragged on and not a single person had spoken treason; Ahmed's eyelids grew heavy. The words of the zealous herald lingered in his mind, especially the descriptors he used for Gurmians. After having met Will, he had continued to wonder how true all those words were. Will had not been what he expected an infidel to be, far from it. He even tried to escape and Ahmed respected him for the attempt. It was Will's duty to do so and Ahmed held duty in high regard.

Ahmed turned back to the herald to check if he was going to say anything else. The crowd had fully dispersed and now gave way to regular traffic but through those people a new man approached and whispered to the herald. They exchanged something then the new man stepped away. Suspicious, Ahmed shifted in his seat as the herald started anew,

"Hear me good people of Ortie, good people of our divinely favored land of Saomarhad! I stand here to deliver to you a warning! This war will only continue if we do not tell our leaders we are sick of it. I implore you to pray to the lord for guidance in this matter. If you have heard as I have heard then you will know that Alhurah wants peace. Our leaders will only bring more war! These men will implore you to fight and die for no other reason than their greed. We should not curse the infidels; we should extend to them a hand of peace. We must recognize the good characteristics of the Gurmians! They are the most able to cope with tribulation, they are the quickest to recover from disaster, they return quickly to battle, and are the best at treating the poor, weak, and orphaned. Greatest of all they do not allow themselves to be oppressed by their kings as we have allowed our sultan to do!

"Let them see how great our civilization is and convince them to convert so that under Alhurah we may learn what good is in them! Show them the asha and clear from them druj. Against those who would continue this war pick up arms, the pen, or any other tool and show the sultan you will not continue to suffer!"

Ahmed shot out of his chair and looked around the square for the mystery man he'd seen. Mere minutes after the herald had spoken in favor of the war, he had changed his opinion. The man had been bribed right in front of him. Ahmed cursed his inattention. He caught sight of the mystery man as he exited the square onto a narrow street. Ahmed tailed him for several minutes, walking south, the crowds thinning until only a handful of people were present. The man stopped and turned, prompting Ahmed to move to the side and turn onto a side street. Satisfied no one was following him, the man continued and Ahmed continued to follow.

Ahmed followed him up a curving street flanked by wooden and fabric overhangs, stairs turning into smaller alleyways, clotheslines and lanterns hanging overhead, and mashrabiyat. On the curve of the street the man stopped, prompting Ahmed to move to the side. He waved up at another man and a woman on a flat roof.

The man turned a corner and a few seconds later Ahmed did the same, but all he saw was two adults walking down the street and two young beggars loitering in a doorway, a boy and a girl. Leading from this street, three others twisted in different directions; which street the man took Ahmed did not know. He scanned minds, searching for someone nervous or hateful or any state that would be a lead. He sensed tension in the beggars. Ahmed wiped his brow of sweat and approached the children.

"Did you two see a man turn off down one of those three streets just now?" Ahmed asked. The girl opened her mouth but the boy stopped her.

"The hungry don't give anything for free." The boy spoke through dry, cracked lips.

"The man I am looking for is a traitor to the sultan. If you know something, but refuse to say it, then you are defending a traitor…" The boy didn't seem to relent but looking at the worried expression of the girl, and the way she wrung her tattered abaya, Ahmed tried a different approach. "…Maybe she is working with him. That means she is a traitor too. She will be arrested, put in chains, and thrown in jail." Ahmed left out the fact traitors were executed; he did not need to scar the girl, but the girl's face lost colour and the boy held up his hands. Ahmed's mouth dried, guilt coming over him.

"O-Ok! I will tell you. P-Please don't take away my sister!" The boy nudged his frightened sister behind him.

"Why are you both here alone? Where are your parents?"

"Gurmians killed them. We've only been begging, I swear!"

"Calm down and tell me where that man went and I will let you two be."

"He took the road on the right, towards the eidgah."

Ahmed pictured the location, on the opposite side of the city. He dug into a pouch on his belt and produced some fulus. "Here take these," Ahmed offered. Calming, the boy accepted with a shaky smile. Ahmed couldn't look away from the girl. "I'm sorry… I have a very important task to fulfil." Ahmed smiled. The girl nodded.

These two in front of him were an example of the casualties of this war. With their parents gone, Ahmed could not imagine how their lives had been trying to survive on the streets. He could only guess the things the boy had done to protect and provide for his sister, a task he had no idea how to do properly perhaps. What had the girl done to keep them alive? Ahmed frowned; he wished he could do more for these children.

Ahmed took the street on the right towards the eidgah. The man turned into the dense residential neighborhood and Ahmed followed him into an intersection of four streets that formed an irregular rectangle with a tree in the center. The man stopped to bribe another herald before descending through an arch and into another square with numerous arched entrances and exits. A woman laughed, speaking to another from her window which looked into the square and the trees at the center. The sky was blocked off by a wooden covering spanning the space between the buildings and from which lanterns hung. The sun shone through the cracks.

The man suddenly turned around and looked back. Ahmed moved under an overhang, leaning in the shade. Gently weaving through people, Ahmed grew tired of keeping up. Despite seeing the second bribe Ahmed started to doubt he was following the right person. Through a narrow street he followed under clotheslines and shade-bearing fabrics. The man abruptly turned into an alleyway. Ahmed made the same turn and… he had vanished. Ahmed swore. He passed a street where one flank exited into a series of downward angled stairs and arches to the end which was more secluded. How could he have lost the man? He could not have fled so quickly.

He sensed a person. The individual was worried but determined and coming closer from behind. Ahmed spun around and flashed a pulse of magic at the man. He stumbled back, tripping over his thawb and dropping his knife. As he tried to regain his footing, Ahmed extended a length of rope nearby, and thrust them forward. The rope coiled around the man's waist, arms, legs, and neck binding him and pulling him towards Ahmed. He fell on his knees and looked up hopelessly.

"You're a…" the Saomardrim man started.

"I know," Ahmed cut in.

"You followed me! Who are you?"

"You bribed heralds into speaking ill of the war and the sultan. Who are you working for? Who told you to bribe the heralds and where are they?"

"I-I don't know anything about that."

Ahmed didn't like that answer. He wanted the straight forward truth. "Don't lie to me! You bribed the herald and then he changed his opinions. I can make you speak the truth!"

"You can't!"

"Who do you work for and where are they? What do you get out of spreading lies about the sultan?" Ahmed's anger was boiling beneath the surface now.

"The sultan is a mad man; his mind is no longer his own! He surrounds himself with men who keep him fighting this war. We need to depose him and start anew!"

"The sultan wants to protect his people; he told me himself. He has our best interests—"

"Best interests? How much grief has this war wrought? People are dying every day and our country becomes e'er weaker. Generations of young people have been thinned."

"If we do not fight then the Gurmian king will destroy us. Peace is not possible."

"Peace is possible if the sultan extends the branch but he will not."

"Why should he do that and not King Duggan?"

"Boyish logic, pathetic." The man spit at Ahmed but with fire in his eyes Ahmed waved his hand in front of his face and the spit fell short. Then funneling his anger into his right hand, a black fire ignited in his palms.

"I will MAKE you tell me!" Ahmed growled. He pushed his hand onto the man's forehead and chanted something he heard of vaguely, long ago in his studies.

"Zilyumi vitalif mrtallat," Ahmed chanted. In a second, the man began to scream. All the man's life absorbed into Ahmed; he tasted the addicting power. He enjoyed this. He did not grow tired; the magic he performed was self-reinforcing his energy, like this man's life-force re-energizing him.

Master Mahad's voice echoed through him, *Never Ahmed! Never! To control free will of any living thing is a path that will open what we call the Dark Magics. They are uncontrollable and dangerous. A dark mage must be purged straight away!'* Then a strange almost mute voice whispered to him from the back of his mind. For a moment, a calm and a rush of excitement took him over. He inhaled and realised what was happening, he was using dark magic. He felt a sudden quake as if Alhurah had noticed his misstep. Ahmed retracted his hand and collapsed on to the ground. His head pounded. Looking at his victim, who was cowering in front of him, Ahmed reached out but the man held his arm out and slid back. The bonds that held him were broken.

"Y-You stay a-away! I will tell you everything just let me go. I-I won't come here e'er again!"

"I am sorry I did not know what I did. You're hurt. Let me help."

"N-No stay away! I was sent by al-Haij Ziyad Sufran ibn-Ra'ed al-Ortie, chief scholar of Ortie. He leads the largest madrasa in the city and wants to spread the truth. He has restricted postal services and has banned certain types of books."

"Ok, but let me…"

"No! I am not…" He got up and ran out of the alleyway. Ahmed stood and looked down at his hands. What had he done? What could he do? He had never even thought he could use such magic. His actions opened a section of his brain, one that longed for him to do it again, No, he'd never.

Ahmed walked east and through a gatehouse towards the souk. Before crossing the river into the souk, he turned southwest and approached the madrasa, an impressive building. A shadirvan stood in the dark marble courtyard before the arched entrance carved into a large rectangular iwan flanked by two large domes for roofs. Tessellated designs decorated the walls broken up with more arches, windows, or overhanging mashrabiyat. Ahmed entered into the main room of the madrasa where scholars rushed around sorting books and scrolls into piles.

"Where can I find Ziyad?" Ahmed asked one of the scholars.

"Take those stairs up." The scholar pointed. "But Ziyad is in a meeting."

"Then I will return later." Ahmed lied; he had no intention of leaving. He approached the stairs seeing a worried scholar rush down towards him. When the man noticed Ahmed, he hurried forwards and handed Ahmed a book, looking back over his shoulder to ensure no one was there. Stunned, Ahmed looked at the book's cover. A round object, like his pearl was engraved on the cover, with a four-pointed, diamond inlayed, star overtop the circle, and a flame engraving burning out of the top of the symbol. It was the symbol on the relic box from Al-Motros.

"Take that out of here, quickly! Get it to the grand vizier if you can." He spoke hurriedly, eyes pleading with Ahmed to go.

"What is this?"

"Ziyad has gone mad! He won't let anyone keep at least one copy." The scholar spoke with disappointment in his voice. "It is an ancient text, written in an archaic language and the results of my efforts for research ordered by the grand vizier. He must have it."

"My friend." A calm voice addressed the scholar from behind. The scholar turned to face Ziyad. Flanking him were four janissaries. Janissaries used to be an elite royal guard, like Sultan Yazid's Immortals. Now, the janissaries protected scholars, and religious affairs. Ahmed tensed, fighting such elites were beyond his skill and he'd have to if Ziyad was the traitor and he realized Ahmed shouldn't be here.

"Friend? You do not listen to me Ziyad! Why have you ordered the destruction of all this knowledge?"

"Because these texts, un-regulated as they have been under Sultan Yazid, can be dangerous. It is from these works zealous people convince us to fight a jihad against the Gurmians and thus continue this war. It is from these works Sultan Yazid is emboldened and finds justification for his want of vengeance at the expense of hundreds of lives. They must be destroyed, all of them," Ziyad spoke with passion.

"But much of these books and scrolls contain great wisdom recorded from our ancestors. This we do not repeat because we know of them now. Things that inform us about our future because we read what comes before. These works can bring peace," the scholar urged Ziyad to reconsider.

"By the time the common people understands such a notion, the primitive passages that promote violence and justify vengeance and jihad will have infected them. By then you cannot change their minds and they will become extremists. I too am saddened by this, but it is a necessary price to pay for a chance at peace."

It pained Ahmed hearing the potential destruction of any knowledge.

"You only wish to control the narrative!" the scholar raised his voice. "I have heard how you manipulate the flow of information in the city. You restrict the post and have your closest scholars review private letters only to destroy those you do not agree with. You spread propaganda through posters and heralds such that it turns the people to your whim. What do they speak of, the posters and the heralds? What are you trying to accomplish? You are bordering on treason, my friend! What happened to you? Before you cherished knowledge and now you destroy it." Some of the scholars around them looked their way, Ziyad noticed.

"It is a necessary task. None of you even stop for a moment and think about what you hear or read. You assume each word is the ultimate truth and never ask yourself where it is from or who has written it and why. If we want an end to the war then we must control the narrative and steer people in the right direction."

"D'you hear yourself? This is wrong!"

"I thought you of all people would understand. I was wrong it seems. Seize him." Two janissaries strode forward and each took hold of one of the scholar's arms. They pinned them behind his back.

"Wh-What is this? What are you doing?"

"You've betrayed the sultan my friend. I was shocked to hear that you stole quite a number of the palace's records when you last—"

"God curse you! I have committed no such thing!"

"That's not what the evidence says."

"You forged evidence. Ziyad you've gone mad!" The scholar struggled against his captors.

"Take him to the shurta." Ziyad ordered the janissaries. They nodded and dragged the resisting scholar away. "Return to me at the eidgah where we will put an end to all the dangerous texts in the city." The chief scholar finally noticed Ahmed. He brought a hand forward. Ahmed stared at him, hesitating. "The book, son." Ahmed looked at the book his master wanted, the one that might say something about the relic, maybe even his pearl. He didn't want it destroyed but if he defied Ziayd then his janissaries might dispose of him too, and Aarif had to know that he'd found the second traitor. Ahmed clutched the book tight and reluctantly brought it forwards. Ziyad took it and smiled.

"Join us in the eidgah son. Learn the truth."

"I will t-try to… sir." Ahmed nodded then fled the madrasa without another word, his heart thumping against his chest.

The shadows cast by the buildings of the city grew long to the east now that the evening brought some small measure of cooling. Ahmed had informed the rangers of what he'd learned and was told that heralds were inviting citizens to a bonfire at the eidgah. Ahmed followed the rangers under a horseshoe arch and the riwaq arcade into a wide-open sparsely green courtyard surrounded by the riwaq. Ahmed realised how he had missed places like this, coming here with his family when it held thousands of people for elaborate ceremonies and festivals.

Now dozens of people were crowding the center where a large bonfire roared and several scholars threw books and scrolls into it. There was a nervous unease among the people. The scholars accepted more books and scrolls from the members of the crowd and tossed them into piles to the side, which Ahmed assumed were destined for the fire. He scoffed. How could such learned people as the scholars of Ortie, the chief scholar included, commit to destroy so much knowledge, to destroy any knowledge. Most of his life thus far had been in study, to value it and to respect it. To see what these scholars were doing now sickened him.

The rangers and Ahmed pushed through the crowd. Aarif ordered his men to spread out so that they surrounded the bonfire. He nodded to Ahmed and pointed at him to take a spot near the front. Ahmed nodded back and took his position. He made a brief glance at the entrance to the eidgah. There a number of shurta filed in. Aarif must have known interrupting this bonfire might send the crowd into a panic and rightly figured he and his rangers would need backup to control the scene.

Ziyad strode forward with his two janissaries at his sides. He walked onto a raised step to address the crowd.

"I am glad so many of you have heard my most urgent call and have come here to rid yourselves of sinful and hurtful knowledge." Ziyad began his speech. "I see the look in your faces and I can hear the uncertainty in your voices. You have been taught such destruction is disrespect to the wisdom that might be contained in these volumes. I understand and you can take comfort in knowing that I do not do this lightly. I have read these texts and I know they contain not the wisdom of our ancestors but the words that encourage us all to pursue violence, war, and jihad.

"Some among you may even think jihad against Gurmanis is ordained. I do not fault you, for in this war Gurmians have committed many atrocities.

They are animals, barbarians who know only the way of violence. Their land is cold, dark and disfavored by God. We should pity them!"

"Pity? No. We should curse them! They have burned our farms and our homes; they have raped our wives and daughters and they want only to eradicate us!" a man shouted from the crowd. The rest of the crowd shouted in agreement. Ziyad held up his hands for silence.

"Are we not the people chosen by God? Is our land not divinely protected? Are we not superior? Then I ask how could God let our wives, sons, and daughters, our brothers and sisters fall to Gurmian swords?" He tried to persuade them but the crowd mumbled unsurely.

"We have erred in the eyes of God!" a veiled woman answered.

"Perhaps, but that is not what I have seen. I have seen our people flawless. Am I not your chief scholar? I speak with the authority of truth!" Ziyad continued. The crowd continued to mumble. "No, what I see is that God has sent us these poor Gurmian barbarians as an opportunity. We have been given a chance to guide them to God, to show them how to live peacefully and civilly. There is potential. Some of these infidels have culture even we must credit them with. Some of them follow the rule of law, not a sultan's whim as Sultan Yazid would have us do. Some have economic skill even we could learn from and slavery is largely minor in their lands so as to have all free and pleased men. They have good characteristics among their faults. Let us expand from this potential and show them the proper way of living so they are no longer ignorant."

"But the books? Why burn the books?" a man asked.

"Ignorance is not only the lack of knowledge but also the learning of incorrect knowledge. These texts speak words not of understanding but of hate. They would encourage us not to make peace with Gurmians and teach them the proper way but instead they would teach us to be like our sultan and lead us into endless jihad. Sultan Yazid is a man filled with hate. He would have law be replaced with his command alone and with it he will ensure all of us and our offspring would continue to fight and die. His quest for vengeance has made him ignorant. Today, those of you here reject our sultan. Once we open our doors for peace, for those we once called our enemies, only then we will be free."

Most of the crowd seemed to cheer in agreement but Ahmed could sense the tense unsure state of those closer to him. Not everyone agreed with the chief scholar. Ahmed did not agree either. Ziyad left out the fact Sultan Yazid's father was savagely killed and his body humiliated by King Duggan. Sultan Yazid had a personal reason for vengeance yet the sultan was a leader of a sultanate and Ahmed knew all his actions would affect many people. Was it right then for the sultan to put his personal vengeance ahead of protecting his people? The impending mass execution of the Gurmian prisoners-of-war never sat well with Ahmed. He was convinced it would cause more problems than it would solve. But then again, Gurmanis refused to negotiate and refused to cease their attacks. Could the sultan really outrage them into surrender, it didn't make sense.

Ahmed took a deep breath and clasped his sword hilt. He waited for the signal from Aarif. One loud whistle threw the rangers into action. Along with Ahmed, they pushed through the crowd to the front and drew their swords, surrounding the bonfire and preventing any escape for the scholars. Their sudden action quieted the crowd and alarmed the chief scholar. His janissaries drew their swords and took a fighting stance. Shurta rushed forward to push back the crowd and obtain order.

"Ziyad Sufran, Chief Scholar of Ortie. You are under arrest for treason against Sultan Yazid. Surrender peacefully."

"Look everyone; see how our sultan suppresses concerned voices. By threatening me you threaten peace, ranger." Some people in the crowd shouted and advanced on the shurta.

Ahmed watched as in a matter of seconds the crowd revolted. It had been too quick, too easy. Did Ziyad seed the crowd with armed men? He'd known about Ahmed and the rangers' task! Chaos erupted in the eidgah. The crowd broke free of the shurta and charged the rangers. In the mess of fighting Ahmed caught sight of Ziyad rushing to the west end of the eidgah with his janissaries. He shouted at his men and pointed to the crowd. Some janissaries surrounded the chief scholar, keeping people back. Ahmed pushed past the fighting, casting pulses of energy to shove people aside. He broke free of the rioters and advanced on Ziyad.

"You were in the madrasa." Ziyad scoffed. "A soldier perhaps, but a mere boy. Do you know who stands in front of you?"

"I-I know who they are." Ahmed shifted, trying to hide his apprehension. Two janissaries put themselves between Ahmed and the chief scholar and leveled their yatagan swords at him. Ahmed realised his foolishness; he'd separated himself from the rangers. He couldn't take on one let alone two. Ahmed didn't get a chance to call out to Aarif. The janissaries advanced on him. One swung at his side. Ahmed blocked with his kilij and countered with his axe. With expert precision, the janissary countered, making a motion to strike Ahmed's leg. Then the other janissary attacked from the right flank. Ahmed corrected to block the new attack then dodged the other. The janissary had feinted and Ahmed dodged right into a strike to his arm. The yatagan bounced off his armor. Ahmed backed away. One janissary attacked his left while the other drew a pistol and made ready to shoot. Ahmed cast a pulse of energy which pushed both one janissary and the approaching bullet back. He cast flame at the pistol wielding janissary, but to his surprise the janissary blocked the fire with his yatagan. Ahmed noticed specks of enchantment pulse on the man's weapon.

"Ahh, you're a mage. It makes no difference," Ziyad taunted.

One janissary swung at Ahmed's neck. Ahmed parried and attacked his side. They traded a few blows, the last cutting Ahmed's flesh. Ahmed grunted and backed away to block the attack of the other janissary. He traded not a half blow before the second janissary attacked his flank. Ahmed blocked the first strike and was cut by the second. He jabbed at the janissary and rushed him with his axe. The man tossed the sword aside and let the axe bounce off his armor. A pistol shot sounded. Ahmed cast out a shield of ice that shattered the moment he cast it, being hit by the bullet. He threw the shattered shards at his enemies. A few hit their armor but nothing more. Sweating Ahmed fell back.

"It's over. Finish the boy," Ziyad growled at his men. Both janissaries advanced. Before Ahmed could react, they ripped his kilij and axe away, pushed him onto the ground, stepped on his hands, and pointed their pistols at his head. Ahmed screamed in pain and looked hopelessly at the elites. Men rushed forwards, engaging the other janissaries. One ranger was shot in the stomach as he attacked, the other pistol shot flew into the air. The rangers cut down the janissaries, overwhelming them. Ziyad fell to his knees in shock and rangers leveled their swords at him. Aarif helped Ahmed stand and two other rangers tended to their dying companion.

"No, it can't end like this. I had so much more to do," Ziyad spat.

"More books and scrolls to burn? Propaganda to spread?" With your words off these streets the people will not be poisoned any longer," Aarif said.

"Poison? The sultan's words are poison. If my words are poison then it is the lesser poison."

"All you have done is exactly what you claim the sultan has done. Like him you spread propaganda."

"Yet I would suggest peace. By controlling the narrative, I safe-guarded all who turn towards the qibla, I attempted to. Sultan Yazid cannot claim the same."

"You have no respect for the texts you burned and the wisdom they had." Ahmed scoffed. "You of all people know their value."

Ziyad laughed. "I could not part with that knowledge. I did not burn any of them."

"But we saw…"

"False texts, blank paper, meaningless scribbles. The text we took from the crowd? Piled up to be sealed away not burned. Many demanded violence, not all but in all of them there was wisdom. Peaceful words alongside passages easy to take wrongly and out of context. I could not destroy them."

"Take him away," Aarif ordered.

Chapter Twenty-One

A LINE OF SHURTA held back the crowds gathered outside the madrasa, who watched the scene unfold with curiosity and confusion. More shurta walked out with boxes of books and scrolls, others escorting shackled scholars.

Aarif had ordered a raid of the madrasa to discover if there were any other plots the chief scholar had planned. They had almost left with nothing until a ranger discovered a letter of some importance. Aarif had agreed and Ahmed found the letter in his hands. He read it;

Ziyad,

God's favor to you this day. Take this as your invitation to my party held at my Ortie estate. All the nobles within the city have been invited. With their wealth under my control, this war will be driven in any direction we desire. I see this as the will of God and the only path to peace. I await your arrival.

Mehmet Özbey

Ahmed folded the letter and returned it to Aarif as he finished explaining its contents to his rangers.

"This letter clearly shows Ziyad is in league with Mehmet. We have to get into that party if we are to discover what his plan to take Ortie's nobles' wealth is," Aarif said.

"Who is Mehmet Özbey?" Ahmed asked.

"The wealthiest man in Ortie and an influential Oghurk. He gained his fortune because his family has always been in close confidence with the sultans, past and present. His family line has suffered; however, he once had many brothers and sisters, aunts, uncles, and cousins but they have all since died. He had a wife but she died when they found themselves trapped in a Gurmanis siege."

"Then this war has hurt him very much."

"Yes. It could be a motive for treason, how strong I don't know."

"We'll call upon our noble contacts for access into the party," a ranger suggested.

"I am not well known in Ortie and my family does not have a strong sway here," Ahmed added.

"Nor do you have an invitation, Ahmed," Aarif said. "Calling our contacts may alert Mehmet to our plans as is why simply demanding entry in the name of the sultan would do us no good."

"God's grace upon you." The shurta chief approached the rangers. Aarif returned a similar greeting. "I bring information. We have a prisoner who was brought in by janissaries accused of burning the sultan's palace's records. It came from the chief scholar but seeing as he is a traitor, I don't think the charges against our prisoner hold up any longer."

"Who is this prisoner?" Aarif asked.

"A scholar. He told us he was sent by Ziyad to obtain a reservation for Hammam Alqibat Aldahabia early this week."

"How is this important?"

"Well he told us Ziyad was intent on going to a party and stressed how much he needed to get ready for it. I thought I should bring this information to you. Here's the reservation slip." The police chief handed Aarif the slip. The lead ranger looked over it then looked up to his rangers.

"Hammams are more than bathing houses, they are also places of social gatherings and as we know, such places are full of potential leads. I say we try this."

The rangers decided that Ahmed and a ranger slightly older than him would enter the hammam as friends. Hammam Alqibat Aldahabia was the most upscale bathhouse in Ortie. Intricate stonework, large, open golden-domed spaces, silks hanging from the walls and the ceilings, carpets, cushions, hookahs; it had everything one needed to detach from the outside to take the most luxurious bath or meet the wealthiest of people. The feeling of only the faintest familiarity grew in Ahmed as he acknowledged that he was still getting used to the luxury he'd lived in before attending the mages university.

Ahmed and his 'friend,' Parvez, walked through the front door and entered into a Qa'a, a reception room, surrounded in an intricate arcade, and with a fountain at its center. They had left their weapons and armor with the others and donned noblemen's kaftans. A man on the other end of the Qa'a, sitting at a reception desk, stood. He turned and ducked his head behind a curtain, calling to someone behind it, then strode towards the boys and bowed. Ahmed used a measured, purposeful tone. It was agreed he would do most of the talking, as the noble boy.

After presenting their reservation slip, modified to accommodate its new owners, the boys were taken deeper into the hammam where slaves undressed them and offered them light drink and food. Parvez seemed to be enjoying the treatment more than duty required. With a towel wrapped around their bare body's lower half, they entered the first room, a large space where men lounged being fed, taking baths and socializing.

"We should split up," Parvez suggested. "I'll go right, you go left."

Ahmed nodded before walking to the left side and observing the scene. They were looking for anything that could help them gain entry to Mehmet's party or at the very least find information about what it entailed. Ahmed stopped at the edge of a pool and looked at the water. He didn't fancy getting wet right now, even though submerging himself in the water and having slaves bathe him was a tempting thought. Instead, Ahmed took a seat along a wall on a low cushion. A cat came up to him and rolled onto its back, stretching. Ahmed stroked its fur as it purred with content. The fastest way to do this task was to listen to many people at once, he figured. Ahmed sat back against his arm, stretched his legs, and closed his eyes. He whispered a spell;

"Sakkhuaya, hear vitalif." The volume of every person on his side of the room increased. He reigned the spell in, not wanting it to extend further and risk tiring himself.

Many men talked about the war, some about work they oversaw. Others talked about their families and a few engaged in inappropriate talk. Ahmed overheard a group of boys sitting in a nearby pool. They mentioned the upcoming party. Most of the nobility here seemed to know about it and were going. What was he to do? Single one out and force him to give them an invitation? Ahmed could gleam little else from the conversations other than the invitations had included lavish gifts. That was not usual. Perhaps Mehmet was ensuring few would decline his invitations.

Ahmed ended the spell and opened his eyes. A slave offered him a drink and Ahmed took it, but before he drank he spotted Parvez wave at him then walk into another room. A lead? Ahmed stood and followed him into a smaller room where a single hot water pool sat under a large domed ceiling. Ahmed brushed aside translucent silks and spotted Parvez lounging in the water. He signaled Ahmed to come forward. Frowning, he'd have to get wet, Ahmed walked over into the water, settling in beside Parvez.

"Enjoying yourself?" Ahmed teased, knowing the boy was enjoying the moment.

"More than you will e'er know." Parvez smiled.

"I'm sure."

"Keep your voice down." Parvez discreetly motioned to a man in his late twenties

Attending to four other men submerged in the pool. He seemed joyful, laughing loudly.

"Who's he?" Ahmed asked.

"One of those men just offered him an invitation to Mehmet's party. He's some minor lord who didn't get an invitation. He wants to make connections at the party."

"So he's our way in."

Parvez nodded. "You follow, I'll tell Aarif."

Ahmed followed the young nobleman through the noble district towards a park in its northwest. He entered the park not far behind his target walking right to a howz at the center. From his vantage point, he could walk directly north, west, or south along the sides of three small canals to three of the four divisions of the park each hosting a variety of trees and colourful floral designs. Sections of the park intertwined indoors and outdoors spaces through courtyards and archways.

Not wanting to lose track of his target, Ahmed stayed close to the path he took going into a secluded section of the park cornered off with jali screens. He watched the young noble wait at the center of a sheltered courtyard as if expecting someone. Ahmed hid nearby behind a jali obscured with plants and vines. A woman wearing a caerulean niqab rushed out to greet the young noble. They hugged then the man pulled away the covering on the woman's face to reveal, to Ahmed's surprise, a Gurmian woman. The two kissed.

"What happened? Did you get it?" the woman asked.

"I did. This will be the chance we need to bring credibility to my family name; then we won't have to live in the shadows like this. With influence back in my hands I can keep any ire off of us."

"I don't want to continue to hide like this."

"It won't be long. I know the people I need to talk to at this party. I know what to say. Do you not trust me?"

"Of course." The two kissed again. Ahmed stepped out of his hiding place and confronted them.

"Stop," Ahmed ordered. The two turned, wide-eyed. They noticed Ahmed's armor.

"This isn't what it seems," the young nobleman said. He stepped in front of the woman who clutched his right arm. "I will not let you part us soldier. I know this is unseemly. Have mercy."

"She is Gurmian. She is the enemy."

"Not her, especially not her. We love each other and we only want to live in peace. You are young, surely you can understand that."

"I can't say I can."

"Why does it always have to be them and us?" the woman shouted. "We want to live our lives here. We are no enemy of yours. We wish not to choose a side. We want to be left alone. It is not our fault that our kingdoms are at war, we had no control over deciding that." The man put his right hand across her.

"I will fight you. I won't let you take her." The woman squeezed the man's arm tighter.

"Before that, and before the rangers with me arrive, perhaps you could tell me about this first. How does a Saomardrim noble fall in love with a Gurmian woman during a war?" Ahmed was curious about this.

"She was captured and bought by my family as a slave. We fell in love and I took her from my home because my family would… could never accept this. I did not care. I married her. She was unlike anything I could imagine."

Ahmed sensed the man's sincerity. It impressed Ahmed more than anything. With all the things he'd been told about the savage Gurmians he had not expected anyone to fall in love with one of them. He thought of Shoran who he freed from slavery. He didn't love Shoran like these two loved each other, but similar emotions must have driven both actions.

Aarif and the other rangers stormed into the sheltered courtyard behind Ahmed. The man and woman tensed. The young nobleman threw up his arms.

"Please have mercy! In God's name let us be."

"That depends how loyal you are to your sultan," Aarif spoke. He stood in front of his rangers and Ahmed to face down the man.

"I don't understand. We have done nothing wrong. We are loyal to the sultan. Did my parents hire you to bring me back? I will not go. She is mine and we will build up our own life if father and mother cannot accept us."

"The party. Talk."

"The party? Of course, I want to go to the party. Did you see me convince that older nobleman to give me an invitation? Of course, you did, you followed me from the hammam. They say all of Ortie's nobility will be there. It's the perfect opportunity to make connections."

"What else do you know?"

"What do you mean what else?" The young nobleman crossed his arms and frowned. Aarif sighed.

"He knows nothing. It's a trap. Mehmet wants all of Ortie's nobles in one place so he can steal their wealth to fund treason against the sultan."

"We know nothing about this. It seems very unlikely."

"But it is likely. We demand your invitation in the name of the sultan."

"This is unacceptable! You can't accost me and take what is mine like this."

"I won't hesitate to lock you up. Think about what would happen to your wife then. She'd be sold back into slavery."

Ahmed looked up at Aarif. He was being heartless. "Wait," Ahmed interjected. "We need that invitation and you need to get into that party. Mehmet may very well be a traitor and dangerous. Will you still go to his party?"

"Yes. It is my only chance."

"Then we can compromise. Help us get into the party. I will go with him as... as your cousin. I am of noble birth as well; I can act the part. Is that acceptable?" The nobleman looked from Ahmed to Aarif.

"It is acceptable if we act as his servants," Aarif said. "We need to control the situation."

"This may be better. I will enter looking of greater wealth. I accept."

"Not so fast," Aarif huffed. "We need to ensure your trustworthiness. Ahmed will stay with you from now until we are in the party and I will have some of my rangers stay with your wife, just in case."

"You rangers are nothing more than thugs," the nobleman scoffed.

"We are genuine," Ahmed tried to convince him. "We need to prevent a treasonous danger, to save people."

"Yes, well you have an odd way of showing it."

<hr>

The nobleman rode at the head of a small column with Ahmed riding beside him both finely dressed and groomed. Behind them, Aarif and two rangers walked on foot wearing simple clothing. Parvez walked ahead of everyone holding a lantern to light the way through the growing night. They'd left Ortie and travelled north to the coastal manor on the rise ahead of them. When they arrived at the manor grounds they navigated through a wide-open garden towards the front door. A line of nobles waited to enter the party. The nobleman and Ahmed approached when it was their turn.

"Welcome to the manor of Mehmet Özbey. Invitations please," the guard blocking entry spoke.

"Yes, here it is." The nobleman presented the invitation and the guard looked it over.

"How many in your party sir?"

"Six."

The guard looked everyone over. "You are allowed three servants max." The nobleman glanced briefly at Aarif who nodded.

"Very well. Any three of you, follow," the nobleman waved his hand. Aarif, Parvez and a third ranger followed the nobleman and Ahmed inside. They walked through a Qa'a and into a large courtyard with a bar in one corner and an elaborate fountain in the center. The entire courtyard was surrounded in riwaq and one end had a balcony overlooking the party below. Tessellations of gold, blue, green, and purple decorated the walls alongside similarly colored fabrics. The space was packed with noble partygoers, their families, and their servants as well as a number of female dancers. Ahmed also noticed there were more guards than might be necessary standing around the edges of the courtyard and in the balconies above. A string instrument, tambur, played an upbeat tune accompanied by the smooth flowing sound of a ney flute and the pounds of a küdüm drum.

"I have done my part. You are in," the nobleman whispered. "Don't think to leave without me. I want my wife freed."

"You have my word. Do what you came here to do but be careful. As we said, Mehmet might be planning something dangerous."

The nobleman huffed then walked into the crowd. Ahmed walked through the party as well. A server tried to hand him a non-alcoholic drink, but he put a hand out to dismiss it. Then he was accosted by a female dancer wearing thin silks that conformed to her body, but Ahmed dismissed her and found a pillar to lean against and wait. That was all he could do right now. He would wait to see what would happen and look for any signal Aarif gave… if he could find him again in this crowd.

Later, Ahmed looked up at activity on the upper balcony where Mehmet Özbey as well as a handful of his armed guards walked out in view of the party. People noticed and cheered. Mehmet held up his hands to silence them with a smile on his face. The man was a large, stout forty-something nobleman. His full beard was neatly trimmed and his clothes were purposefully overelaborate as was his large turban.

"Welcome my most esteemed guests!" Mehmet was given a goblet and he held it up to the crowd. "Drink all of you! Tonight, we must enjoy all the fruits God has blessed upon us!" Everyone cheered and drank. "Tonight, is a special night, no, it is a historic night! Tonight, we lavish in luxury while blood is spilt in the name of God and of the sultan with the dinar you all provide." This got a mixed reaction from the crowd. Ahmed shifted.

"Why the confusion? Is it not your wealth that funds and fuels this war? Do you not relax in your townhouses and manors while countless others fight and die against the infidels? Come now, don't make me a liar! I have seen and I have heard of the dealings the capital's most wealthy make. Dealings that secure your own status and wealth while the rest of the sultanate falls to ruin. I say enough! I say we fund peace. Let us invest in people." The crowd laughed and jeered.

"People? Are you insane? The common people are uneducated rabble," someone shouted.

"You kill the mood Mehmet!"

"You betray the sultan! He knows what is God's will and what is right," a third shouted.

"Peace with the infidels? I'd rather fight them myself!"

"Ah but you won't, will you?" Mehmet laughed. "You speak as if you are strong but in reality, you are impotent and a liar. All of you are hypocrites! You talk of war here but later you will talk of peace when it suits you. You speak of supporting the sultan but you will make a deal or two with a Gurmian lord if it seems the sultan's armies can't conquer the lands you wanted. Afterall, that is what all of you want is it not? You want Gurmian lands that would come from victory in this war so you can gain more wealth."

"Says the wealthiest man in Ortie!" someone shouted followed by the crowd jeering and laughing.

"Yes, and I have seen the error in my ways. The sultan is corrupt and wishes to continue a war that brings nothing but death and suffering funded by all of you who also jump at the first opportunity to betray if it suits you!"

"End this party Mehmet! We no longer wish to stay under your roof." The crowd murmured in agreement.

"Ah but all your plotting must end today. This is why I have called all of you here. Right now, I have mercenaries scouring your homes. They will seize your wealth, and maybe they will also find evidence of your treason. Some I did not even need to falsify. Come morning it will be revealed the wealthy and the noble of Ortie were planning to overthrow Sultan Yazid all along."

"Enough of this!" An agitated noble turned and stormed towards the exit only to be stopped by a guard. More guards rushed out and blocked all venues of escape.

"You cannot leave from here until this righteous work is done. Willingly forfeit your wealth to me. That is the only way the sultan will hear of loyal nobles come light tomorrow." A guard handed Mehmet a vial of blue liquid and he presented it to his guests. "You have all consumed poison. Its effects will start to torture you in half-an-hour. How long will you suffer until you sign over all your wealth to me?"

The crowd shouted, terrified at the words spoken. A noble spit at Mehmet and drew a dagger. He was grabbed by one of Mehmet's guards and run through with a sword. Gasps and screams accompanied the man's fall into his own blood.

"I am serious. If you wish to remain loyal… and alive, do as I say. I have seized what you own anyway, accept it. I'd prefer cooperation for it is easier, however the decision is yours. It shall be a long night." Mehmet laid on a carpet and cushions on a raised section of his balcony and smoked a hookah seemingly unconcerned. The guests were in chaos. People shouted at each other, women and children cried and families huddled together. Ahmed scanned the courtyard for Aarif. He was interrupted by the ranger from behind.

"My two rangers who were not allowed in were instructed beforehand to sneak in," Aarif whispered. "They will bring more men. We will find his store of antidote, but it's up to you and Parvez to keep Mehmet's attention from us."

"How!?"

"Be bold," Aarif suggested, without much thought. He shrugged and strode off. Ahmed found Parvez. The boy had gone pale.

"You drank it, didn't you?" Ahmed asked. Parvez turned to him and nodded. "You couldn't resist?"

"Such a fine taste… I couldn't resist," Parvez admitted. "The suffering will be like a criminal's under Judeicar's Justice… I'm not a bad boy."

Ahmed sighed. "Hold on." Bold? What kind of instruction was that? He had to think of something. Ahmed looked at Mehmet lounging on his balcony unfazed by what he was doing. How could a man be so unapologetic? Ahmed gripped his hands into fists. Mehmet spoke of how wealth drove this war but he was plotting to take all this wealth. What was he going to do with it? Was he going to end the war with it? Did he think he could bribe Sultan Yazid to forget about his father's murder? Then Ahmed got an idea. If bold was what Aarif wanted, bold was what he would get. Ahmed strode to the balcony and glared at Mehmet.

He shouted, "Mehmet Özbey! I want to surrender my wealth to you!" Ahmed waited as Mehmet looked at him and nodded. Two guards approached Ahmed and pointed the way up. He ascended a flight of stairs onto the balcony and stood in front of Mehmet. The man offered Ahmed a seat across from him on some cushions. Ahmed took it, making eye contact with him the entire time. A guard presented a waiver to Ahmed.

"Once you sign, I will give you the antidote. Once everyone has signed or their wealth seized and evidence planted, I will let you go. Do not think to betray me either. I have spent years collecting information on everyone here. I know ways to ensure your statements will be void."

"Actually, I did not drink anything."

"Oh? Then you agree with my view and are willing to sign of your own accord?"

"I cannot waive to you what I do not possess."

"What family do you come from?"

"Sharfi."

Mehmet thought for a moment. "The town Emirate of Hamid. Why are you here? I have no interest in families outside of the capital." Mehmet gave Ahmed a cautious regard.

"Your method of invitation was fallible."

Mehmet grunted.

"Why did you plan this elaborate charade?" Ahmed asked.

"Get off here, boy. I don't even know if I can let you leave my manor now."

Two guards advanced.

"But I agree with you."

Mehmet held up a hand to stop his guards. "Agree?" he raised an eyebrow.

"Yes," Ahmed lied. "This war can only be ended once the wealthy stop funding the sultan's bloodlust. I see now that with that wealth in your possession you can lobby the sultan to end this war."

"The sultan cannot be dissuaded, boy, not by dinar. No, a new order will need to replace him. One that can bring peace. There are those of like mind and with them we can guide Saomarhad to a path that would end this war."

"Was that a promise made by someone?"

"How much do you know?" Mehmet's eyes narrowed.

"They are lying to you. From what I have heard of King Duggan, he will not want peace. He wants to kill all of us."

"I am no fool, boy, nor were my allies. We planned to expel the enemies in our city, assassinate King Duggan, remove Sultan Yazid and establish a council to rule."

"Radical."

"Perhaps, but then you look to the north, to the Republic of Freehold and you see how they govern with a council and you realize it can be possible for Saomarhad. Our ancestors overthrew the caliphs. They fought for the sultan who best represented them. But now, after the countless crusades and jihads in this war, even the sultanate must end. He who controls Ortie, controls the sultanate."

"You give little credit to the emirs."

"They do not benefit from this war. They are exactly the people who want the war to end. Their incomes from trade are lessened because the sultan claims the best imports for the army. Their incomes from their lands are lessened because men are needed to fight. Everyone is tired of the fighting; people are beginning to see through the zealous calls for jihad yet their sultan wants to continue it. That is what they know."

"But your methods are wrong. You wish to kill off all these people, they are innocent."

"Ha! What secrets does the emir of Hamid hide from you boy? Most of these people are guilty of funding death. In my eyes that makes them murderers. Enough of this! I realize now who you really are. You are with the sultan's rangers who undermined the plans of Huzaifa and Ziyad. You have been a nuisance to me..." Before he could finish the crowd below cheered. Mehmet stood and leaned over his balcony. Below Aarif and his rangers had returned and they were distributing vials of antidote to the nobles.

"No!" Mehmet shouted. "Kill them! Guards! Kill all of them!" But when he looked to his guards, he realized many were already dead and others being stabbed by rangers who'd snuck in.

Ahmed stood. The guards advanced on him. Ahmed cast an energy pulse at two, throwing them against a wall. Another jabbed with a spear. Ahmed side-stepped then cast again, throwing him over the side of the balcony. The last guard advanced. Ahmed cast on the vines hanging on the wall behind him. The vines snaked out and grabbed the guard wrapping around him and rendering him immobile then Ahmed turned to Mehmet. The man shoved him aside and ran out the back. Ahmed recovered and tried to pursue only to be punched in the stomach by a tall muscular Zanjī. Ahmed coughed and staggered forwards. The man grabbed him and spun him around and into a head lock, his back pressed against the man's chest. He squeezed and Ahmed struggled to breathe. The man shifted, ready to snap Ahmed's neck. Ahmed tried to focus on his free hands as his vision blurred and dizziness consumed him. He tried to cast, fire, anything! He had to focus. Ahmed's hands burst out a shy fire twice. The man positioned his hands and got ready to twist. Ahmed's hands burst into fire. He shaped the flames into daggers and stabbed at the man. He howled, burned at his thighs, and loosened his grip. Ahmed wiggled free and cast a gale of wind at him throwing him hard against the wall Then ran out in the direction Mehmet had gone.

Ahmed found Mehmet in the garden behind his manor. He had not tried to escape. Instead, he was on his knees weeping over a row of graves. Ahmed cautiously walked up behind him.

"Th-This is my family," Mehmet said without turning. He pointed to a row of four graves. "Those four were my future, my children." He pointed to the grave in front of him. "She was my wife." He pointed to the rest. "My father, mother, uncles, aunts, nephews."

"They're all dead." Ahmed's heart sunk.

"Evet. God has cursed my family. His will has seen to it that every one of the Özbey name died at the hands of some Gurmian attack."

"All of them died because of the war?"

"In one way or another. Those two were adopted, Gurmanis-born, their parents killed by a Saomarhadian attack."

"They were our enemies…"

"Children? No, they were afraid and alone and my wife and I could not leave them to die as we foraged through what remained of our reclaimed lands."

"Your lands were fought on."

"War does not always discriminate between rich and poor. We escaped to the capital but war still found us. Perhaps that is why God took my entire family from me, because he was furious that I spared the lives of Gurmian children. It is ironic. Long ago before this war, Gurmians and Saomarhad's people were friends. We had peace between us. We are far less different from Gurmians than the sultan and zealots would have you think. The Father created us all and if you were to enter a mosque you might see many peoples under one roof. Saomarhadian, Gurmian, sometimes others. I loved these children as my own and they loved me back in equal measure. How is that treason? How is that a sin? They were nothing like what the zealots claim!"

Will entered Ahmed's mind once more. Not like he expected… recently so many things were unlike how he expected them to be.

"I-I have to arrest you."

"I play the sultan's game. He can try to take my wealth once he executes me but I have ensured it will vanish."

"You were deceived by the Gurmian spies as well. They never wanted an independent Saomarhad."

"Evet. We three conspirators knew, so we tried to double-cross them but then the sultan intervened. Boy, go and bring death to those spies. They will be waiting at the largest tavern in the southern dockyard. They will do more harm than good without us to double-cross them." Mehmet turned to face Ahmed. His nose was bleeding. Blood mixed with his tears. He smiled then coughed up blood. Horrified Ahmed took a few steps back. Mehmet collapsed and shook uncontrollably before laying still. Ahmed approached and checked for vital signs finding none. He noticed a large ring on one of Mehmet's fingers. A broken space large enough to hide a pill. Mehmet had taken his own poison.

⚬⚬⚬

Aarif led his rangers to the tavern Mehmet had mentioned, near the main dockyard. Many merchants and travelers used this place; the locals stayed clear. Now, at night, the city was quiet.

A man, the scarred spy, came stumbling out of the tavern and onto the street. He swayed and held a bottle, taking sloppy sips from it. He stopped. Aarif, his rangers, and Ahmed stood in front of him. Blocking his path. Ahmed crossed his arms.

"H-Hey! G-Go out mi way..." the man belched, fumbling with his words.

"You are coming with us," Aarif said.

"You... nah..." he hiccupped. "I-I... am drowning my sorrows... in peace! Can't you let me be!"

"No!" Aarif shot. He and his rangers drew their weapons. Ahmed followed suit. The drunken man laughed.

"Then it's a... p-party!" Gurmian Eyes of the King, as if on signal, walked out on the street, weapons drawn, and took position beside the drunken man.

"This doesn't need to end like this," Aarif warned. "Surrender peacefully. All of you."

"Yooouuu..." —the drunken man pointed at Aarif, almost tripping over, with the hand that held his liquor bottle— "fucked my... my plans..." He hiccupped then dropped his bottle. It shattered into a dozen wet pieces. Aarif sighed.

"Just seize them." The Saomarhad rangers lunged forwards, engaging the Gurmian spies.

Ahmed attacked with his kilij and slashed at a man trying to jab him. Ahmed shoved him aside and advanced but was grabbed from behind. He twisted out of the enemy's grasp and turned. Parvez flanked the attacker, striking his side. The man swung across to where Parvez had stood. The boy ducked out of the way then ran his sword into the attacker's side, cutting almost through. Blood splatter fell across Ahmed's face. As the man dropped Parvez looked at Ahmed with a stern expression and nodded. Ahmed returned the nod.

Ahmed engaged the leader. A lust for blood gleamed in the man's eyes. With an uppercut, he swiped at Ahmed who jumped back. Ahmed followed with a jab, but it was countered. Blocking in high guard, Ahmed ducked as the spy swiped at his head and followed with three fierce diagonal cuts. All three were blocked. He thrust his kilij forward, catching the leader out of guard and ran his sword through him. The leader collapsed, clutching his side. Ahmed crouched to view his face as the rangers were fighting around him.

"B-Blast it. Y-You…" he heaved, his voice drained.

"You are dying now." Ahmed steadied himself.

"I-I need to confess…" the man forced out the words.

"I am the only one here."

"I-I did my duty… k-knowing that twas wrong." The spy gripped Ahmed, coughed, and breathed his last. Ahmed stood, slightly faint. Aarif placed a hand on his shoulder making him shiver.

"You did well, Ahmed," he commented. Around him the rangers were collecting the dead. Aarif followed Ahmed's gaze.

"They will be taken to the palace for the sultan's plan."

<hr>

Ahmed walked down the halls of the sultan's palace to the bathroom. He'd already described his successes, alongside Aarif, to his master and the sultan. They were delighted and showered Ahmed with praise. Aarif also said a special goodbye to Ahmed, telling him he had a place in the rangers.

'Mashalhurah!' The sultan gleamed. 'Once the Gurmian prisoners are dealt with I would have you by my side as my future grand vizier. It will be declared.' Honour and pride surged in him, to be the second most powerful person in the sultanate and it was all because of his hard work and his master. His family would be ecstatic.

Now Ahmed could finally take a bath and let all his worries and adventures with Will and in Ortie be washed away. He entered the bathroom to see it empty. Good, he'd have some time to himself. Ahmed stripped himself and settled into the warm water fed by a fountain, in the shape of a horse. He lit candles. Their smoky aroma filled the small room and Ahmed sat back, relaxing as city dust washed off his body.

He raised his arm out of the water and chanted. The water changed its shape, a dolphin herd jumped forth. The small animals danced as he shaped the water into almost crystal-like forms of animals and objects. Ahmed smiled. His mind drifted and the peaceful shapes became horns and drums of war. The Gurmanis and Saomarhad flags took shape and men marched to fight. An intense yet calming heat came over him.

"True peace is not a luxury given to commanders of war," a powerful voice said. Ahmed clenched his fist and the water dropped. Lowering his arm into the water Ahmed thought on the words. Commander? Him. He was to become grand vizier a position in which he would advise and support the sultan. He would be like those who Mehmet claimed were responsible for the deaths in war because they funded it. Ahmed shook the thought away. He would advise the sultan to find a resolution but he had doubts. In his war room, the sultan had made it clear he wanted vengeance and that meant to continue fighting. He closed his eyes. He was not grand vizier yet.

The candles in Ahmed's room cast a soft and eerie glow as they filled the dark room with a sense of warmth. Across from his bed, Ahmed sat on a desk and examined the two objects before him. The pearls… Seekers' Stones? Their default red colour were richer now that his and Will's pearls were close to each other. They sat perfectly still except for the swirling mists inside the gems. The mists moved towards the opposite stone as if the two were magnets. Ahmed sensed the magic inside them. All he could think was how odd it was that he and Will found the things and why there was little information on them.

Ahmed crossed his arms and examined the objects. Confusion swirled inside him. Why were there only two? Could there be more? They must attract each other out of some common factor. They could be two parts of a whole but then what could two spherical objects combine to make? As Ahmed read the magic between them, the power grew stronger whenever he pushed them together. The magic he sensed in Al-Motros that led him to Will was strong but not as strong as this. As Ahmed had got closer to Will the connection between the two stones became stronger; he knew it. An intense yet calming heat came over him.

"Sometimes what is obvious is true," a powerful voice said. So that meant they were connected. What? Why would he be connected to a Gurmian boy as odd as Will? ***"Duty or truth."*** The powerful voice seemed to be making itself home in Ahmed's mind; he didn't like that. Will was different, unlike what Ahmed expected. He had not expected the reasons why the three traitors betrayed Saomarhad. He had not expected Huzaifa to worry about the Gurmian dhimmis despite sacrificing some of them. He had not expected Ziyad, a man who loved knowledge to get to his position, a man who was devoted enough to go on a hajj, as his full name implied, to want to twist the message given to people. Was he trying to reveal a truth? If what Ahmed saw in Will and other Gurmian people he had recently met were not exceptions, then the sultan and zealots were spreading lies.

He hadn't expected a young Saomardrim noble to fall in love with a Gurmian woman. Similarly, he could have never guessed Mehmet to have adopted two Gurmian children. Things were not what they seemed. This war was not so clear anymore. He was taught to believe that Gurmians, people like Will, wanted to destroy his home and enslave his people but now he found out that there were friends on both sides. Gurmians wanted peace as much as people on this side wanted it. The sultan wanted it, even suggesting it. Then why did he need to plan such a killing as to infuriate the enemy? Because the sultan also wanted vengeance. Even Alhurah spoke of favoring peace over war and vengeance, but when faced with persecutors like the Gurmians, Alhurah spoke defense against such danger.

Ahmed laid awake wondering about everything he'd been through. The entire evening had been plagued with these thoughts. Even the final enemy he faced, the lead spy, said that his work was wrong. Both kings had lied about what the other was like. Why? To make sure neither side would hesitate killing fathers and sons, of course. But if their two kingdoms where the same, then why war? Because of the exaggerated differences.

No, it was Ahmed's duty to serve his state, he had to remain on course for that because it's all he'd ever done and it was all he had worked for. Yet, Master Mahad had always taught the value of truth. It was a scholar's duty to strive for truth, to be just and fair in their study. To ensure all sides were represented. Because they had the power to write the narrative, they had the moral responsibility to avoid propaganda and half-truths. Was this why Ahmed now wondered what the truth was behind this war? Were the Gurmians that bad? That unreasonable? He came to realise from all he'd seen in Ortie, in Kharija, and all he heard from Will, people were tired of this war. More than their leaders they wanted an end but most were powerless to resist.

The sultan wanted to fight until his father was avenged. How long could that take? How many more would die? Ahmed convinced himself that even as grand vizier, he could not sway the sultan with words alone and not in that position. He did not want to become a commander of war to enable the sultan to continue it. There were people even in the heart of Saomarhad, even dhimmis who were unafraid to love, befriend, work with and adopt the supposed enemy. Ahmed knew he was a scholar deep down. In truth the thought of expanding his own knowledge drove him to improve his magic more than the allure of grand vizier ever did. His master was the real politician not him. Will could be his key... if only...

Chapter Twenty-Two

AHMED LOOKED OUT the window of his room at the sunrise. He stood deathly still stuck in place by his indecision. On the windowsill, wrapped neatly, was the brown-gold cloak his older brother had given him long ago. Placed above it was an envelope containing a letter Ahmed had written a few hours ago. It was an apology, a short one, because Ahmed did not know how he could express what he was going to do. Shame colored the thought of how his brother would react to his decision. He promised to return after his studies but now he was going to go further away. He had to. The things he had experienced since leaving Murzq, especially in Ortie and during the time he'd spent with Will had convinced him there was more to this war, and the people involved, than he was told. He could not stand by a sultan who wished to kill so many in the name of vengeance and protection, especially not when those people, it seemed, were as human as the Saomardrim. Ahmed dressed and armed himself, took a deep breath then turned and made his way out.

Ahmed dropped off his letter and the cloak at the palace post office, then proceeded to the grand vizier's wing. Nervousness bit deep into him as he approached his master's quarters with the talisman his master had given him clutched in his hand. He squeezed it. Was he ready to give up all of his fame, glory, and position, just so he could discover the truth? He would be labeled a traitor today, but he knew he had to do this with tact. His master had been there for most of his life, teaching and guiding him.

Master Mahad's door seemed to tower over him ominously as if forbidding him to pass through it. Ahmed's heart thumped against his chest and he fingered his talisman, thinking that he should turn back. Ahmed's feet shifted, threatening to give in to his fear but he forced an arm forward and knocked.

"Enter," his master's voice answered. Ahmed stepped in. His master's quarters was an office full of potions, magic, and papers. A large window was built into the ceiling for use as an observatory. "Ahmed you are always welcome on this glorious day." He was making this harder. "Soon Gurmanis will receive our message and you will become… Ahmed, why so downcast?"

"Master… I am sorry." Ahmed placed the talisman on a table in front of him, across from his master.

"What is this, Ahmed?"

"I can't accept it; I don't deserve it, not after what I must do, master."

"What will you do?" His master raised an eyebrow.

"I cannot become grand vizier. I won't support the sultan in this war when I have come to realise everything we were told about Gurmanis is wrong. I need to go see for myself; I must see the truth."

"I do not understand. What are you talking about?"

"I am going to Gurmanis. I need Will, the boy I brought here, in order to do that."

"That boy, along with the other Gurmian infidels, will be put to death today. In order for you to take him, you will need to kidnap him from the gallows."

"Then that is what I will do."

"That is treason, Ahmed! Where is this sudden insolence coming from?"

"Don't you see that we have all been lied to, Master? We were told we needed to fight this war because Gurmians wanted to kill all of us. We were told they were monsters and demons and that God demanded us to kill them but that's not true. Will has told me of what Gurmians think, and they think of us like we think of them."

"Truth does not matter. What matters is duty."

"What? All those years in university where you and the professors stressed morals, truth and striving for knowledge in all forms. What about the lectures about the responsibilities of mages towards others? Does none of that matter?"

"Not so far as to betray your country!" His master's rising anger was evident in his red, scrunched face. Ahmed's heart sunk seeing his eyes hold this much disappointment. "I will mark this as youthful impulsivity, though I had thought you had better self-control. Do not betray."

"I won't betray my country. I won't kill my kinsmen. But I need to find the truth and… I can't become grand vizier until I do. I now want to know the one thing I have no knowledge of, I want to know what is on the other side of the river. If I knew what Gurmians are really like, if I could reach out to the best among them… maybe we could have peace." Ahmed bowed. "I am so sorry master. I have failed you. I cannot follow your vision for me… not yet." Master Mahad looked at Ahmed in shock then shock gave way to anger. The master mage walked forward, standing closer to Ahmed.

"Traitor! After everything I taught you and guided you through, you'd give all that up for some naïve notion you can single-handedly change the ideology of these states?" Master Mahad scoffed. Ahmed winced at the insult.

"I don't know what I will find but I will find something, something that will change the sultan's mind, inshalhurah, bring him peace, make him realise how much a hundred years of war is wearing away people on both sides."

"You are not of a sane state of mind. Allow me to help bring you back to sanity." The master mage shot his arms forward and a translucent mass rose up and wrapped around Ahmed, ready to trap and constrain him. Ahmed cast back pushing against his master's magic to stop the spell. Rage filled Master Mahad's face. He shifted and cast a shockwave at Ahmed. The boy was thrown back against a wall. He recovered in time to block a swath of flame.

"Master!" Ahmed screamed with shock. He held back tears as he started to feel the gravity of his decision.

"You have become a traitor to the sultan! Traitors are disposed of. Repent and the sultan will spare you."

"I-I can't." Ahmed cast a shockwave forward. His master blocked. He tried to run to the door but Master Mahad cast arms of wind which wrapped around Ahmed and pulled him back. The master mage spun Ahmed around and threw him onto a desk. Ahmed crashed onto it sending books, scrolls and bottles of potions flying to the ground. Master Mahad cast a bolt of lightning at Ahmed. He screamed. Burns dug into his skin, like being torn apart by dozens of blades. Ahmed groaned when his master stopped. Smoke lifted off of him and his skin sizzled.

"The next one can be lethal. Repent!"

"I want an end to this war just as people want. The sultan will not end it; no one will because everyone has demonised the other side. I can see that now! I can go and show Gurmanis we want the same, I will find a way to understand since no one else seems to want to. Will and I… there is something else. He and I have some sort of connection, I can't let him die until I discover what binds us." Master Mahad grabbed Ahmed's neck and lifted him. Ahmed struggled to get air and he tried to pull his master's arms away.

"Excuses! The rationale of a traitor. Do you think you can simply walk into King Duggan's court and appeal to him? Will he listen to a Saomardrim boy? They are heretics Ahmed, as they call us."

"Vitalif qiprana surround push." Ahmed's hoarse voice forced out. Out of his body a blue mist of energy pushed away from him. Master Mahad was thrown backwards. The master mage lifted the spilled liquids on the ground around him and sent a vortex of liquid towards Ahmed. Ahmed grabbed it and forced it into a single stream before him. He cut it in half and sent the two new streams to his left and right, they fizzled, burning things behind him.

Master Mahad did not wait. Pulses of energy sped towards the boy. Ahmed jumped out of the way of the first three, then deflected. Master Mahad grunted and kept the attack coming. The master mage shot lightning out of his hands and Ahmed caught it. He tried to keep his stance but the force of lightning was fierce and produced an intense heat. Master Mahad smiled and closed the distance between them. Ahmed bent back and his foot slipped; he adjusted in time as the master's attack grew stronger. Ahmed cast wind around his master. The master mage was lifted and Ahmed pushed him back into the wall to the left of the window. The lightning was deflected into the roof, punching a hole through it. Master Mahad screamed and sent a large burst of energy towards Ahmed. Ahmed deflected it. The energy smashed into the roof, exploding, pushing both master and apprentice away. As he flew, fragile objects shattered. Dust and smoke filled the space. Landing across the room, Ahmed recovered and ran forward, seeing his master hanging from the edge overlooking the castle courtyard.

"Grab my hand!" Ahmed screamed while extending a hand to his master. His master seethed in pain, the hand holding the ledge swelling. The force of Ahmed's magic had broken it. Master Mahad glared at Ahmed, then a hint of pity escaped his expression.

"T-Take my hand." His insides tightened as if expecting some imminent attack. His world slowed and Ahmed could hear his breath, his heart beat, his— his master cried painfully, unable to hold on any longer. He let go of the ledge, his robes flapping and limbs stretched out as he crashed on the cobbles below, blood splattering under him. Ahmed fell back against the remains of his master's desk and looked forward in shock. Great guilt came over him. He didn't want his master to die. What had he done? Screaming propelled guards into action below. Ahmed forced himself up, holding back tears, and tore through his master's things, finding a sultan's seal. He ran from the room.

Ahmed took two horses to the central city square as quick as he could. If he got there before the guards in the palace did, no one would know of his treason. He galloped hard arriving to see a large gathering crowd, chanting for the glory of God, the sultan, and for death to the infidels. Ahmed tied his horses with others and dove into a sea of people. He pushed past them to the main thoroughfare where the gallows stood. It had three platforms. On the topmost platform hung ten nooses, the second held ten headsman's blocks, at the third ten Saomarhadian soldiers stood ready with muskets. A bloodbath was about to happen. The ultimate end to the sultan's plan to intimidate and enrage Gurmanis. This could not be the way to the war's end. This was why he could not stand beside Sultan Yazid as grand vizier.

Horns and drums sounded. Ahmed turned around and the first of several prison carriages rolled forwards. He stepped to the side, blending in with the soldiers. Ahmed watched the cages packed with Gurmian prisoners-of-war roll forward and stop. He looked for Will, making sure Will was not in the first cage, now being unloaded, then ran further onwards. Louder cheers rang out from the crowd, then silence, followed by the booming voice of Sultan Yazid. Ahmed frowned and shivered, his actions now hurried, his adrenaline spiking.

"Today we take the Gurmian king, King Duggan Chas by the collar and we demand he stop this war!" The sultan spoke and the crowd roared. Ahmed passed several more carriages, the people within, young, old, men, and women. Any prisoner the Saomarhadian troops could capture were stuffed into the carriages, and Ahmed had brought one to this madness.

"We tell him that we will not be intimidated, not when innocent Saomarhadian lives are extinguished by his forces! We all remember the Grand Mosque massacre, the obliteration of the refugee fleet fleeing the burning of the southern jungles, and of course the murder of our previous sultan. For these crimes Gurmanis must be held accountable!" The crowd roared.

As Ahmed passed yet another prison carriage packed with the condemned, he realised he did not know this many people were going to be put to death. The sultan had really gone mad. In truth, he had never known the sultan. Yes, Ahmed knew of the things the sultan spoke of. But this response would only make everything worse. Like other times, Gurmanis would only respond with greater violence, triggering Saomarhad to do the same, perpetuating an endless cycle. He had almost agreed to become a part of it. No! How could he have been so misled? Why had he not been better?

Ahmed stopped. Will was squeezed against the corner of a carriage's cage. He looked lifeless and hopeless, curled up and staring at the cage floor. Ahmed rushed to him.

"Will! Will! Speak to me!" Ahmed shouted. A girl beside Will shook the bars of the cage and shouted at Ahmed,

"Go away! God curse your people for this!" Ahmed looked at the frightened girl, her face wet with tears, her clothes and hair dishevelled.

"Will!" Ahmed ignored the girl and reached through the bars at Will's arm. The girl grabbed Ahmed's arm. "I am trying to save…" Will looked at Ahmed, his empty eyes showing the shell that was left of the boy.

"You're n-not him… n-not the warden…" Will spoke in a defeated broken voice. Ahmed pulled away and found the soldier in charge. The sound of ten muskets firing and the cheering crowd grew loud.

"You have to let that boy go to me!" Ahmed pointed to Will.

"On whose orders?" the soldier asked.

"Grand Vizier Mahad Oman and the sultan."

"Right and who are you?"

"Master Mahad's apprentice."

"Nice to meet you, I'm the prince's attendant. Get back to your post or I'll have you court martialed boy." The soldier grabbed Ahmed and pulled him away from the cage.

"Wait." Ahmed broke free. He pulled out the sultan's seal, remembering he'd taken it. "I have orders to bring the Gurmian boy to my master."

"I hope he experiments on him." The soldier spat at the ground then turned and ordered his subordinates to open the cage. Ahmed composed himself. Another round of ten muskets fired. The soldiers pulled Will out of the cage and shoved him towards Ahmed. The chained boy fell at his feet and looked up.

"A-Ahmed…" Will said, the vacant look still in his eyes.

"Wait, what about me?" the girl shouted. "Wi-Will!"

Will hesitated then looked back. "J-Jillian…"

"We have to go now!" Ahmed took hold of Will and pulled him away.

"Will!" Jillian shouted.

"Stop!" Will pulled away from Ahmed. "Her too. You have to take her too!" Another round of ten muskets echoed. The entire prisoner caravan came forward.

"We…"

"No! We can't leave her." Will glared at Ahmed. Defeated, Ahmed rushed forwards and ordered the soldiers to release the girl.

"I am sending a man with you. I need to be sure of this business," the soldier said upon releasing the girl who rushed to Will's side.

"There is no—"

"Bearing the sultan's seal does not negate your rank. Obey your superiors!"

"Yes, sorry sir." Ahmed led the soldier and the chained prisoners away from the crowd being careful not to be overwhelmed by people shouting, jeering and clawing at Will and Jillian as they pushed through. Ahmed led them to a secluded alley.

"What?" the soldier said. "We made a wrong turn, we…" The soldier grasped his neck and gasped for air. Will and Jillian turned to the man behind them and looked on in shock. Will turned to Ahmed. Ahmed had his arms to his side and was gripping the air as if it were solid. The soldier collapsed. Ahmed turned, with a weary distraught look on his face. He lifted his right hand. The chains on Will and Jillian vibrated, unlocked and fell off.

"D'you kill him?" Will asked.

"No. He is unconscious. Follow me. I have horses not far away." Ahmed led them forward. They ran into view of the horses then suddenly Will stopped and held out his arm to stop Jillian. Ahmed reached his horse then looked back when he realised Will and Jillian hadn't followed.

"Come, we must go quickly if we are to leave the city before the soldiers find out."

"Why Ahmed? What reason d'you have to save us?" Will asked.

"I am saving you. We must hurry! This is not the time to discuss it."

"But you're our enemy. This could be a trap."

"It is not a trap. If you would prefer, I could give you back to the executioners."

"We don't have much choice if we want to survive." Jillian prompted looking cautiously at Ahmed.

"Alright, we will go with you." ·

Ahmed mounted his horse and Will helped Jillian get on their horse. Ahmed turned to Will and gave him his pearl. Will clutched it, hesitating for a moment then stowed in in his tunic. Once Will was mounted Jillian wrapped her arms around Will's stomach. At first her arms hovered over Will's body as if she was unsure of holding him… or afraid to. She made up her mind and held tight.

"What about the others? We can't leave them to die," Jillian said. At the sound of yet another round of ten muskets firing Jillian looked back the way they had come. "No…"

"There is no time! It is impossible to do anything for them now," Ahmed answered.

"So many are being killed. We must do something, can't we…"

"There is no time!" Ahmed shouted at his horse signaling it into a gallop. As Ahmed pulled away Will raised the reigns of his horse and it galloped after Ahmed.

The three rode to Ortie's south gate and left the city without any issues. They distanced themselves from Ortie before slowing down to talk. Will's horse came up beside Ahmed's.

"You saved us, Ahmed. We thank you," Will said.

"I told you not to make me regret my duty, Will, but it seems you have."

Will smiled and Jillian cleared her throat.

"Ah yes! Ahmed, this is Jillian. Jillian, this is Ahmed. Ahmed was the one who captured me and brought me here."

"Should we not kill him and be gone from here?" Jillian asked.

"Unfortunately I am the only one with the knowledge to get you two safely home, and after today, I need a place to hide."

"What happened back there, Ahmed?" Will asked.

"Well I am currently being branded a traitor and being blamed for my master's death."

"Don't think I will trust you so easily, Saomardrim." Jillian crossed her arms. "You might claim you have betrayed your people but it could all be a lie. Still, as you have said, we do not know the way home, so where *are* we going?"

"The south is our fastest option. We go to Jueadi and find a boat to go across the river to your land."

"Across the river is Suthenburg and their cannons will fire on anyone who comes too close. We'll have to land south of the city," Will suggested.

"Well, we should hope to get through Jueadi first before they block the ports."

"This is a foolish plan!" Jillian protested. "You want to ride through an enemy city to reach its port then find a boat? You know how improbable that sounds? We will be captured at the gates!"

"We have time on our side. The mass executions have everyone occupied so we have a head start."

"You must have another plan."

"This is the only plan," Ahmed answered.

Jueadi, the southern half of the city was situated on a large oval protrusion of land with its districts gradually rising in height to the palace, the highest structure. The smaller northern half was lowest in elevation and separated from the southern half by the harbour. This district housed the warehouses, port workers, and the poor. Jueadi received much of the sultanate's boat trade. The harbour was defended not only by canon batteries but also by a long chain that could be raised when required, preventing boats from entering or leaving. The three companions entered without drawing attention and realised the port had been closed, the chain drawn up, and shurta had been ordered to scan the streets for suspicious persons. Ahmed suggested they try to find and launch a boat from below the citadel on the west end of the city alongside the Hertos River, that way they could bypass the harbour chain.

The three rode towards an abandoned dock below the citadel. Before he left, Ahmed examined a map of the city. This small dock was recently closed. Fishermen had used it until they were approved to use an old military marina in the harbour. According to the news sent to the Ortie palace on the military change, the fishing boats were not going to be moved until tomorrow. When they arrived, Ahmed pointed out a small wooden felucca and the three made it ready to sail. Suddenly a horn blared and the three looked to the sky behind them. An airship gained speed and arched towards them.

"They've seen us!" Ahmed shouted. "Quickly!"

"Where did that come from?" Will shouted.

"It may have been patrolling the northern section of the city. We were preparing to sail and did not hear it."

"The boat is stuck!" Jillian pointed to the end where the boat was wedged into a broken section of the dock.

"I can push it free. Get in," Ahmed said. Will and Jillian settled in. Bombs rained from the sky and exploded on the docks. Ahmed was thrown forwards but recovered. He looked at the airship aiming to lower down towards them. How could they outrun that huge thing? If… if Shoran was in there… he had said he would be on an airship moving south. Ahmed instinctively searched for Shoran's presence through the magic around him, forgetting such a thing was useless at this distance. His pearl grew warm and shone. A blurry image took form. Shoran stood on the bridge of the airship.

"Sh-Shoran?" Ahmed said. Shoran turned.

"A-Ahmed?"

"Shoran, help us!" Astonished, Ahmed spoke louder

"Ahmed? Why, Ahmed? Why d'you betray Saomarhad?"

"There is no time. Please, Shoran. They'll kill us."

"You can't be real. This can't be real. No good magic can do this." Dark magic or, Ahmed felt his pearl, Godly Magic. "Get out of my head." The connection was cut. Ahmed frowned. A musket ball whizzed right past him. Saomarhadian soldiers rushed onto the docks. Ahmed turned to run. The airship jerked leftwards violently and plunged over them towards the Hertos River. Shocked, Ahmed scrambled back to the felucca and pushed it off the docks, casting a wind spell to supplement his strength. As he was about to jump onboard, a cloaked man emerged from the shadows and grabbed Ahmed. He drew a bottle and forced the liquid inside down Ahmed's throat. Then he threw the bottle, drew a dagger, and held it at the boy's throat. Ahmed struggled, feeling his legs give away he fell to the ground, still held by the man. He looked up at Will and Jillian.

"Ahmed!" Will screamed.

"Go, get out of here! Don't…"

"Now that the airship is down, they might get away, but you won't traitor." Ahmed recognised the voice. Aarif shoved him to the ground. A wave of dizziness overcame him.

"Wh-What did you do to me?" Ahmed struggled to get up but he lost his balance. Everything was spinning and his stamina withered away. His heavy eyelids closed.

"Sleep now boy so soon you can sleep forever." Ahmed crumpled in a heap.

Chapter Twenty-Three

THE FELUCCA FLOATED to a stop north of Jueadi and Will was the first to storm out. Jillian took her time, carrying off Ahmed's weapons and gear. Jueadi's city walls loomed in the distance under the moon-lit sky. Will had forced them to land here.

Will's falcon soared in circles, calling into the night. Jillian approached Will.

"It's not right! Ahmed had no reason to save us and now…" Will kicked at a rock.

"Maybe, Will, but it was his choice. He knew what he was getting himself into. We should follow his instructions and return home quickly. We are wasting time here," Jillian answered.

"No, he was a nobleman! He chose to save peasants. One more farmer than squire, the other a healer. He will die, Jillian. We have to save him."

"That is foolish, Will! Even if we could save him from the dozen guards guarding him, how would we get out of the city? Much less in?"

"We won't have to face the guards if we take 'em by surprise. We could cause panic an', in the chaos, we would slip Ahmed out."

"That's too risky, Will! Have you lost any sense of feasibility? How would we get in and out of the city? We are fugitives, foreigners in a foreign land, and their enemy!" Jillian glared at him.

"I-I don't know." Will looked away, defeated, and Jillian sighed.

"Ahmed may have saved us but he is still our enemy. Why d'you have sympathy for a person who bound you and dragged you, across the desert, just to be killed?"

"He is different, he also took care of me, healed my wounds," Will argued.

"Sure he did, and only from the kindness of his heart. He kept you alive until you reached Ortie, that's all." Jillian crossed her arms. Will drew his pearl.

"He has this too! Remember I told you about it in Ortie, how I got it, this is not something everyone has. There's a story behind it. It may have been part of the reason he betrayed his people. Maybe we are connected by these pearls!"

"This is far too dangerous. Why do you insist on doing this? Let him go. Be a knight and get us out of here! Sir Robert would do the same thing."

"You know naught about my master! He is a compassionate man who gave me a chance. He would do the same for Ahmed."

"What you propose is impossible. We have no idea where Ahmed is and we have no way in or out of the city." Will looked away and took a few steps forward then crossed his arms. Jillian shook her head and stormed off. Will looked into the sky. Maybe he was crazy, but he couldn't leave Ahmed to his fate because it didn't feel right. Ahmed had given up everything to save him, him, Will. Will cursed. What worth was he to Ahmed? Ahmed didn't deserve the retribution he was to receive for his treason, and they could be friends. He had learned a lot from the young mage, the Saomarhadians weren't all bad.

But Jillian was right after all; what he proposed was impossible. There was only a slight chance of success. An intense yet calming heat came over him.

"A slight chance is still a chance," the powerful voice said. The cold night wind changed; a whiff of hot air streaked across Will's face. He turned and faced that direction. He caught a glint in the grass on the edge of a bump in the land, light reflected off something. He walked over and saw a large pipe embedded into the earth. Water flowed out of it and snaked its way towards the Hertos River. Around the pipe was Saomardrim language but clearly, on the top, was the word: صلمطبیله. Will turned to look south back at the city on the gradual incline and traced the land back to the metal pipe. Will felt around it then after a second of thinking, knew what it was.

"Jillian! Come here!" Will called. Jillian walked over.

"What is it?"

"This is how we are going to get into the city!" Will pointed to the sewage outflow pipe.

"You have got to be kidding me, Will."

"Nope." Will smiled.

⁓

They force fed him a bitter green liquid that popped on his tongue like firecrackers. The substance had sapped his strength, made him dizzy, and stopped Ahmed from using magic. Ahmed shuffled upright in his cell, chains clinking. He was chained to the wall and shackles connected his wrists behind his back. A chain connected those to shackles on his ankles. His wrists had stopped burning and were now numb. The shackles that bound him were made of dimithrite, a rare metal which suppressed magic and was used by some dark mage hunters intertwined with their armor. Maybe they thought he was so dangerous that they needed to block his magic with both the liquid and the metal.

Ahmed had been stripped of all his clothes and was now wearing a dull orange tunic. The footsteps of approaching guards and their jingling keys grew near, but they were not chatting like they normally did; they were silent. The two appeared in front of Ahmed's cell and opened it. They held him by the shoulders, dragging him out on his knees as far as the wall-connecting chains would let them, then unlocked them. They pulled him up, blindfolded him, and dragged him down the hall, deeper into Jueadi's jail. The men brought him to a small cell. They bound his wrists and ankles in clamps attached to a rigid T-bar suspending him against the wall. The metal pressed deeply into his back as his wrists and ankles strained, eliciting a burning pain. They ripped the blindfold off of him and left him. The solid metal door slammed shut.

Minutes passed, the sound of air heavy in his ears, and Ahmed wondered when they would kill him. Other than the beatings Aarif and the guards had given him when they brought him in, they hadn't yet tortured him or anything. Despair filled him. His master was dead; that was all he had accomplished. He wondered about Amir, his father, and his mother.

You will become strong and wise my son; this is for your future,' Baba had said. No, he wasn't wise, he was foolish and impulsive. Now, he would have no future and he had failed his father.

'I will protect you mother. I will keep you happy; I promise.' No, he wouldn't be able to keep that promise. His actions had tainted his family's name. He had probably caused his mother more pain.

'I will come back, then we can play again!' Ahmed almost laughed. He'd naïvely made that promise to Amir. It would never come to pass and he'd never see his brother's smile again. Above all, he hoped Amir of all people would not hate him for what he had done. Shame was all he felt. Shame that his actions had disgraced them. He imagined his mother weeping when she would hear that her son had been put to death. The thought made Ahmed tremble and he blinked away tears.

The door lock clicked and with a loud metallic grinding, the door swung open. Grandmaster of the Immortals, Barbas Abudi, strode into the room. He rushed to Ahmed and grabbed his throat. Losing air, Ahmed croaked and strained. The Immortal forced Ahmed to look him in the eyes.

"Traitor!" Barbas spat. "To think someone so close to the sultan and with much of his admiration would be so wretched." Barbas let go of Ahmed and punched him in the gut. The boy grunted and coughed.

"Enough Barbas." Sultan Yazid stood behind the grandmaster, two of his masked and menacing Immortals flanking him. Barbas turned and bowed. "Leave us. He is no longer a danger." Barbas and the Immortals left the room, closing the door behind them. Sultan Yazid gave Ahmed a hard stare and walked towards him, examining the boy. Ahmed could not make eye contact.

"You look like Sultan Galib the first in the images of his younger self." The sultan sighed. "Except when he brought down the last caliph and started the sultanate, it was for the prosperity of Saomarhad. You, on the other hand, seem to want to side with our enemies. Now, I find myself asking why but I cannot find an answer. I wonder, do you consider me a tyrant as the last caliph was?"

"You are not a tyrant but your idea of Gurmanis has clouded your judgement. I believe you want the best for your people."

"Then why, Ahmed? Why betray me? You had everything, you were the son of an emir, you were affluent, powerful, the finest mage anyone could want and you gave all that away. You betrayed your land, people, family and me. Even your master, you spared no expense into killing him in the most gruesome way possible. Why Ahmed? What for?"

"I did not kill him. He was my master and I respected him. He would not take my hand."

"It does not matter if he fell of his own accord or you pushed him off. The fact is that you drove him to it."

"That's not fair... I..."

"You have no right to talk back to me!" Sultan Yazid shouted. "Look me in the eye so I can see the true image of the boy who murdered my best friend and grand vizier!"

Ahmed hesitated then slowly lifted his head to observe the sultan.

"You were going to replace him to stand by my side, Ahmed. He was my friend and I trusted his assessment of you so I entertained his request, and now he has paid for it."

"I went to him to leave with honour, to beg for his forgiveness. I never meant for his death it was the last thing I wanted."

"And look how that turned out! What surprises me the most is that you did this all for the enemy. You know what they have done, yet you still side with them."

"And what was it that they did? Do you remember exactly how this war started in the first place? Do your commanders know? No one does! They and we are exactly the same. There was no difference, only the lies you have heard from your father and his father. The same lies that are spread through the sultanate."

"What does any of that matter? That is no reason to betray your people. You could have solved this with dutiful action."

"No one wants to hear they have been lied to. No one attempts to try a way to find peace. Your people sultan. Your people are sick of this war. They want an end."

"Oh so it seems then your time in Ortie has taught you treason. What words did the traitors of Ortie speak to you that have changed your view so?"

"It is no change. In Murzq, I was always taught mages and scholars have a duty to find the truth. I have seen your people. Many hate Gurmians with valid reason. They have ravaged so much of Saomarhad in so many ways but many more people are tired. Continuing to fight like you wish to will never solve this situation."

"Perhaps you don't remember what Gurmians did to my father, your previous sultan. Have you forgotten?"

"I have not forgotten but what excuse is that? I understand sultan that he was—"

"You have not lost a father! You do not understand!"

"For years my father was many kilometers south and I could never see him!"

Sultan Yazid eyed Ahmed cautiously, seeming to register the comparison.

"I understand you want vengeance, I would want vengeance, but you are a leader of a state and your actions affect your people. Your drive for vengeance, your wish to continue this war, I have seen, is hurting your people. Sultan, I know you care and you want to protect them, but you are doing the opposite."

"The only way to protect our people is to fight Gurmians! They are vulgar and violent and their king want's our extinction, all the Gurmians do."

"That is a lie—"

"You speak of lies again, do you? Perhaps the zealots exaggerate and the jihadis cultivate the most extreme, but the actions of Gurmians offer them ample proof. Remember, boy, that Gurmanis killed their prisoners-of-war long before I ordered the execution of theirs. Let us not forget the massacres either."

"I have seen the actions of Gurmians in the desert, but this rhetoric will only keep us locked in violence."

"Gurmians see no other way!"

"That can't be true! Will doesn't see it that way; he can't be the only one. He told me Gurmians see us as equally evil as we have been told they are. If they knew we were not, and what if they were not so unreasonable to peace?"

"What treason have you heard? What more proof do you have? Are there really people in this country who think like you?"

"Of course. I have seen Saomardrim caring for the welfare of the Gurmian dhimmis, I have seen a Saomardrim noble give up his plentiful life because he loves a Gurmian woman. I have seen a Oghurk man weep over the graves of his two adopted Gurmian children. These events cannot be isolated. If these people can find peace why can't our country?" Ahmed pleaded for the sultan to understand. The sultan scoffed.

"You have truly gone insane. God has abandoned you, Ahmed; he has scorn for you."

"God cannot have wanted one-hundred years of war and turmoil."

"You cannot claim to know the will of God."

"No, I cannot, but what I do know is that I can't stand beside you and help you continue this war when I have so much doubt. I have a much higher duty to see for myself the truth. This war is built on a foundation of sand, differences and conflicts that never really meant anything significant." Ahmed paused and looked the sultan in the eye. "And I did not expect you to change your mind."

"I came here to try and appeal to your last sliver of sanity Ahmed, but I too realize now you are completely devoted to betraying me. Why did you take the boy and the girl? You could have slipped away quietly."

"I need him. Some sort of magic connects he and I. I need to figure that out and I need him to help me understand Gurmanis. He would not leave without the girl."

"They will be your only victory, boy. Take heart that they have escaped thanks to you because this is your final night of life. I am forced to make an example of you. Your death must disgrace you severely so no one will dare betray me again. You will be put to death. You won't live imprisoned, nor face the tortures that would cleanse your sins not in a cell in the depths of the desert, nor in the crags of the sulfur flats. You will be dammed upon your death and sit by Kalshaimar's side. This is justice for my dear friend.

"Know that once you are gone, I will win this war and the peace you seek will arrive, after Gurmians are utterly humbled by blade and gun. That is the only language they understand." Sultan Yazid took one last pitying look at Ahmed then turned and left the cell. Ahmed dropped his head as the door to his cell slammed shut. He could not hold it in any longer. He started to cry, unable to wipe away the tears. He would never see his family again. Had he hurt more people for some idealistic pursuit of truth rather than helping end this war? He knew one thing, the sultan's way, King Duggan's way, would never bring peace. Not a peace where both cultures got to exist.

The shadows shifted in Ahmed's cell. Through the barred window, grey light shone in. Ahmed, chained and huddled against the back wall, woke. He tried to stretch, his chains clanking, but he could do little.

He stared at the stone floor. A cough echoed, and a door creaked open outside. When will they come? When will they come to kill him? Not knowing when was the worst thing. Ahmed trembled. When?

An hour or two passed, his heart beat in his ears. The click of his cell door lock made him jump. He refused to look up. Two guards towered over him. They lifted him to his knees and bent him forward then unchained him from the wall and stood him up. One guard pulled his jaw open and presented him with the dull green liquid. Ahmed didn't resist. He drank it.

Securing his wrists to the waist chain behind his back the guards led him out of his cell. A guard came forward and pulled a brown sack over his head. Ahmed's hot, moist breath threatened to suffocate him inside the bag and his insides churned. What would dying be like? He had never thought about it until now.

They dragged him down the hall. Ahmed could not see what was happening but he heard another cell door open in front of him and someone being dragged out. He felt a tug on his wrists, the weight of a connecting chain that connected him to another prisoner. The pair were dragged out of the jail to a waiting carriage.

⁓

Scores of people lined the square. They overflowed so much that the lines of Immortals were struggling to keep them back. Yet they managed to keep a lane clear that Will guessed Ahmed would soon come by. Ahmed's execution had been advertised for a few days. Rightfully knowing it would take time to set up this execution, and observing its progress so they wouldn't be too late, Will and Jillian had explored the sewers and found the best path to come by.

The execution platform was a stage. On it two wooden stakes stood upright with some distance between them. A makeshift staircase led onto the stage. Will and Jillian were crouching on the rooftop across the stage, looking over the scene. Will held a bow and arrows he'd found in the boat, and dawned a sword and pistol as well as Ahmed's cloak. He rummaged through Ahmed's stuff until he found a smoke bomb. It may become useful. Will tensed the bow. Beside Will, Jillian noticed this.

"You sure you know how to use that bow?" she asked.

"Yeah, sure, I had a lesson."

"A lesson!? Give that to me. You may well kill Ahmed yourself, making this risky outing very meaningless."

"You know how to use it? D'you have the strength to draw the string back?" Will asked, surprised. He gave Jillian the bow and arrows.

"I've had more than one lesson and this is not some war bow." Jillian smiled. Will nodded. "Go down there and be ready for when I strike. I will protect you, but you will have to be fast to save Ahmed. We only have seconds 'afore the confusion dies out." Will started to climb off the flat roof. "Will," Jillian said. Will turned back. "If you are captured…"

"Then return to the boat and go to Gurmanis. If you can… tell my master I am dead." Will spoke firmly, his serious tone making the girl frown. She nodded.

"You are selfless and loyal, Will. Manis protect you."

Will smiled at Jillian. "He never has." The boy climbed down and off the roof then merged with the crowd, making his way to the stage.

⁓

The carriage jerked to a stop, and the deafening sounds of jeering people surrounded them. Something hard hit Ahmed's arm. Something else hit his head. He heard the door of the carriage cage open and the connecting chain shift and tug. Guards grabbed his arms and dragged him out. More things hit him. Something cut him. A guard yanked Ahmed close and planted his hand over the boy's mouth.

"Traitor! D'you really think a mere sixteen-year-old boy could change the course of a war?" the guard growled centimeters from Ahmed's right ear. He shoved Ahmed forwards into another guard, the connecting chain going taut.

Ahmed was dragged forward barely seeing the outline of a crowd of people. He ascended a staircase then he was shoved, back first, into a pole. The guards chained his wrists, still attached to his waist, to the pole. Another bound his neck and legs to the pole with rope. Someone rubbed at his torso, drawing an **X** on his tunic. The connecting chain tugged at him as the other prisoner was bound to the adjacent stake. Ahmed waited. He gathered courage. He wanted to die with as much dignity as he could salvage, he wouldn't cry. He should, maybe. He didn't prefer to die but he was content with how he had lived so far. He had grown much since he accidentally burned down Hamid's souk. Was he afraid? Should he be? His hands trembled with nervous tension, his ears seemed to perk up, reacting to every noise tenfold the normal. His heart beat in slow rhythmic thumps, his mouth dried, and his muscles tightened. Nausea crept over him. Were these symptoms of fear?

The crowd grew silent as the sultan spoke from somewhere high up.

"Let it be known today the fate of traitors in my sultanate! These two have committed just that. They have betrayed us all and are sentenced to death! May God have mercy on their souls for he is most merciful. God be witness to this day for he is all things!"

"Praise to God! Alhurahu akbar!" the crowd chanted.

Jillian aimed and drew back then adjusted, muscle memory returning to her as quick as wine fills a chalice at a party. She squinted and hoped Will was ready. The tension she created made her break a drop of sweat. She realised how long it had been since she held a bow. Jillian shook the thought away; this was all familiar, that much her body knew. She released the tension and waited until the right moment. Please be quick Will. She looked for him. Will needed to get closer, then she would loose. Too early and they would halt the executions to find the archer first.

She watched as the executioner climbed onto the stage. He picked up a large two-handed scimitar and held it at the ready. He stood near the boy who wasn't Ahmed. The sacks on the boys' heads were ripped off to reveal their faces.

Ahmed shook the sweat off of him. His vision normalized. A herald stood in front of him.

"Condemned to die today is Shoran al-Murzq for the crime of treason. His actions downed an airship and led to the escape of two Gurmian prisoners-of-war thus he had aided the traitor Ahmed Sharfi," the herald announced to thunderous cheers. Ahmed's mind fixated on the name he thought he had heard. Shoran… death… Sh-Shoran. Ahmed turned his head, straining against the rope that bit his neck. Shoran, in tears and looking utterly terrified, was bound to the stake beside Ahmed.

"Sh-Shoran!" Ahmed shouted. Shoran turned to Ahmed, the color in his face lost, but he said nothing. "Sultan!" Ahmed shouted over the crowd. "I beg you! Release Shoran. He does not deserve to die. Please sultan leave him out of this!" Ahmed begged, trying to pull away from his stake. What had he done? He was not thinking when he called out to Shoran, he had not meant to ask for his aid but he had been caught up in the moment. The crowd cheered again and the executioner turned to Shoran. Shoran stared at the scimitar being aimed towards the 𝑋 on his chest. Ahmed struggled. In one swift motion the scimitar pushed through Shoran's torso and the boy grunted. He looked at the executioner with horror and blood oozed from his mouth then he slumped over and lay still. The executioner tore his blade free sending a spray of blood outwards.

"NO!" Ahmed screamed, drowned out by the crowd. "N-No…" he mumbled. Tears teased his eyes. Not Shoran. Not his only friend. His actions had killed or disgraced everyone he cared for. Why had he done it? Why had he allowed his doubts drive him to this? It wasn't supposed to end like this! The executioner stepped in front of Ahmed and aimed his scimitar at the boy's 𝑋. The words the herald spoke about him were muffled, as were the voices of the crowd. Ahmed took a deep breath, sucked up all the courage he had left, and looked his murderer in the eyes.

"The worthiest god is Alhurah and there is no greater god than him, so says the Father," Ahmed whispered. The executioner jerked forwards, eyes-wide, and stumbled away. An arrow was lodged in his back. Another arrow soared through the air, breaking into the back of the man's head.

To Ahmed's right a ruckus broke out in the crowd and he spotted Will forcing his way towards the stage. He approached a guard who collapsed before him, an arrow in his back. The second guard turned to face Will but was shot in the chest before he acted. Right behind him a guard swung a sword at Will but was stopped mid-swing by an arrow. Will jumped to the right, narrowly avoiding the falling sword. Ahmed stood there in a state of shock. Will ran up the stairs. More arrows felled guards. Chaos erupted in the crowd effectively cutting off reinforcing guards from reaching Will. Will fumbled with the restraints and pulled the ropes off.

"Will? I told you to leave me!" Ahmed said.

"I won't leave you to this!" Will tugged the chains.

"You need a key. Leave it and go before you are—"

"No!" Will searched the body of the executioner and found the key. He unlocked the shackles. The two jumped forward onto the ground. Will loosened the chains and shackles on Ahmed's waist and ankles and threw them away. The boys stood up only to be confronted by a group of Immortals backing them into the stage. Sultan Yazid was behind them.

"Kill them," were the two words he spoke. The guards advanced. Will tugged the smoke bomb from behind his waist, breaking it free from its cord. He chucked the bomb at the Immortals and drew his pistol. He fired. The space exploded into smoke, choking the area in greyish white. Will and Ahmed made their escape through a side street blending with the fleeing crowd. Jillian, bow in hand, was waiting for them at a sewer entrance in the city.

———

Will sailed the felucca and Jillian attended to Ahmed who was lying on a blanket near the back.

"What did they feed you?" Jillian asked.

"A green liquid." Ahmed mumbled.

"How do you feel?"

"Dizzy, weak, tired." Ahmed groaned. "It stopped my magic."

"It was some sort of drug used to weaken the senses. I can make a medicine that will counteract its effects with local herbs when we reach the other side, but it must leave your system on its own," Jillian reassured him. Ahmed nodded.

Will turned to him. "Now may not be the best time to say this, but I may have lost your cloak during the escape in the sewers."

Ahmed shifted to look at Will. "It does not matter. What's worse is that they took my pearl. I am glad I had left my things with you."

"Or maybe not!" Will rushed over to Ahmed's things. He dug through and lifted the pearl out. Ahmed stared on wide-eyed.

"But how?"

"Don't know, happened to me once." Will put it back and returned to the wheel. Ahmed paid them no mind. He only saw Shoran's terrified face and his death replayed in his mind.

"S-Sorry," Jillian tried to say. Ahmed looked at her, confused. "Saomardrim understand the concept… I mean…" Jillian looked nervous. "Sorry… we couldn't save him. The other boy. It was too early for me to loose, you may have died." Ahmed looked to the sky. Jillian nodded and stepped away. He'd been too impulsive and he cursed himself for not realizing it. What did all his efforts in becoming so learned matter if in the end his emotions had led him to these bold and sudden actions? It meant he was never who he thought he was. Shoran… I am sorry. You wanted to repay me for freeing you, didn't you? You could not find a way until you were in that airship and you saw what was happening. I did this to you and now you are dead.

Part Four:
The Gods of the World

Chapter Twenty-Four

THEY LANDED AT night, south of Suthenburg, on a beach overlooked by a low hill of grass. To their west, mountains, the Wealdbeorgas, hid the Roywood beyond it.

Jillian and Ahmed stayed with the boat while Will sought information in Suthenburg. Jillian was quick to voice her displeasure at being left with a Saomardrim. Ahmed forgave her caution; it was to be expected. Perhaps after getting to know him some more, Jillian, like Will, might warm up to him.

Jillian and Ahmed set camp on the hill. Ahmed made a fire in the center and Jillian used tarps from their boat to create a tent. She sat beside Ahmed and brought her knees towards her chest, observing him.

"You are staring. Is there something on your mind?" Ahmed asked.

"What I have witnessed about your land, Ahmed, the Saomarhadians." She frowned. "As children they told us that your kind were monsters, that you would steal us away from our parents, bomb and pillage our homes."

"Hostility, all because it is easier to think that way rather than sail across the river and see the truth. We are at war; it makes it easier to kill another person if you think that person will hurt you. Do I look like a monster to you, Jillian? Have I stolen you away?" Ahmed asked, his voice calm.

"No, you brought me home."

"Right, I am not what your people say I am, nor are you what my people said you were. I suppose all Gurmians think like you did?"

"Maybe."

"Tell me, what did you see in my country?"

"People, no monsters."

"Most of whom were not even born when this war began. How can you fault them for this violence? How can you call them monsters?"

Jillian glared at Ahmed. "Your people executed all the Gurmian prisoners-of-war. What me and Will were being dragged to was a bloodbath."

"That was the sultan's plan… I agree… it was wrong, it was a horrific act but it is unfair to blame all Saomarhadians for it."

"A-Ahmed…" Jillian's voice cracked and she rubbed her wrist; Ahmed sensed the air between them thicken. "Saomardrim killed my mother during a raid. I was naught but a few months at the front… my father sent word." Jillian looked at Ahmed, tears welling in her eyes. "I hate those who killed her, I hate murderers of every kind. I'd rather they kill each other. I did hate your people."

"I am sorry, Jillian." Ahmed's insides twisted. A girl crying in front of him was something no one ever prepared him for.

"I know it's not your fault. I am sorry. It's hard for me to trust yo… anyone… anymore."

"I feel the same right now." Ahmed's voice was almost a whisper. "Right now, I feel as if I have landed in an alien place and I am as shocked about it as you had felt coming into my home. I fear I will see monsters just the same as you feared it. I fear Gurmians will stride forth and slaughter me… like my kinsmen did to your mother." Jillian gave Ahmed an understanding nod and by the turmoil Ahmed sensed in her mind, coming in waves, he knew it was hard for her to do.

"You know, Gurmian is a collective term. It includes several peoples united under Gurmanis' flag. There are Franorms, Guelts, Aangsax, Gerio, and Ruvic. It is similar to what Will explained about Saomarhadians. Will and I are Aangsax, though I think I have some Franormish in me."

Ahmed huffed and flashed a smile. "We are so confused about each other's culture that we do not care about nor see this distinction."

"This is all new to me. How was Gurmanis so wrong? How did it all go on like this? Just so we all could fight."

"I agree. I once considered myself wise." Ahmed sighed. "But I realise now I had believed or chose not to concern myself with all the propaganda my country told me. I was accepting lies. For that I am ashamed."

"I see… yes… I feel the same." Jillian sighed and looked away, wiping tears from her eyes.

<hr>

When Will returned he had news to share. He sat beside the fire.

"Sir Robert is at Castle Ochsen. They returned from a three-day battle from Halsburg to Croixville. They won, though Halsburg was captured by the Saomarhadians," Will informed them.

"So, you intend to find your master, but you'd have me taken through people inclined to butcher me," Ahmed said. "Right now, my fate is in your hands… friend."

"If you remain lowkey until we find him, you'll be ok. I will vouch for you an' my master will protect you."

"Can you be sure?"

"He cared for me. I trust him and I hope he trusts me. He won't hurt you or send you back. He's a good man. I don't think I'd have survived in battle without my master's and his allies' instructions." Will frowned.

"From my viewpoint, when I deal with all the wounded, it seems the battlefield is a place of great bloodshed. I don't understand how men can survive it," Jillian said.

"You don't hesitate."

"A healer? What is that like?" Ahmed asked.

"I enjoy the art of herbs and medicines. Maybe that's an odd profession for me but it's the one I grew fond of. I left home; my father was a wealthy merchant. I was given everything to help me learn the craft but never did I have a chance to practice, until I joined the army."

"Odd for a merchant's daughter indeed."

"Well…" Jillian hesitated, unsure if she wanted to share. "We rented out an out-building to an aspiring doctor once. I guess I bugged him enough that he caved and started to teach me the basics." A moment of silence passed between the three.

"We should spend the night here. The roads may be unsafe," Will broke the silence, "That's what the Suthenburg constables told me."

Water lapped onto the beach below and the moon shone a white light. The three youths stayed silent for a while, and only Jillian seemed to be noticing the atmosphere. She sat between Will and Ahmed. Ahmed looked into the fire; Will looked towards the ground. Not far away, on a sandbar risen out of the water, Will's falcon swooped down and landed. It quietly observed the three youths and their fire.

Jillian's eyes set on Will, lingering there for a moment before she turned back to the fire. She ran her fingers through her hair grabbing a strand and dragging down its length then repeating. Finally, she looked around, unable to keep the silence.

"Isn't it so quiet? There is war all around us, yet here it's peaceful."

"Down to its base level… that's all most people want. Peace, contentment, meaning in their lives, and the safety and security of themselves and their loved ones," Ahmed said.

"Yes… I agree." Jillian smiled. Will shivered, despite the fire, he'd longed for what Ahmed described… for years. "There is still much good in this world."

"Thatched over by black straw." Will grimaced, feeling as if the shadows were wrapping around him.

"How could you deny a good thought?"

"For everything good there is something evil."

"And mortals justify what is evil as good," Ahmed said.

"Forget the war for a moment. It's easy!" Jillian frowned.

"It's never easy to forget," Will whispered.

"It's this war that's gotten to you two! There is more than that in this world, do not forget the times of peace." Jillian looked into the fire. "I have stayed home away from the world. When I left, I saw what the world was really like. Despite this war I came across people who wanted to help me.

They'd provided food and shelter even if they had little. I came across kind and unkind people but I can't believe all is bad. If I see a way that would bring fairness, equality, justice, and peace, I want to remember that so I can strive to change things towards that end. I was so ignorant, but now I have learned so much."

"We are three young people Jillian without high positions in society. What we do would change little," Will said, but despite his words he warmed a little inside. He wished such things were possible. He wanted no one to suffer the injustice he had suffered and to hear Jillian convey similar goals made him very content.

Jillian looked at Will as if she was about to retaliate but Ahmed interrupted, "I am more concerned for her lofty goals." Ahmed laughed. "A peasant can do little to enact fairness, equality, justice, and peace."

Jillian's face reddened. "Just watch me; you don't know me," she mumbled, her eyes narrow.

"He has a point." Will shivered. "The powerless can't do anything." That's why at Sir Robert's side he might one day find a way to do something. Jillian seemed to think similarly. They could work together, he'd like that.

"At least we are… are… friends, Gurmian and Saomardrim though we may be." Jillian looked again into the fire. "I had many friends but I was never sure whether father had bought them or if they really were my friends. When I left home, I found a real friend, a girl interested in the healing arts as well. I left her in Sir Robert's camp; I hope she is okay."

"I had many friends…" Will looked into the fire. "The entire village's children because it was us older kids in charge. I had a best friend. In the end he betrayed me… he lied about me… and helped them put me away." Will shivered. "I don't blame Saul, not anymore. I understand he was as young as I was and how he was manipulated into saying what he said. We all came together and beat Lord Jerold' bet." Will changed the topic. "He believed Aldershire's serf children couldn't build their tree castle, but we did! No matter how many times he tried to stop us we outwitted him." Will looked back into the fire, feeling himself grow cold. "Saul? Friends? I ne'er had a real one."

Ahmed cast at the fire pit to strengthen the flame.

"Me and my brother Amir shared friends; we were close. My father allowed any child rich or poor to come into the palace. We didn't always understand how much caution was put onto those kids whom we played with. If one were to accidentally hurt us even in innocent play… he would be punished for it. When I was at the mages university, I met Shoran. He and I had great fun in Murzq, we became best friends. I sent him to his death and I can't go back and change that. I shouldn't have asked."

Silence covered the air between the friends for a while. The thoughts of their lives flooded their minds, how they had made it to this point, sitting over a beach in a secluded part of the world, with people they had once thought were their enemies.

"The world is not all evil; it can't be." Jillian sighed. "We have new friends now, we have each other, despite all that's happened to us."

"You seem to have no problem telling us about yourself." Ahmed smiled.

"What's that supposed to mean?" Jillian blushed.

"We haven't known each other for long."

"I-I mean you saved our lives and that counts for a lot. You had every chance to hurt or kill me… I was afraid. I told you… you know." Jillian frowned.

"Thank-you Jillian. I was afraid too." Ahmed nodded. Will looked from Ahmed to Jillian. What had Jillian told him? "In the moment I had to make the decision to run away, I was filled with great dread. I don't know if I made the right decision."

"I-I feel… comfortable… with you two." Will flashed an awkward smile. Jillian blushed.

"Actually," Ahmed blushed, "since we're sharing so much… I wasn't sure I'd even hold a conversation with Jillian."

"Wh-What do you mean about that?" Jillian raised an eyebrow.

"I've not talked to girls my age much at all."

"You're scared of me!" Jillian laughed. "You?"

"I-I didn't say that."

"Why don't we lie back and enjoy this moment's peace 'afore we all end up embarrassing ourselves further." Jillian giggled and fell back to lie down and gaze at the sky. Will and Ahmed laid down on either side of her.

"See that," Ahmed traced out a long hazy and glowing tail in the sky. "That's our galaxy, beautiful isn't it? Subhanalhurah."

"Those stars look like an arrow plunging into it. What is that?" Jillian asked.

"Oh… it's nothing."

"Come on, it's something."

"That is Kalshaimar's Solution, a constellation. Tonight it is brighter that the other stars which means… it means come morning there will be death and blood."

"Oh." Jillian sighed. "Will, you take the first watch." Jillian turned to her side where Will had risen.

"G-G'night." Will smiled, face flushed in red, his heat thumping against his ribs. He scrambled up. Ahmed covered his face in his arms as Will's falcon arrived to sleep by the fire.

Will, Ahmed, and Jillian approached Castle Ochsen an hour after sunrise. Crowds of commoners were crowded at the gatehouse. Many wept and pleaded with the soldiers on the ramparts to be allowed in.

"By order of Sir Robert you must wait yer turn. Everyone will have a chance to identify your loved ones. Please have patience."

The three walked uneasily through the crowd of distraught people. Ahmed tensed, seeing fear in Jillian's eyes, but they all remained silent. Will waved at the soldier on the gatehouse ramparts.

"I request entry. I am Squire Will with two friends."

"Wh-What? Vagabonds, eh?" The soldier looking down on them scoffed. Will realised he and Jillian were still in their dirt filled, torn and worn clothes. Their hair probably looked no better. Meanwhile Ahmed was in a hooded tattered old cloak. "Is it? Ah! Squire Will! Sir Robert has been worried about you. Thought you went and got yourself captured he did."

"Ah… yeah something like that." Will blushed; he was glad his master did not think he had run away.

"You'd better come in, Manis have mercy." The soldier looked closer at Ahmed for a second before moving to unlock the gate. Soldiers held back the crowd.

The three walked through and Will led them inside the castle, passing through the barbican and up the winding path towards the inner bailey. It was the same path Will had taken with his master the last time he'd come.

The castle, as before, was filled with tents. Soldiers rushed about and Ahmed kept his head low.

As they ascended, what was happening became clearer. People wept, bundles and piles cluttered all the space. They passed a pile of dead bodies being rounded up into carts for burial. Ahmed stopped and realised what it was. Gurmians, the result of the sultan's plan. He noticed more Gurmian dead, a number were headless. Sweat beaded on his skin; had he a hand to play in this massacre? Jillian gasped, giving Ahmed an accusing glare. She crouched towards the pile finding there a dead boy, his eyes still open. On his forehead was a crude hole, its edges crusted in dried blood. It was the exit for the musket ball that had killed him. Jillian took his dead hand in hers and tears teased her eyes. Ahmed was stuck in place. Will came from behind and touched Jillian's shoulder.

"We must find my master." Will remained calm. Jillian stood, wrapping her arms around herself. Ahmed clenched his fists.

"We decided to do nothing. We escaped knowing this would happen," Jillian said.

"We had no choice. We couldn't have saved them all."

"I need to find Ms. Godfrey and Keira. They will need my help now that I am back. Both of you go on ahead. I will see you later," Jillian said. Will nodded and found himself unprepared for the sudden hollowness he felt in her absence.

～

A knock rattled the door of Sir Robert's quarters. "Yes?" He turned around as Will and a cloaked boy walked in.

"Will! Where were you? What happened to you? I feared the worst! Those vile Saomardrim catapulted our dead kinsmen on-masse; I am sure you have seen them. Reports say the same thing has happened all along the front. This is a dark day this…" The knight noticed Will's sombre face and composed himself. He took a deep breath. He was greatly relieved. He'd feared Will had also been killed but upon seeing him a weight lifted off his shoulders.

"At least you have returned, thank Manis." Though Will's shabby appearance gave him pause.

"It's a long story, Master. Sorry I must have worried you."

"That you did, Will. Who is this boy?"

"This is… Ahmed, Master."

Ahmed cautiously stepped forward.

"Ahmed, that is a Saomardrim name isn't it…?" Ahmed pulled away his hood and Sir Robert flinched, reaching for his longsword. Ahmed stepped back. "What is this Will? A Saomardrim!"

"I know, Master. He's the one who captured me. He brought me to Ortie but then he saved me and Jillian, the girl I spoke to you about in Al-Motros, and helped us escape."

Sir Robert tightened his grip on his sword, his heart now hammering away.

"But Will, what will the men say? Especially after what the Saomardrim sent us." His anger broiled inside him as flashes of bodies being catapulted over the walls and pilled onto the beaches below passed his mind. The morning had been chaotic and Sir Robert had maintained his composure, teetering on the edge of breaking.

"I am sorry… I could not stop what has happened," Ahmed said. Sir Robert drew his sword slightly out of its scabbard, prompting Ahmed to move his hand over his sword. Will was insane bringing an enemy here. He'd right his apprentice's mistake by putting this Saomardrim to death.

"Your people not only murdered the surviving soldiers of Al-Motros but also the non-combatants. They showed them no dignity. Is this how the sultan conducts himself? To think I regret killing so many… after this…" The knight's voice was laced with scorn.

"I know, Master but it's not his fault. Ahmed did not agree with the sultan's plan and instead risked his life to save me and bring me here. Otherwise, I would have been in those piles of dead outside. He is considered a murderer and a traitor in his home… like I was."

Ahmed frowned, nodding and Sir Robert loosened his grip. It seemed like there was a friendly understanding between the boys. Will might have been ignorant of the world when Sir Robert had first met him but it seemed to the knight that Will had returned to him with new knowledge.

"I believe my squire." Sir Robert sighed. "You were not the one who killed them nor were you the one to throw their lifeless corpses over the wall. I am sorry but after what your people have done to us in this war, I am inclined to kill all of you."

Ahmed inhaled, leveling his eyes at the knight.

"I know it is greatly unfair to blame or punish you for what others have done. After today however there is great anger among my people. They will call for Saomardrim blood, any Saomardrim blood no matter how innocent or guilty. I should thank you for saving my squire but you must realize as my squire should as well, the complications of you here."

"I understand, sir," Ahmed said, making a slight bow. Sir Robert's anger eased.

"Well, we will have to figure something out. It would not sit well with me sending you back to sure death after what you have done for my squire. Perhaps a servant? Most of your people who made it here are dead. The few free Saomardrim are bullied and discriminated against. Others are interned in prison camps."

"Can't you get the men to trust him Master?"

"No, I can get them to be *ok* with him, but only my own men. For now, he is my servant Will. As squire you have as much say in him as I. Don't leave him alone with the men and keep his presence here discreet. After what they experienced this morning and after the battles they've fought, I fear the worst."

"He is capable, Master. He is also a mage."

"Oh? Well, that's one thing as well and may complicate matters if the men know it too soon, therefore, there must be no magic. Are you a battle mage in the Saomarhad army?"

"No sir," Ahmed started. "I have been studying at Murzq for the entire war. My first experience on the front lines was when I discovered your squire amongst the rubble of Al-Motros."

"I see. I can't rely only on my squire's words for you. Know this one thing: if you hurt anyone here, if it is found out you are a spy—"

"Master!"

Sir Robert shot Will an ireful look. Will frowned.

"You will be punished accordingly. I'll have you fitted in dimithrite manacles."

"I understand your caution." Ahmed frowned. "I… I will accept your conditions. Thank-you." Ahmed looked disappointed but Will didn't understand why.

"Master, what are dimi—"

"For now, the two of you should stay in the keep and rest. I will speak with you both later. Will I want you to tell me everything that happened to you… after you clean up and get yourself a new tunic."

"Yes Master."

"Good. I have much to do so I will get someone to show you to my room. This castle will be deserted in a few days for" —Sir Robert hesitated— "for accelerated plans."

In the afternoon, the next day, on the west wall of Castle Ochsen most soldiers were leaning or sitting against the crenellations. They mingled amongst themselves. The clear sky and sombre mood rendering the afternoon feeling sluggish, to Will at least. Ahmed stayed close, quiet and observing, and Jillian seemed to be waiting to break away from the dullness.

The three friends stood on top of a castle turret. Ahmed shifted the dimithrite manacles clamped around his wrists. The chain between them had been removed.

"I'm sorry... again." Will frowned. "I didn't think my master would be so... distrustful."

"Will." Ahmed chuckled. "Your master has shown me great trust. I do not blame him for binding me to prevent my use of magic. It is natural. Besides, I still have my weapons."

"But they burn."

"For a day or two, then my wrists go numb and it's not so bad."

"I'm impressed..." Jillian smiled, "with you Will."

"M-Me? Why?" Will blushed and his chest tingled.

"It's just that you... you stand up for Ahmed, despite everything we were told about his people and the fact that he dragged you down the length of Saomarhad to have you killed. Ahmed..." Jillian hesitated, perhaps unsure if she should also trust Ahmed readily. "You are proving yourself."

Ahmed blushed.

"Come Will, let's find something to do."

"It will soon be time for afternoon prayer. I will find a secluded place to do so." Ahmed smiled. Will and Jillian toured the ramparts, talking idly and laughing at each other's comments on occasion. Will reveled in her voice as if it had the sweetness of honey in it.

Below, in the courtyard of the castle a number of herders, dog breeders, and their assistants were tending to a dozen hunting dogs. The dogs, puppies and adults, seemed to be tense as if waiting for some opportune moment. The smaller door cut into the larger gatehouse swung open upon a shout from the gate guard. Several hunters entered dragging small mammal corpses behind them. The hunting dogs stood to attention and barked, startling their handlers. Will, Jillian, and a few other soldiers looked down from the wall to see what was going on. One of the handlers shouted as he tried to pull back a larger hunting dog but the dog broke away and charged at the hunters. The hunters dropped their catch and lunged out of the way. The dog grabbed a dead hare and dashed out of the castle.

All the dogs broke away and charged at the pile of forgotten meat. They took what they could then followed the larger dog into the green grassy fields outside the castle, the village of Ochsen visible beyond. Jillian laughed, grabbed Will by his arm, and led him into the courtyard.

"Hurry! We need to round 'em up!" a handler shouted while scrambling to get cages and nets.

"Stop!" Jillian shouted with sudden authority. "Let us go!"

"Who're you ordering us like that?" the handler scoffed. He looked at the boy Jillian had brought with her, recognised the symbol on his tunic, and stood straight. "Squire William." The handler bowed. Will nodded with unease.

"Why did the dogs all run out like that?" Will asked.

"They're the hounds of the Baron of Suthenburg. Been kept in Castle Ochsen for most of their lives. We were ordered to train 'em within the confines of the castle. They never been outside."

"I see; those dogs wanted freedom," Jillian said. "Will let's go after them."

"Those are hunting dogs, girl! Look at them the wrong way and they'll maul you to death."

"We can let them deal with this." Will said, unsure at Jillian's sudden enthusiasm. Jillian shook her head.

"I know what I am doing, come on!" Jillian pointed outside as she urged Will on.

"My young lord. Please wait!" The handler shouted.

"Let's go take a closer look! Come on!"

"Closer… ah, maybe we shouldn't. The adults are very big." Will hesitated.

"It will be fine. I'll protect you." Jillian giggled.

Hey! He could protect himself. Will stepped forward. "Sure, yea, let's go." He followed Jillian out, swallowing. They passed through the west gate and Jillian ran ahead to the grass spinning with her arms out. She laughed. Will smiled wide. As the sun glistened off her skin Will found himself frozen, watching Jillian's travel dress flutter in the air and her hair being lifted by the wind. Jillian stopped spinning and smiled at Will. She stared at him. A battle between warmth and unease raged within him as the ends of his tunic lifted and cooling wind entrained his cloak and hair.

"Join me! Can't you smell the fresh air away from the castle?" Jillian took a deep breath in. "Too close, let's go further!" Jillian ran to Will and took his arm. Their eyes locked for a second, sending a jolt of warmth through Will. She tugged Will forward and Will followed her until they were in the middle of the grassy plain about halfway from the castle and the dogs.

The dogs had all gathered together and were chasing each other for the meat they shared. Jillian ran forward and took in a breath of air. She smiled and turned to Will who was clueless. She hugged Will. Unease surged over him and he tensed at her touch, trying to break free. Jillian's hands shifted to his waist before letting go. She blushed.

The dogs noticed the humans close by and charged them. The adults took the lead, barking angrily, followed by the younger dogs. Jillian noticed, and planted a foot forward. She whistled, the loud sound whirling alongside the wind, and gave the dogs a firm command. Almost immediately the dogs stopped barking, closed the distance at a walking pace, and gathered around Will and Jillian.

"How d'you do that?" Will asked, admiring her actions.

"Do what?"

"Order the dogs to stand down. I was sure the adults would have attacked us."

"It was nothing really."

"It was something. A noble's hunting dogs are strictly trained to obey only their masters, the humans who have been with them since their birth."

"Who d'you think supplies the nobles with hunting dogs? My father was once in charge of a ship load of Free Lands steppe dogs, bred by high orcs. They are some of the most sought-after breeds. My father needed help so he taught me."

"It's a timely thing you remembered what to say." The younger dogs walked closer, pacing around and between the youths and sniffing at their legs. Jillian laughed.

"They like us." She smiled.

"Yeah…" Will tensed.

"There has to be something around here that we can use," Jillian said half to herself. She moved off, followed by the puppies, looking through the grasses. Most adult dogs walked off to a nearby flat, angled boulder to rest. One approached Will and growled. Will stared at it, trembling as it started to bark with force. *Locked up in a lightless cage, a guard holding a growling dog by the leash. It barked at him, centimeters from Will's ear, fury in its eyes. Its saliva finding his face.* Will hesitated then backed away, but the dog approached. Will tripped over himself. The dog still barked. Will's vision blurred; his heart started to race.

Jillian appeared over him, looking concerned. She said something to the dog.

"Shh… Why are you so enraged? Come on, we're all friends." Jillian stroked its black fur. The dog whined happily and Jillian offered Will a hand, smiling. Will looked at her face, comforted by her sight. The sent of vanilla flowed past his nose and the sun behind Jillian seemed to illuminate her. His heart skipped a beat.

He liked being around her. It felt… right to be around her. He could forget so much of the stress of his squiredom and of his past. Will took her hand hesitantly. But what if she didn't want to be around him? What if he lost her? Like he lost his family? Will gripped her hand tightly and let himself be helped up. His chest met the palm of Jillian's left hand. They said nothing for a moment and looked into each other's eyes. Will swallowed, his lips parted. Jillian's skin flushed red.

A puppy bounded forward, stick in its jaws, poking Will's leg with it. The other puppies yapped.

"I told you 'twould be fine," Jillian whispered, removing her hand from Will's chest.

"Yes, you were right."

"And that it would be fun?"

"You never said that!"

"But I implied it!" She smiled and bent down to the puppy with the stick, taking it from him. All the puppies eagerly waited around them, pacing happily. "Then let's enjoy ourselves for this one moment." She threw the stick.

A puppy leapt forwards and landed in a patch of taller grass, shrouding itself from sight. A moment later it poked its head out, stick in its jaw. It bolted forwards and rushed back towards Will and Jillian, sitting with the adult dogs on the boulder. The rest of the puppies mobbed the stick carrier, trying to claim the prize. They dashed towards Will and Jillian, one pup was already on Jillian's lap, resting. Will sat beside her feeling a warmth radiate within him and between them. He watched her hair blow with the wind.

"Your hair's so… light." Will smiled. Jillian looked at him and laughed. She held up the pup.

"He's not amused." Jillian made a playful smile. The puppy yawned and Will's cheeks reddened. A horn blared, angry and demanding. Jillian stood, her lap dog rushing off. Will stood too. The horn sounded again. Jillian's eyes widened.

"That horn… it's… Lord Richrit!" She ran towards the sound and Will screamed her name. He ran after her followed by the dogs. Jillian stopped at the end of the plain where it dropped off to reveal the front gate. She stood there wide-eyed. Will ran over and froze, shocked as well. The puppies came and whimpered; the adults barking angrily. A massive force of Gurmian soldiers marching in formed battalions stretched out before them. Thousands of them, a sea of blue and gold.

Will steadied himself. "I think we should return to the castle."

<hr>

The thunder of horses galloping towards the main gate quieted everyone on the ramparts. Sir Robert made his way to the courtyard. He saw the tents below. Battalions of men and support crew were making camp outside of the castle. In the harbour an armada laid anchor. Reinforcements had arrived. Sir Robert along with his commanders waited as the commanders of the reinforcing army rode in. They dismounted and approached. Sir John, Alex following behind him, shook Sir Robert's hand but he did so solemnly.

"Friend." He nodded. Sir Robert eyed him, sensing an odd tone. Then a regal looking man came forward. He wore blue-gold robes and a black velvet chaperon. A cloak with the symbol of his domain, an impaled man, draped almost to the ground. Behind him were three knights wearing the yellow flowering sun of Manis over a black cross on their white tunics, Knights Teutonic, also coming as reinforcements.

"Sir Robert Gillios you have been a dreadful knight of the realm. I am Lord Richrit of Saalweg. I have come on behalf of King Duggan who has instructed me to supervise the invasion. I have intercepted a letter from one of your commanders, what I read is less than pleasing."

"Lord Richrit." Sir Robert nodded. A thief of letters, but also the man who'd led the Grand Mosque Massacre, stood before him, paler than he'd been described. "The plans for the invasion have already been laid out. There is no need—"

"There is a need!" spat Lord Richrit. "I understand that you are in the company of a fugitive murderer and an infidel. I never thought you would stoop so low, Sir Robert. I always took you for a loyal man."

"I am loyal to the realm, and to the king, however I do hold true to the other tenants of knighthood more than the next knight."

"The *only* reason you are still alive and, I repeat… the *only* reason, is because you and your men are effective. The king deems you valuable but he cannot tolerate what you are doing for long. I know your defence, Sir Robert, and so I am not here to argue but to simply supervise. After the invasion you are to return to Royal Landing with your charges or the king will take it as treason."

"Of course." Sir Robert gestured, the lord's tone irritatingly superior.

"Sehr gut. My army is in need of accommodation; all the commanders will meet in one hour to go over the plans." With that said, Lord Richrit mounted and trotted back to his men. Sir John looked sympathetically at Sir Robert and followed. Sir Robert grimaced, sick of the king's games, and turned to meet Admiral Białek.

"Henryk, you! You scared me there," Sir Robert gasped.

"Tak, Robert." Henryk nodded "This path you are taking is troublesome. Are you sure you want to face the king? He is starting to distrust you. Things are about to get more complicated." The Admiral made off to Lord Richrit' camp, not caring for Sir Robert's answer.

<hr>

Will and Ahmed waited outside the keep's great hall. Two Knight's Teutonic blocked their way into the war meeting. Two of Sir Robert's trusted men stood behind Will and Ahmed, making sure nothing happened. Still, Ahmed kept a hand close to his kilij.

Finally the doors swung open and Lord Richrit strode out. He paused in front of Will and Ahmed.

"It is you two." He scoffed then looked over Ahmed. "Yours is a violent religion with men wishing for death."

"If our neighbors are cruel, it is then we show bravery against those worthless ones." Ahmed smirked, glaring at the lord. He'd heard about what this man had done.

"Ahmed, don't." Will tensed. Lord Richrit laughed.

"And you." He paced ahead of Will. "Kalshaimar's lieutenant. I hope your afterlife at his side will be everything you deserve. I had a son, dutiful and brave. He sacrificed himself for me when a suicidal Saomardrim interrupted our regular mass. My three others now slaughter heretics, heathens, all dangers to glorious Gurmanis."

"The invasion will be a success, Lord Richrit." Sir Robert stepped out of the great hall.

"Klar. The Saomardrim will pay for overstepping their bounds with one swift blow. Some of my men will keep a lookout on this infidel wherever he goes. I do not trust the barbarisch."

Sir Robert did not disagree. Ahmed huffed. Lord Richrit threw his cloak aside then he and his knights brushed past the boys.

"Will. Ahmed." Sir Robert snapped. He strode forwards, signaling them to follow him down the hall. "Leave us Ahmed. Go straight to your quarters. Lord Richrit will only watch you." He stared hard at Ahmed. "Do not do anything to them."

Ahmed nodded and parted.

"Will… keep Ahmed uninformed."

"Master, he's—"

"Will."

"Yes Master."

"We are invading southern Saomarhad. We will be attacking Fort Valki by air to finally dislodge its defenders, but Castle Ochsen will be lightly defended, to confuse the Saomarhad air fleet and draw them away from Fort Valki."

"That's a risk." Will and Sir Robert turned a corner. "If taken, Suthenburg will be vulnerable to attack from behind."

"Ah, you've been learning."

Will smiled wide and stood tall.

"If successful we will have blocked the enemies' support from the north. Fort Valki also provides a direct route to Ortie. They won't take Castle Ochsen; they will turn back.

Lord Richrit and Admiral Białek will also attack the Jueadi air base, keeping the enemy occupied. We will have Sir John's men's support." Sir Robert stopped and sighed, turning to Will. "Get our armor and supplies ready. It is upon the hour of this invasion that will decide this war."

Chapter Twenty-Five

WHEN THE AIRSHIP rose a weight pushed on Will's chest. His stomach rolled and his legs trembled. He leaned away from the edge of the airship, trying not to glance towards the ever-distant ground. Ahmed, on the other hand, crept slowly to the edge of the airship to examine what the world looked like from the sky.

All around them, other airships gained altitude as they flew in formation across the Hertos River towards Fort Valki. Long, boat-like, and attached to a large oblong balloon, it reminded Will of sailing upon the Hertos River. In the middle of the deck, a large engine was kept running by the fire provided to it and the balloon. Smaller propellers kept the ship stabilised. Airships had limited flight time and could not fly too high.

Will's falcon soared through the sky towards the flagship. It swooped down and landed on the edge of the deck a distance from Will. Will gestured towards the bird.

"Uh… could you come closer."

Ahmed stood beside Will and laughed. "Your falcon obviously hasn't forgotten about you. He keeps an eye on you from the skies."

"After you made me shoo him away, I feared he might have abandoned me."

"Well, go get him then."

"I-I… want him to come to me."

"You're afraid to go to the edge."

"I'm not!" He was but didn't want to admit it.

"Prove it then." Ahmed gestured Will towards the edge. Will glared at Ahmed.

Fort Valki's domed keep and towers loomed ahead. Ahmed stood at the edge of the ship when Will came to his side but Ahmed seemed lost in distant thoughts.

"Shoran must have felt so excited and content up here," Ahmed whispered, his voice monotone and limbs lowered. The dullness in Ahmed's eyes filled Will with shame that he had killed Saomarhadians when he wished to prove himself to his countrymen. Will placed a hand on Ahmed's shoulder, remembering back to when Saul was once so distraught and had confided in Will.

The airships loomed over the fort obscuring it in shadow. It rumbled, jerking as it fired bombs, cannon, and fire, all rendering towers and walls to rubble and smoke. The defenders fired back in a valiant defence, but the Gurmian victory seemed inevitable. The defenders looked like mice, scrambling around in confusion. Cannon pounded the flagship while return fire crashed into the frontward airships who'd gotten too low. A quick series of cannon balls from behind sent shrapnel over the deck, making Will and Ahmed rush for cover. The airship lurched and made a sharp dive before the helms man corrected. Will's heart leapt to his throat. Four Saomarhad airships began to surround them in a crescent formation.

"The plan was for that lord to incapacitate the Jueadi airbase." Ahmed tensed. He looked down at his dimithrite shackled wrists.

"Maybe your people defeated him. But don't worry, we won't lose." It surprised Will how confident he was despite the dire odds. Now he had returned to his master, found a friend in Ahmed, and gained the attention of Jillian. All this made him feel just a little invincible.

Saomarhadian airships were more streamlined than Gurmian ones. They also had a large oblong balloon, were fire-driven, and hosted stabilizing propellors, but the space between the top deck and the balloon was almost non-existent.

Gurmian airships countered. One barreled into an enemy airship, pushing it aside. The others slid in-between the enemy and the flagship. Paired one-on-one the airships exchanged fire erupting in air-shaking booms and smoke. An enemy airship veered close to the flagship and positioned itself on the flank, making a pass. Will and Ahmed rushed to the swivel cannons on deck. Ahmed stood close by as Will took a shot. He told Sir Robert and Will he'd not kill his kinsmen. He would only protect Will.

The airships exchanged fire as the enemy's flamethrowers surged to life coating the deck in flames. Several unfortunate men flailed, alight, as others tried to douse them before they followed the few who fell over the side. The enemy's main propeller took three hits, each ripping off a chunk of twisted metal. Bursting and sputtering the airship began to fall. Ahmed helped fight the fires.

A squad of war balloons assaulted the deck with fire launchers and grenades. Sir Robert ordered the pilot to turn. As soon as the flagship's flamethrower came into alignment, it fired a strand of flame into the closest war balloons.

Realising their mistake, the balloons tried to escape. An enemy airship crashed into the flagship and sent it into a nosedive towards Fort Valki. Slipping, many of the crew fell forwards. Will grabbed the closest solid thing he could find and found Ahmed hanging desperately onto the ship's railing.

Sir Robert himself was flailing off the side screaming to the driver to take control. The knight swung back onto the deck and grasped the wheel. The driver moved aside. Sir Robert steered upwards as they were quickly approaching one of the fort's towers. The flagship veered upwards but its lower hull scraped the tower and tore apart. Some men flew out to their deaths on the ground below.

The airship burned wildly as it cleared the fort wall. With a thump it sheared along the ground, wood and metal shred and twist, finally coming to a stop in a smoking heap.

A short second later men poured out, coughing and rolling over the ground in relief. Sir Robert stumbled out and put his hands to his knees. Will and Ahmed came behind him, Ahmed supporting Will. Sir Robert turned and swung his arm around Will's shoulder. Ahmed let go and they looked back at the airship. It burst into a cloud of fire.

Sir Robert coughed, "Remind me never to board an airship ever again boys." The knight laughed. "Great Manis, they are suicidal."

⁂

With the city and fort taken, the Gurmian forces advanced on the Saomarhad capital from two roads over the next three days. They arrived at the crest of a hill. Below them, a dry empty landscape stretched out in three directions flanked to the south and east by hills. They stood in awe at the force opposing them. Archers, crossbow men, gunmen, cannon teams, swords, shields, axes, spears, there were too many to count.

Most frightening was the large oblong, metal plated machines. Not drawn by any horse, these machines were round on their sides, front, and back, sloping towards the domes on top. Its wheels were hidden under the metal. In the front a large cannon faced outward with two smaller cannons directly above it. Coming out of the first revolving dome on top was another cannon, while the same was true of the higher second dome behind the first. There was a small cannon on the back. Around its sides were slits, from which the drivers could see outwards and fire or loose from. The Saomarhadians had designed tanks.

On their hill, opposite the opposing host, the Gurmian forces set up their own cannons and catapults, like the Saomarhadians, wooden barricades, spikes, walls, and watchtowers. The soldiers formed lines.

Near the top of the hill, Will and Ahmed stood and observed all the forces assembled.

"If I go in there," Will started, "d'you think you'll be able to keep your promise that you won't kill your countrymen? You don't have to risk yourself for me Ahmed. I don't want you forced into this."

"I have made my choice to side with you. I would look a fool and a coward if I backed out now. You underestimate me. I can protect you without killing my own people," Ahmed answered. Sir Robert had explained to the boys that this fight would not be like any others they fought in. The Saomarhadians were defending their homes and so they would show no mercy and fight with even greater conviction. They would not stand idle while Gurmians invaded.

"I am under no force except my own. I chose this route because I saw a way our peoples could return to peace. Besides, my pearl connects with yours, that is a question I must answer." An intense yet calming heat came over Will and he noticed Ahmed's sudden reaction and knew that he could hear the voice too.

"Together is the only way forward," the powerful voice echoed in his head. Will and Ahmed looked at each other.

"Perhaps if I remain close to you the mystery of our pearls will soon come to light, inshalhurah," Ahmed said.

"It seems kinda sad now, doesn't it?" Will sighed. "We became friends. Why can't our people." Now back in Gurmanis, was fighting all they were going to do?

"Only Alhurah knows. But maybe I'll figure that out by observing."

"I think you will. I know better now what Saomarhadians are like. You will know better what Gurmians are like."

Near the catapults Sir Robert spoke to the engineers and their commanders, instructing them on what to do when particular signals were given. He'd been organising men since they had gotten here. Lord Richrit could help, but he remained with his fellow Knight's Teutonic and ignored all else. Sir Robert had abandoned his squire somewhere. Sir John would have been livid with him. Squires were meant to help in situations like this.

Admiral Białek rushed through the camp, his face pale and looking like he was going to heave up his insides. Catching Sir Robert's eyes, the admiral approached him, quickly taking him aside.

"You look unwell, admiral. What is wrong?" Sir Robert asked.

"It is Lord Richrit, the king's man. The things he did on the battlefield in Jueadi I will never forget."

"What? What did he do?"

"You should be furious the air base wasn't destroyed! That is only a start to what he has done."

"We did not expect that much aerial resistance. He did not destroy the airbase?" Admiral Białek pressed his hand to his forehead.

"O nie... nie... I mean he did destroy the airbase but he did so too late. He took his time weaving through the streets. We opened the way despite the loss of almost all our ships but he was uninterested in advancing on the airbase immediately."

"That was his only objective, he agreed to that."

"Robert… he ordered the ships to fire upon the city without a care for the people in it. He said this was the opportune moment to take revenge for the execution of our captured men and women. He hit civilian targets. Our men followed him, some out of duty, some out of fear and some out of revenge and zealotry. Others regrouped with me and went straight for the airbase. Lord Richrit decimated the city's population. Men, women, and children lie dead on its streets."

"My God! This was not a part of the plan—" Sir Robert noticed Ahmed standing nearby. Ahmed gritted his teeth, his eyebrows pushed together, and he balled his fists. Will came behind him but Ahmed turned around, pushed Will aside, drew his kilij, and stormed off in the direction of Lord Richrit's tent.

"Stop him!" Sir Robert rushed forwards. Lord Richrit' tent was the largest in the center of the Knight's Teutonic section. It stood in a large oval shape with an extended front entrance and three peaks on top, the middle one higher than the others. Ahmed stormed towards the blue and white striped tent decorated with the crest of the lord lined in golden colour, and the symbol of the Knight's Teutonic.

Two knights tried to stop him, drawing their swords. Ahmed flung out his arms to throw them back but instead his dimithrite bound wrists burned, angrily muffling his magic. Ahmed screamed at the pain. He seethed, glaring at the knights who leveled their swords at him.

"Come out here you murderer! How could you enact such cruelty upon my people! I will avenge them!" Ahmed motioned forward but was grabbed. Sir Robert pulled him back. Lord Richrit came out of his tent tossing a young bloodied Saomardrim girl to the ground. Her pale face and wide wet eyes shattered Ahmed's heart. The pain surged to his throat.

"Demon!" Ahmed shouted at Lord Richrit, he squirmed, trying to rip free of Sir Robert's grasp.

"What did you think would happen after your people slaughtered our captured kinsmen?" Lord Richrit laughed. "Sir Robert. I have been instructed by King Duggan to collect several Saomardrim prisoners to be put on sale in the Rhoathian Imperium's slave markets. I got those barbarisch from Jueadi. You will arrange for their transport to a secure castle."

"Slavery? That cannot be King Duggan's orders. The Church frowns upon such things," the knight answered. Will, confused, walked up behind his master.

"There is no tenant asking us not to enslave the enemy. The kingdom will make profit from this to fund the war."

"You could stop fighting!" Ahmed shouted. "Then there would be no need! Let my people go!"

"Nein. You have no power here." Lord Richrit spat in front of Ahmed and noticed Will beside Sir Robert. "Nor does the fugitive. If you wanted to protect your people then why come here? You should have been in that city defending those you care for so much. You've betrayed your people and abandoned your duty."

Ahmed was unsure what to say. Right now, he was planning to fight his kinsmen. What truth could he find here? What could he see? He didn't know how to even start determining that. So much for his studies, he knew now he'd always be lacking enough knowledge. What *was* he doing here? He'd accomplished nothing and he nor Will had any power or station to bring peace.

Yes, Ahmed would like peace between their nations, but he was also interested in trying to understand Gurmanis and Gurmians. Clearly Lord Richrit was the embodiment of Saomarhad's true enemy, but people like Will, Sir Robert, Jillian, and those who fought as per their duty and not in excess were not equally culpable as men like Lord Richrit.

"My countrymen won't let yours invade so easily. They know if they lose here the road to Ortie will be open. They will not lose!"

"Ah but it could end this war." Lord Richrit laughed. "Imagine that! The Saomardrim who thought he could parlay delivers to us Ortie."

Ahmed froze. What if his actions in betraying his country was leading to the destruction of Ortie? What if that was how the war ended? Ahmed pushed the thought aside. "We will resist from the deserts, wetlands, mountains, and jungles. Alhurah will not abandon us."

Lord Richrit looked down at Ahmed and sneered, "Your people don't deserve peace and freedom. You are all heretics! Manis is the true God and now he will bring his judgment down upon you, through us!"

Ahmed glared at the lord and struggled to get free of Sir Robert's grip.

"What purpose did it have when Saomardrim sent the bodies of our kinsmen flying over walls? I call that savagery. Revenge has been taken by my attack. As the sultan counts his dead, he will understand the gravity of his actions!" Lord Richrit turned and signaled to his men. One of them grabbed hold of the Saomardrim girl and dragged her away. She screamed and sobbed.

"Let me go!" Ahmed growled; his heart broken at the sounds of the girl's cries.

"Your passion does credit to your people but this battle is lost," Sir Robert advised.

"I can't let this happen."

"You don't have a choice right now."

"I will kill that man."

"I can't let that happen." Sir Robert turned to Admiral Białek. "Take him away and calm him down. There will be no more fighting."

"But Master." Will stepped forward, "you can't let Lord Richrit enslave those prisoners."

"I'll see what I can do. Lord Richrit did not specify the castle to send them too. That is all I can promise." Sir Robert gave Ahmed a stern look and he reluctantly nodded, his rage calming and his despair subsiding. A commander ran to the knight.

"My lord, Sultan Yazid wishes to meet you upon the battlefield."

"Prepare an escort." Sir Robert turned to Will. "You will come with me."

<hr>

The sultan's escort trotted out in fine gold, brown and green. Sultan Yazid was at the front on his warhorse followed by two viziers and two rows of mounted Immortals to the left and right of the sovereign. A squad of silâhtar guard and heavily armoured mamluks followed at the rear. Sir Robert and his escort charged forward in similar fashion with various knights following behind, including those from the Knights Templar, Knights Hospitaller, and the Knights Teutonic.

Each party carried their banners, chief among them was the flag of Gurmanis and the flag of Saomarhad, its green crescent moon and star within a yellow sun sat above crossed swords, overtop a half white, half black background and two circles of purple on the upper corners, two circles of red on the bottom corners.

Will rode on Sir Robert's right. The two parties met in the center of the plain and Sultan Yazid stared at Sir Robert, examining him before he spoke.

"Sir Robert Gillios, I have heard of you. You have taken many of my soldiers from this world. I have been to Jueadi." The sultan's gaze was one of measured anger and distrust.

"I have heard of you as well, Sultan Yazid. A wise and dedicated leader, a masterful statesman. It will be an honour to fight you."

"Or you can avoid this fight and the many deaths it will cause. Return home."

"I cannot. This is my duty."

"There have been whispers your resources are strained and your economy drained. Your people will suffer because of that. Is your duty not with your people as well?"

"There have been whispers your country is ailing too. One-hundred years of war has strained both our states."

"I see. In the end it makes no difference. If you intend to fight, we will crush you! I cannot allow any further advancement of King Duggan's armies. Your invasion is an ill mark. I will show no mercy to you and your men upon my victory. What has been done in Jueadi cannot be overlooked."

"We come here today after massacres on both sides sultan. Is more death the only solution to these crimes?"

"Yes." The sultan stood firm.

"I do not wish it. I was outraged and I wanted to kill all your countrymen when I saw what you did to your prisoners-of-war but I stayed my hands."

"This battle will determine who was right and who God favours."

"No. All it will prove is how exceptional we are at causing death. I will try and stay my men from savagery but they have seen what you have done and their minds might take their own path." Sir Robert shifted in his saddle.

"Perhaps you can save many of your men who will die upon our victory. I can lessen the impact of our attack… if you adhere to our terms."

"What terms?" Sir Robert eyed the sultan carefully and the sultan looked at Will.

"I hear Ahmed Sharfi has made it into your care. He is a traitor and a killer of my dearest of friends. Return him to us and maybe many men will be spared." Sultan Yazid directed to Sir Robert.

"Returning him to you will lead to his death."

"The life of a treasonous boy, a murderer, for the lives of hundreds of dutiful men."

"No, I cannot."

"Have you no compassion towards your men?"

"Can you not separate this boy's treason from your whims?" Sir Robert pressed his lips and shook his head, sickened by the man's narrow vision.

"Ahmed Sharfi scoffed at all the honor and prestige bestowed upon him and turned his back on his people. He enrages me. Give him back!" Sensing his rider's rage, the sultan's horse stomped at the ground.

"It is pride that drives you right now, sultan. I don't know how he caused the death of your friend, but other than that, what more evil has he done? He simply wants to know Gurmanis. That is more than any of your people have done in one-hundred years."

"I admit. I think on his treason and his words every day. He lingers in my mind. I wonder what weight his words carry. But then I wake from that foolishness. I remember the grand mosque, Jueadi, and the constant loss of both my father and now, my friend."

"Ahmed's death will solve nothing. None of this death will."

"Says the knight who brings death. You are a hypocrite."

"I am stuck between conflicting duties. King Duggan want's this war, it seems you do as well. Perhaps you are both more alike than you think."

"I am not King Duggan!" Sultan Yazid roared. "Very well then, inshalhurah. We will fight and you will fall! No longer will any foreign army invade us again! This war will be decided on this field once and for all." Sultan Yazid turned his horse and trotted back to his camp. His men followed. Sir Robert did the same.

⁓

After the parlay with the sultan, Will seized a moment to move away from his master and found Jillian. She and the Knights Hospitaller had come across the river after Fort Valki's capture. He approached their tents and adjusted his tunic. He'd cleaned his and his master's armor and hoped he would look the most presentable he had been in a long time. Will spotted Keira outside one of the tents and he approached her. She noticed him, smiled, and curtsied.

"My lord. I have not seen you since Al-Motros. Is everything well?" Keira greeted.

"Everything is well. D'you know where J-Jillian is?" Will asked, rubbing his neck. Keira looked Will over.

"Is your gambeson fitted correctly now? People are saying the battle ahead will be a bloody one. We are the invaders; they will be defending their homes."

"It is on properly now, thank you. Ah… I can see how busy you are."

"That's because we expect many injuries." Jillian, in her Hospitaller robes, exited a nearby tent. Will stilled then smiled.

"I will take my leave, my lord." Keira gave a bow.

"Even after the ordeal in Saomarhad my supervisor refuses to lessen the work I must do. I am not complaining though, whatever I can do to help our men continue to fight is all well and good," Jillian said.

"She is not intending to scold you for yelling at me again, is she?" Will asked.

"She is surprised… I think she's a bit jealous as to my turn around with you. I should say that I am sorry for how I treated you before."

"It is the past now." Will scratched his head.

"There is some worry among the troops, more worry than normal that is. I am anxious… for you."

"For me?"

"Just don't get hurt."

"I will stick as close as I can to my master an' to Ahmed. With them around I won't get badly hurt. They'll make up for my mistakes." Will stood tall, head held high, but he had doubt. He had gone on a lengthy adventure in Saomarhad and had seen many things. He'd gained an unlikely friend in the process. Will knew as a squire it was his duty, but now it felt absurd. Still, he'd made promises to himself that he'd be loyal to Sir Robert, so if Sir Robert was going to fight, he had too as well. He'd made another promise to himself. He would gain influence to ensure others wouldn't have to face King Duggan's systems which imprisoned him, nor Judeicar's cruel justice. But he wasn't any closer to that. Was that even his role?

"I will fight. I will fight by my master's side; tis my duty. I learned much about duty."

"Don't think too much like that Will! You still have to improve. Coming to me wearing newly clean armor and properly styled hair won't make me believe you are a knight just yet!"

"Oh…" Will blushed, "Is that what it looks like."

"I think you look keen." Jillian giggled. "Sir Robert is actually lucky to have you Will, I see that now. You serve him well, with loyalty… I… anyway, I need to finish here and prepare. I will see you after the battle, right?"

"Of course, you will. I'll come find you." Jillian smiled and retreated into her tent. Will hoped he would see her again.

Sir Robert, fully armored, entered a command center built on the side of the hill, halfway down the slope. He stood before a table with a map of the area and refused to look up slope to where Lord Richrit would be observing. He sighed and observed his army tens of thousands proud, all of them in formation to fight against a slightly more numerous foe. Will and Ahmed, also fully armored, stood to the right of the knight and a commander stood to his left.

Smoke rose from the village to the south and distant booms echoed. The advance forces must have engaged Saomardrim defenders. The victor of the engagement would be able to flank the main army of the loser. Sultan Yazid's forces were waiting but the knight knew by making the first move, his army was committed, and soon the main armies would attack.

Around and below him the Gurmian forces stood in formation. On their flanks, behind a row of stakes, archers, crossbowmen, and musket men stood waiting. Closer to the center were regular calvary while the center front of their army consisted of heavy infantry. Behind them, in the center, the heavy mounted knights stood ready. Artillery sat behind him.

Sir Robert ordered a bombardment, waiting no longer. Cannon thundered and trebuchet fired shaking both the air and ground with noise and smoke. The Saomardrim responded. Many shots missed their targets, a few hitting on both sides.

"Commander. What is the composition of the enemy forces?"

"Sir. The new machines, numbering twenty, make up the front two lines with three empty lanes between them. Light mounted archers stand behind them in the center, ranged forces on their flanks, and a mix of light and heavy infantry behind the horse men. Scouts report an insignificant number of mages, mainly healers, like our own mage numbers."

"We have better armor but they do have heavier armoured mounted units like the mamluks I observed with the sultan. What of the ghilman? Where are their heavy armour?"

"I don't know sir. Our scouts do not report anything." A horn sounded from the Saomarhad side and their bombardment stopped. A single horseman advanced through the lanes between the machines while the thunderous cheering of the Saomarhadians urged him on.

"Stop the bombardment," Sir Robert ordered.

"It looks like he wishes to challenge us to single combat." An infantry man from the Gurmian lines strode forward, answering the challenge, encouraged by the cheering of his allies. The Saomardrim dismounted and engaged the challenger. They traded several strikes, the clang of swords drowned out by thunderous cheering, until the infantryman caught the Saomardrim off guard and pushed his sword through the Saomardrim's neck.

In response to the cheers of victory, the Saomarhadians shouted a frenzied war cry and chanted: Alhurahu akbar! Death to the infidels! Drums sounded across the battlefield. Both Will and Ahmed seemed petrified. Sir Robert gave them a knowing smile. He too was easily spooked by such bloodlust at his first field battle. Weaker men and thus weaker armies could rout under such intimidation.

The mounted archers advanced, quickly gaining speed.

"Defensive formations. Pikes out front and shields protecting the infantry," Sir Robert ordered. The mounted archers fired arrow, bolt, and ball into the Gurmian front lines, unable to get too close due to the reach of the pikes. The enemy tried to flank but the Gurmian ranged units held their ground. Sending point blank volleys of arrows, bolts, and balls into the enemy charge. The mounted units retreated behind the tanks, then the tanks crept forwards. Cannon erupted from them as they closed the distance.

"Respond with our artillery." Gurmian artillery returned fire, hitting some tanks but missing many. The tanks widened their formation. Sir Robert watched his front line falling under heavy bombardment.

"Send the cavalry to charge the flanks." The Gurmian cavalry raced out against the tanks. Their speed and maneuverability allowed them to avoid the imprecise tanks but their weapons did little. Grouped calvary fell quickly.

"They must spread apart."

"They cannot find a way past the armor sir." The Saomarhadian mounted archers attacked again catching some of the cavalry by surprise.

"Have the cavalry guide the tanks to the flanks and bring the mortars up behind our ranged units. Have them fire on the machines. It will be up to the calvary to distract the machines and the mounted archers. Once the center is clear have the infantry charge against the Saomarhad infantry. Our superior armor will benefit us."

"Understood, sir." Once the cavalry opened a center path both states' infantry closed the distance and crashed into each other in brutal hand-to-hand combat.

"Everything looks so chaotic from here," Will commented.

"Wait until we get into it," Sir Robert said without looking at him. When the Saomarhad center seemed to be weakening, Sir Robert took his helm, walked forwards to his waiting horse with Will and Ahmed following from behind, donning their helmets. "Commander. Once the Saomarhad center is weak enough, give the order for the infantry to part. Our knightly charge should rout them."

"Yes Sir." Sir Robert turned to Ahmed who held out his dimithrite manacles. The knight unlocked them and handed them off to the commander.

"You will keep my squire safe?"

"I won't let him leave my sight," Ahmed answered. Sir Robert nodded. He, his squire, and Ahmed mounted and rode to join the waiting knights.

Sir Robert shifted on his horse and received his lance. The silence of the men around them did little to make Will feel better about the enemy host. Ahmed shifted nervously beside Will. Sir Robert raised his lance. On his command, all the knights pointed their lances upward. Horns sounded and Sir Robert ordered the charge. The knights barrelled forwards into the chaotic plain ahead of them.

As the knights advanced, they lowered their lances and pointed them straight ahead. Will shifted uncomfortably against the weight of his lance as they rode. He could barely hear his own thoughts, too distracted by the immense rumbling of hooves thundering forward against the earth and the shaking of his horse. They closed the distance towards the enemy. He continued to charge trying to keep formation with the knights and sticking to Sir Robert's side.

The knights crashed into the Saomarhad infantry. Will hit with such a force that it threw him back on impact. He gathered all his strength and courage against his racing heart and fearful body. Don't hesitate, focus, stick close to Sir Robert, were thoughts that raced through his mind. His lance connected with something, or someone, and suddenly snapped in two. It fell from Will's arm. Will was about to draw his longsword but was thrown off his horse by an impact to his side. Disoriented, he scrambled free and was attacked by a Saomarhadian spearman. Will raised his sword, ready to do battle.

Ahmed rushed towards Will, dismounted, and managed to avoid most people. Will was ahead. Ahmed covered his face when a cannonball exploded close by, then another exploded even closer and Ahmed was flung into the air. He landed in a crater. Disoriented, his vison blurry, he stood and stumbled forward. His body was covered in dirt and sweat. His entire body betrayed him as adrenaline and fear fought each other for dominance over him.

Ahmed closed the distance to Will, as Will countered the spearman attacking him. Relief at seeing each other lightened their faces. Will was as dirt covered and sweaty as Ahmed. The fear in his face was equal to Ahmed's. Blood-covered and panting, Will almost fell forwards. Ahmed stabilised him. They gathered courage and stood together.

Two heavily armored soldiers charged at the boys. Ahmed sliced one. His kilij bounced off the man's armor. Ahmed tried his axe, but it had the same effect. He jumped back as the soldier brought his broadsword down.

Will had the same problem with the axeman. Many troops appeared at once and the next thing both boys knew was that they were struggling to dodge the attacks. The men slashed, stabbed, and pounded at them, drawing blood. A cannon shot burst in the enemy ranks and thinned the number charging, throwing dirt and blood onto Will and Ahmed.

Will faced a musket man. His bayonet lunged forward at Will and Will jumped to the side as the man fired. The man lunged again but this time Will blocked the bayonet forcing it to the right. He attacked from the left, his longsword striking the man in his side.

Ahmed pushed two men back with a burst of energy. A spearman lunged downward at Ahmed who jumped, flipped, and faced the spearman. The man jabbed but Ahmed blocked, forcing the spear to arc upward. He forced the earth around the man to rise and entrap him.

A horseman charged both boys. Will and Ahmed toppled to the ground backwards. The horseman turned for another pass as they stood. He charged. The boys raised their swords in dismounting position. They swung and the man tumbled to the ground. Will turned and stabbed him in the back only to be forced to engage a new enemy. He panted, adrenaline threatening to burst out of him. Ahmed looked to follow Will, but was attacked from the flank. He dodged and turned to face his attacker.

"Traitor!" the man shouted, spewing a curse at Ahmed. Ahmed raised his weapons. Barbas Abudi, armored and masked in the Immortal style, pulled his shield closely over his torso and pointed his nimcha sword at high-guard towards Ahmed, then charged him, screaming a war cry. Ahmed blocked the attack, deflecting the nimcha. He swung his axe, hitting the man's shield. Barbas bashed his shield forward, striking Ahmed in the head. Dizzy, he staggered backwards and blocked two counters. He lunged, and Barbas parried, slashing Ahmed on his side. Ahmed grunted and blasted a pulse of energy forward. It hit Barbas' shield and dissipated, specks of enchantment flickering off the shield. Barbas attacked again, drawing blood and bashing Ahmed to the ground. Ahmed scrambled away from a downward cut.

"You should be protecting the sultan!" Ahmed screamed. A cannon ball exploded close by.

"What do you care, worm!" Barbas spat. He advanced on Ahmed who was still recovering on the ground. Will lunged forwards and flanked the grandmaster, surprising him and drawing blood. But the man recovered and countered. Will fell to the ground, bleeding, and Barbas advanced to make a kill.

"No!" Ahmed shouted. He cast against the earth, springing his arms forwards. The earth rumbled. A shockwave of rock burst towards Barbas. He raised his shield and blocked, but was pushed back. Ahmed rushed to Will's side and helped him up. Ten Saomarhadians rushed forwards with Barbas behind them.

"Kill them both," Barbas ordered. The men advanced. The youths raised their weapons. Two terrified boys, gathering the last of their courage, stood side-to-side, Gurmian and Saomarhadian. They were not ready to die but they would stand to the last. The Saomarhadian weapons came down on them. They desperately parried and countered strikes. Ahmed was cut in the side, on the cheek, a mace hit him, cracking part of his armor. Will was bashed with a shield, stabbed with a blade, a mace bounced of his armor, and a sword sliced his leg. Will fell to the ground. Ahmed cast a wind spell against his enemies to throw them back. Some fell back, but a new group of Saomarhadians arrived. They were surrounded.

Then the world grew still and the people in front of them seemed to blur and shake like static. Their pearls vibrated and grew hot like fire. They attracted each other stronger than ever. Will and Ahmed stared at each other wide-eyed. An intense yet calming heat came over them.

"It is time for you both to understand," the powerful voice spoke. A brilliant white light engulfed them.

Chapter Twenty-Six
The Overworld: Palace of the Gods

WILL AWOKE TO a bright warming light tempered by cooling air and a soft mist obscuring his feet. He took a step, swaying as if he'd fallen through the semi-solid cloud beneath him.

A huge gate with a shimmering golden frame and silver barred doors stood before him. Beyond it was a land of clouds. Atop the central clouds sat a massive palace designed with a mix of the many cultural architectural styles used on Erathas. Everything from the thin tall spires and arches of the high elves to the domes and circles of the Saomarhadians were woven into its design. Around the central cloud floated many more each with other buildings designed in one style or another.

One cloud held a great hall made of carved wood and whose roofs were sharply sloped and tiled. Like a set of rectangular blocks, these were stacked upon each other creating a immense hall of towering height. Another held a large building designed in the style of the high elves, demanding presence and order. Yet another held enormous water fountains and a hall built of coral and stone, from which water flowed onto the lands below. An imposing mountain stood reaching the same height as the buildings on the clouds. Large floating rocks accented its peaks. Forests representing each of the four seasons grew on its slopes and a large gate carved into its side lead to something within. Stranger still, milk flowed from one cloud down into another. A sweet sent hung in the air, and a light breeze flowed gently over his face, caressing his skin.

"Wi-Will?" Ahmed's voice cut Will's thoughts short.

"Ahmed, you're here too?" Will looked at him expecting an answer to where they were.

"It's obvious this is not Saomarhad." Ahmed turned. Below the clouds was a vast land of green cut up by flowing rivers and low mountains. In the distance a field of golden reeds stretched far until it became green and mountainous. There tall pillared peaks held waterfalls, palaces, and manors upon their sides. "Are we even on Erathas anymore?" Ahmed frowned. "I have never seen this landscape."

"N-Not on Erathas? Does that mean we're d-dead?"

Clouds rushed towards the space in front of the boys. White mist swirled around a center and a figure took shape. The form solidified into a golden-skinned man wearing long white robes. A set of large white wings protruded from his back. His eyes were pure white, glowing like fire. Will and Ahmed went to draw their swords but discovered them missing. They backed away.

"If you were dead, I would have felt it." The being flexed his wings and checked the unfurled scroll in his hands. "You are not dead and that confuses me. Are you demons? I must banish you to the Void."

"No! We're not demons!" Will said.

"Then explain your presence quickly."

"We came here with" —Will looked through his pockets— "these." He showed him his pearl. Ahmed, watching Will, produced his pearl as well.

"This is exceptional. The last Seeker to have come to the Overworld did so long ago. To feel the living within this place is… it is unique now."

"The Overworld? The afterlife?" Ahmed raised his eyebrows. "We are not dead… Seekers… Seekers could travel to the Overworld while still alive."

"That is correct, Seeker. The arch-gods Manis and Alhurah have called you here. I am Archangel Azriel. Please follow me." The angel turned towards the gate and cast light magic on it. The doors swung open and the angel stepped through. Ahmed followed him with some hesitation through the gate but stopped when he realised Will had remained.

"Come Will. Let's see Alhurah," Ahmed prompted, intrigued at the prospect of meeting him.

"No." Will crossed his arms. "I don't want to see Manis."

The angel stopped and looked back. "You would defy the wishes of Manis?"

"I don't care for his wishes. Will he smite me for disobedience?"

"How dare you speak ill of Manis. No young man, he will not smite you. He will instead weep for you." Archangel Azriel frowned, his tone measured.

"I don't need his tears." Will didn't want anything to do with the one who had betrayed him his whole life.

"Will, why are you so hostile to him?" Ahmed asked.

"You saw my nightmare in Nizid, Ahmed, but you don't know even half of what happened to me in Isen Prison." Will shivered, uncomfortable. "Manis ne'er cared for my plight. He was said to be merciful and cared for the weak an' innocent. My parents said he loved children. When I was a child, my mother told me to always pray to him. When I shuffled into prison like cattle, Manis abandoned me."

"Son, the ways wherein Manis works are more complex than you know," Archangel Azriel argued. "Hear him out."

"I-I don't care to. Please send me back to Erathas."

Ahmed walked towards Will. "I think you should let Manis explain. All of this is confusing. At the very least come with me Will. I need you by my side because you are the only person I can trust in this place."

Will's eyes lit up at Ahmed's words. He was worth something to Ahmed. "Ok." Will sighed. "I'll go for you."

They walked as a bridge of clouds formed under their feet over the paradise below.

"Paradise is experienced differently from person to person. Similarities and differences coexist but what each spirit envisions as paradise, that is what they will experience save the abodes of the gods. This is the Overworld. Below is the Underworld. Your realm is the Baseworld. Though everyone may worship different gods and have different ideas of what these places are, there is but one Overworld, Underworld and Baseworld. All gods originate from the power that is the Father, God of gods, but the arch-gods hold the Father's essence."

A large shining palace stood before them at the center cloud. Its walls white and gold, its gates imposing and each of its keeps floated on several smaller clouds. They entered into a great hall flanked by towering pillars and under a vaulted and domed roof. Before them sat giants on thrones. The gods.

Each one had a glowing aura around them that seemed to invite light and sight towards their figures. Most distinctive were their eyes. a black pupil and grey iris which sucked in all light sat over glowing white. In the boys grew calm, something primal and immutable. It was as if they had achieved a state of complete fulfilment and now had contentment and all the things worth achieving.

Will could recognise a number of the gods, those he remembered from sermons of his village prior in Aldershire, and those depicted on the stone, glasswork, and tapestries of the Aldershire chapel. Ahmed could recognise many more. They talked amongst themselves, intrigued at the arrival of the youths. There, in the center, sat two gods, seemingly more pronounced than the others. Perhaps they were Manis and Alhurah for their aura seemed stronger. Will figured that Manis was surely the truest form among them. He was God, the true essence of the Father.

Brahshartha, god of wisdom, time, and space, who took the form of an old Hrind man, sat on a lotus throne. He was regarded to as the old sage, occupied by an insatiable thirst for knowledge and preservation of knowledge. A historian of sorts, but with a mind to the future as well. Many compared him to Alhurah, who was known as the young sage, an innovator, inventor, a scientist, a mage.

Hertos, god of strength and power, who took the form of an Imperiali man, sat on another throne. His build greater than any mortal. It was for him that the Hertos River was named.

Then there was Judeicar, god of order and justice, who took the form of a male high elf and of whom Will knew well. For him was the dogma of Judeicar's Justice named which most mortals followed, high elf or not.

Will also recognised the goddess of fertility, of agriculture, and the gods and goddesses of the harvest, fishing, foraging, and the hunt. The others, of various species and races, Will didn't know of.

The two gods in the center stood, one stepped forward,

"That is right Will Farmer, the gods," he said, ***"And Ahmed Sharfi, you are right when you think the same."*** They were giants with long silver hair and shining faces. Their robes extended to the ground, one of gold and white, the other of gold and deep green.

"Who are you? Why are we here?" Ahmed asked.

"I am Manis and this is Alhurah. You both are Seekers."

"Mashalhurah! You are most glorious and I will forever be fulfilled." Ahmed fell to his knees and bowed, awe radiating from him. Will figured Ahmed assumed Alhurah was the truest form among them, that Alhurah was God, the true essence of the Father. Stories told of the arch-gods being brothers never confirmed if such a thing was symbolic or not.

"I am pleased at your devotion." Alhurah smiled. Ahmed stood.

"But how do we know for sure?" Will asked.

Manis smiled, ***"Is what you have seen not enough? We will sate your curiosity. Our Imperial Tabernacle forms are those that you can comprehend. Should I or you, Alhurah?"***

"You do the honour." Manis nodded and Alhurah stepped back. Manis took a breath in and raised his arms. Light engulfed him and as it slowly dissipated what was left was something that nearly swept Will off his feet. There was Manis, with four arms and large white feathered wings raised from behind him. His lower right hand held a great golden gada pointed downward and touching the ground, his upper right hand held a cross-bearing orb, aflame in light magic and encircled by a floating crown. In Manis' upper left hand, he held a slender, silver spear taller than he was with crackling lighting jumping around it. In his lower left hand, he held a rose with a long stem. On his right shoulder a bald eagle swooped down and landed, flicking its head.

"I am god of kings and of the Overworld," he started in an commanding voice. ***"I am power and authority incarnate. My gada is the elemental force from which all such force originates. My orb bestows the divine right to rule both mortals and immortals. I hold the great spear Gungnir forged from a single strand of the Mother's hair and the purest of sunlight. This may never miss those who defy my authority. I am the lord of nature for I hold the rose of the Evergarden, the immortal garden."***

Manis smiled as the two humans before him looked up speechless. Alhurah stepped forward and in the same way as Manis he revealed his comprehendible form. In his lower right hand, he held a long staff, interknit with woodwork of a hickory colour, topped off with an emerald head. In his upper right hand he held a spinning blue, green, and red sphere around which revolved a golden disk. The object was engulfed in a light blue flame as it spun in Alhurah's palm. In his upper left hand, he held a book, bound in red leather with gold edgings. A quill wrote in the book, independently. In his lower left hand, he held an ankh and revolving around it were droplets of water, small pebbles, visible pieces of wind, and sparks of electricity. An ouroboros weaved itself between the elements and around the ankh. A young brown-orange and black tabby cat rested on his right shoulder, preening itself.

"I am the god of magic and the Overworld. I am the Wise Lord and the revered for I hold the staff of Divine Magic, the first, present, and last purest source of magic. Without this staff all magic within every mortal would vanish. I am the source of life for I hold all power magical, spiritual, and biological which is needed for life to flourish. My ankh is the key of life and its ouroboros is the bringer of fertility. I hold the power to bestow life. I am the young sage for I hold the Book of Novelty.

"You know our forms now, only the Father is greater for he holds the universe and the Astrals in the palms of his hands."

"Please, we have no doubts now. Revert back to your passive forms," Ahmed asked. Will noticed the tremor in his friend's hands. Manis and Alhurah reverted to their comprehendible forms, sitting down while their companion animals rested beside them, and Ahmed continued, "When we arrived the archangel called us Seekers. Is that—" Ahmed was cut off when Will forced himself forward and glared at Manis. After years of resentment and anger he was unafraid.

"Why?" Will challenged. "Why d'you abandon me? You are no benevolent god!"

"William." Manis smiled. *"You ask such a complex question."*

"Complex? It is simple! You left a ten-year-old innocent boy in a hellish prison. You left me in the hands of the warden, a man who cared only to satisfy his own pleasure. I called to you. I begged you, and I heard nothing from you! My parents were gone. People hated me, considered me worthless and too dangerous to be allowed freedom and dignity. All I could do was waste away and I became empty and distant. I felt so alone and betrayed."

"Do you think in this universe you are the only one suffering as such?"

"Wh-What?"

"Other children, other men and women, an infinitesimal amount of them seek my aid. I cannot 'create' enough solutions and nor am I omniscient as the Father is. Mortals interpret our words and do not know us. You should fault your society that allows the atrocities committed against you."

"I don't understand. Why did they want me to suffer?"

"They follow Judeicar's Justice. In every death a new life would be created with the dead person's soul. But if the soul was sinful the new life would be too. He had no choice but to judge such tainted souls as unworthy of redemption to keep the light and the dark in the universe in balance, as the Father intended. So, he told mortal kind, the only hope for redemption in the afterlife was to purge the sin in a mortal's soul 'before' they died. To do so, mortals read that they needed to imprison, cut, rip, burn, shock, and wear away the mind. In this way mortals' souls would be 'cleaner' when they arrived in Judeicar's court and he could show them mercy. It is this way in most of Erathas. You were punished so severely because your people thought that the crime, they imagined you committed, was so sinful it required the absolute destruction of the self. They wanted to see you go to paradise. Perhaps the warden wanted that too, among his other desires."

"Yet you couldn't do anything."

"I see your entire life. I weep for you."

"So I was selfish? I should have accepted my fate?"

"No, you were right to seek me. I did fail you. We are not without fault, we do err. Can we reconcile William?"

Will sighed. His anger and resentment calmed into a simmer. "Did any of it mean anything? What was it all for?"

"Had you let your friend speak, perhaps you'd have found out sooner."

"I don't think I can e'er reconcile with you, but I will listen an' I will respect your words. It was you who sent that pearl? It was you who helped me escape?"

"Yes. They are the Seeker's Stones. They are a pinch of Godly Magic and the symbol of office for both of you. You are Seekers, chosen to be the last of your kind."

"What are Seekers?"

"Men and women who were holy warriors and scholars," Ahmed explained. "They served as the bridge between the will of God and the will of mortals, and the spirits."

"Yes," Alhurah spoke. *"They kept peace in a time when sin was rampant on Erathas. They have returned in you."*

"For what purpose?" Will asked.

"Ah, but you have that answer. You already know the reason we have made you Seekers." Will and Ahmed looked at each other. Will knew they were thinking the same thing.

They thought back to their journey in the desert, how they had talked and learned so much, and how during and after that journey, they had become friends. Everything they'd witnessed about the war between their countries seemed to build on top of their memories.

"The violence, hate, and suffering," Will started, "all of it is caused by the war and it has been this way for one-hundred years." Will hesitated. "I know what suffering is, what it feels like, what it does to people. Regardless of where it took place, within the walls of Isen Prison or outside them, the same suffering endured."

"I have seen this too," Ahmed said. "Though, I did not realise at first. The suffering the war has wrought is clear in our lands. Furthermore, the people are tired of it, frustrated…"

"That is the reason that fuelled a Priest of Manis and a Grand Imam to swear upon our power saying Seekers would return."

"… Yes. But also, now that our countries have worn each other down, other states look to take advantage. Gurmanis and Saomarhad will cease to exist if the war continues." Ahmed hesitated. "I was… I am more ignorant than I allowed myself to realise. As a scholar, I am ashamed I could not see through the propaganda."

"So," Manis spoke. *"What is your purpose as the last Seekers?"*

"To end this war."

"Exactly. You have come to this conclusion yourselves."

"Why us?"

"I don't understand either," Will said. "What king or people will listen to us?"

"You have already reasoned that out, William. Your time imprisoned is not so unlike both the current suffering due to the war and end result of the war. If one side should win over the other, only intolerance would prevail. You experienced the worst of humanity, and so you will take that knowledge forward to ensure it will never be replicated. We hope."

"Ahmed was ignorant of the true effects of the war," Alhurah started. *"You show that even the most highly educated can err but such intelligent people, and the powerful people who depend on them, need to serve the greater good and not ignorance, bigotry, and selfishness."*

"But how do we do this?" Will asked.

Manis answered, *"If two youths, once enemies now friends, can cooperate and coexist in peace then why can't others? People will see your bond. Talk to the people, they will help you."*

"But why can't you stop this?" Ahmed asked.

"We cannot intervene. It would not be the right way to end this. The people expect an incarnation of us as charismatic and powerful heroes to save them. That would only serve to disable them. They would never think the most unlikely or, in their minds, the most unworthy among them would be their saviours and so they will be challenged to change their flawed views of the world. That is what we want. We want mortals to be independent enough to maintain peace

themselves, without our direct interference. As Seekers you will find a way to guide them. Mortals must grow themselves."

"But why do you care now? The war has been fought for one-hundred years and you've chosen us only now."

"What can we say to you that will satisfy you? What can we say that won't sound like an excuse or would sound selfish?" Alhurah asked.

"I would like to know."

"As you have heard Manis say, we are not omniscient as the Father is. We must select our attention and not always for the best for we have said, we err like mortals do. Perhaps that is one reason. Indeed, those on Erathas worship many gods. Only the Imperium has retained worship of all gods. Other states select their favourite gods and worship them. They respect and show reverence to other gods, but their chief god is supreme. Accordingly, the gods in history have interfered in mortal affairs for those who worship them."

"Worship is validation for you. You reward it," Will figured.

"Perhaps. It was Manis who helped Gurmians long ago when they suffered under Imperium rule. It was my voice that spoke to Saomarhadians of liberation when they suffered under the same rule. Now it is both these nations who fight each other. Avatars and prophets have not worked. Too old and predestined. They preached for worship. You both will appeal to sensibility."

"I see now." Will frowned. "If Gurmanis and Saomarhad were to fall, who would worship the arch-gods?"

"The Imperiali?" Ahmed supposed. "But their worship is polytheistic, split among several gods. It would not be the same."

"Alhurah did say our reasons would sound selfish," Manis said. *"Mortals inflate the prestige of the gods. The Old Seekers eventually understood that too. But they accepted the fact, until one thought he could be better. He corrupted himself, then the other Seekers, then they sought Kalshaimar and became shadow knights. The last time we gave our power to mortals and raised them to Seekers, we were betrayed and Erathas suffered. It took us a long time to decide that new Seekers, the last of the Seekers, was needed."*

"You two must go now," Alhurah said, *"Good luck to you both."*

"Wait!" If this place is the afterlife then maybe… "Are my parents here? Can I speak to them?"

Manis and Alhurah laughed and Manis lifted his arms. Behind each of the boys a door appeared. *"If you must, turn around and see those you want to see most."*

Will and Ahmed stepped through the gates.

Will found himself on a grassy headland. As he stepped forwards the sound of mighty waves crashing against a rocky shore amplified. Two people stood, their backs facing him. Will walked forward, unsure of where he was, the sound normalizing. The sun shone over the land and the air was warm, humid, and left a salty residue on his lips. It was a place of calm and peace, unlike what he'd ever experienced.

Will neared them. They were looking out towards the sea. The salty breeze blew softly over his face, entraining his hair in the wind. He saw them better now. There was a man with his arm around a woman's back.

"Mother… f-father…" The two people turned. They looked at Will, bewildered at first, then they smiled. Will's eyes watered. He stepped forward to touch them. How he had longed to see and be with them again. He wanted to know their touch again, back when his mother would embrace him and his father would hoist him onto his shoulders. Will's hand floated through them.

"N-No… no…" His heart sunk and he stepped back. "No."

"William, how handsome you have grown! How strong. My dear baby." Will's mother stepped forward.

"You're not real. You're ghosts." Will shook his head.

"We are spirits. Images of our once living selves." Trent explained. "Our souls have already gone onwards and been reborn in a new life, but what we once were remains here in Paradise."

"But… I've always wanted to be with you again. I wanted to go home, back to the life I had 'afore you died." Will shivered. "I-I don't want you to be dead. If I'd gotten there faster, if I'd listened to you more, if…"

"Don't blame yourself, Will. What happened was our fate and not your fault."

"I've missed you too much."

"And so have we," Saydie said, clutching her hands together.

"What is most important is that you have grown up well, better than anything we could've done. Despite what you suffered; you've made a life for yourself. A squire." Trent smiled. Will wiped his tears. "You have chosen to serve a good man."

"Your grief is my grief." Saydie said. "We saw you every day rotting away in that prison. We begged Manis to help you, but he ne'er answered us. I may as well have died twice seeing the despair you were in."

Will looked down. Knowing his mother had witnessed his suffering made it worse.

"We spent all our time in Paradise worrying for you," Trent explained, "That was until Manis finally came to us and told us you had been chosen to become a Seeker."

"So, I've burdened you." Will frowned.

"No!" Saydie shook her head. "We love you William. We will always worry for you even in the afterlife. 'Tis our burden, never yours."

"Maybe someday you will learn what that's like my son," Trent added. "You had great strength, strength that allowed you to survive. I am proud you did."

"I remembered many times when you told me to be strong an' when you told me that I had to be resilient against that which would hurt me," Will said, "I fought so hard to keep my time with you in my memories, even when they hurt more than they helped. I *did* die in there. I lost my will to live numerous times. I'm sorry. I tried to end my life even though you told me my life was valuable."

"Don't be sorry. The chaos in your mind overwhelmed you. You were far too young."

"But I did lose my mind. I became silent and obedient to the warden's whims. I only broke free of that when I found my Seeker's Stone."

"But you came back. Not only because your Seeker's Stone helped you but because of your own resilience. We are proud of you William. Because of who you are, you have been chosen for this task of unification and we know you will succeed."

"D'you know you had stolen goods from Lord Jerold?"

"No." Trent frowned. "Of course we didn't and looking back, we should ne'er have made deals with that merchant." Trent gritted his teeth. "We were desperate William. Our savings were running out and that year's harvest was predicted to be a bad one. The merchant seemed so eager to find buyers. I should have known, being a watchman long ago I should have known something was suspicious. I lost my touch."

"I don't blame you for that. It shocked me. Everything that happened to me stemmed from Lord Jerold not simply asking for the necklace and gold."

"Maybe you should blame me, William. I hated myself everyday knowing that what we did, unknowingly, contributed to—"

"It doesn't matter anymore." Will shook his head. Trent nodded.

"Then be smarter than we were. I already see you are on your way there."

"My… sibling…"

Saydie frowned, "Twas going to be your baby sister, Will."

Will gripped his hands.

"I would've helped feed her."

"You overheard that conversation?" Trent asked and Will nodded.

"I love you so much, so so much."

"And we love you very much, Will." They motioned for him to come see the view. Will walked between his parents, feeling warmth, comfort, and as if he had found the place he truly belonged. It was where he wanted to be for so many dark years. Between his parents, safe and loved again. A place where he meant something, where he was full of worth and potential. Where he could be a kid again.

Trent placed his hand over Will's back, though he could not feel it. Saydie brushed her hand over Will's face, as if she were feeling its curves and the shape of his ears. Will admired his mother's compassionate smile.

Will's parents started to disappear, the final strands of light melting away as a soft white mist. Will found himself engulfed in white light. As light as a feather, floating in the calm cool wind, his mind free, empty, at peace.

In his last seconds he saw a young girl not more than three. She smiled in a ghostly way, and Will, in those seconds, realising who she was, smiled back as she disappeared.

Ahmed walked out onto the edge of a mountain. It overlooked the plains of paradise around him, but it wasn't cold. There was no snow and the air was warm and humid, though the strong wind cooled him. Ahmed looked to the edge of the mountain ledge. There a boy stood facing the plains with his arms out wide.

"Where am I?" Ahmed asked. The boy pulled down his arms and turned to face him.

"Ahmed," he said, smiling. Ahmed stepped back, overcome by sadness and guilt.

"They killed you! They killed you because of me!"

"Ahmed…"

"This is my fault! You are dead. If I hadn't called on you, if I hadn't forced you to help."

"Ahmed…"

"Please forgive me Shoran. I will find the spell and bring you back to life, I will—"

"Ahmed!" Shoran shouted. "Ne'er speak as such! No Mortal Magic can bring me back."

"I worried too much about myself to realize in time the consequences. I was selfish."

"Don't blame yourself. I made my choice knowing what would happen, I decided to turn the airship. They arrested me and then you saw them kill me. I remember feeling pain as the sword slid inside me. I felt something twist in my stomach and blood pour out my mouth. Then I remember nothing." Shoran flashed a shaky smile.

"You were living a life as a slave and I freed you for what? So I could kill you later?"

"I don't blame you, Ahmed. You did so much for me. You gave me purpose and meaning. I was afraid when you called on me. I was told you had betrayed us and I was worried for you. I didn't want them to kill you but I was afraid they might kill me. Conflicted, I fought with myself but ultimately, I knew I had to stand by you. What good had Saomarhad done for me? Its people took me from my family and enslaved me. You were the one I owed my allegiance to and you were the only one who cared about me. It would take one-hundred lifetimes for me to thank-you for that. Do not hold yourself accountable." Ahmed nodded though he was unconvinced. Guilt still gnawed at him. "And don't blame the sultan either. It would do no good now."

"So, you're satisfied?"

"Now and forever. I can feel the sky up here and its where I belong." Shoran beamed. A new figure began to take form, this person was taller than Shoran, and his face came into view. Master Mahad Oman.

"Master! Can you forgive me? I..."

"It is I who should be asking your forgiveness Ahmed. The way I left you was horrible; I was blinded with rage. Can you forgive me?"

"It is not right that a master begs forgiveness from his pupil..."

"Nor was it right of me to try and kill you."

"Please Master, I forgive you."

"Good, my mind will be at rest now. You must follow the task set on your shoulders by Alhurah."

"I am a traitor. The sultan will never listen to me nor will my people. I must have brought so much grief and dishonour to my family. If my father will never accept me back then I understand why." Ahmed shivered. He thought about Amir. Might Amir still think well of him, or would he draw his sword and turn on Ahmed. He deserved it. His treason had so far only succeeded in killing his best friend and his master.

"You must bring the honour back to your family name by ending this war. If anything, I practiced you too hard. All those summers when you should have returned home. I understand now, too late, the value of such."

"I feel lost, Master. I still understand so little and I don't know what I can do now. Manis and Alhurah said so much but I don't understand how Will and I can do any of it. Too many people hate us. What do we do? What will happen?"

"Only Brahshartha and the Father truly know the future. In the sultan's mind you have made a stance. A stance that tells him you are not afraid to do what it takes to find the truth that will end this war."

"The truth?"

"There are more important things than squabbling over our differences, more ancient and hidden magic that threaten our world."

"In his mind I am a traitor."

"After the Gurmian invasion he is doubting. He came to me in sorrow not long after his father died. He told me his father praised him for the unity Yazid brought Saomarhad and implored him to hold in defence against the Gurmians. He told him to embrace peace if it came. But Sultan Yazid was distraught by his father's brutalizing, and hate filled that void. You, Ahmed, have reminded him of those words."

"I will be lost without your wisdom master."

"Remember what I have taught you all your life Ahmed, find wisdom in that. You will be your own master now."

Shoran's and Master Mahad's forms faded. Ahmed found himself engulfed in white light. As light as a feather, floating in the calm cool wind, his mind free, empty, at peace.

"Ahmed." His master's distant voice called out. "My talisman will find you again. Keep it. In the future, you will take my place among those who watch as I have always desired."

Chapter Twenty-Seven
The Underworld: Death's Hold

SUFFOCATING HEAT ENCLOSED the boys as they entered a place they hadn't expected to be in. Will and Ahmed stood upon an ash beach flanked by an endless dark sea and on the other side by a looming wall whose gate sat within a river flowing from the ocean. They were in a huge cavern that stretched in all directions disappearing from sight at its lengthiest places. The sky was covered in dark black smog, the air sulfurous, lightning crackling through the clouds.

"This is not good…" Will echoed the thought of them both.

Distant screams, groans, beastly laughter and the shrieks of wraiths capped each word spoken, echoing in the cavern. Along the beach exhausted naked people lay groaning in their chains, little more than animated corpses. Some corpses struggled to climb up the beach towards the river. Others, in the water struggled to even reach the beach. They muttered, begging Judeicar for mercy.

"This must be a mistake! Why would we be here?" Ahmed asked. Then he saw Will pale and stiffen, just his lips twitched. He could sense a hollowness fill his friend. "Will… you're…" He clasped Will's arms. "Focus Will… d-don't" Ahmed squeezed his eyes. "Don't leave me alone in here." The ocean burst, sending burning sea spray onto corpses, rendering them withering upon the beach, but the spray did not affect Will and Ahmed. A huge serpent lunged from the water grasping swimming corpses in its mouth.

"The boy feels what he's been trained to know." A weathered voice cleared itself. Ahmed gasped and scrambled away from the voice. He was a gaunt man with haggard cheeks, an unkept beard, thick sagging age lines and eyes of fire. He leaned on a long ferryman's pole. "I am the watcher of Náströnd, Corpse Shore, keeper of Níðhöggr, and ferryman of the dead. Kalshaimar has called you here."

"This is the Underworld. Let us leave!" Ahmed shouted, his heart racing.

"I cannot do that. Come now, you will not need a coin."

"N-No… Alhurah, this is not happening." Ahmed clasped his pearl, receiving its warmth.

"For the living to travel through the Underworld and witnessing its rivers, planes and realms… they will be rendered insane. Your Seeker's Stones protect you. Bring the other."

There was no choice. There was no place to go. Ahmed searched for Will's pearl and placed his friend's hand over it. Will's eyes glistened and he regained some sense, but remained unresponsive.

They boarded the ferryman's boat and passed the gate under the watch of two towering guards, humanoids, one with an ox-head and the other a horse-head. Will gained sense, only to realise they were going deeper. Down the river they floated past each plane and realm of the Underworld. In each, sinners suffered in a myriad of ways, but the boys remained silent and adverted their eyes even as they could guess the names of the places told to them in childhood.

Through the Silent Labyrinth, the Prison of Winds, the Garden of Thorns, through filth and rot, and the Factory of the Twisted where monsters and demons are made. They passed through the Place of Torrents and Swamps, the Forest of Bile, through intense fires, and a deadland of pits. In the Fields of Madness they were mobbed by the insane and deeper still they encountered demons endlessly boiling corpses in fried oil and blood. That seen in Death's Harem was better left unsaid, and finally they almost froze as they passed through Niflheim, entering into The Core.

Fire and ash fell from the sky, alighting everything. The one structure, standing above pits of screaming people, was a gigantic black castle on top of a huge jagged floating rock.

Below them in the distance was a burning city. Within crevices fires bellowed out and faint outlines of arms and bodies seemed to stretch into the air as if trying to escape. They fought amongst each other in a hopeless survival. From the city, a fiery river of molten rock flowed towards the castle.

Past the castle to the edge of the cavern the snow and ice of Niflheim surrounded the fiery desolation they were in. Below, among the pits was a barren, volcanic rocky landscape. Thick deposits of slime and feces jammed the crevices, locusts swarmed, maggots feasted. A few boiling rivers cut through the rock, reaching a large marshy lake below the floating castle, it's thick surface bubbling with steam.

The ferryman's boat left the water and floated over the pits towards the castle.

"The power of the Seeker's Stones, that's what Kalshaimar wants," Ahmed whispered to Will.

"This is worse than in the stories." Will shivered. He'd clutched his Seeker's Stone for the entire journey.

"There is no rebirth here," the ferryman laughed. "The Underworld is exactly what you see. The dark gods also have their realms here, we passed some. They take from the pool of sinners to their territories and torture them in their own ways. Only eternal suffering or conversion into a demon awaits souls here. People sent to the core of the Underworld are the worst. Lord Kalshaimar, as per his nature, has made this place as efficient in its task as possible."

"This is too much. Why would Manis want this?" Will frowned.

"Such is the hypocrisy of the gods' love and the folly of the Father."

They disembarked and walked under a heavy iron gate and into the throne room of the castle. There on a throne of corpses was the god of death, smiling.

"Well I am glad you made it friends," he hissed, his voice reeking of decay. Red-black dragon scale robes flowed to the ground. His hair was as long as Will's. Parts of his body and face, especially his hair and facial hair, were dissolving into a black mist, dark magic. A force seemed to suck the voice and soul out of the boys, but there was a hint of magic somewhere keeping them from succumbing to it. Will remembered this feeling from being in the presence of the warden. ***"Welcome to Death's Hold, my palace in the Underworld."***

"We are not your friends. Why d'you bring us here?" Will challenged him.

Kalshaimar's face turned red and he jumped from his throne shape-shifting. The god had a dragon-like face with horns coming out of his head and smaller horns out of his arms and legs. The aura around him seemed to suck all light away. His glowing white and slender pupils sat over black misty eyes. His large red-black scaled set of wings from which horns jutted out of the ends stretched wide. His breath smelled like ash and rot.

In his right hand he held a black jagged sword sharpened to two points and made of demonic metal. The fuller of his sword had been hollowed out. In its place sat a thin shaft of solidified blood from which liquid blood dripped in sticky globular clumps. In his left hand he held a long-jagged staff which terminated in several points. Between the points a red-black crystal was alight in a blue-white fire. Twisting around the staff was a hangman's noose. Whiffs of black smoky smog, dark magic, revolved around him. A long grey-green serpent slithered up and around his body, rising its head from Kalshaimar's right shoulder. Will fell back. Ahmed sensed his fear and struggled with his own. They felt something primal and immutable. It was as if they had achieved a state of complete despair. They were like prey facing a predator and knew only imminent death.

"Do not dare challenge me in my own kingdom boy! I am the god of death and the Underworld. I hold the Crimson Blade, harvester of lives. I am the patron of killers and molesters; I am the keeper of the dead of past, present, and future for I wield the eternal flames of the Underworld and the ice, detritus, and corrosive gas therein." He shifted back and sat on his throne. Kalshaimar exhaled, smoky fire leaving his nostrils. A low growl broke the silence. From the shadows behind his throne a large hound came forward to be petted by his master. The hound's three heads turned so that its eyes could lock onto his master's visitors.

Kalshaimar eyed the boys and waved a hand. Red-black, horned, humanoid demons came up behind Will and Ahmed. They wore jagged armor fused onto their skin, and emanated fire and dark magic.

"Now I think it is best if we forget the formalities and get to the point. You see I hate this place in reality, even after I have created it to look this way." Kalshaimar sighed. *"I can only get out if I can remember the Father's name. You see perhaps my brothers did not tell you I swore to destroy the Father's creation when he forced me down here. Surely you could help?"* He spoke in a calming voice, cooling the fear around him.

"They didn't explain anything."

"Well, of course they wouldn't! What vile gods that forget about me in my prison. As they rose in power and importance in the eyes of mortals, I fell. Why? They stole my power bit by bit. I confronted them. I wished only to talk, to come to a compromise, but they had other plans. They tried to kill me and take the last of my power. I defended myself against them. When the Father intervened, they said I tried to kill them! So he banished me to the Underworld for all time. I was deeply wronged. Help me right that wrong."

"What can we mere humans do to help a god?" Ahmed asked. There was a weight consuming him as he stood before the god of death. None of the descriptions or images on Erathas did justice to Kalshaimar's actual aura and the skin-crawling mix between warmth and cold he gave off. Ahmed latched onto the familiar strength of his pearl in order to keep his balance and his mind focused.

"Many things in fact! Become devoted to me, conduct severe penance and meditation in my name, give me my foolish brothers' Seeker's Stones... I like the last one."

"We have no idea..."

"Silence! You think I am a fool? I am God! I know what you are hiding! When the Seeker's Stones were created, I sensed their power emanate through the Three Worlds. I remember their sting long ago in ancient days, now they come again, opening a way for me to be free. The problem is if I touch them, they will not work for me. They only work for Seekers, less you give them to me willingly. So, I require you to help me."

"We would never!"

"So bold you both are to think you can challenge me. Do you think my brothers' powers will protect you here? I interrupted them and brought you here. Ha! Even now they must be scrambling to pull you out, after all, the souls of the dead come here but never leave."

"No, that can't be true! Seekers can travel freely."

"I do not lie. Did they tell you that they fought each other and why? No? After ridding me of my place in the Overworld each sought to take

control from the other. They threatened to destroy creation before I ever tried. I was left in my prison to waste away with the dead. But the Father did not complete this place. There are gaps and cracks, places where I could reach for thin strands of creation. With Creation Magic I populated this realm as I willed.

"Yet even still, after gaining power my brothers could only dream of, I cannot break free of this place. I needed their magic too, when combined with my own I will have enough to shatter the borders of this place. I am a king, yes, but one who suffers in endless pain and sickness. In truth, I am a prisoner here, something you would understand Seeker." Kalshaimar pointed to Will. *"I want freedom. Is that so hard to provide?"*

"I'm not you," Will said. He balled his hands into fists. Kalshaimar was grasping at straws. Though he was on the verge of submitting to the god of death's aura, Will kept his mind focused on the strands of resistance he'd shown to the warden. He accepted that he had resisted his tormentor and if he could do that then it would help him against Kalshaimar. His pearl pulsed, agreeing.

"I did not deserve to be cast down here!" Kalshaimar roared. *"Why is it Manis and Alhurah were allowed to covet and war over power and only I was punished? They shunned me! I had ideas on how to make the Three Worlds better and they laughed them off. They tore down my additions just as they will claim I broke down theirs! I curse the Father for not seeing that!"*

"This is not our fight," Ahmed spoke, boldly stepping forward. "Let us go."

"Go? Go! You will return here. How many have you killed in your lives? What other crimes have you committed? A murder is a murder.

"If you want to be spared from this place you will do as I say! You know not how a person is converted here? First the body is boiled then the flesh is skinned off. Then subjected to great pain within great pressure until the soul withers out. As if I were squeezing him in my hand. Think about the hells that await one here. You may burn endlessly in fire crumbling under the most horrible tortures unimaginable. You could even walk the endless frozen wastes freezing for all eternity. How does being bound to a mirror and shattered into a trillion pieces sound to you or endlessly falling as you are crushed by rocks? If your soul is malleable enough I may make you into one of my demon enforcers."

A blast of brilliant yellow light engulfed Kalshaimar's demon soldiers, burning them in yellow flame. The light formed in between the boys and Kalshaimar. Alhurah took shape.

"You fill their minds with lies Kalshaimar! Their sins if any they have thus committed will be judged upon their deaths. Actions,

reasons, and mentalities will all be judged. The Father is merciful, his children tend not to be. Not all sinners deserve the Underworld; some can be saved."

"No! This is my kingdom you cannot be here. You cannot do this!" Kalshaimar roared.

"This is not your kingdom but your prison." Alhurah frowned. *"Come Seekers it is time we go. We will ensure Kalshaimar will never reach you again."* He waved a hand and a door to the boy's left opened. *"Run through the corridor to the bridge and do not linger."* Will and Ahmed ran. Behind them Kalshaimar growled,

"No! I curse you both! I curse your world! This new age of Seekers has been put into motion and I will not sit idly by while it passes. You will rue the day of my judgement!" Kalshaimar's last words echoed as the door Alhurah had opened, closed.

The boys ran towards a light. They ran past many rooms, demon enforcers advanced behind them.

They turned and Alhurah's voice echoed in the air. *"Run I told you! Have faith, I will protect you. You cannot die in this place."* Will and Ahmed ran. As the demons swung their weapons to strike, lightning rushed down and tore through their bodies. Will and Ahmed ran until they came to a bridge outside Death's Hold. Behind them lightning shattered the door collapsing into rubble and stopping their pursuers. Will and Ahmed took a moment to breathe, Will clasping his knees and Ahmed panting.

"The power within the Seeker's Stones, if Kalshaimar had it, could he really break free?" Ahmed shouted to Alhurah.

"He seems to think so. Coupled with what Kalshaimar knows of creation... I fear what may be possible."

"Can you not do anything? Are you not God?"

"Since Kalshaimar has gained some powers of creation, if the Father were to even try and change this place it may give Kalshaimar the opening to break free. They are in an endless stalemate, the Father and Kalshaimar."

"What Kalshaimar said of you and Manis coveting power..."

"You won't understand such complex things, Seeker."

"You and Manis tried to kill him..." Will said.

"We each had different ideas. One would add something, only to have another tear it down and another add something else. We argued a lot. Kalshaimar ripped down more than he added. He did have ideas vastly different than ours. None evil. But we grew annoyed with him. We did try to kill him. Unable to make his voice heard he tried to deprive us from mortal worship. He'd destroy their temples and shrines, he'd turn them away from seeing us, he'd kill them at times. He simply wanted more recognition of the things he'd contributed,

positive things, but we... we wouldn't recognise his accomplishments." Alhurah's voice seemed pained with guilt and remorse, his sound and aura dull and weak.

"He was banished into a newly created Underworld. Kalshaimar became the god of death. Forsaken and forgotten he refused to destroy evil. With the powers of creation he was able to remould evil souls into his own army, his demons. Like the Father had raised a mortal to godhood, so too did Kalshaimar learn to raise others to the same level. The Dark Gods are the result of this power, made to obtain more Creation Magic for him.

"Kalshaimar became a serious threat to creation and the Father isolated himself, committing to an eternal meditation, isolated from the Three Worlds, to keep Kalshaimar from obtaining more power. The Corruption Crisis, a coming of Kalshaimar on the Baseworld, which occurred in Erathas' past, is the result of this ongoing stalemate."

"So, you wronged him. You shunned and ridiculed and isolated him." Ahmed frowned. Thinking of Amir and the love they shared; Ahmed couldn't understand why the gods were unable to get along. Perhaps the others ignored the fact that Alhurah spoke with the authority of the Father, though a Gurmian would claim none listened to Manis. "I don't know what to believe."

"Let the gods worry about the preservation of creation. Keep Kalshaimar away from our power. The Seekers of old fell to evil, abused our power, and destroyed themselves, to the detriment of the world. In you we risk new Seekers because your lands sorely need it. Worry only about that."

At the end of the bridge a bright mist tore out of the sulfurous air. Will fled first followed by Ahmed, passing through the mist. Light pushed away the dark and once again, like a feather, they were transported out of the Underworld and into the sunlight.

Chapter Twenty-Eight

WILL WOKE ON a soft bed in Castle Ochsen's infirmary. Tattered tarps covered the remains of the walls, preserving the enclosed space. Bandages were wrapped tightly all over him. Turning he noticed Jillian.

"Thank God you are awake, Will! I was worried; I was here the whole time while you were out. The other doctors wanted to bleed you but I kept them away and put herbs on your wounds," Jillian boasted.

"You did?" Will began to sit up, his voice shaky. He winched, sharp pain radiating from underneath his bandages.

"No, stay down Will. You need rest."

"Where's Ahmed?" Jillian pointed across to Will's left to a bed where Ahmed slept.

"He has not woken yet but I had to be stronger with him. All the doctors wanted to experiment on him."

"What happened?"

"Don't worry about that right now. Stay in bed, I'll be right back." Jillian left the room. Will laid on his bed and stared at the ceiling. Images of his visit to the Overworld and Underworld played through his mind. It seemed so surreal now, to have seen the gods and his parents. He smiled. He had been able to say goodbye to them properly. Though he understood they could never come back, it meant a lot to hear they were proud of him. After several minutes Jillian came back into the room and placed a mug on a side table.

"I'll help you up." Jillian helped Will rise, putting her hand on his back. She offered Will the mug. It was filled with a hot, aromatic, light brown liquid.

"What's this?"

"It's a tea. From the far east. It's made of herbs that will help you relax and dull your pain." Will took a small sip. Realising how hot it was, he spit it back.

"It's too hot," Will complained.

"You have to blow on it!" Jillian laughed.

As Will strategized how not to burn himself, Jillian brought her hands to Will's face. He recoiled. "You have cuts all o'er you. I'm checking the bandages." Will hesitated but let her touch him. When Jillian's hands crept to his torso, Will realised he was half naked. His **M** brand stared up at him. Jillian reached to his waist. Will flinched, almost dropping his tea, and suddenly shook Jillian's hands off him. He paled, looking at Jillian with tense suspicion.

"Will… I am not going to…"

"No. It's not that." Will laid back. "This is all uncomfortable." Will traced the **M** brand on his chest.

"I-It's not been applied properly," she said with a nervous voice.

"I got it when I was ten. As I grew it stretched out of shape."

"I see." Jillian bowed her head.

"What happened to us in the battle?"

"I'll tell you and Ahmed when he wakes."

"Thank-you Jillian." Will gave her a shy smile. Jillian returned the smile and moved to Ahmed. Will took another sip of his tea. As Jillian worked, she hummed an old song.

"Treating Ahmed like this reminds me of other Saomarhadians I healed."

"You helped Saomarhadians?"

"Under Sir Robert's command, we try and save the lives of those we can. Mostly friend but we will treat foe. Most soldiers, like ours, are sixteen to thirty-years-old. They fear me when I work on them but once they're healed, they are grateful. Then I see their hopes disappear when Gurmian troops come and take them off to some prisoner-of-war camp."

"What did you think of them?"

"I didn't focus on it. I focused on my job. Before Ahmed, I obviously distrusted and hated them." Jillian sighed. "The Saomarhadians were always kinda like us."

"They are." Ahmed stirred, opening his eyes. He looked at Jillian.

"Welcome back."

"Wi-Will…" Ahmed groaned. He held his head. "Headache."

"I'll bring you some tea for that. Will is behind me. Stay in bed, I'll be back." Jillian rushed out of the room.

Ahmed turned to Will. "What happened to us?"

"We met the gods. They took us out of the battle."

"R-Right." Ahmed started to remember. It seemed so surreal now. He was glad he got to say goodbye to Master Mahad and Shoran on better terms, but guilt still gnawed at him. He let Shoran die. He was happy, but he could have been happy and alive. It was his great failure to such a loyal and appreciative friend.

Those who watch', it was his master's final words to him. What did Master Mahad mean? At the end of this war he'd return and find his master's talisman. Jillian returned with a mug of tea and passed it to Ahmed. She helped him up and he sat and drank.

"This is imported. It's a popular brew in Saomarhad," Ahmed said.

"It was looted before we abandoned Fort Valki," Jillian informed. She stood in front and between the two boys. "You were both injured and knocked out on the battlefield. Sir Robert led four knightly charges into the Saomarhad infantry lines until they were on the verge of breaking. Then everything started to go bad. Our forces, sent to take that hill village to the south, were defeated and the victorious Saomarhadians flanked us. There were not many of them, but Sir Robert had to protect his flank and diverted forces from the attack on the infantry. Then we heard horns and drums from the north. A massive Saomarhad relief force of heavy calvary, mamluks and ghilman as well as robed warriors and battalions of black men were charging our northern flank."

"From the emirates in the deep south, those black men, Zanjī," Ahmed informed. "A land of savannas, jungles and red-orange dirt."

"But there were battalions from eastern Saomarhad too, those robed warriors, a few rode armoured camels."

Ahmed thought for a moment. "Badawī tribal peoples from the Saomarhad deserts. That the sultan was able to bring so many different warriors together meant he was adamant about defeating this invasion, and is a testament to his title: the rightly guided of the faith."

"Sir Robert was forced to retreat and before we knew it, we were in full rout. It was chaos in the camp. I scrambled to remove the injured and Sir Robert made a stand on the hill to give us time to escape."

"Is Sir Robert okay?" Will paled.

"He is well."

"Did the sultan pursue?" Ahmed asked.

"We thought he would and we thought he'd show no mercy. Many in the camp feared it. Some have horrifying stories of seeing people run down by naffatin warriors and burned alive by flaming tar. But he didn't follow us. We couldn't hold Fort Valki because we had bombed it. Lord Richrit wanted to stay but Sir Robert would not risk his men. We looted it and retreated here, Castle Ochsen."

"Really?" This astonished Ahmed. It was uncharacteristic of the sultan.

"He's called a ceasefire."

"What? That can't be!" Ahmed nearly got off the bed, but settled.

"It is. What's more surprising is that King Duggan has agreed."

"These leaders have never wanted peace before. Something else must be in play."

"Maybe. All that matters now is that Sir Robert is being recalled to Royal Landing. He'll take you two. I will come as well." Jillian nodded.

"How d'you find us?" Will asked.

"Sir Robert found you. Actually, you were both glowing."

"Glowing?" Both boys asked at once.

"Yes. I heard it was as if some magic shield had protected you in the middle of the battlefield. It wasn't you, Ahmed?"

"I was with Will in the Overworld. No."

"The—" Jillian cleared her throat. "The what?"

"We are Seekers, Ahmed," Will said. "What do we even do from here?"

"Alhurah told us to listen to the people."

"What does that mean?"

"I don't know."

"You are both talking nonsense!" Jillian shook her head. "Only the dead can go to the Overworld! And what is a Seeker?" They had a lot to tell Jillian and quite a bit of time to do so.

A cart brought Sir Robert, Jillian, Will, and Ahmed through the Roywood towards Royal Landing. The group was met with other soldiers returning from the front. Some were granted leave while others stayed to supervise the ceasefire. They arrived in Serleigh at evening and it was welcome as they had spent the previous night in the woods since the banishment in Burhbarrow was still in effect.

Serleigh wasn't as large or influential as Burhbarrow, but it had its own lord who governed it and the areas around it. The King's Road ran through it. They rented out rooms in the Serleigh inn for the night.

Will could not sleep so he stepped onto a balcony and looked over the Green Swamps. Starting at Serleigh's central square, the road to Charleston wound through the swamp below. Looking into the still night his thoughts plucked at his conscious. He'd woken this time before the nightmare progressed. Will realised he was crying. He wiped the tears away and cursed. Even if he wanted them to stop, his past still haunted him. He still didn't understand what Manis saw in him.

"Watching the swamps, Will?" He turned to see Jillian.

"Yeah, I guess." Will tried to smile, it seemed Jillian noticed but didn't say anything. She was probably disgusted that he cried a lot. He wasn't as capable as Sir Robert or Ahmed, better men than him. "You can't sleep?"

"No. I am worried… anyway… too bad we didn't come on a full moon," Jillian stood beside Will. "You can see the glowing green lights coming from it every full moon. Have you seen it Will?"

"No, I haven't."

"Well they are one of the most beautiful things in the world. There are wisps within the green that seem to dance. Some believe that they are ancient spirits from the time of the High Elven Empire. You can see it in Royal Landing; the lights can be seen for leagues."

The spirit he'd encountered briefly came into Will's mind. "Jillian, you knew I was crying. You must think ill of me."

"What?" Jillian asked.

"Everyone, Sir Robert, Ahmed, have seen it. I am not like other men, not strong like them; the only thing going for me is a little skill I have with a blade, otherwise" —he took a breath— "I am just a boy who only knows how to be miserable, who can't get o'er the memories…"

"The only thing that is wrong with you, Will, is that you believe that."

"What?"

"Will, I don't care if you cry. You *can* get stronger, and who said you were weak? You are not weak." Jillian took a moment to think. "You… you keep fighting Will. Even when you cry you keep living and keep moving forwards. Isn't that strength? To persevere even when everything you do seems in vain or things outside of your control constantly knock you down. Will, I am not about to shun you. You are more than worthy of being anyone's apprentice or friend."

"Sometimes, like tonight, I feel confused. All this stuff is happening to me. I fear it will all go away: you, Sir Robert, Ahmed." Will looked to the ground. "I had a nightmare tonight. The warden came out of the trees and killed all of you. Then he took me and I could feel myself wasting away. Worst of all I lost everything again like I did when I was ten." Jillian came closer and touched Will's face. Will flinched, looking at her cautiously. She wiped away his tears and smiled. "Please don't leave me." Will looked into her eyes.

"I will try not to," she said softly, blushing. "I am starting to understand the things that still pain you," Jillian said.

"Will, why would you think like that?" Ahmed came forward. Will and Jillian turned to him.

"You… what d'you mean?" Will frowned.

"You've proven yourself to us already. We are friends now, aren't we? We won't leave you. You won't be able to forget the memories, I think. You aren't worthless or weak." Ahmed smiled. Jillian nodded in agreement.

"That makes me happy, more than you'll e'er know. Thank you, both of you." Will hesitated, wanting to say more. "I didn't kill my parents… but… I need to know what you think." Will's chest tightened and he rubbed his wrists.

"As a mage I can sense your energies. I can sense your visions, dreams, and memories, like I did in Nizid. After all that, and after getting to know you, I am confident that you speak the truth."

"The answer matters to you, doesn't it?" Jillian frowned.

"Yes."

"Will… I-I still don't know." The boys looked at Jillian. "I'm not a mage so I don't have the ability to look deeper." Jillian looked firmly into Will's eyes. "I trust you Will. I don't say that lightly. In all else, I don't know yet."

"I see." Will's heart sank. He shivered. He didn't want it to be like this, not when he was feeling closer and closer to Ahmed and especially Jillian, day after day. Ahmed put a hand on Will's shoulder.

"We should worry about the coming days," Ahmed said. "I fear what will become of us once we see the tyrant King Duggan Chas."

"He is a man of great temper and cruelty. Even in the north I heard many stories about him and how he enslaved entire villages though this was cast in a good light," Will said.

"Maybe he will be merciful?" Jillian tried, flashing a strained smile. Both boys looked at her. "Well, why can't he?"

"Because he is evil. I am sure you have heard, as we have, the things he has done."

"Even in Saomarhad?"

"Sometimes not all the propaganda they show us is false," Ahmed said.

"I guess it's hard to argue… but… maybe his daughter is a better person! If someone in his family is good then per'aps they can influence his mind," Jillian said.

"What makes you think that?" Will asked.

"My father used to do business with King Duggan. His daughter and his wife used to come by one of our clothing stores for dresses. We catered to the rich, that's why my father became successful. I remember helping her once, fitting her into a new dress."

"As I see it, like father like daughter. The mother was probably as bad as the king." Ahmed sighed.

"That's not true! Both King Duggan's daughter and his wife were very kind to me! His daughter is very agreeable, kind, funny, and thoughtful. Her mother just the same."

"They wanted a dress from you, of course they would be all that."

"That's not the point that's…"

"Face it Jillian, King Duggan and his family do not care about anyone they rule," Will said. The girl looked down, defeated by the two boys.

"Now if you would please go to sleep… you both woke me up." Ahmed frowned.

"Sorry Ahmed." Will scratched his hair.

"Sir Robert said we have to leave early to make it to the next waystation."

"We should go back then." Jillian giggled and embraced the boys but then tears came to her eyes. "Whatever happens in front of the king, we will deal with it." Ahmed left and Jillian followed. Will watched her leaving. Sir Robert's talk came to his mind. How he had regretted not telling Emmeline earlier about his feelings. Will didn't know what to do. Spending time with Jillian had only made those feelings stronger. She still did not believe in his innocence. Maybe all he thought of her was better left unsaid.

"Jillian…" Will spoke, choking on the last syllable. She turned and looked at him. "I… I need to tell you… ask you…" His voice was hoarse and his mouth dry.

"I know what you are going to say, Will, but I can't," she said carefully. Will crossed his arms, making himself look small. He shivered, on the border of withering. Jillian's eyes betrayed the guilt she tried to hide. Maybe she felt something for him too. What was holding her back?

"I-I am not a…"

"It's not because of that. Should we be talking about this now?" She fidgeted with her tunic.

"I just thought…"

"You and Ahmed told me about this Seeker thing and what Manis wanted you to do. Well I also have something to do. I have been away from home too long and I realise I have been selfish this whole time. My parents need me right now. I have to return and help them. That does not mean I will leave you but it does mean that…"

"I think I like you… more than a friend… and it makes me afraid." Will boldly interrupted Jillian. "I know fear… but this fear is different. If I could only know what you think…" Jillian didn't speak. Will looked down. He spoke out of turn, too much, and had misjudged her. She didn't want to hear this; she didn't feel like he did. Of course, she didn't. He was too broken for love. Jillian strode up to Will, making him look up and take a few steps back, and hugged him. Will trembled, tensing, and Jillian hugged tighter. He dared himself to return the hug and against his own comfort, he did just that. Within seconds he brushed her off, breaking a sweat. Jillian didn't seem to mind.

"You deserve love," Jillian said. "I think I like you too." Will's eyes widened, his Seeker's Stone lit up and calmed him. "But if you like me then you will respect my wishes. When I have done what I need to do… then…"

"Friends," Will whispered, giving in. Jillian let him go.

"Thank-you for understanding."

<hr>

The road from Serleigh to the capital took a few days more. After halfway there, they arrived at a resting camp. The journey was uneventful. Will, his master, Ahmed, and Jillian near the back along with five or six mounted troops trekked onwards in relative silence.

The camp was nestled on a main hill to the south connected on the west end by a bridge to a smaller rise, upon which stood a guard tower. On the large hill and in the space below, travellers could set up camp.

When the group arrived Sir Robert was guided to the largest tents. He, Will, and Ahmed did not have to pay for lodging but the troops had to. Many peasants were turned away if they could not pay, forcing them to brave the night on a road of outlaws. The guards stationed there patrolled through the night.

Ahmed yawned on his bedroll and turned from his side to lie on his back. He opened his eyes and was greeted by the tent's roof. Ahmed sat up noticing that Sir Robert was still sleeping in his room of the tent, but Will was gone. He guessed Will had woken early to go relieve himself or something. As

Ahmed stretched, he noticed a used needle lying next to Will's bedroll. No... nothing had indicated to him Will used drugs. The image of Will lying next to a hookah filled with hashish amused him. Ahmed picked up the needle and flicked clear liquid from its point. It had no smell.

Confused, Ahmed wondered if Will was just outside. He exited the tent to rays of dim light seeping through the branches of the trees. A group of people crowded around a spot ahead, mumbling to each other. The camp's commander was trying to clear the area. Ahmed asked what the matter was. The commander turned to face him, frowning, and pointed to the dead guardsmen on the ground.

"Twas the easterner! He did this! He killed these men!" accused a woman. Other guards were carrying some of their dead comrades towards the commander. The crowd made noise at the idea and some started to approach Ahmed but the commander came into their way.

"We can't be sure! Don't care who the boy is, I come from a quiet part I do. We won't accuse without proof," the commander instructed. He gestured to Ahmed who nodded and rushed back to wake Sir Robert. The knight followed Ahmed out and bent down to examine the bodies. Behind him Ahmed had aroused the rest of the knight's men and they armored themselves and came forward. Jillian also woke and stood near the back of the crowd.

"There was no struggle here," Sir Robert said. "These men were killed silently and quickly. They did not know what was coming until it was too late."

"Bandits?" asked the commander.

"Bandits trained with military training. No, this was done by talented men. Besides, bandits do not strike a rest camp in stealth and take nothing. It seems they left in a hurry."

"Crap! I had a flawless record till now..."

"Wait. Where is Will?"

"I woke and he was not there. I thought he woke early," Ahmed said. "There... there was a used needle beside his bedroll." The confused expression on Sir Robert's face confirmed the oddity of the find. Then worry shadowed over the knight and he looked around, screaming Will's name. There was no answer.

"Sir!" A guard rushed towards the group. "The greenery on the forest floor's been trudged through. They came from the trees." A bird screeched in the sky, flying in circles above the camp. Ahmed looked up and noticed Will's falcon. Sir Robert followed his gaze. "Something's happened." Ahmed frowned.

"Quickly. Men. Arm yourselves. We're following the beaten greenery and that bird!" Armoured up, the knight led his men into the forest.

Will woke to unfamiliar surroundings. He saw the sky above him, and the rising sun shone through a nearly destroyed stone vaulted roof. He was in some sort of small, ruined chapel. Will took stock of himself. His arms were pinned behind his back with a set of shackles and his feet were shackled as well. Will was grabbed by two men who dragged him forward, on his knees. The sides of the chapel were crumbling, and standing there were cloaked men with the Gurmanis symbol on their tunics. The uniforms were altered but it was clear what Will saw; the three black stripes of Isen Prison.

Will struggled but the men holding him held firm. His heart thumped against his chest and his body seized up. He could only look straight ahead at a man with a scar, a man Will knew all too well, the warden.

"My job, my wealth, my castle, everything I have lost, and because of you!" the warden said. "When word of your escape hit the king's ears, I was promptly cast out of his service. He put in a new warden because he claimed I was useless since I had let a sixteen-year-old boy escape. I left with a handful of my most loyal men. I was ruined all because of you, because you wanted to rebel against me." growled the warden. He stepped up to Will.

"LOOK AT ME! You always had that problem huh? LOOK!" Rage filled the man's eyes and Will forced himself to keep eye contact. It hurt him to do so but he fought back the tears as his eyes burned. The warden was now looking much like the interrogator who questioned Will when he was ten. The man's face was dissolving into black mist and one of his pupils was narrowed into a vertical line. The warden smiled his evil smile and slapped Will across his face. Will spit out saliva as he forced himself to stare at the creature.

"D'you think you can run away from everything you have done? Did you think that pitiful knight could have redeemed you? Have you redeemed yourself? No! You have not! Not in anyone's eyes. You are a monster and a murderer." Will winced at the familiar words. Images of prison flooded him, but still, he held back tears and stared at the warden. "Now it is personal. You will die today, Will Farmer, like you should have long ago. You will first feel the pain I suffered when I lost everything, and then you will hang. I will have peace." The warden stepped aside to reveal a noose hanging from the rafters above the ruined altar.

Sir Robert's group trodded through the forest as quick as they could, following Will's falcon and any sign of the kidnappers' presence. They froze when they heard a boy's painful scream; Will's voice. Fear ran Sir Robert's face almost colorless as he led on to find his squire.

An arrow whizzed down from the trees and missed a soldier. They took cover. Ahmed and two other crossbowmen fired into the sky. Ahmed took down one man with his crossbow. A soldier took out another. The men in the trees retreated, but Ahmed hit one in midair.

The group ran after the retreating foes. They came to an open area flanked by five huge trees. A ruined chapel was in view. Will's falcon screeched. It flew around the chapel's ruined spire then landed at the tip.

Sir Robert's men stopped in the center. Will's scream rang out again. Isen Prison guards rushed forwards, surrounding them. Sir Robert charged two with his sword and shield.

Ahmed raced forward, following Sir Robert's lead, kilij and hatchet in hand. Ahmed spun around taking out two guards at once. He faced a flail man. The man swung the heavy spiked ball at Ahmed's face. The boy ducked. Moved back. He countered as the weapon came low, swinging forward with his sword and catching his blade on the flail's chain. The flail man pulled away and Ahmed's kilij was ripped from his hands. Ahmed jumped back to avoid the man's counter. He cast a fireball as the flail man came around for his next strike, consuming him in flames.

Ahmed retrieved his blade and turned to see Sir Robert take out two more guards, his men dealing with three. Panicking men ran from the ruined chapel and joined their comrades. His's Seeker's Stone glowed. A force tried to pull him towards the chapel. He rushed forwards to engage the enemy.

<hr>

Blood dripped from Will's face, arms, and back as he withered on the ground. He was not sure what did this; he didn't see any tools, only suffered pain. The warden laughed a sneer sadistic laugh as he satisfied himself. He motioned to his men to take the boy. Will was dragged towards the altar. He struggled to get free, the best he could, but to no avail. The damming clink of his chains sealed his fate. The men wrapped the noose around Will's neck and tightened it. Another guard held the free end of the rope, and at the nod from the warden he pulled down, slowly at first, but then tighter. Will gasped, air escaping him, as he choked and squirmed. Suddenly his pocket burned and a red light shone from it. A guard close by ripped it out from his tunic. The stone blazed red flame and the man threw it, blowing his fingers as he did. The warden looked on mystified, broken from his enjoyment of watching the suffocating boy. The Seeker's Stone rolled down the stairs leading to the altar and stopped.

The stone shone a rage-fuelled red. Waves of magic and red electricity flamed and zapped forward as it threatened to lose control. A tingle ran through Will as the closer waves attracted him. His sight was darkening and he couldn't focus, but his memories flashed through him and Will thought to the moment Ahmed had tested his pearl and when he'd maybe produced magic. Will flexed his hands, mimicking what he'd done before, it was a vain hope. The magic of the stone directed towards him. He didn't know what he was doing, yet the stone seemed to understand what he pictured in his mind. Red electricity split into two streams. One sliced through the noose. Another hit the hangman and he fell in a smoking heap.

Will collapsed to the ground as the Seeker's Stone burst out a shockwave. The warden stood in the center; his cloak blew back. Will gasped for air. To the warden's amazement Will stood shakily, his bonds broken and he took the sword of the fallen guard.

Will walked forward, bending down to pick up his Seeker's Stone, and put it into his pocket. He stood to full height, staring down the warden through wet eyes. His heart raced and every cell in his body fought against the urge to submit and wither.

"Impossible! What is this?" the warden growled as he drew his sword. "You were dying and now…"

"I will ne'er die by your hands warden," Will said with a new sense of bravery. "You have failed."

"Ha! I owned you and I still do now. You were mine."

"Not any longer. D'you know why you failed to break me? Why I was not an empty body like the other prisoners? Because I was not like them. I was innocent and young. The thing that kept me from becoming empty forever was that I always remembered one image; home. 'twould bring me both pain and comfort but it kept me from becoming yours. Now I have found new friends and I don't have to be afraid anymore."

"I can read you Mr. Farmer. You still fear me. After all those years I helped you through, you betrayed me by escaping."

"You never helped me. You hurt me! I hate you and I hate myself for allowing it."

"It was for your benefit."

"No!" Will roared. He winched at sharp pain, his injures protesting his screams.

"I did what needed to be done to ensure your soul would have a chance to be vindicated and pure upon your death."

"There was no need, there was ne'er a need. Mercy is another path, one Manis prefers. All you did to me was so you could satisfy your own desires, but you never broke me." Will stepped close.

"Are you really so ignorant that you cannot see what is clear to me? The way you acted when you saw me, the way you reacted when I used dark magic on you, now. You may not be empty, Will Farmer, but you have been broken. You have been a thorn in my side for too long, now die." The warden charged Will, poised to stab him. Will moved to the side and swiped but the warden turned quickly, countering and pushing back. Will blocked three of his strikes in succession and attacked. The warden blocked Will and countered. Pain diverted the would be parry and the warden cut Will's arm. Will winced. He lunged in middle guard. The warden parried. The man thrust his blade forwards and Will moved to the right, the altar at his back.

The warden attacked again, catching Will off guard. He sliced Will's sword hand. Will screamed and dropped his sword then the warden grabbed hold of Will's neck. He pushed Will downwards and squeezed, rage in his eyes.

"You. Are. A monster. Animals like you need to die a slow and painful death." The warden derided through clenched teeth. Will suffocated, losing air. He tried to find his sword. "What you did was cruel and unusual. You kept stabbing them as they gasped and begged for you to stop. You were naught but cold and callous as you killed your helpless victims. In you is an irredeemable depravity that you refused to face! You should have died in Isen Prison, but I will make do with this place instead." Will struggled, trying to get free. His vision blurred.

Finally, Will's hand found his sword. He grabbed and swung it, striking the warden's side and drawing blood. The warden shouted and let go. He stumbled back, then charged forward. Will barely had a chance to recover. He blocked the attack, pain almost making him drop guard. The two traded blows. Will countered a strike and pushed the warden back. The warden roared and swiped Will who stumbled back to recover. The warden adjusted and thrust. Will blocked, attacked, countered. He saw a weakness and struck the warden's legs, toppling the man. Seeing this, Will bought his sword in an ark. He screamed as he slammed again and again, ignoring the vicious pain from his wounds, until he was able to loosen the warden's grip on his sword. The weapon slid across the floor and Will plunged his sword into the warden's chest. He fell to his knees on top of his ex-torturer and panted.

The warden looked up at his killer, "Congratulations Wi-Will Farm-mer, but I s-still broke you." The warden smiled as he closed his eyes and his breath stopped. From his body black mist surged out and disintegrated in the air. The mist engulfed Will, rushing up his nose and eyes. Will let go of his sword and collapsed backwards onto the altar stairs. Images of his past cluttered his brain and involuntarily, Will curled up, laying on his right-side muttering and whining. All Will could feel was the dark; all he could see was the dark. He only knew he was in a cell so small he could not even stand in it. The walls were closing and a voice was repeating, *'Mine.'*

The moldy door to the chapel burst open and Ahmed, Sir Robert, and his men rushed in swords drawn. Upon seeing the scene, they sheathed their weapons and Sir Robert rushed towards the withering form of Will, while Ahmed examined the dead warden. Sir Robert collapsed to Will and shook his arm.

"Will, what demon has come over you? It's me, your master, Sir Robert. Wake to sense Will!" If Will acknowledged his master's voice he did not show it as he lay there muttering nonsense.

Ahmed approached and placed his hand on Will's forehead. He whispered words then said, "Listen to my voice Will, come back to us, you are alive and you are free." Will's eyes widened and he coughed. The boy looked like a three-year-old might when accused of stealing from a cookie jar. Unseen to the group a single strand of thin black mist disintegrated in the air.

Back at the rest camp, the sun now higher in the sky, Ahmed conversed with Sir Robert, who looked deeply concerned. Will was sitting, head facing down so that his hair covered his face. Jillian was holding him, beside him on his left. Ahmed walked over and took a seat on the log opposite Will.

"Will," Ahmed said. Jillian looked up at Ahmed then at Will. Will lifted his head only slightly. "I need to know what happened before we found you. We all know by now that man was a shadow mage. From what your master told me, King Duggan was in league with at least two of these mages. One is dead, the other is lost. These were men becoming shadow mages even though they had no magic because evil and darkness had corrupted them. The man you killed, it seems he was not always a shadow mage, not when you… you were his prisoner, though I suspect dark magic was in the process of influencing him. His deeds finally caught up to him. What happened in there?"

"Is this the time to ask Ahmed? Will is beat, he just went through…" Jillian began.

"I am sorry but not much is known about these shadow mages. I have to ask now so Will can remember the events that took place. I had to pull his mind from him to get him to come back. What I was pulling it from is something I do not know unless you tell me what happened, Will."

"He hurt me not with physical tools but something else," Will's voice hoarse. "When he died a black mist covered me."

"Perhaps this in combination with your memories of prison caused you to lose your mind and wither."

"I don't know. All I know is he was right, I am broken, he broke me and now I am just glad he is gone."

Part Five:
End of a Century

Chapter Twenty-Nine

A S THEY PASSED under a gatehouse into Royal Landing a swath of noise, shouts, laughs, carriage wheels, neighs, and barks surged over them riding the masses of people. Royal Landing was as large as Ortie, and people worked, traded, and entertained. Will shifted his grip on his horses reigns, looking aimlessly ahead. Memories assaulted him: through the bars of the pig cage he'd been brought in he'd gazed upon the unfamiliar as he was swallowed by the King's Jail.

Will pressed his thighs against his horse to prevent himself from falling over, battling with his thoughts.

People stared as Sir Robert's entourage passed. Will and Ahmed stayed close as the knight stood tall against the judging eyes. Jillian stared at her horse's mane as if hiding from sight.

The finery of the main street on which they travelled served only as a veil to the real state of the city. Its merchant stalls along the road and clotheslines and bridges above displayed flags and ribbons. Sir Robert had told them about the city's poor and it's deprived, many of whom were displaced by the war and had made the treacherous trek from the front to the capital. On arrival, they were quickly stuffed into a ghetto and forgotten. Now even the main street with all its colour and flora could not veil the poor and the forsaken who were bleeding into the nicer parts.

They rode between the stalls and the stone, wattle and daub houses flanking the main street, under a line of banners. The citizens crowded closer while others peered out their windows. A girl ran ahead of them hopping and pointing.

"Look! Look! It's the boys in the prophecy!" she shouted. "They've come to end the war!" The crowds around the knight's entourage clustered, forcing them to slow down. Sir Robert ordered his men to protect the flanks. The girl disappeared, running out of view.

"It is them! The boys with the Grand Marshal," someone shouted.

"Our saviours!"

"He's one of the enemies. I don't believe it. Expel him from the city!" a man shouted.

"They will negotiate with King Duggan and the sultan; they will listen to Manis' chosen!"

"That one's a murderer. He killed his own mother. Bah! Manis curse him! He can't be God's chosen," a woman shouted. Will and Ahmed shifted with unease.

"They're too young! Too unimportant. We need heroes like those of the past. People with courage, bravery, and strength. Not mere boys!"

"Keep your heads," Sir Robert advised. "All we need to do is get to the keep."

Will and Ahmed kept their eyes on their horses. Being called out so suddenly was not what they expected. They looked at each other, confusion evident in both their faces. What prophecy were the people talking about? They pushed onwards.

⌇⌇

They passed through two gatehouses and two city squares, the crowds observing them all the way. They passed under a stone archway into a boulevard, its centerline decorated by flowers. Flanking them were statues, heroes and kings of the past, guarding the road. The castle was perched on a high hill overlooking the city. A moat extending from the Golden Inlet separated the castle from the rest of the city. The four approached the gates, which were closed and its drawbridge up. Five armored men stood there, donning gold-plated armor and long gold-white capes, the King's Guard. A guard dog stood beside them. Sir Robert and his company stopped and the guards demanded Will's and Ahmed's weapons. By the knight's direction, both complied.

Along a raised walkway over the bailey, they approached the courtyard where servants of many barons and lords were walking among tents and their knights converged to hear developments of the ceasefire, some knights were still at the battlefront. Many examined them as they passed including lounging King's Guard from a side keep. Ahead, the imposing Palace of Kings stood tall.

A steward guided them into the throne room where all the barons and lords were seated. Sturdy circular pillars held the roof aloft, flanking the entering group. It was between these pillars that the barons sat on large chairs lined up to make a central path, covered in a blue and gold carpet, to the king's throne. Bright rays of light entering from a tall window behind the throne, luminated the room. Stairs led from the throne to the window and up the flanks to balconies on the left and right where court ladies stood. The flag of Gurmanis flew off the pillars and above the throne where King Duggan sat on a higher platform, flanked by his standard bearers. A richly dressed male high elf whose long brown hair neatly framed his light skin and green eyes, a lugahon, occupied the chair closest to King Duggan's right, and the grandmaster of the King's Guard stood to the left, a helm over his face.

Behind the king and barons, King's Guard and fief knights stood watching with interest at the group entering the room.

King Duggan's expression shifted. He wore a fine fur-lined blue tunic with a cloak and a large golden crown. The wrinkles that defined his face gave him a weathered and experienced look, contrasted with his neatly trimmed and combed facial hair, stuck closely to his jawline and around his lips. Will recognised Lord Dillon amongst the people as well as Lord Richrit. Both lords frowned.

"Sir Robert! You have done a great deed for me!" the king spoke, smiling. Sir Robert stared, confused at the remark.

"My King." The knight and his companions bowed, Ahmed's bow slighter than the others. "What deed is this?"

"You have returned my daughter to me. She stands behind you!" the lords and barons of the room gasped and Sir Robert's eyes grew wide. Sir Robert looked over Jillian in detail, quickly seeing the resemblance. Until now, Jillian had been a name in the knight's mind, a girl Will fancied. The knight realised she had always put distance between herself and him so that he'd not fully looked over her. Indeed, Sir Robert could never imagine Princess Elizabeth in peasant clothes. The king laughed.

"I can recognize my own daughter. Yes, it is a clever disguise! A peasant? No one in all of Gurmanis would believe my daughter would dress as a peasant! Come daughter, enlighten everyone; you have been exposed now." Jillian looked back at Will's shocked face and her face pleaded for forgiveness. She stepped forward, placed a hand on Sir Robert's arm and gave him a remorseful look, then stood before her father and addressed his court.

"My lords, I am Princess Elizabeth Chas, daughter to King Duggan Chas." She stood straight and tall, her chin pointed slightly up. Elizabeth sounded very regal now. Sir Robert bowed to Elizabeth, and sensed the shock and despair coming from Will in waves.

"My Princess, had I known I would have taken better—"

"Have no unease Sir Robert, you are forgiven. I did well to conceal myself from you and thus it is entirely of my doing." This new girl's actions guarded her true feelings well, a slight frown was all she revealed through her regal demeanor. King Duggan smiled and motioned to his daughter to approach. Elizabeth walked towards him and he brought her close in a hug.

"I don't blame you for running away. I missed you, Elizabeth. Tell me all that happened later and I swear if anyone has laid a hand on you, I will punish them severely. And tell me why you left, all will be well now."

Elizabeth nodded then took an empty seat beside her father's throne sitting straight and with perfect posture.

"Well, you have brought her here safely Sir Robert," the king started, "and you have earned her forgiveness, but have not earned mine. These boys behind you must be the Saomardrim and the criminal. Step forward so I may see your faces."

Will and Ahmed did so and looked away from the king, careful not to make direct eye contact.

"My king, I…"

"I don't want your excuses Sir Robert! It is most shameful a knight as revered as you would associate with these people."

"My king, they have not broken my trust thus far."

The king hissed, "this insolence and disloyalty is why you never made it to the King's Guard Sir Robert. Or climbed higher in the hierarchy of the nobility. I have enough reason here to call you a traitor but be lucky you have friends here."

Lord Dillon glanced at Sir Robert then focused on Will.

"Nevertheless, my king I would never think of being disloyal!"

"Then why do you train a criminal and harbor an enemy?" The king rose and stepped down to the boys. The rest of his court stood too. King Duggan first approached Will and inspected his face.

"What does my knight see in you, boy? You are a peasant and a murderer, nothing more. You don't deserve any of this." King Duggan huffed and walked past Will, standing before Ahmed. "And you. Why are you here? What do you hope to accomplish? Lord Richrit makes it clear that your kind are a blight. I am inclined to agree. Your people, your sultan assassinated my wife!"

Elizabeth shifted, grasping an armrest of her chair.

"For that, I will never forgive. Seize him!" Two King's Guards strode forward and grabbed Ahmed's arms. Ahmed didn't resist, stiffening to show bravery against the king.

"You are no more than a savage." The king drew his longsword. The weapon emitted a green mist that gave it a green glow underneath. He pointed the tip inches from Ahmed's throat. "Do you know what this weapon is? It has killed many of your kind in the name of great Manis. This is Heretic's Bane, a blight on your people that brings honour to whoever wields it." Ahmed recoiled from the intoxicating smell given off by the green corrosive poison. He turned back against the sting to glare at the king.

"Ahh I see it in your eyes, the anger, the hate. I could kill you myself, right here, but your blood would taint my hall. Have the Saomardrim beheaded!" The guards propped Ahmed up to take him away. King Duggan returned to his throne.

"No, my king, this is not right. He is a boy!" Lord Dillon spoke.

"Lord Dillon, I am king and this is my court! What I say happens."

Lord Dillon slouched back.

Elizabeth placed a hand on her father's shoulder. "No, father, don't."

The king looked back to the defiant Ahmed. "Well, it looks like the princess favors you, Saomardrim. I will spare you, for now." Ahmed was released by the guards. The king debated what to do. The barons and lords were talking amongst themselves.

"The grand bishop and Lord Richrit have told me about what happened at the Grand Mosque. The traitor priest and the grand imam prophesied some vague arrival of Seekers. It is simply meaningless. It is a false story to discredit and dethrone me. No one thanks their king for driving back the Saomardrim threat!"

"But my lord, the truth is the people have been ever weary. They adore the idea God is helping them. In contrast they don't think you care for them. This is a dangerous atmosphere," a bold baron commented.

"We must not let that scare us. The Saomardrim have murdered our people and will continue to do so until we drive them away!" another said. Suddenly the entire throne room was erupting in bickering lords, those in favour of the war counter to those against it.

"SILENCE!" King Duggan demanded. "I did not permit anyone to speak in my throne room." The room fell silent. The king scratched his bearded chin. "I am not afeared of any prophecy, nor the people, and not God, for Manis is with me in this fight. I am Gurmanis' rightful king, appointed by God by virtue of my bloodline. I fear no uprising. What say you, boys? Do you think you both are some sort of Seeker? Whatever such a thing means." Will and Ahmed hesitated. They didn't know what to say, especially Will, he didn't know how to speak with a king. But also, because they didn't know there was a prophecy people knew about.

"Sultan Yazid wants peace," Ahmed spoke. "King Duggan, you should accept it."

The king laughed. "Peace? There will be no peace until Sultan Yazid steps down from his throne and throws himself at my feet. He must be punished for murdering my wife. He sent Hashashin to kill her!"

"My sultan never sought their services. I have heard of the queen of Gurmanis and she died of sickness."

"How dare you! In front of my daughter as well!" the king roared. "I will entertain Sultan Yazid. If he repents, as Manis instructs mercy, I will show leniency. But to achieve peace I, the rightful king, must rule all these lands."

"You wish only for power, wealth, and control. Having royal blood does not make you lord of everything. That position is only the Father's," Ahmed argued. Will was amazed Ahmed had spoken in such a way to the king. The king scoffed.

"And you, peasant. What have you to say?"

"I don't wish for any power, my king. I just… want a decent life. Sir Robert is kind to me."

"His mistake; for that I am sorry."

Gaining courage from Ahmed's words, Will challenged the king. "Y-You are wrong, my king. Manis is not with you. You and the sultan have the power to end this war but all you both do is continue to fight. Your people suffer for it. If you want to keep your kingdom and rule, you must end this war." Will observed King Duggan. This was the man whose governance had him imprisoned. Ahmed had confirmed that King Duggan allowed shadow mages to work for him. He or his officials probably hired the warden. He advocated Judeicar's Justice. The king was partly to blame for everything that happened to Will. But the king was like Aldershire's lord, a man too powerful for Will to challenge any more than he already had.

"You dare threaten me? The Saomardrim, at least, has wealth and power. That is respectable. You? You have nothing, you are nothing!" King Duggan scoffed. Will winced. "I see now these two are no heroes, no challengers. Have these boys confined within the dungeons and starve them to death! Throw them into the pits, the oubliettes!" Uproar thundered through the throne room, some siding with the idea and others not.

"My king, why do that? Let them go with Sir Robert. What will your people think if you do this?" Lord Dillon demanded. The king thought on it.

"Amis! Friends! Please quiet yourselves." A man who occupied a chair among the barons and lords closest to the king said, as he stood and lifted his hands into the air, asking for silence.

"Duke Célestin, newly come from your domain, you have something to add?" King Duggan invited the duke to speak. The man walked forward, in front of the king, his blue cape swishing behind him. He wore an elaborate set of armor, engraved with gold outlines and with blue sleeves, and a skirt of blue over mail. A small shield sat over his heart, engraved with a castle over a field of wheat both backed by crossed swords.

"Once more Lord Dillon oversteps his bounds and interrupts his majesty. However, I do believe he is right. While it is inconceivable to think that these two should be allowed freedom, might I remind this court that the people believe these two to be special and if we harm them, it is only going to harm us."

"You believe they should be excused, duke of the Franormish?"

"Not without its consequences. I suggest we ban Sir Robert from this palace until his majesty can determine a suitable way to deal with this matter." The man looked at the boys. Will noticed his sharp face, the wrinkles snaking over his brow. His brown hair fell to his shoulders, but not over his ears. A short beard traced his jawline and his two-part disconnected moustache followed the curve of his upper lip.

"I agree with Duke Célestin. Furthermore, Sir Robert, your command of my army is suspended. You are no longer grand marshal. You can take them… for now, until I decide what is to be done with them. The people should support me."

Sir Robert bowed and motioned the boys to come with him. Will looked at Elizabeth who avoided his gaze.

———∽∽———

Sir Robert's unease wore away at his mind. The king would most likely want the boys dead, so why had he agreed with Duke Célestin and Lord Dillon so

359

quickly? It was a confusing thought. As the knight and his pupils made for their waiting horses in the courtyard, a lord who was present in the king's court strode out towards Sir Robert.

He stopped the knight. "Sir Robert I must speak with you; it is urgent." The man was Lord Gregor Thorne of Swordspire, a brown-blond haired man, tall and proud, next in like for the Dukedom of the Aangsax. Sir Robert motioned to the boys to get ready then turned to Lord Gregor.

"Lord Gregor I assume you were sent by your coalition?" Sir Robert asked.

"I was and you know we are worried about King Duggan's current leadership."

"So, what do you have to say?"

"We are troubled about the king's acts towards the people. They have been taxed too far and oppressed too much. The king has not even sanctioned a public building to be built or restored since the death of the queen, and now the people think he does not care for them. Our people look to their local lords to lobby the king. However, our cries and requests are unheard by him. He refuses to listen to reason and plans only for battles.

"He lets that elf observer from Eldarun into his court oblivious to the fact elves only wish to expand their own power. They're not here for diplomacy. King Duggan continues to take out loans he cannot repay, and similar to the high elves, is thinking of making alliances with those who could easily become our enemies. All so he can fight against Saomarhad.

"Melvantil Shabrinthir is that high elf ambassador's name. The empress sees opportunity. If this country were to destabilise, as many lords and I fear is already happening, the Dominion could take advantage of the aftermath."

"So, the war no longer benefits the lords?"

"You wound me Sir Robert. My domain is in western Gurmanis, far from the front. I cannot benefit from new land so easily. Besides, King Duggan, since restarting this war has reclaimed all lands the Saomarhad took from us. Many lords are satisfied with that, nothing more."

"Shouldn't the barons and lords speak to the dukes?"

"As you can already guess Duke Célestin is oblivious to our cries. He is married to Duchess Lena; the king's only surviving sister and he tries very hard to stick close to the king and stay within his good graces. My father agrees with me, but his age limits his action. The other dukes have been silent, they have no personal connection to the king, appointed as they were on merit or wealth. I would assume that they will not jeopardize this."

"So why this now? Why me? I am only a knight and do not command King Duggan's armies anymore."

"You know as I do, Sir Robert, that this is not true. You and your family have always been close to King Duggan, even the princess looks up to you as a friend."

"Yet she travelled with me disguised and never told me the truth, nor can I comprehend how foolish I have been that I could not recognise her." It frustrated him. Did Elizabeth not trust her? If she'd explained he would have helped.

"This aside Sir Robert the only reason you have not been elevated to a baron is because the king wants to hold more control over you. King Duggan has always used you, nothing more. Even if this was not the case you would never accept the promotion… not after the loss of your family…"

Sir Robert frowned, prompting him not to linger on the fact.

"Why now you ask? Princess Elizabeth has returned. Now I don't quite comprehend the commoners' insistence that the words spoken in the Grand Mosque apply to your charges. But what the lords *can* get behind is the princess. There have been queens before. Princess Elizabeth is not like her father."

"You'd put her against her own kin? Elizabeth may not wish for that."

"But she is the only one who can keep the lords content. Not the commoner's threat of uprising."

"We must be more practical. The sultan will come here for peace talks; there may be peace."

"There will not. King Duggan will never yield. I have come to ask you your stand on this. Do you agree with us? Manis' laws say we must move to dethrone—"

"No! Dethroning the king would cause a rift and many lords would take advantage of it even if they mean well now. Elizabeth would drown in it all."

"We are with the princess, the ideal person to succeed her father. But the commoners also want a new king." Lord Gregor looked toward Will. Sir Robert followed his gaze.

"You think Will is that king?" Sir Robert turned back.

"It is possible, more so than the idea that the Saomardrim is the one who would rule. It is true, the people are convinced the Saomardrim and he are those spoken of. Royal bloodlines are divine. Manis chooses kings. In their minds, Will has been chosen. His faults forgiven. Though I expect not by everyone."

"This is madness. Wait to see how the king responds to the sultan. We may be in a ceasefire, but we are still at war. Any instability will be exploited by our enemies. By the sultan or by the Eldarun Dominion."

"So then where do you stand?" Lord Gregor expected an answer. Sir Robert sighed. "Are you not tired like the rest of us Sir Robert, like the people? Don't you see that Gurmanis is weakening the longer this war goes? Today King Duggan invites high elves as 'friends' tomorrow those 'friends' will invade our exhausted state and take our freedom away."

"Over the years," the knight sighed, "Over the years I have fought dutifully for King Duggan. I see the fatigue in my men. I see the crimes the king orders us to commit. I understand."

"Then you are with us." Lord Gregor smiled.

"I didn't say that! I think its best to wait before anything drastic takes place."

"Let us hope time does not run out before you decide Sir Robert." Lord Gregor turned and strode back towards the castle.

Will and Ahmed collected their belongings and were readying their horses when Will noticed an unfamiliar man speaking with Sir Robert. Out of the corner of Will's eye another figure approached. Both boys turned to see Elizabeth. She looked uneasily at Will. Behind her, two menacing King's Guard stood with their sword-hand clutching the hilt of their swords. There was a slight pause before anyone said anything.

"Guards, leave us," Elizabeth ordered.

The two King's Guard looked at each other then one of them spoke, "With respect, your highness, you ought to be chaperoned when speaking with a man."

"I do not need to be supervised in my own castle. I gave you an order, you should follow it," Elizabeth spat, not looking at her guards.

"The king would want you guarded against such a man."

"Retreat now!"

The guardsmen made quick bows then retreated to a position further away.

"I will leave you two alone," Ahmed said. Then he too moved out of the way. Elizabeth's regal mask broke and she looked at Will with a remorseful frown. "I am sorry for that man, Will he…"

"So you're a princess now," Will cut her off. "So everything you said about being a merchant's child, everything you kept on feeding to me, it's all fake?"

"Yes… but I had to say these things. If people were to find out I was the crown princess they would take advantage," Elizabeth answered.

"I ken, but why did ya have to hide it from me? From Ahmed? We're your friends and I… how could you do this Jilli… er… Elizabeth?"

"I am so sorry, Will. I couldn't risk anything. I never told this to anyone while I was away, not even to other friends I had made. You have to understand. I became good friends with Keira in the army, there was so much I wanted to tell…"

"So all that time you were highborn and you must have thought of me as a worthless peasant." Will raised his tone.

"No! Of course not! Why would you ever say that?"

"It's what all of your kind think… you betrayed me! You took advantage of the fact that most commoners never see the royal family to trick me!"

"Why are you saying these false things? I had no ill feelings towards you. Will, you are the most genuine person I have ever met, a light in a sea of masked nobles."

Despite Elizabeth's pleading eyes Will brushed aside the complement. "All this time you knew our friendship was for naught. All fake. We could never associate."

"Will, I…"

"Lies. I must go your highness." Will gave a bow.

Elizabeth stood there shocked until Will turned and left. She watched Sir Robert's company leave.

Will sat uneasily on his horse as the world spun for him. He could not handle this betrayal, it felt like he was being ripped away from everything he knew once again like the day he had lost his parents. He started to fall off the side of his horse. Ahmed, beside him, caught Will and straightened him. Will gripped the reins, battling his dizziness. He could not cope with this, he just couldn't.

⁂

Elizabeth made her way past the main hall and strode lower, into the undercroft of the castle. She approached a tall stone door, coloured in dark blue and guarded by two of the palace's men-at-arms. The men stood at attention and gripped their spears as to show they were always vigilant, when Elizabeth approached.

"I must see my mother, let me in," Elizabeth said.

"Of course, your highness, we would never think of stopping you," one man-at-arms answered. He nodded to the other who turned to the left side of the door and pushed a stone into the wall. Grinding echoed off the walls as the door slid opened and the men-at-arms stepped forward to stay out of its way.

Elizabeth stepped in and paused to examine the giant statue of the first king and his queen. King Calis was an Imperiali, son of the governor of what would one day become the city of Monte Calis when the area was a province of the Rhoathian Imperium. Queen Alana was native Gurmian from Northern Gurmanis, at that time beyond Emperor Tertius' Wall. From Monte Calis, King Calis and Queen Alana laid the roots for native rule of Gurmanis.

In these rooms the statues of all the kings and queens of the kingdom were displayed. It was based off the undercroft of Monte Calis' palace, back when that city was the capital. This was a recreation.

On the sides of the statues before Elizabeth, clear water dropped into a pool below. Flower beds lay at the statues' feet and dim sunlight entered through the roof above. The room was adorned with red, blue, and gold drapery. Symbols of royalty were carved into the stone floor and walls.

Elizabeth turned to the right and entered into a large hall. On either side were the queens of past. The hall was decorated in a similar fashion to the main room. She walked forwards and stopped at the feet of a queen. Elizabeth looked up at her mother's statue, beautiful and regal. She would know exactly how to comfort me.

Elizabeth looked around her. She was alone. Sighing she spoke in a low voice, "Loyalty to family is paramount. You are the daughter of a king Elizabeth. You have a responsibility to this kingdom that you cannot neglect. Though kings are preferred the women behind them can wield so much more influence. Think of Queen Mirabella? Would her son, King Frederic have ever become king?" Elizabeth repeated her mother's words. "Yes Mother, I know she deposed the Imperiali claimant." Elizabeth frowned at her mother's statue.

"I failed on all accounts Mother. I ran from home, abandoned my father when I might have dissuaded his attitudes. God knows he never listens to Arch-Mage Jaxson, who's supposed to be the Lord Chancellor." Elizabeth laughed. Then she remembered the day of her mother's funeral. Just a little girl when she rushed down the isle looking for her father. He stood beside the elaborate gold coffin under the altar in Royal Landing's cathedral, the Arch-Bishop beside him. She tugged on her father's side. The king looked at her and knelt. His face was full of hurt and despair, but there was anger underpinning it. She remembered crying and shivering, and feeling afraid and alone. Her mother was dead, she didn't understand why or how, and in that moment the faces of all the strangers and that of her father confirmed the worst: her mother would never return.

"Look who's alone again." Elizabeth sighed. "I made some friends though, Mother, real friends, but you wouldn't approve. Not especially of Will, probably." Elizabeth blushed as she thought of him, then frowned when she remembered their last conversation. "I am sorry, Mother. But because I ran away, I see things clearly now about Gurmanis and Saomarhad. I can't be sure that Saomarhadians killed you, please don't think of it as a betrayal. Ahmed is proof of nuance… I know now I can't blame a culture for the sins of a few among them, nor the actions of one murderer as the archetype for all such people. I will try to fulfill my duties."

A draft knocked Elizabeth out of her thoughts. She flinched, reddening, thinking someone had crept in behind her. "I wish you were here Mother. I wish you could guide me through this madness."

Elizabeth sat on her bed. This was a vast change in accommodations from those of the last several months. Her room was decorated with gold and blue brocades half covering the painted patterned walls. Her king size bed standing in the center, an ornate desk and mirror to the right, a large fireplace in a corner, and a wardrobe to the left was far from the accommodations she'd been used to during her time away. Standing on a floor of the most expensive wood, on the upper floors, she looked out from a large recessed window on the Golden Inlet. It was all so familiar, comfortable, yet also alien.

Elizabeth moved away from the window and sat on the left side of her bed. A maid knocked on Elizabeth's door and the princess called her inside. The maid walked forward then bowed. She was not one of Elizabeth's maids.

"Your highness, Duchess Lena wishes to see you," the maid informed. Elizabeth collected herself, adjusted her clothes and hair, then nodded.

"See her inside." The maid bowed and left the room returning a few seconds later with a woman dressed in a blue and white cote and mantle. Her hair was tightly braided to a short length, netted, and topped with a short henin. She had features in common with King Duggan.

"My dear niece, you are finally safe. Please do not run away again, I was so worried," Duchess Lena exclaimed. She rushed to Elizabeth who stood to embrace her.

"I won't run again, Auntie. I am sorry if I caused you pain." The two women sat on the edge of Elizabeth's bed. "Where are my cousins? I thought they would be with you."

"Th-They are with our most trusted." Duchess Lena stifled a hard breath and her posture tightened. "Y-Yes… they wanted to see you but we thought it best they stay."

"I hope they are well." Elizabeth raised an eyebrow.

"As well as anyone can be in the middle of this dreadful war." Duchess Lena made a shaky smile.

"Duke Célestin has surely made sure they will be safe. Do not fear."

The duchess flinched at the mention of her husband's name, then took a calming breath. "Yes. They are safe. N-Now enough about Célestin, you must tell me everything that happened while you were away, I must know."

"There was nothing interesting really." Elizabeth lied, knowing her auntie would scoff at her adventures. Was her aunt okay? Elizabeth decided to continue hoping to reveal more.

"You were alone, you must have been scared."

"Never!" Elizabeth refuted, head held high. "I handled myself well."

"That's good to hear. I am sure you witnessed many things."

"I have and not all of them unoffending. My father has neglected his kingdom, Auntie. Our people are suffering because my father depletes our resources for war. I witnessed villages burned and destroyed after its people refused to obey my father."

"They are rebels."

"No they were not. I lived among such people when I was away."

"But you can't deny the rebels of this beast of a woman. Manis help her. Lorna they call her, the fiery-headed angel of retribution."

"Auntie, you never take seriously such obtuse nicknames."

"It is not obtuse! Lorna and her rebels have been a nuisance ever since your father restarted this war. And they have even crossed Sir Robert's path when he was looking for you."

"Lorna… she and her rebels are just an expression of the frustration our people have. I observed and heard these things in Windsfield while working as a labourer." The information came out before she could stop it.

Duchess Lena gasped. "By Manis, a labourer? You passed as a labourer?"

"For a while…" Elizabeth remembered the orphan, Jill, who had discovered her disguise. Elizabeth had convinced Jill to help her, thinking back to the politics she so expertly weaved with her mother back at court. Elizabeth took the girl's name; Jillian she called herself. "Sir Robert almost caught me there. I fled to Altan, and from there I needed to disappear." Elizabeth looked to the duchess. She was listening intently so Elizabeth continued her tale.

"I gained passage on a merchant convoy," Elizabeth explained, "to a cottage outside Charleston. I lived with a very nice family there. The youngest in that family reminded me of your youngest daughter." Elizabeth watched for her aunt's reaction.

Duchess Lena laughed, broken by a sudden warped pitch. She coughed and excused herself. "Y-You lived in the marshes? Elizabeth, if your mother… your mother saw you drenched in mud—"

Elizabeth hid a frown. Lena wasn't herself. "I lived with a family who were local traders and labourers. They drain some of the marshes to create farmland. But I couldn't stay there, you are right, too muddy and wet. A recruiter came to Charleston and was looking for army nurses, so I joined the army." Had she realised it would lead her under the command of Sir Robert, the man she did not want to meet, maybe she would have reconsidered.

"Oh Elizabeth. I cannot imagine you in any of this… simple work."

"I would not have thought of that result either, Auntie, but I did it because I couldn't go back. And it wasn't all bad. I met our people, good people. And I made a friend in Sir Robert's host."

Duchess Lena adjusted herself and placed a hand on Elizabeth's arm. Her expression grew into one of concern.

"Tell me why you ran. I know your father wanted to marry you to the Imperium prince, and you knew one day you'd marry a noble."

"But not that prince. Mother would have never accepted it. She would prefer a Gurmian noble. He wasn't a faultless person auntie. He did not respect me and… I don't want to talk about him." Elizabeth frowned. Yes, the Imperium prince was a bloated and obtuse boy who wished only to show her off to his friends. To him she was his entire world and he felt she should be humbled that *he* was allowing this union. No. The emperor and her father were allowing that union, and her father ignored her concerns.

But she was still a fool. An alliance with the Imperiali would have secured their victory against Saomarhad who would never dare to go against the might of the Imperial legions. But now as Elizabeth knew, it would end the war in the wrong way. Her father would have used the wealth and power gained by the alliance to destroy the Saomarhadians. It was not only that, however. She had run away from all her responsibilities and her duty as a princess, and the possibility of preventing her father from madness, so the kingdom suffered doubly.

Duchess Lena embraced her. "You are safe from harm now, and I know at the time your father ignored you, but things will be better now, I think."

"I really hope so." The female figures in her father's life had left him by disease or betrayal. She'd left him too, for a while. Elizabeth wanted so much to believe that her father was not too far gone. Had she not left; would she really have dissuaded her father from madness without knowing what she knew of the kingdom now?

"I can't imagine how Sir Robert could not see *you* for who you were when you came face to face with him."

"For a moment I was afraid he may have recognised me. It seems perhaps in the time he knew me, he'd never have imagined I would be wearing the clothes of a peasant and had the face of one."

"Yes! By God yes! The dirt filled, malnutrition, grim face of serfs will never suit you, my child."

"Yet, it is the face of my people." Elizabeth held her reaction at her auntie's lude comments.

"I am glad you were with Sir Robert. Thank Manis a man of honourable repute was there. Thank God he saved you from the heathen land. It must have been torturous."

"It is not all heathen, Auntie. Ahmed is proof of that; he saved me. Tis unbearably hot in the desert and it goes on without end. I can never fathom how so much sand could build up in that place yet it has a unique quality to it. The Saomarhad cities too. There is elegance and density in them." Elizabeth changed the subject, "Auntie, I feel bad for my people. It is my fault for their poverty."

"No Elizabeth, you could not control the laws of your father nor the war, it can never be your fault."

"But things are not right. I have responsibilities as a princess and I let my heart drive me instead of my mind. I abandoned all of this and I was wrong; I am needed here." Elizabeth thought of Will. It hurt her to say all this. She wished to have him on her side but she knew she had to stay here and fix things as was her duty.

"You are sounding like your mother." Duchess Lena scoffed. A knock came at the door.

"Elizabeth my daughter, why have you denied all your servants? What is wrong? Can I come in?" It was King Duggan. Elizabeth stared up as the king entered. Duchess Lena stood.

"Lena, I assume you have caught up with your niece," King Duggan prompted, clearly a signal for her to leave.

"I have dear brother." Duchess Lena smiled at Elizabeth. "I am glad you are home."

"Auntie are you okay? Is something wrong?"

Duchess Lena paled.

"What would be wrong?" King Duggan regarded his sister with worry.

"I-I am fine… of course." Her watery smile at Duggan didn't elicit a response. "I will excuse myself." She curtsied and fled. King Duggan sat beside his daughter.

"Elizabeth why are you so down? Look at you! You are a mess! Why have you dismissed all your servants? You need to look your best for your welcome home feast."

"I have no feeling of a party today Father." Elizabeth looked briefly to where Lena had been.

"But you must! Today you are rid of those monsters and have come back safely."

Elizabeth frowned. "They are not monsters, Father. They are my friends."

"Call them what you will, Elizabeth. Now that the Rhoathian Imperium prince is gone we can forget about making them our allies. You will be free to choose another prince. The faster you get settled here the better."

"I am not some sort of tool to be used! The prince was rude and disgusting, I told you so many times before. He took advantage of me and would never respect me. How could you think to have me marry him? Mother never would."

"As princess of Gurmanis it is your duty to care for the security of your kingdom, which comes before all other things. Moral qualities can be sacrificed for the care of your people."

"Care for my people? You wanted me to marry him so you could access his armies and continue this absurd war! That is not duty, that is folly. You wanted me to compromise and that would result in a horrible life. Would you want your daughter to feel as though she is a stranger with her husband?"

"No, I only want the best for you my dear, and for the kingdom."

"Then you should have never introduced me to that prince." Elizabeth was sickened by her father's greed.

King Duggan frowned. "I am sorry."

"What do you mean?" a glimmer of hope bloomed in her.

"I am sorry I did not prepare you enough." King Duggan rose, a tired look crossed his face. "When your grandfather still lived his kingdom's peace was ruptured by the Saomardrim. I grew up watching their advance across the land, creeping ever closer to the capital under Sultan Yazid the first. The Saomardrim slaughtered innocent Gurmians, ravaged the land, and reduced towns to rubble. They raided and attacked every day. All lived in fear. As a child I was nearly kidnapped or murdered by them."

This Elizabeth knew. Her father had told her before how afraid he'd been and promised to never let her fear such a thing. Well, she did get captured anyway, but she'd put herself in that position, not her father.

"Then we had successes and the Saomardrim were pushed back until my father died, and there was a moment of peace."

"I hated the Saomarhadians. I would have spit on them," Elizabeth muttered.

"And a good thing too, but we hid from you just how close they were to Royal Landing. Gurmanis may have been destroyed. The sultan sent his assassins and killed your mother, breaking the peace."

"You vowed to avenge her…"

"Yes. I had to resume the fight, to safeguard Gurmanis and restore her glory. I gathered the full might of my power, punished the sultan, and expelled the enemy from Gurmanis… but it is not enough… no." King Dugan stood tall. "We treat Kalshaimar's spawn as wholly evil because they follow him, so why should we treat the Saomardrim any different? They follow a demon god."

Elizabeth pushed herself up. "No, you have it wrong father!"

"The only way to ensure the Saomardrim do not ever hurt my people again is for me to humble them completely and expand this kingdom from Royal Landing to Outremer. This will bring peace, wealth, and stability."

"It will only bring death and sadness. I saw what our people wanted and they do not want more war. The sultan wants peace, so do his people."

"So said that heathen to me. He lies."

"He does not. Ahmed speaks the truth."

"He and the criminal have abducted and misled you. Those villains must be—"

"Abduction! You are looking for an excuse to be rid of Will and Ahmed. They saved me father. They protected me, and they should be rewarded."

"Elizabeth! Now listen to me." King Duggan shoved a finger towards her. "Here they deserve to die and it will not fit a princess to consort with them."

"Ahmed saved me and Will from our deaths! And Will… he's… not who everyone thinks he is." Elizabeth would not back down. A deep frown filled the king's face.

"You love the swine!" King Duggan's voice rose to a scream. Elizabeth looked away.

"I don't know what I feel. But I feel something for him," Elizabeth stated, not caring anymore what her father thought.

"I will not have a child of mine betray me like this, You will marry and love anyone I choose. After tonight you will no longer have to worry about that boy, ever!" The king started for the door. Elizabeth stood.

"Father what do you mean? What are you going to do? Father please."
But the king had already stormed out.

This was all her fault. Will would never stand a chance against her father's men. She only had herself to blame; she'd let Will come into a world he could never be a part of. Yes, she was scared and despised him when she found out who she thought he was, but her heart would not let her stay away. It brought her closer to him. In Serleigh, he'd been so sincere and raw towards her. She'd felt happy, warm, not afraid. Never in her royal life did people drop their masks so easily. She had broken his heart, she knew. She was a monster having seen the heartbreak in Will's eyes. What plague had she brought upon him?

Chapter Thirty

SIR ROBERT MADE use of his Royal Landing townhouse on Highhill. It was one of the only things the knight had kept from his old life. To reach it, the three rode up a tight road, its buildings lavishly decorated with flowers and coloured daub, to a hill covered in more houses. Sir Robert's townhouse looked over the harbour and the Golden Inlet beyond. To the southwest, the Palace of Kings towered over the city.

Inside, the front door opened to a hall leading to the kitchen. A room from the kitchen led to the attached stables.

A loud knock rattled the front door as Sir Robert and the boys finished supper. Sir Robert answered the door, greeting Lord Dillon and two of his men-at-arms.

"Robert, I know this may be a surprise but I need to speak with you. And a walk after supper is an excellent way to digest the food."

"Dillon this is a surprise. I did not think you would be seeing me."

"For old times' sake let us have a walk, shall we?"

"I had a carriage saddled with horses. I was going to get supplies."

"This ceasefire may be the only time we can talk without interruption," Lord Dillon insisted.

"And the guards?" Sir Robert raised an eyebrow.

"The city can be dangerous after dark."

"If you insist." Sir Robert fetched his weapons then told Will and Ahmed where he was off to. They walked down the hill and along the harbor front on a road higher than the harbor wall. The calm inlet was on their left, and a half moon hung in the sky, its soft light shining down on the nobles. The entire city seemed quiet.

"Robert do you remember the Monte Calis rebellion?"

"It was a long campaign, and the last time you spent an active role in combat I believe."

"Yes… yes it was. I remember you saved me from the storm of them."

Sir Robert laughed. "Indeed, I did."

"There were prisoners afterwards and our king wanted to have them executed, but you stepped in to save the women and children," Lord Dillon said.

"They were defenceless people; most had nothing to do with the rebellion. Our code of chivalry says as much."

"Yes, but it also says to be loyal to our king, Robert."

"But that does not mean blind loyalty." Sir Robert frowned. The nobles crossed the bridge into the northern parts of the city.

"Give up this protection of those boys, Robert. For your own wellbeing."

"I cannot."

"Will is a murderer and the Saomardrim, an enemy. The boy killed his parents and God knows what sins the Saomardrim has committed."

"I took Will on as my squire because I see he is redeemed. He's only ever been loyal. Nothing like the monster people assume he is. God brought him to me to give him a second chance. And you judge Ahmed too harshly."

"Will deserves no redemption for his crime. It was savage and ungodly."

"Yet you were the one who changed the minds of your fellow judges and spared him a death sentence." He wanted to remind Dillon of the compassion he'd felt at that time.

"I did that only so his soul could be saved. I never wanted him to see the light of the sun again. If he was executed instead, he'd find himself in the Underworld for all eternity." Dillon frowned.

"If you took the time to know the boy, you'd realise what he's really like. It took him so long to trust me at first. It took him longer to not be averse to touch, he still struggles with it now. He is not someone who'd kill those he depends on."

"Nevertheless, you walk a dangerous path Robert, and I will help you get on the right path because I still consider you my friend. The boys will be dead by now."

"What? What do you mean Dillon?" Sir Robert stopped, his limbs tightened.

"Relax Robert, it was for the best." Lord Dillon stopped and turned to Sir Robert. The knight drew his longsword.

"Speak! Manis help me."

"Ununiformed, the king's men and a guide will have by now dealt with those boys. Can you not see that loyalty is the only way to maintain your station and the peace? The king balks at how he called you loyal in his court. He wanted to rip those boys from you immediately, but I convinced him of this plan instead… to help you."

"What peace Dillon? There is none! Loyalty? King Duggan had me in his grasp mindlessly following orders." Lord Gregor's words floated into Sir Robert's mind.

"Don't resist. Let us go back to how things were before. I am ready to fake your death and give you a life away from all this. We are friends."

"You will not hold me here." Sir Robert backed away, intent on rushing back to his townhouse. Behind him, Lord Dillon's men-at-arms lunged at Sir Robert, swords drawn. The first swiped forward which Sir Robert countered, side-stepped, and stabbed his side. The other man lunged. Sir Robert batted his sword aside and pushed him into a house.

The man crashed into a window, shattering it as he fell through. Lord Dillon drew his sword and slashed overhead at Sir Robert who blocked, tilting Dillon's sword up as he shoved it aside with his arm. With the sword point at Dillon's neck the lord dropped his sword.

"What did you do, Dillon?"

"I am your friend, Robert. It is only best," the older man pleaded again, straining against Sir Robert's strength.

"Who did you send to kill them? How many?"

Lord Dillon frowned. "It will be like an accident with a local gang, the king could blame the rebels. Once dead, people will realise they weren't the ones spoken of and you will be free to redeem yourself in King Duggan's eyes."

"King Duggan," Sir Robert growled. His heart raced as he released Dillon and rushed back to his house.

<hr>

Sir Robert had left Will and Ahmed alone. Will was pleased to know the knight trusted both of them now. He'd not put Ahmed in dimithrite manacles again either. They had been cleaning their dishes. Will had opened a nearby window to let his falcon inside.

"Look at us, reduced." Ahmed chuckled but Will didn't answer. Lost in thought, he looked at his falcon, preening itself on the windowsill. Ahmed frowned. "What's wrong Will?"

"I can't believe she lied to me, Ahmed." Will sighed. "She knew all along we could ne'er be friends yet she tricked me. Her kindness was only a ruse, only a way to get back home. I hate myself for trying to get her attention in the first place," Will answered bitterly, feeling ashamed now at how foolishly he kept asking for her name.

"She is noble, a princess, yes, but how can you be sure she never cared for you?"

"It's obvious. The highborn think naught about the peasantry. All my life my family an' I were used by them. They don't care. Her highness is the same, she does not care." Aldershire's lord ordered the death of his parents and cleaned his hands of him when he was blamed for their murder. King Duggan had ensured the warden could operate freely. Will's falcon tilted his head at the boy.

"Will, you need to hear Elizabeth's side of the story first."

"I know her story. She will say that she *had* to and that she *could not* tell anyone and that she is not like the other highborn." Will levied the blame on her to try and suppress the nipping feeling of losing everyone he had found. He was immensely grateful he still had Sir Robert and Ahmed.

"Do you think I hate you? I am highborn." Ahmed dried his hands on a towel.

So was Sir Robert.

"At least you didn't lie to me about who you were. She did."

"You are jumping to conclusions Will. I think Elizabeth's feelings were sincere. You feel you have lost her and that gives you pain."

"Stop telling me what I feel! I don't need your magic to tell me what I know," Will growled.

"I think you need to see how all this has affected her. I think you need to hear her side."

"Forget it Ahmed. She is inaccessible now. She sits on a pedestal oblivious to me."

"I defend her because I believe she is not what you claim her to be. While I detest the lies she has made to us, I won't act like she wanted it this way. There was reason for her to hide her identity and she should have not led us on if later it meant she would break her friendship with us…"

"Ahmed, I told you to forget it. Just STOP!" Will shouted. Will's falcon squawked and batted its wings. "What am I doing? I don't know how to care for a falcon." He sighed. Glass shattered and the bang of the front door made him jump. Will's falcon turned and glided out the window.

"Something's wrong," Ahmed said. They turned towards the thump of boots. "Will, it's the king's men!" The boys dashed to their weapons and drew them as the men entered the kitchen and lunged, waiting no time for formalities. Ahmed blocked a man's attack with his kilij and then swung his axe at him before barely countering the next attack and staggering.

Will faced a man with a shield who easily blocked Will's attacks. Will held his longsword with two hands and put all his strength into a chop at the man's shield. The man faltered, off-balance, but regained his footing quicker than Will wanted. Will missed the opportunity and was pushed against a corner under the man's attacks.

This was going nowhere. The men were too determined, too elite. They wore blank tunics with no standard or symbol and were too skilled to be brigands or gangsters. They must want to kill us in secret. A tall menacing man walked in and shoved aside his allies then raised his battle axe over Will. The man came down with full force. Will fell to the ground in a failed attempt to dodge, missing the axe anyway. Will rolled to the side. The man brought his axe down again. Will hit him with his sword but it bounced off. He turned. Ahmed lunged, causing the axeman to correct, momentarily stunned.

"We have to go! This is a trap!" Ahmed confirmed Will's thoughts. Will nodded and ran with Ahmed to the stables, pursued by their attackers. The boys jumped and ducked as weapons hit tables and chairs. Glass shattered and furniture fell.

Will and Ahmed came to a high walled, open-roofed, wooden carriage that was already affixed with two horses. Ahmed sealed the attackers' entrance to the stables with magic, but as he was about to take the reins, an arrow whizzed by and struck the carriage, missing him. Ahmed and Will turned and Will realised who it was. The bounty hunter who he'd faced when he was sixteen was now pointing an arrow at his head. Ahmed raised his hands and took a place beside Will. Vuko walked out from behind Ugrin and growled loudly.

"You bested me in the Roywood lad but there is no spirit to help you now."

Will remembered his first camp in the Roywood when he was still on the run. He'd encountered some sort of spiritual place.

Ugrin loosed again. Ahmed cast a blue ward causing Ugrin's arrows to ping harmlessly off it.

"Ready the carriage Will!" Ahmed ordered. Will boarded the carriage. Vuko rushed forwards and lunged for Ahmed, breaking through the ward. Ahmed fell backwards and Vuko bit his side, drawing blood. He screamed, sharp teeth sliding across his skin and finding a shallow grip. Ahmed drew his djanbīyya and thrust at the animal on top of him. Vuko jumped out of the way while Ahmed regained his footing and dodged Vuko's next lunge. The wolf hit Ahmed's right side but he shoved him off and Ahmed drew his axe. Vuko growled and barked. The wolf lunged forward. Ahmed ducked and the wolf flew over his head. He turned as Vuko lunged again and swiped down with his axe, hitting Vuko's back. The wolf whimpered, falling to the ground, defeated but alive.

Ahmed looked to see where Will was. Will snapped at the reins on his carriage and sent the horses into a trot. Ugrin blocked the doorway onto the street. Ahmed rushed forwards, leapt on the carriage and took the reins from Will. They charged towards Ugrin. The bounty hunter was about to loose but lunged to the side, avoiding the carriage. He cursed as the boys stormed into the streets.

Soldiers pursuing them scrambled for their horses and followed. Musket balls flew towards the boys. From above, Will's falcon tracked the chase. Will found a musket in the carriage and fired back over the top edge. The men gained on them. From the left a new group of soldiers charged forward, led by Lord Richrit. Will pushed tightly against a side and Ahmed tensed, anger filling his eyes. The men closed the distance and jumped onto the carriage. They climbed over the walls and moved forward. Ahmed swerved right and left, knocking them off. A group of horsemen charged to the right of the carriage. Ahmed swerved right and trampled them. Will struggled with the musket.

"How d'you reload this thing?" Will screamed to Ahmed.

"Pour some of the powder in the hole near the trigger, then stuff the rest in the barrel with the ball, ram them together, then pull the lever back!" Ahmed instructed. He grunted. He needed to pay attention. One wrong turn into a narrow street and their carriage would be stuck.

Will fumbled with what he had. Once he got another shot ready, he aimed and fired. The shot hit a man close to Lord Richrit. The angered lord fired his pistol, the shot pinged off the carriage, Will ducking in time.

A soldier managed to get close enough to jump onto the carriage and grabbed Ahmed by the neck. Ahmed let go of the reins and drew his djanbīyya. He stabbed the man's arm and he let go crying in pain. Ahmed grabbed him and dragged him off the side.

Ugrin rode towards Lord Richrit, Vuko keeping pace with the man's horse despite the wolf's wounds. Ugrin and Lord Richrit shouted at each other.

"Ugrin's back!" Will warned Ahmed. The bounty hunter flashed the reins of his horse and advanced on the carriage. Will reloaded and fired. Ugrin swerved out of the way. He drew his pistol and fired back. The shot skimmed across Will's arm, drawing blood. Will dropped his musket and shouted in pain while Ugrin matched the speed of the carriage.

Ahmed urged his horses to go faster, but they were already at maximum pace, neighing frantically. He turned a corner, the sharp turn throwing the carriage dangerously to one side. Ahmed faced Ugrin, anger in the bounty hunter's face. Ahmed cast towards roadside debris ahead of them. He sent a potted plant flying back at Ugrin, collapsed a merchant's stall in Ugrin's way, brought up the cobbles into a spike, but every hindrance did little to stop the bounty hunter. Ahmed cast a stream of fire at the man. The flames scared his horse and the animal threw Ugrin off, but the bounty hunter expected it and used the momentum to send him onto the boys' carriage. Ugrin barreled onto Ahmed and they wrestled.

Vuko growled at Will. The resourceful creature ran up an incline and jumped on to the carriage. Will drew his longsword but Vuko was faster. Vuko toppled Will and took a bite out of his side, sending blood flying. Will hissed, batting pain as he wrestled with the wolf, grasping Vuko's jaws as saliva flew across his face. Punching its underside did little. Will shoved the wolf off him and scrambled up. A pistol shot skimmed over him. Lord Richrit was still chasing them. The carriage jerked to the side, turning and Will almost lost his balance. Will wrestled with Vuko again, managing to throw him from the carriage. Vuko crashed onto the street below and tumbled into a building.

From the right came another cart with a revolving arrow gun mounted on the back. Large bolts broke through the walls, stopped from flying through all the way. Will took cover behind the walls. The enemy crashed into the boys' carriage, trying to push them against the flanking buildings. Some soldiers on horseback were able to make it into the carriage. Will took his dagger and stabbed one.

Ahmed pulsed an energy wave at Ugrin. He struggled to regain control of the carriage. Ugrin flew backwards but grabbed onto the side of the carriage and swung himself onto the back. Ahmed grunted, clutching his side, He grasped the reins.

Will had no time to react. Enraged, Ugrin drew his falchion on Will. Will retrieved his longsword. He swung downward and was blocked. He swung high but was blocked. Ugrin thrust forward and Will parried. The two exchanged blows. Ugrin caught Will unaware and sliced Will's side, forcing him back. An arrow gun bolt flew past between them. They traded more blows.

A pursuing soldier made it to Ahmed and grabbed him. Ahmed pulled an arrow gun bolt from midair and directed it towards the soldier, hitting him in his back and launching him off the carriage. The enemy cart shoved harder and the horses screamed. Ahmed veered the carriage back into the pursuing carriage, hoping Will was holding on.

Will and Ugrin were thrown to the ground, losing their swords. Ugrin crashed into Will and punched his face. The world spun for Will. He spit and caught one of Ugrin's punches, desperately holding him back. Ugrin drew a dagger and plunged it into Will's side. Blood spewed out and Will coughed up blood over Ugrin's face. Ugrin hoisted Will up.

As the two vehicles came into a wide street, another cart appeared. Ahmed veered to the left and the new cart took the space slamming into the enemy. The men and women from the new cart, jumped onto the enemy cart and stabbed its driver and gunner. The driver of the new cart veered towards Ahmed.

"You're the Saomardrim right? Is Sir Robert's squire in there?" he asked pointing to the carriage.

"Yes, who are you?"

"We're friends. Follow us to safety. We'll locate Sir Robert. See to the squire! Another will take the reins."

Ahmed nodded. Will screamed. Ahmed scrambled up and rushed to the back.

Ugrin held Will at the end of the carriage. He shouted to Lord Richrit, shoving the bleeding boy on the edge. Lord Richrit smiled.

"Throw him!" the lord screamed. Will was delirious, losing blood. He heard muffled shouts but he couldn't move his limbs to resist Ugrin. The bounty hunter dragged Will up, ready to throw. Lord Richrit shot. The bullet lodged itself in Ugrin's side and he screamed. He let go of Will and both of them started to tumble towards the street. Ahmed lunged forwards and caught Will's arm. He pulled his friend away as Ugrin fell onto the street and was almost trampled by Lord Richrit' men.

Lord Richrit screamed commands to his group and advanced on the carts. The commandeered arrow gun prevented Lord Richrit from getting close. They were riding closer to the east side of the city.

Lord Richrit fired again. Ahmed hovered over Will, keeping him low. He cast healing magic over Will, staunching his bleeding. The street widened and the boys' allies had a clear shot at Lord Richrit's horsemen. The arrow gun fired out bolts, hitting two of Lord Richrit's men. The lord cursed and the survivors gave up the pursuit. Ahmed looked at his allies.

"We are safe… for now."

Chapter Thirty-One

UNRAYS OF BRIGHT light cast over the damage done to Sir
Robert's house. The knight had already gone through it for signs of
the boys but found none; they had disappeared… or worse. Sir
Robert exited and looked over the harbor as ships made their way in
or out. How could he let this happen? King Duggan didn't even have the
decency to kill the boys outright, preferring subterfuge instead.

Sir Robert observed the road. Turning, he noticed a grey-black and white
wolf limping towards him. The animal planted itself in front of the knight
and looked up at him, as if expecting something. It held a scrap of paper in
its mouth.

"And what is it you want?" Sir Robert sighed, but amused at such a docile
wolf. His apprentice and Ahmed could be anywhere now. The wolf dropped
the paper on the ground. Sir Robert picked it up and read it.

Knight. I know.

The wolf wined. It turned and limped a little away before turning back.
Unsure, Sir Robert followed it. The wolf led him into a small alleyway and
around a corner. It rushed to the side of a man in a modified King's Ranger's
tunic, who lay slumped against a building, bleeding from a wound on his side.

"You sent this message?" the knight asked, flinging the paper to the
ground.

"I-I did." The man coughed and spit to the side.

"Where are the boys I have been caring for?" Sir Robert demanded, not
in the mood for niceties.

"Help… m-me."

"Where are they?"

"I know. H-Help me. I can't get… I can't show my face. T-They'll be
looking for me."

"Who?"

"The King's Guard. I f-failed the king."

"Failed to do what?"

The man glared at Sir Robert. "To kill your charges." Sir Robert strode forwards and grabbed the man's collar. He lifted the man up and slammed him against the building. The wolf barked from the side and the man gave it an order to stand down.

"I can't trust you." Sir Robert didn't even know this man and he'd admitted to trying to kill Will and Ahmed.

"No, but I'm all you have. Help m-me and I will help you." The man groaned. "I don't know how long I-I have left."

Sir Robert lowered the man to the ground. Seeing no other choice, he drew a vial of healing tonic from a pouch at his belt, the very same he'd knocked out Will with long ago.

"I'll need to rip your cloak."

The man nodded. Sir Robert ripped a piece of the man's cloak, poured healing tonic on it, and stuffed it on his side.

"Hold this there. It will numb your wound enough for you to walk. But you need more attention to it. Who are you?"

"Ugrin Vadász. Your charges are safe; they're with the rebels beneath the ruins of the old Imperial colosseum."

"The rebels?"

"Hear me out, twas profitable to take on this contract, and a way to try and redeem myself. As I fought your squire, I was shot!"

"Did you hurt him?"

"I did, but not badly. That mage with him will manage," Ugrin swore. "Fools' business this. I'm no good for it, being bested by a squire. I did better killing off that spirit. Even as a bounty hunter I still ended up working for that shite king. Lords betraying lords. Bah! Lord Richrit shot me!"

"Lord Richrit shot you? He is loyal to the king. Why would he shoot you?"

"Lord Dillon hired me to work for the king. Obviously, Lord Richrit didn't care about me, or he was shooting your apprentice and hit me, or the king ordered him to kill me. Noble games are above me!"

"King Duggan sending out assassins, using his men to murder others, pitting lords against lords…" Sir Robert shook his head. "He's really changed since I was younger."

"Heck if I care. I'll leave this war-torn country, make for a new life some other place. I heard of monster hunters, the Vanari, I'll join them. The king's men may be watching you too, lose them in the market 'afore you make for the colosseum, they have talented eyes on you. I must take my leave my lord, sorry and thank-you." Sir Robert nodded. He turned and made for the ruined colosseum.

⁓

Will and Ahmed stood shocked when they entered the depths of the old Imperial colosseum. They expected ruins but instead met with an entire hideout. The main round room held benches overlooking a round table. Doors to the sides of the room led to mess halls, sleeping quarters, and an armory.

Their wounds had been treated and bandaged, Ahmed's healing magic had been helpful. A red-headed woman stepped towards the boys. She was armed with a two-handed war axe, and her build suggested she could use it.

"The Imperiali love blood sport, they always have. Under their colosseums are spaces for the gladiators an' slaves to live and prepare for fights. Lucky for us, this place has been abandoned for a thousand years." The woman informed them.

"Who are you?" Will asked.

"Lorna Mason, leader of the rebels. We've been waiting and preparing for the moment you two would come to us. We've long held the prophecy as truth an' you two are proof of it."

"You have been preparing for what?" asked Ahmed. "And what prophecy?"

"Why, the overthrowing of King Duggan of course! With him gone, new leadership can bring peace to our countries."

"And you had to wait for us?" Will asked.

"Of course. To do it without you would be disobeying Manis." Will and Ahmed looked at each other.

"We don't know exactly where we fit in," Will confessed.

"Ah but you fit in everywhere. Will as king an' Ahmed as the sultan's grand vizier. It is as Manis says."

Both boys hesitated.

"But I am a squire; I cannot become king!"

"And the sultan considers me a murderer and a traitor!" Ahmed added.

"But what I say is true. Who better to rule the land? The people want change and that change is you both."

The boys looked at each other, unsure. Other rebels began to gather around them.

"Ma'am!" a man hollered to Lorna. "Sir Robert requests entry. He's found us."

"See! Sir Robert is here as well. Open the hatch!" The elevator that brought Will and Ahmed down, now delivered Sir Robert. His face lit up at the sight of Will and Ahmed. He strode over to them.

"Thank-God you are alive!" Sir Robert exclaimed. He gave Lorna a cautious stare.

"Master they want us to join this rebellion."

Sir Robert considered this.

"Sir knight," Lorna started, "I ken some nobles in this country also wish for change. Surely, the grand marshal had been deep in this war for long enough to realise why there needs to be peace."

"Or I am loyal to the king," Sir Robert said.

"After making a serf criminal your squire an' protecting an enemy? With respect sir knight, I feel that you have doubts."

"I know of you Lorna. When I was last in central Gurmanis your rebels attacked our supply convoy bound for the Royal Forces Central Command."

"For the cause. You won't get an apology sir knight." Lorna put her hands together. "But you, grand marshal, have always been a different knight. I lived in the village of your wife's family 'afore I met my husband. I know of your past."

"And you will know no more." Sir Robert glared, uncomfortable.

"So, what now?" Will asked. He watched Sir Robert consider his options while around them the rebels stood.

"There is no force keeping you here." Lorna snapped at her men and they backed away. "All of you can leave. But you take with you our hopes."

Will watched his master contemplate. For a while the knight said nothing, staring into space in deep thought.

"Master, what are you thinking?" Will asked.

"I am thinking King Duggan is not a man worth having loyalty to," Sir Robert admitted. "He's changed from what he once was. Dillon's changed. Henryk and John both have allowed this war to weather them away, though John's done a better job hiding it." Sir Robert laughed. "Lord Gregor and his coalition of lords are all against the king too, leaving men like Lord Richrit, a man filled with hate, to operate freely."

"What now Master?"

"I see now how the winds are changing and how many lords and barons are deciding to turn on the king. I see how unlikely it is for the king to extend his hand to the sultan. I also see how it has affected Elizabeth, how her father morphed from a man she loved into a man who put politics over her happiness. I have been a disloyal knight but not one blind to the peril of this country. I see that now. King Duggan has only ever used me. What do you plan to do Lorna?"

"We'll put him on the throne." Lorna pointed at Will. "You know of the prophecy sir knight? The one spoken at the Grand Mosque Massacre?"

"I know of it."

"And you didn't tell me, Master?" Will demanded.

"I never thought it spoke of you."

"No! I cannot become king. I am only Will, that's all."

"The people demand a king on the throne. The lords would follow a such a king if a queen of noble blood stood beside him. If King Duggan is gone Elizabeth cannot rule alone and many barons will betray her," Sir Robert reasoned. "Elizabeth must also take the throne."

Will's mind was spinning. He never thought he could be a king; this was never part of it.

"N-No!" Will backed away, looking at all the eyes staring at him. He tensed. "Yer are all hypocrites!" Will said, frustrated. "Gurmanis thinks I am a murderer. Gurmanis wanted and did dispose of me. This kingdom's people forgot about me. How can they call me king now?"

"We were wrong," Lorna started. "As a squire you've proven yourself. Ya loyally served Sir Robert. You defended these lands against our enemies, putting them to the sword. Remember your actions at Al-Motros? I ken. You saved that Gurmian column…"

"I saved myself! I was in the column!"

"No… it was selfless."

"It was in the moment!"

"Will." Sir Robert smiled. "When I first talked with you, in Burhbarrow and again in Halsburg, you told me you wanted to prove yourself worthy of being in my service. You told me you wanted to show Gurmanis you were not what they thought you were. Your loyal service has paid off."

"No! You all think Manis has chosen me. That's the only reason you change your minds."

"Your actions confirm Manis' words," Lorna explained. "Know, not all agree with this. Many still think yer crimes unforgiveable."

Will refused to listen any further and walked off through one of the room's doors. Sir Robert started to go but Ahmed stopped him and followed Will. Will sat by the door on the ground in deep thought.

"Will, what is wrong with this king business?" Ahmed asked.

"When I was a little boy sure I would play king with the other children." Will smiled and huffed. "But this is reality, not play. I am no king, I ne'er imagined I would be anything more than what I was in the darkness of Isen Prison. The mercy an' kindness Sir Robert has shown me turned me into a squire, and I was and am happy to serve him in gratitude for what he has done. But that's as much as I am, I am not a leader. I don't know how to be a king. I will fail."

"Yet you wished to redeem yourself in the eyes of your countrymen."

"I wanted people to stop hating me." Will's eyes teared. "I wanted to be thought upon kindly again because I am not what they say. I didn't kill—"

"This is a great honour. Why would the people support your ascension to king if they hated you? If they considered you unworthy? Loyalty to one's people makes the best king. Such a king serves his people and not himself. You have always been loyal Will. You've redeemed yourself. As I see it, you will have Sir Robert and Elizabeth at your side. They won't let you fail.

"Besides, I know, you know, we were told by Alhurah. If anyone thought you were not capable of the responsibility of being king, they are wrong because Alhurah has entrusted you with the responsibility of a Seeker. If God believes you, what is the point of other appraisals?"

"You really think this is all possible? Dethroning the king?" King Duggan surfaced in Will's mind and the vow he made to himself in Suthenburg after he confronted his parent's murderer. To be king meant he'd have the power, to stop the war yes, but to also prevent anyone else from suffering as he had in Isen Prison. It seemed to all fall into place. But Will didn't imagine being a king. That was too much responsibility but, so what? If this was how things were turning, even Sir Robert seemed to see that, he'd make the best of it.

"You forget Will, God is on our side," Ahmed smiled as he clutched his Seeker's Stone in front of Will. Will smiled. He drew his stone and it turned warm. An intense yet calming heat came over him.

"The People have chosen you; fate has chosen you, and I have chosen you. Divine right to rule is taken from the unworthy and given to one whose plans will change history," Manis said. Will and Ahmed came forward to Sir Robert and Lorna.

Will took a deep breath, "I don't understand, how and why?"

"We've been rebelling for a long time," Lorna started, "E'er since King Duggan resumed this war. Its the Eighth Crusade now huh? After the Grand Mosque massacre, survivors claimed to have witnessed a priest of Manis an' the grand imam curse the attackers. They claim the two promised that God would deliver Seekers to end this war. No one's sure what exactly a Seeker is."

Will and Ahmed gave each other a knowing look.

"But the church has declared 'em to be the chosen of Manis. Manis wishes this. The grand bishop and the new grand imam spread rumour they would hold objects of great power. D'you both hold such objects?" Upon saying this, the rebels around them drew closer, eager to see. Will and Ahmed presented their Seeker's Stones. The reddish mist within moved softly around, amplifying its hue. The rebels observed, speechless.

Sir Robert huffed. "The religious institutions of both countries were right, this time, but they also have everything to gain from replacing the leaders who drained their wealth for the war."

"God oft works like this through his servants and truthfully, we are all tired of war. We latched on to this hope that God had not ignored our plight. Now that we see you both, Gurmian and Saomardrim, friends, we know you are the ones," Lorna said, her eyes gleaming with hope. "Not everyone agreed. Many resisted, many did an' could not accept you both. For Gurmians, they could not trust God had chosen a Saomardrim to liberate them and he was to be aided by a criminal. For the Saomarhad, they could not believe a Gurmian, a criminal at that, was to aid their own champion to liberate them. Everyone expected a born 'ero to save us. Someone as legendary as Saint Sir Isen who started life as an honourable and humble priest and who grew into a legend. No one expected their hero to be the enemy, to be boys, and to be a murderer.

"Many within the rebels could not believe it. There was a schism within our group. We purged those who resisted against the prophecy, then we spread the message that you both were the ones. Many have joined us driven to us by fatigue and the hope that in this rebellion, God will be on our side."

"No, you don't understand how much pressure this is." Will shook his head. Sir Robert put a hand on his shoulder,

"But you will have allies through this. It's time for this war to end and for peace to return to this kingdom."

The rebels learned that King Duggan planned to splinter the sultan's sultanate by killing him. Ahmed was especially worried about this and tried to convince the rebels to save his sultan, but they were engrossed in their own matters. To them, it seemed, the sultan was an afterthought. There was still one person who had the ability and position to save his sultan. Ahmed found the people among the rebels who could help him send out a message, sitting at a table of letters and scrolls. He approached them.

"I need to send out a message." There were two men there, one raised an eyebrow, another crossed his arms.

"Go away, we ain't letting you send nothing. Could be you want to contact your infidel friends and have them seize power once we topple the tyrant king." One of them scoffed. Ahmed shook the insults from his mind.

"You don't understand, I want to contact…"

"Shove off! Not all of us are happy bout you." the man's glare made Ahmed flex his fingers, ready to cast, fearing escalation. Suddenly, Sir Robert was between Ahmed and the men, Will close behind.

"Calm yourself now." The knight spoke firmly and calmly. He looked the man in the eyes. The man huffed and turned away. "Will, get Ahmed out of here." Will nodded and led Ahmed away. They moved out of sight.

"Wait Will." Ahmed sighed.

"What happened there?"

"Nothing I should have been surprised about. It is natural that they take their anger out on me who looks like the enemy they cannot reach."

"Enemy they cannot reach?"

"Those who have harmed them. All I can do is prove myself to them. Fight with them and show them I am on their side. I can hope they will warm up to me after that but some may not."

"You…"

"No. There is something more important than me. I need your help Will."

"Anything I can do I will."

"No one is worried that Sultan Yazid may be murdered by your king. These rebels are preoccupied with getting ready to take down King Duggan but when we do; it may be too late for the sultan. I need to contact the one person who has the ability to help me ensure the sultan is safe."

"Who?"

"Elizabeth."

"Oh…" Will frowned.

"I know things have broken down between you and her Will but the rebels won't let me warn her. She could use her position within the castle to protect the sultan from her father. I need you to send her a letter."

"What makes you think she will choose the sultan over her father?"

"I don't know who she would choose, but I do know she understands what would happen to her kingdom and to my home and how this war would continue if the sultan is assassinated. She won't let that happen."

"How would you know what she understands?" Will growled. Ahmed brushed off Will's anger, remembering their conversation about Elizabeth.

"You don't have to write it. I just need you to send it. These rebels trust you more than me. Please help me Will. I am considered a traitor to my state… I feel like a traitor… I need to ensure Sultan Yazid is safe."

Will sighed. "Sorry, yes, I will do it."

"Thank-you Will."

Chapter Thirty-Two

ELIZABETH PACED BACK and forth across her room, dressed in her finest clothes. Today was the day the sultan would arrive. A message came to her the night before, in the most unusual way. Someone had left it for her under her door and in the morning, she had woken before the servants and found it. Waking early had never come easy to her before she had run away. The letter was from Ahmed and it said her father planned to kill Sultan Yazid. Ahmed had quoted something obscure from when they were together alone after arriving in Gurmanis so she trusted it was genuine. How was she to save the sultan from her father's men? This was all so horrible. She wanted to see Will again, but Ahmed did not write about him. Was everything alright? Was Will hurt? Dead? No! A queasiness came over her and she steadied her footing. She would not even think of such a possibility.

"Your highness, I humbly beg you to stop moving around. My fellow ladies and I cannot properly fix your dress." A maid, one of three fussing over Elizabeth, implored.

Elizabeth stopped fidgeting and allowed her maids to properly dress and prepare her. One adjusted the lacing on her dress; another combed Elizabeth's hair and adjusted her braid and the last worked on her face. Elizabeth had finally relented and allowed all her servants to return to her service after refusing them the night before. It made her feel comfortable to have people fussing over her, as comfortable as the present situation allowed her to feel. Despite experiencing peasant life she could not shake the homesickness she realised she'd been feeling. It was so much simpler in the palace to access all the luxuries she had missed. Elizabeth had taken a warm bath this morning with imported soaps and lotions, how she welcomed that. And she had an early meal, the taste of which beat the army rations she had been eating for so long. Quickly, she was getting used to all of this again.

Elizabeth inhaled loudly.

"I am a princess. I have authority. No one will rule my home without my say," Elizabeth said confidently. A multitude of familiar feelings rushed through her giving her ideas as to how to weave through this intrigue effectively. How to play each side to get the right result. This was what she'd been raised to comprehend. A maid looked at Elizabeth in surprise at the sudden outburst. Elizabeth kept face.

"Stop! Off!" Elizabeth waved her hands to dismiss her maids. They bowed low and backed away. Once, she wouldn't think twice about this, but after living differently for so long she felt the cold protocol in it. It would be so much better to have friends to serve her, those she could trust and confide honestly to. A relationship like she had with Keira maybe. A maid knocked on her door.

"The sultan is arriving at the main gates your highness. His majesty requests your presence in greeting him."

"Yes, of course. I will be down in ten minutes." Elizabeth swiftly turned around and walked down the halls toward the main gates with her maids in tow. How was her father going to do it? Stab him in his sleep? Poison his food and drink? How was he going to cover it up? Elizabeth was lost in thought.

"Leave me," Elizabeth directed to her maids.

"We should stay by your side, your highness." One maid bowed.

"No. I know very well how to navigate the palace myself. I do not need you following me everywhere." Once she might have relished the idea of flaunting her power like that, but it seemed while some things of royal life were natural and comfortable to her, others seemed to be less appealing.

"It is our duty to…"

"I will not command you a second time." Elizabeth noticed fear in the eyes of her maids. She then did something she would not have done before, she retracted and smiled. "It is early. Go and eat something and attend to your other duties. I may have need of you at some other time." The maids, puzzled by her lenience, bowed once more before leaving. Elizabeth turned towards a door and sighed. Re-adjusting to royal life was not going to be without some changes.

Elizabeth made her way to the entry gate of the keep. She was allowed through the servants, King's Guard, and advisors, to stand by her father. They were all bundled near the entrance chatting idly about the Saomarhadian arrival. Many had not met a Saomarhadian before. Elizabeth stood a distance from her father as he conversed with Duke Célestin.

"I trust you have the situation with the rebels under control?" King Duggan flicked dirt off his nails

"Oui. They have been bold as of late but I have my men searching. There is talk the rebels may be planning to strike against you. However, it is merely talk."

"They must be emboldened by the arrival of those boys."

"If Lord Dillon does his job, that boldness will die quickly. My men will deal with these rebels."

"Good. The sultan of Saomarhad is to arrive soon. I want everything to go as planned, and there can be no interruptions. Over the past few months you have gained my trust, I know you are on my side and you share my ambitions. Unlike Lord Dillon who is only playing along so he can keep his head."

"Je suis honoré, your majesty. Lord Gregor's coalition I hope will not interrupt. His men—"

"My men, they owe me their allegiance! Lord Richrit has brought enough of the Royal Forces to contend with them. As duke you also command your own army. Where are the rest of your men?"

"Doing their duty at the front of course. If you wish them to reposition as you've told others, I can arrange that."

"I will. Those orders I will draft immediately for your forces.

"Comme tu veux your majesty." Duke Célestin bowed. "The princess has arrived."

"Ah yes." The king looked at his daughter. Elizabeth walked forwards giving a lazy smile, showing no hint that she had overheard her father and Duke Célestin. Though matching Lord Gregor's men and repositioning troops could be call for concern, it didn't seem to her that any of it was related to the sultan's assassination.

"I am glad to see you more up-beat Elizabeth, since our last talk." the king smiled. "You look beautiful in that dress, my daughter. You will be the envy of the crowd. We will work on finding your new suitor after we deal with the sultan." Elizabeth flinched at the word but pushing it to one side she revealed what was on her mind,

"Father I need to talk about the state of the kingdom," Elizabeth said.

"The state of the kingdom? Why now, Elizabeth? The kingdom is fine. The treasury will soon be replenished, the people content. This war is going in our favor."

"No it's not that. The people are not pleased, I have seen it."

"Again Elizabeth? We are about to meet Saomarhad's sultan."

"I have to tell you; it's stuck in my mind."

"Relieve yourself quickly then." King Duggan tapped the hilt of his sword.

Elizabeth sighed and started, "When Mother died, things changed greatly. Not only in the castle, but for the whole kingdom. A war resumed and laws changed. I had thought things were okay. I assumed you had everything under control, and Sir Robert had encouraged that everything was fine. When I ran away, I was at first disgusted the people hated you after you had fixed things, but then I realised that since Mother, everything was wrong. The people do hate you Father. They loathe the unfair laws and taxes and the war. Living among the common folk I came to understand that."

"Do you think I do not know this, Elizabeth? I know how ungrateful the people are after all the protection I provide. Do you think I do not know the rebellion they have created? I am well aware, and I assure you everything is satisfactory."

"It does not seem so; it does not seem right." Elizabeth frowned.

"The peasantry are merely petty. God has given me the right to rule, our blood is divine and so I know what is needed for my people. Manis long ago bestowed his blessings on our people. There will be those who rule, fight, trade and think, the first children blessed by our lord…"

"Then the second children blessed by Manis are those who will craft, labour and serve. So did Manis bless the children of the first Gurmanis born so each shall stay in his place, support the other and work as parts of a body to give function to the whole. I have been taught the story father," Elizabeth said.

"Then you know that all is as God wills it." King Duggan moved onwards. Elizabeth sighed, frustrated.

Duke Célestin approached. "Your highness." He bowed.

"Uncle."

"Excuse my invasion but I share your concerns."

"You heard that?" Elizabeth looked at him. Duke Célestin was always a serious man but today the feeling he seemed to radiate was damper than usual.

"Qui. I too have seen the issues that plague our kingdom."

"Father does not realise it," she said idly.

"He only needs more convincing. He needs you more than you know for I see that you do care greatly for this kingdom."

"You flatter me, Uncle."

"I want to provide you with any help I can give. We should be allies Elizabeth."

"Are we not?"

"Of course we are. I only want to reaffirm that."

Elizabeth resisted the natural urge to show her confusion.

"Whatever comes, I hope to be on your side. We can work together to convince the king to see the harm he does to his people." Duke Célestin bowed.

Trumpets sounded the arrival of the sultan. His entrance party stretched far. The sultan stood in front, flanked by his guardsmen. They all wore the finery of easterners. Behind the sultan travelled a carriage and many servants. His Immortals and their grandmaster, Barbas, stood close to the sultan. As was agreed upon, the monarch had brought one-hundred Saomarhad soldiers, for his protection, who were stationed in the upper city.

King Duggan approached first, followed by his guards and advisors. Elizabeth was placed to her father's right.

"Sultan Yazid. I thank you for coming at a delicate time." King Duggan proclaimed.

The sultan gave the king a hard warning stare. Sultan Yazid stood in front of his father's brutalizer, and Elizabeth imagined it took every bit of the man's strength not to attack King Duggan where he stood. The fact was not lost on the armed men around them who's stature stiffened.

Sultan Yazid remained cordial. "Our countries are at war King Duggan, and we all want peace."

"We all do indeed sultan; we all do. This is a momentous occasion after all! These are the first negotiations in generations. Come let us show you your quarters where you can rest after your long journey. Tonight, a feast in honour of peace. And tomorrow we will negotiate."

"Lead the way King Duggan." Everyone turned to the castle and made their way in. Behind the crowd a young, hooded, Saomarhad ranger followed.

The King's Guard lived in the keep near the east gate. Elizabeth had to see if the guardsmen would help. She knew their leader well, a man by the name of Mercer Gorton, the grandmaster of the King's Guard. Elizabeth hoped the King's Guard had nothing to do with this plot of murder, If Mercer's character was the same as she remembered, he would not be taking part. Still, she would be careful. She passed the guards in the training yard out front and hailed the guards at the door as she walked through. To her luck, Mercer sat, conversing with his men in the common room. The stern faced, lightly bearded, man caught Elizabeth's eye. He was at least five years younger than Sir Robert with black combed back hair.

"Princess." He bowed. "What brings you in here? I am sure your father would need help with his guests."

"My father needs no help at the moment Mercer. Is there a more private place we can talk? I have a concern."

"Anything for you princess." Mercer motioned to his study and Elizabeth followed, walking inside before the grandmaster. He closed the door and walked behind his desk. The man bent down with his hands on the table. "I am sorry I have no seat in here at the moment otherwise I would offer you one."

"That is fine; I will do well without one."

"So what is the problem, your highness?" He gave her a warm smile.

"Did my father tell you anything special to be done when the sultan arrived?"

"Only to increase security around the palace. Nothing else."

"Nothing? He told you nothing about the sultan?" Elizabeth tested him, checking to see if he was in on the plot.

"I am sure your highness… well Lord Richrit flaunted an order from the king to nearly everyone of my men. The king has allowed him to move more of his men into the castle. I assume it's because of the talks."

"Hm…"

"Your highness?"

"Mercer I know you to be a loyal man. You've served my family for years and drill into your men the true mandate of the King's Guard."

"The first king always had a distaste of Imperiali politics." Mercer laughed. "Many times it involved a pretorian blade in an emperor's back. I must say I have the same distaste."

"Then you must know the sultan is in danger. I fear it will be from my father. You cannot let havoc rule this palace."

"I would sooner resign… huh…" He looked unchanged.

"You knew this?" Elizabeth raised an eyebrow.

"No, but I am not surprised. We protect you and the king, but… havoc would spell trouble for that mandate."

"And what if your guard are to be the assassins?"

"How dare they! It is right you came to me."

"I knew it was a sound choice. Can you help?"

"I cannot confront the king with this."

"It would be easier to throw suspicion off of my father if an unaffiliated party killed the sultan."

Mercer's eyes went wide. "An assassin? Here? By the king's mouth? Let it not be a Crimson Blade."

"You must keep an eye on the sultan. I will have my maids be on watch."

"Should we not warn the sultan?"

"No, I don't know how he will react, what if he leaves? Then any peace would be impossible to achieve." Elizabeth couldn't mess this up; it was essential that the negotiations began.

"I see. I will follow your orders princess, and if any of my guard is playing hit man of the king or there is an assassin within these walls, I will find them." Agreement made, the two went their separate ways. Soon the feast would begin and Elizabeth had to get a new dress. She hurried to the keep.

She should have not been travelling as she was in her new dress but there were many worries on her mind, and many questions from her travels to clear up. Elizabeth strode to the castle library and treasury. As she came to its wing a pair of King's Guards waved her through. She approached the main desk and called out.

"Arch-mage Jaxon! Where are you?" A man in mage robes fumbled around with some books at the back then stumbled forward.

"Princess Elizabeth, a surprise, should you not be with your father?" The young man answered. He was clean shaven but lines of stress spread over his face. He was in his late twenties.

"My father is fine without me, and my business here is more important. But first, how are you Jaxon?"

Surprised, the Arch-mage answered quickly, "Well enough, since you left your highness. After your mother, your father left me here as nothing more than a librarian of his archives. I am his arch-mage! I asked if the grandmaster at Schweigendorf could do anything, as he is my superior, but he could do naught."

"I am sorry Jaxon."

"Don't be, your highness, it is my duty. I wish the king could at least let me do my experiments more freely… er… wait! I forgot to bow!" Arch-mage Jaxon started to bow but Elizabeth stopped him.

"There is no time. My father refuses to aid his people and they really hate him. I need to know why. I need to know what my father did to hurt his people in this way. Procure for me all records of all the laws my father has made or changed. Get me everything."

"That is a lot of information Princess. Would your father agree?"

"I can examine this." It was her right.

"I s'pose you are allowed to. I will get all this, but it will take time."

"Please prepare everything and have them taken to my room. I will look through them when I get a chance." Elizabeth was determined to understand what wrongs her people suffered. She remembered Will's disdain for her nobility. She'd show him she wasn't like that too.

The arch-mage nodded. "So much lifting, as you wish."

Elizabeth ignored the jape. First, she had to determine the method her father intended to use for the assassination, then she would worry about the countries' problems.

"Jaxson, I know you dabble in alchemy."

"Yes, it is common for mages to learn it, but I only minored in it at Schweigendorf Mages University."

"But you know enough for what I need. I need a general antidote for poison."

"What!? What need do you—"

"Can you get me that? I don't have much time. Do not worry Jaxson, I'm not asking you for poison." Elizabeth smiled.

"I will see what I have stored for my experiments."

"Thank-you." She had to get herself together as these next days were going to be tiresome. As a princess she knew she would need to worry about these things when she grew up, but now these responsibilities were crashing down on her all at once.

The feast was a step higher than previous ones, but Elizabeth could not calm herself to enjoy it. She fingered the golden chaplet, decorated with fresh pink and blue flowers, around her forehead and hair. At the high table, underneath the elaborate massive carving of a castle and its people conducting their daily lives on the wall behind her, Elizabeth kept her ears attuned to all her father's conversations.

She had her maids check the sultan's rooms for anything out of the ordinary and then kept a close eye on the food going to the sultan. She fidgeted at the high table, glancing over the crowd on the tables below her and the fine murals and tapestries adorning the hall. Her father sat in the middle and she to his right, the sultan to his left. People ate cheerfully, and the sultan asked for a refill of his drink, which was promptly delivered to him. The sultan took a sip and wiped his mouth with a cloth. Well he didn't die.

Elizabeth took a sip of her own wine and watched the jesters now beginning their act. Suddenly the sultan coughed and Elizabeth turned his way. He simply excused himself to the king and continued to watch the performance. What way did her father intend to kill him?

After dinner Elizabeth met with Mercer.

"There are no suspicious persons, Princess, but Lord Richrit and a few of his men have been given a room clearly above his station. By Manis, I should have been more suspicious but with the king inviting Lord Gregor's coalition into the palace, vetting every single person is a difficult task. What if the assassin were to strike the king?" Mercer pondered.

"Calm Mercer." Elizabeth was not calm, but didn't show it. "There may be no assassin. What if my father wants to use—" One of Elizabeth's maids who was checking the kitchen rushed to her. To Elizabeth's horror she presented a vial of liquid to the princess. Elizabeth snatched it.

"Where did you find this?" she asked, her chest aflame.

"By the wine jars my lady," she answered. Elizabeth took a whiff of it and recoiled at the stench of the poison. The wine must have masked the taste and smell of it.

"There is more, your highness. The kitchen staff saw one of Duchess Lena's maids pour the poison into the wine."

"Lena!" Elizabeth exclaimed in disbelief. She shook her head. "Find this maid and dispatch men to capture her. Where is the sultan?"

"Returning to his quarters via the north hall your highness." Elizabeth and Mercer ran off in that direction and as she did, she fumbled with the folds of her dress, feeling for the small vial Jaxson had given her. If the poison was something she had not encountered before, then the liquid in her vial would be the antidote.

Elizabeth and Mercer found the sultan's party in a small secluded hallway. The sultan was coughing and on his knees. One of his immortals lay still beside him, blood trailing from his open mouth and his eyes wide and red. The Immortals were about to call out but as Elizabeth turned the corner, she stopped them. Elizabeth presented the sultan with the antidote. He took it through his coughs and collapsed. The Immortals grabbed Elizabeth and yanked her away from him. Mercer drew his sword and dagger and the Immortals loosened their grip.

"What have you done? You killed him! You and your father are mad people, you want war? We will oblige!" Grandmaster Barbas shouted. "Vile are the Gurmians! We come for peace and this is what the result is." Barbas turned and walked around his men, towards the back.

"No! He is ok. I saved him!" Elizabeth countered and pointed to Sultan Yazid who was trying to stand. An Immortal helped him up and the sultan's guards let go of Elizabeth.

"I am ok. What happened?" the sultan asked.

"You were choking, maybe poisoned. The king's daughter saved you," the Immortal explained. "He was not so fortunate." He pointed to the dead man. "He cleared your food and drink but the poison didn't take effect right away."

Sultan Yazid looked up at Elizabeth. "Poison, a coward's tool! Perhaps your father wishes to continue this war?" The sultan waited for an answer. Elizabeth had no way of knowing for sure if her father was behind this, and if she told him he was, then there would be no chance for peace.

"It was not my father behind this but a band of people who would like to continue this war. Rebels."

"She lies my sultan." Barbas came forward. "Rebels? A convenient excuse." Barbas whispered into the sultan's ear. The sultan nodded.

"Wh-What are you whispering about?" Elizabeth asked, cautious.

"Confine her!" the sultan ordered. His Immortals advanced. Mercer came between them and the princess.

"O'er my dead body!" Mercer challenged. "You will not lay your hands on Princess Elizabeth again!"

"Sultan, please." Elizabeth kept calm. Appearing to beg would look weak; she needed to appeal to the sultan's sense. "I know what just happened makes my father look very bad, but please let us talk. The Gurmian people don't deserve your anger."

"Bah! Gurmians are infidels, they…" The sultan raised a hand to stop Barbas,

"In a way, I do agree. That is why I have sent someone right now to deal with your father."

"What? You were going to kill him anyway! I thought you wanted peace." Elizabeth held her panic in check.

"Your father brutalised my father. Inshalhurah there must be justice!"

"Mercer."

"Yes princess, we need to go." Mercer backed away from the immortals with the princess. From behind, two King's Guard, with swords drawn, approached. The Immortals drew their swords.

"I see King Duggan has sent his men to ensure the job was done." The sultan scoffed.

"So, you two are the ones who disobey our mandate." Mercer hissed. "King Calis would show distain, you two acting like backstabbing pretorians of his time."

"Who even really reads those these days sir," one answered.

"I take offense! You have learned nothing from me. You have lost your senses."

"Please, move aside sir," the second one ordered.

"Not likely." Mercer smiled. The two guards moved forward and in quick action Mercer knocked both of them out with the hilt of his sword and dagger. Three palace men-at-arms arrived, shocked at what they witnessed. Mercer sheathed his weapons.

"Clean this up and keep it quiet."

Astonished, the sultan ordered his men to stand down. "First you save me from poison then you save me from your own countrymen," the sultan said. Elizabeth turned to him.

"And I will save my father next. Then, I want to talk." Elizabeth stood firm.

The sultan smiled. "You are a bold princess. I will be impressed if you can save your father from my assassin. If you do, I will talk to you."

Elizabeth and Mercer ran through the castle towards King Duggan's quarters. They stopped at a crossroads in the hallways.

"You go to the gardens. Check the balcony entrance to your father's quarters, Princess," Mercer suggested.

"I must follow you into his room."

"There is no time to get reinforcements. Trust me Princess. I will keep your father safe."

"Fine." Elizabeth parted with Mercer and ran into the garden, almost tripping over her dress. She cursed. She came out onto a path leading to a junction ahead. Neatly trimmed bushes lined the paths. Displays of flowers occupied the grassy areas. She reached a space ahead of a bench under a small arch, covered in vines. Above her was her father's room and the balcony that led from it. She looked around. No one was there.

Mercer roared. Someone was pushed out to the balcony railing. Mercer appeared. He grabbed the assassin, the enemy struggling to break free. Mercer lifted him and threw him off. It wasn't a far drop, and he fell into a bush. The assassin stumbled out of the bush and ran forwards. Elizabeth stood her ground, noticing the assassin was a young Saomarhad ranger, close to her own age. The ranger glared at the princess, panic and anger in his face, blood dripping down his cheek. Mercer jumped off the balcony and landed behind the assassin, cloak billowing out, weapons drawn.

"Stop!" Elizabeth shouted. The young ranger looked between her and the grandmaster, considering his options. Mercer levied his sword at the boy.

"Surrender," Elizabeth demanded, but the boy lunged. She screamed as he landed on top of her.

"Princess!" Mercer advanced, ready to kill.

"No!" Elizabeth shouted, wrestling with the boy. "Don't kill him!" She managed to punch the boy in the face. Mercer dropped his weapons, growled, and grabbed the boy. He hauled him off of the princess and punched him in the gut. He forced the boy to the ground, disabling him. Mercer looked up.

"Are you alright princess?" Elizabeth stood. She coughed, clutching her side. A little blood stained her dress.

"Don't worry, he missed."

Mercer frowned, looked into the Saomardrim's face, and punched him again. The boy grunted and whined.

⁂

Elizabeth and Mercer left the castle and found the sultan's party in the upper city. They entered a large L-shaped tavern, two stories and of engraved wood and stone, that was surrounded by a mix of place men-at-arms and Saomarhadian soldiers. Inside, Arch-Mage Jaxson was with the sultan's party, speaking to the man.

Mercer pushed the captured assassin ahead of them outside the tavern and past the guards. The boy's wrists were bound behind his back.

"Are they looking for Duchess Lena's maid?" Elizabeth asked.

"I have two men working on it," Mercer said. "Are the bandages on..."

"I am okay." They entered the tavern and were greeted by Barbas, then walked inside where the sultan sat.

Jaxson looked up, startled at the company. "Princess? Mercer? What is going on here?"

"Business Jaxson. Why are you getting the sultan drunk?"

"I am not drinking," the sultan said. "I wished only to see the city and desired to take a break."

"Excuse me sultan." Jaxson bowed. He stood and strode towards Mercer. "He wanted to go suddenly, ordered the palace men-at-arms to take him out. They came to me."

"Then you are doing your job oh so well Lord Chancellor."

"Yes..." Jaxson huffed. "Glad to finally be of use to the king."

"Go back to the palace. We will take over."

"What are you—"

"Go to the king's side. Try not to wake him."

Jaxson nodded and pushed past Mercer and out the door. Mercer threw the assassin to the ground. The boy looked down, ashamed.

"You've failed your sultan, Parvez. Perhaps Aarif was wrong about you." Barbas said.

"I am sorry, sultan." Parvez bowed.

"We will take him back," the sultan said.

"No," Elizabeth refused. "He is our prisoner now. Will all these assassination attempts stop?"

"I have alerted guards I can trust. The king is well protected now," Mercer informed.

The sultan raised his hands and smiled. "I cannot speak for your king, but my attacks will stop. It is clear to me that you two are working against him, why?"

"I am working for my people."

"So am I."

"Yet you'd risk more war. That can't be the best outcome."

"The lands I will conquer will bring wealth to my sultanate."

"The price is too high and too unsustainable."

The sultan smiled. "Why don't we talk alone. Barbas, leave us." The sultan waved his men away. Elizabeth ordered Mercer to go as well. He took Parvez with him. They both sat across from each other. The sultan examined Elizabeth. "I see now. You were with the boy Ahmed brought to Ortie. You were in my dungeons awaiting death."

"You killed many Gurmians in that time." Elizabeth frowned, remembering how she couldn't save them. She had failed them.

"Had you told me you were Princess Elizabeth Chas, heir to the Gurmanis throne, I would have had you treated to better accommodations. You are something to be ransomed."

"I am not a thing! I am a person, and would you have believed me?" Elizabeth asked.

"I have ways to determine the truth."

"And had I demanded the release of my people, all those you put to death, would you have obliged?"

"No, I was in control Princess." The sultan shook his head. "In truth I was uncomfortable about the entire ordeal. I have prayed and thought upon my actions. I was wrong."

"Thank-you… it means something." But didn't feel redeeming.

"In the end your people responded in equal measure. You slaughtered half the population of Jueadi."

"That act was unsanctioned. One lord deviated from our plans and committed mass murder." Elizabeth wouldn't excuse the actions of rouge nobles.

"However, it says something that your forces freely pillaged as they wished."

"Perhaps that's why it is time for peace. Haven't we, as leaders, stroked fires of distrust, hate, and anger in our people for too long? Even now the people are demanding change."

"So I have heard and I have been told yet there are also those who want a war of extermination, like your father. How many raids, massacres, and war crimes have your people already committed? Should they go unpunished?"

"I was ignorant to these things before, but I have learned much since then. We will never negotiate on anything if we use the excuse that they did that so therefore we cannot talk now. We did things many would frown upon, but so did you. We must both repent. Do you disagree?"

"No."

"Then therein lies the problem. We blind ourselves with rage and hurt. Rightly so. How many of our loved ones have been lost to war? Too many. But if we don't boldly put that hurt aside, as is against our nature to do so, we will destroy ourselves. How long will religious fervor and racism fuel war? Can't you see that one-hundred years of fighting is depleting that fuel? If we don't find peace now, a new fuel will take its place."

"You speak well Princess, but an offer of peace has already been presented to me."

"Really? From who?" Elizabeth nodded, tight lipped. Had she underestimated her father?

"A Duke Célestin described to me the offer from the king. He offers the land south of Suthenburg in exchange for the Hertos River Origin region. The region is of some importance in Gurmanis' history, I believe. Land for land to gain peace."

"That would be a fair offer." It seemed too fair for her father's rhetoric.

"I do agree. What would you purpose, I am curious."

"Me?" Elizabeth sat tall. Every conversation and interaction she'd had with her people came to mind. "These lands have been fought over to near exhaustion. The people who live on them bled for them and though they want peace, they do not wish to lose their homes." This she'd heard in her travels. "It is fair, but it is a weak offer. We should not exchange land. This only serves to preserve the division between us. Would there not be a stronger peace if we work together?"

"Would you ask me to pay reparations? I demand the same from you."

"It need not be framed so negatively. I propose we help each other rebuild around the Hertos River Valley, which we share. Let us widen our trade. Most importantly, let us cooperate on the security of the Holy Land and the protection of pilgrims, Manian and Alhurian."

"You want to end this war as allies? Bold if not idealistic."

"Do you not see that it would be better than exchanging land for peace without addressing the tensions and issues between us?"

The sultan leaned back and taped his fingers. "I cannot forgive your father for my father's murder."

"I understand, but I ask you to consider its ramifications. Think about those you have a responsibility to protect, like I do." This Elizabeth knew firmly now. She would never be so foolish as to run away from her responsibilities again.

"I will give you that. I have witnessed traitors and sympathisers among my people. These people who worked against me because they thought they could hasten this war's end. It has hit me personally. Ahmed, the boy my friend and grand vizier was once so proud of, betrayed me."

"Ahmed is a dutiful person."

"He betrayed his people." The sultan scoffed.

"He did something even I refused to do. He risked everything to live with his enemy to see for himself how much was untrue. Never once has he betrayed his people. He has not shared your secrets nor has he killed his kinsmen. Peaceful interaction with an open-mind. That's what brings understanding."

"He shocked me. He gave me much to think about," The sultan admitted.

"I became his friend, along with Will. If we three can be friends, why can't our kingdoms?" Elizabeth hoped the man would see some logic in this.

"Because there is too much turmoil that still shrouds us from each other."

"The only way to clear that shroud is to step through it to the other side. It is not as if there has never been a peaceful interaction between our people. Merchants of both cultures still trade with each other, marriages still happen between us, friendships still form."

"Perhaps."

"So sultan. Can I ask you to consider peace?" Elizabeth really did hope he'd say yes.

"I will never forgive your father, but like Ahmed, I will see what he sees in your people. I called this ceasefire because I considered Ahmed's actions and his words. He challenged me to come myself, so I did."

"Then you will try to negotiate with my father?" Elizabeth kept her joy hidden.

"Despite his unusual offer, I fear your father wants war, Princess. Will he accept?"

"He still may." Elizabeth wasn't confident that her father would change, but she refused to give up hope.

"You are blinded by being his daughter. King Duggan has invested too much, maybe more than I in this war. I will try to offer him peace. I will take the moral high ground and put aside my anger towards him for my people's good. But princess, I am no fool. I do not intend to die here."

"Of course." Elizabeth curtsied and left. Duke Célestin's proposal must be a ploy of her father's. In all her conversations with her father since returning it was clear he would do everything he could to fight. He believed it was the right thing to do after witnessing near collapse of Gurmian civilization when Yazid's father ruled. It was a tragedy in his mind and he also believed he was avenging his wife. Elizabeth feared that when she read the archive records Arch-Mage Jaxson had brought her, she would uncover more things her father had done. He'd even neglected her and tried to force her into marriage, but Elizabeth still cared about him; she still loved him. Whatever would happen during the negotiations, she would not see her father dead.

<hr>

Elizabeth met Mercer and her maid in a dark corner of the castle. Two of Mercer's King's Guard, who he trusted, held Duchess Lena's terrified maid by her arms. When Elizabeth strode up, the maid pushed forward and fell at the princess' feet.

"Princess Elizabeth please have mercy, I was following orders. My lady's children were threatened an' the only way to save them was to kill the king I admit it!" she cried. Mercer and Elizabeth looked on shocked. Mercer grabbed the maid and shook her.

"Treasonous snake! What have you done!" Mercer growled as the woman cried.

"Stop Mercer," Elizabeth ordered. The grandmaster let go of the woman and stepped back. "In your fear of retribution, you have betrayed the loyalty of the woman you serve. Why does Duchess Lena want to kill the king and the sultan? How has she corrupted the King's Guard to do this?"

"Kill the sultan? My lady had no such plans."

"We stopped the poison intended for my father and the sultan. We also stopped the ambush intended for the sultan. Was Duchess Lena planning an ambush for my father? Mercer…"

"You maid," Mercer spoke to Elizabeth's maid. "Alert the King's Guard to rush to King Duggan's side now. Quickly!" The maid nodded and ran off around a bend.

"Where is the duchess?" Elizabeth demanded.

"In her quarters, your highness. What is to become of me?"

"Your treason deserves death, but before I make that judgement I must speak to my aunt." Elizabeth turned to the two guards. "Lock her in a pillory then return quickly to Duchess Lena's quarters. When we are finished you can take this traitor to the King's Jail to await sentence." Elizabeth and Mercer rushed to Duchess Lena's quarters as the two King's Guard dragged the maid off.

Mercer burst through the door to the duchess' room and drew his sword and dagger. Duchess Lena screamed and backed away. Mercer leveled his sword at Duchess Lena's throat.

"What is the meaning of this? Why have you burst into my room in such a manner…" Elizabeth emerged from behind Mercer as a tightness pressed on her chest.

"Aunt Lena."

"Elizabeth…" Duchess Lena tried to advance.

"Stay where you are," Mercer warned.

"Elizabeth why is this happening? What have I done?"

"You should tell us that." Elizabeth looked hard at Duchess Lena.

"Please Elizabeth… have mercy. I had no choice."

"Over?"

"I bought the poison intended to kill the king and I instructed my maid to pour it into the wine."

"He is your own brother!" Elizabeth screamed. "He lost his wife, his other sisters. Now you? How could you!"

"The life of my youngest was threatened, Elizabeth. I would do anything and there was no other way!"

"You could have told my father. You could have warned me! I thought we were close aunt Lena, all my life we were. You helped me cope with the loss of my mother."

"You don't understand… I could not."

"We also stopped a diplomatic catastrophe today as well. Since when did you gain the urge to murder the sultan of Saomarhad?"

"The sultan? I implore you Elizabeth, it was only King Duggan."

"Lies! The wine you poisoned was intended for the sultan."

"I did not know; the wine was meant for the king." Duchess Lena fell to her knees and clasped her hands together. "I swear on anything left between us Princess Elizabeth, I did not know the wine was meant for the sultan. I did as I was instructed."

"Who instructed you?"

"My husband, Duke Célestin."

"Are you telling me that the duke wanted the king to die so badly that he would threaten to hurt his own children? The duke is close to my father and never had a reason to hate him. I find this hard to believe."

"It is the truth. My husband wanted to remove the king and put himself on the throne. On the death of the king he had a plan to discredit you from the throne and use my position to put himself on it. He… he… has always wanted the throne it was… was why he married me."

"And you let him marry you?"

"I only found out well after the marriage. It was not like I had a choice, my father had picked the duke and I had no say in the matter. Initially he did not intend to kill Duggan… but then he changed the plan. I had to save my children."

"All this time you knew of his plots and told no one. Duke Célestin would even hurt his own children to fulfill his ambition."

"I am so sorry," Duchess Lena cried.

"Then my father truly wished to kill the sultan."

"Those treasonous King's Guard must have poisoned the wine first," Mercer guessed. "Duchess Lena's maid arrived after and poisoned the same wine. The wine was intended for the king yet the king must have directed the servants to serve it to the sultan."

"Duchess Lena, where is the duke?"

"I do not know. My husband knows of an impending attack by the rebels on the palace and he intends to use the force to occupy the king while he signals his own army to march on the city afterwards. My husband's men should be half a day from the city."

"He may have gone to signal them."

"He will have a hard time doing so at night when even the skies around the city are watched. I will search for him, Princess." Mercer nodded.

"Wait there is more!" Duchess Lena started. "My husband told me your father intends to kill those in the nobility who do not support him. Then he will send a messenger to the war front and order an invasion of Saomarhad. He accepted the ceasefire and gathered Lord Gregor's coalition with this intent. Most of the knights and high-ranking commanders as well as the Royal Forces have been secretly repositioning along the Hertos River at strategic points, relieving the forces of the nobles he can't trust."

"With the sultan dead, Saomarhad will be in disarray if it is suddenly attacked." Mercer shook his head. "The attack would not be expected by the traitorous nobility either, and by the time they hear that the king had ordered the army to attack, the traitorous nobility would be dead. No doubt King Duggan made deals with the more popular knights at the front, promising them the position of their deceased lords if they invade Saomarhad on the king's command."

"This is madness." Elizabeth held her forehead. Duke Célestin's peace offer to Sultan Yazid hadn't come from the king, it was an offer from Célestin who'd rule as king if all went his way. "How far will my father go to eliminate the Saomarhadians? He wants to throw the kingdom into disarray. We have to find the messenger."

"Should we lockdown the castle Princess Elizabeth?"

"No, Mercer. We don't know if my father has already released the messenger, if he even knows the sultan is alive, or if he has moved on the nobility yet. We need to stop Duke Célestin's message."

"My guess is he will not release the messenger until he is sure the sultan is dead."

"Then be discreet. Search the castle, the city, the surrounding country. Stop those messengers!" These schemes were compounding on her.

"That is a lot of area to cover. I will mobilize the castle guard." Mercer sheathed his weapons. The two King's Guard from before entered the room and took position to either side of Duchess Lena.

"Duchess Lena you will be taken to the place dungeon to await judgement," Elizabeth looked down on her with a sunken heart stabbed by contempt. The duchess cried as the two King's Guards pinned her wrists behind her back and fixed a set of irons on her. They lifted the woman and dragged her from the room.

Chapter Thirty-Three

LORNA SEEMED TO want to use Will and Ahmed as some sort of trophy. She led them through the dark streets of Royal Landing and showed them off to her allies. People reached out, touching them for some sort of blessing and saying, "Thank Manis! Manis cares! Peace will soon come!" Indeed, it seemed the Church had latched onto to the prophecy and spread it among the common people, under the nose of King Duggan.

Ahmed was a little impressed. Aside from preachers and holy knightly orders, one might have thought the religious institutions had forgotten about this war, but they had not. They had worked in the background. For peace? Maybe sections of them, like the attempt at peace in the Grand Mosque. It seemed the Church just needed one thing, them.

Lorna's rebellion had gathered many allies. Once she had toured the boys around the city, Will and Ahmed could have sworn half of Royal Landing and more and half the city watch were on their side. The watch would prevent aid from coming to the palace. Soon they would be ready.

***

"This is an outrage King Duggan! You invited me here to talk of peace. I almost died under your care and now you show the utmost cowardice in this blackmail!" Sultan Yazid hissed as he threw the treaty to the ground. The sultan's party faced the king, his daughter, and Lord Richrit, along with many other servants and guards. They were in the throne room.

King Duggan laughed. "Blackmail? You want peace, and I want peace but the path to it is not effortless! We have lost much to you, much that we need to regain."

"And what makes you think you have the right to Jueadi? To Al-Motros? To Al-Khadra Forest? It is pure insanity that you think we should give you un-challenged control over the Holy Land! I demand we return to a system of mutual protection and acceptance to all pilgrims and citizens within."

"Of course we will. Under my rule all will be protected, but… what is it? Hajj? Logistically it is too much—"

"This is unacceptable!" Sultan Yazid roared. "If you really wanted peace then you would not barter in land and gold. You would not throw the traditions of Alhurians around so lightly. I have brought no such proposal with me!"

"Then perhaps you have a better idea? One we can agree on."

"Only war will satisfy you! We will come up with an agreement, inshalhurah, but no doubt you will turn it into a war plan!" Sultan Yazid's party strode from the throne room. Elizabeth watched them leave; pretty soon, this would all fall apart. The tension in the air was growing and Elizabeth wondered what she could do.

⚬⚬⚬

Mercer, Elizabeth, and a troop of five King's Guard rode hard through the suspiciously empty streets of the upper city towards a tower at its center.

"Stay behind my men, Princess. You should not have come, not when negotiations are still ongoing," Mercer warned. They rode past stone houses covered in creeping green vines and whose upper floor walls were plastered in wattle and daub.

"I will see this through. Duke Célestin… he manipulated my aunt. I won't let that slide."

"I could have handled this alone." Mercer sighed. "You have changed, Princess."

When they arrived at the tower they dismounted and drew their weapons, then ran towards the entrance. They burst in and hesitated upon seeing dead city watchmen on the first floor. They ascended the steps to the top and when they got closer, they heard a watchman's voice and that of Duke Célestin. They crept forward on the landing to see the two fighting.

"I won't let you call aid for King Duggan!" the watchman shouted over the sound of clashing swords.

"Foolish turncoat! I wish to kill the king!" Duke Célestin found an opening and stabbed the watchmen right through his stomach. The watchman spit out blood, stuttered and fell. Duke Célestin turned as Mercer and his men entered, swords pointed at the cloaked duke.

"Grandmaster Mercer, a surprise."

"Stand down Duke Célestin by order of Princess Elizabeth Chas!"

"So, King Duggan does not yet know of my plan, but it is warming to see his daughter works so quickly."

"I do." Elizabeth stepped forward.

"Princess." Mercer tensed. Duke Célestin smiled.

"We can be on the same side Elizabeth, like I told you before," the duke implored. "Tell Mercer and his men to stand down."

"You tried to kill my father!" Elizabeth fumed. "We are not on the same side."

"We both want an end to the war, do we not? King Duggan has given the sultan an unworkable offer?"

"Lena told me how you are willing to sacrifice your own children to gain the throne. How you treated my aunt is unforgivable. I know of the offer you gave the sultan intending you as king, but your rule will be like my father's. I realise now that that is not what this kingdom needs."

"My ambitions are greater than matters of the heart. Tyranny weakens the kingdom whereas I intend a calmer rule."

"By temporary peace and it is no mistake your kin would benefit greatly. You have no care for the damage between Gurmian and Saomarhadian which solved would provide a lasting peace."

"Alas, willingly we could have done so much together. Gurmanis would have been glorieux. As grand as the Imperium."

"Stand down now. I have archers on every rooftop ready to terminate any message you attempted to send. The city gates are already sealed," Mercer warned.

"Non, it won't matter, Mercer. The common folk have betrayed you. The city watchmen are not all on your side; they will reopen the gates."

"Where is the messenger, Duke Célestin? We looked all night and could not find him."

"Dead. Killed by rebels."

"Rebels?"

"In all the time you were chasing me, you were blind to the rebellion that started in the north. It has spread across the kingdom and it has now come here. King Duggan's days are numbered. They will attack him today."

"It seems then, we are one for one in this battle."

"I do not care if our forces attack Saomarhad. The sultan will either die, or if he lives, I, a calmer head, will negotiate with him. Regardless, I will lead Gurmanis in the aftermath," the duke boasted.

"That is only a dream now, Duke Célestin. Stand down!"

"I will not be brought in chains to that fool of a king." Duke Célestin lunged forwards. Mercer and his armored guards all set onto the duke. Even an expert swordsman had no chance against such odds and it was only a few clashes of swords before Duke Célestin was struck. The duke roared. He continued to resist, expertly fending off attacks. Finally, Mercer sliced across his exposed face, leaving a gash. The duke fell to his knees and the King's Guard set upon him, running him through with their swords. Elizabeth turned away. Despite her anger, death was never enjoyable.

***

Rebel heralds ran through the city promoting the people to rise up. Two hundred awaited the signal to spring from their homes and gathering places sprinkled throughout the city, ready to converge on the palace.

Will, Ahmed, Sir Robert, and Lorna were away from their small force. They stood, mounted, overlooking the Golden Inlet on a grassy headland outside the north of the city. In its waters, a dozen Saomarhad ships sailed towards the city. Will's falcon preened itself on Will's arm.

"It seems negotiations did not go as planned," Sir Robert said.

"There must be hundreds of Saomarhad on those ships." Lorna shook her head. "It will be chaos. King Duggan's men against us against the sultan's men."

"The sultan is still in the city," Ahmed said. "They can't attack right now. The sultan will be trapped."

"We need to attack first." Sir Robert turned his horse around and led it away from the Golden Inlet, prompting the others to do the same. "We need to capture the castle before the sultan attacks."

"We can't hold against that force," Lorna said. "Not with our numbers."

"When we take the castle the rest of the city watch should join us."

"I should find the sultan," Ahmed said. "I must tell him to hold off his attack."

"You won't get to him. A Saomardrim riding through the streets alone will attract those who don't support us. Besides, King Duggan's men will never let you through the castle gate. We must have faith that Princess Elizabeth will dissuade the sultan. Let's begin the assault now."

Elizabeth burst through the doors leading to the room where the sultan's party were meeting, with two King's Guard, Mercer's trusted, by her side.

"Sultan, I have seen the ships! Thank Manis my father has not yet noticed. Why have you brought the war here?" The Immortals stood between her and the sultan's party.

"I told you, Princess Elizabeth, I would not die here. That force is here to extract me, that is all."

"It is sufficient to besiege this city!" Elizabeth frowned. Grandmaster Mercer appeared next to Elizabeth and pulled her aside.

He whispered to her, "I have confirmed your father trusted Duke Célestin to deal with the rebels. Instead, the duke maneuvered his way around them. He'd then mop up the survivors with his army. The rebels have captured the east gate. Some but not all of the city watchmen are helping them."

"What do we do?" Elizabeth panicked. This was overwhelming her. "The sultan's one-hundred allowed men are in the castle and in the upper city, and his navy is nearing the harbor."

"This castle will be attacked on all sides. I need to stay beside your father. My duty is to protect him, and you." Mercer's face was twisted with stress.

Elizabeth considered her options. She looked at the sultan. "Pull out. Take your men from the castle and upper city to safety."

"And leave me here?" The sultan raised an eyebrow.

"Halt the negotiations."

"You do not wish for peace?"

"I do sultan, I really do. Right now, King Duggan's other enemies approach him. I ask you to wait and see the result."

"Do you expect an attack?"

"You want my father dead, don't you? Then his enemies may do that for you." Elizabeth hoped she could first save her father from the rebels, then deal with the sultan.

"Who are these enemies?"

"Please, sultan. Send your forces away, halt your navy. Let me take you to a safe part of the castle and wait and see if King Duggan lives."

"This could be a trap," Barbas said. Elizabeth looked at the sultan, expecting an answer.

"We will do as you wish, for now." The sultan scratched his beard, intrigued at what was happening.

⁓

A main road curved through the city running over the King's River and terminating at the gates of the palace. It was a straightforward assault path, but could easily be defended if only the king's men had been aware of the attack beforehand.

As the rebels charged in, some city watchmen were already fighting the king's forces, having thrown open all inner-city gates along the road. From feeder roads more rebels poured in. the city was in an uproar. All signs of normal life had been replaced with smoke, blood, and fury.

Will, Ahmed, and Sir Robert galloped forwards atop their horses, slashing at the odd enemy. They skidded to a stop, forced to dismount due to the density of fighting men and women. Sir Robert rallied the rebels into a shield wall, then they crashed into the bulk of the King's Forces.

Will charged forwards with the crowd, screaming a war cry. His blade slid through someone, forcing him to yank it out, splattering blood. A bayonet thrust across his shoulder, skimming his pauldron. Will adjusted and countered the next strike. The enemy jabbed again. Will blocked from high guard and attacked from middle, kicking under the musket and toppling the musketeer. Will's allies surged forward, trampling the unfortunate attacker.

Ahmed shoved aside an attacker, countered another, then slashed across his face. He looked ahead. Two rows of musketeers lined up behind a barricade and fired. Ahmed lunged behind a building, men in front of him riddled by musket balls. Will and Sir Robert had found cover as well. Ahmed rushed past them and shoved his hands towards the cobbles. The earth rumbled and stone surged forward, crumpling the barricade, striking enemies, and causing the rest to flee.

Will neared the castle hill behind the rebels. He'd fallen behind and Sir Robert nor Ahmed had noticed. A cloaked man swooped out in front of Will and hauled him aside into a small dark alleyway. None of the rebels had noticed. The cloaked man slammed Will against a building and pushed his right hand over the boy's mouth, and his left hand over the boy's sword arm. Will glared at the man, fear overcoming him. He couldn't see his face, it was shrouded in the cloak's long hood, but the man was bleeding all over and it had stained all his clothes. Will looked at the man's armored arms, the metal was engraved with outlines of gold.

"You!" the man spat blood into Will's face. "I know you! Rebels and their ideas. Taking pathetic Church prophecies and calling them truth, bah! Now, at least the mad King Duggan will fall and Gurmanis will have you as king, won't they? Or maybe the sultan has a plan for this mayhem! Ecoutez!" The bloodied man pushed Will harder. Will tried to push back, but the man was far larger and stronger than him.

"This world is full of pathetic leaders. Either mad and tyrannical, lazy and foolish, or indulgent and inattentive. You will be just another one of them. I was going to set this kingdom on the right path. I won't stand idle while all suffer the folly of kings, queens, emperors and empresses!" The man coughed up blood. He shoved Will sideways out of the alley and fled deeper into the side streets, leaving Will dizzy and bewildered, trying to figure out who the hooded figure was.

<hr>

The rebels advanced up the castle hill. Sir Robert, at the front, stopped them upon sight of a large barricade housing three cannons and a large force of men behind it.

Lorna pushed herself forward. "Destroy this barricade. We will not lay down our weapons to return to become slaves of the king!" The cannoneer commander behind the barricade shouted to ready. Sir Robert shouted to find cover as cannon balls slammed into the rebel lines killing and sending many flying backwards. The rebels charged the barricade, some getting shot by arrow or musket, but the enemy could not shoot fast enough and were overwhelmed.

The enemy commander cried out, "Retreat, return to the castle! Retreat!" He and his men ran back, pursued by the rebels.

The rebels set a battering ram at the palace gates and pounded the door relentlessly while resisting projectile attacks from above. Sir Robert protested against the fury, as the small ram was doing little damage. Then the gate suddenly swung open against the smash of the ram, and men and women charged forward, screaming battle cries. Will and Ahmed stayed close to Sir Robert and Lorna. To their surprise, the palace bailey had already erupted in fighting. Royal Forces fought with various men of several different lords from Lord Gregor's coalition. Likely coalition members had opened the gate.

Sir Robert, Lorna, Ahmed and Will pushed through the chaos and neared the throne room to face the king. Will was a little behind Sir Robert when Ahmed touched his arm. Will turned around.

"Will, I must find my sultan. I need to know he's safe," Ahmed said.

"Alone? I'll go with you." Will started to move.

"No. You need to face your king. I will return." Ahmed reassured him. Will nodded and they parted ways.

⁂

Ahmed crept through the palace hallways moving upwards. He figured that's where the royal visitors to the castle would stay. It didn't take long to confirm that. Dead and injured immortals lay ahead of him creating a trail of blood leading to higher floors. Ahmed took a moment to examine the scene noticing a few dead Gurmian soldiers.

He followed the blood. Someone had been led this way, his blood dripping in clumps over the ground. Ahmed reached the next floor. The right side of the hallway opened up to a long balcony overlooking the north side of the castle. Rays of light luminated an injured immortal on the ground slumped against a wall among a handful of dead Gurmian soldiers. Ahmed approached, realising the injured immortal was Grandmaster Barbas.

"N-No…" Barbas said. "A-Ahmed… come." Barbas gestured to him. Ahmed approached, his hand hovering over his kilij.

"Barbas… what happened? I can help."

"N-No… I will live. The sultan is inside… save him," Barbas pleaded, pointing further ahead. "I-I tried to…"

Ahmed nodded and strode past Barbas to the room. He took a step inside and— a pistol shot rung out, making Ahmed's heart skip a beat as the reverberating sound rushed past him. Lord Richrit held a raised pistol, smoking from the barrel, at the sultan. The sultan shouted and kneeled over. Lord Richrit drew a second pistol. Heat rushed to his face, he drew his kilij, then shouted and charged the lord. Lord Richrit turned, startled by the intruder, and swung his pistol around. He fired at Ahmed. It hit the boy and dropped him to the ground. Lord Richrit attacked with his sword, forcing Ahmed to block from the ground. Ahmed pushed him back and recovered to his feet, casting fire towards Lord Richrit. Red hot flames rumbled towards the man. Lord Richrit dodged and glared at Ahmed.

"Fight fair infidel!" he scoffed.

"Fine! I don't need magic to beat you!" Ahmed shouted. They advanced and traded blows. Blocking and countering, Ahmed gained ground. He attacked with his axe, which Lord Richrit tossed to one side, then countered. Ahmed blocked and gave some ground under the lord's next attacks. Lord Richrit feinted. Ahmed was hit on the side while another attack bounced off his armor then he attacked more aggressively, striking hard at Lord Richrit' defence. Ahmed drew blood. The man roared and attacked even harder, forcing Ahmed to give ground. Lord Richrit overextended and Ahmed did not hesitate. He thrusted under the overextension and ran his sword through the lord's side, spewing blood out of the other end. Lord Richrit coughed up blood, a look of stunned disbelief in his face.

"Without men like you, lies, racism, and bigotry will no longer exist." Ahmed growled. He withdrew his sword and let the lord fall dead to his feet. Panting, Ahmed turned around. Sultan Yazid was trying to stand. Ahmed rushed to him and helped him up. Seeing the tear in his side Ahmed pressed his hand over it and cast yellow healing magic, causing both his hand and the sultan's wound to glow. The sultan took a strained breath, almost tripping over Ahmed.

"You fought to save me. Now you heal me."

"I am sorry, sultan. I am wretched, astaghfirualhurah. I caused my master's death, I caused Shoran's death." Ahmed held back his tears, focusing on his healing magic. "I failed you."

"No, I failed you." The sultan smiled and brought an arm over Ahmed's back to stabilize himself. "You were right. My anger for King Duggan led me astray and it warped my intentions. I wanted to defend my people, instead, like you said, I was ruining the sultanate I strengthened. I see I always selected the best and most loyal to serve me. I was wrong about you."

"You only did what was necessary at the time sultan."

"You are too forgiving Ahmed." Ahmed staunched the bleeding, his magic also disinfecting the sultan's wound. He attended to Barbas then he heard shouting. He strode out to the balcony and looked down. In a training field, King Duggan was advancing on Will. Will was struggling. Hoping the sultan and Barbas would be safe now, he rushed down to ground level.

After leaving Ahmed, Will caught up with Sir Robert and entered the throne room with his allies. A line of King's Guards drew their weapons and stepped forward to block their path, Mercer with them.

"King Duggan, Step down!" Sir Robert demanded, "Fighting has broken out in the palace."

"I trusted you, Sir Robert. You have betrayed me!" The king drew his longsword, Heretic's Bane. The blade glowed green with a corrosive, poisonous mist.

"We are with him too King Duggan!" Lord Gregor bellowed as he and a group of lords entered with their swords drawn and some of their men, many stained in blood.

"This is an outrage. All my vassals, traitors!" the king roared, his face red.

"Sir Robert is right. Your rule has compromised the security of our land and ensured distrust amongst your people. Even now, peasants' rebel against anyone who sides with you and your Royal Forces in cities and in towns across the land.

"I am absolute! I am your king. You have no right to dethrone me." He charged Sir Robert. While the two clashed, King's Guard knights surrounded Lorna, Will, and the lords. Strikes came from everywhere.

Will blocked. Lorna was struck by one, but resisted. Will kicked one in the gut who stumbled back. Will approached but was blocked by two guards. He swung his sword but was countered; a sword hit his arm, then face, then leg, the stinging pain staggering him.

Will turned to face Mercer. The grandmaster swung his sword forward and Will blocked while the thrust of Mercer's dagger caught him in his torso. Will fell back to recover, holding his bloody side. Mercer attacked again. Will blocked his quick swipes and jabs, but Mercer's attack was swift and flowing and too advanced for Will. Falling back under the strain, Will tried to advance. Mercer parried Will's attack with his dagger, hardly breaking a sweat.

A second wave of King Duggan's men charged into the room. Their sudden attack broke up the current fights.

Will found himself facing King Duggan. Realising who he was, the king charged Will. Heretic's Bane hissed. Will missed a block and the blade burned one of his gauntlets. Will fell back, blocking aggressive swipes of the king's longsword, finding an opening and thrusted. The king countered and tossed the sword aside. He aimed Heretic's Bane at Will's throat.

"Too easy," the king boasted but was suddenly mobbed by two rebels. Will recovered his sword and advanced on the king. King Duggan ran his blade through one rebel's stomach. The rebel coughed up blood and veins snaked across his face. He looked at the king, shocked and terrified. The other rebel, equally as stunned, froze. Will froze. Heretic's Bane sizzled, releasing smoke of burning flesh and corrosive poison. The king pulled his sword out and swung in at the other rebel, lodging the blade in his side and burning his flesh. The king retracted and glared at Will.

Will raised his sword and backed away from the king, his back towards a side door. The blood drained from his face.

"Come on then!" the king shouted. "Let's fight." They traded blows. The king kept pushing Will back, through the door and across the hallway behind it. Will made a desperate attempt to keep up with the king's swift attacks. His blade groaned with every strike, slowly being burned and chipped away, becoming lighter with every strike from Heretic's Bane.

King Duggan forced Will out into the open. In the sky, Will's falcon soared through the air creaking, sounding like a long wail.

The duellists passed under the northeast wall of the castle, through a small gate, and into a flat area surrounded by buildings. To the northeast, beyond one of the buildings, was a cliff face, that disappeared into the Golden Inlet. The two crossed into the middle of what seemed to be a training field.

The king made an overhead cut. The strength behind the strike pushed Will back when he blocked it. An anger in King Duggan's eyes, he kept swinging with the same attack. King Duggan locked swords with Will, sizzling metal loosened another chunk of Will's longsword. The king reached up to Will's sword and pulled it to the side. He tilted his sword point into Will's chest and pushed lightly through a gap, burning through Will's armor and touching his skin. Heretic's Bane boiled his flesh. Will screamed as his sword was pulled away from him and tossed aside. King Duggan laughed, relishing in his superior skill.

"It's you. All of this is because of you! For years have I ruled this kingdom and I will not be defeated and dethroned by the likes of you! You have no right to rule, you don't deserve it." The king swung his longsword and sliced Will's thighs through a break in his armor. The pain made Will scream and tumble to the ground, his legs started to burn as poison ate his flesh. The king lifted him and threw him backwards into the dirt. Will squirmed. He rolled to his back and looked up at King Duggan. The king held his sword to Will's throat.

"Now you will die and I will rule! Remember this farmer, a murderer does not get chosen to become a king. After this I will kill your Saomardrim friend, and your treasonous master. I will execute everyone who has rebelled against me this day then no one will ever challenge me with this false prophecy again. After that the Saomardrim will fall and they too will beg for my mercy!" King Duggan pushed his sword into Will's throat slowly to draw blood. Second by second the mad king's weapon pierced Will and sucked the life from him. Then a warmth emanated from Will's tunic pouch and he drew his Seeker's Stone. The object shone so bright it was like the sun had landed on top of the castle. The king stumbled backwards, shielding his eyes.

"What magic is this?" he screamed. Will tried to stand but King Duggan thrust forward his longsword. The blade cut across Will's mail, burning metal, got stuck in a ring, then with force, the king pushed. The blade tore through the weakened mail and Will's flesh, lodging itself in his side. Will screamed, tears in his eyes. He dropped his Seeker's Stone and fell backwards. The king removed his blade, his sight restored. Will's falcon swooped down, lunging for the Seeker's Stone. It grabbed it in its claws, unaffected by its power, and took it into the air.

King Duggan raised his sword, ready to make the killing blow. Will was foaming in his mouth and he struggled to regain his vision. The king swung, but his blade was blocked by a kilij. The king turned and looked into the face of Ahmed. He swiped towards Ahmed, shearing the boy's kilij and taking off a layer of metal. Ahmed tilted his sword up, intercepting before Heretic's Bane reached his head. Ahmed moved backwards. Enraged, the king advanced on him, trading blows and backing him towards the cliff.

Will trembled. The wounds in his leg and his neck grew bigger. It was becoming harder to breathe. His vision was growing darker and he choked on his foaming saliva. Will spit it out, unable to do much else. His falcon called to him. It circled in the sky then swooped downwards, landing in front of his face. To Will, the bird's noises were muffled and distant. The bird tilted its head and looked keenly at him. It dropped the Seeker's Stone and pecked it towards Will.

Will flexed his fingers, through stinging eyes he could just see the stone. It shone brightly and a red mist drew towards Will's hand, hinting at the healing it could bring. But it was not enough. Sharp throbbing pain paralysed him, and darkness crept in.

Will's falcon pecked at it again, rolling the stone into his hand. The tip of his finger touched it. Green mist lifted off of his wounds and into the stone, turning it green. When finished, red slowly retook its place.

Will opened his eyes, gasped, still feeling pain. He stood wearingly while his falcon launched itself back into flight and Will drew his dagger.

Ahmed cast a pulse of energy at the king. It threw King Duggan backwards but halfway the king raised his sword and blocked the rest of the spell. He made for a swing. Will shouted behind him and plunged his dagger into the king's sword arm, blood oozed out from the wound. The king screamed, dropping Heretic's Bane. Will withdrew the dagger and backed-up. Ahmed tightened his grip and thrust his kilij at the king's stomach.

"No! Stop!" Elizabeth shouted. Will turned. Ahmed pushed his kilij through King Duggan and turned to Elizabeth. "Ahmed!" She fell to her knees right as her father fell onto the dirt and Ahmed pulled out his sword, the action throwing blood on the boy. Will and Ahmed stood over Elizabeth and King Duggan. Elizabeth glared at Ahmed, tears in her eyes, her body trembling.

"Why!" she cried.

"He's responsible for so much death, pain, and suffering! He refused peace! He almost killed Will." Ahmed shouted, pointing at Will who was looking between the two, discomforted by Elizabeth's grief.

"He is still my father!" Elizabeth shouted. "If only I had known about the kingdom's state beforehand."

"It would not have mattered. He deserves to die!"

"Is that what you want people to remember? That the war ended when a Saomardrim boy killed the King of Gurmanis? What will that say!" Elizabeth shouted. Ahmed paled. His emotions settling, and he realised the significance of Elizabeth's words. What had he done? Ahmed held his forehead and lowered his kilij. "Help him, Ahmed! Heal him! Do something!" Elizabeth cried, her hands on one of her father's arms, helpless to save him. King Duggan spit out blood. Ahmed raised his left hand. He cast yellow healing magic, shining it over the wound he'd given the king. Ahmed closed his eyes.

"I missed his organs." Ahmed opened his eyes, gasping with relief. "We need to stop the blood." Ahmed set to work, but before he could do much, the King's Guard rushed out into the training yard, led by Grandmaster Mercer.

"Step away from the king or Manis so help me I'll kill you both," Mercer shouted. Will and Ahmed backed away towards a building, Will limping from half-open wounds, as Mercer and his men surrounded the king. They raised their swords at the boys. Elizabeth frantically tried to staunch the bleeding. One of the King's Guard helped her.

"The castle is taken!" Lorna shouted. She, Sir Robert, and a group of rebels rushed out of the keep and towards the scene. They were followed by Lord Gregor and his group of rebel nobles. One King's Guard turned to face them.

"Protect the king at all costs," Mercer ordered.

"Wait! The rebels and nobles have made their point. There need not be more blood!" Elizabeth said. "Mercer, my father needs Ahmed… Now!"

"He's—"

"Now!" Elizabeth shouted. Mercer allowed Ahmed to step in and heal the king. Elizabeth stood and turned to face the rebels and nobles. "Please, what more will death do? My father has been defeated; spare his life and those of the guards who protect him."

"He deserves death! We have suffered far too long under his rule an' his lust for war. You know not what we have lost because of him!" Lorna growled.

"Who said I have been defeated?" The king snarled, half delirious. He didn't notice Ahmed yet. "I will not be uprooted by treasonous lords and knights, most definitely not by peasants and filth. Not even by my daughter!" King Duggan spat.

A tense moment passed. "Let the new king decide then!" Lorna concluded. "Shall it be death or not?" Everyone looked to Will, expecting him to make a decision. Sir Robert gave him a sympathetic stare. Will gulped and looked away, not sure what to say and turning red in the face. Elizabeth turned towards Will. Between them was her father.

"Please Will, he is my father. He has done horrible things but he is still my father… Will I am sorry I betrayed you like I had but please… spare him," Elizabeth pleaded. Pain cut through Will's heart seeing Elizabeth so distraught.

"No! You have heard the things he has done. We demand his death!" Lorna growled. Will glanced at her, her seething expression stared back.

In one corner the rebels were in position to attack, in the other the King's Guard stood faithfully beside the injured King Duggan, ready to defend any attack but hopeless in victory. Between them, Sir Robert and the group of rebel lords stood blankly staring at each faction but ready to act if things became chaotic.

The decision was not easy. If he spared the king, pleasing Elizabeth, he may cause the rebels to attack. If he did not spare the king, he could cause the King's Guard to attack. Furthermore, he would hurt Elizabeth by killing her father; she would never speak to him again, she may try to take his life.

Time ticked for what seemed like minutes. Ahmed turned to Will. He expected Will to make a decision as well.

"Will, it is time to decide," Sir Robert prompted. Will hid his anger in hating that everyone expected him to make a decision he knew not how to make. He was and is a farmer, not a leader, not a king. With a final glance at the factions, Lorna's anger, Elizabeth's pain, the King's Guards loyalty, he spoke, "There has been enough death. King Duggan has lost, we can end this peacefully." Will said. Elizabeth dropped her arms and brought them to her chest. Her head bent down and some of her hair fell over her face. She cried, halfway between relief and sadness, breaking her regal armor.

"T-Thank-you Will," she whispered.

"Then we'll respect that," Lorna said surprisingly to the discontent of her fellow rebels, "Be sure he's justly punished."

"If Manis wants this for Gurmanis, then it shall be." Lord Gregor nodded. Will looked to Elizabeth. She wiped her face and regained composure.

"Arrest my father and sheath your swords."

"No… They're all traitors… Kill them! I am your king!" King Duggan raged, helpless. The King's Guards hesitated. Mercer stared at the princess, watching her pleading eyes.

"Grandmaster Mercer." Lord Gregor stepped forwards. "The nobility of Gurmanis stand behind Queen Elizabeth Chas. As is your mandate, your allegiance is to the ruler of Gurmanis. In this circumstance the nobility make that judgement. We have decided. You must decide."

"We serve you now, my queen." Mercer bowed, followed by his guards. The king roared with rage, then coughed. Sir Robert looked at the king with a hard stare. Elizabeth and Will came together and hugged each other. Elizabeth wept silently.

"I don't want you to be angry with me, Will. Forgive me."

Will hesitated, looking at her and feeling both nervous and warm. Only when King Duggan roared again did they part.

⁓⁓⁓

One week later a cloaked figure walked into the dungeons in the Palace of Kings. As the figure approached the guards realised who it was, and stepped aside. The figure entered into a small space with five cells contained behind bars. A guard there opened the barred door then a heavy metal door to one of the cells. The figure looked through a final barred door to the prisoner sitting in the cell.

"Lena." The figure pulled back her hood to reveal Queen Elizabeth. She called into the dark. After a moment of silence, then a clink of chains, a ragged figure appeared at the bars of her cell. Nothing like the duchess she once was, her body was covered in dirt and grime, her once clean and smooth hair now ruffled and filled with mud and the rags she wore were torn. The smell of feces and urine seemed to grow a little stronger. The heavy chains and shackles bound around her, sat uneasily, forcing the woman to correct her balance to accommodate them. The top half of her body was covered in a shawl to hide most of the chains, a privilege, rather unfairly, granted to the wealthy and powerful as if to preserve their dignity.

"I heard of the rebel victory and the Saomarhad withdrawal. The peasant is now king and you are queen from what I hear. It seems you have betrayed your father as I intended, yet I am to be executed in gruesome agony while you shall sit high on the throne," Lena spoke in a broken voice.

"I did not attempt to kill him," Elizabeth reminded the woman.

"It seems such a distinction has made your betrayal righteous."

"Perhaps to end so much death, war, injustice."

"You were always smarter than you looked, Elizabeth. Your mother knew that; sometimes she feared it. Have you come to taunt me before I am to die?" Elizabeth walked forwards and produced a small waterskin. She presented it to Lena through the bars. The prisoner hesitated.

"I heard they have fed you nothing and provided you little water. It is not poison; I do not wish to kill you." Lena took the waterskin and drank.

"You do not wish to kill me? Yet I have been told I will receive no other punishment than a traitor's death. Does the peasant king hold word over you Elizabeth?"

"He does not nor does my word hold over him. We will rule on even ground."

"Revolutionary… change in motion."

"Tell me the truth, Lena; did you want to kill my father or was it really Duke Célestin who held you in contempt?"

"I have pleaded my case before when you arrested me. Nothing has changed. My children; are they dead?" Lena's eyes widened.

"I have ordered the army to seize your estate but harm no one. Duke Célestin's forces will yield when they learn the duke is dead and my father dethroned. We will need a new duke of the Franormish."

"Dead? Then Célestin is dead?"

"He is," Elizabeth said. She would have wanted him disposed of better, in truth, but Mercer's men had dumped his body in the King's River. He couldn't be found again. Lena exhaled, as if a load of stress had been taken off her shoulders. Tears left her eyes and she gripped the bars for support.

"Then I die knowing my children will be safe. I beg you, Elizabeth, send my children, your cousins, somewhere safe and somewhere they will have a pleasant future. Tell them that their mother loves them even to the very end and tell them not to hate me or their father for we made a terrible mistake."

"You will not die and you can tell them these things yourself. I will spare your life. There is an estate south of Monte Calis where you and your children will be confined to. You will never be allowed to leave the estate as punishment for your treason, however, in the future when your children do not harbor ill will to me or King William, and understand why what happened has happened, they may be allowed to leave and lead a decent life. Your maid will remain alive but she will be imprisoned in The Grey Towers Prison for some time before she can be released far from the capital."

"Do I deserve your mercy?" Lena's eyes filled with tears.

"Duke Célestin is the one who is to blame. His ambition led him to abuse his position. He was the mastermind. You were forced into this treason, yet you still had a part to play that cannot go unpunished."

"Thank you, your majesty." Lena's chains clanked as she made a shaky bow.

"When your children are safely in custody, you will be transported to the estate to meet them there." Elizabeth sighed and left the cell.

She walked out and into an identical room, once again allowed to access another cell. Before the guard opened it she took in a deep breath. As the metal door slid open Elizabeth approached the man on the other side of the bars.

"I should be glad you came to see your father after you betrayed him!" Duggan Chas mumbled.

"I never betrayed you. I have always loved you father but what I sometimes feared is that you never loved me," Elizabeth spoke.

"Ha! What have you done then after accepting the rebels and throwing me out?"

"I saved you, father. The path you were going down would have destroyed you. There was no other way; you would not listen to your dukes, barons, or to the sultan or even Sir Robert."

"Sultan Yazid is an infidel and Sir Robert a traitor. Hardly people to listen to." he barked.

"They are valiant men. Wise in their convictions, strong and just leaders."

"So I was not a strong and just leader?"

Elizabeth almost laughed. Her father still could not see his own faults. "You were, then you were not. You oppressed your people and vowed to continue a war no one wanted. Father, I have read all the records kept by Jaxson. They tell tale of horrible things. I cried father. How could you do those things? You burned villages, killed those too young or too infirm or too old, and conscripted children into the war."

"Those communities hid from me their wealth and their able bodied. Both were needed to win the war. The victory would have avenged your mother!"

"The Saomarhadians did not kill her, I know it. I think you used that only as an excuse. A way to justify the vision you wished to fulfil. I let myself believe it and I grew angry, but then I realised the truth both Will and Ahmed showed me."

"What I did was in service of peace. With more land the nobles would have had plenty that they could then bestow upon the commoners. With a kingdom from here to Outremer, the Saomardrim would never hurt us again. Absolute authority is the only way to rule. The people are not smart enough to make decisions so they must be taught how to act and adhere to laws and rules."

Elizabeth shook her head; she could not reason with him. "No, people provide the nobility with food and materials and in turn we provide defence and leadership. That leadership must be just and considering what the people want. A contented society is a productive, united, and strong society. That is the meaning behind the story of Manis blessing the first and second children."

"Only strict adherence will prevail! Look at your impotent criminal King William. The boy will fail to meet his people's expectations then he will fall. What happens when the Saomardrim betray you? When another external enemy brings war upon you?" Duggan shuffled forward and clutched the cell bars. "He will fail, mired by indecision, and Gurmanis will be splintered."

"Duke Célestin thought like you."

"I know now he betrayed me. I trusted he had the rebels under control. I am nothing like that traitor."

"He also wanted power and control. I think he'd rule like you, but with a far more leveled head. I do not believe that forgetting about your people is the strongest way to rule."

"How can you ignore the death the Saomardrim inflicted on us? You lived through the execution of our captured kinsmen, heard and saw it. Do you not care for their lives?"

"I care, but I must let it go. I cannot forgive, but I must accept. If we keep saying that there cannot be peace because he did that, because he is a hypocrite, then there will *never* be peace. The sultan has expressed regret and he works with us. We have to accept that for the better."

"You have an opportune chance, Elizabeth! You are now Queen. Cast away that criminal and rule alone, rule with power and regain honour to the family name."

"Will, he will regain our honour, not your style of rule."

"Then it seems you are not my daughter, for you do not obey me!"

"I am trying to help you father. You don't know how hard it is to hear everyone call your father a radical and a mad man!" tears teased Elizabeth's eyes. What she started to fear now was what could be in her, blood of a tyrant.

"I must carry your crimes now, none will let me forget. Can you not see how insufferable a burden that is?" She and Arch-Mage Jaxson had sealed away Heretic's Bane in the undercroft at the foot of her father's statue. Jaxson had enchanted it. How evil a blade it had become and how many lives had it slowly burned away. Many would recoil at giving Duggan the small honor of a spot beneath the castle.

"I do not need help." Duggan turned away.

"Will and I will rule justly and I will prove to you that just ruler ship can succeed. I always wanted you to be proud of me father but now… perhaps your time in here will allow you to think about things…" Elizabeth pulled up her hood and with a heavy heart she made her way out of the dungeon.

On one hand she felt liberated and powerful, that now she could mend the harm her father had done. On the other hand, she felt like a traitor, ashamed. Questions raced through her head now: what if she hadn't run away? Would all of this have happened? Or she would be in the Imperium now. She would never know.

Epilogue

"SULTAN YAZID HAS agreed to end this pointless war and to begin a new age of peace." Queen Elizabeth addressed the crowd below her from a balcony overlooking a wide square. Two weeks of negotiations had wore away her energy, but the prospect of this speech and finally delivering it re-invigorated her. She wore an ornate fine blue-gold dress and her mother's crown sat on her head, its gold gleaming under the sun.

They were all gathered in the large square, flanked on two sides by statues of Gurmanis' legendary heroes and heroines.

"For a long time, we were shrouded in a war that brought about only losers. It consumed our land, homes, and our lives. Those closest to us died and fought over a reason that was so pointless we all believed or hoped it was worth something. But it was not. So long we held onto old grudges refusing to try something different and it disabled us. Today is a new day. If we'd latched only onto yesterday then today would have never come. We are right to seek justice, but not at the expense of innocence and of our own destruction.

"We lost sight of the unity we possessed long ago against such enemies as the high elves, the Imperium, the Mokerjin Khaganate hordes, and the Corruption during the time of the Corruption Crisis. What is unity? It does not have to be allegiance under one ruler, no, it can be the understanding, respect, and trust, of two peoples within different states. Where we are not unified by government, we are unified by a mutual understanding of each other. One that will help both of our societies. Today marks a dawn of unity between our peoples.

"Much has been lost in this war, deemed the Long Crusades. In our new age of peace, I hope we will regain much of what we lost. Our wounds are deep but with time they will heal. To ensure a greater understanding of our diversity, the river region will see the development of Alhurah mosques on the Gurmanis side, and Manis chapels on the Saomarhad side, emulating our past. For the first time in hundreds, both Gurmians and Saomarhadians will become friends once more.

"Sultan Yazid is older and wiser. His rulership is just. William and I are young but this war has aged us. We will lead this kingdom with the aid of the wisest of mentors, and we will lead it well. I ran from my responsibilities and I was wrong. I have a duty as your princess, and now queen, to see our country strong and peaceful. We will bring new life to Gurmanis and I hope you, the people, will give us place to do it. Let our new age of peace last for hundreds of years more. The Long Crusades have ended!"

Cheers ran wild through the large crowd assembled to Elizabeth's left was King William wearing his own fine blue-gold clothes. Will did not like his new name, however, and he was glad to be called Will by at least his friends and master. His crown sat heavy on his head, not something he was ever prepared to bear. To Will's left was Sir Robert. He gleamed with his polished armor on. To Elizabeth's right stood Sultan Yazid. To the sultan's right was Ahmed.

"That was well said, Elizabeth." Will smiled, admiring how she had weaved her words.

"Yes, and maybe next time you could do it as is custom." The way Elizabeth bit her lip made Will hesitate. Was she nervous?

"I will need to get used to it."

"So… we will need to get used to… this." Elizabeth blushed.

"This?"

"Living together." Elizabeth strode close to Will, centimeters apart. Will tensed. "I don't know… maybe we'll figure it out."

"Figure what out?"

"What you said in Serleigh… about loving me." Elizabeth watched as his face lost colour. "I have been thinking… thinking about it since you left the palace, when we got here… and…" She closed the distance between them and kissed Will. A surge of warmth overcame him as Elizabeth's soft, fruity tasting lips touched his. Her gentle form pressed against him as she leaned in close. His head tilted and he instinctively closed his eyes. His heart pounded in his chest and the fluttering inside him intensified. Elizabeth's arms wrapped around Will, caressing him. Will's own arms refused to move, unsure what to do. Her vanilla sent cascaded over him and time seemed to stand still for one destabilizing yet inviting moment. All tension fled, an expansive weightlessness showered him. Will steadied himself, wishing the moment to last.

A bird's call broke their kiss as it flew in circles above the balcony.

"I-I want to figure… it out." Will blushed. Will's falcon swooped down and Will held out his arm for him. The bird landed and looked around quizzically at Elizabeth and Will. Both smiled.

"It seems that falcon is an expert at escaping the bird tower," Elizabeth exclaimed.

"Like me, he does not like to be locked up." Will took feed from a pouch on his tunic belt and fed his bird. The bird graciously picked at Will's hand. "I like the name you suggested."

"So…"

"Feorhhyrde, guardian protector." Will's falcon chattered then jumped and flew off to join the birds in the sky. "In time I hope to understand this new life. It's all so sudden."

"That will take forever!" Ahmed laughed. The sultan and Sir Robert talked to each other behind him.

"I will miss you Ahmed," Will frowned.

"Not to worry, Will. We will meet again. I hope to return to Hamid to see my family; it's been a long time."

"Yeah well, it's not the same, you know." The three companions smiled.

"I heard the rebels have been disbanded, the men and women returned to their homes. I hope they will be pleased and not… you know… rebel again," Elizabeth said.

"So long as you care for your people, they will be satisfied." Ahmed answered.

"I am queen now; it feels different knowing the new power I have. I will correct the wrongs my father committed." Elizabeth smiled, her mind briefly elsewhere.

"I am sure Alhurah is pleased with all of us."

Sultan Yazid stepped forward with Sir Robert beside him. Behind them, Barbas, Parvez, and the Immortals stood.

"Sultan." Elizabeth stepped forward. The three friends bowed and received a strained return nod from the sultan. His wounds still healing.

"May I be one of the first to greet you King William and Queen Elizabeth. It fills me with great relief and happiness that the war has ended. It would not have been possible had it not been for Alhurah and you three, especially you, Seekers, the word I am hearing that I should call you by," Sultan Yazid said.

"Yet our roles were largely passive. Our purpose was to express God's will," Will said.

"And for a change of heart." The sultan smiled and looked at Ahmed. "Ahmed. When I broke the Gurmian invasion force and routed them I thought about you. At first when I witnessed the tide of battle turn, I was filled with overwhelming pride and rage. I was ready to pursue the rout and utterly brutalize the Gurmian army. Then I hesitated. I remembered you. I remembered what you told me and how boldly and easily you had betrayed me."

"It was not easy, my sultan," Ahmed interrupted. "I was very conflicted."

"Yes. Well, I realised I was becoming King Duggan. That I was warmongering in a pursuit of vengeance you made clear was hurting my people, and that, as you discovered, was rooted in ignorance and distrust. I decided not to pursue the rout because of you."

"Yet, you planned to assassinate my father," Elizabeth said.

"His was the only life I needed to take. Ahmed made me realise the mistake I was making. I was hurting my own people even as I said I was defending them. I will accept that Duggan will spend his life confined. Forgive me Ahmed." The sultan bowed slightly.

Ahmed tensed, "N-No… I mean y-yes, but there is no need to bow to me."

"I still need a grand vizier. Would you consider it Ahmed?" the sultan asked. Ahmed hesitated. He looked away and thought about it. He'd never really wanted the position. He had always gone along with it because it was what Master Mahad wanted for him. Kind of like how Amir had accepted his fate of succeeding his father as emir. He followed along with his master's wishes because, like his brother and the emirate, he thought it was the right thing to do. Now he realised he was most content with knowledge.

"I cannot accept," Ahmed said, looking at the sultan. "This war started from ignorance that fuelled intolerance. Over time we grew apart and forgot how similar we were." Ahmed looked at Will. "I remember when I first found Will he told me how we would see giant snakes and scorpions rise up from the sand to eat us, ridden by dwarves and pygmies." Will blushed, scratching his hair. Ahmed turned back to the sultan. "That showed how absurd our ignorance about each other had gotten. When I travelled through Saomarhad, I observed that ignorance in full display, and when I travelled through Gurmanis I witnessed it again. By making friends with the other, only then I realised that the truth is that we are all more similar than we are different."

"So, what have you decided?"

"My place is to prevent this ignorance from infecting our states in the future. I will create a new organization, with the help of both our countries and the Mages Guild. I will build it at… Hertos Point, right between Gurmanis and Saomarhad. It will be an organization that will collect and examine knowledge. It will spread the message of understanding and unity, as Elizabeth described so well, widely to our people, inshalhurah." The thought of that plan warmed Ahmed. In a way, he'd continue his master's encouragement of teaching and learning.

"I envision that you will have many successes with it. I will support it." Sultan Yazid smiled.

"And so, will we… right Will?" Elizabeth prompted.

Everyone looked at Will again and he tensed. "Uh… Y-Yes… right." Will exhaled. "I will support it."

"It will help both our countries." The sultan smiled and nodded. He turned to Queen Elizabeth. "Your speech was well performed."

"Thank-you." Elizabeth smiled.

"Today we have a moment of peace and celebration but I doubt our struggles are at an end. For generations we have been at war. Not everyone will easily forgive such crimes as massacres, invasions and murder."

"I am well aware. I will try hard to work with you to soften the desire for revenge."

"Building mosques and chapels on either side of the river not devoted to the true divinity that side accepts may sir up resentment and violence."

"I have thought of what we can do to drive our countries in the same direction towards peace. On both sides there is a sense of exhaustion. This is already advantageous. The will of the people to fight is on its way out. What we must do now is promote exposure, cooperation and mutual trade. The people must see how those they have fought against for so long are very much the same. If we can promote Gurmanis and Saomarhad peacefully working together side by side for a common goal then over time, in the people's minds, and very naturally, our cultures will find a peaceful coexistence. Perhaps this is why God makes us share the Hertos River Valley."

"My thoughts exactly, young queen. This war has taught us that separation is an illusion and unity will break that illusion. To promote separation, purity and distinctness is to promote misunderstanding, fear and hatred. If people think of others as only 'the other' then there can be no cooperation and peace. At the base of everything, we are all the same under the eyes of God."

"Yet complete blending risks the loss of unique culture and tradition both of which are just as important. We must also promote the uniqueness of both Gurmian culture and of Saomardhadian culture in a way that respect can grow."

"And what of religion then? For Manians, Manis will always be the inheritor of the Father and the worthiest. For Alhurians, Alhurah will always be the inheritor of the Father and the worthiest."

"Then we should respect that. Let people believe, but we all have to learn how not to impose."

The sultan smiled and nodded. "Inshalhurah. You are very wise, young queen. It has been most enjoyable to discuss affairs of state with you."

Elizabeth blushed. "I have only thought about these things recently. I have witnessed the truth that my people and your people see, that is all."

⁓

Night came over the city and Will looked out over it through his window in the king's study, his study now. To think he was a sad young criminal, now this. Will was glad his name was officially cleared by the courts. Lord Dillon, he who had conveyed Will's conviction and sentence, had fled Royal Landing after failing Duggan. Lord Dillon retreated to Burhbarrow and it was uncertain if he would resist from there. Like Elizabeth did with Lena, he'd forgive Dillon if the lord surrendered his lands and accepted exile. He had only tried to help his friend.

Will thought back far into his past. He remembered the pain, reflecting on the luck that had brought him here. If Sir Robert had not chosen to spare him, he'd be dead. Another voice surfaced. It told him to look at himself. He? There had been nothing special about him. The words of his parents and even Manis surfaced, *'Resilient, strong, loyal.'* Will wondered how much of all this was his personality and actions, and how much was luck.

"You were so young. Every year it seems your face… lost something," Elizabeth spoke, compassion in her voice. Will turned to her. She stood over his study desk, looking at the package of archive papers Will had dared himself to request. He had been too nervous and too afraid to open it. Elizabeth had. Will walked over and looked at what Elizabeth had commented on. She had arranged drawings of Will's face, his mugshots, from the time he was ten to the time he was sixteen, across the table. It was Will's first time looking at his face at those ages, and how it had lost something each year in prison.

"It lost… its humanity." Will frowned. Elizabeth wrapped her arms around him. "I'll ne'er forget. There will be times I wither, I panic, I am taken back."

"I am ready to support you no matter what happens."

"I'll use those experiences. I will make sure such evil never happens again. Manis preaches mercy, that's what the future will be like. First, I will close Isen Prison."

Elizabeth drew him close and rested her head on his chest. Will lost himself in the moment, knowing he loved the girl cradled on his chest. Elizabeth shifted. She opened her mouth to say something, hesitated, then shifted again.

"What's wrong?" Will asked.

"In Serleigh you asked me if I thought you killed your parents," she said carefully, looking to be sure Will was comfortable. Will remembered. Her belief in his innocence was still uncertain, she would never know the truth. Sir Robert didn't care and Ahmed had seen only blurred half-truths, and still made the decision not to care. Why couldn't the girl he loved… not care? "Well… I don't care. It doesn't matter now because I trust you."

Will smiled, relief washing over him in waves.

The pair looked out over the city. The full moon lit the structures below and shimmered off the Golden Inlet. He hoped he would be able to live up to the new expectations laid on him as king. It would be hard he told himself; his life had always been hard, but he could do it. He had to do it, why would God choose him if he couldn't?

Yes, he would make a good king.

Thank-you for reading my book. If you enjoyed it please consider leaving a review at your favourite retailer. Reviews help this book reach more people.

Explore the World of Erathas, view concept art, get access to expanded chapters and short stories, and more! Connect at:

My website: https://nitishsharmabooks.com

Follow my Goodreads author page:
https://www.goodreads.com/author/show/22690886.Nitish_Sharma

Watch my Deviantart page: https://www.deviantart.com/boundlesshero

Thanks!
Nitish